STORY II

The Library of Wales
Short Story Anthology

PARTHIAN
LIBRARY OF WALES

STORY II

*The Library of Wales
Short Story Anthology*

Edited by Dai Smith

PARTHIAN
LIBRARY OF WALES

Parthian
The Old Surgery
Napier Street
Cardigan
SA43 1ED

www.parthianbooks.com

The Library of Wales is a Welsh Government
initiative which highlights and celebrates Wales' literary
heritage in the English language.

Published with the financial support of
the Welsh Books Council.

www.thelibraryofwales.com

Series Editor: Dai Smith

Story II first published in 2014
© The authors and/or their estates
Introduction © Dai Smith 2014
All Rights Reserved

ISBN 978-1-90-894643-0

Cover photograph From *Cardiff After Dark* by Maciej Dakowicz
Cover Design by Marc Jennings

Printed and bound by Gwasg Gomer, Llandysul, Wales
Typeset by Elaine Sharples

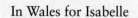
In Wales for Isabelle

INTRODUCTION

If Wales down to the 1950s had too readily been a crucible for common heroism, that tragic condition which so often requires the comic to transcend its inhumane demands, so in the past half-century the mock-heroic, as boastful and contemptible in public life as it can be self-conscious and subtle in private reflection, has been the confused tonality of a country increasingly cut adrift from accustomed mooring points. Not that, all tied up safe to welfarism and communal warmth, it seemed exactly like that at the beginning of this period. And nor, in truth, does it seem quite like that now. Our relative prosperity, certainly relative to what had been our previous lot, and our comparative stability, as expressed despite a few dips and troughs in our politics and society, have been duly reflected in the short stories which have fingered our increasing diversity and our looser identity. Yet this very emphasis on a more individually wayward contemporaneity has struggled to cast off the shadows of a radically different past. We cling, it seems, whether in folklore or historiography, to lifelines of explanation. Our imaginative writers have also tacked and tacked about, in style and in genre, to probe for deeper means of discernment.

This sense of things, of kicking off and yet still treading water, has been grounded in a self-reflexive perception largely absent from the earlier fiction of observation and re-counting. Now, we move into the columns of double-accounting where what we thought and dreamed as much as what we said and did, is held, as if altogether, to assess the accuracy of our tabulated lives of diurnal bookkeeping. Those stories which had, in our actual past, not been directly touched by the world of work, on the land or in industry, could seem fey in their removal from the pressing realities of most Welsh lives. Even Dylan Thomas at his most suburban and surreal kept one eye knowingly cocked for those other Welsh worlds, which he admitted he did not know. Soon, neither would most people, whether directly or not. The absence of heavy industry as an overall definer first came not as a loss of numbers but as a diminution of collective impulses. Since lip-service, culturally and politically, was still paid to this lingering social phenomenon it did not fully impinge on a wider consciousness. When the numbers crunched to a halt via closures and end-games, from the 1960s to the 1980s, Wales was less distinctive economically, and so socially, than it had been over the preceding century. In compensation, perhaps, from the 1960s the tendency was to emphasise our intellectual and cultural definition.

In this, especially, the Welsh language became a rallying force which extended significantly beyond the linguistic fate of Welsh itself. Across key areas of Welsh life coherent networking, generational and familial and ideological, ran ahead of sluggish representative politics. At the same time as collieries and steelworks and nonconformity and communism began a disappearing act, so did a majoritarian culture, one which was largely Anglophone but stubbornly Welsh in origins and aspirations, swing between the extremes of a mythical heritage and the complexities of its unfolded history in an attempt to anchor itself in the contemporary. In literary terms the cultural flux was not content anymore to be labelled 'Anglo-Welsh'. It was never meant other than as a literal description of the language used by those who did not, or could not, write in Welsh. But in the 1960s, when equivalence was to be insisted upon, it was depicted as a lesser and uneven term. For some of Wales' English-language writers it was not sufficient recognition of their straightforward identity. For others, notably a younger generation of poets also writing in English, the desired equivalence could only be won through the forthright expression in their verse of those patriotic values signalled by contemporaries writing in Welsh. The *kulturkampf* was, in truth, largely mild, certainly tolerant, but it remained persistently present because, patently, society-at-large in Wales could not be captured, let alone witnessed, in one tongue only. And the witness from those who did not 'see' in Welsh would need prose fiction and empathetic identification if their windows were to be clear for sight.

This would not prove easy when only the vanishing past, disturbingly enough, seemed to validate the hard-fought values which were being, so uneasily yet so readily, lost to common view. Somewhere along this cultural spectrum respectful obeisance to that past was simply not enough if the witnessing was to reach deeper. It would be Ron Berry, born in the Rhondda in 1920, who quizzed the History as a Shitstory. His irreverence, allied to the conviction of his stylistic break, cracked open the code of *omertà* by which one Wales had silenced another. The voice, he showed us, would need to be sardonic as well as engaged, even cynical if fierce, above all original through its demotic distinctiveness. Berry was ahead of his time.

During Ron Berry's productive lifetime – and one could add that of his fellow bullshit detector, Alun Richards, too – the material production of Wales was the virtual creation of burgeoning cultural institutions. A simulacrum Wales, generally more comfort blanket than intellectual hair shirt, was being spun out of museums and media, in books and through artefacts, on the airwaves and in galleries. Our best storytellers had to equip themselves with rather more than the microscope or telescope viewfinder of their predecessors: literary radar alone allowed for the detection of an insidious mission creep out of a history being simultaneously cleaned-up for consumption. The innocently self-serving and the calculatingly hypocritical in the Wales that twitched helplessly into the 1980s, unlike the human remnants of our industrial leftover communities, bled only on the page. *Story*, Volume Two, is replete with stories whose scalpel-wielding authors document and expose the making and faking of Wales in our time.

Part of the counter to a widespread cultural rodomontade was a determined insistence on the worth of individual differentiation in a society long committed, in every sense, to a collective of clichés and labelling. We hear constantly in the work of younger writers an existential refusal of, practically a scream against, any process of pinning the butterfly to the social wheel. Less and less was written about work and its definers, or even the anthropological fascination hitherto reserved for working-class otherness. More and more, our writers centred on their own angst, on the close analysis of personal relationships, on sexuality or ethnicity as key markers of experience, and they manipulated fantasy, myth and the surreal as a defensive slap against the pain of having to have a common history at all.

This volume of *Story*, therefore, starts and ends with the contradictory notes we begin to hear struck, insistently and unceasing, since the 1950s. The memories of childhood, and of an accompanying world lost to the touch, were not fake but they could soon be dismissed, necessarily perhaps, for their own wistful nostalgia and, contradictorily, by the actual memory of the brute facts of how so many had worked merely to get by, to spend time, their only truly liquid currency, before unlamented death. For many Welsh writers, at their peak in these years, Wales became a country they could only locate, to any real desire or generational need, in a past they could no longer literally inhabit. The sheer, melodramatic weight of that past, the lived history of their earlier selves, oppressed the mind but yet directed the pens of those writers who had escaped via the professions, into public service and teaching, or even exile. The pattern can be traced in the manner in which an appetite for Welsh fiction, particularly in the short story form, would be met by a flurry of anthologies from the 1970s. Yet, at the same time, the assertions of purpose-made manifestos, almost in echo the one of the other, by editors of previous anthologies from the 1930s onwards, now gave way to a wider range of lesser certitude. By the 1970s earlier awe yielded to a perspective on achievement.

When Sam Adams and Roland Mathias brought out their collection of just twelve short stories, in 1970 in *The Shining Pyramid and other stories by Welsh authors*, they were making quietly insistent statements of fact. To begin with, their book, the fifth anthology to appear since the 1930s, was the first to be published in Wales. And, they said in their note to the volume, its emphasis was to be strictly on perceived quality. This was, too, the first collection to place its stories in the chronological order of dates of composition not publication. A kind of tradition was being claimed, and it was no coincidence that this was also the first volume to include nothing that was translated, whilst proclaiming that all the chosen writers were Welsh. Or rather that all the authors were Welsh men, for no woman found her way in.

A year later, in 1971, the doyen of 'Anglo-Welsh' Letters, Gwyn Jones, would claim that the new anthology he had co-edited with the Welsh language writer, Islwyn Ffowc Elis, was the first 'with any real claim to be true to its title or representative of its subject'. This was because *Twenty-five Welsh Short Stories* included ten that were in translation from Welsh. There were four women writers included, three in translation. This tandem, a genteel partnership rather than either a full-on affair or agreed separation, continued up to the 1990s. Alun Richards followed the principle, if not the full practice, of the Gwyn Jones model in his two influential collections: *The Penguin Book of Welsh Short Stories* in 1976 and in 1993 in *The New Penguin Book of Welsh Short Stories*. The former had twenty-four stories by twenty-four authors, of which seven were in translation and the latter had, with some repeats, twenty-eight writers of whom seven were in translation. There were five women writers in 1976 and seven in 1993, two of whom were in translation from Welsh. Richards' editorial comment from the fraught, if still recognizably connected, 1970s echoed the past:

> These stories have been chosen to fulfil such requirements [i.e. 'being at the core of another life...through the mind and the world of the central character']...but they are, in addition, of a place and a time. The place is Wales and the time is this century, since the short story is a comparatively new arrival here. They reflect Wales, not always flatteringly, as it is and has been.

The trouble was that a cusp point was approaching where all that had been seemed to be in danger of losing its way. Affirmation of what the short story had been about to that point, allied to a vigorous defence of its historical contextualisation, was the task Robert Nisbet shouldered when he edited his collection, *Pieces of Eight: Contemporary Welsh Short Stories* in 1982. The editor was clear, though his crystalline note of what was fundamental would soon crack under manifold pressures, that the short story:

> working...with places and people, idiom and local detail, will be much more [than poetry] a product of its time and place, [and this]...will inform a story, in a fairly fundamental way, will penetrate to moods and awareness, even when the world's concerns seems to be substantially elsewhere...[For] Wales now...a sense of community and a sense of the past are fundamental to our way of looking at things...[that] past which informs and gives the communities [of Wales] much of their meaning.

By the next time Alun Richards took up his pen as an editor of Welsh short stories, Wales was no longer what it was or had been. Its very 'meaning' was, for many, in doubt. In 1984-5 the Miners' Strike had, in its travail and defeat, tolled the death knell of that South Wales culture and society which Alun Richards knew best and admired, at its best, most. By the mid 1990s Wales was set to overturn the 'No' vote overwhelmingly registered in the 1979 Referendum on devolved government.

In 1997, albeit by the narrowest of margins, a 'Yes' vote would bring in a Welsh Assembly, institutional government for Wales, which South Wales' pre-eminent post-war writer bitterly opposed, then and in 1979. Already, in 1993, he looked on at the unfolding development of events with his baleful eye and noted the divergent truths all around him:

> The success [of the previous volume] lies...in the variety of stories as much as the badge of nationality...Wales... is a diverse and small country...The collective experience of its writers reflects the diversity and in selecting the stories [in both languages], I have tried to represent all Welsh writers, including those whose work belies the idea of Wales as a homogeneous society.

It was clear in which camp he stood himself. Paradoxically, convergence around 'the idea of Wales', in the civic and public sphere, was not mirrored by any lessening of cultural and literary diversity. Indeed the latter, in both Welsh and English, was often trumpeted as the strength of necessarily parallel strands. Necessary, that is, if the fiction of national homogeneity was only to be allowed into the mind as rhetoric, a mode rightly shunned by the best fictive explorers of our strange new ways. Diversity, transparently so, was the position on the literary native ground, even as the eagles of ideology mapped out a homogeneous national framework. Many chose to navigate by their own compass.

Emphases, by editors and writers, in the two decades to the end of the millennium became noticeably more assertive, chippier even, about the autonomy of their own custom and practice and, from that time to this time, its quite tangential relationship to anything which might, or might not, be being depicted of the real or the historical. The poet, John Davies, collected twenty-five stories from twenty-five English-language Welsh writers in 1988 in *The Green Bridge: Stories from Wales*. The anthologist was bullish:

> A good story offers a past and a future that aren't there...
> Nor is there, was there a Wales as it exists in most fiction.
> It is not social realism that has stimulated the best Anglo-Welsh short stories...they have invariably been mythopoetic...fusing the two known places, the actual and the dreamscape.

On the sliding slopes of Wales at the end of the 1980s this was a view widely disseminated. A known world, the hitherto actual, was slipping away, and occasionally at landslide pace. On such shifting ground, intellectual balance could be all if only we could reach for it. Within the scholarly Humanities or Cultural Studies a welcome critical apparatus, both in historiographical and literary criticism, began to mine the meanings held within our fiction. But current practitioners were not so ready to be transfixed. In 1993 the fantasy writer, Phil Rickman, introduced *Tales of Terror* with the gleeful scream that '...while virtually all the tales are set in Wales, most of them could easily be set anywhere in the UK. Or, indeed the world'. The dis-, or mis-, location, earned via a clamant universal aesthetic, appealed a few years later, in 1996, to Robert Minhinnick when he assembled both poems and stories in *Drawing Down the Moon*. The poet-editor, understandably enough, wished to champion the kind of artistic insight which once, at our beginning, had no apparatus of support outside the writer, and since then had, he thought, acquired clumsy interpretative friends:

In the critical vacuum created by the [post-structuralist, post-modernist, and therefore irrelevant to creative practice] English departments, it has been Welsh historians who have read and interpreted and championed such writers as Alun Lewis and Gwyn Thomas. The trouble with this school of criticism is that its texts, composed by writers who were unique and possessed of individual and difficult things to say, have been perceived as barometers for social and historical change...Such writers wielded scalpels. But their words have been appropriated and used as blunt instruments to make historical points.

If this was the case then it might well be conceded now that, in critical terms, our university departments of English have, in key instances, produced over the last decade or so essays and monographs more subtle, nuanced and alert to the sensitivities of autonomous texts. It is, too, an act of cultural intervention by the Welsh Assembly Governments elected after 1999 which gave us, for the first time, a sustained body of texts, written in English for Wales, which can be so quizzed. That is, of course, the Library of Wales series, of which *Story I* and *Story II* are the latest volumes to be published. If we are then able to place these texts, enjoyed and explicated, into the context of that scholarly historical enquiry which has transformed, through its historiography, the intellectual life of Wales since the 1960s, then we may well return to that intricate and inter-relationship between author and subject which is, indeed, the creative starting point of any imaginative outcome.

That will be a better place to be in than any throwback to any false dichotomy between 'individual' and 'society'. Such a dictum was the solipsistic nursery chant of the socially corrupt and intellectually bankrupt 1980s, a decade that eventually sharpened the Welsh mind by being so out of kilter with any concept, historically derived or culturally aspirational, of what Wales was and could yet be. The vigour and conviction with which the latest generation of Welsh story writers are now addressing their Welsh subject matter is a compound of local sensibility and global awareness which holds their Wales in an embrace as warm as it is guarded. Our story had been stalled for a while, but now it is again kick-started into fresh meaning in language that is fashioned, as speech and description, to bear the mark of our originality, and of our sameness with others. We can detect the voices in chorus in the various collections made from the early 1990s on, and especially in the three made up of the winning stories in the Rhys Davies Short Story Competitions sponsored by the eponymous Trust which has as its aim the fostering of Welsh writing in English. We can taste through their prose the overwhelming engagement this particular Wales has made, for good or ill, with its post-industrial destiny in *Urban Welsh: New Welsh Fiction* edited by Lewis Davies, and in the teasingly entitled selection *Wales Half Welsh* chosen by John Williams, both the editors tellingly being themselves novelists whose own work is as much at ease beyond the borders of Wales as within its boundaries. New horizons can arise, too, from the rescue of neglected traditions as in Jane Aaron's edition from 1999, *A View Across the Valley: Short Stories by Women from Wales*, and in the celebratory *All Shall be Well: A quarter of a century's great writing from the women of Wales* which Stephanie Tillotson and Penny Anne Thomas brought together in 2012. Great writing, from many pens and minds, and laptops, too, of course, has been a real feature of an emerging Wales in the first two decades of devolved policy, of cultural drive and the proper grounding of an institutional life for Welsh-based publishers and national arts organisations. So it would be insidious to single out any particular writer to make an emblematic point; and yet it would be purblind not to do so if the concatenation of the given and desired, the twin poles of the Story I have assembled in this volume, appears so obvious in two instances. For me, then, there is no coincidence that the winner in 2006 of the inaugural Dylan

Thomas Prize for writing from anywhere on the globe by a writer under the age of thirty, should be the phenomenally talented Rachel Trezise, born in 1978 in the Rhondda, nor that this volume ends with a masterly story by Wales' pre-eminent living novelist, Emyr Humphreys, born in 1919 in Prestatyn and a bridge, in both of his chosen languages, for all writers fated to write of their native country with a semblance of his unmatched passion and his cold clarity.

Fortunately therefore, looking back with this *Story* ready to hand, we can see that the intricacies expressed and revealed in our diverse and multiple Welsh stories overrides any simplistic settlement. The range of outlook and insight upon which we can draw reaffirms the galaxy of individual identities, across region, gender, class, age and opinion, whilst, together, proving to be part of a common universe, a tradition perhaps, of the specifically Welsh short story whose motto could come, both near and far, from the American writer, Richard Ford:

> Stories should point to what's important in life...secular redemption...through the opening of affection, intimacy, closeness, complicity [so that we might feel like] our time spent on earth is not wasted.

Our story is certainly not ended for we always get to choose how it might end. That is the promissory note of all fiction whose dreams resolve our lives. Not all will have happy endings, of course, but they will invariably be just. We do not have the choice to escape judgement. We do have the human privilege of standing up before it. *Story* is our testimony at that bar. It is a witness from Wales to the full weighing of human endeavour in this our place over their time.

Dai Smith

THE STORIES

MEMORY

GAZOOKA

Gwyn Thomas

Somewhere outside my window a child is whistling. He is walking fast down the hill and whistling. The tune on his lips is 'Swanee'. I go to the window and watch him. He is moving through a fan of light from a street lamp. His head is thrown back, his lips protrude strongly and his body moves briskly. 'D-I-X-I-Even Mamee, How I love you, how I love you, my dear old Swanee...' The Mississippi and the Taff kiss with dark humming lubricity under an ashen hood of years. Swanee, my dear old Swanee.

The sound of it promotes a roaring life inside my ears. Whenever I hear it, brave ghosts, in endless procession, march again. My eyes are full of the wonder they knew in the months of that long, idle, beautifully lit summer of 1926.

By the beginning of June the hills were bulging with a clearer loveliness than they had ever known before. No smoke rose from the great chimneys to write messages on the sky that puzzled and saddened the minds of the young. The endless journeys of coal trams on the incline, loaded on the upward run, empty and terrifyingly fast on the down, ceased to rattle through the night and mark our dreams. The parade of nailed boots on the pavements at dawn fell silent. Day after glorious day came up over the hills that had been restored by a quirk of social conflict to the calm they lost a hundred years before.

When the school holidays came we took to the mountain tops, joining the liberated pit ponies among the ferns on the broad plateaux. That was the picture for us who were young. For our fathers and mothers there was the inclosing fence of hinted fears, fear of hunger, fear of defeat.

And then, out of the quietness and the golden light, partly to ease their fret, a new excitement was born. The carnivals and the jazz bands.

Rapture can sprout in the oddest places and it certainly sprouted then and there. We formed bands by the dozen, great lumps of beauty and precision, a hundred men and more in each, blowing out their songs as they marched up and down the valleys, amazing and deafening us all. Their instruments were gazookas, with a thunderous bringing up of drums in the rear. Gazookas: small tin zeppelins through which you hummed the tune as loudly as possible. Each band was done up in the uniform of some remote character never before seen in Meadow Prospect. Foreign Legionaries, Chinamen, Carabinieri, Grenadiers, Gauchos, Sultans, Pearl Divers, or what we thought these performers looked like, and there were some very myopic voters among the designers. There was even one group of lads living up on the colder slopes of Mynydd Goch, and eager to put in a word from the world's freezing fringes who did themselves up as Eskimos, but they were liquidated because even Mathew Sewell the Sotto, our leading maestro and musical adviser, could not think up a suitable theme song for boys dressed up as delegates from the Arctic and chronically out of touch with the carnival spirit.

And with the bands came the fierce disputes inseparable from any attempt to promote a little beauty on this planet, the too hasty crowding of chilled men around its small precious flame. The thinkers of Meadow Prospect, a harassed and anxious fringe, gathered in the Discussion Group at the Library and Institute to consider this new marvel. Around the wall was a mural frieze showing a long series of clasped hands staring eyes, symbolising unity and enlightenment among such people as might be expected to turn up in such a room. The chairman was Gomer Gough, known for his addiction to chairmanship as Gough the Gavel. He was broad, wise, enduring and tolerant as our own slashed slopes. He sat at his table underneath two pictures, one a photograph of Tolstoi, a great shaggy lump of sadness, and the other an impression done in charcoal and a brooding spirit, of the betrayal and death of Llewellyn the Last, and as Gomer Gough had often pointed out, it was clear from this drawing that Llewellyn had never had much of a chance.

It was on a Tuesday evening that Milton Nicholas took my Uncle Edwin and myself down to the emergency meeting of the Discussion Group. As we walked down the bare corridor of the Institute we could hear the rustle of bodies and the sough of voices from the Discussion Room. We were solemnly greeted by two very earnest ushers who stood by the door week in, week out, whether they were needed there or no. They had heard so many hot, apocalyptic utterances from the Group they just felt it would be wiser to stay near the door.

'Here, Edwin,' said Milton; 'and you, Iolo, here in the second row.'

'Stop pulling at me, Milton,' said Uncle Edwin. 'Why so far down?'

'This is the place to catch Gomer Gough's eye for a quick question. Gough's eye will have to be very alert tonight.'

'What is this crisis, anyway? Show me the agenda, boy. I don't want to be mixed up in anything frivolous.'

'You know me, Edwin. Always earnest. Uriah Smayle, that neurotic anti-humanist from Cadwallader Crescent, has prepared a very bitter report on the carnivals and bands. Uriah reckons the bands are spreading a mood of pagan laxity among the people and he's out to stop it. I've heard you put up some good lines of argument against Uriah in the past, so just tell your mind to gird up its loins and prepare for its sternest fight. He's a very restrictive element, that Smayle. Any stirring on the face of life and he faints.'

'He's dead against delight, and no doubt at all about it.'

'All right, boy. I'll do what I can. Oh, this is a fine gathering, a room full of people, keen, with their minds out like swords to carve their name on the truth.'

'If that article ever gets as far as this on its travels.'

A man of about forty, ravelled by wariness and rage, looking as sad as Tolstoi but shorter and with no beard and a blue suit, came to sit in the vacant seat just in front of us. He gave us no glance, no greeting.

'Hullo, Uriah,' said Uncle Edwin.

'Good evening,' said Uriah Smayle.

'You're looking very grey and tense tonight, Uriah,' said Uncle Edwin. 'What new terror is gnawing at you now? If life's a rat, boy, you're the cheese.'

'Well put,' said Milton. 'I've always said that if anybody's got the gift of laying on words like a poultice it's Edwin Pugh the Pang.'

'Mock on, Edwin,' said Uriah, half rising in his seat, his arm up at angle of condemnation. 'But some of my statements tonight are going to shake you rodneys.'

'Good,' said Uncle Edwin. 'Set the wind among our branches, Uriah, and we'll make you a bonus of all the acorns that fall.' His voice was soft and affectionate and he had his hand on Uriah's arm. He was known as Pugh the Pang because he operated as an exposed compassionate nerve on behalf of the whole species. We could see Uriah's spirit sliding down from its plane of high indignation. But he shook himself free from Edwin's arm and got back to form.

'Who's the chairman here?' he asked. 'I've got a meeting of the Young Men's Guild to address at eight on prayer as an answer to lust and it'll be a real relief to have a headful of quiet piety after the chatter of this unbelieving brood.'

6

'I'm in the chair, Mr Smayle,' said Gomer Gough, who had just walked in followed by Teilo Dew the Doom, our secretary, who had early come under the influence of Carlyle and very tight velveteen trousers. Gomer paused gravely in front of Uriah before turning to take his seat under the face of Tolstoi. 'I'm in the chair, Mr Smayle,' he repeated, 'and I don't rush things. This Discussion Group is out to examine the nature of mankind and the destination of this clinker, the earth.'

Teilo Dew raised his head and winked at Tolstoi and Llewellyn the Last, very sadly, as if suggesting that if he had been a less gentle man he would have told us the black and terrifying answer years ago.

'These are big themes, Mr Smayle,' went on Gomer, 'and we favour a cautious approach. We try not to be hysterical about them, and the best thing you can do is to set a dish of hot leek soup in front of your paler fears.'

'Stop putting yourself to sleep, Gomer,' said Uriah, 'and get on with it.'

Gomer raised his enormous baritone voice like a fist. 'All right,' he said. 'Brothers, at this extraordinary meeting of the Meadow Prospect Discussion Group we are going to hear a special statement from Brother Smayle. He thinks the epidemic of carnivals and costumed bands is a menace and likely to put morals through the mincer. And he says that we, serious thinkers, ought to do something about it.'

'Mr Chairman,' said Uncle Edwin, 'I want you to ask Smayle to tighten his dialectical washers and define this mincer. Tell him, too, that there never has been any period when the morals of mankind, through fear, poverty, ignorance and the rest of the dreary old circus, have not been well minced and ready for the pastry case.'

'Begging your pardon, Edwin,' said Gomer, 'just keep it simmering on the hob, if you don't mind, until Uriah has had his canter. Carry on, Mr Smayle.'

'Mr Chairman,' said Uriah, but he had his body turned

and he was speaking straight at Edwin and Milton Nicholas. 'Since these bands came decency has gone to the dogs. There is something about the sound of a drum that makes the average voter as brazen as a gong. The girls go up in droves to the hillsides where the bands practise, and there is a quality about these gazookas that makes the bandsmen so daring and thoughtless you've got to dig if you want to find modesty any more. Acres of fernland on the plateau to the west left blackened and flat by the scorch stain of depravity.'

Uriah rocked a little and we allowed him a minute to recover from the hubbub created in his mind by that last image. 'And as for the costumes worn by these turnouts, they make me blink. I am thinking particularly of the band led by that Powderhall runner there, Cynlais Coleman the Comet, who is sitting in the fourth row looking very blank and innocent as he always does but no doubt full of mischief.'

We turned around to greet Cynlais Coleman, whom we had not seen until that moment. He was craning forward to hear the whole of Uriah's statement, looking lean, luminous and virgin of guile. Cynlais had aroused wrath in Uriah during his active years as a foot-runner shooting through the streets of Meadow Prospect on trial runs in very short knickers. After he had given us a wide smile of friendliness he returned to looking astounded at what Uriah had just said.

'Who, me?' he asked.

'Yes, you.'

There was a rap from Gomer's gavel and Uriah addressed the chair once more.

'I've always known Cynlais to be as dull as a bat. How does he come to be playing the cuckoo in this nest of thinkers, Gomer? What sinister new alliance is this, boy?'

'Keep personalities out of this, Mr Smayle,' said Gomer.

'Do you mind if I ask Cynlais a few questions about his band?' said Uriah. 'Mr Ephraim Humphries, the ironmonger, has been requested by some of us to serve as moral adviser at large to the carnival committees of the area and he wants me to prepare a special casebook on Cynlais Coleman.'

'Do you mind being questioned, Cynlais?' asked Gomer in his judge's voice.

'Oh no,' said Cynlais. 'You know me. Gomer. Very frank and always keen to help voters like Mr Smayle who are out to keep life scoured and fresh to the smell.'

A lot of voices around Cynlais applauded his willingness to undergo torment by Uriah's torch.

'Now tell me, Cynlais, my boy,' began Uriah. 'I have now watched you in three carnivals, and each time you've put me down for the count with worry and shock. Let me explain why, Mr Chairman. He marches at the head of a hundred young elements, all of them half naked, with little more than the legal minimum covered over with bits of old sheet, and Cynlais himself working up a colossal gleam of frenzy in his eye. He does a short sprint at Powderhall speed and then returns to the head of his retinue looking as if he's just gone off the hinge that very morning. Cynlais is no better dressed than his followers. His bits of sheet are thicker and whiter but they hang even looser about the body. He also has a way, when on the march, of giving his body a violent jerk which makes him look even more demented. This is popular among the thoughtless, and I have heard terrible shrieks of approval from some who are always present at these morally loose-limbed events. But I warn Cynlais that one day he will grossly overdo those pagan leaps and find his feet a good yard to the north of his loin cloth, and a frost on his torso that will finish him for such events as the Powderhall Dash, and even for the commonplace carnality that has been his main hobby to date. His band also plays "Colonel Bogey", an ominous tune even when played by the Meadow Prospect Silver Jubilee Band in full regalia. But Coleman's boys play it at slow march tempo as if to squeeze the last drop of significance out of it. Now tell me, Coleman, what's the meaning of all this? What lies behind these antics, boy? What are you supposed to be, and I ask with a real fear of being answered.'

'Dervishes,' said Cynlais Coleman. 'We are dervishes, Mr Smayle.'

'Dervishes? What are they?'

'A kind of fanatic. We got the idea from Edwin Pugh the Pang there. When we told him that we were very short of fabric for our costumes and that we'd got no objection to going around looking shameless, out he came with this suggestion that we should put on a crazed, bare, prophetic look, as if we'd just come in from the desert with an old sunstroke and a fresh revelation.'

Uriah was now nodding his head and looking horrified as if his finger, eroded and anguished by a life's inquiry, had now found and fondled the central clod from which all the darkness of malignity flowered.

'You've been the tool of some terrible plotters, Cynlais. And is that leap to show that you are now shaking the sand out of your sash?'

'Oh no. I'm not worried about the sand at all, Mr Smayle. This leap in the air is just to show that I am the leader of these Dervishes, the Mad Mahdi. I got a lot of information about him from that very wise voter who never shifts from the Reading Room downstairs, Jedediah Knight the Light.'

'I'm here,' said a voice from the back. It was Jedediah Knight, resting his eyes in the shadows of the back row and looking, as he always did, shocked by understanding and wearied by the search for things that merit the tribute of being understood. 'But I told him that the Mahdi would never have advanced against the Empire playing so daring a tune and with so little on.'

'What do you say to these charges, Cynlais?' asked Gomer.

'Fair enough, Gomer,' said Cynlais. 'When we get enough

money for new costumes we'll come in out of the Middle East at a fast trot.'

'Any more, Mr Smayle?' asked Gomer.

'A lot more. I have a pint of gall on my mind about that woman's band organised by Georgie Young but that will have to wait.'

He made for the door with long, urgent strides and the two ushers fell back.

'Goodnight,' we all shouted, but the sound that came back from Uriah was just a blur.

'Come on, Edwin,' said Milton Nicholas. 'Let's go and have some tea and beef extract at Tasso's.'

Later that night, at Paolo Tasso's Coffee Tavern, my Uncle Edwin was a lot less serene than usual. Over a glass of scalding burdock, which he drank because someone had told him it made a man callous and jocose, he admitted that he'd been thinking a lot about what Uriah Smayle had said. He made it clear to us that he was in no way siding with Uriah. The pageantry of life had long passed us by in Meadow Prospect and he was glad of the colour and variety brought into our streets by the costumes worn by some of the boys. It would help us, he said, to recover from the sharp clip behind the ear dealt us by the Industrial Revolution. But all the same, he claimed, he could see dangers in this eruption of Mediterranean flippancy and joy.

'We have worn ourselves over the years bald and bandy trying to bring a little thought and uplift to this section of the fringe. Not even a Japanese shirt shrinks more swiftly than awareness. It's been cold, lonely work trying to push the ape back into the closet. Now with all these drum beats and marching songs the place could well become a mental boneyard overnight.'

There was such a plangent tolling in his voice that the steam ceased to rise from his burdock and Tasso offered to warm it for him again, but Uncle Edwin said that at that moment a stoup of cold cordial was just the thing for him.

11

But few of us agreed with Uncle Edwin. For all the young a tide of delight flowed in with the carnivals. At first we had two bands in Meadow Prospect; Cynlais Coleman's Dervishes and the Boys from Dixie. The Boys from Dixie wore black suits and we never got to know where voters with so little surplus to buy bottles ever got the cork from to make themselves look so dark. They were good marchers, though, and it was impressive to see these one hundred and twenty jet-black pillars moving down the street in perfect formation playing 'Swanee' in three lines of harmony.

There were some who said it was typical of a gloomy place like Meadow Prospect that it should have one band walking about in no tint save sable and looking like an instalment of eternal night, while another, Cynlais Coleman's, left you wondering whether to give it a good clap or a strong strait-jacket. But we took some pride from the fact that at marching the Boys from Dixie could not be beaten. Their driller and coach was a cantankerous and aged imperialist called Georgie Young the Further Flung, a solitary and chronic dissenter from Meadow Prospect's general radicalism. Georgie had fought in several of our African wars and Uncle Edwin said it gave Georgie some part of his youth back to have this phalanx of darkened elements wheeling and turning every whipstitch at his shout of command.

Most of the bands went in for vivid colours, though a century of chapel-bound caution had left far too little coloured fabric to go around. If any voter had any showy stuff at home he was well advised to sit tight on the box, or the envoy of some band would soon be trundling off with every stitch of it to succour some colleagues who had been losing points for his band by turning out a few inches short in the leg or deficient in one sleeve. We urged Georgie Young that the Boys from Dixie should brighten themselves up a little, with a yellow sash or even a scarlet fez, a tight-fitting and easily made article which gave a very dashing look to the Tredomen Janissaries, a Turkish body. But Georgie was obdurate. His phobias were down in a lush meadow and grazing hard. It was black from tip to toe or nothing, he said. However, he relented somewhat when he formed the first women's band. These were a broad-bodied, vigorous crew, strong on charabanc outings that finished on a note of blazing revelry with these elements drinking direct from the petrol tank. Their band had uniforms made roughly of the colour and pattern of the national flag. The tune they played on their gazookas was 'Rule, Britannia'. They began well every time they turned out, but they were invariably driven off-key by their shyer members who could not keep their minds on the score of 'Rule, Britannia' while their Union Jacks kept slipping south with the convulsive movements of quick marching on sudden slopes. They had even called in Mathew Sewell the Sotto as musical adviser and Mathew had given them a grounding in self-confidence and sol-fa. But they went as out of tune as ever. Jedediah Knight the Light, fresh from a short brush with Einstein, said that if they got any worse they would surely reach the bend in musical space which would bring them willy-nilly back to the key first given them by Sewell the Sotto on his little tuning fork. Nevertheless, both of Georgie's bands, the dour Boys from Dixie and the erratic Britannias, had a smartness that completely eclipsed Cynlais Coleman's bedraggled covey in their flapping fragments of sheet.

So it was decided by the group that met at Tasso's that the time had come to arrange a new deal for the Dervishes. It was agreed that they were altogether too inscrutable for an area so in need of new and clear images.

It was left to Mathew Sewell, who knew more about the bands than anybody else and had operated as a judge in half a dozen smaller carnivals, to put the matter to Cynlais.

Cynlais came along to Tasso's one Thursday night for a talk with his critics. It was still July but Tasso had his big stove on full in the middle of the shop because he had a

13

group of older clients who had never been properly warm since the flood of 1911. Tea all round was ordered and Mathew Sewell stood in the middle of the room, with his hand up, ready to start, but he had to wait a few minutes for the hissing of the tea urn and the rattling of teacups to abate. As a specialist in the head voice, he hated to speak in a shout.

After a sip of tea Sewell summarised for the benefit of those who were new to this issue of Cynlais' band the findings of Smayle and the other censors. Then he addressed Cynlais directly:

'So you see, Cynlais, there are no two twos about it. You've got to put a stop to this business of going about half nude. It's out of place in such a division as this. I speak as an artist and without malice. But it's about time you and the boys dressed in something a bit more tasteful. Something soft and sensuous, that's what we want.'

Cynlais drank his tea while Uncle Edwin stroked the back of his head, encouraging him to be lucid. Then Cynlais put up his hand to show Edwin that the message had worked and he said:

'I say to you, Mathew, what I said to Uriah Smayle and Ogley Floyd the Flame and those other very fierce elements. Get us the costumes and we'll all be as soft and sensuous as you like. Like cream.'

'That's the spirit,' said Mathew. 'Think it over now, and when you're fitted out consult me about the music and I'll prescribe some tune with a lullaby flavour that you can march to.' Mathew threw such hints of the soporific into the word 'lullaby' that some of the people in Tasso's looked disturbed, as if afraid that if Sewell were given a free wand Cynlais' band would be the first in the area to wind up asleep on the kerb halfway through the carnival. Mathew saw their expression and, always averse to argument, said: 'I've got to go now. Bono notte, Signor Tasso.'

'So long, Mathew,' we all said, feeling a certain shabbiness on our tongues. Cynlais was staring at the door that had just shut behind Mathew.

'Did you hear that?' asked Cynlais. 'Oh he's so smooth and operatic, that Sewell the Sotto. A treat.' He turned to Tasso, who was leaning over the counter in his long white shop coat, his toffee hammer sticking out of the breast pocket, his face grey, joyless but unwaveringly sympathetic. 'Don't you like to have Sewell come out with these little bits of Italian, Tasso?'

'It is true, Cynlais,' said Tasso. 'More than once Signor Sewell the Sotto has eased the burden of my old longing for Lugano.'

Gomer Gough the Gavel got order once again by tapping with his cup on the cast-iron fireguard.

'Now let's get down to this,' said Gomer. 'We've got to fit Cynlais up with a band that will make a contribution to beauty and keep Uriah Smayle out of the County Clinic. We can't leave the field undisputed to Georgie Young and his Boer War fancies.' There was a silence for a minute. Hard thought scoured the inside of every head bent towards the stove as history was raked for character and costume suitable for Cynlais and his followers. Tasso tapped *on* the counter with his toffee hammer to keep the meditation in rhythm. Then Gomer looked relieved as if he had just stepped in from a high wind. We all smiled to welcome his revelation but we stopped smiling when he said:

'Have you got any money, Cynlais?'

'Money? Money?' said Cynlais and our eyebrows backed him up because we thought Gomer Gough's question pointless at that point in our epoch.

'Forget that I asked,' said Gomer. 'But I think it's a shame that a boy like you who made so much at the coal face and at professional running should now be whittled down to a loincloth for the summer and a double-breasted waistcoat for the winter.' Gomer's eyes wandered around the room until they landed on Milton Nicholas. 'Come here, Milton.

You've been looking very nimble-witted since you were voted on to the Library committee. How do you think Cynlais Coleman could get hold of some money to deck out his band in something special? I mean some way that won't have Cynlais playing his last tune through the bars of the County Keep.'

'Well, he's still known as Coleman the Comet for his speed off the mark. Wasn't it Paavo Nurmi, the great Finn, who once said that it wouldn't surprise him if Cynlais Coleman turned out to be the only athlete ever to be operated on for rockets in the rear?' We all nodded yes but felt that Milton had probably never heard of this Nurmi until that morning and was only slipping in the name to make a striking effect. Gomer urged Milton to forget the Finn and get back to the present. 'Let him find somebody who wants to hire a fast runner,' added Milton.

'In this area at the moment, Milton, even an antelope would have to make Welsh cakes and mint toffee on the side to make both ends meet. Be practical, boy.'

'I'm being practical. I heard today that a group of sporting elements in Trecelyn with a definite bias against serious thought are going to stage a professional sprint with big cash prizes. Comes off in three weeks.'

'Don't forget that Cynlais is getting on a bit,' said Teilo Dew, 'for this high-class running anyway. I've heard him wheeze a bit on the sharper slopes.'

'Trust Teilo Dew the Doom to chip in with an item like that,' said Milton bitterly. 'Whenever Teilo talks to you he's peering at you from between his two old friends, Change and Decay. In three weeks Cynlais could be at his best and if you boys could take up a few collections to lay bets on him we'd have a treasury.

'That's a very backward habit, gambling,' said Uncle Edwin.

'Remind me to hire a small grave for the scruples of Edwin Pugh the Pang,' said Gomer. 'Right. That's how we'll raise the cash. Off to bed with you now, Cynlais. You've got to be as fit as a fiddle for the supreme test. No more staying up till twelve and drinking hot cordial in Tasso's.'

Cynlais had heard very little of all this. He had been staring into the fire and pondering on what Mathew Sewell had said. He was shocked when he suddenly found supporters coming from all over the shop and helping him to his feet and leading him with half a dozen lines of advice at the same time.

'Don't sleep crouched, Coleman; it obstructs the pipes.'

'Keep even your dreams chaste, Cynlais; if the libido played hell with Samson, what mightn't it do to you?'

'An hour's sleep before midnight is worth two after.'

'Slip Coleman some of those brown lozenges, Tasso, the ones that deepen the breathing.'

'A foot race is a kind of battle, Cynlais. Make a plan for every foot.'

Then Teilo Dew the Doom waved them all to silence and started to tell Cynlais about some very noted foot runner in the zone who had raced and died about two hundred years ago after outpacing all the fleeter animals and breaking every record. Everybody was glad to hear Teilo Dew opening out on what for him was a comparatively blithe topic but expressions went back to normal when Teilo reached the climax of his tale. At the end of this man's last race his young bride had clapped him on the back and the runner had dropped down dead.

'I know that you are not married, Cynlais,' said Teilo, 'and that you have few relatives who would want to watch you run or do anything else, but there are several voters in Meadow Prospect who would find real relish in hanging around the finishing tape and giving you a congratulatory whack just in the hope of sending you lifeless to the ground.'

Cynlais shook himself free from his supporters and was going to ask the meaning of all this fuss but Tasso just raised his toffee hammer solemnly, which is what he always did when he wished to say that he, too, was foxed.

17

We all joined in the task of helping Cynlais regain his old tremendous speed. We got him training every night up on the waun, the broad, bleak, wind filled moorland above the town. Sometimes Cynlais was like a stag, and our only trouble was to keep up with him and give him tips and instructions and fit his neck back when he went flying over molehills. At first he was a bit stiff around the edges owing to a touch of rheumatism from standing in too many High Street breezes in the role of dervish. Milton Nicholas got some wheel-grease from the gasworks, where he was a leading fitter, and Uncle Edwin, whose sympathy of soul made his fingers just the thing for slow massage, rubbed this stuff into Cynlais until both he and Cynlais got so supple they had to be held upright for minutes on end.

We looked after Cynlais' nourishment, too, for his diet had been scraggy over the last few months. Teilo Dew approached that very sullen farmer Nathan Wilkins up on the top of the hill we called Merlin's Brow, and asked him for some goat milk. Wilkins took pleasure in saying no loudly for as long as Dew was within earshot, and even the goat was seen to shake its head from side to side. So Teilo bypassed Nathan Wilkins and approached the goat direct, and in no time we had Cynlais growing stronger daily. But there was still something jerky and unpredictable in some of his movements. So Gomer Gough and Uncle Edwin decided to consult their friend Willie Silcox. He was called Silcox the Psyche because he was the greatest tracker in our valley of those nameless beasts that roam our inward jungles. If Silcox saw anyone with a look of even slight perplexity on his face he would be out with the guidebook and fanning them with Freud before they could start running. He had analysed so many people into a state of dangerous confusion that the town's joint diaconate had advised him to go back to simple religious mania as being a lot safer and easier on the eyes because you could work up to full heat without reading a word. Silcox had just told the joint diaconate that he was watching them closely and making notes.

A week before the race at Trecelyn we met Willie Silcox at Tasso's. Silcox was leaning over the counter and we all saw as we came in that he had never looked or felt more penetrating. Tasso, who was all for indirection and compromise as the right climate for the catering trade, had shifted away from Silcox and was standing very close to the urn. People claiming to be forthrightly wise frightened the wits out of Tasso. At the sight of us Silcox waved us to stillness while he finished off a quick note he was giving Tasso on what he thought the joint effects of exile and the cash nexus would be on a middle-aged Italian. Tasso said nothing but put his head right against the urn for greater comfort.

'Have a beef extract with us, Willie,' said Gomer. 'Glad you were able to come, boy.'

'Thank you, Gomer. What mental stoppage have you got for me to disperse now?'

'Oh I'm all right. My pipes were never more open. It's Cynlais Coleman I'm worried about.'

'Look, Gomer. Before we go any further, let me make this clear. To prescribe a pill for the mentally ill the patient must have a mind. That's in the rule book and that's the first smoke signal I would like you to send out to Coleman. That element, mentally, is still unborn. What makings of a mind he might still have had he not dropped into the bin years ago by trying to outrun the wind, and setting up as a great lover in an area that favours a slow humility in affairs of the heart.'

'Don't quibble, Willie. Cynlais isn't running as well as he should and we want the cure.'

'All right. Take me to where I can see him and if I can find a pole long enough to reach the end of Coleman's furthest cranny I'll give you a report and charge you for the pole because I'll never get it back after a journey like that.'

The next night we went with Willie Silcox up to the waun.

Cynlais and a group of supporters were already there and Cynlais was finishing a trial sprint. We could hear as we approached shouts like: 'Come on, Cynlais.' 'Let's have you Coleman.' 'Don't look around, boy.' 'Show us your real paces, Comet.'

Then we heard Cynlais run headlong into the group around the tape, sending several of them spinning, and we could see that he himself was lurching and gasping painfully. 'Well done,' said Uncle Edwin without conviction.

Cynlais was making noises like a pump, and writhing. Milton Nicholas was standing over Cynlais and looking as if the campaign had reached some sort of crisis.

'Put your head between your legs and squeeze hard, Cynlais boy. That'll cool you off.'

Cynlais tried to do this and went into a brief convulsion. Several voters told Milton Nicholas to mind his own business, which was gas fitting. And there were a few very shrewd elements in the group who said they would not be surprised to find that Milton Nicholas had laid a week's wages on all the other runners but Cynlais in that race at Trecelyn.

'The aim of Nicholas,' I heard one of them say, 'is to get Coleman into a knot and let him choke.'

Gomer Gough turned to Willie Silcox, who had not taken his eyes off Cynlais.

'Well, Willie. What's your diagnosis?'

'Easy,' said Willie, and from the offhand, flippant way in which he said it we thought he was going to suggest that Cynlais be saddled in harness with Wilkins' goat and told to forget about foot-racing. 'Easy. Do you notice the way he seems to pause sometimes in his running and look back?'

'He does it all the time,' said Uncle Edwin. 'He hardly ever looks straight in front.'

'That's a habit he got into while acting as the Mad Mahdi. All fanatics are persecution maniacs and anybody who introduces Mahometan overtones into the Celtic fringe was bound to hit some kind of top note. Cynlais has now got into the way of looking over his shoulder even in the middle of the waun where his shoulder is about the only thing in sight. And again, that band of Cynlais' contains some torpid boys even for gazooka players, and Cynlais is so fleet he has to keep turning to make sure that he and they are still in the same town. But Coleman's real trouble is love.'

'Love?' asked Gomer Gough and Uncle Edwin and it was clear from their tone that they were now both sorry that they had brought Silcox up the mountain at all.

'Love,' repeated Willie Silcox in exactly the voice of a sanitary inspector making a report to the borough surveyor.

'But Cynlais told me only two days ago that he was no longer worried about this impulse.'

'I've only got to look at a man and I can sniff the urge to love and be loved, however deep and quiet it flows. For months Cynlais has been hopelessly in love with that girl, Moira Hallam.'

'Moira Hallam? That dark, blazing-eyed girl from Sebastopol Street?'

'That's the one. The thoughts that that girl inspires in a single day would fill a whole shelf in the Institute and you'd need a strong binding to keep them in the case.'

'And she's turned Cynlais down?'

'She looks at him with disgust and treats him with contempt.'

'But wouldn't this make Cynlais run even better, to show off?'

'You don't know, Gomer, what a cantankerous article the mind is. Even as he runs Cynlais looks down at the fine, big chest under his singlet and becomes aware of his frustrated passions. It's a wall, a cruel blank wall. His heart breaks his nose against it. His limbs wince and they lose pace.'

'Willie,' said Gomer, 'I can never listen to you without feeling that you put a new and terrible complexion on this planet.'

'Anything to oblige. And let me warn you about this Moira Hallam. She is an imperialist of the flesh, very ruthless. You know that old widower, Alfie Cranwell. He had money saved to provide the deposit on a headstone for the grave of his deceased wives. Blew the lot on a watch for this Moira Hallam. But he would have found the headstone softer. She works in that cake shop they call the Cosmo. Cranwell kept hanging about the shop nipping in and wolfing cakes despite strong warnings about sugar from his doctor. Died of a surfeit. All this Moira did was boast about the bonus she had from the manageress of the Cosmo on the brisk selling she had done to Cranwell in the last weeks of his passion.'

Gomer and Uncle Edwin tut-tutted as if this girl was just another in a long series of obstructions they had found giving life a dark and strangled look.

'Well, thank you, Willie. We'll bear your report in mind.'

But Willie Silcox was not listening. He was staring past Gomer at some member of the group around Cynlais, beneath the apparently bland surface of whose days Willie's dowser had sensed some concealed runnel of trouble. This man was smiling quite broadly at something Milton Nicholas had just said and he did not know how lucky he still was with Willie Silcox standing at a safe distance from him.

Later that evening I was walking along the main street of Meadow Prospect with my Uncle Edwin, helping him to make a casual check on the number of people who seemed to be at ease on the earth. The first person we found who really seemed to be so was Gomer Gough the Gavel, and before Edwin could tell Gomer about this Gomer was hurrying the both of us down a side street.

'Where to now, Gomer?' asked Uncle Edwin tartly.

'Moira Hallam's.'

'What for?'

'To talk her out of this nonsense of frustrating and slowing down Cynlais Coleman the Comet. You heard what Willie Silcox said. Between being a dervish and a disappointed lover, it's a wonder Cynlais can walk, let alone run at his old Powderhall lick.'

'Oh leave me out of this, Gomer. Here were Iolo and I, on a serious social beat, staring at the voters and trying to estimate how many mental inches separated them from the County Clinic. Leave us be. I'm not interested in Cynlais anymore and I don't know this Moira Hallam, except to feel vaguely grateful to her for having helped to shuffle off Alfie Cranwell, who was, as a ram, indiscriminate, irrational and a nuisance.'

'I want you to come along to Moira's house for the very reason that you're called Edwin Pugh the Pang. You are so full of pity the sight and sound of you would bring tears even to the eyes of Nathan Wilkins, the only gorsedd stone ever to opt for hillside farming and working in trousers of heavy corduroy. You can play on the feelings of this Moira. Don't be surprised if, at the door of the Hallam home, I introduce you as Cynlais Coleman's father, who took up thinking instead of sprinting.'

Uncle Edwin was on the point of opening his mouth to tell Gomer Gough to go and jump into the deeper reach of the Moody, our river, when Gomer stopped outside one of a long row of identical houses and said: 'Here we are.'

I was about to move off but he held me back and said he preferred a mixed delegation.

'If we need a statement from the youth of Meadow Prospect, Iolo, to support our own pleas, we'd like to have you on hand. Just turn a possible statement over in your mind while you're waiting.'

The door opened to Gomer's knock. Mrs Hallam, the mother of Moira, was a big, vigorous woman whose eyes and arms gave the impression of being red and steaming.

'Oh good evening to you, Mrs Hallam,' said Gomer, with what he thought was a courtly bow copied from

Cunninghame Graham, whom he had once seen at a socialist rally, but Gomer was at least a foot too short to make this gesture look anything but an attempt to duck for safety. Mrs Hallam sprang back into the passage, thinking that Gomer was going to butt her.

'What do you want?' she said. 'If you are after my husband to join that old Discussion Group again you can save your wind. The last time he went the topic was capital punishment and hanging and so forth and he had the migraine for a week. Anything about pressure on the neck and the poor dab is off.'

'No, we are not here about that. It's about your daughter, Moira.'

'All day long there's a knock on the door and it's the same old tale. Moira, Moira, Moira. But you are the two oldest performers to turn up so far, I'll say that. Why don't you two boys stick to debating?'

Uncle Edwin groaned and came to flatten himself against the patch of wall against which I had already flattened myself trying to think out what the youth of Meadow Prospect might have to say to Mrs Hallam. Uncle Edwin spoke in a dramatic whisper:

'Here am I, my senses in this field of carnality out for the count since 1913, and I have to stand here and listen to this prattle.'

Gomer pulled Edwin back into the field of play.

'We are here, Mrs Hallam, on behalf of that fine runner, Cynlais Coleman.' It was clear from the drop of Mrs Hallam's jaw that she had never heard a sentence she had followed less well.

'What's he running for? Whenever my husband runs he gets the migraine.'

Gomer slipped into his voice the fine bel canto effect he used when he quoted the Bible at public meetings to support social change.

'Mrs Hallam, Cynlais Coleman loves your daughter.'

Uncle Edwin groaned again and I, hoping it might help us to get off that doorstep, groaned with him. There was also a short whimper from beyond the dimly lighted passageway which I took to be Mr Hallam switching on to a fresh track of his endemic migraine. But Gomer went straight on: 'He's losing sleep and health over her, Mrs Hallam. We were wondering if you...'

'Not a hope,' said Mrs Hallam, and she seemed triumphant that after thirty years of indeterminate and depressing interviews at that front door she had at last come across one topic about which she could be utterly final. 'Moira was in the Trecelyn Amateur Operatics last winter. They did *Carmen* and now she's daft about that baritone Moelwyn Cox, who took the part of the toreador. You ought to see his velvet coat and his satin breeches. So tight, so shiny, a treat.'

Edwin pulled strongly at Gomer's coat.

'Gomer,' he said, very softly, 'could I make a short statement here that would cover both love and bullfighting?'

'No,' said Gomer, so quietly Mrs Hallam thrust her head forward to keep a check on what was going on. 'Sebastopol Street is no place to be discussing ethics. You know that, boy.' He raised his voice and then said to Mrs Hallam in a voice that came as close to the bedside manner as Gomer would ever get on the street side of the front door: 'Mrs Hallam, how is your husband's migraine now?'

Mrs Hallam looked at Gomer suspiciously. She was probably marshalling in her mind memories of some of the gloomy specifics for mankind's many ails which had been recommended at the Discussion Group of which her husband had been a transient member.

'Oh, not bad,' she said. 'Twice a week he wears a turban of brown paper soaked in vinegar and it's like having chips in the house. A treat.' She raised her arm and smiled as if wishing to convince Gomer that she regarded this turban motif as the last word, and she wanted no hints from him or Uncle Edwin.

'Will you put in a word with Moira for Cynlais Coleman?'

'I'll mention it. But only because you asked about the migraine. Sympathy is what matters. But I can tell you now, Moira is daft about Moelwyn Cox.'

We made our way back down the street. Darkness had fallen. Our steps were loud and had a flavour. Gomer Gough was staring at the great-looking shape of Merlin's Crown. Uncle Edwin was shaking his head in desperation and warning me in general terms not to get mixed up in anything, not with Gomer Gough or Silcox as a partner anyway.

On the day of the Trecelyn Sports a large body of us left Meadow Prospect to see Cynlais run. There was a huge crowd and the sports field, converted by the flimsiest manoeuvres from being an ordinary field, was full, well-flagged and happy. Cynlais was right in the middle of us and he had been on edge during that walk to Trecelyn by having Uncle Edwin sidling up to him on the pavement and giving him a little supplementary massage.

'Stop doing that, for God's sake, Edwin. You never know what people will think.'

He broke away from us as we entered the field, glad, for a few seconds, to be rid of us.

'How do you think Cynlais is feeling, Gomer?' asked Uncle Edwin.

'Fine, Edwin. Can't you see he looks fine?'

'Frankly, I think there is a very lax, bemused look about him. He doesn't seem too solid on his pins to me. Milton Nicholas says he's been over trained and worn down to the canvas by having to dodge those molehills up on the waun while travelling faster than light, and making sense of the axioms of Willie Silcox the Psyche while travelling mentally not at all.' Uncle Edwin thrust his lips out to show that he was sick and tired of giving consideration to Cynlais. Then his face lit up. 'They've certainly enjoyed full employment, those moles up on the waun. What the hell is their motive in shifting all that earth?'

Milton Nicholas, a nature lover, was going to explain when Gomer Gough broke in roughly:

'Don't go saying things like that to Cynlais. The race is due in twenty minutes and I don't want to upset him. For temperament he's worse than any tenor. I told him that Mrs Hallam was going to do all she could for him. That'll buck him up a bit. But I'm taking no chances. You know how upset he was last Monday?'

'Last Monday?' Edwin for a week had been busy preparing a monograph for the Discussion Group proving that the Celt must at one time have been half drowned in ale and half crazed by lust to have been so busy scalping the drink trade and the flesh ever since.

'What happened last Monday?'

'Cynlais' band and the Boys from Dixie went to the carnival at Tregysgod and Georgie Young didn't finish last only because Cynlais was there before him. It's enough to drive Matthew Sewell the Sotto off his head notes. Cynlais' band lost points for obscurity and brazen indecency, so the judges said, and Georgie's platoon was denounced as too sombre, too austere. It was a terrible day for Meadow Prospect. So I went to Kitchener Caney.'

We drew closer. We were all astonished. Caney was a whimsical mixer of simples, a most inaccurate herbalist and healer.

'Caney the Cure?' asked Uncle Edwin. 'Caney the Herbs?'

'That's him. Compared with Caney, Merlin was a learner. He was most interested when I told him about Cynlais. He says that slowness and sadness are both great evils and that somewhere in fields is some tiny plant that has the full answer to them both.'

'And Caney's the boy to find it. And when he spreads it around there'll be no one around to be sad or slow.'

'He gave me a herbal concoction for Cynlais. He made no charge although the bottle he gave me was the largest I've seen containing herbs. It's called "Soul Balm". That's what it says on the label. It makes the heart serene and oblivious and it sounds to like the sort of thing most of the voters ought to be belting at the livelong day.'

'Cynlais is certainly oblivious,' said Edwin. 'Look at him over there now. He looks as dull as a bat.'

'I got Tasso to slip Cynlais the balm in his last cocoa and for the next few hours his mind will be sunlit.'

Cynlais came towards us. He was dejected and he was shooting his limbs perversely in different directions.

'Here he is now,' said Gomer, very cheerfully. 'Just look at him, Edwin. I've seen taller men, wiser men, but fitter and faster, never!'

Cynlais gave us all a plaintive, pleading look. 'I've just seen Moira over there, by that flagpole.'

'I see her. Eyes made to glow like headlamps by some artifice or other and her skirt three inches shorter than it was last week. Is this blatant provocation or is she tucking the thing up for wading?'

'Could I nip over and have a chat with her, Gomer?'

'Not before the race. She's got even the flagpole bending over for a look. Keep your mind on the job in hand and think of the prize money that will get you out of those shameful costumes you wear as dervishes.' Gomer scanned the field. 'I see some very keen-looking athletes here. Boys who pause only to breed and feed. You'll have to stay calm as a rock and sharp as a knife to win the prize against this competition. If you linger for any traffic with that Moira Hallam we'd have to launch you from the starting line on a stretcher and the Trecelyn Silver Band over there would have to switch from "Anchors Aweigh" to that very slow piece from Saul.'

Cynlais took one look at Moira Hallam. It was too much for him. He went bouncing towards her, using the same clownish and ataxic gait as before.

'Come back here, you jay,' shouted Gomer. 'Oh, dammo!'

'Caney the Cure is at work here,' said Uncle Edwin. 'He

probably put some ingredient in that mixture that blows every gonad into a flame. In a moment you'll see that Moira Hallam shinning up that flagpole and Coleman will be just one hot breath behind her scorching off the paintwork.'

Gomer took me by the shoulder and told me to stay close to Cynlais and keep reminding him of his duty to Meadow Prospect, and Uncle Edwin gave me a few discouraging things about romantic love to pass on to Cynlais if the chance arose.

Cynlais stood a modest five or six feet from Moira. I stared at Moira, my senses candent and amazed. Her eyes had the searing, purposive lustre of opened furnaces and in the hem of her skirt, almost as far away from the ground as the flag on the pole, a new dimension of arrogance was given to sex. Moira's body and urges were meant to last and it was a relief to turn from her to study the resigned limpness of the flag, from which the starch of a dynamic tribalism had long since been laved.

Cynlais just stood there with a dropped jaw and I had to give him a nudge to remind him that if he did not want Gomer and Milton Nicholas and the other fanciers to be closing in on him and applying violence, the best thing he could do was to deliver some simple message to Moira and marshal his thoughts for a bit of foot-racing. Cynlais pulled his jaw back into position and a beauty of longing settled on his face. In that mood he could have come out with a splurge of words that would have struck a new top note in bedroom rhetoric. But all he said was:

'Hullo, Moira. Oh, it's good to see you again after so long.'

'Don't talk to me, Cynlais Coleman,' said Moira. Her voice was sharply impatient, but even Moira's wrath had an edge of lubricious softness. 'You ought to be ashamed of yourself. First of all jumping about like a madman at the head of that band, half naked and putting the preachers on edge, then sending those two jokers to my front door to get around my mother, indeed. What kind of serpent are you developing into, Cynlais?'

'They didn't tell me they were going, honest. Gomer and Edwin were working off their own bats, and you know what a pair of terrors they are for being deep and unexpected. Can I see you tonight, Moira?'

'Not tonight or ever. I'm meeting Moelwyn Cox in front of the Gaiety at seven. Plush seats, back row, one and three, made to measure. Have you ever seen Moelwyn in his bullfighter's uniform? After that you'll always look very colourless to me, Cynlais. Has your heart ever been in the orange groves of Seville?'

'Never. You know that, Moira. The furthest I've been is that bus trip to Tintern Abbey with the Buffs.' The last word came out like a sort of groaning gasp, as if someone had knocked all the wind out of Cynlais from behind. I thought this a very poor augury for the race and I was on the point of giving Cynlais a monitory kick on the shin when Moira let out a laugh that was so loud, contemptuous and yet passionately stimulant it put her instantly under the same shawl as Carmen. Gomer Gough was making that very point when we got back into earshot of the Meadow Prospect group.

'You hear that laugh?' Gomer was asking. 'The sight of Moelwyn Cox's satin breeches has got that girl into a state where she could give a night-school course on lust as a tactic. Come on, Cynlais. Forget about Seville and get your knicks on. The only answer to Moelwyn Cox showing his cloak to the bull is you showing your butts to all humanity by leading the field here today.'

'I don't go all the way with Nietzsche,' said Uncle Edwin, 'but the only recipe is the brutal force of triumph for that sort of girl.'

Cynlais looked puzzled by that statement and Gomer had to explain. Then Cynlais looked downcast again.

'I couldn't look at my knicks today, Gomer, not after that. I haven't got the heart. Not after that.'

'Come on,' said Milton Nicholas. 'Think of the prize money.'

'Aye, and the stinging way those judges spoke to you last Monday,' said Gomer. 'One of them said that your band had undone a whole century of progressive work by the Sunday School union. And he said, too, that as soon as they could raise the fare to Africa the whole pack of you would be on the boat addressed to the jungle.'

Uncle Edwin was staring into the further distance and following the movements of a very large man who was clearly an official and wearing the type of multilateral hat worn by Sherlock Holmes, but this hat was in a kind of tweed material and untidier than the hats we have seen on Holmes.

'Look over there,' said Edwin. 'There's that big auctioneer, Erasmus John the Going Gone, wearing a cloth hat and shaking his gun to show that he's the starter.'

'He's a very cunning boy, that Erasmus John,' said Milton, 'and not only at auctions either. I hear he's got a favourite of his own competing here today.' Milton jumped forward and frightened the wits out of the abstracted Cynlais by urgently grasping his sleeve. 'Keep your eye on Erasmus John the Going Gone, Cynlais. Watch that he doesn't confuse you. Politically and morally that man has for thirty years been master of the false alarm. See that he keeps his auctioneering slogans out of the formula used for starting this race.'

'All right then. For your sake that's all. That Moira... Just one look from her and she scoops the heart right out of me, leaving not even the wish to whistle.' Cynlais straightened his back and gave his head a little shake. 'But I've got it in for that Erasmus John. He was one of the judges at Tregysgod last Monday. He came to see us after the judging, sneering and laughing.'

'I was there,' said Milton. 'I heard him and the things he said were a disgrace for a man who's supposed to keep an open mind. He said that he would like to lay Cynlais as a

31

wreath on the grave of General Gordon who was speared to death by dervishes in the unlimited phase of our imperial adventure. He also said, that as a Christian, he was arranging to have the final mark won by Cynlais' band announced direct by muezzin if the Tregysgod council could throw up some sort of rough minaret. You can imagine how all these references foxed Cynlais and the boys and made them feel that they were standing in a chilling draught of contempt and rejection.'

'Hellish things for draughts, those bits of loose sheeting,' said Cynlais. He waved his arm in goodbye and made his way towards the ramshackle pavilion where the athletes were to change.

'Good luck, Cyn,' we all shouted.

'And watch that Erasmus John,' said Milton Nicholas 'With that length of gun and that style of hat he won't consider today complete until he's shot somebody. Somebody from Meadow Prospect for preference who turns out in carnivals in an overtly anti-British costume. So watch out.'

'I will,' Cynlais shouted back. He tried to make his voice cheerful but we could see that not even his little spurt of rebellion against the insolence of Erasmus John had given him back anything like his usual vim.

'That soul balm of Caney's is wearing off,' said Uncle Edwin.

'Caney should have doubled the dose,' said Gomer, 'but he said it was a tricky mixture. Misery, said Caney, who is a fair hand with an axiom when he tries, has been our favourite tipple for so long it will take a thousand years of experiment with applied gladness to dispel the flavour.'

Uncle Edwin was pointing again. His eye had the aptitude of hawks for singling out significant figures in crowds. 'Isn't that Caney the Cure over there now, Gomer? He's waving at you.'

A man with the hair style of Lloyd George at his bushiest was making his way towards us, holding aloft a stick carved like a totem pole. He had prodded a few voters with this stick to get them out of the way and a few of these people were following Caney with angry faces and telling him to be careful. Caney was gasping and agitated.

'What is it, Mr Caney?' asked Gomer.

'The stuff I gave you for Coleman.'

'The balm,' said four or five voices.

A grimace flashed across the face of Caney the Cure of which we could all taste the unhappiness.

'Balm, balm,' he said, as if trying to reassemble the fragments of a dream that had that very instant been kicked to death. 'I'll tell you about that. The stuff I gave to Coleman wasn't the soul balm after all.'

A wreath of grave expressions formed around Caney and the deep, cautionary voices of the Meadow Prospect group rolled out like drums: 'Buck up, Caney.' 'Have a care there, Kitchener.' 'This is no talk for a magician.'

Caney chuckled but there was no hint of amusement or flippancy in it. We could see that Caney meant this chuckle to be symbolic, a hint that this kind of idiot laughter was the last kiss and farewell of the tragic impulse, that all things, death, love, the senseless plume of space and stars, would all at last come to rest in some kind of cut-rate giggle.

'My wife made a mistake with the gummed label on the bottle. We have a lot of labels and my wife does a lot with the gum because my tongue tickles. She's a fine woman, my wife, but the taste of gum makes her giddy.'

We were all nodding in the most compassionate way because the mention of anyone in a fix even with stuff like gum brought us running up with our sympathy at the ready and fanning away for all we were worth. We urged Caney with our eyes to go on with his statement.

Caney chuckled again, but Uncle Edwin told him that he had our permission to remain sombre.

'That was some very funny stuff that Coleman took actually,' said Caney.

Uncle Edwin put his hand on Caney's shoulder as if to tell him that we were with him all the way, that if Cynlais should now drop down dead before he should even hear the starting gun of Erasmus John the Going Gone, the fact was simply that the angry rat that paces around and around at the heart of the life force had just given Caney one with its shorter teeth, that Coleman and that wrong mixture had been speeding towards each other through space since the moment when the absurd had decided to mould a whole species in its own image. Uncle Edwin tried with very quiet words to make these ideas plain to Caney. But either his words were too quiet or Caney had been too long in traffic with herbs to operate properly in a social context. He looked blank.

We all looked to Gomer Gough. We expected him, after a minute or two of preparation, to peel the ears of Caney with a jet of Old Testament wrath. But Gomer was just looking towards the part of the field where Cynlais and the other runners were reporting to Erasmus John and a clutch of other voters with badges and bits of paper. When he spoke it was in a voice of such softness we were glad that our cult of hymn-singing at all hours had left us with pity sleek and trained as a greyhound on the leash.

'Cynlais is out there, Mr Caney, faced with the hardest race of his life. His running knicks are ill-cut and will expose him to ridicule if not to prosecution. He is flanked by a biased and malevolent body of starters and judges who are not above giving orders to have Coleman strangled with the finishing tape if he should happen to come in first. On top of that, the libido of Coleman is tigerish and currently his head is between the tiger's teeth. His girl is that element with the red blouse standing at the foot of that flagpole. She is five square feet of licence and her name is Moira Hallam. A few minutes ago she gave him a laugh that for sheer contempt and coldness would have frozen a seal. Now you tell me, very jocose, that he has some sinister herb under his belt. What is it?'

'A stirring draught for lazy kidneys,' said Caney, very softly.

'Speak up, Caney,' called the voters on the outer fringe of the group, and Caney repeated what he had said, taking off his slouch in case this might be muffling some of the sound.

'How will it take him?' asked Gomer. 'This draught, how does it operate?'

'It varies,' said Caney. 'Sometimes when it begins its healing work there is a flash of discomfort, and I have known surprised clients come back to me hopping.'

'Hopping? What do you mean, hopping? Let's have the truth, Caney.'

'One leg seems to leave the ground as if trying to kick the kidneys into a brighter life.'

We all drew more closely around Caney and said very quietly: 'Duw, duw, duw!', which was a way we had of invoking God without committing ourselves unduly.

We turned to the part of the field where the sprint was shortly to begin. Erasmus John was entering into the brutal phase of his life as an official. He was dissatisfied with the rate at which the athletes had been coming out of the pavilion and he was prodding the various runners into position with his gun. He was putting some of them, including Cynlais Coleman, on edge and they were threatening to go home if Erasmus did not point the barrel of his weapon the other way.

'The only boy he isn't prodding with that flintlock,' said Milton Nicholas, 'is his own favourite, Keydrich Cooney, that red-thatched, chunky element on the side there, with a scalloped vest and the general bearing of a tamed ape. His speciality used to be cross-country events on muddy terrain and a chance to shove slower rivals into lonely ditches. But he emerged as a runner in sprints when he outpaced two bailiffs who were trying to shove an affiliation writ into Cooney's pocket. Erasmus John will handicap Cooney forward until he is practically biting the tape when the gun

35

goes. See how he's edging on now while Erasmus keeps the other runners in a sweat of anxiety. What Herod did for child welfare Erasmus John will do for foot-racing.'

The gun went off. The crowd surged forward around me and I could see nothing of the race's details. Then there was a shout and a groan and I saw Cynlais Coleman shoot into the air, well in sight even above the taller heads around me. I jumped, too, to see if there was any sign of fresh smoke from Erasmus John's gun because Cynlais looked to me as if he had been shot. For a second the crowd broke and in the gap I saw the red head of Cooney flash past the tape.

It was not until that evening that I learned with any accuracy what had happened. We had led Cynlais home between us. He had refused to get out of his running costume and he looked shattered. He refused to say a word. After we had delivered him to his home we met at Tasso's Coffee Tavern.

Normally when we went into Tasso's the conversation was in full cry even before Tasso got his hand on the hot-water tap. But that night every topic seemed to be lying dead just behind us. Gomer Gough and Uncle Edwin stared at each other, at Tasso and then at themselves in the gleaming side of the urn. Tasso was very much slower than usual getting to work on the taps. He took down a large bottle, fished into it and brought out a wrapped toffee.

'Accept this rum-and-butter toffee, Mr Gough,' said Tasso. 'It will sweeten your mood.' He waited until Gomer had the sweet in his mouth and the first traces of softening in his eye as the sugar struck his palate. 'And what was the foot-race like, Mr Gough? What befell Mr Coleman the Comet?'

For a few moments Gomer could not marshal his words. Then, as the voters of Meadow Prospect often do when they have some outrage to describe, he highlighted some of the principal incidents of his story, with gestures as broad and dramatic as the size of Tasso's shop and the position of the urn would allow.

First he dropped into a crouching position on the floor to invoke the image of Cynlais making ready for the start. Tasso leaned over the counter, concerned, and Uncle Edwin had to tell him that Gomer was all right, just acting. Then Gomer jumped erect, with a cruel, arrogant look on his face to imitate Erasmus John. Gomer's arm was outstretched and his index finger was working violently on an imaginary trigger. He had his hand pointed at the door. Three customers outside peered through the door's glass panel, saw Gomer, and moved up the street, at speed, thinking that Tasso had now had what for a long time had been coming to him, encouraging such clients as Gomer Gough and Uncle Edwin. Tasso told Uncle Edwin that he thought Gomer had now made his point and would he please point whatever it was he was supposed to have in his hand at some other part of the shop.

'In their long history, Tasso, the Celts have done some dubious and disastrous bits of running, but this thing today opened up a new path altogether. Erasmus John the Going Gone, that auctioneer who acts as an official at these events, fired his gun. Cynlais flashed into action and for five seconds he went so fast everybody thought he had left by way of Erasmus' gun. Didn't he, Edwin?'

'Fact,' said Edwin. 'He seemed to be in flight from all the world's heartbreak and shame.'

'Then Caney's cure struck,' said Gomer, and you could almost see the rum-and-butter toffee parting in his mouth to make way for the bitterness of his tone. 'Have you, Tasso, ever seen a man trying to finish a hundred-and-twenty-yard dash on one leg?'

'Not on one leg. Always in Italy both the legs are used.'

'It was a terrible sight. Cynlais gave some fine hops, I'll say that for him. On that form I'd enter him against a team of storks, but against those other boys he was yards behind.

And that Erasmus John the Going Gone running alongside and asking sarcastically if Cynlais would like the stewards to do something about the leg he still had on the ground. I fancied I also saw Erasmus taking a few sly kicks at Cynlais as if he wished to further desolate the parts of the boy's spirit that hadn't yet been laid flat by Caney.'

'And where is he now, the Cynlais?' asked Tasso.

'In bed, trying to explain to his kidneys, which are still moving about inside him like jackie jumpers, about Caney, Caney's wife and her reaction to the gum on the labels that plays such hell with her.'

'It was Moira Hallam that did it,' said Uncle Edwin, sounding as angry as a minor key human being ever will. 'Compared with this business of physical love the Goodwin sands are a meadow. I'd like to make her sorry for the way she flicks acid over the hearts of boys like Cynlais.'

Gomer seconded this, and Tasso did something to set the urn hissing, which was his way of saying that he was behind the motion too.

The following night Milton Nicholas came into the Library and Institute and after a short spell of walking about among the bookshelves and thinking hard about the carnivals, went into the small anteroom where Gomer Gough and Teilo Dew the Doom were locked in a game of chess that seemed to have been going on for several winters.

'I've been thinking about Ephraim Humphries the ironmonger,' said Milton. Gomer Gough and Teilo Dew did not look up or seem surprised. Humphries had for years lived out on a kind of social tundra and his fiats against the pagans of Meadow Prospect were always high on the agenda of the Discussion Group. Ephraim was very comfortably off and he had a great weakness for budgerigars of which he had a front room full. He had three of these birds that could do rough versions of temperance hymns and missionary anthems like 'Row for the shore, sailor, pull for the shore, Heed not that stranded wreck but bend to the oar.' And he had one bird, a very strong, loud performer which had learned the first two bars of the 'Hallelujah Chorus', but this had done something to the bird's tail feathers and it had died. Ephraim's cordial urges had been cooled long since by handling so much cold metal in a shop full of draughts, and he really didn't see why the average human should want to eat, wander or love more than the average budgerigar.

'You know that Ephraim is moral adviser to the carnival committee,' said Milton.

'Yes, we know,' said Gomer. 'Those two bruises on his brow he got from two faints he had when watching Georgie Young's women's band, the Britannias.'

'That's it. He ranks nudity above war as a nuisance. I was at a short meeting tonight after tea. The regional carnival committee. Ephraim was there with a cutting edge. Most of what he said was about his visit last week to the Tregysgod carnival. If he ever gets the sight of Cynlais Coleman and his boys out of his mind his mind will go with it. As for the Britannias he says it's time Georgie Young changed their costume to that of women in purdah so that they can operate from behind some kind of thick screen. But his main phobia is about Coleman, because Willie Silcox the Psyche kept interrupting that Ephraim's obsession with the way the wind kept blowing the Union Jacks against the bodies of the Britannias and showing up their shapes meant that Ephraim was working up to the sexual climax of the century, and that as soon as he caught the Britannias without their gazookas he would proceed to some act of massive ravishment and he would spend the rest of his life dancing on Calvin's grave. At this point that lecherous and bell-like baritone, Dewi Dando the Ding and the Dong, said that if Ephraim did any dancing on Calvin's grave after a session of roistering with those girls in the Britannias it would be strictly by proxy through four bearers. This enraged Ephraim and you could see from his face that his mind had been wallowing a bit in the notions sketched forth by Silcox so he changed tack and stuck to Cynlais Coleman. He's convinced now that what Fawkes was to parliament Coleman is now to morals, a one and fourpenny banger waiting for November. That gave me an idea of how we might get Ephraim to help us.'

'Put a light to Coleman's fuse and shock Humphries out of his wits, you mean?'

'No, no, no! Nothing like that at all.'

'But isn't Humphries dead against the bands? Isn't his task to morally advise them clean out of existence?'

'Not altogether. He says that while they strike him as pretty squalid, if they take people's minds off class rancour, agnosticism and the Sankey award, he's for them, always hoping for the day, he says, when the people generally will find the same release he does in a good funeral or a long argument about Baptism. So why don't we approach Humphries and explain that Cynlais and his boys are puritans at heart and want nothing better than to get hold of some decent, God-fearing costumes so that they can turn out looking less repulsive and frightening to the pious. We could also add that Cynlais has given up his old promiscuity since he came across Moira Hallam and swallowed that draught of Caney's cure. Then we can tap Humphries for some cash. He must have a soft side to his nature or he wouldn't keep all those birds in his front room.'

Teilo Dew and Gomer stared at the chessboard and the stagnant pieces as if they found this game as inscrutable as they had always found Humphries.

'Your mind's just singing, Milton,' said Gomer. 'From what I know of Humphries he probably keeps those birds in his front room just to test for gas. When the birds die Humphries changes the potted shrubs and chalks up a new cautionary text on the wall. He was the grumpiest boy I ever met behind a counter, although I will say that iron at all levels is a pretty sombre trade. He was the one ironmonger who sold paraffin that put out the match. But let's go and see him anyway.'

Gomer and Milton left Teilo to brood over the blockage in the chess game and picked up Uncle Edwin who was sitting in the Reading Room humming a mossy old funeral chant over a brassily authoritative leading article in a national paper that was open in front of him. He invited Gomer and Milton to scan this article. They rushed their eyes down it. The writer had been dealing with the carnival bands and frankly felt that there was something potentially threatening to the State in having such masses of men, with nothing better to do, moving about the streets in march time. He suggested that a monster carnival to end all carnivals be organised, set it in motion with a strong platoon of Guards in the rear to ensure no getaways, then keep the whole procession in motion until it reached the South Pole where they could swap bits of political wisdom with the penguins. When Gomer and Milton finished reading the article they joined Uncle Edwin in humming the last verse of the funeral chant, coming out clearly with the words of the last line which praised the dignity and cheapness of the grave.

'But never mind about that now,' said Gomer. 'Milton has an idea that Ephraim Humphries might supply the money to drag Coleman and his band up into the temperate zone.'

Edwin was not enthusiastic. He said about the only thing he could recommend in the case of Humphries was a load of hot clinker for the man's bleaker and colder urges, but he responded to the glow of enthusiasm in Milton Nicholas' face and we started the journey across the town to the house of Ephraim Humphries.

Humphries lived in one of a group of larger houses on some high ground just outside the town's west side. There was a diamond-shaped pane of dark blue glass in the centre of his door which created an effect exactly halfway between sadness and intimidation. After our first knock we could see Humphries and his wife take up position in the passageway. They peered out at us and it was plain they felt no happiness or confidence at the sight of us. There was an open fanlight above the door through which we could hear most of what they said. They were speaking in whispers but whispers bred on long years in oratorio.

'I count four,' we heard Mrs Humphries say, 'but there may be more arranged on either side of the door.'

'Stop fearing the worst, Harriet,' said Humphries. 'You've never been the same since that lecturer told you your great-grandfather had had his bakehouse cooled in the Chartist troubles. Who are these fellows?'

'Can't tell for sure. There's a shady look about them.'

'That's the blue glass. My own father, seen through that diamond, looks as if he's just come running from the County Keep.'

'I told you you should never have accepted that invitation to go to those carnivals as adviser on morals. These are probably some louts you've offended with your straight talk about how bruises have now taken the place of woad as a darkening element on the moral fabric of the Celt. These men are very likely a group sent here by Cynlais Coleman, the leading dervish, to do you some mischief.' Her tone became strained and sharply informative. 'Do you know that the very word assassin comes from the Middle East where Coleman has his spiritual home. Let's bar the doors.' She made a quick move towards the door and there was a shifting of iron such as we would never normally hear outside a gaol.

'Stop being such a teacher, Harriet,' said Humphries. 'And throw those bolts back. I'd never have had them if they hadn't come to me cheap through the trade.'

The door was opened.

'What is it?' asked Humphries, showing only his head.

'We'd like a word with you, Mr Humphries,' said Gomer, and he gave us the cue with his hand to start smiling in the broadest, most unmalicious way we could manage. This performance was so out of tune with the mood of the times that Mrs Humphries, thinking from the lunatic look of us that we were out to kill them on more general grounds than she had imagined, tried to drag Humphries back into the passage and ram the bolts back home. He threw her off.

'Come on into the front room,' he said, his voice rustling with caution.

We moved slowly behind Humphries into the most tightly packed front parlour we had ever seen. On the wall, frame to frame, as if a broad gap would only aggravate the loneliness that had tormented and killed them on earth, were huge photographs of the most austere voters, a lot of them bearded and all of them frowning and staring straight at Humphries and us.

'Beloved pastors on the right-hand wall and irreplaceable relatives on the left,' said Humphries as he saw us trying to map the great patches of gloom created by those faces. It struck us that with all these elements speaking up for the Black Meadow and the County Assizes on his flank he must have been driven into the ironmongery trade by centuries of inherited ill-feeling about the species. The furniture of the room, and it seemed from the amount of it that Humphries and his wife had both thrown a front-room suite into the marriage chest, was thick with plush and chenille. It made the whole chamber look like the hidden badge of all the world's outlawed or discouraged sensuousness. Our fascinated fingers kept reaching out and stroking the stuff until Humphries, looking convinced that we were all going to unpick and make off with a length of chenille to eke out the costumes of a carnival band, told us to stop it and get to the point. Around the room were eight or nine birdcages and we watched the birds inside with great interest. There might have been a time when the budgerigars had thought of trying to give some light relief to those divines and relatives in the photographs but they had broken their beaks on all that ambient gravity and lost. They now sat on their perches looking as sad and damned and muffled as the gallery of perished censors. Their singing had been soaked futilely into the layers of plush and they had shut up. As we squeezed into the tiny areas of free floor space, with Mrs Humphries pushing hard at Uncle Edwin because she did not fancy the idea of any of our delegation being left with her in the passageway, one of the birds let out a note. It was not gay or musical. It was like the first note of the last post in a low-grade military funeral, heard through rain and trees. It sounded as if the bird thought we had come to bail him out.

Humphries looked up at the bird and said:

'You hear that? You hear that? They might come yet.'

'Oh, nice birds,' said Milton Nicholas with real rapture in his voice. We admired Milton for this because we had never before heard a word of interest, let alone praise, from him on the subject of birds. Once in the Discussion Group he had gone so far as to praise the habit of migration and wheeling off south at the approach of autumn as a tactically sound approach and one which, he hoped, would be copied when man resolved the last cramp of tribal idiocy and took the whole world as his available playground. Milton won his motion that night on the rheumatic vote alone, because there was a whole fleet of voters present stiffened up by winter rains and as badly in need of a stronger sun as of a more encouraging government. Later, Milton qualified those words of approval about birds by saying that he considered pigeon fancying, which at the time was running neck and neck with sex as a life form among the more torpid prolies, a very lulling activity and worthy to be classed as opium for those people who had somehow managed to emerge awake from under the long, soporific cone of our traditional prescriptions.

Humphries let his eyes go right around the room, nodding at each of the cages.

'Would that men were more like them. So bright, so brief, so harmless, and no sorrow in their singing.'

'You're right, boy,' said Milton. 'Good and deep as the singing has been in most of our chapels, I think we've overdone the note of death and desperation in certain types of cadence.' He pointed at the cage of the bird that had let out the solitary note. 'Give us the same seed and the same sure accommodation and we'd be there with the budgies.'

Milton's reference to the chapel singing and the slightly demagogic tilt of the last sentence had made Humphries very wary again.

'Your business, gentlemen?'

'We want to thank you,' said Gomer, 'for the fine stand you made at Tregysgod and the remarks you made about Cynlais Coleman's band. We think the same. Those home-grown dervishes have cancelled out the landing of Augustus. We are collecting among ourselves to fit Coleman and his men out in such a way that they will not cause the very hillsides to blush as they do now. Could you help us?'

Humphries stood stock still for at least two minutes, his lips drawn in and his eyes fixed hypnotically on the most forbidding of the portraits. Uncle Edwin muttered to Gomer that someone should give Humphries an investigatory push in case he had chosen this moment to die just to put us in the wrong. But Humphries came suddenly back to life, shaking his head as if recovering from some spell laid upon him by the granite features of the voter in the portrait.

'That was my uncle, Cadman Humphries,' he said, his voice still a little muffled, uncertain. We remembered Cadman. He had been a quarry-owner, the only quarry owner whose face had made his employees think they were working double time or made them constantly doubtful about where they should place the explosive charge.

'As a matter of fact I could and will help you,' he said. His voice was now loudly vibrant and overwhelming. Four of the birds came rushing to the bars of their cage and Uncle Edwin pressed his body against the plush flank of a settee to mute the effect of Humphries' outburst. 'It will be my great pleasure to do so. I am vice president of a committee which is gathering funds to supply wholesome entertainments for the valley folk during this emergency. Just in case these carnivals should become a permanent part of our lives we must at least see that minimum standards of decorum are accepted, and that the marchers are decently covered against both wind and temptation. As for Coleman, whose first appearance before my wife gave her such hiccups as would take a lagoon of small sips to cure, I will leave it to you men to think out an alternative costume for this buffoon and you may leave the bill, within reason, to me. Nothing too royal or lavish, of course.'

'Of course,' said Gomer. 'By the way, Mr Humphries, have you seen Georgie Young's women's band, the Britannias?'

Humphries' eyes became a twitch of embarrassed guilt and he whipped back around to face Cadman Humphries and to salute the need for a really stony ethic in a softening world.

'I'm afraid I haven't had a good look at them. I've heard about them and I've had some good reports of Mr Georgie Young's excellent work as a driller. But I haven't really seen them. Last week at Tregysgod, for some reason they didn't arrive as far as the judges' stand.'

'Take a good look at them, Mr Humphries. When you see them you'll lose what is left of your hair. Then you'll start another fund to have Young hung and the bands-women treated with balsam of missionary.'

Milton tugged at Gomer, thinking that any more talk that Humphries might construe as being morally double-jointed and we would be getting the boot. But Mr Humphries did not seem put out. Through his eyes I thought I could now see a film of comfortable steam above his thoughts. We said thank you and goodnight.

'Goodnight,' said Humphries. 'I'm surprised to find you men so helpful, such watchdogs in the cause of wholesomeness.'

'Just let us catch a whiff of anything that isn't wholesome, Mr Humphries,' said Milton Nicholas, 'then watch us bark and bite.'

We went straight from the house of Ephraim Humphries to that of Cynlais Coleman. Cynlais' mother, a ravelled woman whose fabric, even without Cynlais, would not have stood up to too much wear and tear, took us instantly to Cynlais' bedroom, glad to be sharing her problem. Cynlais was in bed, flattened under the load of his grief and a big family Bible, trying to reassemble the fragments of himself after the two disasters. We were puzzled by the Bible and were going to ask Mrs Coleman whether she had meant it just to keep Cynlais in bed and off his feet, but she explained that she had given it to him to read the Book of Job to help him keep his troubles in proportion, but Cynlais had kept flicking the pages and referring to Moira Hallam as Delilah, and saying that Job seemed to have come right out of one of the blacker Thursday night sessions at the Discussion Group in the Institute.

At the sight of us Cynlais drew the Bible and the bed-clothes up to his face as if to hide.

'Hullo Cynlais,' said Gomer. 'Big news, boy. We've got the money for the new costumes. What fancies have you got on this subject, and for goodness' sake keep inside Europe this time because we're hoping to have enough to cover you all from top to bottom.'

There was now nothing of Cynlais except his very small brow, and he had his hands clenched over the sides of the Bible as if he were thinking of throwing it at Gomer as a first step to clearing the bedroom. Uncle Edwin, at the foot of the bed, knocked solemnly on Cynlais' tall foot as if it were a door.

'Come on, Cynlais,' he said. 'Buck up, boy, and stop looking so shattered. This isn't the end of the world; it's only the first crack.'

Cynlais' whole face came into view. It was grey, shrunken and lined. Uncle Edwin said that between Caney's kidney-whipper and carnal wishes it was clear that Coleman had been through the mill.

'I keep thinking of what Moira told me,' said Cynlais, with a look in his eye that made Milton Nicholas say that Caney should be held on charges of making a public mischief.

'What did she say?' asked Gomer.

'She said, "Cynlais, has your heart ever been in the orange groves of Seville?"'

We all tried to relate this statement to the carnivals and the news we had brought from Ephraim Humphries.

'You can't possibly have a band of marching oranges,' said Gomer. 'Just drop this greengrocery motif, Cynlais. You can be too subtle in these matters. Look what happened to those Eskimos from the top of the valley. You remember their manoeuvre of shuddering at the end of every blast from the gazookas to show extreme cold and the need for blubber, no one ever understood it. They shuddered themselves right out of the carnival league.'

'I don't mean oranges,' said Cynlais. 'I mean bullfighters, with me dressed up in the front as an even better bullfighter than Moelwyn Cox.'

We had to move away from the bed at this point and explain in low voices to Milton Nicholas about Moelwyn Cox and his appearance with the Birchtown Amateur Operatic company as the matador Escamillo. Milton's first impulse on hearing Cynlais make this reference to bullfighters was to think that Cynlais, between the weight of that Bible and the bushfires of his lustful wanting, had been flattened and charred into madness. Cynlais, with a glare of one hundred per cent paranoia, told us to stop whispering or get out of his bedroom.

Gomer went back to the bedside and shook Cynlais gravely by the hand.

'That's a wonderful idea, Cyn,' he said. 'Come over to Tasso's tomorrow night and we'll talk it over. Do you think you can manage it?'

Cynlais said at first that without some word of

encouragement and hope from Moira Hallam he would never again leave that bedroom except to show the rent collector that he was not a subtenant. But we got him out of the bed and marched him around the room a few times, taking it in turns to catch him when his legs buckled. We all agreed that he would be able to do the trip to Tasso's on the following evening with a few attendant helpers on his flank.

Willie Silcox was in Tasso's the next day. He was interested when we told him about our visit to Ephraim Humphries, and he made notes when he heard about the various quirks of body, face and thought we had noted in Humphries when we mentioned the Britannias.

'One of these nights,' said Willie, 'Humphries will draw a thick serge veil over the portrait of Cadman Humphries, the quarry owner whose eyes and brows keep Ephraim in a suit of glacial combinations, and he will slip forth into the darkened street, just like Jack the Ripper, but knifeless and bent on a blander type of mischief altogether than was Jack. And you say he's going to foot the bill for a new band for Coleman? That will bring him closer to the physical reality of these carnivals and allow his senses a freer play. What is this new band going to be called?'

'The Meadow Prospect Toreadors, Willie. What do you think of that?'

'Very nice, very exotic. It will help to show what little is left of our traditional earnestness to the gate but good luck to you all the same. We are headed for an age of clownish callousness and we might as well have a local boy as stage hand in that process as anyone else. These bullfighters will bring the voters an illusion of the sun and a strong smell of marmalade, both much needed.'

Gomer turned to Mathew Sewell the Sotto who was putting Tasso's teeth on edge by beating his tuning fork on the counter and bringing its pointed end sharply into play on the metal edge of the counter.

'What about the theme tune for these boys when Cynlais

49

gets his new band started, Mathew? What do you suggest?'

Sewell thought for a whole minute in silence, then brought his tuning fork across his teeth as if to bring his reflections to the boil.

'Something Spanish, of course,' said Sewell, and Gomer told him to try his tuning fork on his teeth again to see if he could come out with something more cogent.

'Try to. make it something operatic, Mr Sewell,' said Cynlais Coleman, who had come in five minutes before wearing a long raincoat and the visor of his cap hiding the most significant parts of his face. It had taken some major wheedling to get him to shed this disguise. He sat now by the stove looking overt and edgy.

'What did you say?' asked Gomer.

'Something operatic,' said, Cynlais. 'I want to show that Moira Hallam that I'm as cultured as Moelwyn Cox. What about that Toreador Song? That's a treat. That was what Moelwyn made such a hit with. Let's have that.'

Mathew Sewell ignored Cynlais except for a short glance that told him to pick up his cap and get back out of sight.

'It will have to be something Spanish of course. There are strong affinities between Iberian music and our own and I don't see why we shouldn't exploit this. I can make it marks for you if ever I'm one of the judges. Did you know, Tasso, that we were once known as Iberian Celts?'

Tasso said no very politely, but we could see from his mouth that he was tired of having Sewell pitching on him with questions that were so well outside the catering trade.

There was a long silence from Sewell and Tasso worked the urn to cover his embarrassment.

'What about the Toreador Song?' asked Cynlais again.

'Just sing it over,' said Sewell very casually, as if to say that we might as well have something going on while he picked down the one he wanted from a hallful of Iberian alternatives.

Cynlais started in a tenor so thin he had us all bending over him to follow the melody. Cynlais had never been a vigorous singer, and his collapse had caused his cords to dangle worse than ever. We all gathered around him and tried as briskly as we could to give him support in the bullfighter's song.

Tasso tapped with his toffee hammer on the counter and smiled broadly at Sewell as if to tell him that this was just the thing, especially if played or sung without Gomer Gough, who was lunging at the melody as recklessly as he would have done at the bull.

'No,' said Sewell. 'I don't think so. It's a little bit too complicated to play on the march. We want something a bit witless, something everybody'll know.'

'What about "I'm One of the Nuts of Barcelona"?' asked Gomer Gough, and the title of this piece sounded strangely from the mouth of Gomer, which had been worn down to the gums by the reading of a thousand unsmiling agendas.

'What's nutting to do with bullfighting?' asked Uncle Edwin. 'Let's lift the tone of these carnivals. I'm for the operatic tune. Let's go through it again. It's got a very warming beat, although I still think a nation that has to make the fighting of bulls a national cult is just passing the time on and trying to keep its mind off something else.' Uncle Edwin gave Cynlais a nod and raised his hand to lead the group back into Bizet.

'Don't make difficulties, Edwin,' said Gomer, and he was clearly torn between two conversational lines; one to censure Edwin for hanging a little close to the boneyard spiritually, second, to explain to us how he had come to spare enough time from the dialectic to find the title of such a tune as 'I'm One of Nuts of Barcelona', one of the least pensive lyrics of the period. But Willie Silcox nipped in before Gomer could make his point.

'There's another thing, too,' said Willie. 'Do you still want Cynlais to win the esteem of Moira Hallam?'

'Oh definitely. It'll give Cynlais that little extra bit of winning vim. What are you hinting at now, Silcox?'

'This girl has got some sort of Spanish complex.'

'No question about it,' said Mathew Sewell. He turned to Tasso. 'I expect you've heard, Tasso, that the adjective Spanish is often used in connection with various sexual restoratives and stimulants.' But he got no answer. Tasso was not looking. 'She's even got me feeling like a bit of a picador, and I haven't felt that sort of urge very often since I conducted the united choirs of Meadow Prospect in the *Messiah* three years ago.' Sewell paused and his thoughts dived into waters that were not instantly visible to us. 'Do you remember those sopranos in their snow-white blouses? Do you remember the big dispute about my treatment of the last six hallelujahs?'

We remembered the sopranos, the steep, tumescent tiers of gleaming satin, the last great outlay on sheet music and cloth in the pre-bath-chair phase of the coal trade in the third decade. But we could recall no dispute about Sewell's interpretation of that particular score. His hallelujahs had seemed to us orthodox, even flatly so.

Gomer became annoyed at this backwash of recollection in which we had politely allowed ourselves to become involved. He accused Sewell of egomania, of putting his own and Handel's past before Meadow Prospect's future, of creating confusion and making our thinking bitty. Cynlais Coleman, at best a staccato thinker, and always prone to be hypnotised by Sewell, queried this.

'Anyway,' said Gomer, 'carry on, Willie, with your remarks about Moira Hallam.'

'What better than to have her walking right in front of Coleman's new band, dressed up as Carmen?' asked Willie.

He addressed his question to Sewell, but there was no reply from him. He was in the cold mental vaults of his memories of the *Messiah*, that white acreage of banked sopranos, and his treatment of those shouts of praise.

'That's a first-class notion, Willie,' said Gomer, 'Paolo,' he said to Tasso, 'give Willie Silcox another raspberry cordial. He's the Livingstone of our mental Congo.'

During the next week the bullfighting uniforms for Cynlais and his band were stitched from cheap cloth and rough recollections of *Blood and Sand,* a film which had been screened at one of our cinemas, The Cosy, a year before. On a reasonably flat part of the waun the band practised its marching and playing. The wind came down to us scalloped by the sharp, quick step beat of 'The Nuts of Barcelona'.

We were full of hope for Cynlais and his boys. We needed that hope. A week before the great Trecelyn carnival at which Cynlais was to make his first appearance with his matadors, the Sons of Dixie had registered their tenth total defeat in a row at a town called Elmhill. They had gone to Elmhill with an arrogant faith in themselves and sure of triumph. Georgie Young the Further Flung had drilled them more ruthlessly than ever, and at their last rehearsal he had wept with pride at the sight of their speed and precision. Under heavy pressure he had decided to abandon his phobic faith in an all-black turn out and the wives of the Dixie's had laundered their trousers and shirts into an incredible snowiness and that gentle, theatrically minded voter Festus Phelps the Fancy, who was in general control of décor in our stretch of the valley, had blackened their faces with an especially yielding type of cork down to the very soul of sable.

So confident had we become in the Sons of Dixie before they set out for Elmhill that all the people in Windy Way, the long, hillside street that pushed its grey, apologetic track right up to the summit of Merlin's Brow, got candles and lighted them as soon as darkness fell on the day of the carnival. The candles were placed on the front windowsill of most of the two hundred houses in Windy Way and as the street, seen from the bottom of Meadow Prospect, seemed to go right off into the sky the small flames made a beautiful and moving sight, and we all thought that this would be a fine way of greeting the Sons of Dixie when they drummed and gazookered their return in glory to Meadow Prospect.

But they lost all the same. 'Unimaginative.' 'Prussian and aesthetically Luddite.' 'Naïve and depressing.' These were just some of the judges' verdicts, and Georgie Young was carried back on some sort of litter a full hour before the band itself returned.

The Sons of Dixie came back in the darkness. Some sympathisers had staked them to a gill or two. They marched through the town and halted at the foot of Windy Way when their leader, Big Mog Malley, so erect even in the florescent melancholy of the moment he looked as if he had done a spell of training with Frederick the Great before moving under the baton of Georgie Young, raised his gigantic staff and told them to break ranks. Their mood as they stared up at the long legion of triumphant candles was for some bit of self-defensive clowning. They found they were quite near the work-yard of our undertaker, Goronwy Mayer the Layer. The lads pushed open Mayer's gate. The locks and bolt were brittle because Mayer believed that everything connected with death should be friendly and easily negotiable. They commandeered a hearse. An unbelievable number of them managed to clamber aboard and they began their journey with that erratic reciter, Theo Morgan the Monologue, at the wheel and keeping his head bent in comical sorrow until the hearse hit the kerb and jerked a couple of the Dixies on to the roadway. Some gazooka players fell in behind and struck up with a funeral hymn so magical in its scope for sensuous harmony it had caused many a mourner to forget the body. Mayer the Layer came out of his house full of fury at the sight of his burglared yard but he had to follow behind saying not a word because he had taken a vow never to interfere in any way with the singing of that particular hymn because it had sent up the figures for funeral attendance a hundred per cent. Mayer even joined in loudly in the lower register. He had always said that had it not been for the excluding nature of his trade he could have done something as a baritone.

And with every yard advanced by that strange cortège a candle on its windowsill was extinguished by a housewife eager not to waste the tallow on an empty midnight and wishful not to seem to mock the Sons of Dixie in their hour of hollowness.

That memory made us all the more anxious as we watched Cynlais and his followers practise up on the flat moorland. It seemed that Cynlais' hour had come. The toreador role lifted him on to a plane of joyful release, and once the slower bandsmen had been persuaded that with this move into Spain 'Colonel Bogey' would be definitely out of place the musical side of it went well. Festus Phelps the Fancy created a bit of confusion during the early stages of preparation. Festus' attitude to the bands had been becoming steadily more antic as his power and influence as artistic adviser had increased. He had been delighted when Cynlais and his band had decided to become bullfighters because he had read many books about the bulls and rather fancied that he himself had the shape and style to have done well at this exercise. He felt this all the more keenly because a few years before Silcox and a group of fanciers at the Institute had told Phelps that he had the shape and look of Carpentier. He had one fight. He went into the ring, superbly handsome but totally inept in the use of his hands and attended by two of the least aware voters in Meadow Prospect who were to be his seconds. They believed that Festus would win by grace of footwork and they were still massaging Festus' feet when the first bell went. The opponent's opening view of Festus was a figure falling on his face for no reason that he could see. He helped Festus to his feet and set to work. Festus was in the ring twenty seconds, but that was only because the referee was a slow counter even when not doing it over the form of a man as prone and still as Festus was at that moment. Since then Festus had felt that in a sport like bullfighting he would find the right field for the passion and solitariness he knew to be his, without having the clumsy folly of his fellow men clogging the pipes of his talent every whipstitch. So he tackled his advisory job with the Meadow Prospect Matadors like a crusader.

At a full meeting of the bandsmen at the Institute he explained to them the main movements of the bullfight, comparing them with the phases of a symphony to which he applied the proper Italian terms. Then he told them about the moment of truth, the moment at which the bullfighter faces the bull with a tension of courage that makes life imperishably resonant, when he slaps death's both cheeks and dares it to try on him any of the infamous betrayals whereby it had made shoddy and shuffling fools of the whole race of men. Festus, on the platform, looked right into death's eyes, taking a little time off now and then to throw looks of freezing contempt at the bandsmen whom he saw as the sweating, treacherous, contumelious ticket holders in the sun and the shadow. He rose on tiptoe to deliver the stroke of death to the grave-ripe beast which only he could see. The bandsmen, few of whom had heard Festus' talk from the beginning, were confused as never before and they thought that Festus' mind, without question one of the most sensitive in the division, had now been submitted to one aggravation too many and had broken loose from its last hinge. Some pointed end of revelation had jabbed Festus on to a high apocalyptic peak. All around him on the stage walked every privation and mishap that had ever driven him into his tight and terrifying corner of self-awareness, one last rubbed nerve between himself and the relief of a frank lunacy. 'What can be the flavour on the tongue of death, daft death?' he had shouted. 'What was that again?' asked a few of the bandsmen in the front row, and they started to fidget a bit as they got a glimpse of death as an articulate but loutish imbecile met casually in a lightless lane. Three committee men of the Institute, who were sitting in the back row, reminded Festus that questions of the raking, rattling sort he had just put to the matadors had to be reserved for the smaller, quieter rooms.

Then Festus, overcome by the beauty and mental nakedness of the moment, had broken down and was led weeping off the platform. Gomer Gough and Uncle Edwin were sent for from the Reading Room and were told of what had been going on. They got hold of four bandsmen, lined them up on the stage and told them to run through 'I'm One of the Nuts of Barcelona' twice. It took that and a short statement from Gomer Gough on the dangers of emotionalism to get the matadors back into mental motion.

Festus even then had not quite shot his bolt. Up on the practice ground he made a last effort to give an authentic Sevillian edge to what he thought the rather clomping approach of Cynlais' boys.

'The day of straightforward marching is done,' he said. 'In these carnivals we have the seed of a great popular ballet. You see into what ruin you run if you stick to the stolid conventions that have governed the carnivals so far. The Sons of Dixie marched with the dour determination of iron collared serfs and what did it get them. Half an acre of bunions and a threat of police court prosecution from Goronwy Mayer for dragging the paraphernalia of death into a context of gross buffoonery. No, what we want is a leap of imagination.'

He got his leap. It was built around the moment of truth.

At the end of the theme tune the band would stop dead and every gazooka would blow a long, loud, low note. That was supposed to be the final defiance of the bull. Then the matadors all stood on tiptoe and held their gazookas as if for the thrust of extinction. This manoeuvre was looked on with astonishment by all the supporters who watched the band rehearse up on the moorland. Either the matadors were a naturally flat-footed lot, or they held their gazookas too low, or they did not realise how tall a bull can be, but their posture was ambiguous and created a lot of unfavourable talk among those supporters who were anxious to keep the goodwill of the chapels.

Two days before the Trecelyn carnival we were walking down the hillside with Cynlais. About twenty yards behind us Festus Phelps was talking fast and passionately to half a dozen matadors who still did not know what he was supposed to be getting at. Of these voters there were four who had never been able to stand on tiptoe without a feeling of crucial absurdity, and they were telling Festus that after two efforts to rise like that and deal with the bull they would never again have the nervous calm to find the right note when the band struck up again with 'Barcelona'.

'That notion of stopping and lunging with the gazookas is going to play hell with the marching,' said Cynlais Coleman. 'I think that that Festus Phelps the Fancy has just been sent here to hinder us. Why didn't you tell him to leave us alone, Gomer?'

'Patience, Cyn. We can't afford to offend Festus yet. He's doing splendid work with the costumes. He's got the touch and the women who are doing the stitching say that he's got a peerless hand with the needle. But we mustn't allow him to overdo this mania for the ballet or we'll be badgering Ephraim Humphries for another grant, this time to have Festus removed. If he's going to develop fresh art forms for the people he should have a better team to play with than the matadors. There are some very bandy-legged boys among them and they seem to be even more so when they get up on their toes and get poised for the thrust. The bull would run right through.'

'What about Moira, Gomer? When is she going to start walking in front of the band like you said?'

'We're keeping her as a surprise. Don't worry, she'll be ready for the day. We've given her the beat of "I'm One of the Nuts" and she's been practising around the table in her front room. Sewell has been coaching her. The first time he walked in front of her round the front room table to give her an idea of the type of slink and wriggle he mentally associates with this element Carmen. The second time Sewell went around the front room table behind her, and he felt his reserve ravelling and he had to sit down at Mrs Hallam's harmonium and play that version of "Abide with Me" that leaves no room for laughs. And don't forget, Cynlais. In the carnival you'll be walking behind her, too, and your gonads are still fresh-faced compared with Sewell's. So if your mother has any cooling herb in the house fill up on it before the big day.'

Cynlais stopped, opened his eyes wide and raised his arm. 'In that matador's uniform, Gomer, I'll be like a monk. Honest to God.'

The next night there was a big excited crowd in Tasso's Coffee Tavern. They had come there straight from the practice ground where Cynlais and the boys had rehearsed for the last time, in full Andalusian rig. It had been an exultant occasion and the committee men had marched alongside the band, keeping step and humming the theme tune. Gomer Gough was breathless as he leaned over Tasso's counter. He was in moderate funds after the sale of thirty bags of coal from his tiny unofficial outcrop mine near the top of Merlin's Brow. He gave Tasso a complicated order of fruit drinks for about half the bandsmen. Then he said to the whole shopful of matadors and supporters: 'Well, tomorrow's the day, the Trecelyn Competitive Inter-valley Festival.'

'What are the prospects, Mr Gough?' asked Tasso, leaning away from the urn, which was in top fettle.

'Never better,' said Gomer. 'You should see Cynlais. Sideboards down to the chin, little moustache, a stiff, flattish black hat like Valentino but even flatter, I fancy, than that hat we saw Valentino wearing in that film down at The Cosy. And his every glance is a search for a bull. It took him a bit of time remember that he was no longer the Mad Mahdi and to stop looking demented, but he's fine now.'

'And the Signorina Hallam?'

'You wouldn't believe! Carmen in the flesh. Red shawl, and we've collected so many combs to stick in her tall black hair there isn't a kempt head on our side of the Meadow. We've kept her dark so far because we don't want Ephraim Humphries to see her and start accusing her of goading the poor to ruin. Ephraim paid for most of the costumes and on questions of decorum he's touchier than a boil. Let's hope it's a very fine day tomorrow. Then Ephraim can put Moira down to a shimmer of heat.'

Tasso raised himself and spoke over the heads of the people who were standing in the shop.

'And how, Mr Sewell, are the ladies, the Britannias?'

We hadn't noticed Mathew Sewell sitting in the far corner and he advanced at our call from the corner and towards the counter with a cup of some dark, cold-looking liquid in his hand. He gave a deep groan. Just behind me Willie Silcox was whispering to Uncle Edwin that this groan we had just heard from Sewell was without question an echo of what Sewell had gone through in Moira Hallam's front room when he was getting her posture up to the mark.

'It's a fatal thing, Edwin, a fatal thing.'

'What is, Willie?' asked Uncle Edwin, who was exhausted by watching the final rehearsal and talking with Festus Phelps about the crass, anti-cultural attitude of Gough and Coleman. Uncle Edwin had not been listening at all attentively when Gomer had explained the day before about Sewell's visits to the home of Moira Hallam to give her secret instruction in being a Carmen. So Willie Silcox had Edwin foxed. 'What is, Willie?' he asked again, hoping that the blankness on his face would send Willie whispering to someone else. 'Playing "Abide with Me" on a small harmonium right on top of a mood of intense longing. I've known it bring down the whole mental scaffolding of voters before this.'

Uncle Edwin asked Tasso to turn up the steam of the urn

to a point where it would blot out Silcox. Then we resumed our study of Sewell.

'Tasso,' said Sewell, 'slip another beef cube in this cup and warm the water up while I tell you about my troubles with those women, the Britannias. I've spent weeks trying to find out why they go so out of tune on "Rule, Britannia". If they were all brazen and defiant like their leader, that heavy, fierce woman, Maudie Gordon, I don't think they'd have any trouble. But there's a core of very shy women there, I'm sure, who must have been in a mood of strange brief frenzy when they signed up in the Britannias in the first place, and who still feel horrified when they find themselves out in the street with little more on than a single layer of thin Union Jack. They play out of tune to take the public's mind off how much they're showing. I've got five members of my madrigal group to march on each side of them, singing the melody loud and plain to keep them on the pitch, but I don't know how the judges will take to that tactic. I've chosen madrigal singers who don't open their mouths very wide and we'll have them edging in towards the Britannias from time to time as if they were members of the public, not to make the thing too obvious.'

Sewell took a quick, painful sip at his now quite hot drink, and while he blew loudly to cool his lips everybody in the shop chatted about the Britannias and what could be done to keep these women in tune. But Sewell waved them to silence as if that issue had now ceased to be important.

'But my biggest trouble now,' he said, 'is that drummer, Olga Rowe. I told Georgie Young from the start that he should have given Olga a much smaller drum. But he said it made a nice touch of pathos that made up to some extent for the many faults of the Britannias on the march. It's fine, he said, that big drum advancing on you with hardly anything of Olga in sight except her arms.'

'I've seen it,' said Uncle Edwin. 'It's uncanny. What's the matter with her?'

'She's been driven hysterical by the new pattern of vibrations set up in her by the drumming and now she gets a laughing fit every time she touches the pigskin. She keeps her husband out on the landing at nights because she's so sensitive and so easily set off. Her husband is that complaisant, uncomplaining little voter, Mogford Rowe. He says he doesn't mind sleeping upright and alone if it means getting away from Olga's tremors and being beaten black and blue to the rhythm of "Rule, Britannia". Even in sleep this Olga is on duty in the back row of the band.'

'A brisk tune, "Rule, Britannia",' said Gomer Gough, 'and damaging to marriage when heard without warning in bed.'

'Is Willie Silcox the Psyche here?' asked Sewell. 'Oh aye, there you are. Tell me, Silcox, what psychological approach would you recommend for a woman in such a fix as this Olga Rowe?'

'I don't know,' said Willie. 'I know this woman only from afar by the racket she makes banging on this instrument. And Freud, not often foxed, is silent about women being driven mad by their own drumming.'

'Never mind, though,' said Mathew. 'Of one thing at least we can all be certain. Whatever happens to Georgie Young and Olga Rowe, tomorrow will be Cynlais Coleman's day.'

But it was not to be. The prize was not to be ours. It was a day of oven heat and the wet hills under the unaccustomed shimmer seemed to be laughing with surprise. But the sun meant little to us for calamity trailed like a flag behind us all day long.

Georgie Young had been persuaded to let the Sons of Dixie have one last fling before hanging up their gazookas. Georgie had been hyper-tense for days and his daughter had alerted Peredur Parry the Pittance, the Public Assistance official who was charged with the task of keeping an eye on the twin field of destitution and dementia among the voters. Georgie had been watching with a yellow eye the proud strut of Cynlais Coleman and the matadors and he was heard muttering to himself as he wandered around the bookshelves of the Institute looking for books about his idol, Kitchener:

'I'll give them bull. I'll give them toreador. I'll show that bloody Coleman. I owe it to Kitchener.'

So between resentment and a touch of late summer madness Georgie decided on a bold stroke. He told the Sons of Dixie to shed their white suits and fitted them with a tip-to-toe covering of cork stain and a kind of thick straw sash made from a thoroughly looted little rick on the land of Nathan Wilkins, the farmer. This was to give the effect of African warriors of the Lobengula epoch. The straw sashes were not easy to fasten and had the hard, abrasive quality of Wilkins himself. Besides, Wilkins had turned up with a shotgun to stand guard over the rick as they were helping themselves to material for the last twenty sashes, and there was a big feeling of insecurity among the boys wearing this last batch of coverings. The bandsmen were in trouble after the first dozen steps and overtly scratching in ways that the judges were bound to consider insanitary and ungracious. On top of that Georgie had decided that the Meadow Prospect Matabele, as he now called his followers, would march barefooted. He said it would be a tour de force to have them march with the same fury and dash as of old with nothing between their feet and the County Council highway, which could, in patches, be rough.

But the day of the carnival was against him. The sun had started to melt the macadam on the road by eleven in the morning and the marchers behind Big Mog Malloy were leaving a significantly deep spoor behind them. After the first mile the Matabele had a four-inch sole of asphalt, and those who were not actually keeling over were slowed down to a pathetic stumble and urging Mog Malloy to take his feather headdress off and use it and kill Young. To make things even cooler, council officials were up and down the flank of the warriors demanding their arrest for playing such hell with the road surface and making a rough assessment of the weight of macadam being carried by each bandsman. The Dixies were disqualified for holding up the carnival by sitting down on the roadside and using knives to chip off the macadam. They were disqualified under Rule 17 of the carnival code which stated that offensive weapons were not to be used on the march even to get back to bare feet. Sweat and anguish had streaked their cork stain into a dramatic leopard pattern.

The Britannia were early thrown into confusion by Olga Rowe tickling herself into the loudest laughing fit of this century. She had not been helped by having Sewell and the madrigal singers going up to her at short intervals arranged by Sewell and telling her: 'Olga, what you feel inside you, Olga, is joy, just joy.' And they would laugh in a way which for Olga was the cherry on the trifle. She was last seen drumming at forty miles an hour, down a side street, followed closely by a short old man with very fast legs. Some said this voter was the owner of the drum and off to get it back; others said he was a noted amorist out to take advantage of Olga Rowe's confusion.

The day had started well for the matadors. We had formed in a crowd outside Moira Hallam's house. Then Cynlais' band, a moving wall of red, yellow and black, giving out 'I'm One of the Nuts of Barcelona' with tremendous brio on their gazookas, had marched into the street. They blew a sort of fanfare which was Moira's cue. She came out of the front door like a sensational shout from a mouth. The crimson shawl set the whole street flaming and Moira's management of her body did as much for our senses. Moira had had her hair bunched up in a way that made her stubby body look rather top-heavy, but no one looked at her hair for long. Moira took up her position in front of the band.

Gomer Gough and the committee men led a little burst of clapping and this was the cue for that well-known gardener, Naboth Jenks the Pinks, to step forward with a rose of deep, red and the biggest petals ever seen in Meadow. Jenks moved out of the crowd too abruptly and Moira stepped away from him thinking that Jenks was merely out to commit some act of sexual bravura. Then she saw the rose which Jenks had been holding behind his back and while she was marvelling at the size and perfume of it Gomer Gough, in his role of tireless chairman, was proposing a formal vote of thanks to Jenks for having evolved a rose with definite cauliflower overtones. Then Gomer told Moira to put the rose in her mouth and keep it there. At first Moira did not like this idea and Mrs Hallam went right up to Gomer and told him about some uncle of hers who had been driven mad by nibbling at flowers. But Moira was persuaded that no one had ever seen an authentic Carmen without the rose in her mouth and very gingerly she placed the bloom between her big, strong teeth. The sight of her had a great effect and even Teilo Dew the Doom said later that even he, upon whose love life a heavy ice cap had fallen in the autumn of 1922, found himself gulping with desire as the red of the rose and the white of the teeth made their first impact.

Then there was a whistle from Cynlais and a flourish from his drum major's staff. The bandsmen raised their gazookas to the ready and on the down beat from Cynlais they began to play and moved off in the direction of Trecelyn. On the pavement the only professional gambler in Meadow, Kitchener Bowen the Book, was taking small bets favouring Cynlais to win against all comers and at that moment we all agreed with Bowen.

But the sun and all the baked ironies it propagates on this earth were already hard at work. By the time we reached Trecelyn the last petal had dropped from the red rose that Moira Hallam held in her mouth. Moira did her best. She was upset once or twice by Cynlais who in his excitement kept ramming his drum major's staff into her back to remind her that she was not alone. One or two of his thrusts were wild and almost sent Moira hurling into the crowds on the side-walk. Gomer Gough and Uncle Edwin went on to the road and told Cynlais firmly to cut out this manoeuvre with the staff. Moira kept chewing at the bare stem of her rose and tried to make up for the lack of petals by making more challenging the fine, fluent swing of her body beneath the lovely shawl. Jenks the Pinks had been on the point of making some remark about the lack of stamina of his petals but he just looked at Moira and said nothing. But it was a new band, not much older than our own Matadors, the Aberclydach Sheiks, that did for us in the end.

A few furlongs outside Trecelyn one of our scouts, Onllwyn Meeker, came tearing along the road to give a report on what he had found to Gomer Gough. Onllwyn Meeker had been running hard and he had to be held up and dosed from one of the lemonade bottles that had been brought along for the harder-pressed marchers before he could make a reasonable statement. Meeker was an alarmist and Gomer had been cautioned against making him a scout, and it seemed from the way he shook his forefinger and rolled his eyes that he might well go off the hinge before he managed to tell us what he had seen in Trecelyn.

'Gomer, Gomer,' he said. 'This is a wonderful band you've got here. The Matadors are a credit to Meadow Prospect, but I've just seen the Sheiks of Aberclydach and you've got a surprise coming to you.'

'What's up, Onllwyn?'

'I've just seen them. They're wearing grey veils and dressed like they think Arabs dress in Aberclydach. They're playing some slow, dreamy tune about Araby and swaying from side to side with the music, looking and acting as warm and slinky as you please and promoting a mood of sensuous excitement among the voters.'

'Come on, boys,' said Gomer. 'Let's run ahead and see these Sheiks. I don't like the sound of this. Ephraim Humphries is one of the judges today and by all the rules of nature he should be in favour of the band whose uniforms he helped to buy. But he might well operate against the Matadors on the grounds of discouraging self-pride. And did you hear what Onllwyn said about these Sheiks wearing veils?'

'To keep the sand out of their mouths,' said Onllwyn. 'I was puzzled about these veils and I asked their secretary why sheiks should be wearing veils and he said that about the sand.'

'Ephraim Humphries is going to like the idea of those veils. In everything except his doctrine of damnation for the great majority, he is against the overt. A wholly concealed humanity, beginning with these Aberclydach sheiks, would be quite welcome to Humphries.'

'No doubt indeed,' said Onllwyn Meeker.

'And when he takes a look at Moira Hallam, with that stem in her mouth and the shapes she's making, he'll think she swallowed the petals of that rose herself to keep fresh for some new round of sinning.'

The word 'fresh' seemed to remind Gomer of something and he told Cynlais to break ranks for a few minutes and take a rest on the grass bank that flanked the road.

'They can sit down if they like, but carefully and primly so that there won't be any creases in the uniform. They've got that old Colonel Mathews the Moloch, the coal owner, on the panel of judges, and they say he's a hell of a man for spotting creases.'

Cynlais passed this warning on to his followers as they were taking their places on the grass bank, and there were a lot of interesting postures.

'There's another thing,' said Uncle Edwin, sucking at two blades of some healthful type of grass that had just been passed to him by Caney the Cure, who was with us as a supporter and because there was never much doing in the herb line during the summer. 'There's another thing. Don't forget Merfyn Matlock.'

'Explain about Matlock,' said Gomer.

Uncle Edwin explained. Merfyn Matlock owned the department store in Birchtown and by the standards of the zone he was a kind of Silurian Woolworth. Merfyn had served in the Middle East with Lawrence of Arabia, dressed as a Bedouin and blowing things up, and he had been flat and sad and bitter ever since he had come back to Birchtown, blue serge and verbal negotiations.

'Remember what he said in 1923.'

Everybody had forgotten what Merfyn Matlock had said in 1923 and Uncle Edwin was asked to remind us.

'We had been having a chat about Matlock and the eager, wolfish way he had of stalking about Birchtown showing contempt for the voters. When he was in the Middle East he believed in explosions in a way that had little to do with the Turks. He made the Bedouin twice as nomadic as they had been before, largely to get out of Matlock's way. So we debated a motion in the Discussion Group that "The shadow of the Boy Scout, with all the attendant ambiguities of his pole, lies too heavily on British society and politics." Many references to Matlock were made in the debate and there was not a single vote against. Matlock commented on this. He said that given a supply of dynamite and a few helpers to keep the matches alight he would deal with the dialecticians of Meadow Prospect in under five minutes.'

'And you say this Matlock is a judge.'

'He is a judge because he is the donor of the silver cup for the best character band. Mathews the Moloch is donating the cash part of the prize.'

'Why not make it plain that we have given up all hard thoughts about Matlock and politics. Why not have a kind of placard carried in front of the band just saying "The Matadors. Above Party. Above Class".'

'Any kind of placard or slogan in front of the band would clash with Moira in that fine romantic costume of hers. But the slogan you've just mentioned would put the judges out for the count. We'll have to rely on the goodwill of Matlock and the others. We'll have to convince them that through these carnivals we are now making our way towards the

New Jerusalem by a blither route, thinking no thought that cannot be played on a gazooka. Now, that's enough defeatist talk for one morning. I'm going to get a new rose for Moira. She makes a wonderful picture with that flower hanging from her lips.'

Gomer looked around. The only dwelling on that part of the road was an old cottage in which lived an ancient couple, secluded and somewhat petulant, still closer in spirit to the peasantry of the distant country of their origin than to the loud beetle-browed valleys where they had come tetchily to settle. If they had seen any of the carnivals' bands pass their cottage they had probably taken them as being quite seriously a part of the crudescent lunacy they had always spotted at the heart of the life around them.

In the front garden of the cottage were hundreds of roses in full bloom and of as deep a red as that which had been given to Moira by Jenks the Pinks. If Gomer had had a less sonorous approach to living he could have put his hand over the fence and helped himself to a handful. Instead, he went up the garden path and knocked on the door. The woman appeared and peeped out. She looked as if Old Moore had been keeping her prepared for the coming of Gomer for years. Gomer held out to her the unpetalled stem of Moira's first rose.

'Since the beauty has slipped from this,' he said and gave a light laugh which did not help, 'could I prevail upon you to furnish the lips of Meadow Prospect's Carmen, Moira Hallam, with a rose on a par with that grown by Naboth Jenks the Pinks?'

Every reservation she had ever felt about her days on this earth crowded on to the woman's face. She slammed the door shut and started crying out for her husband, who was somewhere in the back of the cottage. Then the woman's face appeared at one of the front windows, her eyes two pools of shock. A few of Cynlais' matadors, hearing the bang of the door and wondering what Gomer was up to, strolled over the brow of the grass bank and came into view of the cottage. The woman behind the window saw them and the door was instantly locked and barred. Gomer left the garden and picked up a rose on the way.

The band fell once more into line. At the sight of the fresh rose and after a round of servile attendance from Cynlais, Moira had picked up her spirits and the first notes of 'I'm One of the Nuts of Barcelona' had a swirl of optimistic gaiety as the matadors set forth on the last lap of their journey.

'Now let's hurry ahead and see about these Sheiks,' said Gomer.

We reached the centre of Trecelyn at the double. We had passed a group of bands all dressed in chintz, unstitched from looted curtains in the main, and all playing sad tunes like 'Moonlight and Roses', 'Souvenirs' and even a hymn, but those latter boys were wearing a very dark kind of chintz and from their general appearance were out on some subtle branch line of piety. Then we saw the Aberclydach Sheiks and they stopped us in our tracks. What Onllwyn Meeker had said was quite right. The grey veils worn high and seen against the dark, rather fierce type of male face common in Aberclydach, high cheekbones, eyebrows like coconut matting, was disquieting, but in a tonic sort of way. But it was their style of marching that hit the eye. They played the 'Sheik of Araby' very slowly and their swaying was deep and thorough. Their leader, in splendid white robes and a jet black turban about two feet deep and of a total length of cloth that must have put mourning in Aberclydach back a year, was a huge and notable rugby forward, Ritchie Reeves, who in his day had worn out nine referees and the contents of two fracture wards. The drummers also wore turbans but these were squat articles, and it was clear that Ritchie Reeves was making sure that it was only he who would present the public with a real Mahometan flourish. Gomer Gough went very close to the boys from Aberclydach and then turned to us.

'The boys between Ritchie Reeves and the drummers are not sheiks at all. They are houris, birds of paradise, a type of ethereal harlot, promised to the Arabs by Allah to compensate them for a life spent among sand and a run-down economy, but I can see three Aberclydach rodneys in that third row alone who wouldn't compensate me for anything.'

Teilo Dew was staring fascinated at the swaying of our rivals.

'If these boys are right,' he said, 'then the Middle East must be a damned sight less stable than we thought.'

'They are practically leaving their earmarks on either side,' said Uncle Edwin. 'They are wanting to suggest some high note of orgasm and pandering to the bodily wants of Ritchie, who has made it quite plain by the height of his hat that he is the chief sheik.'

We looked at Ritchie. His great face was melancholy but passionate, and we could see that between his rugby-clouted brain and carrying about a stone of cloth on his head his reactions were even more muffled than usual.

'Where are the judges?' asked Gomer, pulling a small book from his pocket.

'Over there in the open bay window of the Constitutional Club.'

We looked up and saw the judges. Right in front was Merfyn Matlock, very broad and bronzed, and smiling down at the Aberclydach band. At his side was the veteran coalowner Mathews the Moloch, and he did not seem to be in focus at all. He was leaning on Matlock and we could believe what we had often heard about him, that he was the one coal owner who had worked seams younger than himself. Behind these two we could see Ephraim Humphries in a grey suit and looking down with a kind of hooded caution at Ritchie Reeves and the houris.

Gomer stood squarely beneath the judges' window, slapped the little book he was holding and shouted up in a great roar, 'Mr Judges, an appeal, please. I've just seen the Aberclydach Sheiks. They are swaying like pendulums and I'm too well up in carnival law to let these antics go unchallenged. The rules we drew up at the Meadow Prospect conference, which are printed here in this little handbook, clearly state that bandsmen should keep a military uprightness on the march. It was with a faithful eye on this regulation that we told our own artistic adviser, Festus Phelps the Fancy, to avoid all imaginative frills that make the movement of the Meadow Prospect Matadors too staccato. And now here we have these Aberclydach Sheiks weaving in and out like shuttlecocks in their soft robes. This is the work of perverts and not legal.'

Merfyn Matlock pointed his arm down at Gomer and we could see that this for him was a moment of fathomless delight. 'Stewards,' he said, 'remove that man. He's out to disrupt the carnival. Meadow Prospect has always been a pit of dissent. Here come the Sheiks now. Oh, a fine turnout!'

We turned to take another look at the Sheiks as they moved into the square and as we saw them we gave up what was left of the ghost. The Sheiks had played their supreme trump. They had slowed their rate of march down to a crawl to confuse the bands behind them. And out of a side street, goaded on by a cloud of shouting voters, came the Sheiks' deputy leader, Mostyn Frost, dressed in Arab style and mounted on an old camel which he had borrowed from a menagerie that had gone bankrupt and bogged down in Aberclydach a week before. It was this animal that Olga Rowe caught a glimpse of as she was led back into position on the square. It finished her off for good.

At the carnival's end Gomer and Cynlais said we would go back over the mountain path, for the macadamed roads would be too hard after the disappointments of the day. Up the mountain we went. Everything was plain because the moon was full.

The path was narrow and we walked single file, women, children, Matadors, Sons of Dixie and Britannias. We reached the mountaintop. We reached the straight green path that leads past Llangysgod on down to Meadow Prospect. And across the lovely deep-ferned plateau we walked slowly, like a little army, most of the men with children hanging on to their arms, the women walking as best they could in the rear. Then they all fell quiet. We stood still, I and two or three others, and watched them pass, listening to the curious quietness that had fallen upon them. Far away we heard a high crazy laugh from Cynlais Coleman, who was trying to comfort Moira Hallam in their defeat. Some kind of sadness seemed to have come down on us. It was not a miserable sadness, for we could all feel some kind of contentment enriching its dark root. It may have been the moon making the mountain seem so secure and serene. We were like an army that had nothing left to cheer about or cry about, not sure if it was advancing or retreating and not caring. We had lost. As we watched the weird disguises, the strange, yet utterly familiar faces, of Britannias, Matadors and Africans, shuffle past, we knew that the bubble of frivolity, blown with such pathetic care, had burst for ever and that new and colder winds of danger would come from all the world's corners to find us on the morrow. But for that moment we were touched by the moon and the magic of longing. We sensed some friendliness and forgiveness in the loved and loving earth we walked on. For minutes the silence must have gone on. Just the sound of many feet swishing through the summer grass. Then somebody started playing a gazooka. The tune he played was one of those sweet, deep things that form as simply as dew upon a mood like ours. It must have been 'All Through the Night' scored for a million talking tears and a disbelief in the dawn. It had all the golden softness of an age-long hunger to be at rest. The player, distant from us now, at the head of the long and formless procession, played it very quietly, as if he were thinking rather than playing. Thinking about the night, conflict, beauty, the intricate labour of living and the dark little dish of thinking self in which they were all compounded. Then the others joined in and the children began to sing.

A Christmas Story

Richard Burton

There were not many white Christmases in our part of Wales in my childhood – perhaps only one or two – but Christmas cards and Dickens and Dylan Thomas and wishful memory have turned them all into white. I don't know why there should have been so few in such a cold, wet land – the nearness of the sea, perhaps. The Atlantic, by way of the Bristol Channel, endlessly harried us with gale and tempest. Perhaps our winds were too wild and salty for the snow to get a grip. Perhaps they blew the snow over us to the Black Mountains and Snowdonia and England.

Most of the Christmases of my childhood seem the same, but one of them I remember particularly, because it departed from the seemingly inexorable ritual. On this Eve of Christmas, Mad Dan, my uncle, the local agnostic, feared for his belief but revered for his brilliantly active vocabulary in the half-alien English tongue, sat in our kitchen with a group of men and with biting scourge and pithy whip drove the great cries of history, the epoch-making, world-changing ones, out of the temple of time. They were all half-truths, he said, and therefore half-lies.

I sat and stoned raisins for the pudding and listened bewitched to this exotic foreign language, this rough and r-riddled, rolling multisyllabic English.

'"There is only one Christian and he died upon the Cross," said Nietzsche,' said Dan.

Nietzsche, I thought – a Japanese. Perhaps he can speak Japanese, I thought. It was said that he, Dan, knew Latin and Greek, and could write both of them backwards.

'Can you speak Japanese, Mad Dan?' I asked.

'Shut up, Solomon,' he said to me.

'"Workers of the world, unite! You have nothing to lose but your chains,"' he said. 'Irresponsible rubbish. Cries written by crabbed fists on empty tables from mean hearts.'

'"*Dulce et decorum est pro patria mori.*"'

'What's that?' I asked

'Latin, Copperfield,' he said, 'meaning it is sweetly bloody marvellous to die for your country.

'"Man is born free and is everywhere in chains" – golden-tongued, light-brained, heedlessness of consequences.'

'"I think, therefore I am" – Descartes.'

'French,' I guessed.

'Right, Seth,' he said. 'Thou shalt have a Rolls-Royce and go to Oxford and never read a book again.'

'"I think, therefore I am,"' with scorn. 'Wallace the fruiterer – he who sells perishable goods after they have perished to Saturday night idiots – might well say of them, "They do not think, therefore they are not, they buy perishable goods after they have perished."'

Out of the welter of names and quotations (Mad Dan's 'My personal leaden treasury of the human tragedy') the cries, the references rolled out endlessly. He said that Martin Luther should have had a diet of worms. Why, I thought, why should the man eat worms?

'Can you eat worms?' I asked.

'Not as readily as the worms will eat you,' he said.

He roared with delight at this incomprehensible joke. He had become more and more burning and bright. He said he had a cold, and took some more medicine from a little bottle in his pocket.

This was as it should be. Uncle Dan had been talking ever since I could remember. Until this moment Christmas was

Christmas as it always had been. But then my sister's husband, cheekboned, hollowed, sculpted, came into the room.

'All right, boys,' he said, 'off you go – take the boy with you.'

'Where to?' I asked.

'Just go with Dan and behave yourself,' he said.

'Where's my sister?' I said.

'Never mind,' he said. 'Go you.'

I went out into the night with Dan and the other men.

Why were they sending me out at this time of night on Christmas Eve?

My mother had died when I was two years old, and I had lived with my sister and her husband ever since. I had had lots of Christmases since my mother's death, and they could already be relied on, they had always been the same. There was the growing excitement of Uncle Ben's Christmas Club (you paid a sixpence or a shilling a week throughout the year), and the choosing from the catalogue – *Littlewood's Catalogue*. There was the breathless guessing at what Santa Claus would bring. What was in those anonymous brown paper parcels on top of the wardrobe? Would it be a farm with pigs in a sty, and ducks on a metal pond, and five-barred gates, and metal trees, and Kentucky fences, and a horse or two, and several cows, and a tiny bucket and a milk-maid, and a farmhouse complete with red-faced farmer and wife in the window? And a chimney on top? Pray God it wasn't Tommy Elliot's farm, which I'd played with for two years and which I feared – from glances and whispers that I'd caught between my sister and Mrs Elliot – was going to be cleaned up and bought for me for Christmas. It would be shameful to have a second-hand present. Everybody would know. It must be, if a farm at all, a spanking-new one, gleaming with fresh paint, with not a sign of the leaden base showing through.

And I would spend an hour singing Christmas carol duets from door to door with my friend Trevor, picking up a penny here and a ha'penny there. And then home at nine o'clock, perhaps to gossip with my sister and eat more nuts, and be sent to bed sleepless and agog. And now, at the time of getting to bed, I was being sent out into the night with Mad Dan and his audience – all of them with Christmas colds, and all of them drinking medicine out of little bottles kept in their inside pockets.

We went to the meeting ground of our part of the village. It was called 'The End'. It was a vacant stretch of stony ground between two rows of cottages – Inkerman and Balaclava. Both the Inkerman people and the Balaclava people called it 'The End'. Insularity, I realise now, streetophobia – to each street it was 'The End'. It should have been called 'The Middle'.

The miners had built a bonfire and stood around it, burning on one side and frozen on the other. Chestnuts and – because there had been plenty of work that year – potatoes were roasted to blackness, and eaten sprinkled with salt, smoky and steaming straight from the fire. And Mad Dan, making great gestures against the flames, told the half-listening, silent, munching miners of the lies we had been told for thousands of years, the mellifluous advice we had been told to take.

'Turn the other cheek. Turn the other cheek, boys, and get your bloody brain broken. Suffer all my children. This side of the river is torment and torture and starvation, and don't forget the sycophancy to the carriaged and horsed, the Daimlered, the bare-shouldered, remote beauties in many mansions, gleaming with the gold we made for them. Suffer all my baby-men, beat out, with great coal-hands, the black melancholy of the hymns. When you die and cross that stormy river, that roaring Jordan, there will be unimaginable delights, and God shall wipe away all tears, and there will be no more pain. Lies Lies! Lies!'

The night was getting on. Christmas was nearly here. Dan was boring now, and sometimes he didn't make sense, and he was repeating himself. What was in those parcels on top of the wardrobe, and why had I been sent out so late on Christmas Eve? I wanted to go home.

'Can I go home now, Mad Dan?'

'Shut your bloody trap and listen,' he said, 'or I'll have you apprenticed to a haberdasher.'

This was a fate worse than death for a miner's son. There was, you understand, the ambition for the walk of the miners in corduroy trousers, with yorks under the knees to stop the loose coal running down into your boots and the rats from running up inside your trousers and biting your belly (or worse), and the lamp in the cap on the head, and the bandy, muscle-bound strut of the lords of the coalface. There was the ambition to be one of those blue-scarred boys at the street corner on Saturday night with a half a crown in the pocket and, secure in numbers, whistle at the girls who lived in the residential area. The doctor's, the lawyer's, the headmaster's daughter.

And Dan roared on. He said be believed nothing and believed everything. That he knew nothing and knew everything. He said that be was the Voltaire of Aberavon. He wept once or twice, and the silent miners chewed and stared uneasily. Crying was for women, or for preachers when talking of God's magnanimity, his mercy, his love. Miners did not weep – not even gabby miners like Mad Dan, who evaded work whenever he could. Mad Dan, with passionate eloquence, had long been an advocate of frequent and lasting strikes. Life was too rough to cry about.

I tried to sneak out of the circle around the bonfire and make my way home, but one of the miners caught me by the ear and brought me painfully back. 'You'll go home when we go home,' he said.

Dan didn't *speak* any more – he chuntered on – that is to say he would have been mumbling into his beard, had he had a beard. There came out of the grey embers of his dying oratory occasional flashes of coherence.

'Who sent the slave back to his master?'

'Was St Paul a Christian?'

And, with snarling sarcasm, 'There was an Israelite indeed in whom there was much guile.'

'"Give me liberty or give me death."'

'"Thou hast conquered, O pale Galilean; the world has grown grey from thy breath."'

The wind, tigerish, now crouched, now circled, now menaced the bonfire. And the bonfire, now rearing back from, now roaring back at the wind, would send showers of sparks and smoke and coloured flame up the endless open chimney of the night. I was bored and bewildered. I pondered on some of the half-baked things that Uncle Mad Dan bad been saying – he talked like a book, they said of him. What did Mad Dan mean about cries being lies? Anyway, his cries didn't sound much like cries to me. They sounded like sentences. Cries were screams and things like that when somebody twisted your arm or busted your nose. How could 'Turn the other cheek' be a cry? Or 'God is love' or 'The wages of sin is death'? I dimly guessed what time in mist confounds. Why was the Twenty-third Psalm a poem of incomparable beauty? The teacher in school had said it was. I puzzled about this, too. It didn't rhyme. How could it be a poem if it didn't rhyme?

What were cries? How could something be a half-truth? Why were cries lies? Why couldn't I go home? Why was I kept out so late on Christmas Eve, when Holy Santa was due any time after midnight? I dimly guessed what time in mist confounds.

Why had my sister been upstairs all this night on Christmas Eve when I was home? Why wasn't she peeling potatoes, or something? Why were two of my aunties sitting in the parlour, and with them Mrs Tabor TB – she who wore her husband's cap on back to front? Why did they talk low? I dimly guessed. Was my sister dead? Dying? I loved my sister – sometimes with an unbearable passion.

I suddenly knew that she was dying.

'Is my sister dying, Mad Dan?' I said.

'We are all dying, Nebuchadnezzar,' he said.

'Even your growing pains are reaching into oblivion.

'She'll last the night, Dyfrig,' he said. 'She'll last the night.'

Now my sister was no ordinary woman – no woman ever is, but to me, my sister less than any. When my mother had died, she, my sister, had become my mother, and more mother to me than any mother could ever have been. I was immensely proud of her. I shone in the reflection of her green-eyed, black-haired, gypsy beauty. She sang at her work in a voice so pure that the local men said she had a bell in every tooth, and was gifted by God. And these pundits who revelled in music of any kind and who had agreed many times, with much self-congratulations, that of all instruments devised by man, crwth, violin, pibcorn, dulcimer, viola, church organ, zither, harp, brass band, woodwind, or symphony orchestra – they had smugly agreed that there was no noise as beautiful at its best as the sound of the human voice.

She had a throat that should have been coloured with down like a small bird, and eyes so hazel-green and open that, to preserve them from too much knowledge of evil, should have been hooded and vultured and not, as they were, terrible in their vulnerability. She was innocent and guileless and infinitely protectable. She was naive to the point of saintliness, and wept a lot at the misery of others. She felt all tragedies except her own. I had read of the Knights of Chivalry and I knew that I had a bounden duty to protect her above all other creatures. It wasn't until thirty years later, when I saw her in another woman, that I realised I had been searching for her all my life.

Why had I been sent out? When would they let me go home? Why were my aunties there, and Mrs Tabor TB? (She was called Mrs Tabor TB because she'd had eight children, all of whom had died in their teens of tuberculosis. She was slightly mad, I think, and would mutter to herself, 'It wasn't Jack or me. TB was in the walls. The Council should have had that house fumigated. The TB was in the walls.')

Mad Dan was silent now. His stoned eyes stared into the fire. A little spittle guttered quietly from the corner of his mouth.

'Let's have a song, boys,' he said slowly. 'Stay me with minims, comfort me with crotchets.'

The crag-faced miners sang with astonishing sweetness a song about a little engine.

> *Crawshaw Bailey had an engine;*
> *It was full of mighty power.*
> *He was pull a little lever;*
> *It was go five miles an hour.*
> *Was you ever see,*
> *Was you ever see,*
> *Was you ever see*
> *Such a funny thing before?*

They sang a hymn about what you could see from the hills of Jerusalem; they sang a song about a saucepan; of a green hill far away, without a city wall; of a black pig and how necessary and how dreadful it was to kill it; of the Shepherds and the Magi. Mad Dan stared, and I sang soprano.

There was a disturbance outside the fire's night wall and my auntie Jinnie came suddenly into the tight. Mad Dan stood up.

'All right?' he said.

'Lovely,' she said. 'Nine pounds – a wench.'

'Come, Joseph of Arimathea,' he said to me.

'Santa called early tonight. Home we go.'

We walked a few steps.

'Oh!' he said. 'Any of you boys got a piece of silver? A tanner would do, but half a crown or a florin would be tidier.'

One of the men threw him a florin. 'Tell her it's a happy Christmas from Nat Williams, and all that,' he said.

We went home. Mrs Tabor TB was downstairs in the kitchen, husband's cap on back to front. My brother-in-law was whistling at the hearth, with the flat iron and the nuts, working steadily. My auntie Jinnie and my auntie Cassie, spinsters both, were arch and coy, and spoke to me as if I were demented and slightly deaf.

'Santy Clausie has brought Richie-Pitchie a prezzy-wezzy for Christmas. Go upstairs and see what Santy has brought you.'

I went upstairs with Mad Dan. As I went, Mrs Tabor TB said to my breath-whistling, nut-cracking brother-in-law, 'Talk to the Council, Elfed,' she said, 'get them to fumigate the whole house.'

I dimly guessed, of course, but there was still a chance that there would be a fire engine, loud-red and big enough for an eight-year-old to ride in. The prezzy-wezzy was a furious, red-faced, bald, wrinkled old woman, sixty minutes' old.

'Try this for size,' said Mad Dan, and pressed the florin into the baby's left hand. She held the money tightly. 'You've got a good grip,' said Mad Dan to the baby. 'She'll never be poor,' he said to my sister.

My sister looked washed-out and weak. She smiled at me, and I gave her a kiss.

'Well, what do you think of your Christmas present?' she said.

'Fine,' I said. 'Is this all I get?'

'No, there'll be more in the morning.'

'OK,' I said. 'Goodnight, then.'

We went downstairs together, and the baby screamed.

'There,' said Mad Dan, 'is the only cry that is true and immortal and eternal and from the heart. Screaming we come into the world and screaming we go out.'

'Well, what do you think of your new sister?' they asked in the kitchen.

'New *niece*,' I said. 'Fine.'

I went to my bedroom in the box room. The bed was old, and the springs had long ago given up, and sleeping in it was like sleeping in a hammock.

My brother-in-law blew out the candle. 'Sleep now,' he said. 'No lighting the candle and reading.' He closed the door and went downstairs.

I pulled the clothes over my head and made a tent, felt for my Woolworths torch, and with *John Halifax, Gentleman*, propped against my knees, began to read. The Atlantic wind, wild from America, whooped and whistled around the house. The baby choked with sobs on the other side of the bedroom wall. I listened. Well, at least, I thought, it isn't Tommy Elliot's farm.

NATIVES

Ron Berry

Levi Jones swung away from the bar, a mindful slew on his stiff right leg. He returned to the table. 'Referring back,' he said, holding out the tray, Martin and Felix taking their drinks, 'it's my opinion we have been discussing the modern disease mobility of labour, royal commissions examining this and that, it's a disease of the soul.'

Felix said, 'I've had politics up to here.'

Martin said, 'The rot set in when they closed Fawr and Fach colleries.'

'We're leftovers from the regime of King Steam Coal,' said Levi. 'But listen, the best human stuff comes from roots, from inheritance. Put bluntly, a man can't, he *can't* renege on the way he's made, his birth-given packet. Where people don't belong, that's where they go doolally. Therefore, boys, culture, civilisation, these are ours until Upper Coed-coch becomes totally extinct.'

Martin spoke to Felix. 'He's still librarian in the Institute, knocked down about eight years ago.'

'Time has reduced this village,' conceded Levi. 'The old cramp of time, in conjunction with economics, the great falsehood, the gospel of men who worship privilege. We are governed by twenty-four carat fakes disguised as civil servants.'

'Rubbish,' said Felix.

'Profitability,' argued Levi, 'comes before people. Whole

85

families have left, drifted away from Wales forever. Every time a house falls empty, the council start demolishing.'

Martin said, 'Train service killed by Beecham, bus service every three hours, our doctor emigrated to Australia, my grandchildren travelling eight miles each way to school...'

'We are living in a ghetto,' pronounced Levi.

'One pub, used to be five,' said Felix.

Levi grimaced, firming his false teeth. 'Boys, truth is we're on shifting ground, similar in miniature to the biblical Jews except there's no redeemer, no flesh and blood God's-son guaranteed to unite the masses. We need a big name figure, a kind of phoenix ready to spurt up from our ashes.'

'Politically powerless we are,' said Martin.

'Cultured decadents,' explained Levi, 'short of a prescribed saviour.'

'We're well past middle age, we're on compo and hardship allowance,' said Martin.

Felix added, 'Knocking back scrumpy five nights a week, beer on Fridays and Saturdays.'

Levi raised his glass. 'We are the immovables, financially deprived, dauntless, capable of social sweetness, murder by degrees, slow suicide, humility, even visions. Anything at all on the graph of human behaviour.'

'Bar earning a living wage,' grumbled Felix.

Martin said, 'Being disabled, the three of us on the books in Hobart House, London SW1.'

'Sacrificial victims to the old black diamonds!' crowed Levi. His friends nodded.

'King Coal, the rotten waster,' said Felix.

Levi rolled three cigarettes and fingered a single match from the ticket pocket of his jacket. 'Aye, Upper Coed-coch has been renamed Isolated Area by our country planning experts. Consequently the Forestry Commission has taken over. Surface pillage succeeding subterranean rape.'

'Mountains around here,' said Martin, 'they'll be like the Western Front when these trees are cropped.'

Felix went into a controlled bout of coughing. Then he apologised, 'My sixty per cent dust from hard headings down the old Fawr Nine Deep.'

'Me, I'm seventy-five per cent pneumo,' said Martin.

'We shan't witness the millennium,' promised Levi.

Martin looked angry. 'Nor roam the mountains on Sunday mornings. You need a can-lamp and knee-pads to crawl under the bloody Christmas trees.'

Levi dipped a finger in his beer, swam it humming around the rim of his glass. 'Economics, the name of the game.'

Martin coughed, paused, steadied his breath to mutter, 'The daft sods.'

Felix suggested, 'Let's shift from this corner. Sing-song out there in the back room.'

Levi launched into chicane prophecy. 'By the year two thousand and eight, every infant will slot-fit instant social service before he's off the breast, his poop conduited to manufacture manna, his water piped to produce energy from the earth's magma, and at the end, at the very end his processed corpse will magic blossoms from gravel!'

'Talking like the Bible again,' said Felix.

Levi lowered his head, presenting tanned baldness, whispy eyebrows and the blue-scarred ridge of his heavily boned nose.

'My prerogative, Felix. I'm one of your stall and heading examiners who filled out coal on a diet of Spinoza, Immanuel Kant, Nietzsche, Voltaire and Charles Darwin, with Walter Whitman and Johnny Keats for after.'

'Some fuckin' collier,' vowed Felix. 'C'mon, let's see what's doing in the back room.'

'He dropped in clover after his kneecap was busted,' said Martin.

Levi sniggered like a schoolboy. 'Twenty years in the Institute library, franking the date on Westerns, Thrillers, Ethel M. Dell, and Charles bloody Dickens. Righto then, we'll join the entertainers. As from tonight universal literacy is a curse, a cancer spread by Fleet Street.'

They left the public bar.

There were less than a dozen customers in the large back room. Friendly atmosphere, greetings, the compo and hardship allowance trio settling at a table near the serving hatch.

Martin whewed disgust. 'This used to be the Singing Room, crammed to the doors every Saturday night.'

'Blind Goronwy tonking the keys as usual,' said Felix.

Goronwy played 'When the blue of the night meets the gold of the day', with Mrs Charles crying temolo fragments from her small mouth.

'Fierce, she's a fierce old bird,' Levi said, remembering Crad Charles, killed, crushed between fallen rock and timber, circa 1959.

'Her and Mrs Sen-Sen James, they've messed up a few marriages,' said Felix.

Levi tutted amiably. 'Mrs Sen-Sen looks fey, a lady born and bred not to lift a finger to help herself. Black hair from a bottled greying out from the crown of her head. She's well matched with Mrs Charles, they're close, spur and stirrup since burying their husbands.'

'Fawr pit widows both,' said Martin.

'Queens of deception,' said Levi.

Felix humphed a noise in his nose. 'Young Billy Tash could do with a bath.'

'Scrap merchants make their contribution to the community,' contended Levi.

'Glenda put the snaffle on him good and proper,' said Felix.

Levi supplied details. 'She's the brainiest woman in Riverside Terrace. Glenda used to fill in Billy's income tax forms. One morning last summer he found her what they call *en déshabillé*. Billy, well, his eyeballs came out like gobstoppers. And then, boys, human nature. Short jump and long hop to their wedding before the end of the taxable year. Glenda's old enough to be his mam.'

'True,' agreed Felix. 'She's older than Jesse Mackie' – Jesse was sitting with Billy and Glenda.

'Orphan,' said Martin. 'Underpaid labourer for Billy Tash since Billy went into collecting scrap.'

Levi hoiked himself upright in his chair. 'Jesse never knew adolescence as a time of pomp and arrogance!'

Martin and Felix pretended they were deaf.

Goronwy played 'Sixteen Tons and What Do You Get, Another Day Older and Deeper in Debt', encouraging Hopkin Morgan, who cuffed Whitey, his pale grey alsatian. The animal dropped couchant like a dog-faced sphinx. Hopkin sang 'Sixteen Tons', stanced in profile, occasionally shovelling imaginary coal.

Felix called, ''Core, encore!'

Martin was clapping. 'Not bad for a man who never filled a dram of coal in his life. Oil-boy and haulier since he was a kid.'

'Pack of dogs these days and he's on his third wife,' said Felix.

'Sound Coed-coch stock,' maintained Levi. 'Head of a druid, muscles bulging below his armpits, chest like a barrel, hands like grappling hooks, and now he's redundant, probably never work again.'

Felix scowled. 'Bloody Hopkin, he'll thrive where the crows' beaks'll drop off.'

Pamela Pryor (BA Aber.) came to the serving hatch. She bought a bottle of stout for Blind Goronwy.

Levi said, 'Evening, Miss Pryor. Visiting Mam and Dad for the weekend? Nice too. If there's one thing I admire it's families sticking together.' He saluted Idris and Maisie Pryor. 'Shwmae, Id! Hullo there, Maisie!'

The Pryors smiled, tucked at their table by the piano.

'I'm driving back tomorrow night,' said Pamela.

'Smart little car, Fiat,' said Martin.

Felix winked at the scholarship girl. 'Ask Goronwy to give us a number.'

She swayed a little, reflective, left knee dipped, her tummy sagging. Pamela taught English and history in a Surrey boarding school.

Felix recommended, '"Your Tiny Hand is Frozen", that's Goronwy's favourite.'

Pamela sighed, 'Goronwy is a lovely old character. Excuse me.' She walked to the piano, poured Goronwy's stout, then went to every table, collecting glasses on her tray, and returned to the hatch, innocently imperious, beckoning to Levi, Martin and Felix.

Martin said, 'Straight beer, please. Ta very much.'

Goronwy lifted his thin, true eunuch's tenor through 'Your Tiny Hand is Frozen'. He followed this with a chorus piece from *The Desert Song*.

Martin said, 'Something I'd like to do, buy drinks all round. I couldn't afford to, not even when I was on yardage down in the Red Vein district.'

'Why bother! You can't make such comparison,' declared Felix.

'Neither is she at all like her father,' Martin said. 'Idris Pryor's a tight man, always was.'

'Similar to her mother,' said Felix.

Levi prolonged his, 'Aaaah.'

They stared at one another, brief, silent, glinty scrutinies.

From Felix, 'Aye.'

Martin, 'Well, yes, same as Maisie when Maisie was Maisie Beynon.'

Levi, 'Undoubtedly.'

Goronwy spun around on his stool, plump face utterly impassive, his blindness shielded, sunk in rolls of pinkness. He spun again, pudgy fingers roving, tinkling 'Rock Around the Clock'.

Stan Rees and a blonde woman began dancing.

'Go-go, that's your real go-go,' said Felix.

Rising from the table, Levi waggled his stiff leg. 'Old style, boys, handed down from Africa! Or from Iolo Morgannwg. Come on, have a go-go!'

They trucked awkwardly to the beat. After the dance Maisie Pryor hurried across the room, a trim woman in her late forties. She said to Levi, '"Lonesome Road" please, for our Pam.'

He made the announcement. 'Ladies and gentlemen, by special request, "Lonesome Road" from Martin Davies and Felix Mathias! Give them a big hand!'

Male voice partly baritones, they achieved Gregorian purity, singing directly at each other, solo phrases given each to each, balanced, the harmony of instinct.

Mrs Charles and Mrs Sen-Sen James sent high piercing squeals above the applause. Pamela Pryor brought three whiskies from the hatch.

'Years ago,' Felix said, 'we were near enough perfect. Right, Martin?'

Levi intervened. 'Water under the bridge. On short notice you boys did very well.' He caught Pamela's wrist. 'See, Miss Pryor, time goes by. My butties are out of practice. Can we expect a number from you?'

'Contralto,' said Martin. 'I remember this girl in a school concert. St David's day it was.'

'Oh, I wish I was back in Upper Coed-coch,' confessed Pamela. It's depressing where I am now.'

'Aye, the hiraeth,' said Levi.

'Hiraeth won't pay the rent or keep grub in the pantry,' said Felix.

Martin carefully pummelled himself on the chest. 'Hold on! Got it! "Greensleeves"! I'll pass on the word to Blind Goronwy.'

'Oh, no no no!' Suddenly Pamela's pleading collapsed to enigmatic composure.

Martin waited for her at the piano. He held up his arms. 'Quiet one and all, right 'round the room, please! Thank you!'

Pamela sang 'Greensleeves'.

Said Felix, 'Her head's screwed on the right way, different from Maisie at her age.'

'Meticulous, despite the fact she's half pissed,' said Levi.

Martin downed his whisky. 'Strong contalto. Sheer quality.'

Felix chuckled in delight. 'Us three, we're all of us half pissed.'

'As we are *entitled*,' stressed Levi.

Their heads close together over the piano, Goronwy and Pamela quietly chanted snatches of 'Myfanwy'. Stan Rees had his hand up the blonde's skirt. Billy Tash gave some money to Jesse Mackie. Glenda seemed lost in daze. The widows Charles and James were watching Stan and the blonde. Hopkin Morgan eyed the clarity of his seventh pint, and lowered it to a third. The dog Whitey remained motionless. Idris and Maisie Pryor smiled at themselves.

Goronwy lifted the lid of the piano. 'It's in there somewhere! My Joseph Parry music sheet!'

'"Myfanwy"! "Myfanwy"!' yelped the widows.

'In public,' muttered Felix. 'Stan Rees better leave that girl alone or she'll spew her guts up.'

Levi raised his fist, 'Boys, rapture is on the loose tonight! Blind Goronwy and Miss Pamela Pryor are about to unlock the paradox of paradise! Entrancement of the species! A throbbing pore in the flesh of flux! Aye aye! Reality grinds behind the gargoyles of our humdrum dementia!'

'Husht, man,' said Martin.

Miss Pryor and Goronwy sang 'Myfanwy'.

'Up, Wales,' growled Felix.

'You bloody cynic,' Levi said.

Martin added a rider, 'Fel, don't be a shit all your life.'

Goronwy banged hard for silence. He turned his blind head. 'We call upon Levi Jones for a monologue!'

Stan Rees came over with his blonde. 'How about it, Levi? Give us "The Green Eye of the Little Yellow God".'

'"If"!' shouted Hopkin Morgan.

Felix and Martin said, '"If".'

'"Dangerous Dan Magrew"!' screeched the widows.

The blonde's mouth hung open. 'Well a' bugger me, let 'im make up 'is own mind for Chrissake.'

Stan threatened her. 'Watch you language in company.' He grinned at Levi. 'Take no notice, she's been on the vodka and lime since seven o'clock. Tell you what, Levi, recite "The Green Eye of the Little Yellow God" and I'll buy you fellas a pint.'

'"If", insisted Martin.

Stan's grin fell sour. 'No offence.' He steered the blonde way. 'C'mon.'

Levi limped across to the piano. 'Ladies and gentlemen, some Rudyard Kipling. These days old Rudyard is seen as a bit of a flag-waver before Britannia turned constipated on her throne. I must ask you to make allowances. My memory is not so good. I might get stuck here and there.'

'He's on form,' said Martin.

Goronwy spun delicate chords, pacing Levi's elocution. Afterwards he recited 'The Green Eye of the Little Yellow God'.

Martin approved. 'Nice performance, Levi. You held 'em in the palm of your hand.'

Stan Rees refilled their glasses.

Eira came into the back room, Hopkin Morgan's third childless wife. The alsatian trailed her to the piano. Blind Goronwy celebrated Eira's faded reputation, playing 'Blue moon'.

'Torchy girl from days gone by,' said Levi. 'Duw, the scorched christs and creamy lucifers of long ago, long before they even sank the bloody pits.'

'*Blue moon, I see you standing alone,*' sang Eira, her arms reaching out to Hopkin, his stubbed teeth grinning pride.

Sprawled at their feet, Whitey dreamed along his nose, sensitive quivers plucking the roots of his cocked ears. Jesse Mackie went to sit beside Mrs Sen-Sen James. His forearms were on the table, each side of his pint. As Eira pecked a thank you kiss on Goronwy's forehead, Mrs Sen-Sen went to the hatch for a Scotch egg and a packet of crisps for Jesse.

'Eira's over the hill like the rest of us,' said Martin.

'Liberation, emancipation,' cried Levi faintly. 'Freedom from anxiety and remorse. We're aeons from the jet set, light years from lotus delirum!'

'Quiet, man, talk sense,' warned Felix.

Levi pulled up the leg of his trousers. Howling softly, he slapped his misshapen knee. 'Boys, Charity blows her snot in the bandage off the eyes of Justice!'

Goronwy played 'Calon Lân'. Everybody sang. Billy Tash followed Glenda to the serving hatch. She bought a bottle of brandy. Goodnight, Mrs Jones,' she said. 'Goodnight, Mr Davies. Goodnight, Mr Mathias.'

'Party?' enquired Martin.

Billy slid the bottle into his pocket. Glenda's features squeezed disdain. 'It's for Billy, he's not feeling well.'

'Touch of the 'flu I think,' Billy said.

Glenda edged herself in front of him. 'And besides, he works outdoors in all weathers.'

Levi held up his open hands. 'Say no more! The man who succeeds in business starting from scratch, he deserves nothing but the best!'

'So long as you don't cast sneers, Levi Jones.' Glenda's eyes were green, glacial. She caught Billy's arm, leading him from the room.

Mrs Sen-Sen bought three hot pasties wrapped in doilies. Jesse Mackie sat between the widows. They mothered him competitively. Eira bought a pasty for Whitey. Maisie Pryor and her daughter visited the Ladies. Stan Rees and his blonde were kissing. She drooped limply in her chair, eyes wide open, empty as sky.

'Whoor-master, he's nothing but a whoor-master,' growled Felix.

'Ordinary greed,' muttered Levi.

Out in the public bar, the landlord rang his handbell.

'Can't be!' Martin said.

Felix drained his glass. 'Bloody well is! Last orders. My turn.'

They rose together with fresh pints as Goronwy hammered the opening chord of the national anthem. But the widows and Jessie Mackie wound up the night, singing 'We'll Keep a Welcome In the Hillsides'. Blind Goronwy was leaning on two pillars in the Gents.

Levi, Martin and Felix stood near the door. They shook hands with everybody. Outside the pub, moon glow chilling the forested hills, they huddled for a few minutes, talking, then strolled home, still arguing, comparing, marking boom-times, tumults, struggles, the rising and falling histories of Upper Coed-coch.

MEMORYSTICKS

A ROMAN SPRING

Leslie Norris

I have this place in Wales, a small house set in four acres of pasture, facing north. It's simple country, slow-moving. I look down my fields and over a narrow valley, green even in winter. I go whenever I can, mainly for the fishing, which is splendid, but also because I like to walk over the grass, slowly, with nobody else about. The place is so silent that you discover small noises you thought had vanished from the world, the taffeta rustle of frail twigs in a breeze, curlews bubbling a long way up.

It's astonishing the old skills I find myself master of when I'm there, satisfying things like clearing out the well until its sand is unspotted by any trace of rotten leaf and its water comes freely through in minute, heavy fountains; or splitting hardwood with a short blow of the cleaver exactly to the point of breaking. I've bought all the traditional tools, the rasp, the band saw, the edged hook, the long-handled, heart-shaped spade for ditching. After a few days there I adopt an entirely different rhythm and routine from my normal way of living. Nothing seems without its purpose, somehow. I pick up sticks for kindling as I walk the lanes; I keep an eye cocked for changes of the weather.

We went down in April, my wife and I, for the opening of the salmon-fishing season. The weather had been so dry that the river was low, and few fish had come up from the estuary, ten miles away. I didn't care. We had a few days of very cold wind, and I spent my time cleaning the hedges of old wood, cutting out some wayward branches, storing the sawn pieces in the shed. After this I borrowed a chain saw from my neighbour Denzil Davies, and ripped through a couple of useless old apple trees that stood dry and barren in the garden. In no time they were reduced to a pile of neat, odorous logs.

They made marvellous burning. Every night for almost a week I banked my evening fires high with sweet wood, and we'd sit there in the leaping dark, in the low house, until it was time for supper. Then, one morning, the spring came.

I swear I felt it coming. I was out in front of the house when I felt a different air from the south, meek as milk, warm. It filled the fields from hedge to hedge as if they had been the waiting beds of dry ponds. Suddenly everything was newer; gold entered the morning colours. It was a Sunday morning. I walked through the fields noticing for the first time how much growth the grass had made.

From some neighbouring farm, perhaps Ty Gwyn on the hillside, perhaps Penwern lower down the valley, the sound of someone working with stone came floating through the air. I stood listening to the flawless sound as it moved without a tremor, visibly almost, toward me. 'Chink,' it came, and again, 'chink,' as the hammer chipped the flinty stone. I turned back to the house and told my wife. We had lunch in the garden, and afterward we found a clump of white violets as round and plump as a cushion, right at the start of the road. They grew beside a tumbledown cottage which is also mine, at the edge of my field where it meets the lane. The cottage is called Hebron. It wasn't so bad when I bought the place – I could have saved it then, had I the money – but the rain has got into it now, and every winter brings it closer to the ground. It had only two rooms, yet whole families were raised there, I've been told. We picked two violets, just as tokens, as emblems of the new spring, and walked on down the hill. Ruined and empty though it is, I like Hebron. I was pleased that the flowers grew outside its door.

As we walked along, a blue van passed us, and we stood in the hedge to let it through. Our lane is so narrow that very few people use it – the four families who live there, and a few tradesmen. But we didn't recognise the van. We heard the driver change down to second gear as he swung through the bend and into the steep of the hill, outside the broken cottage. We had a splendid day. In the afternoon we took the car out and climbed over the Preseli Hills to Amroth, in Pembrokeshire. The sands were empty; the pale sea was fastidiously calm. It was late when we got back.

The next day was every bit as perfect. I got up in the warm first light, made some tea, cleaned the ash from the grate, and went into the field. I took a small axe with me, so that I could break up a fallen branch of sycamore that lay beneath its parent in the bottom field. Beads of few, each holding its brilliant particle of reflected sun, hung on the grass blades. I pottered about, smiling, feeling the comfortable heat between my shoulder blades. Over the sagging rood of Hebron I could see the purple hills of Cardiganshire rising fold on fold into the heart of Wales. I listened idly to my neighbour, whoever he was, begin his work again, the clink of his hammer on the stone sounding so near to me. It took me a little while to realise that it *was* close at hand. I was unwilling to believe that anyone could be away from his own house on so serene and beautiful an early morning. But someone was. Someone was chipping away inside the walls of Hebron.

I ran through the wet grass, reached the cottage, and looked through a gap where the stones had fallen out of the back wall. I could see right through to the lane. The blue van was parked there, and a thin, blonde girl stood beside it, her long face turned down a little, her hair over her shoulders. The wall was too high for me to see anyone in the house.

'What goes on?' I said. I couldn't believe that my ruin was

being taken away piecemeal. The girl didn't move. It was as if she hadn't heard me.

'Who's there?' I called. 'What do you think you're doing?'

A young man stood up inside the house, his head appearing opposite mine through the hole in the wall. He was dark, round-faced, wore one of those fashionable Mexican moustaches. He had evidently been kneeling on the floor.

'Just getting a few bricks,' he said, his face at once alarmed and ingratiating. He waited, smiling at me.

'You can't.' I said. 'It's mine. The whole thing is mine – cottage, fields, the lot.'

The young man looked shocked.

'I'm sorry,' he said. 'I've had permission from the local Council to take stuff away... They say it doesn't belong to anyone... I'm sorry.'

'The Council are wrong,' I said. 'This cottage belongs to me.'

I felt stupid, standing there, talking through a ragged gap in a wall three feet thick, but there was no way of getting around to him, except by walking back up the field, through a gate, and down the lane to the front of the house, where the white violets were. The thin, silent girl was standing almost on top of the flowers, which made me obscurely angry. I turned around and hurried off, alongside the hedge. As I went I heard the van start up, and Hebron was deserted when I got back. I opened the door. They'd taken the frames out of the windows, the wooden partition which had divided the little house into two rooms, and an old cupboard I had been storing there. I was incredulous, then furious. I looked down at the floor. All my marvellous quarry tiles had been prised up and carried away. I could have wept. Nine inches square and an inch thick, the tiles had been locally made over a hundred years ago. They were a rich plum colour, darker when you washed them, and there were little frosted imperfections in them that caught the light. They were very beautiful.

I ran up the road, calling for my wife. She came out and listened to me, her obvious sympathy a little flawed because she was also very amused. She had seen me stamping along, red-faced and muttering, waving aloft the hatchet I had forgotten I was holding.

'No wonder they vanished so quickly,' said my wife. 'You must have looked extraordinary, waving that tomahawk at them through a hole in the wall. Poor young things, they must have wondered what sort of people live here.'

I could see that it was funny. I began to caper about on the grass in an impromptu war dance, and Denzil Davies came up in his new car. As far as Denzil is concerned, I'm an Englishman, and therefore eccentric. Unmoved, he watched me complete my dance.

But I was angry still. I could feel the unleashing of my temper as I told my story to Denzil. 'They had a blue van,' I said.

'It was a good market in Carmarthen last week,' said Denzil carefully, looking at some distant prospect. 'Milking cows fetched a very good price, very good.'

'Took my window frames, my good tongue-and-groove partition' I mourned. 'My lovely old cupboard.'

'I believe the Evanses are thinking of moving,' said Denzil. 'Of course, that farm is getting too big for them, now that Fred has got married. It's a problem, yes it is.

'A young man with a moustache,' I said. 'And a girl with long, fair hair. Do you know them, Denzil?'

'I might buy one or two fields from old Tom Evans.' Denzil replied. 'He's got some nice fields near the top road.'

'They stole my quarry tiles,' I said. 'Every bloody one.'

Denzil looked at me with his guileless blue eyes. 'You've never seen my Roman castle have you?' he said. 'Come over and see it now. It's not much of an old thing, but professors have come down from London to look at it. And one from Scotland.' Kitty excused herself, saying she had some reading to catch up on. I sat beside Denzil, in his new blue Ford, and we bumped along the half mile of track that leads to his farmhouse. I'd been there before of course, Denzil's farmyard is full of cats. After evening milking he always puts out an earthenware bowl holding gallons of warm milk. Cats arrive elegantly from all directions and drink at their sleek leisure.

We left the car in the yard, and climbed through the steep fields to a couple of poor acres at the top of the hill. Although high, the soil was obviously sour and wet. Clumps of stiff reeds grew everywhere, the unformed flowers of the meadowsweet were already recognisable, and little sinewy threads of vivid green marked the paths of the hidden streams. Right in the middle of the field was a circular rampart about four feet high, covered with grass and thistles, the enclosed centre flat and raised rather higher than the surrounding land. I paced it right across, from wall to wall, and the diameter was nearly seventy feet. There was a gap of eight or nine feet in the west of the rampart, obviously a gateway. It was very impressive. Denzil stood watching me as I scrambled about. Everything I did amused him.

I took an old, rusty fencing stake to knock away the thistles growing on top of the bank and forced its pointed end into the thin soil. I didn't have to scratch down very deeply before I hit something hard, and soon I uncovered a smooth stone, almost spherical and perhaps two pounds in weight. I hauled it out and carried it down to Denzil. It was grey and dense, quite unlike the dark, flaky, local stone used for building my own cottage. And Hebron too, of course. I scored my thumbnail across it, but it didn't leave a scar. It was incredibly hard. Faint, slightly darker parallel lines ran closely though it, and a small irregular orange stain, like rust, marked its surface on one side. Denzil nodded. 'That's it,' he said. 'That's what they made the walls with. Hundreds and hundreds of those round stones.' My stone had been worn smooth and round in centuries of water, in the sea or in a great river. We were nine hundred feet high and miles from the sea or any river big enough to mould such stones in numbers, yet the Roman walls were made of them.

'They're under the road, too,' said Denzil. 'The same stones.'

I looked down from the walls of Denzil's castle. It was easy to see the road, now that he'd said it. A discernible track, fainter green than the land around, marched straight and true, westward from the Roman circle, until it met the hedge. Even there it had defied nearly two thousand years of husbandry. Generations of farmers, finding that little would grow over the stones, had left its surface untilled so that the road, covered with a thin scrub of tenacious blackthorn, went stubbornly on. We saw it reach the road two hundred feet lower down, halt momentarily, and then continue undeterred until it was out of sight. I knew it well, on the other side of the narrow road. It was the boundary of my fields. I had often wondered why I should have had so regular a strip of difficult and worthless shrubs.

'Just wide enough for two chariots to pass,' said Denzil, 'That's what one of those London men told me. But I don't know if he was right.'

We looked with satisfaction at the straight path of the Romans.

'I've got new neighbours,' Denzil said. 'Down in Pengron. Funny people, came from Plymouth.' He looked gently toward Pengron, a small holding invisible in its little valley. 'They hadn't been here a week,' he went on, 'before they cut down one of my hedges. For firewood.' He let his eyes turn cautiously in my direction. 'Young fellow with a moustache,' he said, 'and a fair-haired girl.'

'How interesting,' I said, with heavy irony. 'And do they have a blue van?'

'Strange you should ask that,' said Denzil mildly. 'I believe they do.' We smiled at each other. 'Can you see,' Denzil said, 'that the Roman road must have passed right alongside Hebron? There must have been a house on that spot for hundreds and hundreds of years, I bet.' He was right. The old cottage sat firmly next to the dark accuracy of the traceable road, its position suddenly relevant. Carrying my stone, I walked back through the fields to have my lunch.

In the afternoon I drove over to Pengron. The house, its windows curtainless, seemed empty, but a caravan stood in the yard. The thin girl came to the door of the caravan, holding a blue plate in her hand. 'Good afternoon,' I said, but she didn't answer.

I've never seen anyone as embarrassed as the young man when he appeared behind her. He jumped out and hurried toward me. 'I know,' he said. 'You want me to take everything back. I will, I'll take it all back this afternoon. I certainly will.'

I felt very stiff and upright, listening to him. I could see all my tiles arranged in neat rows, six to a pile, on the ground. He must have taken over a hundred. He'd been at it for days, chipping away with his hammer while I wandered round in happy ignorance.

'I can understand,' I said in the most stilted and careful manner, 'that someone surprised in a situation as you were this morning is likely to say something, as an excuse, which may not be exactly true. But I have to know if you really have permission from the local Council to remove material from my cottage. If this is true, then I must go to their offices and get such permission withdrawn.'

He was in agony, his face crimson with shame. I felt sorry for him as I stood unbendingly before him.

'No,' he said. 'No, I don't have any permission. It's just that someone up the village told me that he didn't think the old place belonged to anyone. I'll take everything back this afternoon.'

I looked at my tongue-and-groove partition, my window frames. Unrecognisable almost, they formed a heap of firewood in the corner of a yard. Waving a hand at them in hopeless recoginiton of the situation, I said, 'It's not much use taking that back, but the tiles, yes, and my cupboard, and anything else you haven't broken up.' I walked back to the car, and he followed, nodding vehemently all the way. I was glad to leave him. When I looked in at Hebron later on, the tiles and the cupboard had been returned. I didn't enjoy myself that day. It's stupid to be so possessive. The old cottage is unprepossessing mess, not even picturesque. I ought to have been pleased that someone was finding it useful, but I wasn't. The lingering remnants of my anger pursued me through the night, and I was pretty tired the next day. I took it easy.

I can't think why I went down to Hebron in the cool of the evening. I walked listlessly down the hill, becoming cheerful without any energy when I found a wren's nest in the hedge. There never was such a place for wrens. They sing all day, shaking their absurd little bodies with urgent song. It was a good evening, cloudless and blue, a little cool air tempering the earlier warmth. I began to whistle. At quiet peace with myself, aimless and relaxed, I approached the cottage. When a man pushed his head and shoulders through the gaping window I was totally startled.

'How much for the house, then?' he said. He withdrew from the window, and stepping carefully, reappeared at the door, closing it slowly behind him. He was a very small man. Despite the mildness of the evening, he wore his reefer jacket wrapped well around him, and its collar high. He couldn't have been a couple of inches over five feet.

'It's not worth much,' I said. He pushed his tweed cap off his forehead and smiled at me, a sweet, wise smile, but incredibly remote.

'No,' he said, 'not now. Oh, but it was lovely sixty years ago.'

'Did you know it,' I asked, 'all that time ago?'

'Longer,' he said. 'More than sixty years ago. Since I first saw it, that is.'

He stood outside the house, his hands deep in his pockets. He stood very carefully, protectively, as if he carried something exceedingly fragile inside him. His breathing was gentle and deliberate, a conscious act. It gave him a curious dignity.

'Know it?' he said. 'For ten years I lived in this house. My brother, my mother, and me. We came here when I was five years old, after my father died, and I was fifteen when we left. I'm sixty-seven now.' We turned together to walk down the hill. He moved slowly, economically. We had gone but a few yards when he stopped, bent down, and picked up a thin ashplant, newly cut from the hedge.

'I've been getting bean sticks,' he explained. 'I've left them along the lane where I cut them, so that I can pick them up as I go back.'

We talked for a long time, and I warmed toward him. He was a great old man. We stood there, the evening darkening around us, and he told me of people who had lived along the lane in the days of his boyhood, of his work as a young man in the farms about us, of the idyllic time when he lived in Hebron with this mother and brother.

'But there's no water there,' I said. 'How did you manage for water?'

'I used to go up to your place,' he said. 'To your well. Times without number I've run up this road, a bucket in each hand, to get water from your well. We thought it was the best water in the world.'

Slowly we moved a few yards on, and the old man lifted the last of his bean sticks from where it lay. Then he turned, faced resolutely forward, and prepared to make his way back to the village, perhaps a mile away over the fields.

'I've got to be careful,' he said. 'Take things very slowly, the doctor said. I'm very lucky to be alive.' He placed his hand delicately on the lapel of his navy coat. 'Big Ben has gone with me,' he said. 'Worn out. He doesn't tick as strongly as he used to.'

'Let me carry those sticks for you,' I said, understanding now his deliberate slowness, his sweet tolerance, his other-worldliness. He was a man who had faced his own death, closely, for a long time, and he spoke to me from the other side of knowledge I had yet to learn.

'I'll manage,' he said. He bundled his sticks under one arm, opened the gate, and walked away. It was so dark that he had vanished against the black hedge while I could still hear his footsteps.

In the morning I went into the field below Hebron. It's not my field, Denzil rents it from an absentee landlord, and keeps a pony or two in it. There's a steep bank below the hedge, below the old Roman road, that is, and Hebron's garden is immediately above the bank. As I had hoped, the ground there was spongy and wet, green with sopping mosses. I climbed back up and into the garden, hacking and pushing through invading bramble and blackthorn, through overgrown gooseberry bushes. In the corner of the garden which overhangs Denzil's field, everything seemed to grow particularly well; the hedge grass was lush and rampant, the hazel bushes unusually tall. I took my hook and my saw, and cleared a patch of ground about two yards square. It took me most of the morning. Afterward I began to dig.

It was easier than I had expected, and I hadn't gone two spits down before I was in moist soil, pulling shaped spadesful of earth away with a suck, leaving little fillings of water behind each stroke of the blade. By lunchtime I'd uncovered a good head of water, and in the afternoon I'd shaped it and boxed it with stones from the old cottage, and while it cleared I built three steps down to it. It was a marvellous spring. It held about a foot of the purest, coldest water. I drank from it, ceremonially, and then I held my hand in it up to the wrist, feeling the chill spread into my forearm. Afterward I cleaned my spade meticulously until it shone, until it rang like a faint cymbal as I scrubbed its metal with a handful of couch grass.

I knew that I would find water. For hundreds of years, since Roman times, perhaps, a house had stood there: it had to have a spring.

I put my tools in the boot of the car and drove up to the village. If I meet my old friend, I thought, I'll tell him about my Roman spring. I saw him almost at once. He stood, upright and short, in front of the Harp Inn. There was nobody else in the whole village it seemed. I blew the horn, and he raised both arms in greeting. I waved to him, but I didn't stop. Let him keep his own Hebron, I thought. Let him keep the days when he could run up the hill with two buckets for the best water in the world, his perfect heart strong in his boy's ribs. I had drunk from the spring, and perhaps the Romans had, but only the birds of the air, and the small beasts, fox, polecat, badger, would drink from it now. I imagined it turning green and foul as the earth filled it in, its cottage crumbling each year perceptibly nearer the earth.

I drove slowly back. The next day we packed our bags and travelled home, across Wales, half across England.

A VIEW OF THE ESTUARY

Roland Mathias

It was a narrow cul-de-sac set at an angle upwards, with a mere pretence of a turn-round at the top, and I made a poor job of parking, shuttling to and fro feebly for more than a minute and bringing the car only very slowly to point downhill. For once Celia wasn't there to get worked up about it and my nylon shirt collar didn't get as sticky as it usually does. Mair sat quite still. And when the gear-pushing was over and the wheel was turned in against the curb, I sat too and looked.

Over against us, and seen haphazardly rather than clearly through the old fly-spots and the oily residue on the windscreen, was a reach of grey water, river broadening indistinguishably into sea. Behind it was the long black shore of Gower, cliffed just high enough to cut off any view of eastwards and beyond. The stacks on the nearer shore tipped and barred the water like organ pipes, dropping to trebles and sizes smaller, it seemed at first sight, as the water broadened away above them in the distance. At an angle lower was the scurry of roofs, slate-grey and slithering after the recent shower. It was a scene not meant to charm. It was full of the commonness of man, rugged, makeshift, tricky, work-stained, attaining any sort of peace only insofar as it avoided self-justification. There was sea if one cared to notice it, but a sea of silted-up harbours and derelict tramp ships. A sea which was one with the red flowers of the tropics only in the sense that there are different months in the same year, and a different moon in each of them. I dwelt on the scene for some minutes, neither expecting beauty nor finding it. The pull was one of verity, of life lived. It was years since I had seen the Llwchwr, as many years as would carry me back to boyhood, and yet there was nothing to wax sentimental about. 'How've you been, mun?' was the brusque greeting it gave me. And I to it. The question was unanswerable, anyway. 'Working,' I might have said. 'Working' might have been its nod too. Times were easier but we had long memories: my working day would long be over before the river, in its turn, could show a face that made believe that it too, had, forgotten.

What impression this scene and the odd silence that accompanied it made on Mair I did not enquire. She had been born away and outside the generations of rigour and needed no excuse to continue sitting. At my signal we got out and opened the gate from which paths splayed to both halves of the bungalow which presented its length above. There was a dilapidated terrace with posts and roofing that had not been painted for years, and the door into the leftward half looked little used. On one of the posts to its right it was possible to make out the name GLANABER in a spidery Sunday black, two of the letters weathered away but easy enough to guess. I knocked at the door once: then again after an interval.

'Uncle's very deaf these days,' I said. 'Or else he's out in the garden.' I knocked again, louder and more insistently.

Round the corner of the right-hand bungalow and up onto the covered terrace came a woman on the young side of middle age, plump, bespectacled and a little short of breath.

'Mr Evans is shaving,' she said. 'Besides, he never hears anyone at the door nowadays. You should go round the back.'

She stopped, taking in my rumpled but obviously formal suit. 'Wait a minute.' She thought while I could have counted three. 'I'll tell 'im.' Still puffing slightly, she disappeared the way she had come.

After what seemed an infinitely longer count, the woodwork opposite us began to shudder and give inwards at the top. The shuddering increased in dimension: there were sounds of heaving inside. Then the door was flung open with a violence its obstinacy had deserved, and in the gap, half carried away by his own impetus, stood my uncle, once cheekbone shaved but soap still adhering strenuously to all other portions of his face. Over his left arm was a towel which he had obviously meant to apply before the priorities got confused. He was wearing three pullovers, the longest of which left a couple of inches of greyish woolly vest showing above the dark-blue suit trousers, which had wide out-of-date bottoms and were frayed in several places. His braces hung down from the sweat-darkened turned-back tops.

'Well, well. Couldn't think *who* it could be. Dewch i mewn!' And again, 'Well, well.'

He stood, towel now in hand, overcome by the crisis. His hand went up as though to wipe his face, but another thought got there first. He smiled with his eyes and forgot about the soap.

'Who's this then, bachan? Which of your daughters is this? Mair, did you say? *Mair.*' He rolled the 'r' around his tongue and savoured the name as though it were a new word. 'Never seen you before, have I, Mair? No? I like to be sure.'

He remained standing on the threshold, looking at us, his perfunctory invitation to enter forgotten. 'Well, well,' he said again, using the towel now to dab at his eyes. 'Your aunt will be surprised. She will indeed. Sara!' he shouted turning at last and disappearing down the passage. 'Sara, look who's here!'

Left to ourselves, we made our way into the dark little kitchen, which was plainly the hub of confined life of Glanaber. 'I was just getting your aunt up when you came,' Uncle Ben shouted from the next room.

'I thought you were shaving,' I said with an amused face that I knew he could not see.

'Eh, what's that?' he asked, coming out. 'What's that? What did you say?' He was watching my face. 'Oh, chipping me, is it? I always had to watch you, didn't I? Always up to something you were. I remember! Not changed a bit, have you?' His dark face, topped with greying scalp-curls as tightly rolled as an African's and fronted by the great nose that looked as though it had grown up too ambitious for its station, was crinkled with laughing. The flecked brown eyes, which all six brothers (my father amongst them) had had in common, were liquid and friendly. Just to catch a glimpse of them turned the years back and made me a child again.

He remembered the towel at last and rubbed off most of the soap from the unshaven cheek and jowl, forgetting that he hadn't really finished the other side. 'Eisteddwch i lawr,' he said. 'Sit down, sit down.' His hands and arms were dark, tanned in the way holidaymakers dream of, but there had been little sun and leisure in his past. His fingers were thick and clumsy now, the joints stiffened and the thumbnails broadened and turned in towards the quick.

'You mustn't mind me,' he went on. 'I'm a bit slow now. Don't hear very well either. So Auntie and me, we don't do a lot of talking. Can't be helped, though, can't be helped. But I'm glad to see you, bachan, indeed I am.'

Mair was sitting quite still, waiting to understand. She had never really known her grandparents, who had died long ago, outside the first unthinking decade of her life. This was the first time she had been really close to an old age that was linked to her in blood. Sensing a little constraint, I stood up to close the gap and rally Ben a bit. I peered in the glass beside him.

'The older generation of Evanses may not have been handsome, but they were certainly distinctive,' I said. It was true. Six brothers and three sisters, some round-headed and some long-, three of the brothers and one of the sisters dark as Spaniards, and all of them with the haughty, sometimes digressive, nose that looked as though it were a child's attempt at distinguishing a Roman patrician. Ben's nose was the best of all, the most digressive and outrageous, achieving by stature what it lacked in accuracy. And it was the only one alive too.

'Should have some value as a museum piece, shouldn't I?' he queried, amusement leaping from crag to crag of his face.

'Scarcity value. Very hot on that these days, I'm told. Eighty years old and a craftsman's job. Nothing like it round here now.'

'Mair,' he said, turning, 'don't take any notice. Your father's always rude to me.'

'I don't,' she said. 'He's always rude to me too.'

'Well, well,' he murmured, recovering his grasp of routine. 'Time to get Auntie out.' With that he disappeared into the adjoining bedroom. I had been in the bungalow just long enough to notice how cold it was, and trying to suppress a first shiver in action, I got up to see whether I could help. At the door of the bedroom I stopped: Ben was already coming towards me with a bundle in his arms. There was condensation on the top panes of the only window.

'Take her a minute, will you, while I get the chair ready.' I caught my aunt under the armpits and held the poor four stone of her, clothes flouncing and dangling, nothing visible except the head lolling against my chest. From this burden came up a foetid smell, the smell of incontinence, of clothes lived in like a burrow. I was sickened momentarily, revolted. I tried desperately to hold my breath. Then Ben was taking the burden from me and tucking it down in the chair. On what looked like a child's face, pink and white and unlined, was a feeble smile, made of parted lips and something, just something, in the eyes.

'There, Sara. You didn't believe me, did you? But here's Gerwyn, as I said. And Mair. You've not seen Mair before, but I've told you about her, haven't I? You remember. She's

115

at university now.' Mair and I in turn felt for the limp fingers hidden in the end of the long woollen sleeve.

'How are you, Auntie?' I asked, my voice sounding louder than necessary. The lips moved, but no sound was detectable at the range of formality. Bending down, I picked up the burden of the whisper as it was repeated. 'All right, boy. All right but for this ol' complaint.'

'Good, good. That's it, that's the way.' I followed with other meaningless heartiness, of which I was ashamed even in the saying. I did not know the end, let alone the way. And to have known something of the beginning seemed at that moment of very little help. It was a mercy that these dishonesties elicited no further reply beyond the barest parting of the lips.

But my uncle was not one to leave me in difficulties for long. Never getting any answers, or none that he could hear, he had long been accustomed to a rhetoric of his own devising, which bounded forward at quick irregular intervals, as though, having played his ball onto a wall or an angle of his private fives court, he had to jump in and slash it back, or missing, take it another way on the rebound. He appeared to know that he could afford a second or two for plain inattention, but must then make some immediate, possibly violent, move.

'How's Celia, then, bachan?' He did not wait for an answer, his dark face animated. 'Our Rhian's won a scholarship, did you know? To university, yes. Clever girl, she is. There's not many can say they've got a granddaughter that's won a university scholarship, now is there?

'When...' I began. 'When...' But my thought had already been distracted by the movement that I sense rather than saw. I was conscious of some urgency in the doll-like figure in the chair. Looking more closely, I realised that the lips were moving.

'Photograph.' The word formed slowly and whisperingly. 'Ben, show them the photograph.'

Ben was talking hard, rallying Mair now and pushing her shoulder back with the blunt ends of his extended fingers. He had taken no notice of my attempted question, let alone his wife's tiny excision of her envelope of silence.

'Uncle,' I said. '*Uncle*! I see I shall have to do some bullying too.' He looked at me in surprise half thinking I resented his familiarity with Mair. 'The photograph. Auntie says what about the photograph.'

For a second or two he still looked at me blankly. Then, realising and turning almost concurrently, he disappeared into the front room and came back with it in his hand. 'There,' he said triumphantly. 'Isn't she a fine girl, our Rhian?'

I looked at the photograph carefully. There were the features again, unmistakeable. The dark, handsome, almost negroid face with the distended nostrils and the mass of little scalp-curls. Idwal to the life, all but the squint she had against the brightness of the light. A fine-looking girl, by any standards.

'Taken in Adelaide?' I was trying hard to avoid the real questions.

'Yes, Adelaide. That's the university in the background.' It was a slab of white wall. It could have been anywhere, provided anywhere was sunny enough.

He took the photograph back slowly, keeping his eyes on it as though there were something about it that he had not really seen before. Then, turning away, he put his arm round Mair's shoulders with sudden boisterousness. 'Come on, merch fach i, let me show you the bungalow. Great place we've got here, you know. Extensive. Room for twice as many.' His voice swept down the passage and into the front room. I was at a loss. The invitation had not seemed to include me: indeed, I had some sort of sense that it was important to Uncle Ben that I should not tag along. 'At all costs,' said a cowardly urge, 'don't get left here, mun. Don't be left with Auntie. What will you say?' I went down the passage far enough to be out of sight of the invalid chair and stood still. Uncle was talking photographs in the room beyond, pointing out each individual face. Mair was mute, probably muddled by the many names she did not know and afraid to reveal her ignorance. They wouldn't be out for a minute or two yet. I stood in this transit-place, aware that I had deliberately walked out of life and all ears not to be caught doing it. I stood with both palms against the clammy wall and thought.

That photograph. Shaking really, that anybody could be so like. The past living again, but in Australia. Something about that transplanting was a wound, even to me. It was an end and a cutting-off, whatever life was in it.

I found myself pressing against the wall, for no reason that I could name. Perhaps I had walked out of time too. I was possessed by that utterly alien feeling that one has only in childhood, that sense of seeing and understanding and not being at home. I was back forty years and the wall was cold behind me. Uncle Ben was an ironmonger then and Aunt Sara, in her cold, composed way, was queening it among the locals. An inexorable social aspirant, Sara. Her good looks, broad brow and closely curling hair didn't hold the attention long. The hardness came out like a ratchet to fix one exactly in one's place, and it had to be a very special occasion for me not to be conscious of being pinned down, not so much intimidated as powerless to escape the measuring tape with which her square hands were so constantly occupied.

Whatever Ben and she were did not so much matter. It was for Idwal, her son, that she planned and drove. Ben must work harder, make all possible. Ben must immolate himself on the altar. Ben must not question the unspoken contract she had with the greatness of her son's image. It was a hard, cumulative story that had cracked now as iron cracks. It was all so old, and unbelievable. And yet it had produced Idwal, if only for a time. Idwal was in some ways a replica of his mother, only handsomer, with black, curly hair and dark, almost negroid features with wide-spreading nostrils. How poor Ben, with his digressive nose, could have had a part in such symmetry was at first hard to see. But he had given the boy his colour and the black scalp-curls too. I remembered going down to the river at Llanybyther once to find Idwal. He was about twelve then, bare feet and jam pot for tiddlers and all, and I was two years younger. I went to the river because I had been sent. The truth was that I was a bit afraid of Idwal: he was tougher than I, more confident as well as older. Not at all prissy and sensitive as I was. Idwal laughed when I arrived and showed me off to a lot of other kids. 'My cousin, look,' he said. '*My cousin*. Down from the Valleys.' He laughed again, as though daring any comment. I quivered inwardly, wishing myself anywhere else in the world, knowing that the next step would be a dare. Across the river by way of the stones, many of them awash. What would my mother say? And my best shoes too!

Later, more than five years later, Idwal proposed to follow a course in medicine at a London hospital. Ben, at Sara's bidding, sold his ironmonger's shop and bought a dairy business in Cricklewood at a price that crippled him financially – just to save lodging money for Idwal and to keep him in Sara's sight. We met occasionally in the next few years, Idwal and I – I was a clerk in the Aldgate branch of Lloyd's Bank for my first permanent appointment – and once in a while we foregathered at Stewart's or Pritchard's in Oxford Street or at Hyde Park Corner. These meetings would be on Sunday nights when I had come across for the service at King's Cross Chapel, whether for my cousin's sake or to hear Elvet Lewis I never quite knew. Idwal had the same confidently jovial manner then as that day by the river, but enlarged as perhaps only London could enlarge it. He slapped me on the back and patronised me happily to his fellow students. 'Our banking member', he called me. I didn't feel much larger on these occasions than if he had dared me to wet my shoes again. Rotund, earnest and vulnerable, I reserved my wit for those who were a bit slower than I was. I knew I cut no figure beside Idwal's broad sholders, and dark, authoritative head.

Once or twice, too, I visited the dairy at Cricklewood looking for my cousin. Uncle was always dead beat with work, cycling the last rounds himself in plimsolls with a few bottles on the tray of his bike. Up at four in the morning, working sixteen hours a day at least and grey in the face with fatigue. My aunt kept a prim house behind the shop and welcomed me with only the briefest of smiles. She regarded me as a hanger-on, an amiable nobody who could not, even if he would, help her son in any way. I didn't like facing her on my own. Give Idwal his due, when he was there he brushed past all this, jollied his way in and out. And then even my uncle would joke for a minute or two, till his arm dropped off my shoulder with weariness.

Idwal failed his exams a couple of times, but the power behind him was inexorable. In the end he passed. Six years – or was it seven? He could hardly do anything else. And then he suddenly said he wanted to join the Army, become a doctor in the RAMC. I say 'suddenly' because I'd never heard of it until it happened. I was over at the dairy one night after the results of his examinations were known – this was not the celebration: we had had our junketings at Stewart's and in The Coal Hole and other places too many to remember – and I sat down at the piano to play for Idwal to sing. He was no singer but he liked to have a bawl now and again, a concession to the Welshness of his youth, and Sara approved my pianistic skills (which didn't really go much beyond knocking out a tune by ear) because they were a means for Idwal to make more noise than I did. She sat in the background, a faint smile on her face, intervening only to suggest that we might drop some of those ol' Welsh hymns and sing something a bit more refined. Ben came in once, in his plimsolls, and joined in a verse or two, singing in a resonant voice that was nearer the note than Idwal's. But

Sarah's was impatient, waving him away. 'Get finished, Ben, before coming in here. You know very well it'll be ten o'clock before you've finished with those bottles. Go on.' Almost as the door closed, Idwal switched his bawl to the sort of conversational tone that he thought wouldn't ding my ear in. 'You know I've decided to try the Army, don't you? In my astonishment – partly at the news and partly at the unnecessary drama of the decibel-drop – I let fall my hands on the keyboard in an unspeakable disharmony of sound. Sara's patience with me, always thin, broke at that, and it was no more than a perfunctory few minutes before I was on my way out. I didn't really need to work for my bank exam – I'd been at it both the nights previous – but it was the quickest thing to say.

It was some months before I heard the news and many years before I understood that I should never see Idwal again. The rigorous medical examination he had been given by the Army Board had revealed a kidney complaint at a stage already advanced: he had, in the doctors' opinion, six months at most to live. It was suggested to him, however, that his life might be prolonged if he could make up the salt deficiency somehow, perhaps by going on board ship and crusting it in by wave or wind all hours of the day and night. The hope was not much but he seized it; he signed on as a ship's doctor and, war breaking out within the next few months, sailed back and fore to the Far East in troopships – at least till Singapore fell, and after that on voyages more devious but always fresh with the winds of continuance. So nearly eight years passed: the war was over, and Idwal, still journeying back with the repatriated and out with the emigrant hopeful, strengthened his hold on life. So much so that he ventured on marriage to Margaret, a nurse of Welsh descent who had been brought up in Australia (where her mother still was), and steeled himself to take a post ashore. For nearly a year the omens held: Rhian was born of the union, Idwal managed as a houseman in a Liverpool hospital. Then the end came, and suddenly: he went blind and was dead within the month, prescribing for himself with full medical competence at each deteriorating and terrible stage of the disease. It was an exercise in doggedness, the tight-lipped parries of a man who had counted out his days for more than a quarter of his life.

It was the end, all this, of more than Sara's hope in Idwal. Margaret went back to Australia to her mother, taking Rhian with her: later she married a schoolmaster named Robertson, a colleague of hers in the boarding school where she served as matron. So all that was left of this flesh and blood was in the Antipodes, a slip of a girl with an Australian accent and a name that her acquaintances would most certainly mishandle. And that photograph! – the likeness was uncanny. The hatpeg nose would die with Ben, but his colouring and the curled wool of his hair had been transplanted successfully. A whole culture off and yet a biological survival.

It would be ridiculous to suppose that all this flashed through my mind's maze as I stood with my back to the wall in the passage of the bungalow. And yet it was all there, colied, uneasy in my consciousness. It had been collected from letters, the chatter of an ageing female cousin, and just two visits, the last one more than ten years ago. Truth to tell, I hadn't wanted to see Sara. Why should he survive, I could imagine her saying: why should he survive who never had anything about him, when Idwal, with twice the presence, could not? An aircraftman, that's all I'd been, and a pretty poor one at that. And if I was a bank manager now, was it due to much more than a ready smile and a terrible fear of doing the wrong thing, socially and financially? But there was really no need any longer for this reluctance of mine to visit Ben. Sara had Parkinson's for upwards of six years and for the last three or four she had said nothing. Nothing that was readily audible, anyway. And yet I couldn't face her, couldn't produce tenderness for one who had needed fear of old. And pity? I was suddenly uncertain of my motive for coming at all, though I had thought it a matter of conscience that had been nagging me for months, years.

It was at this uneasy moment, when I had begun to lose myself as well as time and place, that I heard Ben's voice growing louder. He had been the round of photographs and was shepherding Mair back to the kitchen. I had no time for a new posture: all I could do was advance with an air of happening to be on my way to look for them and to meet them in the doorway.

'Nice bungalow we've got here, haven't we, Mair?' Ben said when he saw me. 'Too big for us really. You must come and stay some time. Leave your old Dada. He doesn't appreciate you. Only thing he cares about is counting the coppers. He won't notice you're gone even.'

Unease or no unease, I couldn't help rising to this. The Evanses could always spark off the present, whatever past or future might say. 'Go on, Uncle. You set too much store by that unique beauty of yours. Unrepeatable value and so on. There's something to be said for bank managers, you know.'

'Something, but not much,' said Uncle Ben, his eyes wrinkling with a friendliness that took all the sting out of words. 'Come and look at the garden,' he added, fumbling with the back door, which had a piece of sacking nailed to the bottom to keep out draught. An overlapping piece was stuffed down the side, too, and it was this which made necessary what looked like furious efforts on my uncle's part. 'All these damn doors stick,' he muttered, suddenly flushed about the temples. The garden, when it finally came into view, was a large kite-shaped patch with the length of it dragged steeply uphill to a point where two other gardens nipped it with brick walls and shrubbery and held it there, immovable. In the middle distance were some old brussels sprout stalks, bare to the palm-plumes at the top. Nearer were one or two lumps of squitch and a great deal of groundsel. 'Too much for me now,' Ben said heavily. Good soil, too. But it can't be helped.'

Goodbyes came a few minutes later, despite Ben's unwillingness to let us go. Tea was something he could manage, part of the old code of hospitality. 'You could stay long enough for that, bachan,' he said wistfully. 'Auntie would like it. Wouldn't you, Sara?' I couldn't be sure whether the shapeless little doll in the chair moved or not. Perhaps there was something minutely different about the expression. I tried hard not to think so as I took the powerless hand and came for a moment again within the foetid arc. 'Goodbye, Auntie! Look after yourself.' The ridiculous words came out before I could stop them. I rushed out after the others, fearful that Mair might have heard. I knew Ben would not.

But they were standing by the gate looking at a small yew cut like a bear. It had an empty tomato tin upturned on one paw. 'His honey pot,' said Ben, simply and without excuse. 'Who did it? You?' I asked breathlessly, anxious to purge myself by saying anything, anything. 'Yes,' he said, waving a hand as though expansively. 'I can't draw any more, but still like to make things.'

'You'll come again, Mair, won't you?' he asked. 'You're not too far away, half an hour on the bus at most. Never mind what your Dada says. He can't stop you from where he is. Come now.' His grip on the girl's arm was urgent and his face serious.

'Yes, I'll come,' she said. We got into the car and slid away quietly down the cul-de-sac. I could see Ben in my mirror: he was standing outside the gate with one arm upraised, motionless. The stacks against the Llwchwr dropped quickly out of sight, and the sea's dull grey was lost behind the rising angle of the roofs. What elevation there had been, and it was just enough for us to see the river as it debouched, had disappeared, and near-sightedness, the care of the crowded road, took over again.

THE INHERITANCE

Sally Roberts Jones

To the child Mari, the tea service was the most beautiful thing that she had ever seen. It sat in splendour on its own particular shelf in the glass cabinet, as remote and magical as the crown jewels. And yet splendid was not really the word for it. Chaste, perhaps; elegant, refined – she had no words adequate to describe how it rested there among the painted jugs and the souvenirs of Sunday School trips to Aberystwyth to Tenby, alien and yet quite at home.

Once Mari was allowed to handle it, during the ritual washing of the 'best' china. Her aunt laid a padded sheet on the carpet, and Mari took the twelve cups out of the cupboard one by one, then the twelve saucers and the twelve plates, the two square bread and butter plates, the milk jug, the sugar and slop basins and last of all the rectangular fluted teapot, setting each one in its own place as delicately as though she were handling egg shells. The china was a clear, shining white, its decoration an austere pattern of ivy leaves in pure gold; each plate and saucer had an outer rim of the same delicate gold leaf.

'It has never been used,' said Aunt Anna. Mari nodded. It was almost inconceivable that there would ever be an occasion on which it would be suitable to use the tea service. Even for the Queen herself…

'One day it will be yours,' her aunt told her. 'After I am dead. It goes always to the eldest girl in the next generation, and I have only sons. If you have a daughter then it will go to her, but if not, then it will go to your brothers' children. First Gwilym's eldest daughter, and if he has no girls, to Huw's. You must remember that. It's not written down, you see, for the service doesn't belong to me or to you or to any of us, but to the family. Everyone knows. It won't be in my will, but your mother understands. I've left you the cupboard though, so that you'll have a proper place to keep it. That's written down, of course.'

Mari listened gravely, a small acolyte being instructed in the ritual of worship. The directions seemed to refer to a future beyond knowledge, and the idea of Gwilym, a noisy three-year-old, or the still-swaddled Huw being themselves married, with children, was almost laughable. Aunt Anna picked up one of the plates and dipped it into her bowl of soapy water, moving it gently under the bubbles. Then she took it out again and handed it to Mari, to be dried. Last of all, when the non-existent dust had been washed away, and the glass shelf wiped, the tea service was put back, each piece placed with the utmost delicacy and precision. Then the cupboard door was closed for another year.

Aunt Anna lived for many years after that, and when at last the tea service came to Mari she was already a married woman with children of her own, living in a small town in a South Wales valley. She put the bow-fronted cabinet in her front room and spread out the white and gold china inside it like an exhibit in a museum. Then she took her daughter, Siân, by the hand and led her up to the cabinet.

'Pretty!' said the little girl, laughing with pleasure. 'Pretty flowers!'

'One day it will be yours,' said Mari, and smiled for joy in her two treasures.

When she was five years old, Siân caught diphtheria, and not all Mari's devoted nursing could save her. The child died, and was buried at home in Bryncader with the rest of her kin.

'She will be less alone there,' Mari told her husband, knowing as she said them the foolishness of her words.

'Well, no doubt we'll join her there one day,' he agreed. He too came originally from the little village on the banks of the Teifi.

As time went on, the glass cabinet filled up once more with Welsh lady matchbox holders, flower vases, jugs, all the garish ornaments that her son gave Mari on her birthday each year. The tea service withdrew once more to its one special shelf, where it seemed to Mari all the more beautiful against the surrounding bric-a-brac of human affection. Sometimes, when she had a moment free from the pressure of washing and cooking and mending, she would go into the front room and sit, just looking at the golden tendrils of the ivy, until she heard the banging of the back door and went back to the kitchen to see what was wanted, oddly refreshed by the few minutes of contemplation. In a strange way, it seemed to her, the tea service was the source of her strength; while it was there she knew who she was; it linked her to the long generations of women before her, and their courage and purpose were hers. But these moments were rare. Work and the lack of it, the husbanding of their small resources, these were the framework of life.

Mari's husband died in an accident at the steelworks where he worked, not long before he was due to retire, and Mari was left alone. Their son was an architect and lived in London with his wife and family. He had married well, the daughter of a London Welsh family in comfortable circumstances, solid, chapel-going people, and his home was modern, elegant, a showcase for his success. Since he could not hide his Welshness, he used it as an accessory, like the decorative harp which no one in the family could play, but which stood prominently in the lounge. There were many heart-searchings before he and his wife agreed to ask Mari to come to live with them. Her quality was less amenable than the harp or the Welsh tapestry covers on the chairs.

Mari would have preferred to remain in her own home, but her health had finally shown the effects of the years of overwork and poor food, and though she was not ill, her doctor urged that she should not live alone if there was an alternative.

'You'll have your own room, Mother,' said Ivor. 'You can have your own things about you there.'

'Nothing too big, of course,' said his wife Ceridwen, hastily. 'The rooms are too small for this heavy old stuff, naturally.'

'And you won't get much for them in auction,' said Ivor, regret in his voice. 'Still, they didn't cost much, I suppose.'

'Not much,' agreed Mari. Much though she loved her son, she was aware of a certain lack of understanding, an inability to appreciate what fell outside his own experience, and she did not expect her new life to be one of unalloyed delight.

In the event, it was better than it might have been. At the least she was useful to Ceridwen, and if she soon saw that she was not expected to join the company in the lounge when visitors called, there were always the children. Ceridwen was bringing them up according to whichever theory was most in vogue at the time, and they came to cling to Mari's firm but unvarying kindness as a fixed point in the continual movement between strictness and softness.

Mari's room was small, but pleasant, and it held the one piece of furniture that she had kept when she left her old home. The glass cabinet took up more than its fair share of space, but the tea service stood out as perfect as ever against the distempered walls of the bedroom, shaming its bareness into elegance. She had considered giving it once to Bronwen, Huw's eldest daughter who was heir to the white and gold china. But Bronwen and her husband were living in two rooms in Cardiff, and had two small children to care for; just now her inheritance would have been more of a burden than a pleasure to them all. Still, Mari made it clear to Ceridwen that the service was held in trust, and should anything unexpected occur, it must be passed on to Bronwen with due ceremony. Ceridwen was not pleased. Something drew her to the heirloom – perhaps the very fact that it *was* an heirloom – and she would have liked to display it on Thursday afternoons when her friends came to drink tea and play bridge.

'It would be such an attraction,' she told Ivor. 'But your mother won't hear of it. Anyone would think it was the finest Sevres or Dresden. And it really should be yours when she dies. The oldest daughter indeed! The whole thing's positively tribal.'

'If I land the commission for the Delano offices, you'll be able to buy yourself a solid gold teaset if you want it,' Ivor assured her. 'Take no notice of Mother. You know what she's like. Too long in the land of her fathers. Now if she and Dad had got out a few years earlier, come down here instead of hanging on in that godforsaken terrace—'

'Oh, it's easy for you,' sniffed Ceridwen. 'And she's your mother.'

When the War began, in 1939, the children were sent back to Wales to stay on the farm with Huw and his family. Mari was happy at the thought, remembering her own childhood in the green fields above the Teifi. She would have liked to go herself, but the farms were not large, and Ceridwen, involved with endless committees and voluntary good works, had a greater need of her now that servants were no longer so easy to find. (Not that either of them put it so baldly, even in their most private thoughts.) Ivor, unfit for military service because of the angina that had come with success, made up for this by becoming a fire-watcher, and though they suffered all the inconveniences of the Blitz and the years of war that followed, the tragedy passed them by. Mari lived to see bonfires on VJ Night, but after that, the need for her help being past, she drifted gently away into a death that seemed as welcome as it was peaceful, and in due season was buried beside her husband and her child at Bryncader.

It was some three weeks after the funeral when Ceridwen, turning at last to the depressing task of clearing out Mari's room, became aware once more of the tea service.

'Shall I pack it up for you?' asked Siân, her eldest daughter. 'Then we can take it up to Auntie Bronwen next time we go to the farm.'

'No, no,' murmured Ceridwen, staring at the cabinet. Its veneer was beginning to flake, and in the harsh light from the uncurtained windows its contents looked as pitiful and shabby as the leftover rubbish after a jumble sale. Only the white and gold cups and plates caught the light and seemed to grow more translucent, more glorious with it.

'No,' Ceridwen had decided. 'Bronwen can have the cupboard and the knick-knacks if she wants them but the tea service belongs to Ivor. He's his mother's heir, and this is the only thing she had worth inheriting. I won't give it away just because of some archaic nonsense.'

'But Mummy, it belongs to Auntie Bronwen. *We* can't keep it.' Siân knew very little of her mother after the years in Wales, but Mari had had more success with her granddaughter than her daughter-in-law, and Ceridwen saw that the matter must be handled carefully, or Siân would ruin everything.

'Well, we'll see,' she temporised. 'Now, what about the clothes? The next parish appeal, I think. There's nothing here worth keeping, even for the material.'

For the moment Ceridwen left the glass cabinet untouched. Then, a few days later, Ivor came home with the news that he was on the point of landing the biggest contract of his career.

'After this I could retire,' he said. 'Get away somewhere, out of this country, somewhere there's warmth and light and no austerity. The Bahamas, perhaps.'

'Will you get it?' Ceridwen was already lounging in thought beside a crystal-clear blue sea.

'It's in the balance. Look, you could help. You've met Sir Iorwerth Thomas through your welfare committee. He's on the Board— if he supported us—'

'What do you want me to do?' Ceridwen was doubtful.

'Well, he's obsessed with tradition. Can't stand anything more recent than 1900. If you could invite him to – tea, say— and impress on him that Evans and Hartlepool are as traditional as Yorkshire pudding and Beefeaters— or cawl and Welsh cakes, I suppose, in his case? It couldn't do any harm.'

'I'll try. But I can't promise anything. You know I'm not good at all this leeks under the toenails stuff.'

The lure of the Bahamas was strong, however, and in due course Sir Iorwerth received and accepted his invitation to tea. The afternoon of the visit saw Ceridwen putting the last touches to a table on which the white and gold tea service was laid out in all its splendour. Beneath the china was a spotless lace tablecloth borrowed from her sister, who lived nearby; on and around it was an array of sandwiches and cakes all with an appropriate Celtic flavour.

'Be careful of that cloth,' said her sister, who had just dropped in to see how things were going. 'It belongs to my mother-in-law, and it's priceless.'

'Don't worry. The children are all out for the afternoon. We don't want any wrong notes, after all, and they *will* keep on about that wretched farm. Sometimes I wish they'd go back there if they like it so much.'

'They'll settle down in time. Now they're getting older they'll soon come to appreciate the advantages of city life.' Her sister was as complacent as only one without the same problem can be. She gave the table a last inspection before taking her leave. 'You know,' she commented, 'that tea set really is rather fine. It must be quite valuable.'

'Well, from what I heard, it's never been useful. Never been used since the day that Ivor's great-great-great-great-grandmother got it.' Ceridwen shrugged her shoulders irritably. The whole business was somehow awkward, like a stone in an old, comfortable shoe.

She saw her sister out, and waited. Soon Sir Iorwerth arrived, together with the other members of the committee, whose presence made the party legitimate. After tea they were to discuss plans for a charity concert.

'Do have a scone,' Ceridwen urged, taking her place by the teacups. She lifted the teapot and noted with some annoyance that is was damp; fortunately the pottery teapot stand had protected the tablecloth from any damage. Carefully she poured the tea into the glistening cups. Slowly, one after another, the white shells darkened and turned brown as the hot liquid seeped gently through the china and overflowed on to the lace cloth. After a century without use and five years of constant bomb blast, the cups could hold nothing, and were as porous as filter paper.

'How very strange,' said Sir Iorwerth. 'And such a perfect service. I remember seeing one very like it in Swansea. Ah well! Now, about the soloist—'

After the committe had gone, Siân came in to hear her mother rejoicing over Sir Iorwerth's discreet hint that the contract was Ivor's and to help clear the table. Ceridwen was triumphant, but the near-disaster rankled.

'Well, after all the fuss, your grandmother's old tea set wouldn't even hold the tea! We'll have to throw the cups away, I suppose, they're dreadfully stained, but the plates will do for a while. Just look at Jenny's cloth. She'll be furious.' She dabbed angrily at the stain.

'It was so lovely,' said Siân. She picked up the only undamaged cup and cradled it in the palm of her hand.

'Lovely is as lovely does,' said Ceridwen, tartly. 'If you like it so much, you can keep it. I'm sure I don't want it, and I doubt if your Auntie Bronwen will think much of it now. Neither ornament nor use.'

'It wasn't meant to be that sort of useful,' said Siân. 'Can I have the cabinet if Auntie Bronwen doesn't want it? To keep it in?'

'Do what you like,' said Ceridwen. 'I'm going to soak this cloth. Heirlooms! You can keep them, for my money.'

But Siân was not listening. She was looking at the unblemished bowl and the curving golden tendrils that caught and concentrated the light as though they were on fire.

'It never was a *useful* thing,' she said. 'Only beautiful.'

THE WAY BACK

Tony Curtis

Pugh squinted through the wedge of his crossed shoes—a stone circle by Rauschenberg; Leda turning wistfully from the Swan; Leonardo's drawing of a giant crossbow, a great engine of war cocked back ready to hurl its shaft into some stone wall; below and to the left a miner strutting across the wall, twisted side-on to the shoulder bulged in profile, narrowing down an arm like a piston.

The noise of feet down the stairs and along the corridor signalled the hour and Glyn flexed his legs to bring the feet down from the edge of his desk. Midway, caught in an absurd position, between slouching in the low chair and hinging himself up with enough momentum to stand, he held the position for an instant, imagining how some of the students passing might look in and see him as a figure landing clumsily from a height.

But no one looked in and the voices passed by, blurred and greying in the dulled noon time of a bad March day.

'Er, come in,' he answered the knock with an almost convincing tone of surprised reverie: you should study in a study. But the yale was engaged and his pose was broken by the necessity of rising to open the door. It revealed a young woman of twenty-one, too boyish in her check shirt, wearing her hair cropped, to be thought of as a girl, but with an open, smiling face which sent Glyn back into his room bumbling about, setting the chair opposite his desk to rights and shovelling unnecessary books up to the far end until they stockaded his phone.

'Excuse the mess, Jane. There really is a sort of order here.'

'Underneath it all, no doubt, Mr Pugh,' her tone was friendly and familiar for her final year dissertation meant that their tutorials brought her regularly to Glyn's pokey study on the arts block's busy ground floor at midday on Thursdays and they had a good working relationship.

The work was going well, but her approach to the poetry of R. S. Thomas was simplistic, seeing the man as some romantic recluse, peering out at the small tragedies of the north Wales hill folk like an eagle, head bunched into moulting neck feathers, beak curled round on itself as if aiming at its own breast.

'But what about politics, Jane? The suspicion of the English, and their eventual canonisation as Lucifer's mechanised aggressors bludgeoning the Celt and Celtic nature into a uniformity that's the real bloody pain of Hell.'

'I plead innocence and ignorance of all that,' she replied.

'And you from Middlesex: acres of the Fallen.'

'Staines,' she said.

'Damned by your own admission.'

'What's in a name?'

'Enough!' and he held up both hands in mock surrender. 'But you will have to watch your approach you know, sticking to sensible limits for a 5,000 word essay is essential. And with Thomas, this one as much as his namesake, you've got to avoid distractions. Here's a mystic with his feet in wellingtons and wearing a grey suit.'

They both laughed at the prospect of this vision, Jane easing back into the low armchair he'd sneaked over from the staff room in the Christmas vacation, one of her legs, in jeans just losing blue and fading into the right shade, hooked over the end of the armrest.

'D'you know, Jane, all we need is a kettle and some coffee and we could have really productive sessions here.'

'Remember what happened to Miss Jean Brodie though.'

The phone rang and Glyn, before he could get out a 'I'm in my prime,' ploughed a hand through the books to lift the receiver.

'Extension 219, Pugh here. Hello Liz. Yes, well a tutorial really. No that's OK. Yes. And when did they call? Hospital… Gwili… last night. And they were sure it was the heart? Well why didn't they phone before? OK. I'll get back and decide then. Bye, love.' He replaced the receiver, clumsily failing to fit it cleanly back into the cradle.

'Look, Jane, I'm afraid I'll have to cut our hour short. My grandmother's been taken ill and I'll need to get home and possibly travel down to Caer. Anyway, now you can ease that hunger with an early lunch.' He managed a smile as she patted her flat stomach.

When she'd gone, Glyn took a minute in his chair. On the largest wall were Alun's splashed paint shapes from playschool, and next to the window his favourite: almost becoming figurative, blue, mauve and yellow in a large blob, and underneath, a sheltering shape of paler blue. Paint trickles from these two like legs and beneath an ochre sun, finger marks becoming flowers in the hands. Rorschach. A student that week had seen it as St Francis of Assisi. On the side of his filing cabinet an LP sleeve of Thomas reading his poems: the vicar, hands joined across his waist, low and to the left of a photograph filled with sea and an horizon island humped in blue.

On his way to the car park, Glyn registered that in his room he must have seemed calm and sensible.

He cut across country, using the narrow lanes of the Vale with their high hedges reminding him of Pembrokeshire, to reach the main road west. From Cardiff the A40 pushes beyond Bridgend with stretches of three-lane highway which draw out the most maniac driving from people. The fatalities among time-cutting commuters and overloaded holidaymakers escaping to the west makes the route a battlefield.

To his right, in a field adjacent to the road, the area's TV transmitter thrust a huge needle towards the low clouds, threatening to burst them. Glyn's eyes turned from the back of the tanker which had forced him to change into second gear and traced the lines of the aerial's supporting cables down to their bolted hooks and sunken concrete cubes in the meadow grass.

Back in the house his son Alun would be sprawled on the carpet or the settee soaking in the television's images, resting before an afternoon chasing and kicking and fighting in the garden. Liz would be getting Bethan down in her cot, fingers crossed for an hour's relief, time off from being Mother before the afternoon swung on towards teatime.

This ordering of the day into tasks and meals, the organisation of each day, each week to roughly the same pattern was one of the things that Glyn sometimes felt was grinding him down. The easiest thing was to let oneself be carried through the year like that; putting all the small acts and decisions into order. That way the pains were small too. You had to live with the claustrophobia of such a life, house-tied, time-tied, family-tied. That was what had caused the first and only period of conflict between himself and Gran. He'd been granny-reared.

They'd lived with her from the beginning—his beginning, for as an only child he'd always had difficulty in imagining his parents living without his presence, just as it now seemed that Bethan and Alun were the gravitational laws without which his life with Liz would fail to make sense. And with his mother going out to work and his father putting in overtime and back shed fiddles it had been Gran who held the timescale in his childhood with her meals. Though he could genuinely remember ration books and toast and dripping, the terraced council house which seemed so pokey and shabby now, had fitted snugly as any home around any child.

There were, though, constant quarrels and bickerings with the neighbours; four years ago, Gran had spoken to Mair Evans for the first time properly since five-year-old Glyn had ended a fight with Mair's Alwyn by sending a broom-handle past Alwyn's head and through the Evans' back-door pane. After twenty years of sour memory the two women had come together over their bins and talked of Mair's Ron, dead a month back, two years short of retirement. Liz thought that Gran's concern with the movings of Nott Street, the way she seemed to be able to swivel and catch the passing of anyone on the pavement beyond her low privet hedge, was, if not exactly a raison d'etre, then at least some tangible function of involvement in life, as hers was becoming smaller and tighter.

'That's why she's glued to *Coronation Street*, *Crossroads* and the rest of the soapy shows, isn't it? It's sublime. An all-seeing camera beats the slit between curtains doesn't it? At eighty-six d'you think she'd be as sprightly if she'd no one to peer out at and nothing to complain about?' argued Liz.

'Well, I'll only really start worrying about Gran when she doesn't know what Mrs Rees' social security cheque is and who's the real father of her Ruth's youngest.'

The old woman's omniscience in her niche of the universe was one of the features of her character. Glyn had never felt deeply involved with the bulk of the members of his family. He would tell apocryphal stories about them over meals at friends' houses, or whilst teaching *King Lear* 'Nothing will come of nothing', or in a lull in the Friday lunchtime bar. It was a convenient safe fiction as he lived a two-hour drive from the town of his childhood; and anyway, wasn't a colourful, close family background the one shared Welsh heritage?

He pushed the throttle firmly down and drew away from the tanker and its tail-back as the dual carriageway carried the traffic at speed towards the dull-reddish brown pall in the sky over Port Talbot.

All that cosy fiction was slipping away now. She was ill, in grave danger, found collapsed on the path by the privet hedge at dusk the previous evening. A neighbour, old Mrs Matthews from opposite, seeing the front door of No. 34 open to the evening's damp, had wrapped a raincoat over her bony shoulders and, torch in hand, crossed the road to check. Gran lay prostrate after a heart attack and the cackle of *Opportunity Knocks* audience was coming from the corner of the front room.

Glyn's first kiss had been interrupted by Mrs Matthews. It was 1959 in the Palace with a plain girl who limped and hardly spoke a word. He'd been left with her by Bryan Hughes who was nearly fifteen, wore suede shoes, could click all his fingers. He fancied her sister and Glyn was a convenient partner.

Mrs Matthews patrolled the aisles at the Palace like a floating lighthouse, a beacon of vigilance against penknives in the upholstery and groping hands in the dark: the torch lady.

Glyn had no experience of death. His other grandmother had died at the tea table on a visit to Wales, but he'd been a young child, four at most, and that had been a strange dream—running to Mrs John's back door and babbling for help. She was beyond help though and had faded out of his life as surely as if the train had carried her back to that mill town in Lancashire.

Gran's sister Rosie had died in the back-bedroom; two deaths in a childhood. She'd become too ill to keep herself in the rough-stone Pembrokeshire smallholding and had been persuaded by his father to come up to the market town to rest and recover. Glyn remembered the journey, in an old Alvis built like a tank, the warm softened seat-heater against his bare legs; her moans and grunts coming from the layers of blankets across from him in the back seat. He had left a new Dinky armoured car in the footwell sunk into the great car's floor behind the driver's seat. The well was his secret fort on the journey down, and for twenty winding miles back home he'd worried whether the khaki car would be still there, whether Rosie, who smelt of farmyards and bran, would have trod on it.

Away from the geese, the fields and her pining collie, she quickly lost hold on life. Her breathing creased the old parchment of her weathered face, narrowing her eyes and slackening the folds of skin around her neck. When she died they kept him from the room until the men had come for her. Her wooden clogs stood like sentries at the foot of the bed.

Six years back, just after he had started teaching and was full of the new creativity, Glyn tried to write a poem about the tough old woman. There was no suitable ending though, and the mutual irritation there had been between the leathery farmer's widow and the milk-sopped town boy drove cracks through the structure of his writing.

In health Rosie and Gran could have been twins. The move to town had softened Catherine though over the years. As a girl in her late teens, she had left Jobstone farm which was obviously doomed to pass out of the family with her father's death and she and her five sisters losing their older brother to the lure of farming fortunes in Canada. Living in the minister's house as a housemaid had been harsh and illiberal but the Great War had reshuffled society and three years after she married a Berkshire man brought into west Wales by work on the Great Western Railway.

He died a matter of weeks before Glyn's birth. 'A life for a life,' she'd said, peering out of the small panes of the front room window at the drifts of snow: Glyn's father remembered that. It was one of the coldest winters on record. People froze to death, their heavy, black cars smothered in huge drifts of snow. The thaw revealed hill sheep in crevices and beneath hedges as sodden heaps of dirty wool.

Further west, beyond the great steelworks, the slag heaps of the mines, only an Indian file of high voltage pylons marred the rich green of the fields. Glyn drove down towards Garw. Four miles and two spread, rolling hills away from Caer, past the old mill beside the bridge.

When he was eleven or twelve, he would ride there on the new bike given to him for passing his eleven-plus. The school holidays seemed to stretch open endlessly in the sun. The hedgerows were full of birds and wild herb smells.

It would have been good to have had a grandfather then. A man with time to spare, becoming crotchety perhaps, but on hand to help with fishing ties and punctures.

Sentiment, he thought, I don't ever remember missing him. What vague feeling of loss there had been was due to the prompting of the grown-ups around me. 'A shame the old man died, you'd have had some times with him, Glyn boy. Knew all about railways. Well, he travelled every mile of the GWR. Every mile.'

But Ralph Pugh had remained that slightly out of focus, portly man in the sideboard's photograph, with his younger self in a group picture in the hall. There were posed the bell-ringers of St Mark's and his grandfather next to the slight figure of the vicar who was one of Toad Hall's weasels, imagined the boy Glyn.

Around the roundabout and slotting into the line of a dozen or so cars held back by lights. The council had worked on the bridge every year of Glyn's life, and every summer the stream of holiday coaches, cars and caravans had swollen to grind down at the road's surface and throb through to the huge foundation slabs buried in the silt and centuries of the Tywi.

The town was clustered on the far side of the slow, wide river, like a growth of buildings with the bridge as its stalk. Glyn remembered coming back to Caer after three years away from Wales, he in his mid-twenties, and for the first time realising how small the place was and how fine; the way it held to the hill running up from the river with a rightness that was a form of beauty. The sleepiness of west Wales that had irritated and exasperated him and his fellow sixth-formers was now what the world craved for, getting away from the loud, pressing matters of the world. The projected motorway would mean a fast lane from London to the Celtic Sea linking the colour supplement city of their early '60s dream with the harsh, vital coastline they'd taken for granted: Carnaby Street to Caldey Island.

To the north-east the river wound back up the broad valley to its source in the mountains. Gwili and the hospital lay in that direction, but when the traffic began to flow again, instead of entering the one-way system and bypassing the narrow shopping streets, Glyn swung the car left and to the west.

He had phoned through to the ward from home whilst Liz packed some sandwiches and a flask.

'She's comfortable, and doing as well as we can expect. It's been a great shock to her system and—'

'And her independence?' said Glyn.

'Yes, Mrs Pugh is a strong-willed woman. She's taking food and sitting up now. Visiting hours are between seven and seven-thirty.'

The staff nurse had sounded young, but confident in her manner. Coming all that way from the other corner of Wales, he could, she was sure, ignore the strict hours and pop in on his arrival. At eighty-six Mrs Pugh was in less danger there, tucked and resting in bed, than lifting and bending to her chores at home.

Somehow, arriving at Caer, with the sun finally breaking through the turning clouds, he felt the need to take in some of the memories of the place where he'd spent the first thirteen years of his life. He would give himself a half-hour and then drive over to the hospital to arrive after tea and before the visitors.

The curve into town from the dual carriageway going on to the west pulled up towards the mart and Nott Street. To his left was the park where he'd spent almost every summer in from the time he could run. There he had perched on his father's shoulders and watched the cycle races, afraid for the lean, wiry riders in their skull caps that reminded him of skulls, strapped by the feet to their pedals and pushed off at the time start by men in cloth caps and raincoats. Then thrilled by their cambered speed; there was always the guilty hope that there'd be a crash coming down off the last slope. In that park he'd learnt to tackle, the round ball and the oval, and lastly, to smart-talk to the gang from the Girls' Gram, who met the lads from his school (as if predestined) on neutral ground; a Garden of Eden with swings, a crumbling bandstand, benches peeling in the sun and rain.

Those last two summers before they'd moved to Rosie's old house in Pembrokeshire were formative, his body expanding and contracting by turns in a new awareness that excited and bewildered him. He'd moved away from the family, further into himself. His father had taken to drinking more heavily and his mother returned home smelling of starch from her long hours at the laundry. Gran's world had shrunk into Nott Street and the Llandeilo Café; tatws a pysgodyn served hot and greasy to the farmers across from the mart auction, ordering double fish in their rough Welsh. By that time she had stopped the Sunday ritual of walking over to Ralph's grave in St Mark's. Glyn often went with her, enjoying best the changing of the water for the flowers and the fierce pressure of the tap at the rear of the church. He would pick up handfuls of the white chippings, like crystals, so pure and dead, and trickle them through his hands like fossilised snow. They crunched and squeaked when you put your whole weight down on them and as his grandmother fussed and busied herself around the headstone and vase, the boy pressed his feet into the white surface, wary but defiant of the body beneath.

One of his bad dreams was of the chippings erupting, forced upwards in a shower as the dead man lurched back out into the world.

Being there in the graveyard was never frightening though. There was a fir tree near to his grandfather's plot and he would collect the dropping cones for missiles. From this spot you could see too the backs of the houses in St David's Street parallel to his own, and beyond, the hills stretching back inland to the remote farms. On windy days clouds would sweep quickly up the river from the bay and move the weather like a clock.

Glyn pulled across the line of traffic coming into town on the back road and drove through the wrought iron gates, parking on the gravel of the V-shaped drive. The church looked smaller and nothing like as old as he'd remembered.

It must be twenty years since I bothered to look at this place, Just drove past every time as if it were nothing at all to do with my life.

He sat there in the car looking out to his right where the graveyard fell away to the backyard walls of a row of terraced houses. There the graves were as old as the church itself, ornate Victorian angels, doves and floral crosses in stone for the comfortably pious dead. Most of the statues and markers had inclined with soil movement and the wind away from the true upright and the previous hot summer's drought had brought the grass up as high as the grandest angel's wings. They'd begun burning the stuff and it looked like stubble in a fired harvest field, as if Christ had come in blazing judgement and half done the job. Rain began to pattern the side window and he contorted himself behind the wheel to pull on a weather proof anorak over his jacket.

The driving seat and facia took a shower of water as he got out of the car. Without wasting time over fumbling with the keys he walked quickly for the shelter of the church, hands in the zippered pouch of the anorak, slamming the car door behind him with one foot. He stood there for a moment, shoulders bunching up and drawing his head down from the rain. There was no break in the downpour so he made his way around to the rear of the church, holding as close to the wall as he could. The blackened mass where they'd fired the long grass stopped short of the path and the plots at the rear of the church were still overgrown. There was the tap, its water pipe loosened and bending away from the green lichen of the wall. The niche smelt of decay, the previous weekend's pile of dead flowers blackening in a wire bin alongside the top.

His grandfather's grave was close surely; forward to his left and a matter of feet from the tap. But the sodden, matted grass seemed to blanket out all the graves' edgings and chippings. Only the grander headstones had any permanency; it seemed from the path that the earth had drawn into itself all trace of those whose relatives could not afford the hackneyed art of the monumental mason.

Jane Thomas   1862   18 years
Calm on the bosom of thy God, Fair spirit rest thee now
Ever while thy footsteps trod, His seal was on thy brow

and

Severed whilst in bloom

The rain stopped and the fir tree's soughing died with the wind. Glyn moved under the deep green of its lower branches and put his hand out to the trunk. The bark was hard and full like an exotic cork cut into vertical channels. He was aware of the town's traffic noise building up to the later afternoon.

This church is like a bad film set, he thought. The tree is wrong, it's not Wales, more a Japanese ceramic, though the houses surrounding the place are tight and comfortable in the way they hem in the graveyard. He remembered last summer's holiday on the Lleyn and visiting Aberdaron. R. S. Thomas' church, older than this one by centuries; small and simple, banked up from the sea and dominating the village's cottages and narrow, winding road. Linking by death the hills and the waves.

Here at this moment there are two points of focus; as surely as the traffic and the land's produce are drawn in towards the mart and market, so the neat townspeople who have built the town around that trade, are always moving in towards the graves at the end of their gardens and yards.

Two other churches: at Enbourne in Berkshire, a Norman squatness that had sunk lower into the earth over the centuries of its life, holding the dead generations of Reeves who had led to Ralph and John and Glyn's father and himself.

And the village church in Pembrokeshire which rose above Jobstone Farm, directly across the road from the farm's yard, that held the Barrah family and the Coles and Williamses and Vaughans who all formed Catherine and Rosie and the sisters and Matthew who'd taken a ship across the North Atlantic and disappeared in Canada.

The Church of England, the Church in Wales, the bell-ringing, the vestments and litany, the railway joining the two and letting the blood bypass the centuries of Welsh-speaking Wales, leaving him with a tongue outside the language yet stirred by the sense of being Welsh, of belonging here and nowhere else and wanting to understand his place, how Caer and west Wales had made him feel that way. A hybrid needing to draw diagrams of the twisted and confused roots that fed his life. He walked forward into the longer grass, feeling with his feet for the rise of graves, the hard edge of a stone kerb. There were two he located at the end of a row that must have extended beyond the tree. The first held James Davies and his wife Martha –1938 and 1945 – *Cofio Rest Eternal* on a black marble book laid open with ridged pages frozen at the place. Next to it the rectangle he could trace under the matted grass with his foot.

There were the beginnings of brambles curling through the grass and he scratched his hands in pulling back the thick covering. The vase had slumped to its side into the dulled gravel and it shocked him to find the decay of remembrance so complete. How many years was it since Gran had tidied the grave of the man who was her husband? When had the Sunday ritual become redundant? Glyn could not remember her ever going to church or chapel. His memory of her refused to conform to the hat, gloves and Sunday best of the proud, little women shuffling their way to heaven past their house and the green flecked gate he'd swung upon.

You learned to cope with death by developing a numbness, was that it? What am I doing here? he thought.

With loving memory of Dad
from Mam and the boys

What sense am I trying to make of all this, when Gran herself is lying in a bed two miles from here?

Why here? Why didn't I drive straight over to her? What sort of concern was that? Are the dead and our memories to hold sway over the living, the daily dying of ourselves?

Glyn picked up one of the grave's loose chippings. Trying his hand against its sharpened end, he threw it towards the fir tree and he walked back to the car. Here was the unifying image that could bring the generations to a point: this churchyard, the grave and its rain-polished chippings, this town with its pubs and chapels, and tired cinemas; this place, shaping all their lives like a funnel down which he fell. The novel he would start seeded and swelled like propagation in a speeded-up film as he joined the traffic and drove across town to the hospital.

A Sort of
Homecoming

Tristan Hughes

It flashes into view, hard and clear like waking, after the winding, cocooning green of the bends. The point is called Gallows. Masts are packed in the air over beached boats, a confusion of crosses, clicking, tinkling, whirring in the breeze; mad clockwork sounds that measure a chaos of time that runs not just forwards but backwards and sideways too. Crosswinds. Ropes hang everywhere, rocking like nooses. From the point (of no return, he can't go back now, can't run from this or here) the sea wall curves gently inwards while opposite, across the straits, the mountains bulge outwards into the horizon and are reflected down into the sea as though the whole scene is made out of mirrors. Seagulls swoop in distorted space towards the summits of the mountains in the sea. On the other side of the little bay the shore is a bright phalanx of colour where a Georgian terrace laps the water, painted pink and yellow and green; candy houses with marzipan walls and icing roofs, like those gaudy, confectionery cottages in fairy tale woods that lost and orphan children look hungrily towards.

'There's a message for you Robert, I think its kind of urgent.' His boss retreats instantly, the onerous task performed, meandering past computers and their cables that sprawl, disemboweled, across the floor. Robert Llewelyn looks down towards his screen: 'In *De-Scribing The Savage*, Professor Larkin, one of America's finest critics, offers both a brilliant analysis of the colonial discourse on savagery and a major contribution to postcolonial theory. Concentrating on the textual representation of encounter Larkin unravels the...' He feels himself unraveling, as he has felt for years now, stretched and dislocated as though all the hyphens he has had to rescribe in these fucking blurbs has hyphenated him. Yes, I'm Ro-bert, very good to meet you. They always give him this stuff to do. Ato, who works in the same office, is half Nigerian but they think it might be too obvious if they handed it to him, stereotyping: give the black guy the colonial material, he's sure to be interested. They're still a bit guilty for it all, he sees – sorry about our empire fucking up your country, we feel terrible about it, we know better now. But as for a Llewelyn, well that happened seven hundred years ago, who even remembers, lots of time to get over it. Only a name, not even a skin, to remind them of ancient borders overthrown. To remind himself. They like it at dinner parties, it's a good conversation starter: 'Llewelyn, that's Welsh isn't it...You are...Where from...Can you pronounce that place with the really long name?' A hint of ethnicity, very fashionable in London now. Savage, from the French souvage, a dweller in woods and forests; wild, uncultivated. When he first arrived he didn't know how to use the underground or what wine to buy or where exactly Soho was. Everyone was surprised he wasn't even more of a hick. Barbarian, from the Greek barbaros, to babble, meaning those who do not speek Greek. 'Llanfair-pwll-gwyngych...', low murmurings of amusement ripple into the room as the impacted double *l*s and rasped *ch*s dance through the air like performers in a circus.

There is a small memo pad in the corner of the room with one line scrawled upon it. Nobody is around, they have left him alone with this. He reads it slowly, trying to make it last:

'Robert, can you phone home immediately – your father has passed away.' It is the full stop he notices most, thinking how he has never really felt a full stop before. They have helped him catch his breath but they have never taken his breath away. A life drifts around him in the room, his own, his fathers', pieced together with a less harsh punctuation, a dash here and there, the odd semicolon, a mix of exclamation and question marks; clauses that seem to run on forever and forever... And then this little dot stares up at him, prohibiting extension, whispering that syntax isn't going to help him here, that grammar is full of what is lost and irredeemable. It is a cruel sentence to be handed. It is.

Outside on the street the letters on the signs seem to have lost their coherence, their fixity, and returned to some primordial condition where they are just strange shapes stuck together. The alphabet has exploded and lies strewn in charred fragments all around. Everything is unraveling now and beneath it all is death. What did they expect? What did he expect?

Past the candy houses and around the corner and he has arrived. Castle Street is bustling beneath drooping banners that proclaim some town festival, looking exhausted with the burden of civic happiness they bear. A torn poster on the window of Edith's Newsagents announces that there will be a Lithuanian jazz quartet playing at the Bulkley Hotel on Thursday, followed by Misty Twilight, 'a world-renowned' four-piece Celtic rock band. Looking down the sidewalk Robert wonders if this might all be too much for the slow-bobbing blue rinses that hover everywhere on the verge of the road, perched, as if on the very edge of eternity, while they wait for the traffic to recede so they may cross over to the Castle bakery and buy 'authentic Welsh raisin bread'. They come all year, shipped along in gleaming metallic tubes – Fringe Express, World's End Motors, Dragon Coaches – sealed off from the attritional, scouring rains and winds that arrive interminably from the Irish Sea; they have little left, more to preserve. Pensioners from everywhere, mostly women – the men die earlier – come to look at the castle as though it offered some vision of corresponding decay, of crumbling, rock-strewn endurance. He had grown up pushing impatiently between them and, returning, notices a faint aroma in the place that he has forgotten, an invisible patina that floats like scum upon the air, the scent of composty earth and slithery autumn leaves; a detritus of perished cells – the smell they have left over. Twilight: everywhere it is misting through their eyes, the light failing, falling, beneath it is... He is home.

Robert has not been back for years. Not since he began to feel his life spinning out of the orbit he had imagined it following, become sidetracked in an unmapped constellation that he knows now is failure, where the starlight shines at different angles as though viewed from some other hemisphere. This readjustment in space has made him shifty, furtive, a guilty interloper in the place where his dreams had formed. Coming back he feels a traitor, a betrayer of some earlier self that had formed out of this small island world a promise of undefinable vastness – of tundras, steppes, prairies – that would pulse and tremble behind the hedgerows and fields and houses and sky. That prior self and the quivering landscape that surrounds it will not leave him now, even in London, they are like an albatross hanging upon him, a hanging judge. What he has been and what he is are two places, two countries; borders that will not be broken. Outside Evans' Funeral Parlour he sees John and Bev Roberts and ducks away down Church Street to avoid meeting them. It's a reflex action, the traitor's instinct: avoid eye contact, speaking, explanation, they might see it in your eyes, hear it in your voice. He knew their daughter Tracy in school, they were friends, lovers too he remembers now. Why are they here? Her grandmother, he thinks, looking back a decade to a liver-coloured old woman who lurked in a house, upstairs, an inconvenience to them both. He waits for them to walk past and prepares to see his father.

Mr Evans, tender of the town's dead, meets him at the front of the parlour. Inside it is slatey-cool, refrigerated by a cold stone through which the spring sun cannot obtrude. 'This must be a terrible time for you Robert, coming out of the blue like that. Nobody could have expected it.' Evans speaks with professional graveness, the voice gently assuaging an unspoken indictment: he died alone, he died without you here, why didn't you visit all these years? His father had nobody else, no other family in a family country. Robert's mother had died in childbirth and become an invisible woman who lived in the melancholy glinting of his father's eye. There were no aunties and uncles and cousins. They came from meager stock his people, barrens; producing even him had been too much, a fatal taxing of their paltry fertility. He thinks of this often during sex, imagines the deficient rush of his briny sperm as though it were some dead sea tributary trickling by in sterile, salty streams, not coming but departing. 'You must have made good time to get back so quickly,' says Evans, making small talk as they walk towards the room where the body is stored, the pronunciation careful, camouflaging the other language that lies behind it, the other accusations: why did you leave us, why did you forget what was yours? Evans knows that Robert has lost much of his father's first tongue. Does it matter now? he thinks. Surely the dead cannot speak any language. There can be no bilingualism to link those in the grave with the living. Alone with his father, in a cold room full of slightly chemical smells that remind him of dissecting frogs in school, Robert is shocked by the silence. In his memory there is noise everywhere: the crackling, spluttering sounds of fat boiling in his dad's chippy (what will he do with it now); the drunken, exaggerated loudness of the lads jostling around the counter on Saturdays; the gruff hwyl of farmers come by for a midweek treat of oozing, oily sglodions; the droning of an old radio set amongst plastic bottles of sauce and vinegar. His father is at the centre of all this noise, sharp-eyed and watchful, thick eyebrows arching over gleaming metallic edges that frame glass cases in which lie crusted slabs of fish, shriveled lengths of sausage, flaking pies. He is waiting in that noise, always waiting, for what Robert could never guess. Maybe for his wife to return, to materialise out of the frying, fat-sparkling air, her bones once more coated in a batter of pink, living flesh. Or maybe he had simply been waiting for the noise to stop. He had been a farmer's boy and never forgot the corner of land his father had sold to buy the shop, the quiet fields he had worked as a child with only the rushing wind around him. He had been most cheerful on those Saturday afternoons when the farmers came to sell him potatoes, arriving in rickety vans and unloading coarse, bulging brown bags that smelt of fresh earth, moist and fecund. They would stand together at the back door, speaking raucously in Welsh, elated by the small harvest that sat on the pavement. Afterwards his father would linger by the open sacks, inhaling the scent of clinging dirt like it was a perfumed emissary from paradise. They were his link with the patch of ground where he had been happiest, where his wife had not died, where his son would not leave.

The skin on his father's face looks waxed and pallid as though covered by a layer of cold, congealed grease, and Robert half expects to catch the familiar aroma of stale chip fat drifting towards him. But there is nothing, there is not even the grief he felt welling within him when he first read the note. His father died then, this body is no confirmation, no accentuation of that moment; death cannot be extended, even by a body, its leftovers. The features are almost the same as when he left: the high cheekbones, the drooping nose, the little heart of a mouth. He has aged well. Only the slackness of the skin along the jaw and the extra layer of collapsed flesh beneath the chin acknowledge the intervening years, but perhaps that is what happens to corpses. How should he know, this is the first he has seen. In the stone-chill of the room he feels the desire to hide slip away, his betrayal is safe with his father, entombed. The past is comfortable here, with the dead. Suddenly he is a boy again, wandering along the shore of the small bay, picking his way through twisted clumps of seaweed, looking out onto the winking scintillation of the straits and the mountains beyond which loom darkly and flare into green luminescence as the clouds scud over the sun, a panorama of swift shadow and light. The world is hovering, fluttering like a hummingbird's wing, its airy transparency irradiated by some great immanent space in which his heart expands until it is huge, until it could almost break. A promise, a secret, a revelation, given to him by this little postage stamp in the sea, that he carried with him always, that he went away that he might learn to translate it, to return it as a gift of thanks, but instead let wither and fade, finding in its vacated place an emptiness of unspeakable, mute vastness, a world in which he will always be lost. The cold eyelids of his father stare up at him. 'I'm sorry,' he whispers, tears wetting his lips, 'I am sorry fy nhad.'

Inside The George the afternoon has been hidden behind musky floral curtains. Jack Tacsi and Doreen are sitting in the corner beside an empty fireplace fringed by brass ornaments that look dull and pallid, yearning for the absent flames to light them. They look up and see Robert at the bar, sloshing a pint of Stella with hands that are trembling; it has been a difficult day and he cannot shed the coldness of Evans' parlour from his skin. 'Rob lad,' calls Jack, 'wot the fokk are you doing back?' Rumbled at last Robert walks nervously over to join them, steeling himself to hide his failure once more. But after a few pints it has retreated, receded into some distant corner that is another country, far away from here. Jack and Doreen are reminiscing about Rob's old man and slowly, as the appropriate, comforting earnestness with which death introduces itself begins to fade into familiarity, they begin to laugh together. Jack is telling a story about how he and Rob's father had collected a load of fish in his old van and stopped off at The Sailors Arms for a quick one, which became a quick eight or nine, after which they forgot about the van and staggered off leaving the fish to the mercy of the hottest August day anyone could remember. '...it wos fokkin stinkin like a bastard when we went back, I'm tellin ya, you could smell it in fokkin Llanfairfechan...' Jack's face is alive with laughing, though the years of drinking have puckered it inwards, like the vortex of water that is sucked finally down the plughole. He had once skippered a charter fishing boat that trolled tourists out past Puffin Island and into the ocean. Robert remembers its name, *Starider*, and imagines Jack at its helm plunging through a sea of stars. They are in his beer now, percolating silver orbs floating in a golden milky way, stellar, a beautiful space where time is stilled and softened, it binds them here – him, Jack, Doreen – they are watching the stars from the same place. 'Did you hear about Tracy Roberts,' Doreen asks, taking silence as an answer, 'poor thing was killed in a car crash about three days ago.' The heavens are shifting again, nothing will stop them.

Outside he knows where he is going. Down the street and around past the castle walls that stand in crumbling watchfulness, looking out into the surrounding woods that have receded over the centuries into long fields dotted with vestigial oaks; this ancient anglo-island put up to keep its eye upon the unruly natives that lurked beyond its perimeters, behind the trees, babbling in an alien tongue. He walks up the sloping fields towards the undiminished clusters of forest that still remain, passing beneath the shadows of the single, lonely, leftover oaks. They had hidden in these little cocoons of green once, Tracy and him, finding refuge here from the liver-coloured presence of the grandmother. They had lain on the gentle, leafy grass, her black hair falling about above his head, the slight chill of evening upon them, damp and dewy, and then the sudden hot wetness of her, almost stinging him, enclosing him in a moment of frantic, slippery warmth. Afterwards the slight sadness, the intimation of a small emptiness returning, the light fading under the cushioning branches. 'Did you come in me?' she had whispered here. 'Yes,' he had said, 'I came.' She has gone now. Somewhere, he thinks, her body lies crumpled and broken. Perhaps beside his father's. He digs his fingers into the earth, gathering it in his hand and pressing it into his face, tasting its fecund decay, smelling its bountiful rotting. Twilight is descending now, covering him, and below the town is dissolving in an evening mist; the castle walls, the dreaming, delicious houses, the tranced water, the still and silent masts, the mountains insubstantial as clouds, all are dispersing into a vapoury darkness, hanging on the borders of night.

BREAKDOWN

THAT OLD BLACK PASTURE

Ron Berry

He dealt the clerk a fast, wristy backhander across the mouth. There were witnesses too, standing behind him in the queue.

The clerk yelped, anguished as a girl.

Inside the office, the tubby cashier strutted like an April bantam cock. 'Lloyd, what an earth are you doing?'

Pushing his head through the hatch, 'Gabe,' he said. 'Gabe Lloyd. None of your Lloyd to me. Shut up a minute, you crabby-minded bugger. This isn't the first time I've been swindled. My water allowance, five bob a day, so dish it out or I'll be right in there with you.'

The cashier exploded with authority. 'You can't treat my staff like this! If it's trouble you want, rest assured you'll get it, oh yes, I'll warrant that!'

'Not before I bust you one,' he said.

'Leave off, Gabe,' warned a greyed old miner. 'You'll cop the worst end of it.'

Way back in the queue they were yelling, 'What we waiting for?'

'Keep moving boys!'

And, 'Same every bloody Friday! Dried-up gravy on my dinner!'

The clerk dabbed blood off his lip. He had overlooked the

water allowance. Simple matter to put right. Next Friday, two water allowance payments. The cashier tutted confirmation, having survived twenty years of payday tantrums before nationalisation. Precedence, truth, ironed his brow as he paraded, quick white fingers tap-tapping his waistcoat buttons.

Gabe lunged through the hatch, grunting as he missed the clerk. Colliers hauled him away, sympathising, pacifying him at the same time. He shook free, glaring at the cashier. They made a triangle. Cashier, clerk and Gabe, his cheekbones shining baby pink beneath coal dust, tight grey eyes menacing above the meaty splodge of his nose. He snorted, coughed abruptly, alerting his wits, then held out his hand. 'My money, I want it,' blunt chin outslung, oddly offset by the puffy innocence of his mouth.

The cashier saying, 'I shall rectify the error,' plucking out his fountain pen, bottle-rounded figure leaning over the red-spined ledger. 'Petty cash.' The clerk sniffed, sorted twenty-five shillings in half-crowns and slid the money across the hatch counter, and from the cashier, 'You haven't heard the last of this matter, Lloyd.'

'Very good of you. Big laugh. You pair, you couldn't fill enough coal to boil a bloody egg.' He was cocky now, grinning triumph. 'Perhaps it'll teach him a lesson. He isn't the first been slapped in the teeth. You sods fiddling in this office, you'd raise the bile in any man. What d'you know about what it's like down under? Bloody experts you are, on the Consultative Committee an' all!' He jigged on the balls of his feet, haranguing the queue, 'Harmony between workers and management? Load of ballox! Only management can afford to renege. Don't take my word for it though, just remember my old man.' He shook his fist. 'Mansel Lloyd did more than his whack to improve conditions in Black Rand! What for? I'll tell you. Bloody wreath from the NUM when we put him in Tymawr cemetery.' Gabe punched the stack of half-crowns into the

palm of his other hand. 'These slashers in the office, they
never cleared a top hole, never filled a dram, couldn't pack
a gob wall, never cut up a rib face, they'd be smothered in
yellow working a low seam with the top pouncing like
bloody Guy Fawkes' night. How can they think like us, ah?
They don't *feel* like underground men. Same things, thinking
and feeling.' He let the half-crowns fall in a clacking, flashing
current before dropping them into his pocket. 'Never trust
'em,' he said.

They bantered, 'You like stirring it up.'

'Lloydie know-all.'

'Not a patch on his old man.'

'Amateur,' they said. 'Three-rounder.'

He walked away. I'm different from my father and
grandfather. They believed in rank and file. I say, bugger the
rank and file. It's all mouth, always was, always will be. This
life is for Gabe Lloyd, to do as I want with it, mine from the
beginning. Some men are born slaves. Not this kid. Never.
It'll take more than religion or politics to alter things too, for
definite. All I've heard is jaw-jaw. Bosses and workers, jaw-
jaw. Good people, bad people, all yapping like costive
poodles. I'm different from my old man and my grandfather.
They broke Mansel's spirit, but he kicked the bucket sitting
up in bed not flat on his back like those who spend a lifetime
squashing their arses in offices. As for Grancha Tommy, he
worked on sinking Black Rand in the first place. They repaid
him by breaking his leg in the '21 strike. Lovely people,
great, these stupid sons of workers coming here to Golau
Nos, bashing hell out of the strikers. Marvellous, the rank
and file, wonderful they are. Shove them into uniform, give
them orders, then they'll make Holy Christ out of some
government creep. Next minute they'll hammer him to
pieces. Following orders. That clerk I flipped across the puss,
by tomorrow he'll have two shiners and teeth missing.
There'll be more rumours floating 'round than bum paper.
His name's lousy in Black Rand. They all detest the stingy

bastard. Rumours and a bit of glory for Mansel Lloyd's son. Course you know him. Fists up before you can say boo. He's like a match. Aye, working a stent off Lower North heading. Decent enough if you catch him in a good mood, except you rarely find him in a good mood. Gabe Lloyd, he isn't just a mug either. There's that chip on his shoulder all the time. Got it from Mansel. Give the boy another ten years, let him settle down with a wife and kids, that'll tutor him. Sure to, aye, always does. Women, they cure rebels.

Chinking the half-crowns in his pocket, he vowed, Gabe Lloyd comes first, second and last.

July sunshine from naked blue sky glittered the compact saucer-cambered town. Slanted windowpanes dazzled, denied staring at, and slate rooftops on the far slope shone like the flanks of battleships, TV aerials sprouting from every chimney stack. He passed two punters faithfully posed outside a betting shop, heads lowered, the shabby street invaded by the hard suavity of a Peter O'Sullivan commentary. Everywhere the same 3.30 race from Goodwood, accurate, factual as Gospel, the hullabaloo crowding down to a laconic summary. And Gabe was thinking; another week wrapped up, shan't see coal till Monday morning. Too warm for fires this weekend. Short week of short shifts. *Man's* job so the adverts reckon. You'd think all the bints and pansies in the world had dabbled in the face and cried off. But it's worth sticking for the short week. Anyhow, blokes down under are better men, better for me. True, there's a fair quota of trychs in Black Rand. Where won't you find a trych here and there along the faces? Some bladder-brain who'd graft the heart out his young butty. They tried that on me, the fascist bastards. If you can't check your wages, too bad. You'll get robbed, diddled, up, down and sideways. NCB 'll never pay us enough, but the job's worth sticking for the short week. You won't dodge a wet shirt anywhere off Lower North, water cold as lollipops melting down the back of your neck. Some shifts you're wetter than others. Sheer luck. Useless making a song and dance. By grubtime you're sweating from eyebrows to ankles. But it's a good pit, no doubt at all. Decent pit, decent blokes... as he entered the house of his only sister.

She placed his dinner on the table. Arms folded, she looked down at him.

'What's up, girl?'

'Silly bugger you, Gabe. Why'd you go and bump that chap in the office? Her from next door came on the run to tell me.'

'Sharp of the mark, Sue.'

'Her two sons are in Black Rand Colliery premises, you couldn't have picked a worse place to lose your head. Time you used some brains for a change.'

Sue Preece served lamb chop and vegetables for herself, clipping the oven door shut with her knee. She was thirty-four, severe from adjustment, her straight black hair cut for utility, the same principle affecting her clothes. She refused to primp herself as female. Her husband lived with another woman in a caravan site with a dozen others behind Golau Nos cricket pavilion. Sue despised him. She always had, reconciled deep in her insular spirit. She practised loyalty by deed towards Gabe or anyone who sought it from her.

'Makes no odds,' he said. 'They won't do anything, not for a little smack across the mouth. I was twenty-five bob down on my money.'

'There's the Lodge, you pay dues every week. Let them sort it out instead of taking the law into your own hands, specially with your record.'

'Our committee's a right shower,' he said.

'Point is, boy, you can't go 'round hitting people. You're not a snobby-nosed crwtyn any more.'

He glanced at the travelling clock tilted up in its plush lined leather case on the middle shelf of the dresser.

Below the clock, framed photographs of their parents, each quarter-turned inwards to a larger photograph of Sue and himself. Twice his size then, she had one arm around his shoulders, his hair boy-rough while hers surrounded her head in a stiff aura of permed waves. He wore a willing grin. Sue and their mother showed the same expression, humourless.

'Fetching that clock home don't give you the right to take a poke at the least one who upsets you.'

'I must have been pretty handy, Sue, couple of years ago.'

She jeered bleakly, 'Bullheaded, and you wanted to turn professional. By now you wouldn't know if you was coming or going.'

'I can still do a bundle.'

'Ach, act your age.'

'I beat everyone in the area for that clock.'

'Novices. Be quiet and eat your dinner.'

'I'm going out for a swim afterwards,' he said. 'Listen, lots of girls come out to the Lake, all you do is mooch around indoors as if there's nothing left till cowing doomsday.'

Passively regarding him, 'Never you mind about me.'

From a crystal stream Melyn Lake ballooned to smooth, straight sausage shape. Vandalised trees and brambles wound in and out by pickers' footpaths covered the far bank. He approached aslant down a steeply turfed hillock, moving up the shoreline to level ground where sunbathers gossiped among romping kiddies. He stripped off, taking his time, the comfort of the dinner heavy on his stomach. Gabe's toenails were black, and dull blue scars hung like tattoo streaks behind his left shoulder, ending in a pink crinkled indent over his floating ribs. He wiped his armpits draped his towel and looked around for company. Nearest were boys and girls, all gush and giggles. He returned a straight-armed salute to some young colliers entering the water, pushing and tugging at each other.

'See you later.'

Then he sat down, elbows on widespread knees. Flat as

glass Melyn Lake, ripples catching his eye in fits and starts, dwindling to flatness again. He dreamed himself behind the wheel of a brand new Standard Eleven car, Sue sitting beside him. Nearby ripples – a frog sculling close to the bank before circling back to cover. Gabe's tongue tipped out his lower lip while he groped for a pebble to lob at the spot where it disappeared. Spiky turf on bare clay, so he flipped his cigarette butt, heedless now, then laid back on his towel. He felt supreme, prepared to luxuriate while the weight of his meal subsided.

Twenty minutes later he walked slightly knock-kneed into the water and plunged his mountain stroke (half trudgen, half breast stroke) to join the gang of young colliers.

'Here he is, best clouter in Black Rand,' they said.

'Gabe's al'right.'

'How's it going, Gabe-boy?'

'I had my money,' he said. 'Anybody been across to the other side yet?'

'Let's all have a go!'

'For a pint!' shouted the fastest man, foaming into crawl-stroke.

But forty yards winded them. They milled around, treading water, saying, 'Nob it.'

'Too much like graft.'

'Leave it there.'

Hard-muscled face workers, they gleamed white skinned from daily scrubbing under the pithead showers.

'Hey, know what, Gabe, they might give you your cards on account of this afternoon.'

'Aye, and I might bang a one-two on Monte Leyshon for a so-long present,' he said.

'Only once you'll do that, brawd. They'll rush you inside, your feet won't touch the ground.'

He relished foolish bragging, saying, 'Fair enough, once will do me.'

'They'll shove you down Cox's for months, man!'

The crawl swimmer said, 'I heard they called a doctor to the office. What you bash him with, your bloody water jack?'

'Up your jacksie!' he said.

'You'll hear more about it. They'll get a certificate off the fucken doctor, see!'

Grunting, he rolled over for a relaxed float back to his clothes. The sun was hot, the water mellow. He floated. Forget about Black Rand. Why worry? Ruination of a man, worry.

Rumours ceased, verified by reality two weeks later when a police sergeant came to the house with a summons.

He said, 'Seems like I got to attend the ceremony then.'

'Plead guilty, say you're sorry,' advised the sergeant. 'Understand this, fella, you've assaulted a person while he was under the protection of his employer, namely the National Coal Board. It's worse than pub fighting in the eyes of the law. Not that I blame you personally; worked in the pits myself years ago. Say you're sorry, lost your temper, won't happen again, and hope for the best.'

'What about the times I been booked in the past?'

Grave, furrow-faced, the sergeant hooked his thumb in his breast pocket. 'They'll go down against you. How many times, fella?'

'Once for scrapping outside the Workmen's, one for foul language, once for pissing in a gwlli, once for obstruction as they called it, and there was the time you blokes locked me up.'

'Drunk?'

'More or less, aye, suppose I was.'

The sergeant offered, 'Good luck, fella.'

'Same to you, Sarg.'

Due to appear in Dove Street Court at 10 a.m. on a thundery morning. Sue was harshly critical while they were having breakfast, softening at the last moment, fussily adjusting his tie and smoothing his hair. She sent him off with a stroke of her palm on his chest, tenderly, like a blessing.

After Black Rand's cashier's evidence, judgement came within five minutes. Gabe was fascinated by the magistrate. Monkey Lips whispering to colleagues on the bench. They nodded together, at each other, dumb as marionettes.

'Lloyd, stand upright.' The flat, dead-sure God Almighty legal voice.

He slid his elbow off the ledge of the dock, removed his other hand from his pocket and held his fists to his thighs.

Monkey Lips glanced from the cashier to the police inspector. 'Young man, we have sufficient evidence of your lack of discipline.' He paused to extend, slide down his upper lip, concealing the lower one. 'You have appeared in this court before but obviously you aren't prepared to learn from experience. The National Coal Board is determined to protect its staff from brutality and insults.' Incurable neurosis writhed his lips again. 'We fine you thirty pounds, and you shall remain on probation for a period of two years.'

Thought Gabe, bloody old chimpanzee.

The clerk of the Court bawled out, 'Will you pay now?'

Leaning over the dock, 'Give me a few days, sir?' – *Sir* granted as part of Dove Street rigmarole.

'Seven days to pay,' announced Monkey Lips.

Chin tucked aside, he smirked to himself as he climbed down. That old stuff-pig, him telling me I'm short on discipline. Discipline's for goofies who can't think for themselves. Shitten-ringed old bastard, he scraped his way to where he is. They're all scrapers. Justice, by the Jesus, more justice in the weather.

The probation officer beckoned him into a room below the court. A scrawny man, thin hair fighting off a centre parting along his flaky sunburned head. Gravestone teeth in his mouth, and, 'Cigarette?' pleasant as a visiting uncle.

'Ta very much,' he said.

'Did you enjoy hitting that chap?'

'What d'you mean enjoy?'

'Were you infuriated or simply using the incident to hurt someone?'

'I don't get you, mister,' he said. 'Look, why not leave it there? See, they paid my water allowance, so I'm satisfied.'

The probation officer led him to a side door exit. 'Gabriel, I would like you to appreciate my position. The less we see of each other the better I shall be pleased. That's the best for both of us. All you have to do, stay out of trouble.'

There's loads of luck in it, he thought. For two years I'll have to watch my step. They can pick me up for twp things like crossing the railway line or fiddling a bus ticket. Any-fucken-thing. When I buy my Standard Eleven next Spring I'll have to learn the Highway Code backwards. Soon they'll pinch us for not pulling the chain in the lav. LAW? Double rupture the law and every chimp-brained magistrate since the one who played crafty with the Jews. They're still chopsing about him and all, every Sunday in chapel.

He dry-spat on his palms. Anyone with a black cap in his pocket or a black staff dangling against his leg, he's a menace to society. My kind of society, when I find it.

Four days after the court hearing, a Lower North fireman came up the conveyor face. Gabe knew he was coming, word having passed from collier to collier.

'How old are you now?' says Iago Eynon, resting on his knee-pads and aiming a chameleon's tongue of tobacco juice at a roller carrying the rubber belt.

He hunkered closer to Iago, his cap-lamp killing the glare of the fireman's at halfway. 'Why then, any bother?'

'No-no, boy. They're inquiring in the office.'

I'll be twenty-three next October.'

Iago poled slowly to his feet on his safety stick. 'Manager wants to see you in the top pit cabin, near enough ha' past two.' He jabbed at the coal, 'Lovely face slip that. Hole under a few inches and she'll spill out like a bag. You can't beat Lower North coal. S'clean!' Iago gently toed the seam. 'Righto, boy, don't forget, ha' past two in the cabin.'

He watched the fireman crabbing up the face. Another brilliant NCB official, he thought. Otherwise ignorant. Streamers from the roof glinted ahead of Iago's lamp but he ploughed on, hooped forward, trailing his safety stick. The buggers are up to something. They'll be waiting in the cabin. Gog-eyed Monte and his clique. Brainy Monte, his missis no thicker than a T-head rail. Poor dab always looks flummoxed. She's in a worse state than Sue. But Monte Gog-eye, what he doesn't know about production isn't worth knowing. I expect he'll warn me to keep my hands quiet. No choice, Monte, I'm on probation.

He stepped out of the cage seconds after 2.30 p.m. hooter skirled from the roof of the winding house; echoes were still pounding around the gullied mountain above Black Rand as he crossed directly to the officials' cabin.

Iago Eynon and two other firemen stood behind the colliery manager. Gabe grinned amiably. They were like a photo from *COAL* magazine. As if they went grouse shooting together. Monte, you clever sod, something's hatching behind that shiny snake-eye.

The manager removed his white pit helmet, decorous as an undertaker doffing at a funeral. He placed it on the table, folded his hands upon it, friendly, smiling. The off-centre pupil of his left eye swole behind his spectacles.

'Shwmae there, Gabe. I suppose you're wondering why I wanted to see you?'

Iago rubbed the underside of his chin. 'Don't jump to conclusions now, boy. Mr Leyshon don't intend victimising you at all.'

He licked coal dust off his lower lip. 'Aye, right, OK, no messing about, ah, let's hear the news.'

The manager accentuated some downright nodding as if saying *Here we are, man to man*. Then, 'Gabe, I'd like you to drive the cutter in Lower North. As you know, Billy Holly drives the cutter by night. I want you to help him behind the Longwall until you get the of it.'

'*Behind* the cutter, Mr Leyshon?'

'Exactly, until you can drive the machine. In due course you'll be more or less your own boss. That's important, Gabe, surely? It's a damn good job anyhow, one of the most skilled jobs in the pit.'

He said, 'I'm happy filling out coal.'

'Colliers are two a penny in a conveyor face. I want a reliable cutter operator.'

'Find someone else, Mr Leyshon.'

'Now listen, Gabe, I won't have you dictating to me...'

'Nights! Bugger night shift.' He felt the eyes of the firemen ganged behind the manager: Keep your dagger looks to yourselves.

'I'm afternoons regular,' complained a wizened official.

Gabe shrugged. This little short-arse with about nine kids, afternoon shift was good enough for him. 'Your problem, man. Maybe it suits your missis.' He regretted the insult, but when you speak out of turn you either back down or bash on regardless, so he jerked a reverse V-sign at the fireman: Up your pipe.

The little fireman ranted, 'I know what I'd do if I was Mr Leyshon!'

The manager waved his hands for peace. 'Look here, I'm afraid you'll have to go on night shift until I find another man.'

He said, 'For how long?'

Monte Leyshon returned superior irony, dry brown hair puffed across his forehead, his strange eye starred behind his glasses. 'Until I find another man.'

'I'll see our Lodge sec.' he said.

Iago rolled his chew to his jaw teeth. 'What kind of talk's this? Don't sound a bit like the Lloyds, boy. Lodge can't do nothing for the simple reason Mr Leyshon isn't down-grading you at all. My own son, he spent a few years behind the cutter.

More's the pity he smashed his elbow that time, put paid to him proper. By now he'd be on cross shifts with Billy Holly, cutter-man himself.'

He hardened his stomach against rebellion. They had him back-pedalling. Troublemakers never lasted on day shift, not without blessing from the Lodge. Committeemen carried *constitution* on their tongues. Before nationalisation troublemakers were sent up the road. Principle older than the NCB. These officials were a breed, connivers from their socks up. They had him where they wanted him. Reading the situation as true, nevertheless, 'You can stuff the job,' he said.

'Fortnight's notice, that's the alternative,' confirmed the manager.

Old Iago Eynon cluck-clucked. 'It's a bad thing to sack a man, Gabe-boy. Means they'll stop your dole for six weeks. Paid up your fine yet? If not, how you going to? Use a bit of common, that's all I'm saying.'

'Well?' from Monte Leyshon.

Gog-eyed bastard, he thought, he isn't bothered either way. Me neither. There'll be a Standard Eleven outside our house next Spring. 'Right, I'm on for a quid a week extra,' he said, 'on account of the night shift.'

'Ten shillings. Consider yourself lucky.'

'Make it a quid, Mr Leyshon.'

'Ten shillings.'

The puny afternoon shift firemen protested again, 'Bloody big-head, I wouldn't have him in my district.'

And, 'Thinks he's chocolate since he boxed for the Coal Board,' said another official, confident beyond need of malice.

The manager rose from the table. 'I don't expect the cutter to run up and down the faces like clockwork. There are sure to be snags occasionally, resulting in overtime. You'll make a pound a week over and above the rate.'

He conceded, 'Fair enough.'

'Good, start Monday night.'

Soaping himself under the shower, he thought, Christ, I must be easily led. It's the bloody probation. By the time I buy my car I'll be down on my knees every night. Ah, by the loving Jesus…

Still carping at himself, he met Iago Eynon on the steps outside the baths. 'I'm on night shift reg'lar myself next week,' says Iago. Getting on a bit now for rushing about the place. 'My legs it is, aye, bloody rheums.' Wry self-regard crossed Iago's blue scarred face. 'See, boy, I'll be overman by night.'

'Give us a fag then, Iago. Might be I'll do you some favours once I'm on the cutter job.'

The fireman upended a solitary kinked Woodbine. 'Genuine now, Gabe, you and Billy Holly will make a go of it al'right. Like Monte Leyshon said, Billy's his own boss, y'know, give and take now and agen.'

He grinned his teeth, 'Come off it, you fucken old hypocrite. Why didn't you tell me when you came up the face this afternoon?'

'Not my place to, boy. Mr Leyshon says where and when in this pit. He's paid for doing it.' Iago unstrapped his knee-pads. 'Fair do's Gabe, you took it better than I expected.'

He pressed a derisive thumb lightly on the old fireman's nose. 'See you Monday night on top pit.'

Nationalism brought new washery plant, pithead baths, canteen, ambulance centre, and a crescent of brick buildings, the kind of neat, spartan administration compound attached to light engineering factories. Situated at the upper left corner of a quincunx of pitshafts, Black Rand held favour for wages and generally safer conditions. All five collieries bore the stamp of a power industry planned for the millennium. At Black Rand, mown sward bordered a tarmacadamed road out to the motorway, the grass perhaps symbolising greater permanence than red ash footpaths to the canteen and pit-head baths.

Airgun slugs had pocked the large green and white sign:

NATIONAL COAL BOARD
BLACK RAND COLLIERY
NUMBER THREE EASTERN AREA

The designation irritated Gabe. His first shift on nights and he felt readier for bed than changing into pit clothes. Eastern Area be buggered. They've organised everything, these NCB experts. Whole country's floating on paperwork. You could paddle Wales across Europe on a raft of pulp. Call it democracy, more expensive than pee-tee actresses standing in a queue from Golau Nos to Scotland. Dent somebody's teeth for trying to swindle your earnings, then you cop two years' probation plus £30. Plus you're shoved on nights. All paperwork for the blue-eyed cuthberts. More mistakes are made on paper than with bombs. Me, I'll make plenty. Twti mistakes though. We're ruled by paperwork. Words and figures, out-and-out killers. They finish off kings, popes, politicians, millions of ordinary people, aye, even God up there. Some day I'll have my cut price quota in Tymawr cemetery, along with Tommy Lloyd's and Mansel's and Martha Lloyd's. Number Three Eastern Area: Rubbish. As if the pit got lost somehow, until the NCB went popping along to find it again.

He met Billy Holly in the lamp-room. A lean man, pale, auburn haired, Billy had deformed feet and dire righteousness, the kind of spleen which succumbs to raging temper. Billy was respected for his outbursts. He drove the longwall coal cutter. He could 'make it talk' they said, but, handicapped from birth, Billy was merely concerned to spare his frailty. When conditions were bad he served colliers a skimped undercut which had the appearance of a good clean cut to the full extent of the jib. After a couple of feet, colliers were hand-cutting, cursing Billy Holly, but dispassionately, because a 4' 6" undercut might have collapsed the roof. Puncher, mandrel and shovel work with a chance to make money was better than day-wage clearing and packing roof muck. And safer.

'Howbe, Cochyn' he said. 'I'm supposed to learn about the cutter from you.'

'I heard Cochyn enough when I was a kid.'

'Doesn't mean a thing, man.'

Billy explained, rocking thoughtfully on the heels of his stumped feet, 'Point is, if you're going to be bloody chopsy, well, see, I can shake you up good and proper if I've a mind to, only we got to work together.'

'No argument, I'm on your side.' He lifted the sack of sharpened cutter picks off Billy's shoulder. 'I'll lug these.'

Billy's neat pursey mouth exuded complacent grunts. 'Been hoping you'd offer, though I wasn't going to ask, not first shift.'

The top pit banksman opened the gate. They stepped into the cage behind Iago Eynon and a group of repairers.

'Last bon down as usual,' from the banksman as if talking to himself.

Billy told him politely, the way of rebuking a pest, 'Mind your own poxy business.'

The banksman passed it off, having no authority bar the safe, standby grumbling of his job.

Then a fireman came running from the officials' cabin. The banksman grimaced false teeth. He swung the gate open again.

Angry, wheezing short, scrapy breathing, the fireman shouldered around to Billy Holly, accusing him of negligence – the cutter was in the fireman's district, buried under a fall. No spare labourers to clear the machine.

'How much muck is there?' asked Iago.

Billy's forbearing gesture with womanish, claw-fingered hands, 'Wait, listen, before carrying on any more, let's find out who shifted the cutter since last Saturday morning.'

'Bloody cutter's where you left it up near the gate road. Who's going to drive it? No bugger, not till young Gabe here takes over on afternoons.'

'Ah, now I think I can explain...' began Billy.

'Fucken dead loss you are,' said the fireman.

He saw Billy's eyes retreat, glitter inside slits. The bones seemed to contract under his brow and cheeks. Billy's steel tipped boots went *Tap-tap-tap tap-tap-tap* like the disregarded menace of metallic beetles. Proud Cochyn, he thought, bending his knees, tightening his legs as the cage slowed to ear-filling pause then glided delicately to pit bottom.

They stepped out, the firemen rowing Iago, demanding to know who was going to clear the fall. Iago chewed tobacco, waiting for his colleague to finish. Meanwhile the pit bottom hitcher hand-pushed a full tram of debris into the cage, clanged the gate shut, pressed the green button and the thick heavily greased guide ropes squelched as the cage lifted into darkness. Suddenly the sack of cutter picks was snatched off Gabe's shoulder; Billy Holly held it dangling at arm's length, the weight of it canting him as he hobbled around the two officials.

'Watch out,' warned Iago, stepping aside.

Snorting from his small hooked nose, Billy advanced, crouched over, wild to land a swinger with the sack of picks on the fireman's head. The fireman backed away, between the guide ropes and beyond, to the brink of the pit bottom sump.

'Stop him!' ordered Iago. He pushed Gabe. 'You! Get on, boy, quick!'

He yelled. 'What am I supposed to do, crack him on the chin? Do your own dirty work, Iago!'

Iago appealed, 'Just stop him.'

Taking for granted that he wasn't personally involved, entitled to dramatise, he charged past Billy, then a sharp about-turn, 'I'll take care of him!' and he grabbed the fireman's lapel. 'Move! Out on the main or you'll be in that sump and you won't come up again.'

The fireman blustered, 'This all you're good for, hitting a man old enough to be your father? Carry on, you'll land in worse trouble!'

He realised the man feared Billy more than himself. Sample of guts, at least for a Black Rand official.

Billy was screaming, 'Lemme gerrat him! I'll show him who's a dead loss!' He dodged the loaded sack, but Billy missed anyway. The fireman wriggled free, running around to the wide, traffic side of pit bottom. Billy almost fell into the sump with the momentum of his attack. He lost grip on the sack of picks. They leaned over, watching it bubbling to the bottom of the sump. Sixty sharp picks in four feet of black water. It took them an hour to hook the sack out with a length of wire, guaranteeing the event as legend in all five Golau Nos pits.

Iago Eynon brought labourers from another district to help clear the fall. Three o'clock when Billy started the longwall cutter, Gabe behind the machine, scooping away hot, fine gumming as it churned out from the jib, thinking, we'll never get 'round to a bust up, me and old Cochyn. One thing, this is slightly cushier than filling out coal. Unless I cop pneumo. Or bloody deafness. What if a paratrooper worried about diseases? He wouldn't learn to live rough and kill without warning. Similar down here. You can't have coal and pure spit. You can have House of Lords, you can have the House of Commons, two loads of crap for sure, so why respect? Why respect any system? I'm a Lloyd, therefore I'm against respectfulness. Definitely too. Us Lloyds are entitled.

He shovelled, musing, dreaming, squaring his manhood.

In front of the cutter, shuffling backwards, bent kneed, bent backed, Billy Holly kept his right hand on the bull-nosed machine, near the control chipper. He watched the roof, overhanging coal slips, timbering, and he dragged the heavy electric cable ahead as the cutter crept forward, steel tow rope lapping on its drum housed in the nearside of the Longwall. Billy would listen, chipper raised, stalling the machine, listen for wrong-sounding creaks from the roof, the jib clearing itself under the seam, its snarling roar diminishing as the picks spun free, chaining around at constant speed like rattling bracelets above the heavy drone of the electric motor.

Coming up behind, watching, listening, he hung poised over his round-nosed shovel. By knocking-off time they were established butties, but it took him a few shifts to orient himself to the Longwall. It was something to cope with. Night shift soured him. He slept poorly by day, split in two parts, morning and late afternoon. Grouchy at home, 'Like a bear to live with', in Sue's opinion, her dourness tormenting him. There was no yielding in her. Home had always nourished his morale. Outside the house he made his own way, following the only rule: Fight to have and hold what's yours.

He learned how to doze while standing, hanging forward over his shovel, a wafer of consciousness sensing the roof and crackling, sagging coal. Sometimes the cutter crept on and on, leaving him drooped, duff spreading out in a thick level carpet behind the jib. Six inches deep and deepening, the Longwall ploughing slower, groaning, burning the picks. Unless conditions were suspect, Billy left him alone. He'd chip hauling speed to zero until the jib cleared itself. Gabe repaid by taking on heavy work. He dragged the cable when they moved to another face, he heaved, levering the crowbar when they flitted out of the seam onto the cutter trolley.

No question of guilt regarding bouts of dozing. He awoke easily, muttering, 'Night shift be buggered, I'll never acclimatise myself. It's only good for owls and fucken grave robbers.'

Most shifts they catnapped for a few minutes at grub-time. Billy nominated dry sections of conveyor face.

After sandwiches and mouthfuls of water they settled down for a little sleep, breaking mining law, liable to prosecution. Billy's alibi: 'It takes a sneaky bastard to spy on a man when he's at his grub.'

Comfortable on warm, powdery gumming, he agreed. The waster deserved a running kick.

'What I mean to say, once a bloke's on top of his job, see?' insisted Billy.

'Right, let's take five.'

He relied on Billy to rouse him. Billy prolonged groaning yawns, or clanged the lid on his tommy box or raised his water jack for loud echoing gargles. Or related dirty jokes to spurt his consciousness. Cruel at four o'clock in the morning, wrenched between conscience and the flesh. Billy affirmed *duty* with rectitude, while ever concentrating on making it as light as possible.

One night they were in D face off the main heading. Broken roof had fallen behind them as they were cutting down. One of those bondage shifts when everything went hellish. The tow post pulled loose three times, the picks blunted from chewing through a rising roll of slag inside the coal, and Billy Holly swore he was in the throes of tonsillitis. Sweat streaked his haunted face, coalescing with icy streamers from the roof. Damp globules highlighting his pale gingery eyebrows, dripped off the tip of his small, beaky nose. This hard, grubbing shift, aggravated by visits from Iago Eynon who preached responsibility. Fevered Billy lost his cutter man's caution. He took risks. Iago squatted with them at grub-time shooting tobacco juice and quoting estimates per man hour, per length of stent if day-shift colliers had no ready-cut coal waiting for them in the morning.

He felt harassed behind the cutter, the onus on himself to keep the jib clear. The Longwall ripped quickly under dangerous sections of roof. He crouched from one steel prop to the next, his fears eased by cold metal against his ribs. Often he shovelled one-handed at full reach of his arm. On ahead of the cutter, two repairers were chopping and fixing extra timber props. Behind them the whole face pounded, coal crashed down, grinding roof fissures fractured, buckling timber flats above the props. Time after time he scurried to safety in front of the machine.

It was a normal conveyor face squeeze, temporary,

worsened by the longwall coal cutter. Self-protection hinged on experience gambled by chance.

Worn by fever and strain at the end of the shift, Billy tottered back to pit bottom. The following night however, saw him riding down in the last bon, thick-speaking from his inflamed glottis, yet steadfast, saying, 'We'll change the picks first thing. Won't take us long.'

'Righto,' he said. Didn't think you'd be here tonight, Coch. Missis boot you out of the house?'

'Mine's a good un, don't you fret. Seen Iago?'

'Went down earlier.'

'Hear the way he carried on last night? Notice how he gets his pound of flesh out of the daft likes of you and me? Crafty bugger, Iago is, on the quiet.'

'We won't see much of him this shift. They're re-laying the double-parting on Gomer's heading.'

'Better not, or I'll be fast into him.' Billy rocked promissory *Tap-taps* on his heels.

'You're a bloody hog for punishment,' he said.

They found Iago waiting for them, dollops of his tobacco juice glistening on the flat, steel clad Longwall.

'News for you, Gabe. Monte says you're ready to cross Billy on afternoons. I told him you could handle this cutter.'

He dropped the sack of sharpened picks. 'Leyshon reckoned I'd only be on this job till he found another man.'

Sliding his backside off the machine, Iago crawled on hands and knees until he was able to stand up in the roadway. 'Gabie-boy, you're in the same position as five weeks ago, as I understand it. Either drive the cutter or take fourteen days notice as from tonight.'

'Al'right, al'right, on your fucken way then, don't rub it in,' he said. And he realised, here's the discipline. Old Monkey Lips in Dove Street, he put the jinx on me when he yapped about discipline. Monkey Lips should have been with us when we cut down through D face last night. Born and bred bloody chimp, he'd cry for mercy.

Billy shouted after the retreating cap lamp, 'Switch the power on, Iago!' and, 'Now then, boy, told you he was a proper bastard. Him and Monte, they make a cowin' pair.'

'No rush, take our time changing the picks,' he said.

'Course! We got a pretty dry run in front of us tonight too, thank Christ.'

After unlocking the jib he signalled Billy to haul forward a few yards until the jib straightened itself out from under the seam. Billy linked the tow rope to the jib, ready to chip it back at right angle to the machine. He trilled a pigeon fancier's whistle for Gabe to start changing the picks.

Reaching for the sack, he dabbed his hand on Iago's tobacco juice. Minutes later Billy did the same thing. From shared animus they cursed the official and his family. Straining wits, blaspheming him almost respectfully in the manner of miners, sailors, soldiers, prisoners, slaves. Language alien to domesticity, inane to the eye, the ruination of dialectic, gross heaped on dross, idiom of tongues obeying harmless, subtle phantasmagoria. He changed the picks one at a time. Short stubby picks locked in the chain by a single nut-headed grub screw. Simple, just tug on the spanner, remove the blunt pick from its socket, tighten in the sharp pick. Blunt picks were bagged ready for the blacksmith next morning. Billy hunkered at the controls. Heeding the word from Gabe, he chipped the chain around the jib. Between times he oiled the machine. He sloshed half a pint on Iago Eynon's trade marks, covered them with duff and scraped it all off with a shovel. And Billy sang a doleful *O more and more, I adore you. Gianina mia* in thoughtless bath-tub tenor.

Cochyn kidding himself as the great lover, he thought. Him hopping on his bad feet, crooning from that little mouth under that hook of a nose, hair the colour of apricot jam sprouting over his lugholes. He's like a bloody tropical parrot. God Almighty, you'll only find his kind here in Golau Nos or some similar place where the spunk of every man's ancestors has taken a lambasting from trying to prove himself stronger in the goolies than in the gumption. I bet Coch's a sticker on the nest. He's the goods all right. Found himself a woman, which is more than I can say. After I buy my Standard Eleven I'll be on the lookout. Bloody chronic, not having a regular girl. I'll end up like our Sue. Least she gave it a try before chucking the towel in. First buy the car. Afternoon shift... by Jesus, best shift invented for saving a few quid a week.

He moved away from the jib. 'Right, Coch' – there weren't many picks left to renew.

Billy tipped the chipper, inching the chain around.

'That'll do butty.' The chain stopped. He shuffled in close again on his left knee, right leg outstretched, dragging the spanner and sack of picks with his left hand.

Then it happened. Perhaps a lump of coal fell on the controls, or a flake of roof. Later, Billy pledged on the lives of his children that he hadn't touched the chipper. The chain roared around, the tow rope began hauling the jib into the coal, and a cutter pick jabbed through Gabe's right boot, thinly slicing skin where the arch curves under. The leather held. His boot rammed against the coal and the cutter *stalled*, power to mince granite whining, raging from the motor. But the chain stopped dead. Miracle, luck, anything beyond reason.

Billy cut the motor, he unlocked the pick and loosened Gabe's bootlace.

His foot pulsed fire on Billy's lap. 'My jack, Cochyn, pour some water over the fucken thing.'

Billy fingered the reddened underside of his sock, 'Bleeding, man, best take a look at it.' Removing the sock, 'Ah, good Christ,' said Billy.

He brought his foot up high across his left thigh. It felt worse than it looked.

'Bruised and that bit of a cut. Fetch my jack.'

'Bones all right, Gabe?'

181

Flexing toes and ankle, 'Aye, bound to be.'

'We ought to keep it warm. Can you hang on here while I fetch Iago Eynon?'

'No option. Gimme my jack before you go.'

At this point, handing him the tin jack, Billy again vowed he hadn't touched the controls. How could he while lodging the empty oil can on the gob wall?

'Jonnack now, I didn't touch the chipper. Honest, boy, honest!'

Said Gabe, 'I'm not blaming you, for Christ's sake.'

'What's the pain like? Can you walk out?'

'I'm staying. Those mean bastards, they'll crop me half a shift.'

'Sure now, Gabe?'

Who laughed, 'Bugger off, get me a bandage.'

It was late in the shift when Jobie Lewis asked them if they would help one of the heading miners.

'What's it worth?' Billy said.

Jobie unclipped his lamp, hit the glass bullseye with a tiny squirt of tobacco juice, wiped it clean with his thumb, offering, 'I'll book it down now,' says Gabe. 'Next time you plant your filthy gobs on the cutter I hope your tongue blows out as well.'

They walked the two hundred yards to the development heading. NCB planners were reopening an old supply road to exploit a new district. Jobie left them at a junction off the main, 'I'm only asking you blokes to give Stan Evans a hand with a pair of rings, that's all. It's pinching a bit in there, but do your best. See you on top pit.'

Gabe and Billy entered the mouth of the old heading. 'Stan's making four quid a yard,' said Billy. 'Us two, boy, we'll be booked in as dead-work. Stan'll gain the benefit.' He paused, teetering on his heels, singing, 'Tell me the old, old story,' then 'Bullshit baffles brains. Members of the working class, we been fed bullshit since day one.'

'You remind me of my old man, except you're fucken vulgar,' says Gabe.

Far ahead, flickering like a glow-worm, they saw the heading man's lamp.

Gabe held Billy's wrist, 'Hush a minute. Listen. Hear that? Wouldn't mind betting it's a proper crib in there.' He flung his arms around Billy, 'Butty, you bolt up the fishplates. Got your skyhooks handy?'

Billy tilted his head back, gazing at twelve foot rings arching the heading. Some were twisted, fishplates gaping, held by skewed nuts and bolts. Thin puffs of dust jerked down through mildewed timber lagging lapping from ring to ring. They heard their own breathing and the persistent whispering of moving earth. 'It's pinchin' al'right,' Billy said.

'Pinching! It's all on the bloody move. Steady, hold on, Coch, plenty of time.'

Small rivulets of grained rubble drifted down behind the drystone-walled sides of the heading. They dribbled, stopped abruptly like scatterings from the claws of watchful rats. High up inside the roof, booming rolled, nagging on and on, echoing distant as fading thunder. Billy sniggered, stepped backwards, impelled by the tension of his neck, his raised chin exposing the jig of his Adam's apple. A fist-sized piece of rock thumped muffled on the overhead canvas airbag which ventilated the reopened heading. Dust shone innocently, swirled away to nothing. Another stone fell on the airbag. Billy darted, tucking himself close to the roadside, one boot resting on 2" compressed air pipe column clipped low down on the rings. 'Long way off yet,' said Billy.

Says Gabe, 'Aye, hope it stays a long way off.'

They walked in fifty yards, halted, hearing harsh tearing of timber, like crossed branches strained by winds. Common enough, the way it creaked slow and steady.

Billy said, 'Old ground, she'll settle by and by.'

Gabe spat superficial anger, 'Let's put this bloody ring up and clear off out.'

The heading man grumbled, 'Where the hell you been? I asked Jobie for help hour an' a half ago.' Bulky Stan Evans, middle-aged, wearing a half-sleeved woollen vest, badgerly hair like lathe shavings bushed on his chest. A cud of tobacco seldom left his nibbling front teeth. Brown stain crystallised on the rims of his pink lips.

Gabe said casually, 'Go easy on the mouth, Stan. We came straight off the cutter.'

'Where's your reg'lar butty?' inquired Billy genially.

Lifting off his helmet, Stan wiped his bald skull with a hairy forearm. 'Christ knows. Youngsters these days, they chuck money away like it was dirt.'

'No worse than miserable old buggers like yourself,' said Gabe. 'C'mon, let's shove this ring up.'

'Keep your eyes open,' warned the heading man.

4½' posts stacked near Stan's last pair of rings, new timber for lagging, and a level-bedded tram of muck, sprags locking the front wheels. Both halves of the new roofing ring sloped against the sides of the tram. Small, meaningless puddles and shattered rock from previous shot firing concealed the end of the tram rack. A narrow seam of rider coal glistened damply some ten feet above the rubble.

Stan indicated the rider, 'When she runs out we'll be into four feet of clean coal. She's causing all the trouble, that dirty little rashing of mum-glo. Wouldn't be so bad if there was something solid up above.'

Back in the roadway, stones cascaded, echoed on the overhead lagging.

Billy screwed up his small mouth, 'Coming closer.'

Stan tossed a pair of fishplates and four nuts and bolts on the tram of muck. 'Who's fixing?'

Billy clambered up off the hitching plate. 'Let's have the bloody spanner.'

'I'll fetch it once you've got the bolts through,' said Stan. 'It's on my toolbar.' He and Gabe lifted one half of the new twelve-foot ring, resting the butt on the thick wooden sill. They raised the other half. Billy drew the crowns flush together. Gabe and Stan held perfectly still. Skinny, dextrous on the tram of muck, Billy slotted the fishplates in position and sent the bolts through. He gave the nuts a few turns by hand.

Stan's toolbar was ten yards back in the road. He lumbered hesitantly as timber squealed, rending across the grain, followed by sibilous roaring soft shale pouring out from a break in walling between the rings. 'Damn and blast, couple of drams of muck back there,' complained Stan, plodding out for his spanner.

Billy looked down at Gabe, still humped against his half of the ring, 'Slacken off, butty, she won't topple now.'

'Where's he off to, for Jesus' sake?' says Gabe.

The heading man was near the fallen shale, his cap lamp dancing as he examined dry-rotted overhead lagging. They heard his furious shout before the roar of the next fall drifted mazy curtains of dust. Stan's light disappeared. From his perch on top of the tram, Billy saw it again, moving away, and Stan's bellow rang up the tenor screaming, 'Come on out!'

'Get moving,' urged Gabe, offering his shoulder for Billy to jump down. Billy landed like a thrown bundle, rose to all fours, unhurt. He set off, trotting out. Gabe's jacket hung over a corner of the tram. He snatched for it, saw Billy stop suddenly, heard heavy stuff rumbling farther out in the roadway, lags snapping, and Stan's light disappeared again. Billy came backing away, soft stepping away like a wary primitive.

'Keep going!' yelled Gabe, glimpsing the heading man's lamp shining far out, a small white glitter in blackness.

'Can't,' Billy said.

'We gotto make it,' Gabe nudging him forward. 'C'mon, Cochyn!'

They were a few yards beyond Stan's toolbar. Another fall spewed out from the left side of the road. They waited, cursing, praying for it to stop. Fishplates squealed like bats, releasing shrapnel-pinging stones. Gabe reasoned from his gut. There's a bloody huge cwmp on the way. He said, 'Let's get out from here.'

Baulked by frailty, his boots scuffling dust, 'Back to the dream,' said Billy.

'We'll soon be out on the main,' argued Gabe, bundling him over the rubble. But there were no more falls. Every few yards the walls burst open. Softly roaring slides of crushed shale spilled out. Overhead rock cramming down on the rings broke the lagging, jagged stones smashing through, pelting like volcanic hail in the roadway. And not a flicker of Stan's cap lamp.

They were isolated, the earth rolling original chaos.

A small stone struck Billy's shoulder, up near the neck. As he pitched sideways another bigger stone skidded off his left buttock, ripping his trousers. The torn cloth flapped down. Gabe saw Billy's underpants spread loose over his lean shape. Billy yelped to growling, rolling himself into a hedgehog ball. Gabe grabbed him beneath the armpits, hauled him towards the base of the rings until his grip was broken by chuting stone deflecting off his forearms. Gabe crouched low, tight to the rings. Floods of rubble continued, burying Billy's head and shoulders. Grazed hands shielded between his thighs, without realising Gabe heard the sickening knock of stone against bone. The bones of his butty's skull.

Frenzy quelled Gabe Lloyd's fear, gave him the blind power of heroes and agonised cowards. He caught Billy's boots, dragging him clear, the cap lamp trailing on its flex from the battery clipped to Billy's belt. Unbuckling the belt, Gabe hitched it over his own. He thrust Billy's lamp into his jacket pocket. With Billy dead in his arms, he lurched back to the tram. Seconds into minutes later came the biggest fall in memories of Bothi Number Two. Forty yards of heading blanket crashed, leaving eight new rings, strained but upright behind Stan Evans' tram of debris.

Head bent against slow-surging clouds of dust, Gabe sat on the hitching plate with Billy across his lap. He's muttering, 'You were right, Coch. Man, you were right.'

Pain registered. He dangled his right arm. There were lacerations along the back of his hand, blood clotting, glints blackening. Fist clenched, he tightened the forearm muscles, a sense of wonder beguiling him. It was OK, the arm, proved by digging his fingernails into his palm. Gabe waggled his bandaged foot, feeling it tolerably sore. The soreness comforted his existence.

'Cochyn, hey, Billy…' Widening the spread of his thighs, bending over to lever up Billy's head and shoulders, he saw a blood bubble film out of the small mouth, burst soundless, the lips set still.

He's crying, 'Billy, Billy, Billy,' and staring at the pulped flesh behind Billy's ear, bone punched inwards, all of it wet black, minute highlights shrinking, fading to overall matt black. 'Ah, Christ, Billy,' he grieved, wrung bankrupt, desolated, and lowered him over his thighs again, letting the slack head loll down.

Gabe didn't know what to do. He sat on the hitching plate, listening to the roof sounding off. High up air pockets imploded in rock molten and sealed for three hundred million years. Tension drained away. Reveries surfaced, disconnected, the mixture unstoppable: Sue's wedding day, her new husband bragging in the kitchen, already half pissed, confetti peppering his curly hair. Flabbergasted Sue. She dapped him in his place before the first week was over. Very likely banned cock on him. No doubt, aye. Sue, she's a Lloyd. Married a runaway husband. Mansel's big welcome for Martha when she came home from hospital. Martha created ructions. Carpet clashed with the wallpaper and they hadn't bought stair rods. Last round of his match against Nobby Graham. Two straight lefts smack on the point, then Nobby fetched a right-hander from nowhere and they wobbled back to wrong corners like in a comedy. Shoni Joseph's gang of boys racing up the old big tip incline, Shoni in front with a new wristwatch. Shoni's record for running up the incline. He could gallop along like a milgi. Crumped-up Grancha Lloyd showing newspaper cuttings, reports about pit owners who refused to allow food sent down the shaft when colliers were on stay-in strike. Police on guard around the pithead, batons keeping away wives and lodge committeemen. Grancha Tommy's walking stick bouncing off the mantelpiece, him reciting olden times, his voice quavery inside his chest, 'Durrty swines, they'd leave men rot so as to make their profits!' The winter weekend of twenty-foot snowdrifts, top-pit horses sledging groceries from the shops. Everything altered. Hedges vanished. Bank manager's bungalow just a white trump. Sheep down off the hills, they'd crash into your pantry. Lucy last night... up there in the canteen, blonde hair like Goldilocks. Lovely Lucy.

His breath groaned for himself stranded alone. Muttering, 'One-two-three,' he staggered lop sidedly to his feet, hoiked Billy over the rim of the tram. Thus Gabe laid out his butty on the rubble. Didn't matter anymore. Cuts on Gabe's hands were burning, his fingers stiff as he unclipped his cap lamp. He tried the pilot bulb. The faint glow swung his head, stare pop-eyed at the full glare of Billy's lamp. Gabe switched it off, waited, adjusting his eyes to the dim light: 'Give a bloody rabbit nystagmus.' And he switched it on again.

He drained his water jack, the last capful chilling inside his chest, then he settled down on his heels, tired but sure of his strength, compelled to dismiss Billy Holly, dead. Concentrate on himself, trapped in his heading. Air for instance. Aye. Christ, aye! The big canvas ventilation bag from the main was under the fall, smashed to smithereens.

Gabe went searching for the 2" compressed air pipeline which powered Stan Evans' boring machine. It was buried.

Hunkered in the roadway, Gabe felt confident, untested yet confident, conscientious, talking to himself as if discussing pit work over a beer, 'Pipe column finishes this side of Stan's toolbar, blast hose connected to the column and the valve's turned off. Must be turned off because Stan's drills and boring machine are stacked behind his toolbar. There's roughly four yards of fall between me and that bloody valve. Eight, ten drams of muck if I can timber up as I drive through. Big IF. Umpteen drams if the heavy stuff starts shifting again. It won't move though, not if I go careful on the timbering.' Gabe climbed to his feet. 'Hey, any case it's shit or bust.'

Stan's shovel, pick and hatchet were propped against the side of the tram. Testing the blade with his thumb, he remembered the other hatchet buried under the fall. He carried the new 4½' posts to the edge of the fall. Three journeys and he was sweating. He sniffed for air. There wasn't much circulating. None at all, maybe. The canvas ventilation bag was in ribbons, some twenty yards out from the tram.

Filling his water jack from a thin streamer glinting below the high, narrow seam of mothering-coal, he kept his eyes averted from Billy Holly. Pointless examining a corpse. First things first. Drive through to the stop valve. Knock on the pipe column. Remind anyone at the other side that he was alive and kicking. Time enough to worry about Billy when they could bring in a stretcher for him.

Gabe worked hard, careless of his durability, following the left-side tramrail, intent upon digging a low burrow between the rail and slewed butts of the collapsed rings. Every shovelful had to be thrown well back. The muck would have to be handled twice. At least twice. For a couple of hours he cleared sliding rubble. No alternative. He had to reach the solid, stone packed fall. Again Gabe counted his posts. Thirteen. One extra, Welshman's luck. Flats, he thought, I'm without flats. Strong flats, else I'll have muck tamping off my bloody helmet. Can't expect to hold big stuff up with these thin four'n halves. He cooped on his heels, expectant, waiting for ideas, thinking, I shan't travel far trimming these lagging timbers. Flats? Bloody flats... Sleepers! Yes, by Christ, sleepers. Rip the lot up.

He prised out rail cramps from the end sleeper. Slackening the wheel sprags, he pushed the tram forward over the loose rails. Then he removed four more sleepers. Pleased with himself, he said, 'Now for the real fucken graft.'

Massive slant-locked stones were his enemies. Gabe tackled them cautiously, loosening rubble with his pick, his head always protected by a half-length of sleeper flatted across short props. He chopped 18" off the posts, using off-cuts for wedges. His small burrow meant less digging. Less muck to clear. Twice the service from his sleepers.

Seven hours after Billy Holly's death, Gabe sounded a steeply-raked slab of rock with his pick-head, and he put the pick aside. Groping upwards, he finger-tipped delicate fern shapes, rippled tracings etched in the edge of the stone. They signified naught. He crawled out. Rest, *think* – instead he wondered about the rescue team working into the fall from the other side. Jammy sods, plenty of timber and steel flats. 'Few six'n-half posts would do me al'right,' he said. Two six-and-a-halves, that's all I need. There're thousands mouldering on collieries all over Wales. Fuck Wales. Fuck the mines. How would Mansel and Tommy perform, stuck in a crib like this? No-answer bloody question.

Then, straightening out his legs, instinct crowed from him, his bootstuds scraping on the nearside rail. 'Just the job,' his touch of joy. Gabe knew he'd found a way to work under the big stone. Plant a couple of 2-yard rails up against it. Rails and heavy wedges.

Prolonged toil wearied him. He struggled, hooking out shovelfuls of packed shale inside the line of rings, working back to a firm base upon which to slope the tramrails against the slab of rock. God knows how many feet of broken ground above the slab.

Muttering, 'So far so good,' he came kneeling out for a drink of water. And tired, weary, the gristle of his bones fiery. Sleep, he decided, save light, save my battery. Precious cap lamp held to his stomach, he slept in the dark. Dull pain from his bruised foot and grazed hand failed to message his senses.

Gabe awoke fearfully, conscious of time spent. How much time? He inhaled, testing the air. It smelt familiar, the stale atmosphere of abandoned districts. Stale, like a dead-end airway road before knocking through to a ventilated coal face. Not *too* bad. I can stick a lot of this. Besides, doesn't seem to be any gas here inside the fall. No killer gas, thank God.

Head turned from glancing at Billy Holly on the tram of muck, Gabe returned to his burrow.

He plodded now. Fatigue centred his body. He fiddled with the mandrel instead of hacking debris loose enough to shovel away. And his shovelfuls fell short. Crawling out, he remained stooped until he fell sideways, his limbs creeping to slumped rest. Rest, peace.

Often he simply listened. Surely to Christ they were working on the fall from the other side, day-shift colliers fresh from the kitchen table. Rescue teams from all over this bloody Number Three Eastern Area. Working side by side in pairs, under new rings, turn and turn about every few minutes. Slash into it, you dim-witted buggers. Bang on the pipe column, you bastards, let a man know you're getting stuck into it.

Gabe crawled out.

Clear sterile water dripped, spun candlewick streamers from the high, narrow layer of impure coal. Small puddles spread around the grey heap of rubble. Water seeped back under the tram, dampness invading dust in the shallow indent left by the far side rail, swelling half an inch wide to surface-coiling current where it leaked beneath the fall. Resting outside his burrow, Gabe thought. Thank Christ it's over there, otherwise I'd be soaked to my knees in this bloody dugout. I've shifted tons of muck. Few more hours should put me by the stop valve, near as damn it, I hope. By then I'll be knackered. Just about knackered as it is. There's old Cochyn my butty, he's out of it. He's finished. His missis'll go off her rocker when she sees him. As Mansel would say, here's the price of the old black diamonds. He was never stuck in a crack like this. Stan Evans' heading, right place for trying out our NCB office staff, our collar-and-tie brigade.

Gabe's mind feathered as drift around himself and Lucy Passmore, finally vanishing, become phantasmal. He drank from his jack before crawling into the hole.

Raging, 'Anyone back there?' careless insanity promised to protect him. He slaved briefly, desperately. Exhaustion and stale air drained his spirit. He threw muck twice, clearing the burrow. He dragged in his last two props. When they were fixed in position, Gabe crawled out and slept. Cap lamp in his hand, consciousness settled greyly peaceful. *Stop valve*, get on to the pipe column or you'll wind up a deader like Billy Cochyn, which sparked defiance. *Never*. But torpor held his unfeeling body.

He hacked slowly at the rubble, levering away larger stones, rolling them behind him. The rail was his base for shovelling, screwing aside, turning every shovelful over his left thigh.

As in dream, impacting like divine insight, a streak of black low down in the debris, Gabe scrabbled with his fingers, freeing a loop of rubber hose. The blast hose connected to the 2" pipeline. Confidence swam warmth, magic hurrahs singing his blood. Uncoiling the tough rubber hose, scratching forward through rubble, he found the smooth iron pipe. Gabe turned the stop-valve wheel, clung to it with a searing wrench of strength as compressed air whined, howled from a leak at the hose connection, purging the burrow with pricking dust and grit. Sobbing breaths, he eased back the knurled wheel until gentle air purred out, consistent, like a soft chimney draught drawing a fire. Gabe lashed his muffler around the leak. He crawled back to the tram. He felt convinced. All he had to do now was rest, wait for rescue teams to work through the fall.

Sprawled in the roadway, cap lamp and helmet held to his stomach, he listened to cool, flowing air. Memory fragments bobbled like spawn. His fight-training days in the basement below the Institute. Sweat and snobs. Hard. Nothing like this.

Few minutes rest, relax all over, then start banging on the pipe column. Battery's just about flattened. He switched on as he stood upright. Glimmer focused on Billy's studded bootsoles projecting above the rim of the tram. And Gabe's throat lamented, 'Poor old Cochyn.'

Whispery, human-sounding air flowed out from the threaded nozzle of the blast hose. Gabe pulled on his jacket, feeling his bones worn, feeble. He dragged Stan Evans' hammer-headed hatchet into the burrow, poised it over the 2" pipe and knocked six hard bangs. He waited, eyes shut, his mouth open. Six far-off signals resounded faintly. He hammered aggressively until he realised the danger of dislodging stones above his head.

As before, answers came softly pecking along the pipeline.

He's mumbling, 'Christ... Christ-man, it'll take 'em ages to cut through.'

Gabe huddled at the end of his burrow. The banging clacked on and on, all the time far, far away. He couldn't calculate how far. Head wrapped in his arms, he lapsed into misery worse than any physical beating, worse than the deaths of his father and mother. He was reduced, flawed in power, Gabe's secret faith where he lived heroically.

Frightened, he skulked around the tram to peer at Billy Holly's shrunken face, 'Billy Coch,' he said, mawkishly superior, 'we're trapped inside a bloody big dose of it, heading's blocked right out to the main, way they're knocking through on the blast pipe. Trapped, see?' He reached over and buttoned Billy's jacket, tidily, the way Sue straightened his tie before he went to Dove Street court. 'But you're safe, Cochyn, lucky man you.'

He circled around the tram. Cracked saucepan tappings were still coming from the burrow, endless, and he thought, they've put a youngster on the job, just bashing the pipe column. Monte Leyshon's back there, Monte the gog-eyed wonder, in charge of operations. He'd better be. I hope he is for Christ's sake. I'm relying on more than brains to get me out from here.

When the knocking ceased, he stilled himself in listening. Abruptly then, with blind certainty, Gabe leaned over the tram and rifled Billy's waistcoat pockets. Jacket pockets never carried anything except water jack and tommy box. A harmless WHUMP froze him in the act. He gazed up at the new untightened ring. Shot firing on big stuff back there.

The distant explosion shook down diminutive whiffs of dust. He crouched into the burrow. Billy had small change and a return bus ticket in a Zube tin, a piece of hacksaw blade attached to a wrist loop of baling string, pair of pliers, box spanner to fit nuts on the longwall cable pommel, and two sticky boiled sweets wrapped in paper. Gabe switched off his cap lamp, lowered his mouth to the sweets, sucked, a king of clockwork suck-suck-suck, then crunched, savouring fragments to his upper palate, draining juice out of them, twitchy like a rodent. Hours later he replaced the articles in Billy's waistcoat pockets.

He licked buttery crumbs off greaseproof paper which had wrapped Billy's sandwiches – Sue Lloyd always packed his sandwiches in a plastic bag. Sleep, he thought, for the time being, sleep. She's heard the news by now, odds are Sue's on top pit, blinding holy Jesus out of officials. Sue and Cochyn's wife, that queer little sprat of a woman. Strange little piece, Mrs Holly, busy-busy like women with kids are supposed to be.

Gabe examined ground around the tram for a dry, shaly

place to sleep. Knock first, he thought. Ease off the blast or I'll freeze.

He clanged the pipe six times with the hatchet, returned to the driest side of the tram and curled up with his head tucked inside his jacket. Nine hours later, when he roused feeling broken, nerves snapped beyond cure, a fourth rescue team were beginning their work on the fall.

Gabe drank too much water, felt it grip his insides like colic. The worthless mystery of his heart said, 'I'm starving.' I'm starving. Jesus Christ, I could eat now, put away the eggs and heaps of rashers. Forearms pressed to his stomach, he see-sawed from the waist, defending himself against gnawing chill. Bound to wear off, he thought. Gripe. I'll have to go steady on the water. It's easing already. Must keep warm. At a pinch I'll borrow some of Billy's clothes. Dead cert there won't be any grub. Set my mind on that. God help me if I can't go without grub for a couple of shifts.

Insectile vibrations plagued along the metal. He's squawking, 'Slash into it!' the same dumb answer along the compressed air pipeline.

Idle bastards, he thought, they're not putting their backs into the job. Every man in Bothi Number Two should be out there, all the rings, timber and flats they want coming up right behind their legs. Everything to hand for the asking, while me, I'm...

He rubbed his eyes, quenching tears. The knockings were punishing his mind. But tears flowed as crawled from the hole, clogging runnels in his blackened face. Gabe sobbed, warning himself, 'Hang on, gotto hang on to my nerve. Once my nerve goes I'll be useless. I won't lose my nerve. *I won't.* No matter what, I'll stick it out. Must hang on, thinking if it takes them a few shifts to clear the fall, I'll be al'right. Just hang on, stick it until the first lamp comes up the heading.'

By way of inane authority, he shouted, 'Cochyn, I'll stay company with you.' Then mumbling defeat, 'Ah, poor old Cochyn.'

On in front of the tram, waxily black against grey rock, the rider seam of inferior coal wheezed airily, handfuls spraying down over the rubble. Gabe hunkered motionless, chin on his chest. He was failing to estimate how long he'd been cut off in this bloody deathtrap of a heading.

Like a drugged man he scuffed his shape in the shaly rubble. Gabe laid flat on his back, Billy Holly's jacket wrapped around his legs. Staring at darkness, cap lamp clipped to the front of his belt, he invented tactics: The longer I'll sleep, less I'll panic. There's enough strength left in me. I'm a long way from beaten, hell of a long way yet, as I'd show if Lucy Passmore was here. I could use a good woman, put some life in my guts. She'll be waiting. Lush blonde. I had the green light off her again last night. Last…? How long since the fall? We'd finished cutting when Jobie came. Say around six o'clock in the morning. *Saturday*. I worked at least a full shift digging through to the stop valve. Then slept. Slept three, four times. Making it Sunday evening. Sunday night at the latest.

He drowsed, hungering, cuddling his privates for warmth, the only wistful reach of life in his humanity. Subsequently through his drowse, emerged a large amorphous female, soft concubine of dream to give succour, dissolving benevolence throughout his bones and flesh. Instantly losing her. Afterwards deep sleep, peaceful, and all lost forever in the spastic rigor of his awakening.

The pilot bulb glowed like a cigarette, outlining its single filament. Gabe stared, his other hand reaching for the lamp on the tram of debris. Now he curled himself with Billy's lamp ready between his knees. He gazed at the slender curve of reddened wire, waiting for the glow to die but the glow remained, ceasing when he was already blind, tranced from staring at it. He thought, I should be working from this end. No timber, nothing, nothing. Nothing left. Despair chuckled, 'I'm not a fucken mole.' It's me, Gabe Lloyd… NCB champion two years ago.

He switched on Billy's lamp and briefly wept, pleading, 'I can't last much longer. My butty, he's dead in here.'

Water trickled under the far side of the tram, spreading outwards to Gabe's shaly bed. Unclipping his own lamp and spent battery, he placed them beside Billy Holly's feet, 'Mine for yours, Coch-boy. You don't need light any more.'

The fragile corpse stank, stained teeth bared inside tightened, spread-away lips. Like a foolish, sentimental child, Gabe caught up the nozzle end of the tough rubber hose and he fanned softly purring compressed air over Billy's face, saying, 'Can't bury you, Coch. Pointless even if I could, same it would be, the stink. I'm taking a real bloody hammering. I'm weak as a kitten. Aye, weak.'

He dropped to his knees, complaining as he crept into the burrow, 'God knows how long I've been in here.'

One knock on the pipe brought immediate ringing reply, nearer, urgent, distinct, as if the rescue teams were a couple of rooms away. Gabe clanged the pipe with the blade of his shovel. Someone answered furiously, loud kettledrum syntax, reverberations thrumming the narrow burrow. Stupefied, Gabe crawled out. Unable to lever upright, he kept moving, hands and feet each side of the rail. Face down on the shale, light switched off, Gabe breathed shallowly across the back of his hand. Asleep, he lowered into disintegration. Eighteen hours later, chewing and swallowing pellets of greaseproof paper, ugly jeering taunted as a threat: *Jibber, you're jibbing, Gabe.*

'Nuh,' he said, sinking away.

He lay there to the eighth day, curled in darkness, small pieces of leather bootlace inside his mouth. Total blackness no longer disturbed him. There weren't even any terrors. Billy's broken hacksaw blade hung from his wrist. Short lengths of bootlace clustered meaninglessly in his stomach. Like an infant he licked the dried, coal-grained cuts on his hand, puckered skin cold against scant warmth of his tongue. He moaned to sighing, very, very slowly creeping his thighs to his belly, sighing, sighed into the coma which sustained him on ebb until Monday evening, when the first rescue miner found him.

Crouching out from Gabe's burrow, he came bowling forward on hands and feet like a grounded ape. Pausing short of the team, hand clamped over his nostrils, the beam of his lamp shone on Gabe. He shouted into the hole, 'Come on! Safe! We're too late by the looks of it!'

Rescue miners were grouped around the tram. Saying, 'Right now,' they lowered and covered Billy Holly's body on a Stokes stretcher. Heads shook, twisting aside, 'Ach,' they said against the foul smell. The ambulance man trickled diluted brandy down Gabe's throat. He convulsed, jackknifing trembles from his groins. They wrapped him in blankets.

'Carry Billy out to the main,' ordered the team leader. He spoke quietly to the ambulance man. 'Open the flask.'

The ambulance man spooned patiently, 'Good on you, son, you're all right, you're safe. Slow now, slowly does it.

Gabe strained for consciousness. Neural tics plucked his face. His tongue felt huge, wooden.

The ambulance man laughed up at the team leader, 'He's ours! Aye, great!'

Monte Leyshon finger-wiped his nose, inquiring, 'Where's Jobie Lewis?'

'Top pit cabin,' they said. 'Old Jobie's knackered, been working too many doublers.'

The manager kneeled into the burrow. 'Bring Gabe out to pit bottom when you're ready. I must speak to Jobie. He'll have to let Mrs Holly know about her man.'

A miner said, 'Don't forget Sue Lloyd, for Christ's sake.'

Another miner said, 'Sooner Jobie than me.'

Gabe's speech broke through whining, 'I was licked. Billy Coch, see, it kill't Billy.'

The ambulance man wiped his mouth with cotton wool. 'We're taking you out, Gabe.' He cautioned the miners each end of the stretcher, 'Gentle, lads, lift altogether.'

Gabe moaned as they dragged him through the hole, 'Ah, Christ, I was all in, I was beat.'

'Talking bloody daft,' said a man at his feet. 'I saw you fighting Nobby Graham. Guts, boy, you won on guts.'

Out on the main, Stan Evans leaned over him, 'Gabe, I didn't expect it to come in like that, indeed to God I didn't. Whole place fell in. I couldn't do anything, couldn't warn you in time.'

The team leader pushed at Stan's chest, 'Be quiet. No call for you to take it on yourself. Nobody's bloody fault.'

They lifted Gabe on his stretcher into a tram, men squatting each side, easing jolts as they journeyed back to pit bottom. A chatty young GP examined him in the ambulance centre. Gabe swallowed more soup. Sue was holding his hand. Befuddled, Gabe grinned at her and the world before sleep collapsed his senses. He fell away, emptied into warmth.

Mid October and after-dark chill scuttling customers into the public bar. Gabe stepped to the curb as Lucy Passmore's little car circled outside the prototype Edwardian Great Western Arms.

'I didn't expect to see you so soon, Gabe.'

'Me neither,' he said. 'How's trade in the canteen?'

'Pard'n?'

He gripped her knee, squeezing hard. 'Knocking somebody else off these days, girl?'

'You're hurting me!'

He rolled his shoulder against hers, saying, 'Dyffryn Lake, let's find out if it's the same as it used to be.'

'My knee! You're cruel Gabe, cruel.'

He said, 'Aye, I know that too.'

'Everyone kept saying you were dead. Morning, noon and night in the canteen, Gabe Lloyd is gone, he's bound to be dead. Even Mr Leyshon, he believed you were dead.'

He jammed his fists into his pockets. 'OK I don't want to hear any more.'

Lucy turned into a lane at the lower end of Dyffryn Lake to the gate of a derelict sheepfold.

He loosened his shirt collar, 'We'll stay inside tonight.'

Her lips found his mouth, 'I'm trying to be nice to you, Gabie-love.'

'You were in my mind, Lucy. *That* was cruel.'

'I missed you, darling.' Carefully moving away from their kiss, she opened her handbag, 'Cigarette?' Her lighter spurted flame. She puffed contentment, glow-'puhh' glow-'puhh' glow-'puhh', her plump, perfumed body sagged behind the wheel. Awkwardly in the cramped space, the seats creaking, pulling closer to her, his hand reached down between her thighs. Lucy sat motionless. Cigarette smoke whoofed softly at his ear, preceding benign fatalism, 'Poor Gabeie, you've picked the wrong night.' Crossing her legs, she embraced him affectionately, 'There, that's better. Now we can have a lovely cwtch.'

'Jesus Christ,' he said.

'You're ever so greedy. For one thing you're not fit yet. They kept you in hospital for ages. I mean to say, I had no intention of meeting you tonight, only you insisted. You did, Gabe, after all you've been through.'

He said, 'You should have told me straight off.'

'Dear God, what a way to talk, as if I'm some kind of um, well, y'know Gabie you're only concerned about sex.'

'Lay it on, girl,' he said.

'I'm telling the truth.' Strange to his ears, Lucy giggled, 'Matter of fact the under-manager, he asked me, offered to make a date.' She pressed her knuckles over his mouth, 'Sshe, wait till you've heard the bleddy story. It was for Rosser's sake. The undermanager promised he'd try to find Rosser a job in Bothi stores. My husband can't do heavy work, his chest being the way it is. By damn, I've kept our home going for years and years!'

Gabe said, 'Been out with him?'

'Once. We saw a show in Cardiff.' She gushed nasally,

'Bleddy Kairdiff. Lousy it was, I couldn't follow it myself. As for him, he was really chuffed.'

'What about after the show?'

'We had a meal. Oh, shurrup, Gabe. No reason for you to criticise. Stop quibbling. Honest to God, you're narrow-minded like all the rest. 'Tisn't as if there's any future. Where's our future? Least we can do is be friends. Don't make bad blood between us.'

It was a serene Autumn morning when Sue went upstairs to Gabe's room. She stood beside his bed.

'C'mon, move, it's eleven o'clock.'

'Be right down.'

'When you starting work?'

'Monday, day shift an' all, my own stent.'

'Wake up, you loafer.'

'Al'right, al'right.'

After breakfast he walked alongside a feeder stream to Dyffryn Lake. Drought-weather fog capped the low hills. Dark-mossed stones were drying out above the water level and still green clods of sedge tufted vagrant pointillism. His first long ramble since rescue teams stretchered him from Bothi Number Two, Gabe making the most of it, scorning his sloth, the flabbiness of his belly muscles. He broke into jog-trotting, leapt to and fro across the brook, made short sprints, and turned, setting himself a brisk homeward pace.

Near the village football field, Gabe met Rosser Passmore.

Riven-faced, tormented by sickness and conscience, Rosser stamped by his walking stick, 'Glad to see you out and about, my boy. Must have been terr-rrible for you down there in the bowels of the earth. Remember the proverb, The finest blades are tempered in the fiercest fires. Oh yes, our time of trial will come. Tell me true, you prayed to the Lord when you were trapped down there.'

Gabe stroked his nose, 'Can't say I did.'

Rosser made high, shaky baton strokes with his stick.

'There isn't a man alive who can afford to neglect the Almighty in his hour of need. Every day of the week Christian lives are saved by prayer.' Climbing to the Pentecostal fervour Rosser hovered his stick above Gabe's shoulder, 'Without prayer our sins mount up higher and higher! There can be no salvation…'

Gabe snatched the end of the stick, Rosser blinking skywards, gulps of irritation stringing his throat. 'Excuse me,' said Gabe. 'If you don't mind, Ross, You're spouting to the wrong fella.'

'Then you are blind and proud!' accused Rosser.

'Doesn't matter about that for now,' suggested Gabe, ready to appease. This man was a wreck, old Bible-puncher not far short of his coffin. He says, 'Cheerio, Ross. My dinner's waiting for me.'

'Hear the word of the Lord!'

The walking stick whiffled above his shoulder again, victimising him.

'Don't fucken-well do that,' snarled Gabe, attack glinting his grey eyes. He flung down the stick. 'Belt up, you drippy old bastard. Buy a pair of working boots and get your missis to fill your tommy box.' He returned walking stick to Rosser, 'I'm on my way home. Just leave me alone. You go your way, I'll go mine.'

Rosser was gasping, 'God-bless, God-bless, God-bless,' his arms jerking fore and aft, seeking to propel his legs.

Gabe nodded, 'No offence, it's only, aah for Chrissake listen a minute.' And it blurted out, 'Do something about your wife, will you! She's chasing 'round like a bitch on heat.'

Rosser Passmore's head planed forward, vulture hanging.

Short cutting across the field, Gabe cursed himself for a bloody fool. Typical. No better and no worse than Sue. Two beauts under the same roof. What in the name of Christ am I any good for? What? Five bloody stents a week. So he talked to the grass under his shoes, 'Act your age, Lloydie, for Christ's sake grow up, man.'

THE WRITING
ON THE WALL

Raymond Williams

'A liberal man in a liberal place': that had been Evan
Richards' reputation until the events of November 1963,
when, if in different ways, both the man and the place
changed.

The occasion appeared to have little history in it. As
announced and as initially performed it was, rather, the
principal event of the year in the artistic life of the college,
which was not, it is true, especially a centre of the arts, apart
from the occasional gift of sculpture or silver at a death or
a centenary, but which nevertheless, like any other
Cambridge college, had its appointed moments of traditional
celebration and cultural event. Yet this November evening
was rightly seen as exceptional: a first performance, in the
college chapel, of the fifteenth-century miracle play, *The
Feast of Belshazzar,* with new music by Luke Beit, the young
Rhodesian who had been the college's most brilliant organ
scholar in memory and who was already gaining national
recognition as a composer. The inspiration for the music had
been the new college organ, commissioned, after long
controversy, to replace the attractive but failing early
Victorian instrument which for so long had filled the small
medieval chapel and the tiny Chapel Court with its
shuddering music for evensong. Evan Richards, as it

happened, had led the opposition, in Council, to the new organ, wanting the money spent instead on three new Research Fellowships. He had collected a sizeable negative vote, but its grounds had been mixed, ranging from a general unwillingness to spend money on anything to a middling agnostic and small atheist wing who wanted no expenditure of any kind, beyond maintenance, on anything to do with the chapel. The traditional vote for the chapel and for an instrument of divine worship had been significantly smaller, but it was joined by a decisive musical vote, especially among the scientists. The magnificent new organ had been finally installed in the summer, and Beit's *Belshazzar* was to be its first public performance.

'At least,' Evan Richards had said, 'it will, as a Feast, go down well in the college.'

But that was a standard liberal joke, as conventional, in its way, as the College Feasts themselves. There were no hard feelings. Even the close vote – there had been only one closer, in recent years, on a scheme for reforming the gardens – had been taken in the usual watchful, soft-voiced and relaxed atmosphere of all college business: what the young sociology Fellow called 'the "with-respect-Master" bit'.

Certainly this liberal unity in diversity was sustained, at least socially, in attendance at the occasion. Almost all the Fellows were there, with their wives and guests, and the free public tickets had been all taken a week beforehand. The atmosphere in the dimly lit chapel, which converted so well to a theatre auditorium and stage, was warm, appreciative and even, in its way, emotional. Evan Richards and his wife arrived at the low door at the same time as John Forrester, the Senior Tutor, and his wife, and they walked in and sat together on reserved chairs at the front of the nave. The conversation, until the lights were switched off, was, as so often, about examinations.

Belshazzar the king-actor did not dine with a thousand of his lords, but the deep power of the new organ, and the strong singing of the augmented choir, were, if anything, too crowded, too rich and impressive, for the small space of the chapel. Richards noticed that the audience – the congregation, he had momentarily thought – were pulling back slightly from the swell of the music. On most of the faces near him he could see that expression of a strictly guarded interest and an always tentative benevolence which he had learned to recognise as a university habit. An exception was Mrs Forester who, although her husband was Senior Tutor, had as little as possible to do with the college and nothing at all to do with the university: they were, she insisted, uncreative places, deficient in all the emotions to which the arts appealed, lacking the aesthetic sensibility which nevertheless they persistently discussed. Richards guessed that his own face had the standard expression of sceptical attention – a tutorial look – as he watched Mrs Forrester's settled raptness of reception: what he had heard her refer to as her physical openness to the music. But as the chorus ended and the dialogue began his own attention shifted and he listened curiously.

Like many others in that predominantly academic audience he had looked up the fifth chapter of the Book of Daniel before coming to the play. Every story has a version, and the whole point of training is to identify it. What had the anonymous author of the medieval play added to and taken from that chapter? What had the adapter, an English research student, himself added or subtracted (though that could be only inferred; there was no easily accessible text of this relatively unknown play)? It quickly appeared that from one or the other or both there was extra emphasis on the captivity of the Judaeans; on their status, in effect, as political prisoners (but that was surely the adapter). Then there was an elaborated (probably medieval) mockery of the parade of stolen wealth: the gold vessels taken from another people, another god, another land. The court's pride in wealth and in power was made simple and explicit, and the crescendo of organ music which was the climax of its celebration was indeed overpowering. But then it was broken off, with startling effect, in mid-phrase, and above the screen of the chancel, now for the first time illuminated, appeared the known, unknown words: *Mene, Mene, Tekel, Upharsin.* Richards was as little able as the theatrically startled Belshazzar to see quite how it had been done. It must, he supposed, be some effect of fluorescence: the startling successive appearance of each word, on what he could see was black muslin, without even the Biblical part of the hand to write them.

And it was true, a true effect. The strange words were startling. As even with English words, the more you looked at them, in the prolonged silence, and with nothing else to look at, the stranger, the more alien and disturbing, they became. This effect was held, and then, with a sharp change of mood, the dialogue resumed. Astrologers, Chaldeans and soothsayers were busily summoned and interrogated. The adapter showed through in a number of phrases suggesting, rather broadly, a translation class, with special play on the Biblical anomaly of *upharsin* and *peres*. This went on rather too long. Then the Queen came, and her recommendation of Daniel was a beautiful slow song: the first effect of the music that owed nothing to amplification. And Daniel, too, was magnificent – a tall figure accusing the King.

> Whom you will you kill
> Whom you fear you fetter

But to the words, to the words. In another startling effect the words vanished. They were suddenly just not there; there was only Daniel's relentless accusation. It was only at his climax that they appeared again, not now successively but in a single flare. *Mene, Mene, Tekel, Upharsin.*

And then it was in effect an anticlimax as Daniel interpreted them, with full allegorical tendentiousness: the original now a mere trickle through the consequential homily on the inevitable turning of Fortune's wheel and against the pride of worldly wealth and rule. The momentum was not regained until the new final scene, written for the music, in which among flashes in the darkness the court was scattered and the kingdom fell: a rush of disintegration, under the power of the organ finale, until only the words were still visible, in the now wholly dark chapel.

The applause came well before the lights: an applause of relief, it seemed, before it was approbation. But it was long and obviously genuine. The performers appeared and acknowledged it. Luke Beit ducked rather than bowed and at once disappeared. The audience began to get up and to make its slow way out. Richards, standing with his wife and the Forresters, looked up at the muslin, above the chancel screen, to try to identify the technique of the effect of the words.

'Oh blast,' he heard Forrester say, and looked down to see the Head Porter, holding his top hat to make a way through the shuffling exit, bearing intently in the direction of the Senior Tutor.

'I'm sorry to disturb you, sir.'

'Yes?'

'We have some trouble, sir, on the west wall.'

'What sort of trouble?'

'Daubing, sir. The two who did it have been caught.'

'Oh no,' Richards said, as if at an intolerable joke.

Forrester and the Head Porter looked at him curiously.

'Do you know anything about this, Evan?' Forrester asked.

'No, nothing. I was only thinking of the outrageous coincidence. And of the way undergraduates have of making outrageous coincidences happen.'

'What coincidence?' Mrs Forrester asked, but her husband had taken charge. With the Head Porter clearing the way, they went quickly out to the court and round to the west chapel wall. There, under the light from the windows, a group of men were standing: two porters, the verger and two undergraduates. One of the porters had a torch and as he saw the others approaching he swung its beam to the wall. In large white painted letters, on the dark medieval stone, were three words: *Free Nelson Mandela.*

'When was this done?' Forrester asked.

'About an hour ago, sir,' said one of the porters. 'I was on my rounds. I found these two gentlemen actually finishing it off.'

'These two?'

'Sir.'

'Who are you? Come here.'

The two undergraduates stepped forward.

'Lewis.'

'Aitken, sir.'

Richards watched Aitken's face. He knew him well as one of his own students: a normally quiet boy. He was pale and tense, but with an edge of defiance. Lewis, beside him, looked more openly angry.

'You're both responsible for this?' Forrester asked.

'Yes sir.'

'Is it your idea of a joke?'

'No sir, not a joke,' Aitken replied carefully.

'Putting Mandela in gaol is no kind of a joke,' Lewis said, aggressively.

'But you are not Mandela and this is not a gaol,' Forrester said sharply. 'This is a college chapel, which you have defaced like any hooligan.'

'It's a silicone paint, sir,' the Head Porter put in.

'What?'

'You can't get it off, sir. Not like whitewash you can't. It dries hard to the stone soon after it comes from the can.'

'The can?'

'The aerosol, sir.'

Forrester walked to the wall and tested the paint with his

fingers. It had indeed dried hard. He looked at his unmarked finger. Then he turned to the Head Porter.

'Mr Peters, call the police.'

'Right, sir.'

The porter was turning to go as Evan Richards protested.

'For Christ's sake, John, not the police. We can deal with this in the college.'

'Why should we?' Forrester asked. 'If they were street hooligans would they get that privilege?'

'We always have,' Richards said, weakly.

'We always have with practical jokes. But we've just been informed that this isn't a joke.'

'No, but think of the situation.'

'What situation? The South African situation? This college is not responsible for the South African situation.'

'It is in part,' Aitken said. 'It buys South African food. It invests in companies which exploit black workers. It's at the end of the line which put Nelson Mandela in gaol.'

'And for that tenuous connection you deface, perhaps permanently, a medieval wall.'

'Walls are less important than people,' Lewis said, hoarsely.

'You have to do something,' Aitken said, 'to bring it home to people.'

'Well you have,' Forrester said, 'brought it home. To yourselves. Go on, Mr Peters.'

As the Head Porter went, Richards tried again.

'I didn't mean the South African situation,' he said quietly to Forrester.

'What situation then?'

'Our own, don't you see? The occasion they exploited. The coincidence they made happen.'

'I don't understand you.'

'Well for God's sake, they must have lifted the can as the words appeared in the chapel. The writing on the wall.'

'Oh that,' Forrester said.

'I don't understand,' Mrs Forrester said. 'What has the play got to do with it?'

'No but look,' Richards said, remembering the intolerable explicitness of the medieval homily. 'It was writing on the wall, an avenging hand in the name of a conquered people.'

'The hand of God,' Forrester said.

'The play wasn't about South Africa, Evan,' Mrs Forrester said. 'And when I think of all that wonderful music, people creating something beautiful, and then this, this destructive daub.'

'At least Belshazzar was frightened,' Mrs Richards said. 'And wanted to know what it meant.'

Forrester nodded.

'I see your point, Evan. But it's no good. You said an outrageous coincidence. I say simply an outrage. A cheap point scored and never mind the damage.'

'I don't think my own point is cheap,' Richards said. 'We are not Belshazzar and Daniel any more than we are Verwoerd and Mandela, but we are a comfortable society, we were a comfortable audience, and I think we do have to look at the writing on the wall.'

'You approve, Evan, of what these young men have done?' Mrs Forrester asked.

'No. But I know why they did it. And I know we'll look ridiculous if we prosecute the action we've just pretended to respond to, at a safely aesthetic distance.'

'That's just philistine, Evan.'

'I don't think so. But tell me one thing, Mark,' he said, turning to Aitken. 'Did you mean to get caught? Or did you expect to get away with it?'

'We wanted it in the open,' Lewis said, defiantly.

'No,' Aitken said. 'We hoped we wouldn't be caught. We hoped the words would just have appeared, the unseen hand-writing.'

'And why the silicone, which is bound to damage the wall?'

'You'd have preferred whitewash,' Lewis said sharply.

The Head Porter came back.

'They're on their way, sir.'

'Thank you, Mr Peters. Take Aitken and Lewis to the lodge. I'll see the police there.'

Richards turned again to Forrester.

'There are still these few minutes, John. Before the line is crossed.'

'What line?'

'A change in this place. A change in the mind of this place.'

The Head Porter was looking at Forrester. Forrester nodded.

'If you'll come this way, gentlemen,' Peter said to Aitken and Lewis. They went off, with the other porters behind them.

'In the morning, Wilkes,' Forrester said to the verger, 'go to the Bursar's office, get the agent to ring the paint manufacturers, ask for their advice on its removal.'

'Sir.'

Wilkes followed the others. The two Fellows and their wives were left on the damp grass by the chapel wall. As the lights in the chapel went out, the offending words – *Free Nelson Mandela* – were only barely distinguishable.

'You're right, Evan,' Forrester said. 'A line has been crossed, and that generation has crossed it. And none of them will know, for a long time, just what they've lost, what they think they're free to reject.'

'You'll get the police to charge them?'

'Yes, certainly. I'm going to hold back this barbarism as long as I can.'

'Barbarism? For God's sake. A political protest!'

'A political protest by articulate young men who can think of nothing better than to deface walls.'

'Perhaps we need a Daniel,' Richards said, half laughing.

'Are you casting yourself, Evan?'

'An hour ago any of us might have. But we've gone beyond interpretation.'

'What does that mean?' Mrs Forrester asked.

'I'm not sure yet what it means. But, John if it goes to court I shall speak for them. I'll give evidence of motive and evidence of character.'

'And put yourself in their camp,' Mrs Forrester said.

'It's been our habit to defend them.'

'Well habits need changing,' Mrs Forrester said. Forrester was looking unhappy.

'You must do as you think right, Evan. But you're profoundly wrong all the same.'

'I watched the play,' Richards said. 'I think, don't you, it will have a rather large audience.'

'It certainly deserves to,' Mrs Forrester said, with relieved enthusiasm.

They walked away separating, over the damp grass.

BOWELS JONES

Alun Richards

'Mr Bowcott Jones has the gripe,' Fan Bowcott Jones said to the Portuguese guide who had inquired. '*La grippe, n'est-ce pas?*'

'Sardines in charcoal?' the guide said with a charming smile and a fey waggle of his braceleted wrist. He was young, dark, and beautiful, with neat hips swathed in scarlet flares like a girl's. 'Cook in charcoal, no? Just the peoples from the hotel?'

'No, he's not feeling well. *L'estomac!*'

The guide persisted in not understanding.

'In a boat with fisherman's, Portuguese style?'

'I shall come.'

'But of course...'

'But Mr Bowcott Jones is inconvenienced.'

'*Vour parlez français très bien,*' the guide said, and took out a handsome red purse. 'I shall require two hundred escudos for the two.'

They stood outside the bedroom door on the fourth floor of the Hotel Lagos in the Algarve. The guide had come all the way up the stairs since the lift was out of order, but Mrs Bowcott Jones could not make herself understood. The Portuguese were simple and charming, but the confidence with which they assumed they understood everything was profoundly irritating. They were grave and serious, more attentive than the Spanish, and the food, if you ate it in reasonable quantities, was infinitely more value for money. But this year, like the last, Bowcott had found a pub where they gave the impression of listening to him, and once again, it had led to excess.

Mrs Bowcott Jones sighed, searched her vocabulary, and finally said in a mixture of Spanish, French and Portuguese, overlaid with a sympathetic Welsh valley accent: '*Solamente uno!*' She held up one finger. 'Señor Jones – non! *Pash favor, uno?*'

'Ah, jest one?' said the guide, flashing his teeth.

'*Pash favor,*' Mrs Bowcott Jones said again, returning his smile. They were extraordinarily sexy, these nut-brown boys. If you gave your mind to that sort of thing.

'One hun'red escudos for je..st the one?'

'*Momento,*' Mrs Bowcott Jones went into the room and closed the door firmly behind her. Now her expression changed and her voice became harder as she looked down at the gross, fleshy bulk of her husband who lay motionless in bed, his chin bowed and thick knees doubled up over his comfortable belly in the attitude of an elephantine embryo. Bowcott was bilious again.

'No good asking me for sympathy. You're fifty-six years of age, very likely Chairman of the bench next year, but the moment you're abroad, you're like a sailor off a tanker or something,' his wife said sharply. The neat figure of the waiting guide had irritated her, and now the lump of Bowcott's heavy form reminded her of the white rhino in Bristol Zoo, the highlight of school trips when she was a child, and later a primary-school teacher.

Bowcott attempted to speak, failed, and said nothing. Years ago, he had thought his wife a little common, but it had the effect of increasing his self-importance. He could condescend from time to time. But now he could just moan and was in danger of being sick.

'Oh, Fan… Oh, Duw…'

'Whatever you think you're doing, I'm going on the sardine trip.'

He opened his mouth once more but realised that his lips were partially stuck together, and gave himself an intelligence report. Booze *and* fags, he thought. He'd meant to stick to cigars.

'Just the people from the hotel. It's a deserted beach,' his wife said with some emphasis. 'And there's no need to make a face like that. The people on the tour are very nice people. English, of course, but they all asked after you at breakfast.'

Bowcott gave a little belch. He was getting old. One night on the tiles meant that there were days that got lost, slipped past the memory, notching themselves on to his stomach, however, like knife slashes on a branch.

'Where's your wallet? The guide is waiting.'

That was another thing. He couldn't remember where he'd put his wallet. He rolled over in a pool of sweat and felt under the pillow, but it wasn't there. He could not remember what he'd done with his shirt and shorts for that matter. Avoiding his wife's eye, he slid a glance in the direction of a nearby chair. But his shorts and shirt were missing too.

'I washed them,' Fan said darkly. 'Well, I couldn't send them to the laundry. I daren't. And your wallet wasn't in them. Oh, for goodness' sake, what have you done with it?'

She had been asleep when he had eventually got home in the early hours of the morning. He had been in the English Tavern in the village, a place he privately referred to as a hot spot, but things had got a little too hot, and now an extraordinary phrase kept repeating itself in his mind.

'*For Chrissakes, the bogey's got his shooter out!*'

It was such an alarming phrase for a man like him to have heard at all. There was a note of hysteria in it, but as he tried to fit it into place, he recalled incidents from the previous night, images floating into consciousness like the interrupted trailer of some incredibly seedy film. What had happened this time?

His wife turned impatiently to the dressing table drawer where they kept the passports. The wallet was not there either, but his passport was. Hidden between the folded pages, there were a number of high denomination notes which she knew he kept there for emergencies. They had always smuggled a little currency out of the UK. You never knew when it would be needed with Bowcott. She took two five-hundred escudo notes and snapped them in his face.

'I wouldn't be surprised if I didn't really *spend* today. Some of that ornamental silver is expensive enough,' she said punishingly. She folded the money into her purse, put on the pink straw hat which she'd bought for the occasion in San Antonio, picked up her Moroccan handbag, and finally the Spanish stole from the package holiday four years ago, and then marched to the door,

'The mixture is beside your bed,' she said at the door.

'Mixture?' he said hoarsely. He sounded like the victim of a pit disaster.

'The kaolin compound you had from Lucas Thomas the Chemist. Four spoonfuls a day,' she said getting it wrong. *Two spoonfuls four times a day*, the instructions read, carefully written in Lucas Thomas' feminine handwriting. 'Although what Lucas Thomas knows about conditions here, I can't imagine. Portugal is not Dan y Graig.'

Her last words. She slammed the door which did not close and he heard her brave Spanish once more.

'*Vamos a ir. A los sardinhos*,' she said to the guide who had remained.

'*Senhora* is multi-speaking?' the guide said politely. 'In your absence, the lift is working.'

'*Obrigard*,' she pronounced carefully. She went to the first three lessons of the language classes in the Women's Institute every year. It gave her enough to be going on with, apart from prices which she insisted on having written down.

Still immobile, Bowcott heard the lift descend, feeling like an overworked seismograph. His stomach was so distended that each part of his anatomy seemed now to distinguish sounds, as well as record its own special suffering. Although by now the Bowcott Joneses were veterans of the short quick trips all along the Costas, he always forgot himself sooner or later. If it wasn't the sun, it was the food or the wine, and although he usually reserved the big bust-up for the end of the stay when he could at least be in flying distance of Lucas Thomas' healing potions, this year he had gone over the top on the second night.

Perhaps it was a mistake to come to the Algarve? In one week last year, he seemed to get to know the town, and they had returned expecting to be celebrities, only to find that last year's crowd had moved on. But it wasn't only that. The trouble was within Bowcott himself. As his wirey, ninety-three-year-old mother said, 'Wherever we go, we take ourselves with us', and it applied absolutely to Bowcott, just as much as did her other countless sayings: 'He would go too far… Beyond,' as she said, using the word in its dark, Welsh sense; and she was right.

This year again, there was the extraordinary feeling of Welshness which came upon him abroad. At home, the valleys being what they were, if you'd had a dinner jacket before the war, and there hadn't been a lavatory 'out the back' for three generations, you were almost minor nobility. Not to have had anything to do with the pits was blue-blood itself, and since the Bowcott Joneses had been wholesale fruiterers for years, he was a man of property and substance, and had always been so. But get him abroad, and the old ilk was still there, a wildness of spirit and a capacity for living recklessly that was now beginning to shake his fifty-six-year-old frame as much as it delighted his image of himself at the imbibing time. Fan, fair play, was as good as gold normally. A collier's daughter wasn't going to moan about a drop too much, or the occasional accident, hygienic or otherwise, but this time, there were additional complications. The world was changing, Portugal and Wales, and Bowcott had suddenly become caught up in a sea of feelings, even ideas, that were strange to him. If only he could remember, he was sure it was all very frightening. Something had happened which placed him on the map. But what was it?

It was not simply that he had taken too much to eat and drink. Not this time. And he doubted whether his condition could in any way be attributed to Lucas Thomas' fawning habit of dispensing without prescription. Both of them regarded the valley's solitary Indian practitioner with some reserve, and for matters of the bowels, Lucas was very good on the whole. But perhaps the streptotriad tablets, advised and dispensed as a prophylactic against gyppy tummy, were too strong. For Welsh mams with filial problems and an aversion to the smell of alcohol, Lucas actually kept animal chlorophyll tablets of staggering breath-cleansing propensities. Perhaps the strepto-what's-its were also out of Lucas' VIP draw? Perhaps between them, they had been too clever by far? Was the thin, anaemic figure of Lucas Thomas, pinhead ever bobbing and smiling obsequiously behind his affected Douglas-Home lenses, *a guilty figure*?

In fairness, Bowcott did not think so. Lucas had seen him right through a number of marathons in the last two years, Twickenham, Murrayfield, Dublin and even the Paris trip which was an exploder, a real gut-buster, yet Bowcott was still standing after sixty-four hours of playing and drinking time when former Welsh rugby internationals had gone under the table, Triple Crown Championship notwithstanding.

Talk about Bowcott and you weren't talking about a cauliflower-eared colliery fitter. As Lucas Thomas said, 'Old Bowcott knows his Raymond Postgate. Hell of a *bon viveur* ackshually.'

But others put it less delicately.

'By God, you've got a constitution, Bowcott!' a former Welsh centre had said when he walked off the plane at Rhoose before they drove into Cardiff. Alone of the party, Bowcott arrived clanking with duty-free booze, fags and perfume for Fan, and walked, what is more, despite an inflamed eye or two, with a spring in his step. He might have been bringing the mythical Triple Crown home in his back pocket.

'I just keep in with Lucas Thomas,' he usually said with a snide tug at his clipped moustache. 'One needs a chap to look after one.' What he really meant was that he couldn't abide that Indian ghoul who didn't seem to understand the need for a blowout or the demands of a palate like his own.

But now he was knackered. The wogs had got him in the guts. He slipped into the vernacular when he felt sorry for himself, and he lay on the bed like an infantry officer who'd been bayoneted against the trench wall. He felt as if they'd done for him good and all, his Triple Crown constitution notwithstanding. Once again, the hoodoo was down below the belt. It felt like snakebite and gave him second thoughts. Perhaps he should have gone to New Zealand anyway and followed the Lions? He would have, but for Fan, although when he read the advertisement, 'Six hundred pounds and two years to pay', he'd felt tempted, but then decided against it. It wasn't so much that he couldn't afford it, but with payment on the never-never, it meant that a right lot would have been going on the trip. Of course, Bowcott was no snob on a rugby trip but, sport apart, he had a position to keep up as a magistrate. 'Out of town, we South Walians are all much the same,' he used to say with a twinkle whenever he addressed the Lodge or the Rotarians, but the truth was, New Zealand was too far for Lucas Thomas' ministrations. Lucas had always been his secret weapon.

His former adviser, he now thought bitterly. He wanted to think of anything rather than the muddied events of the previous night. But that damned voice returned. That incredible sentence...

'*For Chrissakes, the bogey's got his shooter out!*'

It was a common English voice, but for the moment, he could not put a face to it. He knew the police were involved too, but fortunately not with him. That was a relief. He closed his eyes and tried to trace back the roots of his involvement, but his mother's voice came back to him. She was always uncannily present after remorse-begetting situations.

'*Bowcott, you will always be judged by the company you keep.*'

'*For Chrissakes, the bogey's got his shooter out.*'

That was duologue for the record books.

'*Your father was a man of substance. Admittedly, he marched with the miners in '29, but of course, they were a lot of rodneys, half of them, not Welsh anyway.*'

'Welsh... Welsh...' he groaned. What memories on a Portuguese morning! Roots were always a problem, had bothered him when he and Fan had taken up their position at the bar near the swimming pool yesterday. Fan had put on her sundress and he wore the khaki shorts and short-sleeved bush shirt which he still affected on these occasions. He'd also worn a straw fedora and the thick leather belt he'd bought in Malaga two years before. There was, as ever, the District Commissioner look that he cultivated before he let his hair down. Commissioned in the RASC, he'd been in Imphal later in the war and, now and again, let the phrase 'Wingate's mob' drop. It gave an impression that was not strictly accurate, but now most people did not remember, and he'd just qualified for the Burma Star so sucks to anybody who challenged his credentials. He was President of the local British Legion anyway, and his knees were brown enough in the old days. He's been around, as they said, quite long enough to look after himself.

Why then, had things gone wrong?

He cast his mind back to early morning. A shaky day had begun beside the hotel swimming pool where English from Romford had arrived in large numbers. Previously, he and Fan had always found what Fan called 'a good class of people' on holiday. She meant rather far-back, posh accents, persons verging on county stock, justices of the peace at least. These, the Bowcott Joneses either accepted or did not. Ex-

Indian Army people, they got on well with anybody military who drank an occasional excess if you wanted a definition. In previous years, they'd met a very engaging old boy, Sir Philip Somebody-or-Other, and his wife from Bushey, and she'd also been nice with it. Nice with his full-time drinking, that is to say. In fact, on that holiday, she and Fan had had two spare-time drunks for husbands if you wanted to put it in an unkindly way. It was what they had in common, a circumstance that immediately rose above geography and class. But now both these veterans of the bottle were dead, and over the years, the Bowcott Joneses had noticed that the people who went on package tours had changed, and that was the start of it yesterday by the pool, a decided lowering of the tone.

The irony was that they could have tolerated a Dai Jones, or a couple of Rodneys. In the previous year, they had taken to an Irish couple and been pleased to show them the ropes, but the Romford English were quite impossible. They were careful with their money, always checking their change, wrongly suspecting the waiters of robbing them, often shouting with those whining Home Counties accents, sometimes leaving the best part of the asparagus, drinking beer with meals instead of wine, moaning about tipping habits, and making no attempt to speak the language. Bowcott who always called all foreign currencies 'chips', tipped lavishly, and when tight, insisted he was *Pays de Galles*, and had little jokes with the waiters, like announcing as he came into the dining-room, '*El Presidente arribe!*' or '*Voilà la Chef de Policia!*' in shoni-foreign language, and the fact that he attempted to communicate delighted everybody. It told everybody that he was a large jokey man, and not mean, and the waiters gave them better service and huge, daily smiles. As at home, he felt a character and was richer for it, but yesterday, for the first time, the Romford lot had put the kybosh on it, and more than anything, their voice infuriated him.

There was a child with freckles who did nothing she was told and whose parents could not stop talking. You did not take an early morning gin by the bougainvillea to listen to them.

'Emma... Emma, don't go into the pool.'

'Emma, you'll get orl red.'

'Emma, if your brother's bein' a berk, there's no need for you to be.'

'You tell him, Dad. If he think's he's goin' to get away with that for change of a hundred 'scudos, he've got another think comin'.'

'Go on, Dad, tell him. You was in the Army.'

'Pardon? Pardon? Isn't the toilets' system rotten? Pooh... Raw sewage, I could smell. Reelly...'

Listening, Bowcott had never felt more snobbish. And years ago, if anybody had said Tom, Dick or Harry were coming abroad, he would have protested valiantly, but he sadly realised that now it was true, and felt vaguely ashamed. Unless they were careful, they were going to have a thin time of it. Very well, the thing to do was to cut loose from the package tour and investigate the terrain.

'*Emma! Emma, come and put your nix on!*'

That bloody child... To get away from Emma, and Emma's red-necked parents, Bowcott anchored himself permanently in the far corner of the bar, leaving Fan to snooze under the sun shade. He ordered a second gin and tonic (large), and looked philosophically at the glass.

'*Bom dia,*' he managed to the barman.

The barman smiled, and in response, Bowcott showed him a trick with Worcester sauce. A minute drop cleared the rime from a grimy escudo and the barman was suitably impressed. Thereupon, for devilment, Bowcott sprinkled a little sauce into his third gin and tonic, no more than a drop, but enough to give the teasing, iron-man impression that broke the monotony of the morning. And, after that, he had to have another one to clear the taste away. Then there was the sun.

Although his body was shaded by the canopy of the bar, his legs were burning, but the moment he decided to take a dip to cool off, what amounted to a Romford water-polo team arrived and made that impossible.

'To you, Georgie! Georgie! Not out of the pool! Oh, shit, you've knocked a bottle over.'

Bowcott woke Fan under the sunshade. She was a marathon sleeper.

'I think I'll have a stroll down the Vill'. I don't think I shall spend much time here.'

She blinked amiably.

'Be back for lunch?'

'Of course.'

'I should cover the back of your neck if I were you.'

She sounded like his mother. He nodded, found his fedora, buttoned his wallet pocket, and marched away, four gins down. The hotel, a hastily completed building especially created for the package trade, was surprisingly elegant with marble vistas and lavish copper fittings, reminiscent of the Spanish paradors. It would have been splendid if it weren't for the people at present in it, Bowcott thought. He now saw the Romford mob flitting in and out of it like fleas, their twanging voices affecting his nervous system so that he actually twitched once or twice. Getting old, he thought. Getting old and finding Buggins everywhere. He was pleased with that phrase. It was rather Army.

So it was in his District Commissioner mood that he walked down to the village, fat legs, heavy buttocks, belted girth and thick arms swinging as he affected a military gait along the rough, cobbled track. Several *burros* drawing carts passed him, their aged, black-shirted drivers eyeing him inscrutably. It was a poor country, he noted once more. Every piece of woodwork needed a coat of paint, plaster flaked from the walls of the narrow cottages, and the burnt, arid soil behind them was lifeless and without green. There was not a flower to be seen, and the children ran about bare-footed in the streets while mangy dogs stretched out in the shade, and, here and there, a caged bird sat lifelessly outside the houses. The few Portuguese pedestrians he saw, lowered their eyes when they passed him, or else paid no attention. They were neither surly nor obsequious, just there, passive spectators of the doings of the Lisbon speculators who'd brought the tourists there.

Poor peasants, Bowcott thought. Sad old men and women in black, unaware of the world that was changing about them. He felt vaguely sorry for them, but he was too much of a man of the world to entertain the idea that anything could be done for them. Two soldiers came around the corner, their shabby red berets, lounging gait and lacklustre boots catching his eye. For a second, he half expected them to salute, but they were just peasant soldiers, homesick boys without a spark of life left in them. He felt sorry for them as well, and at the bottom of the hill where he passed a small infirmary for the tubercular, he felt that half the soldiers he had seen might well have been garrisoned there. Once again, he felt sorry. Fair play, he thought, the old wogs never had much of a chance and didn't even look inclined to do much for themselves. Perhaps it was the heat?

By now, the back of his neck was burning. It was August and the wind that blew from Spain stayed there for the month, but he walked on masterfully, tipping the straw hat back. He never wore sunglasses on principle. You could never see what a man was thinking in sunglasses, and he detested people who wore them indoors which was scarcely reason for not wearing them ever, but he did not. The sahibs never did, he seemed to remember, so he did not either.

Presently, he came to a little square where there was a First World War memorial, and for no accountable reason, he stood for a moment and doffed his hat in memory of the dead. If you'd asked him, he couldn't remember on whose side the Portuguese had fought in that war, but memorials always affected him. His father's two brothers had been with the tunnellers of Messines and had not returned, and Bowcott had an immense respect for military ceremonial, often stating that in the period of the two minutes' silence on Armistice Day, he resolutely attempted to remember faces of the dead he had known. It was somehow always an intensely moving experience to him, coupled with the thought of lives that might have been.

He stood for a full two minutes holding the straw fedora to his chest, then strode to an adjoining bar whose proprietor had noticed his little vigil.

'*La Guerra*?' the proprietor said curiously.

Bowcott gave a stiff military nod and sat astride a bar stool as he ordered a beer. From Omdurman to Mametz Wood, from Monte Cassino to Caen and back to Vimy Ridge, his mind had strayed to the accompaniment of ghostly bugle notes. The faces of the dead... How young they were... Callow boys for the most part, legions of them with no chance of living, the missing generations.

He switched his attention to the proprietor, erupted into two languages simultaneously, capping them with stern valleys posh.

'*Las guerras lo mismo todo el mundo*,' he said portentously.

'*Ah, si*,' said the proprietor with a wise nod.

A few more words, a few more beers, a good tip, and Bowcott was off again, feeling rather better. It always paid to communicate with the locals. He passed the cobbler's shop where last year the cobbler had encompassed his extravagant paunch with a specially made belt from horse leather. 'Got a little chap I know in Portugal to run it up one morning,' he told Lucas Thomas the Chemist. 'Did it on the spot. There's such a thing as service left in the world.' ('That Bowcott Jones has been around,' Lucas told his wife.)

Bowcott looked in through the cobbler's doorway, but a different face greeted him, and rather than inquire, he backed away. There was still the same smell of leather and sawdust in the air, but the old man behind the counter was not half as jolly as the jester the previous year. It might have been an omen. But Bowcott went on up the street. He was heading for the English Tavern where an old Kenya Planter had set up a pub, English style, and where, the year before, he had drunk copiously with much good-humoured joss in the company of like-minded fellows of his own age. They were exiles for the most part, chaps who had got out of England for one reason or another. He liked them best because they had given him the opportunity of playing up the Welsh side of his nature. 'Wouldn't think of living in England myself!' he had announced, and with his jokes and quips, the alacrity with which he bought his round, he was eminently acceptable, and indeed, the nights had passed in much the same way as they did in his local at home. The bonhomie of drinkers was an international thing, a safe and comfortable world in which to float.

The taverner's name was Matt, late King's African Rifles, a Kenya wallah with a prodigious thirst, and a joker into the bargain. Then, Bowcott had been *Bwana Mc'wber* Jones, and Matt was *My man*, and they'd done a little Forces number, *Ten cents a dance, that's all they pay me!* to the delight of the Portuguese waiters. The company of old soldiers was the best in the world, Bowcott proclaimed, and what is more, Matt kept a good house: cockles on the bar on Sundays, always beef sandwiches to order, and it was a cool, clean bar with white-aproned waiters who knew their place, and a Victorian air to the china pumps with engraved fox-hunting scenes and vintage dirty postcards in apple pie order on the notice board. More important than anything else, except the beer, was the lavatory, the cleanest in the Algarve, a shaded white light, English paper and the wholesome smell of disinfectant and none of your damned scent. Eight pints down and you knew you were safe with a beef sandwich to build up your bowels when seafood got a bit too much. Bowcott, like an army, marched on his stomach, and in the previous year, he prided himself that he'd found the only place on the continent where you could drink like an Englishman and not rue the day. He'd told this to Matt who'd made him write it in the visitor's book. Last year, the lavatory, the pub, the fresh cockles and delicious beer and the primed ale had made it the best holiday Bowcott had ever had and he'd come back with the same expectancy.

Fatal...

District Commissioner Jones, *Bwana Mc'wber* Jones, Jones the Gauleiter of Romford had made a cock-up in coming back.

'*For Chrissakes, the bogey's got his shooter out!*' the voice returned.

As did his mother's: 'Figs and pancakes, Bowcott?'

Yes, by God, he'd done a burster. No wonder he had a mouth like an acrobat's jockstrap. Perhaps he'd swallowed a fig stone? Perhaps it was the oysters? He must be alive with shellfish. Shake him and he'd rattle.

'*You will suffer, my boy. Yes, you will, you'll live to regret. Thank goodness Colenso isn't like you.*'

Colenso! That was it! Now he experienced total recall. Colenso, his moody nephew. Pertinent point! As well as his guts and the wogs, the Welshy-Welsh had knackered his holiday. Trust them!

The Bowcott Joneses had no children of their own. ('Lack of greens,' his mother said.) But he had a nephew, Colenso, whom he'd attempted to take under his wing whenever allowed, a small, thin, bespectacled, intellectual boy who had got into the wrong set at one of the lesser Welsh universities and emerged a rabid Welsh nationalist with Honours Welsh and an interest in his country that amounted to fetishism, in Bowcott's eyes. Despite all the gifts, the golf clubs, the fishing rods, the use of a salmon stretch, the wretch had become one of the interrupters of her Majesty's judges, a demonstrator, a non-road-tax payer who disappeared for weeks on end to summer schools and folk festivals where they ate, slept, breathed and dreamed Welsh, a way of life and habit which Bowcott found incomprehensible and which irritated him more than he could say. In his aversion to this recently reborn element in his country, Bowcott was quite unreasonable. There was something sickly and introverted about it, he was sure. There was nothing for the people in it, just milk and honey for training college lecturers and the like, another bloody cottage industry from which the few profited and exploited the many. Moreover, it excluded Bowcott entirely, with his long-forgotten Welsh and what he called his international outlook. Fan, who was easy-going, said live and let live, but if it were possible, Bowcott would have been a hanging judge as far as Colenso's lot were concerned. A number of the young were quite taken with it, even protested a patriotism that made Bowcott into a kind of quisling and that set him off to boiling point. A quisling! After the scraps he's been in while in the Army, even going so far as to thump a paymaster and risking a court martial after one guest night.

'Welsh bastards,' the paymaster'd said. That was enough. Bowcott found a right cross that would have made Dancing Jim Driscoll cheer in his grave, and the paymaster had gone down in a heap in the corner by the ornamental-silver cupboard. The Adjutant had made enquiries and Bowcott had told him straight out.

'Can't have that, sir. It's not the "bastard" I object to, it's the slurring use of the adjective!'

'The Adj had told the Colonel, and the Colonel (who was from Abergavenny) had a good laugh about it as it happened and everything had been quite all right, even lent a certain kudos to Bowcott's reputation and the paymaster'd emerged as a shit anyway. Bowcott had struck a blow for his country, but it didn't register with Colenso one little bit. When he'd told him with a certain pride, Colenso's face had kept its intelligent, precious, rabbit look, and then he'd gone off and married a girl who was even more immersed in the Welsh business. They were like a pair of folkweave Ghandis together, often spoke Welsh in front of him, and brought him to the boil more quickly than if they'd taken drugs in public. All through the Investiture (to which, naturally, he'd been invited and now kept his red, ornamental chair in the hall) he'd been on the lookout for violence, but the fact that Colenso's lot weren't violent made him dislike them all the more. Roots versus roots... It was a Welsh conundrum.

But to meet it here in Portugal! That was it, he'd gone into the tavern to find that Matt had left, packed up and gone to Ibiza. A youth stood in his place, a dirty, bearded, London wide boy.

'Trouble wiv the Missus, so he scarpered.'

'Scarpered?'

'I bought him out February.'

Matt gone... The place was no longer the same. The china beer pumps with their engraved fox-hunting scenes, exact replicas of a pair in the cocktail bar of the Norfolk Hotel in Nairobi, were missing, so were the comic postcards, the cheery publican's greetings cards from home, the little saucers with crisps and olives in them, even the waiters' crisp white aprons. Where there had been a jar of the precious beef sandwiches, now there was a machine for dispensing salted peanuts, and, as soon as he found out, in the best lavatory in the Algarve, there was now a contraceptive slot machine and a notice by the management proclaiming, 'This gum may taste a little rubbery'. Not graffiti; by the management!

Worse still, there was Hair in the bar, by which Bowcott meant, the young. Previously, it had been the middle-aged who had congregated there, giving the place the atmosphere of a cheerful, senior officers' mess. But now girls in hot pants and semi-naked boys, looking like aborigines in Bermuda shorts, draped themselves about the place and the girls. There was not a soul in there his own age.

'What'll it be then, Chief?'

'A pint,' Bowcott said, fragile suddenly.

'Sagres?' the new proprietor said, referring to the local beer.

'Anything else?'

'I keep a few Guinesses for the old boys.'

The old boys... For some reason, the first phrase that came into Bowcott's mind was a Welsh one, *Bechgyn y Bont*, one of the few he knew. Translated, it meant 'Boys of the bridge', referring to a group of old soldiers from his home town, survivors of near-decimated regiments who had congregated together after the First War. They met once a month, growing older over the years, finally attending each other's funerals until they were virtually non-existent. Each of the boys of the bridge had a touching habit of leaving a tenner in their wills, a tenner 'for behind the bar', when the survivors would raise a number of solemn pints in memory of the departed. But the time had come when they could not exhaust the tenner and the change was stuffed into a charity box. In the end, the change exceeded the money spent. Farewell the Bechgyn y Bont.

Now Bowcott felt like one of them, and once again, seemed to hear the Last Post sounding in his ears.

'I'll have a large scotch,' he said in his most cultivated voice.

'Right you are, guv. Old Matt had all the big spenders here, eh?'

The big spenders... Bowcott sat dismally upon a stool. No one paid any attention to him. A young couple, draped around each other at the end of the bar, changed hands soulfully. Why they had to feel themselves in public, Bowcott would never know.

'Drop of splash, mate?'

Mate... But he nodded. It looked like a morning on the scotch, a morning of silent reverie seated at the corner of the bar. He felt like a colonial planter, recently returned home and completely out of things. But it was not in his nature to sit maudlin anywhere, and he soon struck up a conversation with the new proprietor, only to find there was another blow to the stomach.

'I thought you was Welsh.'

'I beg your pardon?'

'Iacky Da, I gotta few Taffees comin' here.'

Bowcott did not reply.

But he was to have no peace. Like a light-skinned negro passing as white, he had been spotted, and when he had downed another scotch in stony silence, a newcomer entered the bar, nodded at the proprietor who promptly sidled up to Bowcott and made the unwanted introduction.

'Major Bowcott Jones,' Bowcott said grimly.

The newcomer was young, with dark, curly hair, a pale, nondescript face, and a slight stoop, unmistakeably Welsh.

'It's hardly possible, but I don't suppose you're related to...'

Colenso, of course. Anything was always possible with bloody relatives! But to come a thousand miles to Portugal to have the dismembered limb of the family regurgitated. Bowcott could not supress a dismal nod.

'I have a very great admiration for him,' the young man said.

Bowcott would have said, 'Good chap!' not, 'a very great admiration.' It sounded so fawning.

'Why?' Bowcott said sharply. His temper had risen immediately.

'His general militancy.'

'On whose behalf?'

'Why, the Welsh people.'

'He's never met any of 'em,' Bowcott said unreasonably. 'But for Christ's sake, let's not go into it, I'm on holiday.' He felt so annoyed at this extraordinarily unlucky encounter that he was in danger of letting himself go. Questions of Welsh nationalism affected him in the same way as a wholly English counterpart might be similarly provoked by encounters with advocates of illegitimate birth, CND, or permissive television. He cut short the conversation as soon as he could.

'Young man, if you don't mind... Look here, why don't you have a drink?'

231

'No, thank you,' the young man said. He turned away, but did not go.

Bowcott sighed. It was absurd to be standing in a Portuguese bar in the presence of obvious riff-raff, boiling about Aberystwyth University and its environs. He was on holiday, and now it was as if two worlds had collided in one person, and back his thoughts went like tired homing geese to the perennial open sore – Wales. It was a country of permanent ills, four countries rolled into one, and if you didn't get away from it now and again, you choked in the backbiting and rancour. Thanks God he was a South Walian anyway. Thank God for coal and the Marquis of Bute. And a pox on the Ychafi Welsh and their road sign campaigns and eternal bleating.

He ordered another whisky and, by habit, asked for the morning paper, but when it came, it was in Portuguese.

'Haven't you got the *Express*?'

But they had not, and the young man smiled, Bowcott thought. He could not see, but he was sure he was smiling, smiling a young Welsh smile, and it was dark and foreboding, Bowcott was sure. Unreason leads to unreason, misunderstanding to further misunderstanding. Where prejudices foster, rancour is rife, and Bowcott now felt a wave of self-pity as he recalled that, sitting on this very stool the previous year, he'd felt like a proconsul. He and Matt had gone shark fishing with a drunken Dutchman, and with the wind in their faces, the rolling Biscayan swell beneath them off St Vincent, they had drunk whisky and eaten meat and recaptured a piratical feeling of freedom that had lasted a year. They'd brought in an ebony black Mako shark, its jaws snapping as they gaffed it, and later proudly laid it on the beach where the peasants came to inspect the day's catch. Bowcott had insisted on its being given away for fertilizer and then they'd drunk late into the night, wearing cowboy shirts and cutting slices of dried cod with sheath knives. It was a holiday of holidays, a reversion to primal living that had given him a new image of himself as an international outdoorsman.

All to crumble if he didn't shake off this Welsh depression. The young man had moved to another corner of the bar so Bowcott finished his drink, and with a curt nod to the proprietor, wandered out into the street where he bumped into an acquaintance of the year before.

'Jake!'

'Bowcott!'

'My God, that place has gone off since Matt left.'

'How long are you over for? When are you going back?'

They soon found another bar. Jake was large, sad and dyspeptic, a remittance man, odd-jobbing for the tour operators, an ex-professional wrestler with a villainous broken nose but with the temperament of an obliging spaniel, an expert hanger-on. He had gone native in Singapore when the Japs got in, had stayed out of captivity, a valuable workhorse worth hiding. But now he was ulcerated and hungry, occasionally delivering new cars from Lisbon, picking up what he could here and there. But an old soldier down on his luck could not wish for better company than Bowcott.

'How've you been?'

'So, so…'

'You don't say?'

'Place has got too full of people from home. Got very tight, it has. You haven't eaten by any chance, have you?'

Jake wanted a meal. Nothing but the best then. Jake had been around, that was the cardinal point.

'You had to get around,' Bowcott said happily, the moment they seated themselves in a restaurant.

'All over,' Jake said. 'All over.'

They ate through the afternoon and into the early evening. They ate oysters and clams, the fruits of the sea, and then gorged themselves on spiced meats and oiled salads. And they had to have a swallow with it, didn't they? And after the wine, the brandy – a 'tween course pick-me-up – they started on the fruit and figs. Bowcott had a passion for figs, as Jake had for *Crêpes Suzette*, so that they did themselves proud, 'going round the buoy twice' whenever there was a course or a glass that took their fancy. By the time they lit cigars, Bowcott had shaken off his depression. Once you got a drop inside you, the world was a different place, no matter whether the drop included the anti-Romford gins, the War Memorial beers, the anti-Welsh whiskies, or the old soldier's litres, it was all a drop taken, and by the evening, he felt he just could not leave without a final pint at the English Tavern. Just to show there were no hard feelings. Jake did not mind, had looked wistfully at the tip which Bowcott left in the restaurant, but no matter, they'd have a chaser at the bar and drink to the vanished Matt.

But when they got there, the tourists had given way to the locals, including a uniformed Army picket from the fort. The proprietor had his eye on the winter custom and encouraged the locals whereas Matt had closed in the winter, but a whisky drinker was a whisky drinker, and he greeted them cordially. Bowcott responded with a nod, at the same time aware of a certain tension in the air. Was it sixth sense that warned him of an atmosphere amongst the Portuguese? Jake and he were the only two foreign customers and it seemed as if people had stopped talking when they entered. Bowcott gave Jake a wink, lowered his District Commissioner's ear and raised Special Agent Bowcott's other antennae. He ordered two whiskies and chasers, sized up the bar.

The army patrol were standing uneasily in the corner, their glasses empty, but on the other side of the room by the panelled mantelpiece, there sat a large muscular young man with the stump of an arm protruding from his sports shirt. He was dark and thick-necked with an insolent flushed expression that separated him from the two nervous youths who were drinking with him. He wore his hair short, and from the way he put his good arm to the side of his head, seemed to have suffered a head injury as well. He kept tapping his head with his fist, a sombre demonstration indicating that there might be something inside which had gone wrong, and which he could not forget. But for the stump of his arm, his heavy, dark face might have protruded from the back row of a Welsh pack, Bowcott thought. It was absurd, but many of the larger Portuguese looked South Walian. They had the same quality of brooding, not quite surliness, but an air of threat. There were even waiters in the hotel with aggrieved Tonypandy walks, hacking 'dust' coughs, and bad feet. But here no one spoke. There was definitely an imposed silence, but the bar was so small, it was impossible to say anything without being overheard. Insanely, Bowcott wished he could mutter a few words in Welsh to Jake because no one else would have understood. The fixed glances of the army patrol in the corner left him in no doubt that their arrival was an embarrassment. There were so many things that it was better the tourist did not see.

The proprietor switched on the taped music and an ancient pop number came up loudly.

'*Quizas! Quizas! Quizas!*'

The atmosphere seemed to lighten momentarily.

'*A situarzione?*' Bowcott whispered inquisitively.

Jake shook his head nervously as if to compel Bowcott to say no more.

But Bowcott was curious.

'Punch-up, d'you think?'

Jake leaned forward and whispered with a convict's side-of-the-mouth grimace.

'The guy with one arm's loco.'

'Eh?'

'Mozambique.'

'What?'

'Caught one in the head. Bullet. I shouldn't say anything if I were you. Now he breaks up bars for a living.'

Bowcott looked around him with a distinct unease, and

suddenly, the afflicted Portuguese rose unsteadily and wandered over to Bowcott who rose instinctively.

'Engleesch peoples very good peoples,' the Portuguese said.

His eyes were troubled, perhaps unfocused. His breath was sour. He was very drunk and swayed once more, 'Naice peoples, no?'

'Well,' Bowcott said. It seemed a little inappropriate to insist on '*Pays de Galles*' as he often did.

The Portuguese put his only arm on Bowcott's shoulder and leant heavily upon him. He spoke with difficulty.

'Engleesch peoples fair peoples,' he nodded and smiled with all the air of definitive scholarship of an extremely drunken man.

Across the bar, the proprietor and the soldiers were tense, but Bowcott put his arm around the young man, gulping as his eyes met the obscene stump of the amputated arm. The flesh was red and puckered and strangely disturbing, a real wound beside all those phoney memorials.

'*Soldado?*' Bowcott said.

'Ye...s,' the young man gave a bitter smile.

Bowcott puffed out his chest.

'You'd better have a drink with me,' he said in a fatherly voice. 'Beer?'

The young man nodded, but the proprietor shook his head nervously. Bowcott ignored him. He knew he had skills with drunks.

'Two beers, *pash favor?*'

'I don't think...' the proprietor began to say.

'Nonsense!' said Bowcott. 'If two old soldiers can't have a drink together, what's the world coming to?' He was pleased he said that. A Buggins would have run out of the bar at the first sign of trouble. Even Jake was sitting there like a Methodist Sunday School superintendent.

The Portuguese lurched dangerously against Bowcott. The stump of his arm was barely concealed under the short-sleeved sport shirt.

'Steady the Buffs!' Bowcott said. He gave a friendly man-to-man wink, but it did not register.

The Portuguese looked into Bowcott's eyes.

'Me – crazy,' he said. It was a phrase he seemed to have learned to say, apologetically like a beggar's set piece.

The proprieter put the beers on the bar. The patrol had not moved and the sergeant held an empty glass in his hand like a weapon.

'We all have our off days,' Bowcott said, short of words suddenly.

The Portuguese nodded, deeply and mysteriously to himself, swayed again, then lurched from Bowcott's friendly arm and picked up the fresh beer glass defiantly, spilling half its contents as he raised his arm in a toast.

'A Che Guevara,' he said loudly with a sideways glance at the patrol. He said it with reverence, a name that meant something, that was dangerous to say, but would be said always, secretly and in the open, a name for such young men to conjure with.

But Bowcott sighed dismally, reverting to his earlier feeling of dismay. Politics again... The bastards were everywhere, excluding him from their enthusiasms, waving ideas like flags, but always beating a hollow drum as far as he was concerned. It had taken him fifty-six years of his life to know his way around and learn the ropes of living, so why should he want to change anything?

The patrol sergeant, older than the boy soldiers beside him, was corase faced and muscular, his leather shoulder-straps worn and comfortable, and the little gold wheel insignia on his beret was almost polished away with years of cleaning. He snapped a word of warning in Portuguese across the bar.

The young man spat on the floor.

'A Che Guevara,' he said again, raising the glass and spilling the remainder of his drink.

Two young Portuguese customers left hurriedly, a sweating

youth tucking his shirt into his trousers as he went out through the door without a look behind him.

In order to quieten the situation, Bowcott raised his glass. 'A *Pays de Galles*,' he said, clicking his heels to attention. 'No, *Che Guevara*,' the young man said. '*Che! Che! Che!*' It was a tense moment.

A policeman appeared in the doorway. The flap of his holster was unbottened. He was a small, wizened, untidy policeman with the stub of an unlit cheroot stuck to his lower lip. His blue-grey uniform was shabby and his collar was unbuttoned below a podgy, unhealthy face. He drew his revolver apologetically like a tired male nurse producing a thermometer, but when the revolver was drawn and the safety catch removed, he beckoned at the young man and said one word.

'*Vivaldo...*'

The young man swayed uncertainly and turned towards him, putting down the empty beer glass. At that moment, seeing their chance, the patrol rushed the young man from the rear, the three soldiers, sergeant in the lead, coming around the corner of the bar like wing forwards. They knocked Vivaldo head first out into the street and as his head hit the cobblers below the doorstep, the policeman brought his boot down in a tired little kick that caused blood to spurt from Vivaldo's nose. But the damage was done by Vivaldo's head hitting the cobbles and he was unable to rise.

Across the street, a woman screamed.

Bowcott stared. The kick infuriated him. He drew himself up, brushed aside Jake who had risen to stop him, and marched to the doorstep, staring haughtily down into the face of the policeman.

'Look here,' he said importantly. 'There is no call to kick a man when he is down.'

It was then the proprietor called frantically.

'For Chrissakes, the bogey's got his shooter out!'

'Be quiet!' Bowcott snapped.

The policeman looked up at him confusedly. What business was it of his?

A sedan had driven up the street. At the wheel sat a large elderly man, deeply sunburnt behind dark glasses, the elbow of his light grey suit casually resting in the opened window. He lifted his arm slowly, a gold watch bracelet glistening then disappearing behind his shirt cuff. He seemed completely relaxed but as if by prearranged signal, the soldiers now picked up the semi-conscious body of Vivaldo and dragged him across to the car, bundling him into the rear seat and closing the door. The man nodded and drove away.

For a moment Bowcott was tempted to run after the car, but the proprietor had joined him.

'Come inside!'

'I demand to know where they are taking him.'

'That's his old man, you git.'

'What?'

'Come in before the bogey gets shirty.'

Bowcott hesitated. There had been no mistaking that kick in the face.

'Never interrupt the bastards when they've got their shooters out. If you was in the Army, you ought to know that.'

Bowcott turned away confusedly. The soldiers were dusting themselves down in the gutter and the policeman lit his cheroot. Bowcott's interruption had been brave and meaningless, like a donkey braying in the dark.

'That Vivaldo,' the proprietor explained. 'The moment he's got a load on, it's Che Guevara day and bloody night.'

'But...'

Course, you can't normally do that in Portugal, but the joke is, see, his old man's in the police himself. So they come and get him once a month.'

'You mean, his father...'

'In the Chevrolet. Full up to here wiv him, he is. Must be.'

'You mean, they're doing his father a favour?'

The proprietor nodded.

'But what about the kick?'

'I 'spect the bogey's full up to here wiv him too.'

Bowcott could hardly believe it. But it was a village scandal and a village story into which other worlds had intruded, other worlds, alien ideas. The last thing Bowcott remembered before he mooched back to the hotel, were the Portuguese women drawing their black shawls over their heads as they came out into the street to discuss the matter, their sharp tongues cawing away like crows. He remembered enough to know that everybody's sympathies were with the father. An ordinary Portuguese would, of course, have been locked up at the mention of Che Guevara, but Vivaldo apparently had connections.

'Influence,' Bowcott thought moodily. When he got down to it, the whole bloody world was like Glamorgan.

But how much had he understood? Had he behaved ridiculously again? He found his wallet finally, stuffed for safety on top of the Westinghouse air conditioner, then examined Lucas Thomas' handwriting on the medicine bottle, '*Two x 5m spoonfuls to be taken four times a day*'.

'Good old Lucas,' he said, forgetting his earlier animosity. He had a sudden intolerable nostalgia for grey skies, grey faces, grey terraced streets, the bustling conviviality of teeming football grounds and men's four-ale bars, and as if to salute them, he suddenly removed the cork from the medicine bottle, upended it, and drank copiously from the neck. He reverted to the vernacular finally, grateful for its protection. Bowels was buggers of things when you came to think of it. It was as if there was a particular danger that this slightest disturbance might make you think.

And he was spared nothing.

'Emma… Emma…' the voices began outside, floating up from the swimming pool as the Romford lot began to colonise it. '*Even if it is abroad, you can't run around without your nix.*'

He belched. There were days when it seemed as if his stomach was pressing against his eyeballs, and the way he now felt, it had all the signs of a real clogger. Lucas would eventually have to get the arrowroot out again, and Fan would probably enjoy herself for a day or two, mostly on her own.

STRAWBERRY CREAM

Siân James

I was eleven that summer, but according to my mother, already moody as a teenager, 'What can I do?' my constant cry. 'I'm bored. What can I do?'

'There's plenty to do. What about dusting the front room for me? Your grandmother and your Auntie Alice are coming to tea on Sunday.'

I hated our front room which was cold and shabby, the furniture old-fashioned, the ceiling flaking and pockmarked with damp and the once mauve and silver wallpaper faded to a sour grey and wrinkled at the corners. Our whole house was depressing, each room having its own distinctive and unpleasant smell, the front room smelling of mushrooms, the living room of yesterday's meat and gravy and the back-kitchen of Oxydol and wet washing.

'Dusting doesn't alter anything,' I said.

I expected my mother to argue with me, but she seemed too dispirited. 'I know it doesn't,' she said. And then, 'Just get yourself a nice library book and pretend you live in a palace.'

Was that what she did? She was always reading; two and sixpenny paperback romances with fair-haired girls standing on windy hills on the covers, their skirts gusting out prettily around them, their long tresses streaming behind, but their make-up immaculate.

Once I'd tried reading one of them. *Caterina breathed in*

as Milly tugged at the corset strings around her waist. 'Tighter,' she commanded sharply.

'Yes, Miss Caterina,' Milly murmured in a humble voice. She loved her mistress with a blind adoration and wanted nothing but to serve her.

I continued the story in my own way. *Milly squeezed the juice of the deadly nightshade into her mistress' drinking chocolate and chuckled as she imagined pulling the strings of the shroud tighter and tighter around the tiny waist.*

I was fiercely egalitarian. My dad was a farm labourer and he had the same attitude, speaking to his boss with unconcealed disdain. 'You want me to do... what?'

'Don't you think that would work?' his boss would ask.

'Of course it wouldn't bloody work, but I'll do whatever you tell me. It's all one to me.'

My mother served in the village shop for two pounds ten a week and she was pretty cool too. I don't think she ever demanded a decent wage, just helped herself to groceries to make up the deficiency, mostly items that fitted neatly into her overall pockets. We were never short of packets of jelly, cornflour, mixed herbs, caraway seeds. Or bars of chocolate. That summer, Cadbury's Strawberry Cream was my passion and she brought me one every single lunchtime. And every afternoon I'd snap the bar into eight squares, sniff every one, bite a hole in the corner and very slowly suck out the oozy pink cream, afterwards letting the sweet chocolate casing melt on my tongue. Sometimes I could make it last a blissful half-hour.

My father's boss, Henry Groves, had a daughter called Amanda who was three or four years older than me and went to a boarding school in Malvern. I'm sure she wouldn't have chosen to spend any time with me had there been any older and more sophisticated girls in the village, but there weren't; she'd knock on our front door and stand there silently until I condescended to go out with her.

We usually walked along by the river, kicking at stones

and muttering to one another. 'What's your school like?'

'Deadly. What about yours?'

'Deadly.' We had nothing to talk about.

We could never think of anything to do either. What was there to do? The sun beat down on us mercilessly every afternoon, the hours stretched out long and stagnant as sermons; I felt dusty and dried-up as the yellowing grass on the verge of the path.

'Don't you have any adventures at your school?' I asked her one day. 'Don't you have midnight feasts and so on? Pillow fights in the dorm?' I wanted some sort of conversation; lies would be fine by me. Her eyes narrowed. 'What rubbish have you been reading? How old are you anyway?'

'Thirteen.' She looked across at me. I was tall and sturdy for eleven. She was small and, I suppose, rather pretty; a turned-up nose and so on, floppy hair and so on. My God, she looked a bit like the lovesick girls on the covers of my mother's Mills & Boon. Why was I wasting my summer afternoons with her?

'Well act your age then. Pillow fights! For God's sake!'

I tried again. 'Do you have a boyfriend?' I asked.

She gave me a friendlier look. 'That would be telling.' I was definitely on the right track.

'I'll tell you if you tell me,' I said, trying to recall conversations I'd overheard on the school bus; a fierce, fat girl called Natalie Fisher, who was about fifteen I suppose, but looked thirty, who was always whispering loudly about 'doing it', I could pretend I was 'doing it' with Joe Blackwell who sometimes helped me with my science homework.

'You go first,' she said.

'I've got this boyfriend called Joe Blackwell.'

'And?'

'He's tall and he's got red hair and millions of freckles. Quite attractive.'

'And?'

'And... and we "do it" sometimes.'

She was suddenly looking at me with alarming admiration; her eyes dilated and her lips moist. 'Go on,' she said.

'Nothing much more to say. Your turn now.'

'Let's cross the river. It's more private in the woods. We can talk better over the other side.'

We hadn't seen a soul all afternoon, but if she wanted to cross the river I was quite prepared to wade across with her. It made a change.

We took off our sandals and splashed across. The sky was white and glaring, the stones in the riverbed were hot and sharp.

'These are my father's woods,' she said.

There was no answer to that. I knew as well as she did whose bloody woods they were. 'This is where Joe Blackwell and I... you know.' I said. It seemed a way to get even with her.

'Show me what you do,' she said, moistening her lips again with the tip of her small pink tongue. 'Show me how you do it.' She sat on the ground and pulled me down with her.

'I can't do it with a girl,' I said, my voice gritty with embarrassment.

'Yes you can, of course you can. Don't you think I know anything?' She was opening her dress and pulling me to her.

'Do you like my breasts?' she asked, tilting them up towards me.

I hated breasts. My Auntie Alice was always getting hers out to feed her baby, great mottled things, large as swedes, but more wobbly; I hated having to see them, the shiny mauve veins; the pale, wet, puckered nipples.

Amanda's breasts were different, small and delicate, creamy as honeysuckle, pink-tipped. She snatched at my hand and placed it over one of them. It seemed like some small, warm animal under the curve of my palm. 'What now?' she asked. 'What do we do next?' Her voice was creaky like the hinge of a gate.

Her nipple hardened under my touch. I felt shivers go down my body like vibrations in the telegraph wires. I closed my eyes as my fingers circled over and over her breasts. 'We have to do this part properly first,' I said.

I peeped at her face. Her eyes were closed. She looked like the picture of St Winifred in church; as though she was seeing angels.

'Now what?' she asked again. I lowered myself onto my elbow and licked her nipples, one after the other. Her eyes flicked open in surprise. 'Licking?' she asked.

'Licking,' I said firmly. 'Don't you like it?'

'I think so. Do you?'

The shivering started up again, it was lower now, my belly seemed to be fluttery as a nest of fledglings. 'Yes, I like it.' I tried to sound non-committal, but suddenly I was lifting her towards me and sucking, sucking her little round breasts.

'That's all I know,' I confessed at last. Other images which were beginning to besiege my mind seemed altogether too bizarre. 'I don't know the rest of it,' I repeated.

I thought she'd be annoyed, expected her to fasten up her dress and flounce off. She wasn't, though, and didn't. 'Well, we can do this part again, can't we?'

And we did. We did it again and again all through the last dog days of that summer. Every fine afternoon we'd set off wordlessly along the same path, crossing the river at the same spot, lying down under the same trees, finding the same stirrings of pleasure.

At the beginning of September, it got damp and cold, the leaves lost their lustre, the birds grew silent, the woods began to smell of rust and wet earth and we realised that our time was running out.

'I'm going back to school next week,' Amanda said one Friday afternoon, 'so I suppose we'd better say goodbye.'

I raised my mouth from her breast and sat up. 'Goodbye,' I said. I felt something almost like sadness, but wasn't going to let her know.

'Perhaps we'll do the other part next year,' she said.

'Perhaps.'

I never saw her again. Before the Christmas holidays my father had found a better job and we'd moved from our horrid old house to another that wasn't quite as horrid, and my mother worked in an office instead of a village shop.

I went to a different school and forgot Joe Blackwell. But I never quite forgot those afternoons with Amanda: my strawberry cream summer.

WHINBERRIES

Deborah Kay Davies

From where she stands, duster in hand in the twilight of the landing, Tamar's mother watches her daughter drooping around in the garden. It seems as if she's spent years of her life doing this. Spying, glancing, checking through nets and blinds and half-open doors. Trying to understand *something* she's actually reluctant to know about her daughter. Tamar is doing the sort of thing she always does when she's been sent out into the fresh air and she's bored – scuffing her sandals in the gravel, snapping little shoots off her mother's flowers. Just now she's sitting on a wooden bench intent on sucking her hand. She has cut the fold between her thumb and finger. Tamar's mother watched her running her hands through a clump of asparagus ferns. She watched as she'd held tight to the damp fronds for a moment. She's not surprised now that Tamar has this cut. She sees the wound streaked with green sap.

She turns away to flick her duster at spiders. Then she pauses again to peer through the nets. She automatically dusts the windowsill and sees Tamar grimace as she sucks her hand. She remembers the childhood taste of warm blood, cut through by bitter fern-juice. She knows the juice will make the insides of Tamar's mouth tighten; its sour taste will cause the blood to feel creamy on her tongue. Tamar still goes on sucking though; probably it's something to do. Her mother rearranges the drapes and moves away from the window.

As she sucks, Tamar looks up behind the house to the mountain. Although the mountain is near, she has never walked there. Today's gently rounded summit is the colour of her mother's bunches of dried sage. Every day she looks at the mountain and notes its changes. It sits above the house – both unreal and part of home. Up till now she has never thought of going there, but today, suddenly, she realises there is nothing to stop her. She could just go; walk and walk and eventually stand on the very top. The possibility flashes briefly, and then Tamar looks down and studies her hand. She thinks really it's too far.

Later that evening, her mother, dry-eyed, will remember seeing Tamar hunched up in the garden. She'll hold her daughter's summer cardigan tight against her body and tell her husband how Tamar looked out there, sucking. How every now and then she'd shake her hand and then put her thumb back in her mouth, how just once she looked up and gazed at the mountain. She'd looked as if she had never seen it before. The mother thinks if only she'd gone out into the garden then, taken a little strip of plaster, or called Tamar in to bathe her hand, perhaps given her some ice cream. She remembers how she'd paused to look through the bedroom and then the landing windows, and how irritated she'd felt to see Tamar so absorbed, messing about on her own in the garden, her socks loose around her bony ankles. Spoiling the flowers.

Tamar had known all along how her mother was watching from above. She'd shaken her hand as if the pain of the cut was unendurable because her mother watched her, but she wouldn't look at her. More than anything she wanted something to happen. Something exciting and different. She didn't even mind if it wasn't nice, just as long as it was something. Her mother always said little girls had no business wishing their lives away. Enough unpleasant things happened every day without wishing for more. She'd grow up soon enough and know these things for herself.

Tamar watched her mother as she pursed her lips and talked on and on. She listened to her mother but didn't believe a word she said, not for a moment. Even waiting in the garden it was possible something could happen. Knowing her mother watched through the window made things exciting. It was like being a closely-guarded prisoner, and mother was the warder. Tamar knew that really her mother would love for her to go out and play with the other children in the street; she was always arranging little visits with children she thought were her daughter's friends. She never gave up trying to make Tamar play with her older sister, even though she must have known it was a waste of time.

Tamar turned her back on the windows and walked toward the back gate, scuffing the stones, raising little puffs of dust. The gate was tall and locked, smelling darkly of fresh creosote. As Tamar walked nearer, the smell intensified. The gate would be tough to climb, impossible with Mother looking through the window.

Tamar's mother has made her another healthy lunch; a hard-boiled egg, some crackers, a stick of celery. She tells her if she eats her egg and celery she can have ice cream. She knows Tamar won't be able to. Her mother watches as Tamar cuts the celery into tiny crescents. Tamar hears the clink her mother's spoon makes in her ice cream bowl. She eats very daintily. Ice cream is all she is eating for lunch. It is variegated ice cream; tenderest pink, creamiest yellow. Tamar has eaten her egg and managed, though she was careful, to put some bits of eggshell into her mouth. They grate between her teeth. No matter how she tries, she cannot eat the wet celery moons. No ice cream for you then, says her mother, as she whisks off the table cloth.

Later, around about midnight, still holding the cardigan, Tamar's mother thinks about lunchtime. She could have offered her soft bread and butter and cheese. It would have been so simple to give Tamar that. Tamar would have loved to eat a bowl of raspberry ripple ice cream. She finds it hard to think of how she ate hers slowly, exaggerating each movement of the spoon. Tamar had sat quietly without looking up. The silence in the kitchen was so complete she could hear the crunching of eggshells as her daughter chewed.

She's baffled now, unable to keep still, suffused with a wincing, stark regret. Why hadn't she relented, pretended it was all a friendly game? She imagines herself back in the kitchen, but this time telling Tamar to shut her eyes tight while she places a bowl of pink and white ice cream before her. She could have sprinkled it with hundreds and thousands, poured a gleam of scarlet sauce liberally into the bowl. Instead, after listening to the crunching sounds Tamar made for so long, she'd said calmly and deliberately, go upstairs and clean your teeth. Don't stop till I call you.

An hour after lunch, Tamar's mother reminds her it's time to call on Tom. This is one of the arranged things her mother does. The afternoon is drifting slowly up and away in a dusty haze of hot tarmac and wilting roses when Tamar gets outside. Her mother had insisted she carry a cardigan. There seems to be no possibility of anything happening in amongst the small, red-brick houses of Tamar's neighbourhood. The hard surfaces make the air so hot and heavy it singes the insides of her lungs. The glaring warmth of everything makes Tamar think of leaves and water. She hopes Tom will want to go fishing.

Tamar's friend lives near the canal. Tom thinks fishing will be a good idea. He has a fishing net and says they should see if they can catch some sticklebacks. Tamar is to carry a jar for holding the fish. She waits on the porch as Tom gets ready. She can hear Tom's mother; she has some friends around. They're laughing; there is a smell of cigarette smoke. Tom's family has a television. Tamar can see the strange flashes and bars of light coming through the open door to the lounge. No one is watching, but the women in the kitchen are all humming along to a song a dancing man is singing on a show.

When he shouts '…What's new pussycat?' the women all sing along. 'Woh ooo, woh ooo woh oo' they hoot. They are holding imaginary microphones, though Tamar doesn't know it. Then they stop and laugh at themselves.

Beyond the singing women the back door is open, and Tamar can see clearly through the house to the little children playing on the swing and slide in the garden. There is even a paddling pool. Tom's mother shouts up the stairs. She tells him to get a move on or his little friend'll start taking root. She's not angry at all. Such a slowcoach, she says, walking barefoot to the front door, smiling at Tamar. She rests against the door frame. 'D'you want an ice lolly, lovey,' she says in a cool, casual voice and ruffles the little girl's hair.

Tamar has to be very still. She wants to reach up and hold the hand down onto her head; it feels like an absent-minded blessing. Instead she says no thank you. She thinks about the silent kitchen and the eggshells. Her mother eating ice cream. The way things are. Tamar sits down on the porch tiles. The floor is a rich brown, smooth and chilly against her skin. The tiles don't shine like her mother's porch. She would like to live in this house. Tom has three brothers and a baby sister; his gran is always around, giving him sweets. They have a television that everyone can sing along to. She supposes this is what makes the house so different.

From where she is sitting on a stool in the kitchen, Tom's mother can see Tamar in the porch. The following week, when it's all over and she sees her friends again, she tries to tell them how she'd felt as she watched the little girl play with a cut on her hand. She'd looked so self-contained, so intent on what she was doing. Tom's mother tries to tell the listening women about Tamar crouched out there in the shadowy porch, how she seemed far too eager for a smile, like a little puppy. As she sits smoking, one leg crossed over the other, she can't put into words how she'd wanted to do something, make some gesture, somehow include Tamar. She sips her coffee and tells the other women how Tamar's never included in anything much. They all sit drinking in the sunlight, and no one says a word.

On the canal bank it is cool. The nearly-still water smells of weeds. Tamar lies on the bank and dips her forehead in. The water is brown; she can't see the bottom. She imagines two thin, hairless, pale-green arms snaking their way up from the oozy mud. She thinks she would gladly hold on to them and fall in, her body hardly making a ripple on the surface, her bulky clothes slipping away as she slides down, down. Tom doesn't think this sounds nice. Think of all the dangerous stuff down there, he says; lots of rusty cans, and old prams. Big eels too. They decide to walk on and find some part of the canal where the water is clear. Tamar trails her cardigan in the dust. Tom walks on ahead; he's eager to catch something in his net. 'Come ON,' he says over his shoulder. I'm not hanging around for you. Tamar walks slowly. It's shivery but airless near the canal. The trees meet overhead. On the path in front of her she can see blobs of quivering sunlight. As she walks they surge up and over her, as if the sun is melting and dropping from the sky. The bank nearest the hedge is sprawling over the path, luxuriant with wild flowers. She stops to watch a huge black and amber butterfly open and close its wings as it rests on a drooping foxglove spear. It looks like a velvet brooch pinned there. No one seems to be awake for miles around.

Tamar walks on. She has no idea how long she has watched the butterfly. She doesn't care where Tom is. Each step has become a huge effort. She has a blister on her heel. As she walks she stoops occasionally to pick up a stone. She puts each one carefully into her shorts pocket. Soon her pockets bulge. She walks to the place where the canal slips under the earth for a stretch. Above there is a little rise and some open ground. The hedge is broken by a stile.

Tamar notices someone is resting against the stile. She walks towards the person and then stops, standing quite near. She wonders if she should say hello. The person resting there is a man. He seems old. The sort of old man who would still wear a cap on a hot day, and a tweed jacket buttoned up. Tamar thinks it's funny how old people never seem to get hot. The man turns and smiles at Tamar, gesturing for her to come nearer. It's as if he's been waiting for Tamar to arrive.

Tamar thinks she recognises the old man; he seems so friendly. 'Do you know me?' she asks. The old man smiles again. Tamar climbs up and sits on the top plank of the stile. She can smell tobacco and mints from the old man's coat. It seems familiar. She and the old man just stand, looking up through the fields to the mountain. Tamar realises it's the same mountain that hides behind her house. From here it is easy to see how anyone could climb up from the fields. She can almost make out a narrow path. The man starts to talk to her about the mountain. He tells her there is an enormous lake up there, just over the other side. Hardly anyone knows about it. No one ever goes there nowadays. He tells Tamar that there are the most delicious fruits on the mountain, called whinberries. He says they are dark purple and holds out his thumb. They're as big as my thumbnail, he says. Tamar looks at the old man's nail. It seems huge, ridged and very tough. Tamar touches the man's nail and tries with her fingers to bend the nail over. I'm far too strong for you, says the man, and smiles.

Moving a little nearer he rests his arm on Tamar's bare leg. The tweedy jacket scratches her skin. The man's arm feels heavy, too heavy for Tamar to lift off. The man is gazing at the mountain. Would you like to climb the mountain and pick those berries? he asks, not turning to look at her. Tamar gazes hard at the mountain top. It looks like everything she's ever wished for. She imagines lying down among the short, springy bushes and tasting the berry juice. She pictures the smooth, deep lake, brimful of clouds, like a milky eye. She would like to paddle in it. The old man climbs slowly over the stile and stands in the field. Come on, he smiles, let's go now. He holds out his arms for Tamar to jump into. Tamar leaves her cardigan on top of the stile and leaps down, sure that she'll be caught. She slips her hot hand into the old man's cold palm. Then they walk together up the narrow track toward the waiting mountain.

STONES

Grace slips out through the back door after the police call around. The sight of her mother is too much. She stays long enough to see the officer put Tamar's cardigan down on the table. She'd looked at the mound of soft yellow knitting from where she stood half hidden behind the lounge door. She tried to make sense of the cardigan. She tried to read the signs. She saw some sticky buds stuck to its waistband. She watched her mother's blue eyes slip down to rest on it. Everyone, the two policemen, her mother and father, were all motionless in the small kitchen. And on the table, near the sugar bowl, Tamar's cardigan, like a discarded skin.

Grace runs through the woods that rear up at the edge of the playing field. She runs along all its little dirt paths. She visits all the places she can think of. The beech canopy above her deepens to a secret green as the summer evening progresses. She runs through the pain of her stitch, through the undergrowth, welcoming its cuts and blows, until she falls down the steep side of a stream and comes back to herself in a luxuriant clump of dead-nettles. The palms of her hands sting; she has lacerated them on the drooping ferns that loll across her running paths. She sits in the silted margin of the stream and dabbles her raw hands in the water. Her gingham skirt sucks up mud. She thinks about her sister's cardigan and shakes her head like a pony troubled by flies.

Grace pushes open the front door. Her mother sits on the stairs covered in shadows. Her father is leaning against the wall. No one shouts at Grace for being out late. No one notices her injuries. No one asks if she is hungry. Grace pushes past her mother. She sees again the cardigan, now in her mother's arms. In her room the darkness is soothing. She climbs under the covers fully-clothed, and rests on her side. She looks across at her sister's empty bed. The room seems different now. Better perhaps. Her own. She's drifting through sheets of half-sleep, dreaming her little sister is never coming back. Grace thinks she is to be the only one again.

Then the bedroom light snaps on. Grace can hear talking; there is a sense something has happened. The house is full of people. Grace does not move her position in the bed. Her father comes in carrying Tamar. He places her carefully on her bed and tucks her in. Your sister's back, he says, and goes out. Grace and Tamar stare at each other. What happened? Grace asks. She looks at her sister's golden head resting on the pillows. Her hair stands out like a fluffy ruff. She's had a bath. What happened? she says again.

Tamar puts her thumb in her mouth. Girls your age don't do that, Grace says. I do, Tamar whispers around the sides of her thumb. She turns to lie on her back. I went walking with someone, she said. An old, old man. He was my friend from the canal. We went to pick mountain fruits. Grace asks, did you know him? There is no answer. We walked a long way, very hot, Tamar says, and he made me hold his hand all the way to the mountain top. Grace imagines her sister holding hands with an old man she doesn't even know. She can see her trying to pull free. The man would need to be very strong to hold on to Tamar, who never wants to hold hands with anyone.

I liked him, Tamar says very quietly. Grace has to sit up to hear her. He gave me sweets. He said there was a lake. So? says Grace. There is a long silence. Grace can hear her sister's even breath. You are so stupid, Grace says suddenly, and falls back on her pillows. To go with someone you don't even know. Tamar says, but I had my stones. As if this makes the

difference. Grace imagines Tamar perspiring at the side of
the old man, her pockets weighed down by stones that had
taken her fancy earlier on the canal bank. She is always
finding nice stones. It drives their mother mad. When they
are all out together she makes Tamar empty her pockets
periodically, ignoring her screams. Now Grace imagines
Tamar with the man. She sees her pulling away. Not
frightened, but wanting to run in the grass. She sees the two
figures walking purposefully up the shrubby mountainside,
the only movement in the silence. What difference does
having stones make? Grace asks.

Tamar says, as if in answer, I needed a wee. I told him not
to look. He said we were nearly there at the lake, but I
couldn't wait. Grace knows the brow of the mountain, the
little blind lake behind its shoulder. She has been there with
her friends. She imagines Tamar squatting down to wee, her
blue cotton shorts bunched around her bare ankles. The
immense, scraggy mountain all around her. The skylarks
singing up in the clouds. Incurious sheep chewing sideways.
Grace sees Tamar's figure hunched down, trying to move her
feet out of the way of her own jet of warm wee. Where was
the man? she asks. Grace finds it hard to imagine the man
there while her sister goes to the toilet. He said he would
stand guard, Tamar says. I told him not to peek.

The bedroom curtains move in the midnight breeze. Behind
the house Grace knows that the mountain waits. He touched
my bottom, Tamar says, and smiles at Grace from her nest of
pillows. Grace can see her sister's tiny oval buttocks, pale
amongst the scratchy ferns. She imagines the old man leaning
down to cup them in his big hands. It's not funny at all, Grace
says. Tamar doesn't stop smiling though. She puts her thumb
back in her mouth and concentrates on sucking for a while.
What did you do next? Grace asks. Tamar uses her fingers
across her bedspread and mimes running. Then what? Tamar
mimes climbing a tree. Grace knows Tamar is a good climber.
And she runs fast. She sees her streaking away, and pulling

herself up out of reach. The old man would never have been able to catch her. Tamar says, he tried to get me, but I threw my stones down on him. He fell over.

Grace can see it. The old man caught in a hail of sharp stones. Tamar throwing her stones down hard on his upturned face. Tamar untouchable in the tree's crook. Her sandals splattered with wee, her hair standing out in sweaty points. Tamar tells her that, when he was on the floor, she climbed down. She was going to run home. But when she saw him lying there with his head all bleeding she picked up a heavy stone and hit him with it to make sure he didn't get up and catch her. She says, I hit him a lot. He was bleeding more. After a while he stopped making sounds. Grace feels far away, listening to the small voice. She looks at her sister sitting up in bed. She is acting out hitting the old man's head with the big stone. Grace's eyes are so wide she feels they will split at the corners. Her scalp is twitching. Then what did you do? she asks. Then I ran down the mountain, Tamar says, but I was lost, and I fell and cut myself.

Grace gets out of bed and moves across to her sister. She pulls back the bedclothes. Tamar's legs are heavily bruised. She has stitches in both knees. Her face is cut. Black suturing snakes away up into her blonde hair. Tamar holds Grace's hands. There was blood on his lips, she says. Lots of blood on my big stone too. Then she pulls Grace towards her. Why are your clothes still on? she asks. I was waiting to see if you were coming back, Grace says. Tamar sits up and helps Grace take off her blouse and skirt. When they get down to her vest and pants, Grace says, that's enough. Don't your stitches hurt? she asks. Tamar is sucking her thumb again, and just shakes her head. Grace puts her feet up on the bed, and they each unbuckle a sandal, Tamar using her one free hand. Come in my bed, Tamar says, and lifts the covers. She smells of talcum powder and antiseptic.

Grace gets in stiffly and lies with her eyes open. She listens as Tamar starts telling about her dream. She says that they have a little baby to look after, in their own big house. But we're children, Grace says; we can't have a baby to look after. But soon she's sucked in; it seems so nice, and she's tired. They lie in the narrow bed and tell each other what their baby looks like, what they have in their house, what they eat. Eventually they fall silent. Grace stares at the ceiling, while Tamar snuggles up and goes to sleep, sucking her thumb.

November Kill

Ron Berry

As if talking to himself, 'More guts than sense in this bitch,'
Miskin said. Hunkered over the belly-up bedlington, he
caressed her ribs with his knuckles. Lady wheezed sighs,
slaver glistening her teeth inside slack lips. Miskin had three
hunting dogs, two rough-coated bridle lurchers, Fay and
Mim, and the slaty-blue bedlington.

Beynon's terrier, Ianto, was a long-jawed black and white
mongrel.

Miskin's small, clenched mouth accentuated the bumpy
profile of his broken nose. He screwed two short vertical
furrows up his forehead. 'We'll cover Dunraven Basin this
morning.'

'Good,' said Beynon, who had the closed face of a weary
spectator. Tall, lean, deliberate in style, he squatted beside
Miskin. 'Saw you coming out of the Club last night. Any luck?'

'She's solid as asbestos,' said Miskin curtly.

'Thought so.'

'Come off it, how would you know?'

'I've tried Glenys.'

'Real kokum you are, Beynon.'

'You were slewed,' Beynon said.

'Same as most Saturday nights,' conceded Miskin.

Beynon levered himself upright. 'Set? Let's go.'

Miskin thwacked his trouser leg with a thin stick. 'Come
in, dogs, *in*.' The lurchers fell to heel with the bedlington.

Beynon clipped a lead on his terrier.

'Train the bloody animal,' jeered Miskin.

Beynon winced mock alarm. 'Ianto's like me, he's uncontrollable.'

'You! There's more temper in a dishrag.'

'I'll frighten the crap out of you one of these days,' said Beynon.

'I'm pooping already!'

'Take it easy, Miskin.'

They grinned, gently grinding shoulders, appreciating a bond without malice.

Eight o'clock Sunday morning, quietness everywhere, two milkmen bypassing each other in whining electric floats, the Beynon held Mim's scruff. 'Good bitch, Mim. Stay now.' He waited while Miskin climbed to a sheeptrack winding midway around the cirque. Then they kept parallel, rounding inside the vast bowl Dunraven Basin. The dogs hunted systematically, the lurchers higher, leaping ledges sure-footed as goats, Lady and Ianto nosing holes and crevices.

Miskin came down at the far end.

A buzzard hung like an emblem above the horizon, standing still in the updraught. Harsh *kaark kaark* calls from the two ravens, weaving low over the glacial bog.

Miskin rubbed mucus off his nose. 'I thought we'd raise one this morning.'

'We've seen some good chases this time of year,' Beynon said.

The lone buzzard drifted back over the skyline. A mallard squawked. Beynon spied through his glasses. He saw the drake shooting up from the narrow glittering stream emptying from the bog. The ravens planed and wheeled.

'Something's down there, Miskin.'

'Great. You sorted that out all by yourself.'

'Mouthy bastard,' said Beynon equably. 'Hey, reynard... left hand side of the brook, on that stretch of mud.'

'Glasses!' Miskin snatched, he hissed through his teeth,

sighting the fox trotting its sidelong gait, front and rear legs inswinging, four pads straight-tracking in the peat-stained silt, then rippling tremors of rushes and tall, fawny grass blades snaked diagonally across the bog. Light-footed over cropped turf and up to the scree spillage below a gully, the fox climbed swiftly, skittering over stones like a squirrel.

Miskin pushed the glasses at Beynon.

Beynon said, 'Ta.' He sharpened the focus, thereafter he supplied a commentary: 'Long in the leg, sure to be a dog fox. He's in perfect nick, white tip on his brush, black on his ears, white on his breast. Man-o-man, he's a beaut. What a pelt, aye, wrapped around the neck of a girl by the name of Glenys. Bet you a pint he's heading for the same old bury.'

Miskin gulped snickering. 'Much too far away to send our dogs after him,' he said.

Beynon said 'Four hundred yards.'

'More like five.' Staidly polite, Miskin accepted the glasses. 'What's he doing out and about in daylight, ah? There, you're right enough, Beynon, he's just gone to ground.' The dogs milled around Miskin's legs. He flipped neat backhanders.

'Quiet!'

Beynon put Ianto on a lead.

Miskin leashed the bedlington with a choker. 'OK, let's bolt the bugger.'

The foxhole angled down through raked stones. Lady whined, ceaseless shivers quivering her slingy body. They searched for another exit from the bury. Miskin looked worried. 'There's no place for him to bolt. This little bitch, she's onto a pasting.'

'Send Ianto in first,' Beynon said.

'He won't go far, too big around the chest. Fox'll chop his face to ribbons.' Miskin stroked the bedlington. 'Steady, gel, relax.' Reluctantly, muttering concern, he slipped Lady into the hole.

Ianto bayed like a hound. The brindle lurchers weaved to and fro on tiptoe, wetly black noses twitching, ears full-cocked from their sheepdog sire.

They heard the bedlington barking, a rapid burst followed by growling. 'Christ, she's in deep,' vowed Miskin. Kneeling, he poked his head into the hole. 'Shake him, gel! Meat off him!' He sat back on his heels. 'She's cornered him. It's a block end.'

'Put Ianto in,' said Beynon.

Ianto howled underground for fifteen minutes.

'Call him out, Beynon.'

'Right, he's this side of the bitch, can't get on, and he might make things worse for her.' Beynon shouted at the hole, 'Hee-yaar Ianto! Hee-yaar Ianto!' The terrier came scuttling out, one of his front paws bleeding and a flesh graze on his shoulder. 'Good dog, good dog,' Beynon said.

The November Sunday waned to lifeless evening. Miskin and Beynon shared cheese and ham sandwiches. Without animosity, they argued pros and cons. At dusk they left the basin, Miskin cursing, effortlessly cursing the bedlington bitch.

'Take it easy, we'll dig her out,' promised Beynon. 'Hard graft, but we'll do it.'

'She's in deep, man.'

'I know, I know.'

'Listen, Beynon, tomorrow morning: mandrel, round nosed shovel, hatchet. We'll need a hatchet to make the place safe.'

Beynon said, 'I'll bring a crowbar and a bowsaw. Plenty of timber on top. Those bloody Christmas trees.'

Miskin nodded grunts.

Short-cutting on lower ground, returning to Nant Myrddin, they reached their home village as the first white frost of winter rimed roof slates.

'Half seven, early start,' said Miskin.

'See you,' agreed Beynon.

They felled three sitka spruces, trimmed the six-inch boles and chuted them down grassed gullies to the fox bury. The lurchers punced, jostling around the hole, kneed and clouted by Miskin. He listened at the cavity. Very faintly, the snarly growling of the bedlington. 'Beynon she's in deeper than last night.'

Beynon said, 'Sounds like it.'

Miskin organised the work, his authority from five years at the coal face. Taking turns, they hacked and shovelled surface debris, starting a vertical dig above the trapped fox – Miskin's calculation. By late afternoon they were prising out big stones with the crowbar, from the jumbled bulk of the old rockfall. Interlocked layers of blue pennant sandstone governed the shape and the size of their hole. When they were a yard down – a massive, inclined slabstone. Miskin stamped on it. He flung curses.

Mim, Fay and Ianto snoozed, curled on the trampled soil outside the fox bury.

'We'll be here tomorrow,' said Beynon.

'Maybe. Depends on the bastard gravestone.'

'Work around it,' Beynon said.

'No option, man!'

'Anyhow, she's still all right down there.'

'Sheer bloody guts.'

'We'll dig her out, Miskin.'

Evening came, chilling the sweat of their bodies. Their ragged hole was like a shell crater. Props and stayers held the slab of rock. As they trudged home in darkness, Beynon heard Miskin groaning misery. 'Take it easy, butty,' he said quietly.

By Tuesday night they were twelve feet down, hauling up rubble with a bucket and a rope. Less often now, Lady's growling sounded hoarse. She responded instantly, feebly, when Miskin yelled at the mouth of the bury.

On Wednesday morning they felled four more sitka spruces. They fixed horizontal timbers across the dig, with props and heavy wedges at each end. Beynon relied on Miskin. He felt safe doing his stints down below, leavering his weight on the five-foot crowbar, heaving stones up on the cross-timbers.

Mim, Fay and Ianto were thirty yards away, tucked on a wind-trapped mattress of dead molinia at the base of a buttress.

'Weather's changing,' Miskin said. 'Time for some grub. Catch hold.' Gripping wrists, he helped Beynon out of the hole.

Beynon hated failure. And he felt troubled for his mate. 'Miskin, what d'you say we sink a few pints in the Club tonight. Do us good, right?'

'Nuh.'

'We're much closer to the bitch. She's not far below us. Tomorrow she'll be ours.'

Miskin argued, 'Listen to me! If it rains the sides of this bloody crib are likely to start slipping!'

'So we shift the bastard muck again!'

Miskin thrust his hand into the foxhole. 'Lay-dee! Lay-dee! Hee-yaar bitch!'

She barked for seconds, then silence.

Miskin chewed a sandwich, 'Weakness, Beynon, she's weakening.'

'But she's safe. We'll get her out.'

'Too bloody true,' said Miskin.

'That's settled then. Tonight we'll have a few pints.'

Hospital charity dance in the Social Club on Wednesday night. Beynon and Miskin sat in the snooker room. Very soon, as usual, they speculated about their runaway mothers.

Miskin: 'She never felt anything for me when I was a kid. As for my old man, he was on a loser from the start.'

Beynon: 'Before my old lady went off, she treated me and my sister and me as if we were nuisances in the house. What do they call it, maternal instinct? It's a load of bull.'

Miskin: 'D'you think all women are the same, I mean selfish?'

Beynon: 'Christ knows. They go their own way like cats.' On and on, the same unforgiving rancour, the same helpless groping for motive, a reason to shed guilt, absolve themselves and their mothers.

Beynon said, 'My old man's a worrier, he's a clock-watcher taking tablets. Duodenal ulcer according to the quack. Knock it back, Miskin. My turn.' He crossed over to the serving hatch with their empties. Happening to glance above the hooded glare on a snooker table, he saw Miskin brooding, his powerful shoulders humped forward, chin pressed to his chest. Beynon thought, she's been four days without food and water. It'll break Miskin's heart if Lady dies underground in Dunraven Basin. He'll quit. Sell the dogs. No more weekend fox-hunting. By the Jesus, we'll have to dig her out tomorrow.

Miskin raised his full glass. 'Cheers. Before stop tap we'll manage a few more.'

Beynon watched the beer glugging steadily down Miskin's throat. 'Bloody sump you are, comrade.'

They were cheerfully drunk leaving the Club, moodily determined next morning, wading through sodden, crimping bracken. Drapes of mist scudded across towering Pen Arglwydd mountain.

'Showers forecast, dry this afternoon,' said Beynon.

Miskin hooted disgust. 'It'll tamp down all day over in the Basin.'

Beynon said, 'Sure to, butty.'

9 a.m. at the fox bury, Miskin ducking his head into the hole. Silence. 'Lay-dee! Lay-dee!' Far-off husky whining from the bedlington. Silence again. The lurchers and Ianto cringed away, sensing viciousness. Miskin raged despair.

'Hey man, take it easy,' warned Beynon.

Sheltering from the rain, the lurchers and the long-jawed terrier clumped themselves together on accumulated sheep droppings below a cavernous overhang at the foot of a buttress.

Using the head of his mandrel, Miskin tapped protruding boulders in the sides of the fifteen-foot crater. 'Sounds OK so far. Nothing loose.'

Sweating inside oilskin coats and leggings, they continued hacking out stones, rubble and clay. Rising wind lulled the downpour to sheeting drizzle driving around the bowl of Dunraven Basin. It was one o'clock. They fed the dogs and themselves. Miskin kept three faggot sandwiches in a canvas bag.

Beynon cooled a pint of tea in his big flask. He said 'I'll dig for a spell,' clambering down on the cross-timbers. He listened, his eyes tightly shut. 'Lady! Hee-yaar bitch!' Then suddenly, he punched up his arms, shouting, 'She's below us! We're right on top of her!'

Miskin swung down like an ape. He elbowed him away. Beynon spreadeagled himself against the sides of the pit. Balanced on one knee, Miskin placed his ear close to the clay-slimed rubble. Low snoring, like someone sleeping in another room.

'Lay-dee!'

She yapped briefly. The snoring seemed to come in fading spasms.

'Careful, Miskin!'

'Goddam, Beynon, shurrup! I know what I'm doing!'

'All right, all right,' Beynon said.

The wet rubble concealed another tilted stone flat as a table. Scrabbling with his fingers, Miskin clawed down, searching for the edge of the stone. It was a foot thick, lodged in the sides, immovable.

Beynon climbed up across the cross-timbers. Miskin filled the bucket, Beynon hauled the rope, flung the debris, lowered the bucket. They worked for less than an hour, until Miskin saw clay-water whirlpooling down a cranny below the underside of the big stone. Delicately, slowly, Miskin corkscrewed the crossbar at a shallow angle into the fissure. The water swilling away. Like jigsaw trickery, the bedlington's snuffling, mud-smeared nose appeared. Miskin's yell screamed to castrato.

'She's safe!'

'Thank Christ,' muttered Beynon.

'Those sandwiches!' cried Miskin.

The lurchers and terriers came bounding down from the overhang. Ianto threw his echoing hound baying. Miskin clubbed when she sprawled into the pit, her hind legs flailing in sliding rubble. 'Get away! Out, gerrout!'

The brindle escaped, curvetting zig-zag leaps on the timbers.

But Lady was still trapped under a crack between two stones bedded like concrete lintels. Beynon squeezed the width of four fingers in the slot. He strained a grin at Miskin, 'Three inches, mate.'

Miskin spoke to the bedlington while dropping her pieces of faggot sandwich. 'Good bitch then, good bitch. You're in the way, Lady. I can't bash these stones if you stay there. Use some sense now, gel, back off a bit, back off the way you came in.' Frustrated after several minutes, he stood up, ranting, 'It's like talking to that bastard shovel!'

'Take it easy,' Beynon said.

'For fuck's sake you've been saying take-it-easy take-it-easy since last bloody Sunday!'

'Shh't, leave it,' Beynon said, head bowed, not looking at Miskin. 'You're blowing wind and piss, you're hysterical, like my old woman, like yours an' all.'

They laughed at each other.

Miskin slid his hand edgewise into the crack. He fingered Lady's head while Beynon wrenched on the crowbar, creeping the stones another inch apart. Exhaustion slumped Beynon on his backside. Miskin had pulled her out. She wriggled. She snorted ecstasy. Her floppy ears were scagged with cuts, tooth-holes through her upper lip, clotted blood on her feet, clay matted in her fur. Miskin mumbled, cradling the bedlington in his arms, 'You daft bloody thing you, bloody daft, daft...'

Beynon let the shakes drain from his limbs. 'She's stinking of fox,' he said, probing the cavity with the crowbar. 'Aye, he's in there. Lady killed him.' He picked shreds of fox fur off the chisel tip of the crowbar. 'Definitely, she finished him.' He slumped down again. 'I'm knackered.'

Miskin said, 'Thanks, butty.'

They climbed out. Lady lapped the lukewarm tea, then Miskin carried her all the way home, shovel, mandrel and hatchet roped across his back. Beynon carried the bowsaw, crowbar and bucket, a steady plod in cold drizzle, trailed by the brindle lurchers and the long-jawed terrier.

BREAKOUT

FOXY

Glenda Beagan

Into the cornfields of the Philistines the burning foxes run.
Red gold of the foxes. Red of the flames. Gold of the corn.

I've decided to be me. I know it's living dangerously but I've made up my mind. This is me as I really am. All the highs and all the lows. Intact.

And almost immediately the dreams start. Ordinary daytime things become extraordinary night-time marvels. Fine. So far. It's when extravaganza of sleep slips into the hours of daylight that the trouble starts. This time though, when the storm comes, I intend to ride it.

I'm an artist. Well, I used to be an artist. But the marvels became terrors and my well-meaning husband Giles persuaded me to get expert help. Those were the words he used. Dr Drysdale's expert help was very expensive but his prescriptions worked well. I had no complaints. For peace of mind I was prepared to jettison every creative atom in me. I was thankful for the calm.

And then I met Foxy.

I'm jumping ahead of myself. I must tell you how I came to this outpost in the mountains, this cottage at the end of a narrow valley in north Wales. Our home is called Cae Llwynog. Foxfield in English, but it sounds so ordinary in English. And there's nothing ordinary about this place. Its signature is slate. Look one way and you see nothing but the old quarry workings, the great heaps of slate waste that are almost mountains in themselves. It has its own kind of beauty. Its light and shade, its cloudscapes. I never knew there were so many shades of grey.

I didn't want to come here at all. We had our rural retreat in the Rodings, so easy to get to and from London, so charming too. We still own it, but for the most part Giles rents it out to friends. And friends of friends. But why Wales, I said, nearly seven years ago when he bombarded me with estate agents' brochures and I met Foxy. Well, it was her cub I met initially. He stepped out of the bracken like a little ginger puppy. I nearly fell over him! And he held up his paw as if he wanted me to shake hands with him. You know sometimes things *are* just too cute to be true. Ghastly word cute, I know, but there you are.

The fox cub was there for just a moment and then he seemed to dematerialise back into the bracken. I scanned the bare grassy part of the hillside beyond and sure enough a little while later they emerged, a vixen and three cubs. She stopped and stared at me, at a safe distance, admittedly, but quite without concern.

And that was my first encounter with Foxy.

As I said, I'm an artist. And what I'd hoped would happen, happened. Even before I'd stopped the tablets completely the dreams came back. And the ideas, weird ideas sometimes, but I welcomed them all. Not that my first drawings were in the least bit weird.

One of the things you can't help noticing when you come to Wales is the chapels because even the smallest village has at least two of them. I reckon there must've been terrific competition between all the denominations, Baptists and Wesleyans and Calvinists and Congregationalists, all of them striving to build the grandest and the best. Not terribly Christian that, perhaps, and now as the increasingly elderly worshippers decline and die the chapels do the same. More and more you see these often huge places standing empty.

The quintessentially Welsh scene for me is one of an ornately pillared and porticoed chapel set behind railings and wrought iron gates, with, in the background, a hint of mist and fir trees. And then there are those heaps of broken slate glinting in the rain.

Anyway, I started to draw chapels.

I went looking for them. Since I lost my nerve with driving I've taken to the buses in a big way, bizarrely irregular and infrequent as they may be. My chapel studies started as strict architectural drawings. It was as if I had to re-educate my eye. And hand. There'd been a time when I could execute the finest precision drawings with ease. Not now. It was painstakingly hard work. Then, as I grew more confident, I started to sketch more loosely, more in my original style. It was as if I'd had to get back to the mechanics of drawing itself and be sure of that before I could allow myself a freer rein. When Giles came up one weekend after I'd managed to produce quite a portfolio, I showed him them and was pleased for two reasons, first that he liked them and was glad that I'd revived my former skills, and secondly, and most importantly, that he still had no idea that I'd stopped the medication. There was no real reason why he should have guessed it, since I was perfectly relaxed and contented, but in a way it did indicate how little he understood me. He didn't seem to make the connection. It didn't occur to him that it was strange I should suddenly take up my art again, after years of not even thinking about it.

Cae Llwynog stands on its own at the end of the valley facing the village in an oblique sort of way, looking out on the hugest, grandest chapel you ever saw. Engedi. It was the first chapel I drew, naturally, as it was right on my doorstep. It's been closed for some years now. The few remaining members of the congregation must have rattled about in its vastness, and running costs must have been punitive. I'm not surprised it had to close its doors for the last time and perhaps there's a moral to the story after all. Of the three chapels in the village, this, the biggest and most grandiose, was the first to close, whilst the smallest and most modest of the three, the plain whitewashed Gosen, is now the only one in use.

Engedi is still an extraordinary monument, its façade being so over-the-top ornamental it takes some getting used to. Frankly, it's ugly, but so confident in its ugliness as to be almost endearing. I tried to imagine how the original worshippers must have saved and saved to build it, how they must have pondered over the builders' style books of the day before deciding on this dubious combination of Classical pillars and Gothic stained glass in windows incongruously like portholes, except for one quasi-rose window dominating all. The whole thing looks sad now. It's emblazoned with FOR SALE signs, and more recently, and more desperately, MAY LET signs as well.

There was never a dull moment at Cae Llwynog. I augmented my chapel sketches with landscapes, moody monochrome things that wouldn't please the tourist but reflected the mountains more truly than sky-blue prettiness and sunshine. And I took an increasing interest in the wild life of the area, sketching that too, especially the birds, kestrels and buzzards and the wonderful ravens, nesting high up on the quarry terraces. They're so talkative, constantly chattering amongst themselves. In spring and way into our brief summer, I would listen out for them calling to each other as they soared. And how utterly different were these calls from the harsh croaks we commonly associate with ravens. They were notes of joy, clear as bells.

And all the time I was getting to know Foxy. If a day came and went without my catching at least a glimpse of her I felt quite bereft. I would often go walking up in the hills behind Cae Llwynog, looking for her in a way, I suppose, though at first it hadn't seemed that straightforward. I had only recently acquired this confidence, to go walking on my own. To make me feel really safe though, I always took my grandfather's walking stick along with me, my talisman. It had been kept all these years as a thing of beauty rather than for its practical application, but practical it most certainly was nonetheless and I loved its smooth dark wood, its shape, its fine sense of balance and the band of enscrolled silver on it. I reckoned it brought me luck.

I'd been reading about Australian aboriginal art in one of the journals I'd started subscribing to again. The article was a bit of a hybrid, part artistic critique, part anthropology, but I was fascinated by what it said about the way those truly native people acquire totems. They don't choose their totems. Their totems chose them. Surely Foxy had chosen me. I found this whole idea thrilling. I watched her and her little family with growing fascination. I found places where it was easy simply to sit and wait for her to come by. I never tried to hide from her at all. I got to know her body language, what I can only describe as her gestures, her means of communication and believe me, she did communicate. She was not in the least bit afraid of me and though I never tried to get too close to her and her cubs, I knew that on some level she accepted me. I was not an outsider, not to her. One evening I remember in particular, one of our special September sunsets turning the mountains into a paintbox. I sat there quietly watching Foxy at the edge of the woods. We were both perfectly still, looking sort of sideways at each other. Then as the lightshow moved slowly across the sky the glory of it caught her magnificent white bib and turned it pink, no, more a deep cochineal. She was thin, crumpled and shabby after all that breeding and nurturing, but still with her rich brick colour. Now she was regal. Just sumptuous. And still we watched each other. A mutual frank approval. I felt I accessed her pure intelligence.

I was conscious though, and, not for the first time, that despite the proximity and acceptance of my totem, I could never be a true native. Love of a place is not enough. But even if my ancestry and my language debarred me from really belonging in human terms perhaps I could be redeemed by knowledge. I determined to get to know this land and the creatures of this land in the deepest way possible. It was not going to be just a matter of enjoyable country walks any more. It would involve a proper thoroughgoing study. I would keep a nature journal. I would observe more rigorously, not simply to enjoy the sights and sounds around me but to understand their interaction, their constant interplay. I would become a true ecologist.

The next time Giles came up he seemed to be rather amused by my acquisition of binoculars and reference books and my new interest in his ordnance survey maps. I thought he was being patronising and told him so, my earnestness alerting him for the first time that there was, maybe, a difference in me. He began to look at me rather quizzically, keeping his thoughts to himself, though, because Adrian knows what he's talking about so when he suggested I choose the best of them and write a little history of the chapels, explaining the relevance of each name, for instance, and then send them off to *Resonant Image*, I was all ears. And then he said something about the name Engedi, and how it struck him as strange.

It sounds really Welsh, he said. Don't you think?

And it suddenly struck me too. Yes, it did sound Welsh. It was also unusual. The Horebs and the Salems and the Seions might be commonplace but Engedi was different, special, and, as far as I knew, a one off. I had no idea what it referred to either, so next time I went on the bus to Caernarfon I found myself in the library poring over a Biblical concordance. Here it was, in the Book of Samuel, the story of David and Kind Saul, their enmity, and Saul's spies informing him that David was hiding in 'the strongholds of Engedi'. I liked the ring of that, and how, while Saul slept in a mountain cave with all his men about him, David crept up from within the cave's depths and cut off a section of his garment, challenging him later by holding up the piece of cloth to prove how easily he might have killed the sleeping king. Why did this story appeal so much to our valley's quarrymen that they named their proud new chapel after it? I was none the wiser, unless they too thought the word had a Welsh sound to it, and liked, as I did, the idea of 'the strongholds'. For surely these mountains were still a language and a culture's strongholds even today. I kept repeating the phrase to myself. It had an appropriately bleak, astringent music, did the strongholds of Engedi, with paradoxically, at the same time, a kind of friendliness.

As I sat there in the library the concordance flicked open to a nearby page and I saw the word 'fox'. Quite casually I looked up the reference in the Book of Judges and read on, intrigued by an astonishing story of lust and violence and horrible revenge. I read with horror and incredulity about Samson gathering together three hundred foxes (now quite how did he do that?) setting fire to their bushes (the implication being that he did this rather as a chain-smoker lights one cigarette from another) and then letting them run loose, the poor panicking things, into the Philistine fields. It was the time of the harvest.

Red gold of the foxes. Red of the flames. Gold of the corn.

I felt that this was my image, that these were my colours. I can't explain it. I was exhilarated, appalled too, but I have to say mostly exhilarated. Something rushed up and out in me, like a logjam breaking. I knew with growing excitement and conviction that this would become a painting, by far the best, by far the strongest thing I'd ever done. The background of it was there in my mind immediately, familiar as breathing.

Here was my stronghold of Engedi. Here was the view from Cae Llwynog, the row of quarrymen's cottages with the circlet of hills behind, the stark geometrics of the quarry, the heaps of waste and then the chapel itself, handsome and new, a congregation descending its front steps following a sermon, a nineteenth-century congregation dressed in all their Sunday finery. A woman is prominent amongst them. She stands a little apart, pointing out across the valley, the foreground of the painting. It was one expanse of wheat. And it's starting to burn but you guessed that. The painting has a split personality, half painted entirely realistically and with meticulously detailed control, half executed as a Dionysian welter, violently surreal. Half is grey, dark, wet, sombre. You can see the fronds of fern amongst the stones, the individual bricks in the wall. You can smell wet bombazine, wet gaberdine and serge, and the wet leather of hymnbooks. Half is an inferno, of stalks and seedheads, smelling horribly of burning leaf and grain, of singeing hair and fur. And amongst the corn run the glorious flaming foxes, consumed by their own fire, the colours of the sun.

I bought my acrylics, my boards. And I couldn't wait to get home. Did I know then that my latest craziness had begun? I think maybe I did, but if I did, I know, too, that I embraced it.

CHARITY

Clare Morgan

At the wedding she had said 'Yes', and 'Until death'. That was a long time ago and her hair was quite grey now, and her eyes were marooned in a sea of little wrinkles.

Alessandro saw them, the eyes and the wrinkles, when he knocked at her door. She was a typical, timid woman who answered his knock, too many years without a man, too many days and nights in the long bed (bought to accommodate her husband, surely, because she was a very short woman) alone.

Alessandro held out the collecting box, and seeing the refusal begin to form in her, the tensing of the muscles in her neck and the start of the side to side movement of her head that would send him back down the steps empty-handed, he said,

'It's a good cause.'

What he really said was, 'Ees a good cau-sa', because he found English difficult, having only recently, and reluctantly, given up a long-standing career at sea.

'I deen wanna', he said to his one friend Elis, who was also an exile, having settled by accident in the county after spending most of his life in the North.

'I deen wanna.'

But what else, his accompanying shrug seemed to indicate, can a man do?

'Ees a good cau-sa,' he repeated, standing on her top step with the wind that funnelled up the street, and before that, up the valley that became the street, lifting the blunt ends of his straightish hair.

He shook the collecting box and the coins inside rattled. The wind brought with it the smell of living in a strange place. He knew many of the smells of the different places in the world. Rio, Santiago, Durban, Qatar. Now he smelled the particular smell of this small part of a small country. It had nothing to do with politics. The smell of a place was made up of its weather and its history. That was how he wanted to think of it. It wasn't as simple as that but he wished it to be simple, because he had led a complicated life and it had tired him, and now he wanted to lead a simple life, and feel the tiredness leave him, and sense himself to be at peace.

He shook the box again and said,

'Anything…'

She moved her head from side to side, very firmly this time, with just the right balance of decision and condescension, lengthening her neck a little so that the large lapels of her flowered blouse could assert themselves.

'No,' she said, in a soft voice that was definite too. He thought that she had probably been a schoolteacher. Either that, or a district nurse. He could imagine her quelling unruly children with a look. He could imagine her too in uniform, closing her front door at dawn or before dawn, pulling it to behind her with a click and getting into her dark little car and feeling the hem of her gabardine raincoat rasping her stockings as she adjusted her legs.

He was going to say something more to try to persuade her but she had already closed the door, almost, and the only thing that was left of her was an eye.

And what an eye it was, he said to himself afterwards, walking along with the collecting box hanging by its two strings from his wrist. It was an eye that was ageless and placeless. It was Eve's eye. It was the eye of every woman he had made love to, and most of those he had fucked.

Alessandro (it was a nickname, he had been baptised Guiseppi) was widely experienced in women. He had fucked women in most of the countries of the world. He had made love to women rather more selectively, perhaps in only two or three countries. There had been a few boys too, Morocco had been bad that way, for temptation, but he did his best to forget about those experiences. There were things it was better not to let in, they cluttered up your life, they made it difficult for you to be at peace.

That evening, when he was sitting on the bench by the war memorial waiting for Elis (it was a warm enough June, and girls with their legs all bare and little cotton tops that their breasts pushed out of were walking up and down) he thought of the woman again. She was fifty, or more than fifty. He thought of her body and knew what it would be like, because he had measured the decay of his own. He had measured the decay and hated it. His own age, other people's age; he hated the fact that youth was naturally fuckable and age was not. If he had been a different kind of man he would have taken to drink. As it was he confined himself to moderation and maintained a certain terseness in his dealings with his inner and regretful self.

When Elis came he asked him who the woman was, knowing already, because he had asked at the shop, that she was Miss Thomas, Gwynfryn. She was a relative newcomer and kept very much to herself.

'They say she came from Pontypridd,' Elis said. 'But then, I've heard too, that she came from Abergavenny.'

Elis said it rather mournfully. He was a mournful man, recently widowed. There was loneliness in the angle of his cap. They sat on the bench talking quietly and irregularly for half an hour or an hour, watching but not watching the girls walking up and down and the boys, who sat on the wall together and swung their legs, and pushed their hair back off their foreheads and then, after a suitable interval, let it fall forwards again.

283

The only thing left of her was an eye. It was the eye that he remembered throughout the following day, as he went from house to house with his legs getting heavier and his heart feeling large under his ribs.

'A good cau-sa', he said, again and again. And most of the men and women agreed.

At the end of the afternoon he climbed the steps to the Town Hall and went in past the Corinthian pillars (too grand entirely for the building, and the building itself too grand for the town, but that was how they had done things in the old days, you could see it in all the big old buildings, the sense of getting ahead of yourself, the idea of somewhere big and important where, with a little effort, anyone could go).

He offered his collection box to be counted, and sat down to wait. The room, which was a large room with high ceilings and a cornice, contained, as well as the tables where people were counting out the money, displays of all the uses the place had been put to over the years. There were photographs of it turned into a hospital during the war. Then in the first war, as a recruitment office. Alessandro recognized a picture of Kitchener. Then there was a faint, yellowy-looking photograph, the steps packed with people and a banner with Welsh words on it that he couldn't understand, and a banner with English words that he could.

'That,' Elis said when he asked him about it later, 'was the investiture of the Prince of Wales. Nineteen hundred and two, I think it was. Anyway. A long time ago.'

Then there was tea, at the Coronation. A party for the Silver Jubilee. Brass band competitions. The crowning of Miss Miskin, a plain little girl with hair straggling on her shoulders. A rally, during the miners' strike. Boxing contests, and wrestling, on a Saturday afternoon.

The wrestling held Alessandro's interest. The other pictures had bored him. It was not, after all, his country, and all the pictures seemed to be of grey, indistinguishable faces.

But the last picture of all was of two women wrestling, and it held his attention because it reminded him that once two prostitutes had pretended to fight over him. He had forgotten, because it was a long time ago, exactly where. Perhaps it had been one of the Mediterranean ports, but he thought not. It had more the feel of South America to it. Anyway, they had pretended to fight over him, and his shipmates had been envious. He couldn't remember which of the women had won. One had been darker than the other. One had been very thin. Had the dark one been thin? Or had the thin one had lighter hair, almost a reddish kind of colour, which grew down onto her forehead in a peak? It was odd how you remembered sometimes, the littlest of things. Afterwards he'd had both of them, the first in a proud way, offering his body as a kind of prize. The second he'd treated more gently, feeling for an instant an unfamiliar desire to console.

He hadn't thought about it from that day to this. But he thought about it now, and it made him restless, and he leaned forward and looked at the photograph closely, the one woman, fleshy and blonde-looking and with a lot of black stuff around her eyes, the other, darker and more wiry altogether, with her hair cut off short around her face, and a defiant look as she stared at the camera, the corners of her mouth pulled in tight. 'Mad Marge' the caption under the photograph said. 'Mad Marge *v* Jinny the Giantess. September 1963.'

And when I said 'Yes', Marged said (going to the window and looking out to where the grass was growing on the landscaped part, very green indeed all the way up the hill, but too smooth to be a real hill, and with a few black bits showing however much they tried to hide them, in between).

When I said 'Yes', I hadn't meant yes in the way people mean it, the forever kind of yes that lives with you and becomes part of you and you can't get away from. I meant the *for now* yes, this minute, today, this week. But Yeses had a habit of catching you. Noes were safer. And all that time ago she'd said yes, just for the sake of it, really.

'Marged,' he'd said looking very sorry for himself one night, sitting in her mam's back-kitchen on the way home from the pub. And she'd said, almost without meaning to, it was strange when she heard herself say it,

'Very well, Ifor.'

It was a grown-up thing to say.

And after they were married, he stood at the foot of the bed and took his clothes off, one by one, his tie, his shirt, his socks, his underpants (she had looked the other way when he unbuckled his belt). He had stood at the foot of the bed, at last with nothing on at all, and his body rather thin and drab, and a thin streak of shadow under the curve of every rib, and almost directly under the electric light, so that his body looked elongated a little, although it cast no shadow, which was strange because everything else in the room had a rather black shadow attached to it. When she had seen him like that, she knew the true nature of the mistake she had made, and knew also that it was not something she could put right, not ever, because now she had done it it was part of what she was, and yourself was one thing you couldn't get away from, no matter how long, or how earnestly, you tried.

In the event, it was Ifor who had got away from her. Not that even *that* was true, really. He had never been hers, although he might have liked to be. And she had certainly never been his, except in the exchange of her body for his name, and in doing the things a wife does, like a maid really. Her mother had been a maid before the war, up at Canal Head House. Marged had seen a photograph of her with her hands clasped in front of a little white spoon-shaped apron, and another little bit of something white, with primped-up edges and a visible kirby grip, settled precariously in her hair.

'Ifor not back for the weekend?' her next-door neighbour

Eirianfa said. (Eirianfa came from Dolgellau originally, and went back there not long after, the South never really suited her, it was impossible to settle, somehow, in the strange, pale air.)

'Ifor not back?'

Marged had said to herself, when she was child, that she would never be anybody's maid. There was an old snapshot, quite bent around the edges, of her in a sunbonnet, staring out fiercely from the deep shade the brim cast across her face. She was waving a stick at the camera, and the little cluster of lumps that was knuckles stood out.

'Fierce, by God', Ifor had said when she showed it to him, the only time, really, she had showed him anything. The way he said 'Fierce' troubled her. He said it with that look she didn't like in men, the mouth too relaxed, and the pupils of his eyes taking on a dark look, and the muscles in the neck tightening and then going slack again.

When Ifor had left, eventually, not letting her know beforehand, just not coming back, and getting a friend to write her a letter, an English friend, they were working on the new road near Ross (the letter had a Hereford postmark), when Ifor had left she felt strange, and separate, and missed for a few nights the idea of him taking his socks off at the bottom of the bed.

'Ifor not back, then?'

Ifor will never be back. Ifor will never lift the latch on the gate, and take the three steps you have to take to get to the door, open it, and come in, bringing with him the smell of the outside, the town in his coat and in his hair, the smell of exhaust fumes, the cold wind under his fingernails.

Behind the house where she had a room, in Cardiff, in a small street that didn't lead anywhere, was a dug-up piece of earth, with primroses on one side, and daffodils on the other, and the brown-coloured bits of what was left of the snowdrops in between. (My life has been made up of back yards, and half-turned earth. And the walls of the houses

287

going up very straight, and the roofs, in layers, angling back over themselves.) There was a lot of traffic and the shop windows were very shiny and you saw, as you went past them, your own reflection coming at you from different angles. It didn't seem like you. You were no longer the person you had thought you were, but another person who looked rather like you but wasn't. (And what is this strange sense every morning, waking up, of my self getting smaller and smaller, like an island in the middle of a river rising in flood?)

'You,' the man said, and pointed at you, there, in a line, waiting to see if you were any good at it, looking at you first as you walked up and down in a swimming costume, looking at you very closely indeed as you waited, your turn three away, then next-but-one, then next, and others already there and doing it, or having done it, the grunting and the falling, the pretending, and the odd occasional blow that caught you like a fiery and exploding thing.

The man's forefinger was stiff and straight at the end of his straight arm. 'You!' The finger moved twice, from the joint.

She stepped forward. She felt like a schoolgirl. She felt as she had sometimes in Chapel, on a Sunday. If there had been any excuse for it, that would have been different. If she had done it for any of the reasons women do things, any of the old reasons—

'You!' the man said.

And then she stopped thinking about it and climbed up, with big, fluid movements, into the ring.

Now, Marged. What was it like? (looking out over the landscaped part and counting the black bits, one, two, three, four, see how they all link up and make a pattern, like veins the black bits are, snaking in and out of the green).

When she had first come there, nearly thirty years before, everything had been black still. The wheel had been turning, the spokes of it all in a blur. Strange how memory took away the colour. The sky had been white. She had climbed up into the ring and felt the top rope scrape at the skin of her shoulder, and the middle rope press into the flesh of her thigh and then spring loose again as she let go. She had stood up in that square, free space that took away entirely and for the allotted time her freedom, and felt cut off from everything that she knew and was, from everything that she had ever dreamed of, or wanted to be. And yet, how solid the sweat had felt running down her back, and down her ribs at the sides under her arms. How real the faces were still, and the room, hot and tight on her, and the air thick with the tail ends of words. She never knew for certain whether she had been more herself at those times, or less.

'Stick to what you know', her mother had urged her once, fiercely, although her voice was getting very thin. But sometimes knowing (she had come to understand) can be more of a burden than a relief.

And what do I truly know? (staring in the mirror in the room in Cardiff, with her back to the window, and the patch of earth unturned now behind her, and treacly-looking in the uncentred light).

What do I truly know?

There had been a man she went to bed with sometimes, but intermittently. His body had been solid and his steps definite on the linoleum as he collected up his clothes. And something in it had brought her afterwards back to this half-known place, rather like Eden, the old pictures of it, sketches in Borrow, *Wild Wales*. Eden no longer. (She had heard her mother speak of the boy from Canal Head House riding his pony up on Ferndale, late in the afternoon.)

And yet it was in a way like Eden. Quiet, her house. Peaceful before the fall. The clocked ticked. The flames in her gas fire made little whiffing noises when the wind backed round. She had pointed herself, like a weather vane, in this inevitable direction. She did not long for, she resented rather, the sound of a step on her step, the rasp of the knocker, tentatively yet deliberately raised.

Who is it? she called, in her head perhaps, because it was evening now and the children who played outside in the street had gone in, and a certain thickening in the outline of things told you it would soon be dark.

Who is it?

Alessandro took his hands out of his pockets. The edge of his pockets rasped over his knuckles as he withdrew his hands. A cool current of air wound up the street towards him and threaded itself between his ankles and slid up over his shoulders and around his neck. He put his head on one side at an awkward angle and looked up past the dark shape of the hill rising away. The sky was a colour he had never seen before. It was the colour he thought it would be the first time he crossed the equator. A dark, indescribable colour. He settled his weight back on his heels. Something ticked inside him, like a metronome. The street, where it fell away quite steeply, was dull under the lack of stars. A light came on inside the house, and went out again. He felt the wind lodge in a series of cold little bars under his fingernails. The town was yellow now below him, and the hill black and solid-looking behind. He strained for a sound of something inside the house, but there was only the wind out there with him, and the curious half-darkness lapping the promontories of his hands.

TOO PERFECT

Jo Mazelis

The man and the woman were standing side by side at the marina, studying the new housing development on the other side of the water. He had been expressing surprise tinged with disgust at the sight of the red-brick buildings with their gabled windows and arches and as he put it 'postmodern gee-gaws'. While she, having no knowledge of what had stood there before and no great opinion on architecture, said nothing.

Then into the silence that hovered between them he suddenly offered 'Do you mind?' and before he had finished asking, took her hand in his. In reply she gave a squeeze of assent, noting as she did how large and warm and smooth his hand was.

To a passerby it would have looked like nothing out of the ordinary. He or she, on seeing this man and woman by the water's edge, would assume that this hand-holding was a commonplace event for them. But it wasn't. This was the first, the only time of any real physical contact between them.

Later, still awkwardly holding hands, each now afraid that letting go might signal some end to that which had not yet even begun, they made their way to the old Town Hall, once the home of commerce and council and now a centre for literature. This was the purpose of their trip, the reason why at seven that morning she had stood at the window of her bedsit in Cambrian Street, Aberystwyth, waiting for the tin-soldier red of his Citroen to emerge around the corner.

Each had expressed an interest in visiting the Centre and had behaved as if they were the only two people in the world with such a desire. That was why, uncharacteristically, he hadn't suggested the trip to the other members of his tutorial group. It was also the reason why Claire had omitted to tell any of her friends, why she had agreed to wake Ginny that morning at ten o'clock, despite the fact that she and Dr Terrence Stevenson would probably be enjoying coffee and toast together in Swansea by then.

Terry, as he was known to colleagues and students alike, was a large man, over six feet, with large bones and large appetites, which now as he neared fifty expressed itself in his frame. He had once been lithe and muscular but his body had thickened with age. He blamed too many years at a desk, the expansion of his mind at the expense of an expanding behind. But he dressed well enough, choosing dark tailored jackets and corduroy or chino slacks, as well as the odd devilish tie, which was about as subversive as he got. In colder weather, as on this grey October day, he wore his favourite black Abercrombie overcoat of cashmere and wool mix. The coat hung well from the shoulders and had the effect of tapering his body, disguising its imperfections with a veneer of powerful authority and masculinity.

Claire thought he looked like one of the Kray twins in this coat of his, and to her that signalled a sort of dangerous sexuality. She could not help but imagine herself engulfed in that coat, held willing captive in its soft folds.

Next to him, she looked tiny, even less than her five feet and a half inch. Claire had very long hair, grown in excess to compensate perhaps for her lack of height. It hung down, straight and sleek to her bottom and a great deal of her time was taken up with this hair: washing, combing and plaiting it before she went to bed each night. Most of the time she wore it loose and her gestures, the movement of her head, body and hands were all done in such a way as to accommodate her river of hair. When eating, for example, she would hold the fork in one hand while with the other she held her hair away from the plate. She was very proud of her hair and if asked which part of herself she liked the most, that would be what she would choose. Her last boyfriend, whom she had met at the Fresher's Dance at college and dated for almost three years, had loved her hair; had sometimes spread it over her naked body, Lady Godiva style when they made love; had once even made the pretence of tying himself to her by it.

Claire's body was like a boy's: flat-chested and slim-hipped. And today she was dressed like a boy too, with jeans and heavy black lace-up boots and a white shirt and a man's tweed jacket two sizes too big. Through both her right eyebrow and right nostril she wore tiny silver rings and her eyes and lips were exaggerated with make up in shades of reddish brown. She seldom smiled, but when she did her entire face was transformed into something not quite wholly beautiful, but something very like it.

They had trudged through an exhibition of artefacts relating to the town's one famous poet: the scribbled postcards, the crumpled snapshots, the yellowing newspaper clippings, all framed for posterity like the relics of some dead saint. Terry had begun by clucking and tutting yet more disapproval of the venture, disapproval he'd been nurturing and planning since he first heard of it, but with Claire by his side he found himself softening, growing acclimatised to her open-minded acceptance of all such endeavours.

They spoke in whispers, though the place was almost entirely deserted, this being after all a grey Tuesday in October, and around the back, beneath some engravings by Peter Blake they kissed their first kiss. It did not feel like the world's best kiss for either of them, but did well enough as an awkward, uncertain snatched preliminary to better things. Afterwards Claire had wanted to wipe her mouth with the back of her hand, not from disgust but just because the kiss was a little wet. His mouth had swallowed hers, had not measured out the size of her lips yet.

After the kiss they each felt like a conspirator in some deadly plot; what they would create that day felt as if it might be as deadly as Guy Fawkes' gunpowder, as bloody as any revolution.

The second kiss came as they sat in a deserted bar of the Pump House. The barman, a student, they decided, was propped against the far end of the counter, his head bent over a book. They took turns to guess what the book might be. Terry said it was a handbook about computing, and she thought it was a script of something like *Reservoir Dogs*.

The clock above the bar, a faux-nautical affair, hung with nets and cork floats and plastic lobster and crab, read twelve-fifteen. They had the afternoon and the early evening to spend together. He was thinking about the Gower coast, a cliff walk, the lonely scream of wheeling gulls and the sea a grey squall bubbling under the wind. She was thinking about a hotel room, the luggage-less afternoon ascent in the lift to the en-suite room and the champagne, herself languishing on the sheets, feeling intolerably beautiful under his grateful gaze.

After that second kiss, which was prolonged, they wrenched themselves away and began to speak in a strange language of unfinished sentences and hesitant murmurings.

'Oh.'

'Gosh.'

'You know we…'

'I never…'

'Oh my…'

'We shouldn't…'

'I never thought…'

'Nor me…'

'I mean, I always thought that maybe…'

'Me too…'

Then they kissed again and the barman, who wasn't a student, raising his eyes briefly from his novel by Gorky, watched them with mild interest and thought they made an odd pair.

The odd pair finished their drinks: pints of real ale. She stubbed out her cigarette and they made their way towards the exit, his arm thrown protectively around her shoulders while his broad back wore her tiny arm, its fingers clutching the cloth, like a curious half-belt.

The sky looked by now greyer and darker than before. To the west a blue-black curtain advanced, promising heavy rain and a wind blew up from the east, sending her hair on a frantic aerial dance. They ran across the empty square as raindrops as big as shillings began marking the paving stones with dark circles.

Then she half stumbled and he caught her and in catching her, gathered her to him and they kissed a fourth time, this the best, with the rain splashing their heads and water pouring down their faces.

When they had done with this, this their unspoken moment of willingness and promise and wilfulness, their pact to indulge in what they knew was an unwise thing, he quickly kissed the tip of her nose and then hand in hand they began to run again.

Under the covered walkway, they slowed down and shaking off the worst of the rain from their hair and clothes, barely noticed a man standing close by. He was busy putting away a tripod and Terry muttered, 'Afternoon' and the man, grinning broadly replied, 'Thanks'.

Naturally neither of them made much of this, assuming it to be yet another curious aspect of Welshness. A further example of the strange smiling politeness, the thanking of bus drivers and so on, the chatting to strangers which each of them had at first perceived as alien, but now despite their breeding, accepted and in part adopted.

Later that afternoon, in his car near a field in the north of

Gower, with the day as dark as ever they almost made love. The next day, back in Aberystwyth, they did make love.

She had rung him from the payphone in the hall of her house when she was certain all the other students had gone out. His wife had answered the phone and she'd given her the prearranged message, which was that she'd 'found the journal with the Lawrence article he'd wanted.'

What happened that Wednesday was perhaps rather sad, though not necessarily inevitable. It became clear to both of them that what they sought was a fugitive moment; that there could be no more than this, the furtive opening of the front door, the climbing of the stairs, the single bed dishevelled and cramped under the sloping roof, his glances at his watch, her ears constantly straining for any sounds from down below. Both of them too tense for pleasure, but going through its rigours, him professionally, she dramatically.

Afterwards, when they had dressed again, they sat side by side on the bed like strangers in a doctor's waiting room, each thinking silently about how to end it, how to escape. She took his hand and held it on her lap, then began to speak.

'Your wife...'

'Catherine?'

'She sounded...'

'Yes.'

'She sounded...'

'Nice?'

'She is. I...'

'I don't...'

'I can't...'

'I think that...'

'Me too.'

He sighed. She understood his sigh to mean that he didn't want to leave and she sighed back at the thought that he might cancel his three o'clock lecture in order to stay. He had sighed because he was wondering how long he ought to stay to make it seem at least remotely respectable. He rested his eyes on the small wooden bookcase next to her bed. She had all the required texts as well as a rather unhealthy number of books by and about the American poet Sylvia Plath. This made him sigh again. She was trying very hard to imagine him back in his study, with the coffee cups on the window ledge and the view of the National Library and the letter trays overflowing with student essays and she sighed again because now that she'd seen him in his underwear that ordinary idea seemed impossible.

He stood suddenly, ready to go, but somehow his watch had become entangled with her hair and she gave a yelp of pain as he unthinkingly yanked at it, ripping the hair from her head. They both looked aghast at the tangled clumps sprouting from the metal bracelet of his watch. He pulled at them but they cut into his fingers and stretched and curled and slipped and clung until finally they snapped, leaving short tufts poking out here and there.

Tears had come to her eyes with the sudden pain. He looked at her and seeing this, with ill-disguised irritation as much at himself as with her, said 'I'm sorry,' then bluntly, 'Why don't you get that cut?'

That would have been the end of the story, except that some moments, elusive as they may seem when lived, come back in other guises, unbidden. Theirs was a photograph, unfortunately a very good photograph of a young girl on tiptoes, her long wet hair lifted wildly in the wind and a black-coated man bent over her, his hands delicately cupping her upturned face as their lips met. Rain glistened on their faces and shone in silvery puddles on the paving stones at their feet and behind them the sky was a black brooding mass of cloud.

It was a timeless image, a classic to be reproduced over and over, whose currency was love, truth and beauty. The people who bought the poster and the stationery range and the postcard assumed that it must have been posed, that it was really too perfect.

Barbecue

Catherine Merriman

It's Saturday morning and we're headed north out of Beaufort, out of the Valleys, up on to the mountain. Jaz on his Guzzi, Mitch on his Triumph chop, and me on the Z1000, on our way to Crickhowell for a drink. And to get away from our mate Dai, who's panicking back at the field because the others haven't returned from Glastonbury with the bus, and how the hell is he going to lay on a barbecue this evening without the cooking gear?

Not a soul on the mountain but we can't open up the bikes for the hordes of sheep dawdling on the tarmac, bleating and giving us the idiot eye. They've got half a county of moorland to roam across, up here, but as usual they're ignoring it. Mitch reckons it's definite proof of over-civilisation, when even the sheep are scared of getting lost.

The other side of the mountain, and we're into Tourist Information Wales. Money and horseboxes and hang-gliders and not a derelict factory in sight. The little town of Crickhowell, nestling snug and smug over the Usk.

We get to the pub and down a swift ale, and we're just explaining to the landlord about the bruises on Jaz's face when the door opens and who should fall through it but the bus crowd. That's Wayne, Pete, and the two girls.

'What you doing here?' Mitch bellows across the room at them, making half the bar slop their pints. Short on manners, Mitch is, but the landlord's easy-going. 'Dai's doing his nut, waiting for you.'

The girls duck down the corridor to the Ladies and Pete and Wayne push their way towards us. Pete has got his hair tied back in a dinky plait, instead of loose and ratsy. Wayne is in his He-Man rig, bandannaed blonde mane over acres of leather-strapped, tanned flesh. They stare at the purple lumps on Jaz's face with awe. Sharp little face, Jaz had, when they last saw him. Looks like a plum pudding now. 'Shit, man.' Pete looks alarmed. 'How's the Guzzi?'

Jaz tells him, like he was just telling the landlord, that the Guzzi's fine, but that he had a run-in with a couple of lads from Tredegar. Yesterday, it was. He sold them a Suzi, and it blew up before they reached Ebbw Vale. They wanted the Guzzi to make up for it, but he hid it in his mam's back-kitchen and took a thumping on the doorstep instead.

Wayne claps him round the shoulders, making him flinch – thoughtful type, Wayne is – and says he'd have been safer at Glastonbury, where it was all peace and love and a soft landing on mud.

'You there all this time?' I ask. 'Been more than a week.'

'Na,' says Wayne. 'Trouble in Bristol coming back.' He grins wide. 'This publican, he won't serve us 'cos he says we're a coach party. So I backed over his fence, accidental-like, on the way out. The cops had us for criminal damage. Got a conditional discharge.'

Jaz wonders how many hospital visits it takes to cure a conditional discharge, and I tell Wayne how Dai's got it into his head about this barbecue and wants the bus back pronto. The bus is mobile HQ – as well as the cooking gear, everyone's got equipment and spares stashed in it.

'Be back this afternoon,' Wayne promises. 'It's down the lay-by now. Just got to pick up stuff for the girls.'

They disappear after a quick pint. We don't stay long either, because Jaz's getting anxious about leaving the Guzzi in the car park up the road. It's day-tripping weather and the High Street's already jumping with Valleys' lads.

Nobody near the bikes though, except a couple of kiddies admiring the puddle of oil under Mitch's chop. Brit bikes need to sweat, Mitch says, he's a patriot. We decide we'll head back and give Dai the good news. We set off and I'm in front, revelling in the way the Z1000 powers up the gradients, when I see a dead sheep, lying at the side of the road. Fair-sized corpse, but definitely a lamb, not one of the scrawny ewes.

I flag the others down. There's no one else on the road.

'This fella weren't here when we came across,' I say. 'Did you see him?'

'He weren't here,' says Mitch. 'We'd have noticed.'

Jaz props the Guzzi and squats down to take a dekko. Barbecue, I'm beginning to think.

'How long do you reckon he's been dead?' I say.

'How long you been dead?' Jaz asks the lamb, but it stays stum.

'Stick your finger up its arse,' I say. 'See if it's warm.'

'I'm not sticking my finger up any tup's bum,' Jaz says. But Mitch dismounts and says he'll do it, so he can tell his grandchildren about it when he's old, and they refuse to believe he had a wild childhood.

He pokes his finger into the lamb and says it's warm. He looks up and grins. Jaz and I grin back. We're all thinking barbecue now.

We ponder what to do next. We can't cruise into town with a dead tup behind us – even with a jacket on it won't fool anyone.

We decide to dump it in a shallow ditch a few yards from the road and go back to Jaz's place for equipment. His mam's got a smallholding this side of town. They don't keep stock now, but there's any tool you want in the sheds.

When we get there we find Lizzie all a twitter because the two Tredegar lads have been back. Jaz's mam is Lizzie to everyone except Jaz. She says the boys didn't come to the house, but she saw them with another lad in a white van, parked down the track. Jaz takes her into the front room to calm her down, and so she doesn't see us rummaging in the back shed for the axe and knives and a couple of plastic feed bags.

'She all right?' Mitch asks, as Jaz joins us in the hallway on the way out. It's not just politeness, we all got time for Lizzie. 'Cos she's always got time for us, I suppose. Jaz says she's OK now, no need to worry.

We drive like vicars on mopeds out of town with the gear stuffed down our jackets, and pootle out to where we've hid the lamb.

There's a few cars on the road now. Mitch's the largest and ugliest of us so we leave him by the bikes to glare at anyone who looks like stopping, and Jaz and I scramble over the heather to the ditch.

We don't bother to skin the lamb, because Pete used to work in a slaughterhouse and can do it blindfold, we just chop off the head and feet and gut it. I'd have left the gore there for the foxes, but Jaz's fretting about an old ewe bleating at the edge of the ditch and says it's the tup's mam and we can't leave bits of her baby lying around. I say fine – you can't argue with Jaz about mother love – just so long as he deals with dumping it later. We stuff the carcass into one bag and the head and feet and as much of the guts as we can scrape up into the other. The carcass bag straps across the tank of the Z1000, and Jaz ties the other to the grab bar of the Guzzi. Then we drive, nice and sedate, the three miles through town to Dai's.

The bus is down the field already, next to Dai's collection of rotting mechanicals. But it's changed colour since last week. Instead of blue it's sickly green, with what look like white ticks round the windows. Down the field a bit the ticks turn out to be peace doves. We bounce the bikes over the grass to where Dai, Pete, and Pete's girlfriend Karin are standing by one of Dai's decomposing JCBs.

'What you done to the bus?' demands Mitch, as we prop the bikes. 'Bleeding hell.'

'You know anyone works in a chippie?' Dai asks, not listening. He still looks fraught, despite the return of the bus. He's tugging at clumps of his beard like he's plucking it. 'Need a sack of taters.'

'We got something better than taters,' Jaz says, beckoning him over to the bikes.

'Who painted the bus?' Mitch roars. 'Looks like a fucking playbus.'

'It was to get in,' Pete says soothingly. 'They said we could park it by the Green Field if we let the kids paint it.' He tilts his head and nods at it. 'Looks OK, I think.'

Behind his back Karin pulls a face and twists her finger into her temple. Dai's standing over the Z1000. 'Jeez,' he whistles, as Jaz opens the bag. 'Where'd you get that?'

'What is it?' asks Pete, coming over to look. He peers inside. 'Shit,' he says, stepping back.

'You got to skin it,' says Jaz. 'We done the rest.'

Pete shakes his head and says no way, he'd become a vegetarian. But Karin rips into him and says she's fed up with him flirting with the hippies at the festival and if he wants to become a fairy that's up to him, but he's not sodding well laying it on us.

'OK, OK,' says Pete, with a look that suggests this isn't the first bollocking he's had over this, and agrees to skin the lamb as his last carnivorous act. Mitch gives him the axe and knives and he humps the bag up the field towards the outhouses. Karin follows him still giving him mouth.

'Where's Wayne?' I ask.

'In the bus with Josie,' says Dai. 'Better knock first.'

'My face hurts,' Jaz says, touching his cheek gingerly. 'I need a kip.'

'You got to dump that bag,' I remind him.

'Later,' he says.

I don't push it. He's suddenly looking very weary. He's

holding his shoulders funny, and where the side of his helmet's been pressed against his cheekbone it's made a dent in one of the purple bruises. We walk over to the bus and Mitch kicks the side. Josie sticks her head out of a window, pulling a T-shirt on over her long straggly hair.

'Oi,' says Mitch. 'Jaz needs to kip.'

Josie says, 'Oh, right,' and there's some scuffling and groaning inside. She opens the back door tucking her T-shirt into her jeans. She looks at Jaz's face and winces. 'Better come inside,' she says. 'I got some aspirin.'

As they climb in Wayne hops out pulling on his boots. We start to move back to the bikes.

'You know the boys who did that?' Wayne gives a last hop and jerks his head back at the bus. He means Jaz's face. 'Any of you there?'

'Nope,' says Mitch. 'Just Jaz and Lizzie.'

'Uhuh,' says Wayne. I know what he's thinking. I'm beginning to think it too. It didn't sound so bad, the way Jaz told it, but who likes to tell it bad? And seeing how stiff the boy is, and mess they made of his face... it's out of order to thump a lad, and want his bike off him as well.

'They been round to his place again this morning,' I say, with my eyes on Wayne. 'They're after the Guzzi. Maybe they'll be back.'

Wayne picks up Jazz's helmet and climbs on to the pillion of the Z1000. He grins, patting the seat in front of him. 'Let's go see,' he says.

Lizzie's pleased to see the three of us, especially when we tell her Jaz's fine, resting in the bus. She says she hasn't seen the Tredegar boys again, and doesn't want to, and would we like some chips? Ta, we say, great; it'll be hours before Dai's cooked the tup, if he ever stops bellyaching and gets on with it. We eat the chips in the front room where we can keep an eye on the track outside. Lizzie guesses why we're watching out and says what we do is our own business, but she doesn't want Jaz getting into no more fights. She looks fierce when she says it, and I think it can't be much fun watching your son get beat up on your own doorstep. Wayne says we're maybe saving Jaz a fight, if the boys are still after the Guzzi, and Lizzie mutters that no bike's worth getting hurt for and she wishes Jaz had just given it to them. She doesn't mean it though.

We wait an hour or so, and then Mitch says we ought to get back to Dai's to make sure he's got the lamb rigged up proper. As we leave Wayne gives Lizzie a squeeze, making her go pink and call him a wicked boy, and we tell her to lock up tight and not to expect Jaz back, because the barbecue'll go on all night.

As soon as we turn into Dai's field we know something's wrong. The fire's not even lit, Pete and Dai are shouting at each other in front of the bus, Karin's screaming at Pete, and Jaz's sitting next to Josie on the back step with his boots off and his head in his hands like he just died.

Josie comes running over. 'They got the Guzzi! Just walked down while Jaz was asleep and we didn't know who they were.'

'Fucking left the key in it, didn't I,' wails Jaz. 'Drove it straight off.'

'Just as well,' Karin snaps, coming up. 'Carrying lump hammers, they were. Saw them.'

'Then why didn't you say so?' yells Pete. 'Stupid cow.'

'Thought they were a couple of Dai's mates, shithead,' Karin shouts back. 'There's always blokes in and out of here.' She's steaming with rage.

'What I want to know,' says Dai, scratching his beard and looking bewildered, 'is how they knew to come here?'

Nobody bothers to answer him, it's such a stupid question. Jaz's got the only big Guzzi in town, and everyone knows he knows Dai, and where the bus is parked. I'm thinking about what's strapped to the back of the Guzzi. No sign of a feed bag on the grass. Can't decide if it complicates things or not.

'We'll go get it back,' says Mitch, wheeling his bike round.

'I'm coming,' says Jaz, struggling to get his boots on.

Wayne gives him his helmet back and gets a spare from the bus. I remember what Lizzie said about Jaz staying out of fights, but I reckon it's his bike and if there's four of us no one should get hurt. Wayne gets on behind me, Jaz behind Mitch. I tell Wayne about the feed bag as we bump up the field and he says, 'Uhuh,' like he's got to ponder it too.

We go to Tredegar first, the back mountain way. The way you'd go if you'd nicked a big spiteful bike and needed some easy miles to get used to it, then up into town, round the clock tower, and cruise the streets a while. See a couple of kids on Yams and ask them if they've seen a big Guzzi with two up, but they say they haven't.

We stop in a lay-by the north end of town to decide where to go next. Jaz nods towards the Heads of the Valleys road up ahead and says they'll go for a thrash, definite, they won't be able to resist it. 'Bet they total it,' he moans.

'Which way d'you reckon?' I say. 'Merthyr or Aber?'

'Merthyr,' says Wayne. Jaz and Mitch nod. Aber way the boys'd be heading back on themselves.

We eat up the miles for five minutes or so. Big bare road, the Heads, flattened spoil heaps either side, no trees, no hedges to hide behind. Then, up at Dowlais Top, just before the road sweeps wide of Merthyr, we get lucky. There's a garage at the roundabout and on the forecourt there it is, the Guzzi, and beside it, two lads in helmets. But it's not as lucky as it could be, because parked in front of the Guzzi there's a cop car, and standing by the lads, two flat-top coppers. And shit, the feed bag's still strapped to the Guzzi.

We slow right down to enter the forecourt and park the bikes a distance away. The cops have seen us and we don't want them nervous, so after we've propped the bikes we take our helmets off. I lay a hand on Jaz, to stop him rushing over and saying too much. If the cops know the Guzzi's stolen, and the boys tell them why, it could be in a lock-up for months while they argue about it.

Wayne's thinking the same; as we walk over he hisses, 'Don't mouth off about nothing, right?'

The cops wave us to a halt a few yards from the boys. They don't want us mixing with them till they've sussed us out. I'm trying to see what the lads look like under their helmets, in case we need to find them later.

'What d'you boys want?' one of the coppers asks. He's a big red-haired fella. I recognise him, we've met him before.

'That bike's a friend of ours,' says Wayne, smiling at him easy. 'Just come to see how it's doing.'

The copper stares at us. Not unfriendly-like, just letting his mind tick. I look past him to the feed bag. Feet and head and guts… it's been a hot day…

The copper's eyes settle on Jaz. A moment registering the bruises. Then, 'You,' he says. 'You're Jason Williams, aren't you?'

'Yep,' agrees Jaz.

'This your bike?' He gestures towards the Guzzi.

'Yep,' says Jaz.

'You give these boys permission to ride it?'

Jaz takes a while to think about this. Then shrugs. 'Maybe.'

'That's what they say. That you said they could take it.'

'We said a spin,' I say quickly, before Jaz can foul things up. 'Not all day.'

'So you want it back, right?' The copper's voice says he doesn't believe us, he knows it's nicked, but he's not going to push it.

'Yeah,' says Jaz, after catching my eye. 'May as well.'

'OK,' says the copper, stepping back. 'You take it across to the others. Then you lads go home, right? That's thataway.' He points back the way we've come.

We all smile and say, 'Sure,' and 'Right,' like we're not going to cause him any trouble. As Jaz walks over to the Guzzi I call out, 'Give the boys their bag. They'll be wanting that.'

It takes a second for the Tredegar boys to grasp what we're talking about. Then they glance at each other quick. They don't know how to play it. Hope they're as stupid as they look. Jaz unstraps the feed sack from the grab bar.

'Shit,' he says, acting indignant as he lifts it off. 'You've scratched the paintwork, what d'you want to tie this on here for?'

The red-haired copper narrows his eyes at the lads. He's picked up their confusion, but hasn't read it right. 'What you got in there, boys?' he asks.

Jaz drops the bag on to the concrete. It hits the ground with an interesting squelch.

'It's not ours,' one of the lads says, but it comes out rushed, and even I don't believe him. Jaz says, 'Well, it weren't here this morning,' as if it's nothing to him, and dusts his hands off.

As the red-haired copper squats down to the bag his mate stabs a finger at Jaz. 'Now hoppit,' he says.

We don't need telling twice. Reckon we've got about five seconds. We race over to the bikes and start them up quick, to drown out any shouts, and don't look round as we fasten our helmets. Just a peek back as we roar out of the forecourt. The bag's standing upright and open on the concrete. One of the lads has got a hand to his belly, the other's turned away, pinching his nose. The red-haired copper's on walkabout, arm across his mouth. Wish I had a camera.

We have to take it easy back to the field, we're laughing so much. Wayne keeps hitting my shoulder with his helmet. 'Oh, shit,' he keeps gasping, almost knocking me off the bike. Jaz is arsing around on the Guzzi, circling all the roundabouts twice, punching the sky like he's taking victory laps. Mitch sheepdogs us at the rear, lights blazing, grinning all over his face.

And when we get back, the bonfire's lit, and Pete's got the tup spitted above it. We can smell roast lamb from the top of the field. Everyone jumps up as they see the Guzzi and suddenly it's a celebration, not a wake. The start of a magic night: stories to tell, evidence to eat, cops to watch out for, and scores even. Best barbecue for years.

WANTING TO BELONG

Mike Jenkins

Hiya! I'm Gary Crissle and this is my story, well some of it. I know my name sounds like rissole and rhymes with gristle, but if you're smirking you wouldn't if you saw me, cos I'm pretty solid, as they say round Cwmtaff. I've got boxer's muscles and I'm tall as a basketball star.

Gary is short for Gareth. I like Gary because it's more cool. Gareth sounds a bit naff, though it makes me more Welsh. It wasn't like a passport when I first came to Cwmtaff though. It didn't matter to them.

I got Gareth from my mam, who comes from here originally. She's small and blonde and nothing like you'd picture a typical Welsh woman to be. She met my dad at a disco in Cambridge. It must've been dark cos he isn't exactly John Travolta. More like John Revolter, I'd say!

The Crissle comes from my dad of course, and isn't the only thing he's lumbered me with. There's my teeth, which stick out like a cartoon rabbit, though my brace has trained them down recently. The first month at Pencwm Comp, I had it on. Imagine being from England and having an iron mouth as well. The stick I got was beyond. I never told anybody the name of the village I'm from, as it would give them more ammunition. It's called Horseheath. They'd have me born in a cowpat! So Cambridge was enough for me. When people talk about racism, I know it isn't all black and white.

(I'm writing now when I can. There's a terrible routine to my life, but it helps to get things down.)

It seems that Mark Rees was behind most of it. Sparky they called him. He was a small, scrawny boy into everything he shouldn't have been. Most kids in my class worshiped him, while most teachers couldn't stand him.

Sparky loathed me from the start. He was always nicking my bag and hiding it, so in the end I stopped bringing one to school. He got the others to go 'Oo arr! Oo arr!' whenever I read in class and even called me 'A posh twat' which is a joke cos my accent is real country, though I've picked up some Cwmtaff recently.

The crunch came when Sparky and his gang decided to jump me on my way home. He didn't like the way I was friendly with the teachers. He thought I was a crawler, a grass, but I never meant anything. I just wanted to belong.

Well, my mam was working all hours and my dad's job at Hoover's was under threat. Things were very strained in my house and I snapped at school that day. Although I'm strapping I'm not a troublemaker, but Mark Rees pushed me too far.

We had this supply teacher with a fancy voice, who was also from England. I felt sorry for him but couldn't sit there like a stuffed parrot while our set played up. He tried to make contact when he heard me, and I replied to be polite.

'Who do you support?'

'Cambridge United. They're great!'

'Oo're they? Oo're they? Oo're they?' Sparky started up a chant that all his mates copied and the poor wimpy supply screamed 'SHUT UP!' as sweat leapt from his face.

I lost my head. I clutched the paper in front of Sparky (with only the drawing of a magpie on it), crumpled it up and rammed it into his gob.

'Out!' yelled the supply, 'both of you. Out!'

I suppose he thought he was being fair, but what happened

after was that a Deputy, Mr Lloyd, found us in the corridor mouthing and shoving each other, and he blamed Mark Rees cos he'd got a reputation worse than Ian Wright.

I didn't expect him to get revenge so soon. Him and his mates ambushed me in one of the alleys in Penôl estate, where we both lived. I didn't stand a chance against six of them, though I tried my best.

'Bog off back to bleedin' England!' Rees swore as he kicked me to the ground.

I made out I was hurt more than I was by yelling hell and this woman stuck her head over her fence to give off to Sparky's mob. They gobbed at her and left me blacker than a copper's uniform and bleeding like a beaten boxer. The woman was nice and offered me a cuppa. I told her no and stumbled home.

There were plenty in school who didn't go along with Sparky, who knew he'd end up going down or killing himself in some stolen car. But in my form he ruled like one of the Mafia. His word was law.

I began to really resent my mother for being Welsh and for dragging us back here. My younger brother in Year 7 seemed to be having it easy though, cos he was sickeningly good at everything. He was called Ryan and was a left-winger and they nicknamed him 'Giggsy'.

I wanted to impress upon Sparky and the boys that I wasn't a swot. As my schoolwork went downhill faster than a freewheeling pushbike, my mam got a warning letter home. She threatened to ground me for at least a month that evening.

'I ain't staying in!'

'Go to yewer room, Gary!'

'I 'ate this crappy town and I wanna get back so I can see United every 'ome game. It's your fault!'

'Yewr dad'll 'ammer yew when 'ee gets 'ome. Now do as yew're tol'!'

'Naff off woman!'

I slammed out and ran for my freedom. I ran towards town through streets which were carbon copies. I ran past the bus-shelter where Siân Jones and her friends stood smoking. I liked Siân, but the girls she bothered with bugged me no end.

"Ey Gary, wha's up? Runnin from Sparky agen?' They cackled like demented chickens. Siân looked on, sad.

I didn't have a clue where I was going. All I ever did in the evening was have a kick around with Ryan and his friends. I thought of getting on a bus or train, but I was skint.

(Listen, I've got to go now and leave this for a while. Unfortunately, there are things to be done. Lights to be put out. Promise I'll be back.)

Anyway, what did I do? I carried on striding down High Street, till I heard this familiar voice calling out—'Gary! Gazza!'

Gazza? Was it really referring to me?

And there, sitting on a bench was Sparky, ready for the taking if I'd been in the mood. He was a tiny ant without his gang: could easily be stamped on. I crossed over to him, more out of curiosity than anything. His eyes were glassy and he giggled for no reason. I could see how other kids were attracted to his cheeky eyes.

'All right? Where's the rest then?'

'Revisin f'the exams, o' course.' I could see he was talking bull cos of his grin. "Ow come yew're down yer. Not yewer scene.'

'I've 'ad enough. I'm runnin' away!' Strangely, I found myself speaking like him.

'This is-a cheapest way t'excape, Gary.'

He took out a carrier bag from under the bench and offered it. It contained a flagon. Sparky was a real alkie.

'What is it, meths?'

'Scrumpy Jack. On'y the 'ard stuff. Knock it back!'

He was standing now and practically pouring it down my throat. Before I knew it we were exchanging swigs and strutting through town. 'Lookin' f'action,' Sparky said, though it was deserted as a wet winter Sunday.

'Don' worry Gaz, there's always one fuckin' plank-'ead!'

I didn't know what he was on about, but the Scrumpy was doing its business and I was travelling far enough without spending a thing. I liked the way Sparky had changed towards me, though I couldn't fathom why. Maybe it was the booze. If so, I didn't want to be around when he got a hangover.

As we passed the taxi-rank and the station, he was babbling away like he did in lessons.

'Gary, yew carn 'elp bein' English. Listen! I really liked the way yew stuffed tha' paper down my gob. Yew got style. We could be a team.'

He began to sound like some gangster film. Nothing seemed real till we reached the rough and ready car park near the railway line. Then he spotted something and flung the bag into a tangle of weeds.

'Looks as if someone's missed theyr train from Cardiff.'

His baseball cap was a buzzard's beak, as he clawed in his jeans pocket. What he'd noticed in the distance was one particular car, not a new job, but an Escort GT all the same. I could make that out and I was no expert.

When he took out a screwdriver I was dead scared. In fact, I was nearly shittin' my boxers! The cider hadn't made me bold enough, but I couldn't let on or Sparky would spread it round school faster than teletext. Instead, I made out I was a professional.

''Ow about goin' fer a better one?' I suggested, hoping he'd be diverted.

'No way, Gazza. This one's got no bells. Yew int scared, 're yew?' He stared, grin gone, eyes full of purpose.

'No way! Let's go for it then!'

'Yew wan-oo?' He held out the screwdriver.

'No thanks. You're the best, Sparky. Everybody says.'

I thought of legging it rapidly, but before I could say 'Here come the cops!' he was into the Escort and he even had a key.

'C'mon, Oo Ar ol' son! Le's mule!'

He called me Oo Ar pleasantly now. I felt accepted. As soon as I sat in the passenger seat he put his foot down and screamed away like the cops were chasing us already. I belted up, but didn't feel exactly safe. Joy riding's definitely not the word for it. I'd call it 'mental muling', except I'm not sure what that means.

He drove like a boy possessed, taking the roundabout by the Labour Club almost on two wheels. We flew under the railway bridge and out of town. The cider wore off in seconds. I knew he was more than half gone and though he handled the car like a bucking bronco, I could still see us getting thrown.

'Jus' drop me off at 'ome fer a change of pants!' I gasped.

Luckily, the road was deserted as town had been. Everything was fast forward and my hands fumbled the dashboard for a hold button.

'Where we goin', Sparky?' I asked, trying to sound super cool.

'Oo knows? An oo fuckin' cares!'

Then he lifted both hands and I closed my eyes and—

(Interruptions! There are always people poking their noses in here. I'll start my story again when I can. But with all the commotion going on I don't know when.)

I opened them and we were on the slip road overtaking a lorry. Sparky was yelping and laughing his head off at me.

'I cun smell summin, Gaz, an' it int the engine burnin'!'

'Now what? The cops are bound to find out an' I'll be for it. My dad'll murder me!'

'Right! Jes round Asda's roundabout, through McDonald's fer a burger an 'en ram-raid a gypo camp.'

'No way, Sparky, there'll be a huge great security barrier.'

'I 'ate em!'

'What? Security barriers?'

'Na, gyppos! Worse 'an the English! No offence like.'

He sped round Blaenmorlais top and back downhill again. I saw a white car along the Heads of the Valleys which could've been the police.

'Spark! Look! I'm sure I saw the cops!'

'I'll go up Bogey Road. We'll lose em tha way.'

He took a sharp left and I had to admire his skill. It was a Grand Prix to him.

'Better 'an shaggin, eh? Even with Siân!'

Suddenly, it was all ugly. I noticed the glint in his eyes when he mentioned her. I wondered what the hell I was doing in a stolen car with a boy whose gang had only recently jumped me. I didn't belong here either. He drove frantically towards the unofficial gypsy camp with its wooden fence. My dad had driven past once and my mam told me about it.

He swerved into the entrance and I instantly made a grab for the wheel. He jammed on the brakes, skidded and we hit the fence and a man standing just behind it. He fell with the impact as the car stopped.

Sparky reversed and accelerated up the hill, yelling a series of curses at me. Now he was truly mad and veered off the road onto the moors, our headlights picking out fleeing sheep and small ponies trying to gallop away.

''Orsemeat f' supper, Gary? Yew 'aven 'ad Siân 'en, I take it? Yew mus' be the on'y one!'

The Escort rose, then dipped wildly into a pit. My body jerked like a fit. I couldn't see! Sparky shouted so loudly and painfully it razored my nerves. The car was motionless. I could feel damp spreading. I daren't open my eyes this time. I wanted to wake up somewhere else: at home, in comfort, by the telly. I wanted to rewind the tape and delete what had happened since I met Sparky.

Everything was frighteningly quiet. I kept on seeing that man we'd knocked over like a wooden pole, maybe lying dead.

If only I hadn't touched the wheel. Then I imagined Sparky and Siân Jones at it in the back of a car like this, and dared open my eyes again.

My jeans were blood-soaked. It was on my hands. I wasn't cut. Where was the blood...? Sparky embraced the steering wheel. His head was deeply cut. I whispered 'Sparky' and shook him. No reply. His face was deathly white. I panicked. Releasing the belt, I staggered out. I stumbled back along the direction I thought we'd come, tripping over clumps of reed. Surely the road wasn't far? Luckily, it was a clear night. I swore and swore at Mark Rees, for every step a different word. I nearly crossed the road without realising it. A pile of tipped rubbish told me it was there. I followed it downwards and heard ahead another voice of panic, echoing mine.

I'd have to pass that camp and they could kill me, but it was my only chance of getting help. Maybe Sparky could be saved. I didn't know if I wanted him to be, but I'd have to try.

What could I tell them? What convincing story? I groped in the dark for one.

In the end, I didn't have a chance to explain. As I trudged towards the ramshackle camp among what looked like old waste-heaps, all I could hear was—'Look yer's one! Quick, grab 'im!'

Before I knew it a horde of youths and children were coming for me. I went on, shouting "Elp, 'elp! I need an ambulance, quick!'

There must've been blood on my face as well, cos they held back from attacking me. The young men grabbed my arms, the children my jeans, as if making a citizen's arrest and marched me towards a battered old van, parked over our skid marks. Among cries of revenge like 'Give 'im a boot in the goolies!' I noticed how one man, who was holding open the back doors of the van, managed to pacify them.

'Sure he's hurt. Leave him be!'

His voice was authority. I was chucked like a sack of coal into the back alongside the old man we'd knocked over, who lay groaning between two rolls of carpet. My head hit a sharp jutting edge of metal and began to bleed. I welcomed the pain. I deserved it. Absurdly, I began to wish I'd been injured more seriously.

'It wasn't me! I wasn't drivin'!' I explained pathetically to the man who drove the van, who'd saved me from the mob.

(I can hear someone coming. I'm going to tell those kids to 'Bog off or I'll kick your 'eads in!')

It's later now and I'll tell you what happened. Bri, my Care Assistant came in. He saw me writing.

'Good news, Gar... Oh, sorry! Wha's this then? Yew doin' 'omework? I don' believe it!'

I rolled up this paper hurriedly, holding it tight, in case he decided to investigate. I've got a lot of time for him, but he does want to know everything.

'It's nothin', Bri. Jus' letters, tha's all.'

'OK! Anyway,' he says, eyeing me suspiciously, 'yewer parents want yew back an' I think there's a really good chance of it 'appenin... everyone knows yew've done yewer time in yer. T' be 'onest, it woz an' 'ard deal in the first place.'

Brian put his hand on my shoulder and I had to swallow hard to keep down the tears. I squinted into the mirror and observed myself, thin and puny, for the first time genuine. Perhaps I should change my story? I wanted to hug him and tell him I'd never do anything like it again, but I couldn't be so soft even in my own room with no one watching.

'Thanks, Bri,' I said, thinking of Sparky half dead in hospital and with a chair-bound future ahead of him, and of others like him who'd go from probation, to fines, to prison.

I thought of that old gypsy in his grimy, cast-off suit rattling agony in the van, each moan my guilt. I thought of his family who forgave me while I sat with them all night, willing the monitor to keep on bleeping his life.

I'll end it now, though I'm sure there are bits I've left out. Do I belong more in Cwmtaff? Well, I know where I don't belong that's for sure.

MAMA'S BABY
(PAPA'S MAYBE)

Leonora Brito

Two summers ago, just after I'd turned fifteen, my mother
got ill. One night in our flat on the twelfth floor, she held
her face in both hands and said, 'Leisha, I'm sure I got
cancer!'

'Just so long as you haven't got AIDS,' I said, and carried
on munching my tacos and watching the telly. The tacos
were chilli beef'n jalapeño. Hot. Very hot. With a glistening
oily red sauce that ran down my chin as I spoke.

'AIDS?' I remember her voice sounded bewildered.
'What're you talking about, AIDS? How the hell could I
have AIDS?' She grabbed at my shoulder. 'I'm an
agoraphobic, I don't hardly go out…'

I took my eyes away from the television set and stared
at her face. Then I just busted out laughing. I couldn't help
myself. I was almost choking. Loretta looked at me as if
she didn't know me. As if I belonged to somebody else.
'J-O-K-E,' I said, catching my breath and wiping my chin.
'*Laugh, Muvver!*' But she couldn't do that, laugh. Even
when I spelt it out for her. 'Like, AIDS'n agoraphobia –
they're mutually exclusive, right? So you haven't got it Lol,
have you?' She still didn't laugh. She couldn't laugh or be
brave or anything like that, my mother Loretta.

All she could do was hit me with a slipper and call me

319

stupid. 'Orr, Mama!' I rubbed at my arm, pretending to be hurt. 'You can't take a joke, you can't.'

'No, it's no jokin' with you.' Loretta got angry as she looked at me. 'You're gunna bring bad luck on people you are,' she said. 'With your laughin' an jokin'!'

Bring bad luck by laughing? Such stupidness, I thought, in my own mother. Then I noticed how her body kept shivering as she sat there, squashed into the corner of our plush red settee. And how she couldn't keep her hands still, even though they were clamped together tight. So tight, that the knuckle bones shone through. 'Cancer's a bad thing, Aleisha.' My mother shook her head from side to side, and started to cry. 'A bad thing!'

'Orr Mama, you talks rubbish, you do.' She looked at me through streaming eyes. 'How do I?' she said. 'How do I talk rubbish?'

I shrugged. 'You just do.'

I remembered what she'd said about tampons. Loretta said tampons travelled twice round the body at night, then lodged in your brain. Fact. Even the nuns in school laughed at that one. They said what my mother told me was unproven, unscientific and an old wives' tale. Stupidness!

Now Loretta was sitting there, crying and talking about cancer. I wished she'd stop. The crying made her dark eyes shine like windows, when the rain falls on them at night. There was light there, but you couldn't see in. Not really. It was like staring into the blackness of outer space. And it made me mad.

'Look, why don't you just stop crying,' I said, adopting a stern voice, a mother's voice. A sensible voice. 'And get to the doctor's first thing tomorrow morning and see about yourself?'

Loretta looked at me and hiccuped. Then she started crying again. Louder than before. 'Just phone Joe,' she said through her sobs. 'Phone that boy for me, Leish. I want that boy with me.'

'Okey-dokey.' I took another big mouthful of taco and chewed callously. It was out of my hands now. Now Loretta had asked for Joe. Let Joe deal with it. I stood up. 'Where's your twenty pence pieces then?'

I went off to the call box with the taste of Mexican takeaway still in my mouth. Joe was out with the boys, so I left a message with Donna, who was full of concern. 'Is it serious?' she said.

'Nah.' I burped silently into the night as the tacos came back to haunt me. 'It's not serious,' I said. 'But you know Loretta.' My nostrils burned and my eyes filled up with water. 'You knows my mother, once she gets an idea into her head...'

Donna laughed brightly and said not to worry. She'd tell Joe as soon as he came in. 'Yeah, tell him,' I said. Raising my voice as the time ran out and the pips began to bleep. 'Though it's probably nothing. Something an' nothing. Knowin' her.'

I was wrong of course. I was wrong about everything under the sun and under the moon. But what did I know? I was fifteen years old that summer, and mostly, I thought like a child.

Like when I was six, nearly seven, I found a big blue ball hidden in the cupboard of the wall unit. I brought the ball out and placed it on the floor. Then I tried to step up and stand on it. I fell off, but I kept on trying. Again and again and again. All I wanted to do was to stand on the big blue ball that had misty swirls of white around it. Like the swirls I'd seen on satellite pictures of planet earth.

When I finally managed it – arms outstretched and my feet successfully planted, I felt like a conqueror. A six-year-old conqueror. 'Orr look at this!' I yelled at Joe. 'Look Joe, look!' I stayed upright for another dazzling moment. Then the ball rolled under me and I fell backwards, screaming as my head hit the floor. Loretta came out of the bathroom with a face pack on. She silenced me with a slap. Then she took the comic Joe was reading and threw it in the bin. 'Naw, Ma,' said Joe. 'That's my *Desperate Dan* that is.'

'Too bad,' said Loretta. 'Maybe it'll teach you to look after this kid when I tell you!'

Joe laid his head down on the pine-top table, sulking, while I sat on the edge of our scrubby, rust-red carpet and hugged my knees. I wasn't worried about Joe getting into trouble on account of me. All I was worried about was the ball. The beautiful blue ball. More than anything in the world I wanted it back.

But Loretta had snatched the ball away from me and was holding it up to the light. Palming it over and over in her hands. As if she was searching for something. But what? What magical thing could she be searching for? I watched the ball turn blue under the light bulb. Then not so blue, then *bluer* again. And it came to me in flash – that what my mother was doing was remembering.

But remembering what? Her creamy face was cracking into brown, spidery lines as she looked at the ball. And I got up on my knees, wanting to see more.

'*Bug-eyes!*' Joe leaned down from the corner of the table and hissed at me. 'Fathead,' he said. 'You boogalooga bug-eyed fathead!' Joe's words put a picture inside my head that made me cry. I opened my mouth and bawled until Loretta turned round. Her face had stopped cracking, and she looked ordinary. 'Joe!' she said, 'how old are you for god's sake? Tormentin' that kid. She's younger than you.'

'She's a *alien*,' said Joe.

'Oh don't be so bloody simple!' Loretta looked across the room at me. 'She's your sister.' Joe shook his head. 'She's *not* my sister.' He kicked at the leg of the table with his big brown chukka boot. 'She's my *half*-sister,' he said.

I remember the words were hardly out of Joe's mouth before Loretta had reached him. 'Half?' she said. 'Half?' She started bouncing the big blue ball upside his head. 'Who taught you half? I didn't give birth to no halves!'

Loretta was mad at Joe. So mad she kept banging the ball against his head. As if she was determined to knock some sense in. Until Joe (who was twelve, and big for his age) lifted his big chubby arms in front of his face and yelled at her. 'Get off've me! Fuckin' get off've me. Right!'

I was scared then. I thought Joe was in for a hiding. The mother and father of a hiding. But something strange happened, Loretta suddenly upped and threw the ball away from her – just threw it, as if she was the one who was hurt. And as soon as she let the ball go, wonder of wonders, Joe burst into tears and pushed his head against her belly. Sobbing out loud like a baby, saying, 'It's not fair! It's not fair!' And asking her over and over again as she cwtched him, 'How come *my* father never brought *me* no presents, Ma? How come?'

Poor Joe! I sat in the middle of our scrubby red carpet happily hugging the big blue ball to myself. I realised now that I was luckier than Joe. My *half*-brother Joe. And quicker than Joe and cleverer than Joe – even though I looked like a *alien*. Joe was like Loretta. I looked across the room at them, across the scrubby, rust-red carpet, which suddenly stretched out vast and empty as the red planet Mars.

'You takes after *my* family,' Loretta was telling Joe. 'You takes after *me*.' I felt a pang, but it didn't matter. I had the blue ball – which was big enough to stand on, like planet earth. A special ball, bought for me specially, by a strange and wonderful person called *my dad*!

Of course, *my dad* was always more of an idea than anything else. I never saw my real dad when I was a kid. But I clung to the idea of him. In the same way that I clung to an image of myself at six, triumphantly balancing on a blue, rolling ball. They were secret reminders of who I really was. I held on to those reminders even more when Loretta was diagnosed as having cancer. They helped me keep my distance. And I needed to keep my distance, because once the hospital people dropped the big C on her for definite – cancer of the womb (Intermediary Stage) things got scary. And while Joe tried to pretend that nothing terrible was happening, or would happen, I knew better. And I made sure I kept my distance from the start.

Like when Loretta had to travel back and forth to the Cancer Clinic for treatment. Joe asked if I'd go with her. 'Sometimes,' he said, 'just to keep her company?'

'I can't,' I said. 'I've got tests coming up in school.'

'Tests?' Joe looked at me gone off. 'Tha' Mama's sick,' he said. 'She needs someone with her. I can't go myself cuz I'm in work.' His jaw tightened.

'I've got a biology test coming up, I said. And maths and history...'

'Oh leave it Joe,' said Loretta. 'I'm all right!' She laughed, 'I'll manage.' Joe umm'd and ah'd a bit, then he gave in.

'If you're sure, Ma,' he said. Hiding a little smile, I picked up my biology textbook, *The Language of the Genes*, and began taking seriously detailed notes.

I never did go with Loretta to the Cancer Clinic. Though I could have made time, if I'd wanted. Academic work was easy for me, I enjoyed reading books and doing essays. And tests were almost a doddle. But at home I began making a big thing of it. Hiding behind the high wall of 'my schoolwork' and 'my classes' and my sacrosanct GCSEs, which I wasn't due to sit until the following year anyway.

I also let it be known that I had to go out, nights. Most nights, otherwise I'd turn into a complete mental brainiac.

So when Loretta arrived home weak and vomiting from the radium treatment, I'd already be standing in front of the mirror, tonging my hair, or putting on eye make-up. No need to ask where I was going. I was off out, to enjoy myself. Even though enjoying myself meant drinking (alcopops) and smoking, and hanging with the crowd. All the stuff I used to describe as 'too boring and predictable' for anyone with half a brain. Now though, it was different. Now I became best mates with a hard-faced, loud-mouthed girl called Cookie, who Loretta said was 'wild'.

The euphemism made me smile as I rushed around the kitchen filling the kettle and making the tea to go in the flask. I was happy and focused on what I had to do, knowing that the sooner Loretta was settled, the sooner I'd be out through the door.

Luckily, there was no need to bother with food. Loretta couldn't swallow any food. Only Complan. And Complan made her vomit. So she stuck to tea. Weak tea, and sometimes, a couple of mouthfuls of tinned soup. Which I did think was sad, because my mother was a big woman who'd always enjoyed her food.

Now, she hardly ever went in the kitchen, and it wasn't worth bothering to try and tempt her with anything. But I brought her a cup of tea, and handed it over. And I put the flask on the little table next to the couch.

Taking a couple of sips of tea seemed to exhaust her. And she laid her head back on the cushions, tired, but not too tired to speak. 'This girl Cookie...' she said.

'Yeah?' By now I'd gone back to the mirror and my mascara.

'I don't like the idea of you runnin' round with her.' Loretta pursed her lips. 'That girl's trouble,' she said. 'That girl's hot!' I was watching Loretta's face in the mirror. Her face and my face, side by side. It was eerie seeing us together. Like watching night turn into day or day turn into night. There was no resemblance between us. No real likeness that I could see. And it played on my mind. Who was she, I thought? This big woman lying on a plush red couch, with a green plaid blanket pulled up to her chin? I crossed over to the couch and looked at her, coldly. 'What're you talking about, hot?' I said. 'You're always going on about something.'

Loretta sighed. 'I just don't want you in no trouble,' she said. 'You nor Joe, come to that.'

'I'm not gunna be in any trouble!'

'No?' Loretta looked up at me and smiled. 'Well, God be good,' she said, 'let's hope it'll stay like that.'

'Listen,' I brought my face down close to hers and spoke slowly, deliberately. 'Cookie's ways, are not my ways, right?' My voice grew colder. 'Your ways, are not my ways...' Loretta stared at my face, as if she couldn't understand what I was saying. Then she took a gulp of tea and her eyes swam with tears.

'You little bitch,' she said. 'Anybody'd think I was a bad mother to h'yer you speak!' The sudden energy in her voice surprised me. And I tried to back away from what I'd started. But Loretta was on a roll. 'Did I get rid of you?' she said. 'Did I? No, I kept you. You and Joe. Even though I had no man behind me. And what's my thanks?' Her voice was angry as she spoke to me. Loud and angry. 'Shit is my thanks!'

I shrugged and tried to move away, but she started off again. ''Course, it'd be different if I was posh, wouldn't it?'

'Pardon?' I said.

'They gets rid of their kids in a minute. Don't they, posh women? When they wants to go to *college* or something.' Loretta looked up at the ceiling and laughed. 'An' no bugger ever says a word,' she said, disbelievingly. 'Not a bloody word!'

For some reason I found myself laughing along with her. Enjoying the unfairness of it all. Then she closed her eyes again, tired. 'Look, *get* if you're going,' she said. 'And don't be back yer late.'

When I reached the door, I turned to look at her. 'D'you want this light left on?'

'No, out it.' So I flicked the switch and left her there, in the dark.

It was always a big relief to me when Loretta was taken into hospital.

I was happy then, escorting her down to the waiting ambulance and handing her in. It felt as though we were celebrities, touched by a black and tragic glamour, as the neighbours rushed out of their flats and gave Loretta cards, and waved her off, like royalty.

Back inside, I always walked slowly past the lifts in the entrance hall. Then I'd whizz around the corner and start bounding up the stairs. Two at a time. All the way up to the twelfth floor.

The first few times Loretta went into hospital, I stayed with Joe and Donna in their little two-bedroomed house. But I didn't feel comfortable there. And when Loretta began to spend longer and longer as an inpatient, I told Joe I preferred to stay where I was, and keep an eye on the flat. Joe stuck out his jaw and said, 'If that's what you want, Aleisha. I'm not gunna argue.'

Which was just what I expected him to say. Though I hated him for saying it. After that, it wasn't difficult for me to ease my way out of things, bit by bit.

Whenever I made an appearance at the hospital, I was never on my own. I always came in with a crowd – usually Cookie and her sister, Cherry. Or Cookie and her new man friend, Wayne. I think they liked being with me, because I was fifteen years old and my mother was dying of cancer. It was like something off the telly that appealed to them.

Joe never came in on his own, either. He was always with Donna or one of his mates – usually Deggsie, or a caramel-coloured boy called Chip-chip, whose teeth were brown and white, like popcorn.

With so many young people around Loretta's bed, there was never any time for seriousness. All we could do was lark and joke about. Once, when they were fooling around, Joe and Chip-chip pressed down on the foot-pedals of the bed. Sending Loretta up in the air. And all she did was laugh and say, 'Put me down, boys! Put me down, people can see my old blue slippers under there.'

It was odd, standing under the bright hospital lights, watching Loretta laughing. And Joe laughing. All of us laughing, as if everything was right with the world. Loretta was queen of the show. She sparkled in company, which was the way she used to be, I suppose, when she was young and working in pubs as a barmaid.

One night, Joe and Donna came in carrying a bouquet of flowers between them.

Loretta didn't care much for the white chrysanthemums, but she was chuffed with the card: '*Happy memories, luv from R. (The Rover).*' R. was Royston, Joe's father. And he'd been on friendly speaking terms ever since Joe had left school, and met up with him again.

'Now he sends me the white bouquet,' said Loretta. 'Maybe he wants to marry me...' While we were laughing, Donna said soppily, 'Why didn't you marry him, Lol?'

'Marry Royston? Prrrrf!' Loretta's voice was derisive. 'He was no good, him, Royston.' She looked at us. 'I put his bags outside the door, didn't I? Comin' his little ways. I said goodbye, tara, I'm sorry – I needs my space!'

'Orr, my poor father! I bet you gave that man a hard time,' said Joe, laughing. I was in agonies in case anyone mentioned *my* father. But luckily the nurse came round, ringing the handbell so we had to go. Good job too, because I would have hated to hear Loretta start in on my dad.

As we were leaving, Joe leant over the bed and asked Loretta in a low voice, about her blood count. When she told him it was up a couple of points, Joe looked relieved. 'Good work Ma,' he said. And went off happily with Donna.

Joe never asked the doctors anything. He clung to his ignorance like a baby clinging to a bottle, and I despised him for it.

My own behaviour was more rational. Gradually, I dropped off going to the hospital on a regular basis. Telling everyone I was studying hard for my 'mocks'. Where we lived, no one understood about 'mocks' and when they were due. Instead, relatives and friends of my mother admired my determination in carrying on with my schooling. You keep it up girl, they said. You're makin' your mother proud!

No one, not even Joe seemed to realise what I was up to. Though I saw my mother less and less, I always made sure I phoned the hospital regularly. 'How is she?' I'd ask dutifully. And I'd end by saying, 'Please give her my love.'

But instead of studying, I spent my time lying on the old red couch where Loretta used to lay, dreaming about my life in the future. 'My dad' was somewhere out there, in the future. I knew his name (from my birth certificate) and that he'd cared enough about me to leave me a gift – the beautiful blue ball. These days, the blue ball looked like a sunken moon, stuck on top of the wall unit. But I treasured its memory, knowing that one day in the starry future, I'd meet my dad, and we'd talk about this gift he'd given me. Of course, we'd recognise each other instantly – my dad and I, because it was obvious to me, that his genes were the dominant genes in my make-up. They were there, encoded in the double helix of my DNA. How else could I account for me?

It was strange how pleasantly the time passed when I was thinking like this. Even when I did put in an appearance at school, I didn't let go of the daydreams. And when scary night times came around, I'd turn up the mattress on Loretta's bed, and fish out some notes. Then I'd go off with Cookie and the gang, drinking.

Not that I did much drinking, except for a couple of cans of *Hooch*. Three cans of *Hooch* and I was away. Floating. Doing stupid things. Once, I tried to walk around the side of a mirror in the pub toilets. I couldn't see that the toilet door was a reflection – and I kept banging my head on the faecal-coloured wall tiles, as I tried to go round it. The side of my head was swollen and smarting when I stopped.

'Leisha man you makes me piss!' said Cookie, laughing. 'You really do!' It crossed my mind to ask her why I was so funny. And why was she Cookie, and her sister Cherry, so cool? Both of them wore shiny auburn wigs, like supermodels. And they had the clothes. But Cherry was humungous in size. And Cookie wasn't much smaller. So how come they were cool?

I opened my mouth to ask – but I couldn't fit the words inside the moment. The moment just went by me. Pass. So I opened my mouth a bit wider, and started to laugh.

Coming home from a night out, I'd crash down on the old red couch and fall asleep, happy and floating. But in the morning, even before I was awake, I'd feel the weight of something miserable pressing down on me. My eyes would focus slowly, and I'd remember what it was.

Then one day, I woke up and saw a piece of blue sky through the window. I realised it was spring, and for some reason, that made me feel better. So I went and phoned Joe's house, to check up on hospital visiting times; and to see who was going in that night.

The minute she picked up the phone and heard my voice, Donna broke down in tears. 'Wassamarrer?' I said, suddenly fearful. There was a long snuffly silence. Then Donna managed to tell me what had happened. She said the consultant had called Joe up to the hospital and explained there was nothing more they could do. Treatment-wise, that was it. 'Oh, Leisha! I'm so sorry,' said Donna sobbing all over again. 'But there's no hope for her. There's no hope for Loretta!'

It sounded like the title of a book, the way she said it: 'No Hope for Loretta.' That was my first thought. Then I began to feel empty, as though a stone had dropped inside me. And I needed to sit down, but I couldn't because I was in a call box.

'How're we gunna tell her?' I said, helplessly.

'Oh don't you do anything,' said Donna, quickly. 'Leave it to Joe, Leish. Joe said he'll deal with it.' So feeling especially childish and helpless, I rang off.

I didn't do any of the things I might have done, like phone the hospital. Or actually go in and see my mother. Instead, on a sudden whim, I lifted the telephone book out of the cubbyhole and began flicking through its pages, idly at first, then with more attention. It was gone ten when I arrived in school. Calmly, I sat through classes until lunchtime. Then I picked up my bag and my jacket, and left.

Once out of the school gates I turned right, and onto the high road that ran past the school. I walked slowly, admiring the big solid houses, with their spacious lawns and double-garages. In this area where my school was, all the houses had names instead of numbers. And I said them to myself as I walked along: 'Hawthorns, Erw Lon, Primrose View, Ty Cerrig, Sovereign Chase…' names that were as anonymous as numbers, really. But I didn't mind. It was a lovely day, warm and sunny, and I kept looking up at the blue sky, marvelling at how beautiful a day it was.

When I came to a black and white gabled house, with a big front lawn and a wrought-iron gate marked Evergreen, I stopped. This was the place where the man who could be my dad lived. Blyden, D. H. I'd got the name out of the telephone directory that morning. It was almost the same as the one written on my birth certificate under father: 'David H. Blyden, O/S Student.' It could be him, I reasoned. It could be my dad, living here in a mock-Tudor house with mullioned windows. Loretta had never had much to say about him, except that he was quiet. But he had his little ways, she said, like they all do. Joe had whispered to me once, that my dad was from Africa. But would an African be living around here? Maybe, I thought, if he had money.

The detached house, like all the surrounding houses, was set well back from the road. And on one side there were no neighbours. Only a red-brick observatory and a fenced-in tennis court. It was all in keeping, I decided approvingly. Everything was so quiet, and cultivated and tasteful. Then, afraid someone might be watching from the window, I walked up onto the grassy bank, nearer the observatory, and sat down.

Now I could see the house from the side, facing the sun,

with the dark pine tree towering over it. The pine tree was striking. Its dark green branches seemed to flip out like arrows, right up into the blue sky. As though, I thought admiringly, they were aiming straight into the heart of heaven.

I wondered about my dad, living here. I wondered if he visited the observatory at night, to study the billions of stars in the universe? If he did, he'd understand just how little our lives were, compared to the vast infinity of outer space. Surely he would? He was the man who had given me the blue ball.

I don't know how long I sat there, dreaming and wondering in the sun.

I imagined my African dad, climbing the steps of the observatory, and looking out over the mysteriously empty ball court. Like a priest in ancient Mexico – except that we were in Wales. Our history class that morning had been about lost civilisations – which was a theory connecting Africa to ancient America and to ancient, Celtic Britain. *We were all connected*! I suppose that fed into my mind, and kept my thoughts turning over, magically.

It was late in the afternoon when I heard the sound of car wheels crunching over gravel. Someone was parking a car in front of the house. I got to my feet in a sudden panic. What if it was him, my dad, arriving home? My heart began to pound, and I felt sick. This could be him, I thought with wonder. This could be my dad! Involuntarily, I looked towards the house, and my courage began to waver. Could it be my dad, back there? It was possible, I knew it was possible, but was it probable?

No, I decided, suddenly. No! The sun had disappeared behind the clouds, making everything seem different. Devoid of magic, colder. I glanced up at the observatory, and was amazed to see its structure in a new cold light. Now it was revealed as squat and ugly. Shaped like a red-brick kiln against the sky. I looked again, and saw that its narrow windows or apertures were shuttered over with grey metal grilles. There was a padlock on the entrance door; and weeds were sprouting from the brickwork. The place was derelict!

And there was no mysterious ball court. Just an ordinary tennis court marked out with yellow lines, behind the trampled wire netting. Enough was enough. I swung my bag up over my shoulder, and started walking, fast. I didn't look behind me, not even for a last glimpse of *Evergreen*, with its lonesome pine tree standing dark and arrow like against the sky.

Of course, running away like that allowed me to keep on dreaming. And even before I was halfway home, I'd begun to reassemble my defences. After all, nothing had happened. I could always go there again, I reasoned. Not straightaway, but one day. When I was ready. The choice was mine...

By the time I stepped out of the lift on the twelfth floor, I was actually smiling. It was fun trying to picture myself living with my dad, in a big gabled house, a wrought iron gate and a plaque on the front, marked *Evergreen*.

I was still smiling as I put the key in the lock and gave the door a push. When it swung open, I almost collapsed. Loretta was framed in the doorway, wrapped in a red velvet dressing gown, staring at me. 'Ullo stranger,' she said, in a croaky voice. 'Wassamarrer with you, seen a ghost?'

Inside the living room I was surprised to see how everything had been changed round. The old red couch had been pushed to one side and Loretta's bed had been brought in and placed against the wall. I didn't see Joe at first, hunkered down by the little table, fixing a plug on the lamp. When I did see him, I gave a sigh of relief. 'Oh Joe!' I said, 'you're here!' Joe nodded over his shoulder at me, and carried on with what he was doing.

I watched Loretta move slowly across the room. Twice she had to stop and retie the belt on her dressing gown, as it came undone. Then very gingerly and carefully, she lowered herself onto the edge of the bed, and looked at me. I was terrified. 'What're you doing home?' I said, in a rush. 'I didn't know you were coming home...' Loretta began to laugh. 'She wants to know what I'm doing home, Joe,' she said, looking over her shoulder at him. 'Shall we tell her?'

'Uh, Ma?' said Joe. Too busy screwing a light bulb into the lamp it seemed, to pay much attention. But Loretta didn't need his support. Instead, turning back to me with her dark eyes shining, she leaned forward and whispered, 'I'm home because I'm cured! Ain' I Joe?' she sang out loudly. 'Ain' I cured, almost?'

At that moment, Joe clicked the switch on the table lamp. Throwing a soft, glowing light over everything. Including our faces. 'There!' he said, turning round at last. 'Sixty watts so it won't burn.' He grinned. 'That's better, ain' it?'

A week later I ran away from home, and two days after that, my mother died. I suppose there was something inevitable about the way those two events were linked. But it didn't seem like that at the time.

That last week, I played along with Joe and Loretta as far as I could. What did I care? And on the Thursday night, when I'd had enough, I went out clubbing with Cookie and Cherry. It wasn't really clubbing. We ended up sitting in the Community Centre, because I was broke and Cookie announced, suddenly, that she was saving up for a white wedding.

I asked how much it would cost, a white wedding? 'Thousand pounds,' said Cookie, proudly. 'The dress alone'll set me back a couple a hundred.'

'Wow.'

'That's because she wants one that flows,' said Cherry.

'Yeah, that dress just gorra to be fl-o-w-i-n'!, man,' said Cookie, snapping her fingers and laughing.

I was troubled in mind, but I laughed along with them. Just to show willing. I even asked about the car. What sort of car would they be having? And Cookie said, 'One with wheels, preferably!' And while we were laughing at that, a man came over and asked if he could buy me a drink.

When I said no thanks, he walked away. All nice and polite and everything, but Cookie said I was simple.

'He had a fuckin' big gold ring on his finger!'

'Yeah,' said Cherry. 'And that twenny pound note he was flashing came off've a roll!'

'So?'

'So,' said Cookie, 'anybody'd think you won the lottery!'

For some reason, I lost my temper and started shouting. I told Cookie if I won the lottery, I'd buy *her* a friggin' ticket to Mars. 'And Joe,' I said loudly, 'I'd buy Joe a ticket to Mars, straight off!' Just then a hand tapped me on the shoulder, and I froze. Cookie and Cherry burst out laughing. They knew I thought it was Joe. But it wasn't Joe, when I turned round. Only his best mate, Chip-chip, wanting to say hello. Naturally he asked how my mother was, and I said fine. She's fine. Then Cookie and Cherry went off to the toilets, and Chip-chip pulled up a stool and sat down. He told me he was working part-time, now. In McDonald's, Mickey D's? 'But really,' he said, 'I'm a *player*.'

'A player?'

'Didn't Joe ever tell you?' he said. 'I plays basketball.'

'Oh, yeah,' I said, unenthusiastically, 'basketball!'

'Hey, don't say it like that,' said Chip-chip. He pulled a face at the way I said it, making me laugh. '*Barsketbawl!*'

'I didn't say it like that!'

'Yes you did,' said Chip-chip. 'Still, it's good to see you smiling, I like to see you smiling,' he said. And he went off and bought us both a soft drink, to celebrate.

'Well kiss to that!' said Cookie, coming back to the table half an hour later. 'Lemonade and no major money? An' having to listen to all that stuff about sport is fuckin' boring!' she said. I agreed. But I still thought it was nice for him. Having an interest like basketball. 'His little life is rounded by an O,' I said, half seriously. Then I laughed and got up to dance, when the man with the gold ring on his finger came over and asked me.

While I was dancing, someone tapped me on the shoulder. I looked round with a smile on my face, thinking it was Chip-chip.

But it was Joe. I shied away from him. But he raised his arm and brought his fist crashing down on my back, again and again. 'Where's your mother?' he said, as he punched me. 'I'll tell you where,' he said, punching me. 'She's in the hospital dying,' he said, punching me. 'And where are you? Out!' he said, punching me. 'Enjoyin' yourself!'

Joe only allowed Donna to grab hold of his arm when he'd finished. Then the two of them walked out of the Centre, arm in arm.

Most of the sympathy was on my side. People said Joe was taking everything out on me when I wasn't to blame. Neither of us was to blame, they said; and I knew it was true.

But still, I felt guilty. Before going out that night, I'd brought Loretta her cup of tea and her tablets, and watched her swallow them. Eyeing my outfit, she'd asked if I was going out? 'Yes, I'm going out,' I said, coldly. 'I can go out, can't I? *Now you're on the road to recovery...*'

Loretta didn't say anything after that. And I waited until the tablets knocked her out 'dead' as she always said, then I put on my coat and switched off the light; and left her. An hour or two later, Joe had called at the flat, and found her on the floor, haemorrhaging. I suppose our behaviour that night – mine and Joe's, was totally predictable.

A couple of days later, I left Cookie's house where I was staying, and went with her and Cherry to the hospital. Joe was sitting in the waiting room, munching french fries and KFC out of a carton. Neither of us spoke. Then Joe pushed the carton of chicken across the table, and told me to take some. I did. Then we both went in and sat with Loretta until she died.

Inside the cemetery most of the stones are black marble, with fine gold lettering. I like the homemade efforts best. The rough wooden crosses that you see here and there, with 'Mam' or 'Dad' painted on them in thick white letters.

Loretta has a cross like that, though we are saving up for a stone. Right now her grave has a blanket covering of long brown pine needles over it. Fallen from the pine tree overhead. There's a row of tall pines all along this side of the cemetery – and I see them differently now, depending on the season.

It's late spring and the sky is blue and the sun is shining. Looking up at the patch of blue, through the pines, I notice the little wooden pine cones, tucked beneath the brush of feathery green branches. 'Like little brown eggs,' I say to Chip-chip as we walk away. Chip-chip says it takes two years for these pine cones to mature and fall, as they're doing now, all around us as we walk. Two years! I think to myself, well, that must be about right.

'Hey! Frank Sinatra's dead,' says Chip-chip, as we reach the exit gate. 'Is he?' I say without thinking. 'Then his arse must be cold.' At first, Chip-chip is shocked, then he starts to laugh. 'That's your mother talkin' that is,' he says. 'That's Loretta!'

'Yeah,' I say looking at him and smiling. 'I think it is!'

SOME KIND
o' BEGINNIN

Mike Jenkins

The sound o' voices rises from-a street. More banterin' 'an arguin', but it still brings back tha' night. There's too many thin's remind me. Ev'ry time I see Dave on telly playin' fer-a- the Jacks. Ev'ry time I go out to a club (though tha' int often nowadays) an' there's a barney.

Puttin' on my face, layer 'pon layer, I carn 'elp thinkin' 'ow she must afta dollop it on t' cover over wha' I done. An' there by my mirror is-a cuttin. People might think I'm sick or summin, but I jest don' wanna forget. It's a warnin: NEVER AGEN!

Wish I wuz goin' out with them girls. Theyer jokin pierces-a glass an' ruffles-a curtains. A whool gang of 'em I bet, like we woz in Merthyr: me, Nadine, Andrea an Jayne (with a 'y' don' forget, she'd always say).

I long fer theyer voices now goin' up an' down like-a mountains an' valleys.

Funny tha', it's flatter down yer an-a way 'ey talk ave got the same music to it some'ow.

Mascara, face cream... 'owever much I put on, I could never be like 'er. My teeth stick out in funny ways an' I got ooded eyelids like my dad wuz an owl or summin. I light up a fag an' burn an 'ole jest above 'er ead. I 'member wha ee once said, 'Martine, I'm sorry t' tell yew, but yewer breath's mingin'… yew should try an' give up.' But all 'em months in the Centre I needed 'em so much. I'll never stop now, not even if I seen im agen.

The thin's the papers said, an mostly true, I know. But oo cun understand all-a-goadin'? All-a-gangin up an' pickin' on me er friends done? It woz like Cardiff 'gainst-a Jacks, we all knew it wuz gunna go off sometime, but no one spected I would make it 'appen.

I blow smoke at 'er picture. The 'eadlines blur. I yer my flatmate Chrissie come in from work: tidy job in-a travel agents, all dolled up. She's like me, tryin' t' make a new life. She've 'ad 'n 'ard time, brought up in-a 'Omes. Carn understand 'ow she's so sorted though. TV on, cuppa tea next…

'Hey Martine! D'you wanna cuppa?'

'No ta, Chrissie! I'm off soon!'

She knows all 'bout me, but it don' bother 'er. She reckons er dad done worse thin's than tha' to 'er an' 'er mam.

Tha' bloody burn above 'er air looks like a friggin 'alo! I feel like askin' tha' photo once an' fer all, but instead I stub-a fag out on-a mirror, right where my teeth jut out comical.

Chrissie looks so relaxed in-a sittin' room when I enter, feet up an' sippin' away. As she turns 'er head, fer a moment she reminds me of 'er, tha' beaky nose an' pointy chin, but…

'Martine, you look great!' she says, an' I do feel ready t' face the world, even though I wan' more.

'Aye, but oo cares in tha' poncy 'otel?'

'Well, maybe you'll meet someone tonight. Some millionaire soccer star'll be passing through and propose to you over his lasagne!'

'Soccer star?'

'Oh… sorry Martine!'

I larf an' she wriggles in 'er chair an' echoes me. Soon it's S'long!' and 'Bye!' Me wonderin' 'ow she cun talk so posh with 'er background an' 'ave survived.

The streets o' Abernedd turnin' inta Merthyr by the second. Cack-jumpin an' spottin where yesterday's shops ewsed t' be. See-through windows replaced by-a environmentally-friendly sort, perfect fer graffiti an' posterin. Local bands like Panic Stations an The Pocket Billiards advertisin gigs. I woz inta football when my friends listened t' the Merthyr equivalents o' them. I woz turned on when Merthyr played the Jacks (Dave wern with em 'en) an stood with Dazzy an' the boys loathin an' chantin at them players an' losin' myself.

Wassa time? Shit! Four minutes late an moany ol cow Thorpe'll be bound t' dock me.

Car beeps me. Two boys in overalls, all over painty. Give 'em a V and see 'em mouthin' off at me.

There it is at bloody last, The Dog and Duck, Abernedd's finest, 3 star, AA. Looks real tidy from-a front an' all, but I could blow it open, wha' with ol' Thorpey an' 'is stingy ways... scrapin-a mould off of fruit an' tha' ol' can opener sheddin rust!

'Yer! Wha's this in my peas, waitress?'

'Oh, I believe it's some sort o' garnish, sir.'

When in doubt, call it garnish, tha's wha' ee tol' us t' say.

Just as I'm gaspin' fer a fag an' fumblin' in my pockets, Thorpey 'ops through-a door t' greet me.

'Martine, you're five minutes late again. It'll have to stop, Marteen!'

Sayin my name like I woz 'n alien. Feel sorry fer 'is missis, I do. Imagine 'im on top on the job... 'You've had your ten seconds heavy-petting, dear. Now we'd better hurry up and start breathing faster!'

'Marteen! Stop grinning and get ready, will you!'

Soon I'm all frilled up an' layin-a tables, all-a time chattin t' Michelle oo on'y jes started las' week an' oo keeps cockin' ev'rythin up. She's so nervous an' tryin t' please, but Thorpey give 'er so much jip when she wrote-a orders down wrong, she nearly give up on 'er first day. An' the bloke what 'ad steak 'n' kidney pie 'stead o' steak! I thought ee wuz gonna crack 'er one on-a spot!

Lee, the main chef, ee takes-a piss outa Mich no end. Ee tried it with me when I begun, so I tol' Mich t' take no notice. But she don' know when ee's bullin or not. Ee tol' 'er the correct way t' serve chips wuz with a fork an she believed im. By-a time she'd got 'em on-a plate, they'd frozen agen!

Friday evenin', but it's real quiet. I serve a family with a stroppy veggie wife an' two kids insistin' on avin' adult portions.

'What's this Vegetable Steak Casserole?' she asks.

'Oh no,' I says, 'tha's vegetable casserole with steak in it.'

'But it does say Vegetable Steak, doesn't it?'

This coulda gone on forever, on'y 'er ol' man tells 'er t' ave-a veggie lasagne.

Lee's outa' is 'ead as per usual. I reckon ee's on summin, I do.

'One veggie lasagne, but I reckon there's some rat in it somewhere, Martine... Look! There's its brother!' ee yells, pointin 'is spatula at-a corner of-a kitchen. I twirl round like a ballerina, then give 'im a shove in 'is bulbous beer gut an 'ee makes out t' swat me like a fly. Mich comes in lookin all excited like she seen some lush pop star. She catches old o' my arm, while I'm on-a lookout fer ol' Thorpey, oo always seems t' rush in when we int workin' tidy.

'Martine! There's these really ace boys!... Yew gotta come an' give me an 'and! I'm on pins!'

'Aye, I will, arfta I done this one table. OK?'

So I takes in the veggie lasagne an' the 'usband's 'ome-made pie (what comes straight from-a freezer) an' 'ave a gawk. There's a loada tables put together an', jest as Mich said, a pile o' stonkin' men and boys in posh suits an' flash ties. Then I see Thorpey chattin' to an older man oo wuz with 'em an' ee glares over at me, so I make out I'm busy servin' the famlee.

As I'm dishin' out-a veg, I yer a Merthyr voice an' 'n unmistakable one at tha'. I practically fling-a veg onto the bloke's lap an' spatter 'im with gravy. The back end o' Dave's 'ead, I'm shewer.

'Excuse me!' says the bloke.

'Oh, I'm sorry!' I grovel, in case ee should call Thorpey. I do a rapid runner back to-a kitchen an' grab 'old o' Mich, oo's gotta 'andful o' prawn cocktails.

'Well, Martine, what d'yew think, eh?'

'Mich! Lissen! There's this boy I ewsed t' know there... I think theyr Swonzee football team... I gotta do the next servin', right?'

Coz I'm so 'igh-pitched an' wound up, Lee yers me over 'is sizzlin chip-oil an' steak-bashin. 'Is face is a pumpkin grin.

'Ne' mind the rat, where's the fuckin' poison? I could never stick the Jacks!'

'Don' be darft, Lee. Ee's from Merthyr.'

''Ey, Mart, I thought yew woz a true Bluebird.'

'Tha's all in-a past... Right, Mich, give us them prawn cocks!'

Michelle's nearly creamin' er knicks on-a spot, she's so worked up.

''Ey, we could be on yer... I fancy the big black one, I do!'

'I gotta black puddin' in the fridge, if yew don't get off with 'im,' shouts Lee.

'Shurrup Lee, y' racist dick!' I yell as Mr Thorpe comes bustin' through-a door. Ee's tampin' an' 'is 'ard white face 'its me like a breeze block.

'Martine,' ee whispers snakey, 'just get on with the job or you're out! Right?'

I feel like tellin' 'im t' stuff it, but I 'iss back 'Yes, Mr Thorpe!' I go calm but quick inta the dinin' area an' make a point o' servin' Dave first. I glance over t' see Mich urryin towards the big black fella, oo looks real chuffed. Dave's busy talkin, so I lean right over 'im, cranin' t' face 'im like I wuz goin t' give 'im a peck.

'Yewr prawn cocktail sir!' I says, so deliberate an' sarky ee turns straight away, lookin' curious till ee recognises me. 'Is eyes 'n mouth narrow t' three blades. Then ee turns away with a flick o' is 'ead like ee wuz 'eadin-a ball or summin.

As I return to-a kitchens I yer 'im callin' me back. I don' wanna respond, but thinkin' o' Thorpey's warnin', I decide to.

'Uh… 'scuse me, waitress, but can I 'ave my steak well done, please? I carn stand the sight o' blood!'

An' all-a players larf, like it woz some private joke.

'Yes, of course sir!' I feel like spittin' out-a words, but I control myself, savin' it up. Inside, I'm so angry coz ee treated me like I woz nobody. All 'is indifference brings it back: 'ow ee ewsed me against 'er, 'er against me. I seen 'ow ee wanted us t' be total enemies. An' I played 'is game orright… a Stanley knife I on'y brung fer protection… she wuz 'avin' a go at me all-a time… 'Martine, yew've lost 'im, yew bitch! Le's face it, yewr a loser!'… Blood everywhere. Now I gotta remember. 'Er blood on my clothes an' 'ands: I knew I'd never wash off them stains. An' when Dave says 'bout 'is steak jest then it seemed aimed, like 'is sharp eyes shinin'.

I decide t' take in these special steak knives we 'aven' ewsed frages an' Lee thinks I'm darft.

'Wha' yew wanna bother with 'em for? I need 'em f' choppin up the rats anyway.'

'Lee do me favour an' chop yewrself up, they'll be one less rat then.'

I rub my 'and cross-a blade o' one. I feel scared an' thrilled at-a same time. Mich comes in grinnin' all over 'er body, as if she've orreadly got tha' fella. I 'old up-a knife towards 'er.

''Ey, Martine! Go easy! I never spoke to yewrs. 'Onest!'

'It's OK, Mich. This one's fer 'im!' I clatter-a knives onto a tray, leavin' Michelle stunned.

This time I take it real slow, as if I woz strokin'. I know wha' I'm doin', so I ask oo's 'avin' steak an' watch 'is face as I carefully place each knife. I 'old each one a while before puttin' it down an' I cun see 'is panic risin'. Ee cun see I'm leavin 'im till last an' 'ow much I'm relishin' it all. Looks as if ee's shittin' 'is load when I finally come t' 'im.

'Yew 'avin' steak, sir… Well done, wern it?'

'Er... aye... ta!' ee tries t'act so cool, but 'is 'ands 're fiddlin' with 'is other cutlery, as if ee's searchin' f' weapons!'

I take 'old o' the las' steak knife an' prepare t' show 'im. Now ee'll get the message. I cun take down tha' cuttin'. I cun wash off tha' red. I sweep the knife up to 'is face an ee jerks back in 'is chair, nearly fallin'. At-a same time, Michelle comes in screamin', 'Don' do it, Martine! Don' do it agen!'

An' I says t' Dave, real calm... 'Is this done enough fer yew sir?'

Ever'thin' 'appens so quick, I think I've sliced 'im without knowin'. Is teammates 're laughin', Michelle grabs my arm an' Thorpey's fussin' an' pullin' me back t' the kitchen. Ee drags me outa the door inta the yard. I still gotta knife, but there's no blood anywhere t' be seen.

'This is no joke, Martine! How dare you treat our customers like this? Who do you think you are? You can't...'

I fling the knife to the ground an-a sound severs 'is words, leaves 'em angin'.

'Yew cun stick yewer bloody job, Mr Thorpe! I wozn messin', fer yewr information, it wuz fer real. I owed tha' boy one!'

'I should never have taken you on... I knew about your record, you know... They told me you'd changed... Now, get out of my hotel!'

I undo-a apron an' scrumple it up as ee shoves past me. I fling it in-a bin an' feel a real buzz, though ee never seen me.

As I stride away down-a street, a coach passes an' faces stare at me with a 'Wow!' on theyr lips. All of 'em 'cept one, that is. I lost so much to 'im: my body, my freedom an' now my job. I'll go 'ome an' take-a scissors to 'er photo. Cut it up inta tiny pieces knowin' tha' won' be the end, but tha' problee, this is some kind o' beginnin'.

DAT'S LOVE

Leonora Brito

Dat's love, tra la, la, la, dat's love – remember that song? Well she won't be singing *that* at the funeral. In fact, although the crowds have gathered like moths around this candlelit church, just to hear her sing, Sarah Vaughan won't be singing at Dooley Wilson's funeral at all.

I will, for I am what's known as a 'godly' singer. I sing at funerals. Chapel or Church; Pentecostal or Congregational – I go where I'm asked. Though the Church of the Blessed Mary will always be my funeral-singing home, so to speak. 'Mrs Silva has never put red to her lips, she does not smoke, or blaspheme, or take strong drink. And when she lifts up her voice, it is to sing God's praises in his house.'

Father Farrell is a nice enough man. His face is moist and white as an unbaked loaf, risen and unwrapped for the oven. His face has that unwrapped look, though his eyes are very dark and sincere. When he says his little piece, I go along with it. Shake my head, pull down the corners of my mouth in a little smile. I worry about other things like: are my new shoes too tight for my feet? Did I remember to take the price labels from the backs? Today, especially, I'm worried that the creases will start to show in my costume, which is on the small side for my ampleness. Vanity is mine.

I take my seat about halfway down. 'His Eye Is on the Sparrow', I am hymn number three on the hymn board. A few rows in the front have been left empty for the family –

what family there is. Most of the people have packed themselves in at the back, with the crowds stretching out into the road. In the end, he was one of us; the local entertainer who paved the way for others – meaning Sarah Vaughan – to reach the heights.

I can feel the sway of bodies behind me, hear their breathing, sense the awful hush of excitement. It's the one thing I don't like about funerals today, this excitement over death, the leaning in on grief, and they won't hold back.

I'm getting too emotional; but I knew Dooley Wilson before he *was* Dooley Wilson, when he had a room in my father's boarding house just after the war. He was known as Archibald something or other then and he played piano, wonderful piano, in between features at the Bug-house or up at the young people's club – the Rainbow Club, on the bridge. All the popular tunes of the day, whatever you cared to ask for, he'd oblige. And he could imitate all the stars, with that wonderful singing voice of his. '*I'm the sheik, of Arooby!*' Wonderful voice, wonderful smile. We all admired him, especially us girls.

He was a smart-looking man. Big built, but smart-looking, with a beautiful razor moustache, and a fine blue suit which he always wore on Sundays, when he played piano in our front parlour, with the family gathered round. Old-fashioned songs like 'No, John, No' or quiet hymns and spirituals – 'Ezekiel Saw The Wheel'; 'There Is A Balm in Gilead' – songs which pleased my father and mother especially.

I sang along with the others, but I liked to watch him play. His wide dark hands had pretty fingernails that shone like pearly shells as they struck the keyboard. He used pomade on his hair too, which he kept in a green jar by his bedside, along with a flat-backed hairbrush and four or five lavender coloured tablets of toilet soap. His room had its own, specially-scented smell. We used to argue amongst ourselves, one girl and two boys, for the privilege of cleaning it out on a Saturday – as I've said, we all admired him, but from a distance – I was only a young girl then, and he was a grown man, almost a god in my young, fifteen-year-old eyes.

It was enough for me to lean my mop and bucket upside the chest of drawers and run my fingers over the things that were left on top: the hairbrush, with its smooth wooden back; the green fluted jar; the leather manicure case that opened out to show all the silvery blades and things he kept inside, all inlaid with mother-of-pearl, and strange and beautiful to me, as I held them in my hands.

When he changed his name to Dooley Wilson it was a shock. We'd never heard of anyone changing their name before. Our silence around the supper table made him laugh; and my father, who was a member of the Abyssinian Brethren, said something about the leopard not changing his spots; the Ethiopian, his skin. But that just made him laugh all the more, pleasantly, because he was a same-island man, like my father. Still, he threw back his head and laughed, so that the shirt button came undone at his throat; and I remember how his collar opened up around his wide dark neck, like the white wings of a bird.

After that he became Dooley Wilson. You must remember him – the coloured fellow in the white suit. The one who rolls his eyes when he plays piano in that famous film and sings that famous song, so doleful! As if he already knew, even as he was singing it, poor dab, that he was destined to be forgotten. Except in our dockland part of the city.

You needed an American sounding name in those days, to help with the bookings. And I think it made him laugh, the man lying down there in the coffin; stepping into someone else's shoes and trying to make them fit. Especially as he was a different type of coloured man altogether really – our Dooley was broader, taller, darker – much darker than the light-skinned chap in the film; and with a much sweeter singing voice. Not that anyone seemed to notice; and after a while, I don't think he noticed himself. His act fell into more of a comic routine in the end, and that kept

him popular in all the local clubs, long after the days with
Sarah Vaughan.

Close my eyes and I can see him now. I saw him once, on
my birthday, a couple of years ago. A big fleshy man, decked
out in a white, satiny suit. A real professional, flashing his
teeth in a smile while his fingers plinked out tunes on the
piano: 'You must remember this'. And this – then he'd go
into his act, putting on all the voices, pulling faces:

> 'Dat boy over der, what's his name?'
> 'That boy? Why that's Sam, Miss Ilsa. Sam.'
> 'Dey sho' is goan be trouble, Mister Rick ...'
> 'Play it, Sam! Sing it, Sam!'
> 'Please keep away from him Miss Ilsa; you bad luck to 'im!'

The voice was all honey and molasses as he rolled his eyes,
and drooped his mouth to make us laugh. Under the
spotlights, his black skin had a silky-looking sheen to it, still.
Like black taffeta, cool, under the spotlights. Of course, I
stayed at the back with the girls from work; I didn't come
forward at the end, to introduce myself. From that distance
his eyes looked dull and small, like two black dots on a pair
of dice...

Though what I was remembering was the time he stopped
playing the piano in our front parlour and told me I had a
voice. 'Drink to Me Only with Thine Eyes' I sang, staring at
the flowers inside the glass dome on the sideboard, then at
the black iron archway of the fireplace, with the blue piece
of sugar paper folded inside, because it was Sunday. It was
cold in the room, but the paper seemed to blaze blue when
he said that: 'Gracie girl, you've gotta nice voice!'

He had tossed me that compliment like a flower, and I kept
it for a long time, close to my heart.

Once I start remembering, I can't control things. The
memories spin around in my head like a big roulette wheel.
Black and red, blue and gold, and I can't control them. I

never know when the wheel is going to stop – it drives my old man Frank to distraction.

'Sweetness, don't you go sorrowing for that man. It will only upset you, and for what?'

I was standing in front of the old-fashioned mirror that hangs over our mantelpiece when Frank said that. I didn't say anything, just moved my hand along the mantel, searching for the tortoiseshell combs to put in my hair, as if I'd forgotten where I'd left them, or hadn't heard him right. But I could see his eyes, looking at me through the mirror. They've got the same sort of gleam as the television set he sits in front of, my Frank's eyes. That greenish-grey sort of gleam, when it hasn't been switched on yet.

After a minute or two, when he saw there wasn't going to be an argument, he picked up the newspaper on his lap, and turned to the horse-racing. Frank knows full well I cry at funerals, I always cry a little bit, no matter whose it is. But he's jealous, Frank. He's gotten jealous in his old age. I know how it is with him, that's why I never bother saying much. Except I remembered to ask him what he was having for his tea before I went through the door. He looked up and yawned like a baby, both cheeks bellied out, bright as a brass teapot. But the inside, I thought, corroded. Green.

'Oh don't you worry about me,' he said. 'I'll fry up the fish.'

I had taken the fish out of the fridge earlier. Cleaned them myself, because he says the market girls don't clean them properly. I don't like cleaning them, but I did it. I took the knife with the long shiny blade, and slit open the soft, silvery underbelly, scraping out the wraggle of guts. The blood spilled dark red, like wine, and the fish felt like something carved under my hand. I cut the head off, slicing behind the fins. I was concentrating on how pretty the fish scales looked towards the tail end; they had a pearly sheen on them where they caught the light. The fin opened out, shadowy like a bird-wing, when I picked it up between my fingers and threw the head to next door's cats.

'Are you sure now?' I had to ask, about the tea.

'Sure I'm sure. You go on and bury the dead.'

He looked at me then, and showed his teeth, brown between the ivory, in a smile. 'We've all got fish to fry, haven't we?'

'You come with me then,' I said, as nicely as I could. 'Just to show your face. Frank?'

But he wouldn't budge. So I left him there, sat in front of the television set, waiting for the two o'clock at Sandown. Yet something touched my heart to see him sat, upright, with a hand on each knee of his dark, pinstriped trousers. The trousers from what used to be his best suit, thirty years ago. And I noticed how the hair on his head was like cigarette ash; white and grey and soft as cigarette ash to the touch. Because I had to rest my hand on his head for a moment, before I went through the door.

My thoughts spin round. If the girls on my section could see my eyes fill up, they wouldn't know me.

At work I keep my head down and just get on with it. I'm a roller in the cigar factory. I cut tobacco leaf on the machines. I'm a skilled machinist, cutting the leaf on the metal die as the drum turns round. The drum is as big as a silver wheel, with twenty-four clefts cut into it. Each cleft is filled with tobacco that has been wrapped once by the girl at the other end. My leaf is the second wrapping, the one that shows.

The wheel of the drum turns round and round. The clamp picks up the cigars... *picks up the cigars* and places them in the clefts, on and on. The finished cigars roll down the belt, and I pick them up, five at a time; scoop them up with my free hand, and stack them, row upon row in the tins, without stopping... *without stopping*. None of that stopping and starting. Not for me. It's very rare for me to have to take my foot off the pedal. Very rare. Five hundred cigars per tin, ten tins to reach my target – that's five thousand cigars minimum – and then move on to bonus. And always cutting my leaf to get my number out.

I've been rolling cigars for years, though these days I'm on part-time. It's a well enough paid job, part-time. There's nothing romantic, or exotic, or *steamy* about it, except in other people's imaginations, other people's bad minds, as Frank would say. Sometimes, during the summer months, when it gets really hot – when the machines are roaring and the generator's going full blast – the girls will ask me to give them the lead in a song. 'Grace, give us a song,' they'll say. 'Please!' And I'll often come out with a Christmas carol. Christmas carols have a cooling effect when you're singing them in August... and you're stuck there, in a forest of palm-green overalls, trying to cut your leaf to get your number out.

When I was a young girl, I sang different songs – 'I Don't Want to Set the World on Fire!'; that was one of our favourites, I laugh when I think of it now. We formed a group; me, Baby Cleo and Sarah Vaughan. And practised singing in work-time. Our first and last performance was at the Rainbow Club, one Bonfire Night. Those two hoofing across the stage, doing the high stepping and the 'Whoo-ooh-whoo-oohs' behind me, while I stood still and sang, happy not to have to shake too much, because of my bulk. The three of us wore wrap-over pinnies, yellowy white, and brown berets. We called ourselves 'The Matchstick Girls'.

Dooley Wilson played piano for everyone who was performing. 'Bye-bye Blackbird': that was our encore! It was me and Baby who had the idea for it, then we had to have Sarah in to make the number up.

Hark at me, sat inside this darkened Church with my mind wandering. But that's always the way with funerals, I find. The emotion comes and goes, like God's grace, or the light falling in on us now, from the high windows. It comes and goes. Walking down the road towards the Church, the sun was shining where, a minute before, it had been raining. Warm spring rain. Standing by the kerb, waiting to cross, I saw white cloud and blue sky mirrored in the black water as it ran into the gutter. So clear, it made me think – to see the sky beneath my feet as if the earth had gone.

There were quite a few mourners waiting outside the Church. I counted more women than men, standing under the trees in silent clumps of black. The wreaths had been propped against the funeral car windows. I saw two red hearts and a cross made up of curling, wax-white petals, and I wondered who had sent them, these tokens of love and tribulation, love and trouble.

Baby Cleo came over to talk to me. Old friends, we stood by the black-speared railings and talked a little bit. She said she'd heard a rumour that Sarah Vaughan had managed to telephone Dooley Wilson long distance, just the night before he died. Baby couldn't get over it. 'Imagine,' she kept saying, as we walked through the gate and into the Church yard. 'After all them years, oh God love 'em.' She dabbed her eyes with a hanky.

It's like a film, I thought. But I didn't say anything. People see life down here like a film.

But it's different for Baby. She was one of the girls who joined the dance troupe, the one Dooley Wilson got together and toured the Valleys with, in the early Fifties. 'Jolson's Jelly Babes' or some such nonsense they were called, and Sarah Vaughan made her name in it, blacking her face up and acting comical at the end of the line. If Al Jolson'd had an illegitimate daughter, the paper said, she'd have been it. Baby was one of the girls who came back on the charabanc, while Miss Sassy Vaughan ended up in a London show, swaying in front of a coconut tree, under a pale yellow moon. Sarah Vaughan, the coloured young lady with the Welsh name: 'The Sepia, Celtic Siren,' they billed her as. That was her gimmick: batting her eyelashes and telling reporters she was a native of Cardiff. They had thought she was American, but she didn't have that good a voice.

I was glad not to have been a part of the Valleys tour; the other girls were all a bit downcast when they got off the bus. Proud, but downcast.

I was surprised to see more people crowded around the side entrance as we approached. But Baby said they were waiting there just in case Sarah Vaughan were to turn up. It had said over the local radio that she wouldn't, couldn't; but people still hoped she might appear, unannounced, the way stars do.

He will always be remembered as the man who discovered Sarah Vaughan. That will be his epitaph, discovering her. Like finding something valuable and precious that no one else had ever realised was there before. Mr Columbus.

There's only a month between our birth signs, mine and Sarah Vaughan's. Not that I believe in that sort of thing, but it makes you wonder. We both started out over the cigar factory on the same day; bunching and rolling tobacco leaf on the same machine, getting our numbers out – and singing together, high over the noise of the machinery … all those years ago. We were friends, I suppose. But it wasn't all cosy and sentimental. Oh no, because I was the roller and she was only the buncher. And she didn't like that, because I got paid more. I did more too; but you could never reason with her.

> Stuff it, I wanna go home!
> Stuff it, I wanna go,
> But they woan let me go,
> Stuff it, I wanna go home!

Except that she used to mouth *f— it*, staring down the length of our machine, Number 28, with cheek and daring in her eyes, I used to think, as I scooped up the cigars and stacked them neatly. Always the calm and steady one. Steady and responsible, that was me. And I think it used to provoke her, Sarah, into behaving worse. She was a wild one, one of those girls who wouldn't take a telling, not from the foreman, the supervisor or anyone.

'Keep your eyes off Norman, he's mine!' she was always threatening people. Or, 'Think I'm gonna spend the rest of

353

my life in this place? Uh. Uh. Not me! So what if they pays better than the brush factory or the box factory, so what!' And that was to the foreman. She didn't care, Sarah. Most of the other girls admired her for the way she acted. But I could see it for the put on it was. She hadn't been brought up properly. Her father had left her mother with three small kids, and they were dragged up, not brought up like the rest of us. She wasn't sure about a lot of things: behind the loudness you could see. It was easy to get to her, if you put your mind to it.

Some things she had going for her – she had a good figure, with a jutting bosom and a narrow waist. And she wore her brownish gold hair swept over to one side, in imitation of some Hollywood film star or other – it used to curtain half her face, like the webbing on the mouth of a wireless, unravelled. Sometimes she tied it back, and I thought that looked much nicer, neater. Not that you could tell her anything, though. Sarah Vaughan. She took that name, Vaughan, from the man her mother was living with at the time. Her real name was more common: Jones. Everybody knew that. But; her eyes were brown like toffee, and her skin was bright like tin; and if she wanted to call herself after her mother's fancy man, then she would.

The name-change business came after the performance at the Rainbow Club. At first, she hadn't wanted to waste a Saturday night at home in the dockland. 'The Rainbow Club!' she said when I asked her to make up our number. She curled her lip. 'Run Off Young Girls, Boys In View – it's run by the friggin' missionaries, ain' it?' She wanted to go to the American Base in Brize Norton, where the GI soldiers were. But her mother said no, for a wonder. So she ended up with us, performing with me and Baby down the club, because it was some kind of a 'do' and she knew the songs, we'd sung them in work often enough, and the steps were easy.

It was raining that Bonfire Night. Everything was gleaming black with rain. And I can remember Sarah standing at the end of the bridge just in front of the club, frightened to go inside on her own. The tweed coat she had on was waterlogged and rucked up at the back, and she'd straightened her hair too much in the front, greased it so that the drops of water stayed in her hair and glittered like small glass beads. That's what I remember: and the rain, the sound of it running into the gutters and flowing under the bridge as we walked up to her. And the child's voice, reciting through the club's open door, 'Tiger, tiger, burnin' bright, inna forest of the night...'

On the Monday morning she was late for work.

'A grown man, right? Wants to go out with me.'

All five of us sitting around the canteen table looked at her.

'What would he want with someone like you then, Sair, a grown man?'

But the women on the table were nudging one another and laughing. Sarah laughed along with them, then she pushed a scribble of hair away from her face and took a swig from a bottle of Tizer. 'She knows him.' She nodded in my direction, smiling. 'He's a big feller, ain' he?' She took another swig from the bottle and burped. 'An' he wears this awful blue suit I'd like to set alight to, with a match...'

The women around the table laughed, and someone said, 'Well madam, are you going to meet up with this one or not?' Sarah placed her elbows on the table and leaned forward. 'Oh, I'm definitely going! He wants to give me *breathing lessons*, doan he? Says it'll improve my singing voice, ahem!' She coughed.

They all thought that was funny, and they roared. Even Baby, though she had left the club with me, and must have been as surprised as I was. We did our encore, 'Bye-bye Blackbird', and we left. People were clapping us out, because we'd been a hit. Funny. We were supposed to be funny, but it was Sarah who had been the funny one, going cross-eyed in the background as I sang. She made them laugh, as I was singing. I had to turn round to see what they were laughing at. The piano was slow and lilting. It wasn't him, he played it right. But she made it funny pulling her beret down over her eyes and acting gormless.

I watched her wipe her mouth with the back of her hand. She hadn't said anything nice about him, only nasty. She hadn't even mentioned his piano playing, or his smile, or his beautiful razor moustache. Nothing, only smut.

'An' who d'you think you're looking at?' she asked, still smiling.

'I'm looking at you,' I said in a steady voice. 'You've got no manners, have you? Sitting there with your elbows on the table, drinking out of a bottle!'

The others were embarrassed to hear me coming out with something like that, out of the blue. Everyone stared at the Tizer bottle, mesmerized by the sudden shame of it. And Sarah's mouth opened and closed a few times, before she leaned across the table with a little screech, and dragged her fingernails down the side of my face, once.

Then she clip-clopped through the canteen doors and was gone before I'd even got to my feet. But I remember holding my hands to my breast and screaming after her: 'You tart! You tart, you!'

A storm in a teacup. No one had any idea what it was all about, least of all Sarah Vaughan, who got the sack for it. One misdemeanour too many, or so they said. I was only given a warning, because I'd acted out of character, they said. I saw her later on that afternoon, at four o'clock. She was standing by the fire-bucket outside the foreman's office, waiting for her wages to be made up. I had to walk past her. She was wearing her old tweed coat, with the rucked-up hem. She muttered something horrible as I went past. When I got to the end of the corridor, I looked round; but she had taken her compact out of her bag, and was busy putting lipstick on, pulling her mouth over her teeth, and making her lips look like dark red wings.

If I felt guilty about her getting the sack, the feeling didn't last long, because only a couple of months later she was off with him, touring the Valleys as a Jelly Babe. And the rest, as they say, is history. But not for me, my mind keeps going back to it.

I remember having to go up to his room on an errand, after the fight with Sarah. I knocked at the door, my face still smarting. I was holding the blue suit over my arm. My mother had had it cleaned and ironed for him. I was hoping he'd be out. But he was only getting ready to go out. His hands were slick with pomade, so he left the door ajar and I walked inside and draped the suit carefully over the chair. He had turned back to the mirror. The contents of the manicure case were spread out on top of the chest of drawers, all silvery and pretty, with the mother of pearl inlay along each handle. He'd been trimming his moustache, I could see that; prettifying himself.

He said something about starting up a dance troupe. 'I want you to come with us,' he said, taking more pomade from the jar and smoothing it onto his head like green ice.

'A Jolson Jelly Babe!' He was laughing in front of the mirror. There was a white shirt on the bed, whiter that the one he had on. A tie had been placed alongside the shirt, ready for going out. The tie had a pattern of small red diamonds on it. Flashy, like a playing card, I thought.

'I'm Alabamy bound!' He waved his hands like a minstrel in front of the glass, laughing at his own reflection.

'OK, OK, Grace.' He could see that I wasn't smiling back. He turned away from the glass and faced me.

And I remember him putting his hand to my cheek and stroking it in surprise, when he saw the marks. 'You're a nice girl,' he said, over and over again. 'A nice girl, Grace. Did you know that?' He stopped stroking my face and glanced towards the open door. Then he put his arms around my body, and drew me close to him.

I felt his head against my neck.

'Ma-mmy...' he was crooning softly, singing against my neck, 'ma-ha-ha-mmee...' Leaning into my body, and singing like Al Jolson. I could see us in the mirror. His arms around the dark width of me, his head against my neck.

And I held him to me, young as I was. I put my arms around his white-shirted back and held him. His shoulder blades parted under the pressure of my hands. I felt them opening out and spreading under my hands, like the white wings of a bird. Then still holding him with one hand, I leaned towards the chest of drawers, and picked up one of the silvery blades. It was the one he used for trimming his moustache. When he tried to move away, I brought the blade up against his chest, and stepped back.

I let myself into his room after he'd left us. The blue suit was hanging up behind the door, on a wire coat hanger. I put my hand inside the pockets and drew out a card of matches. The pink had bled on the matches, so I threw them into the empty fire-grate. Looking down, I noticed his passport photo, wedged between a crack in the oilcloth and the clawed foot of the chest of drawers.

I eased the photo out with my thumb and looked at it for a long time, but I didn't see it. The wound was only a flesh wound, that made a small red diamond on his shirt, before it flowered into a buttonhole and had to be bandaged up. He had packed his bags himself, moving in with Sarah Vaughan that same night. But nothing came of it. Their love affair, so called. Which didn't survive her fame, how could it?

And now he was dead.

Love is a bird, that flies where it will, that's what it says in the song. But I think we travel in flocks; different flocks, cut into by our shadowy opposites always flying the other way. And not just for love, but for life.

I tucked the tiny photograph inside the wooden frame of the mirror. I remember doing that then stepping back, further and further into the darkness of the room, until it looked as though his face had been imprinted on my forehead. His eyes were just gashes of black: with dots of light at the centres, like domino pieces. Then the photograph came unstuck and dropped to the floor.

The Lord is my shepherd, I shall not want.

Father Farrell bares his teeth in a pearly-gated smile. A signal, but when I get up to sing, I find that my heart isn't in it. My face is as dry as tobacco leaf, and my lungs feel shadowy and empty like the branches of a tree in wintertime. I picture my lungs like that; and yet. And yet... as soon as the organist pumps out those opening chords... I shift my bulk and sing.

'*And I sing because I'm happ-ee, and I sing because I'm free!*' Vanity, I think, as I sense the congregation perk up behind me. All is vanity. But Baby Cleo is smiling, smiling and crying at the same time; and myself?

I have hoarded my tears like a jewel thief, but one or two steal down my face now, as I look towards the coffin for the last time. Sing! I think, even as my voice veers out of control, and *cr-a-ck-s...*

WOMAN RECUMBENT

Stevie Davies

After a day and a night of lying on bare tiles, shafts of cold penetrating her pelvis, hooping her chest, if human warmth ever came, it would strike like a grenade. Libby set rock-hard, puzzled at her rigidity when she inclined to move. Pain was glaciated, fear glazed. In the old days, the clemency of pneumonia would long ago have commuted her sentence: 'the old man's friend'. That friend had several times tapped lightly at her door, dithered and been turned away by the authorities.

Prone on the kitchen floor, she spasmodically caught (as an eye twitched open) the wink of house keys hung high on a ring. Through the open door to the sitting room her glance angled the faint cream glow of a wall-mounted phone. Once, waking, she thought, *it is never wholly dark. All night round light wanes but never succeeds in failing.*

Otherwise how could the remote keys, the phone hanging as it seemed in space, remain discernible? Men had space-walked on umbilical ropes. They had floated out where there was no height or depth, neither up nor down. In this cold, and with a cracked hip or thigh, which she had heard snap doubly like distant twigs, the kinesis had failed that might power an effortful raising of head, torso, belly, from the tiles. At first there was a dimming, then suspense, now fractional intimation of renewal: on the point of extinction light rallied, to tip dull mist on to dusty surfaces. Her immediate world was bounded by the edge of a dingy mat, inches from her face. How frayed it was, rimmed with hairs like lashes, or a centipede's legs, grease-clogged. For years her soles had worn themselves thriftily thin on this mat, a squalid object if you thought about it, but its proximity now brought a tinge of dark comfort, like some pet, mangy and disgraceful, but known.

She was numb to time. Chill glazed Libby's mind and the long pauses between pulse beats stretched away untenably until the heartbeat (unexpected by now) came with a soft explosive startle of her whole body. There was no horror, none. Only the icy abstraction of waiting in death's antechamber, so near to this familiar mat, with pearls of light dewing the pane of the living room window (for the door was open, ready to walk through with a tray of tea). An idea distilled. *Pull down the drying up cloth, lay your head on that.* It dangled above her, and so did the idea, but though she urged herself to claw, hook, flip, drag it somehow down, she could perform this only in imagination: her body withheld assent. Such baffling impotence impelled Libby to try again and again, enacting her project solely on the mental plane, whilst her hands maintained metal-cold inertia and her head continued unpillowed. Her skull might have cracked open like an egg, and all her yolk slopped out, so concussively hard had she come down.

It dawned on Libby, hearing the sough of early commuting traffic on the Swansea road, that she must have spent her last or penultimate night on earth. They would all carry on threshing in and out of a city that had long been less of a memory than a rumour in her solitude; and she would be out of it. Well out of it. Yet some spasmodic instinct still thrust up towards warmth and life: the quickening sap of hope hurt mortally. Tresses of light wavered on the carpet and against the armchair in the living room, so comfy, so ordinary, holding the shape of Libby's light frame. The curtains remained apart like wide eyelids: there'd been no time to close them before being caught short by this whatever-it-was, this seizure. Or had she tripped on something? A ruck of mat? Had someone got in and assaulted her, how could you know? All around her consciousness the house was open to the light of day. Nakedly open. Strange shame confounded Libby, lying here on the rust-red tiles, at the prospect of being found, her body putrefied perhaps, beyond recognition. How ghastly for them: she hoped it would not be Ceri, her young neighbour, great granddaughter of Libby's decades-dead childhood friend, also a Ceri. *I'm just popping in, Mrs Vaughan. Brought you some baked rice with a cinnamon skin, I know how you like it.*

They would blame Danny for not coming regularly to check on her. For always having excuses: *I've got work to go to, a living to make, I can't be round there all the time, it's just not on, sorry.* Poppers-in twisted the knife in Danny's sullen back. *Ah,* they cooed, in unsubtle rebuke, *she's such a spry soul, isn't it, you must be proud to have such an alert, intelligent mam, 94 years of age, and all her wits about her!*

And he made that face, that (to Elizabeth) highly legible face which had first appeared when he went away to school, a stricken guilty-angry scowl, bending his grey head like a schoolboy and mumbling. He had been the unintended child of her age, his debilitating presence in her belly mistaken for the onset of menopause until he could no longer be ignored as a human burden.

Danny wouldn't come. Why should he? She did not blame him. Not a whit. She should beg his pardon for knocking him down.

Had she indeed knocked him down? On her motorbike? In the war she had sped through bombed-out Swansea bearing letters as a courier but could not recall knocking anyone down, let alone her one son. But he had come a cropper: of that there was no doubt. It was a conundrum and she let it go. Light washed on the green settee; it must be breezy out there. When you peed yourself lying here, for a moment the sensation was warm and comforting, then colder than before. Danny had been a bed-wetter: she had smacked, they endorsed violence to children in those days. And you, criminally, obeyed. A rapture of black impatience quivered through her: why couldn't it be over, the punishment? Why be put on this earth, to rot like this, at tedious length? To suffer interminable resurrections. It is unnecessary, she thought. It contributes and amounts to nothing whatever. It is uneconomic.

Uncle Evan with his healthy brutality, his sense of timing, had given equal weight to economy and mercy. With one clean wring of the neck Evan would slaughter chickens. Shot the tired and gallant mare through the temple. Libby had looked Jenny-Jill in the eye before Uncle despatched her. Trustfully she'd clopped along to her death between uncle and niece, the tumour in her belly pendant as though she were in foal. Elizabeth, gazing into the patience of Jenny-Jill's eye, had fingered her velvety muzzle in awed valediction, the tapering bone so solidly defined; rushed away into the farmhouse at Uncle's bidding and left Jenny-Jill to his canny mercy.

Crack went the pistol shot. And your hip which was friable as a dead twig, porous, its vital juices and calcium leeched, cracked one evening, once, twice. No one came to offer the clemency of a bullet, a shot in the arm, nor had you means to make an honourable, a Roman, end of it. The long freeze perpetuated itself. Libby shut her eyes, to seal out the fringe on the mat, dust-puffs and decaying crumbs, the wanton bloom of light on the couch through the door. Everything drifted down in a fine silt, the leavings, skin-flakes, coffee-particles, dust powdering surfaces like a pall of ash.

In this extremity appeared the most minor of miracles. A creaturely presence. The ant had scurried from somewhere into Elizabeth's field of vision, where it now paused. Her jaw and cheek burned with the atrocity of cold as if her face were one giant toothache, while her eyes took in the visitation. It had roamed far from its nest: perhaps the community sent out scouts, to reconnoitre territory. And doubtless the ant, with its superior senses, intuited as foreign the presence of the mountain range of skeletal flesh that was Elizabeth, the foothills of her skirts, and waited irresolute, so near to her milky-blue eyes. She was herself terrain now.

Libby pondered the ant. The habit of intelligence was tenacious. She felt bound to take the ant into consideration. It was a life after all. A creature at eye level. Nothing to do with her, and what a relief. Inhabiting its own proximate world. You put down poison for the colony. It didn't work, in her experience. A puddle of bleach sometimes did the trick. A cluster of brethren drowned, alerting the corporate mind. Then they'd all decamp. Disappear from the cracks in the tiled sill which was the entrance to their nether kingdom, pouring out to forage, pouring in with supplies, only to reappear on the counter by the bread bin. She didn't much mind them. But she had never before been glad of one. She kept her eye on the ant, until it no longer seemed as miniscule, but a companionate presence which she tacitly saluted.

And there beside it, one human hair. White, curved, single. How come she had not seen it before? It lay in an arc, curving toward the mat with its eyelash-fringe. One of her own hairs, for certain; yet it seemed alien, not pertaining to her as she essentially was, despite the fact that she had been grey for decades. Or rather, pure white, and sparse, so that the scalp showed through a fluffy cloud. But that this should be *her* hair, detritus of *her* head, and not her mother's or grandmother's, puzzled Libby, as if a system had slipped.

Detached, the hair lay there, next to the ant, which appeared to have moved. Presumably as she'd pushed her hair back from her forehead yesterday or the day before, this individual had detached, hanging by a follicle to her jumper, then slipped away into these reaches she had never imagined. Indeed, why should she? What would be the utility? The schoolmistressy riposte rapped out in her head like a ruler on a desk (what attitudinising piffle it had all been, though, the geography and Scripture, the gold stars and the black marks, considering the finality of this perspective, getting down to it, level with this ant, that hair). Perhaps now, soon, she could be quit, make her quietus.

A face youthful at the window, craning. Consternation seizing the face. Not Daniel, because of course Daniel was grizzled now, on the cusp of middle age. The young face was jabbering but she failed to make out the words. His eyebrows worked, his hands flapped. Her heart's sap surged, with painful warmth. If she could have moved, Elizabeth would have shooed Jason the Milk away. Now it was all up, they would resuscitate her. Having got so far, the deathly cold having seized her feet and calves in such a vice that she could no longer feel them at all, certain bones having snapped, her mind having pitched down this cliff, they would abort her journey. They would importune her, *You must rise again, so that you can die again*. Like all acts of public benevolence, this alienation of her rights would be reinforced by violence.

'It's all right, Mrs Vaughan, my love, don't you be scared, darling, I'm coming through the window. Only way, see.'

A fountain of glass smithereened; the morning imploded; but its shock was unregistered until the warm male hand cupped her head, lifting it from the tiles on to her sheepskin. Then she was shaken with grief at the sight of Jason's tears as he stammered into his mobile phone, rushed for a blanket, covered her and chafed her hands with their great knots of vein, so that warmth prickled into her slow-sliding blood.

'Don't you worry now, darling, ambulance is on its way. Thank goodness it's one of your milk days.'

A slight, fair-skinned boy, crew-cut, a ring in one earlobe. Observing the gleaming lobe in the sun-slant, Libby despaired. You ran the egg and spoon race, ran it for safety not for speed, loping on your long legs, plaits bouncing on your shoulder blades, balancing the egg carefully: and though you came in last and all the other lasses had vanished, vanished long ago (because you excelled in caution and stamina, longevity was in your maternal genes, frugality and a spartan diet in your traditions, a brainy, resourceful, bookish girl) – despite all this, you had the tape in sight. And now just within reach, you dropped your egg.

'What was that, Mrs Vaughan, lovely?' The earring bent to her mouth.

'Humpty.'

'Don't you worry now, be here any minute.'

He treated her like a child. Thought she'd gone off her rocker, when in point off fact she had never known such luminous clarity. For (it burst upon her now, with Jason's hand cradling both hers) she never should have had a child. Even the one. Too bony, too hawkish, cerebral, opinionated. She had done wrong by Daniel from the first. Reading Sophocles – Sophocles! – while she fed her baby in the night. *Not to be born is best.* Oh yes, a very nice lullaby when you are hesitantly sucking your rubber teat, a lovely welcome to this world. Closing her ears when he cried. Banishing him to the Siberia of school at the earliest opportunity.

Life means life. When the judge imposed his sentence, he stipulated, *in this woman's case, life must mean life.*

She was raised on the stretcher by men in yellow coats, wheeled out into the mouth of the morning. Her own lips gaped apart and she lapsed asleep.

The intuition reared that Danny had died: that he had lain prone on a cold floor with people kicking him, coiled foetally to hug his head. She'd sent him into this zone of violence, driven him out. For every time he had to go away, Danny had wrung his hands at the station, at which she betrayed him, saying, *You'll be all right, Daniel. Soon as you get there.* And he had begged, every time, *But.* She spoke over his *but.*

They both did. She and Huw, who'd crammed Dan's blazer pockets with sweets till they bulged, not meeting those brimming eyes. She had driven him off, out, away, go, shoo. The train pulled in with roars, hisses, shocks of smoke and the stink of sulphur. Her fingertips poked into the boy's tender back as he mounted the steep steps. Up he must go, up; stand tall, like the other boys. She waited, desperate for the whistle to blow. And he said *But Mam please*. Now he had fallen. Under the train? She wanted to ask the man in the yellow coat but a plastic beak over her mouth and nose, with oxygen flowing through it, impeded speech. No, she grasped the recognition, the reassurance, as it flashed through her brain, it was not Danny who had fallen, thank God, but herself who had been lying on the kitchen floor with the cold kicking up into her slack belly, her pouched cheek.

'Come to see your mam? We were becoming quite concerned, Mr Vaughan, we couldn't get hold of you. She'll be so relieved to see you, thinks you've had an accident. Ah, a lovely lady, your mam. Don't worry, she's doing just great.'

His shoulders sagged. His eloquent eyebrows drooped.

Yes, Elizabeth seemed to hear her son say. *I sometimes think she's immortal.*

'Well, of course, she took a nasty fall. But she came through the operation lovely.'

'Good.'

'Be a relief to you, I know. Mrs Vaughan, here's your son to see his mam. Doesn't say much at present, there's always an element of trauma.'

'Yes, I know.'

'Danny. You needn't have come, I'm quite all right, I didn't want you to fall, you know that. But I should have kept you safe. You should have had an alarm, one of those gadgets with a bleep, it's connected to a carer, you didn't even have a phone, did you, and if you had, how could you have reached, darling, being such a little boy for your age? Actually of course we didn't have a phone either in those days, and if we had, would I have answered? They say my hearing's acute, but is it? I sometimes think I'm congenitally stone-deaf. I was preoccupied, it was my books, you see, but what excuse is that? I don't ask your forgiveness, no, for letting you fall under the train, it was sheer negligence, I can see that now, and you never got over it, never, I can see that too just from the way your shoulders hunch and you duck your head to one side as if someone were going to cuff you. You should have had home helps, you should have had more than just someone popping in to check up on you and breezing out and then I'm convinced you would *not* have fallen.'

She spoke her mind with her usual crackling asperity. Daniel was leaning forward and appeared to be listening intently. His breath came fast and shallow as his hand crept toward hers across the starched linen.

But Mam, he said, and couldn't go on.

THE ENEMY

Tessa Hadley

When Keith had finished the second bottle of wine he began to yawn, the conversation faltered companionably as it can between old friends, and then he took himself off to bed in Caro's spare room, where she knew he fell asleep at once between her clean white sheets because she heard him snort or snuffle once or twice as she was carrying dishes past the door. (She experienced a moment's disrespectful relish, at the thought of his rather ravaged fifty-five-year-old and oh-so-male head against her broderie anglaise pillowcases.) Caro herself felt awake, wide awake, the kind of awakeness that seizes you in the early hours and brings such ultimate penetration and clarity that you cannot imagine you will ever sleep again. She cleared the table in the living room where they had eaten together, stacked the dishes in the dishwasher ready to turn on in the morning, washed up a few delicate bowls and glasses she didn't trust in the machine, tidied the kitchen. In her bare feet she prowled round the flat, not able to make up her mind to undress and go to bed. Tomorrow was Sunday, so at least she didn't have to get up for work.

What was it about Keith, after all this time, that could still make her restless like this; could make her feel this need to be vigilant while he snored? When they sat eating and drinking together she hadn't felt it; she had felt fond of him, and that his old power to stir and upset her was diminished.

He was nicer than he used to be, no doubt about that, and more thoughtful. They had talked a lot about his children; the ones he had had with Penny, Caro's sister, who were in their twenties now, and then the younger ones he had with his second wife, Lynne. She had been amused that he – who had once been going to 'smash capitalism' – took a serious and knowledgeable interest in the wine he had brought with him (he had come to her straight from France; he and Lynne seemed to spend most of the year at their farmhouse in the Dordogne).

None the less, the thought came involuntarily into her head as she prowled, that tonight she had her enemy sleeping under her roof. Of all things: as if instead of a respectable middle-aged PA living in suburban Cardiff she was an Anglo-Saxon thane, sharpening her sword and thinking of blood. Just as the thane might have, she felt divided between an anxious hostility towards her guest and an absolute requirement to protect him and watch over his head.

In May 1968 Caro had turned up for a meeting of the Revolutionary Socialist Student Federation at her university wearing a new trouser suit: green corduroy bell-bottoms with a flower-patterned jacket lining and Sergeant Pepper-style military buttons. The meeting was to organise participation in a Revolutionary Festival in London the following month, to generate support for the Vietnamese struggle for national liberation. The festival was supposed to make its appeal to a broader section of the people than more militant demonstrations, although it was already provoking all kinds of ideological dissent: the Trotskyists thought the whole project was 'reformist', and the Communist Party were nervous at the use of the word 'revolutionary'. The Young Communists were going to appear riding a fleet of white bicycles which they had collected and were donating to the Vietnamese.

Caro had bought the trouser suit because her godmother (whom she had adored as a little girl but had stopped visiting recently because of her views on trade unions and immigration) had sent her twenty-one pounds for her twenty-first birthday. She could have put it aside to help eke out the end of her grant, but instead on impulse she had gone shopping and spent it in a trendy boutique that she had never dared to go inside before. It was months since she had had any new clothes; and she had never possessed anything quite so joyous, so up-to-the minute and striking, as this trouser suit. She knew that it expressed perfectly on the outside the person she wanted to be within. With her long hair and tall lean figure it made her look sexy, defiant, capable (in skirts she often looked gawky and mannish).

The meeting was in a basement room in the History Department as usual. As usual, it was mostly men, though there were three or four girls, bright history and politics students, friends of Caro's, who came regularly. (The girls really did get asked to make the tea: and really did make it.) They sat at desks arranged in a square under a bleak electric bulb with an institutional glass shade, surrounded by maps on the walls that were of course nothing to do with them – Europe after the Congress of Vienna, the Austro-Hungarian Empire in 1914 – but none the less gave the place an air they all rather enjoyed of being a command centre in some essential world-changing operation. By the time Caro arrived the usual thick fug of cigarette smoke was already building up (she smoked, too, in those days). She was greeted, because of the trouser suit, with a couple of wolf whistles, and everyone looked up. It was complicated to remember truthfully now just how one had felt about that whistling. A decade later it became obligatory for women to be indignant at it and find it degrading; at the time, however, she would probably have felt without it that her trouser suit had failed of its effect. She could still recall how the whistle seemed to slice thrillingly through your clothes; and how you met it without making eye contact but with a little warm curl of an acknowledging smile, a gleam of response.

Two men had come from Agit Prop, to talk to the meeting about the festival (Agit Prop was a loose association of activists and artists named after Trotsky's propaganda train and dedicated to promoting revolutionary messages through aesthetic means). That was how Caro met Keith Reid for the first time: when she arrived he had already taken his place in a chair at the centre of things, commanding the whole room. Keith was a very attractive man – it was the first thing you needed to know about him, to get any idea of who he was, then. Not handsome, exactly, but whatever it is that in men is better than handsome: off-centre quirky features held together by a fierce fluid energy, fragile hooked nose, hollow cheeks, a lean, loose, strong body, a shoulder-length mess of slightly greasy dark curls. He had a rich Welsh accent: it was a Valleys accent, in fact – he was from Cwmbach near Aberdare – but in those days Caro had never been to Wales and couldn't tell one accent from another. At a time when left politics was saturated in the romance of the workers, his accent was in itself enough to melt most of the women (and the men).

He looked at Caro in her trouser suit.

'Don't you find,' he said, 'that dressing up like that puts off the working classes?'

She thought about this now with stupefaction. Had she really once inhabited a world where such absurdities were a real currency? She should have laughed in his face. She should have turned round and walked out of the meeting and never gone back.

'No,' she said, calmly taking a place directly in Keith's line of sight, so that he could get his eyeful of the offending item. 'I find it gives them something good to look at.'

Of course she wasn't really calm. She was raging, and humiliated, and struggling with a muddled and not-yet-confident sense of something fundamentally flawed and unfair to do with men and women in what he had said and all that lay behind it: everything that was going to overflow into the flood of feminism in the next couple of decades. And no doubt at the same time she was scalding with shame at her bourgeois depraved frivolity in the face of decent, suffering, working-class sobriety, just as Keith meant her to be. And she was thinking how she would make him pay for that.

They had such energy, then, for all the battles.

After the meeting the visitors from Agit Prop had needed a floor to stay on and Caro took them back to the big, disintegrating old mock-Tudor house, its garden overgrown as a jungle, that she shared with a motley collection of students and friends and politicos. (Later she had had trouble with that house; it was rented in her name, and some of the people using it refused to pay their share. She had to hassle them for it, and came home once to find 'Rackman bitch' scrawled in red paint on her bedroom wall.) They sat up until late smoking pot and sparring; Caro and Keith arguing not about the trouser suit, which wasn't mentioned again, but about the dockers' support for Enoch Powell and its implications for the alliance between left alternative politics and the working-class movement. Caro had been on the anti-racist march to Transport House: Keith thought she was overstating the problem in a way that was typical of bourgeois squeamishness in the face of the realities of working-class culture.

The way Keith dominated a room and laid down the law and didn't seriously countenance anybody else's opinions should have made him drearily dogmatic; but his ironic delivery in that Welsh accent of his made it seem as though there was something teasing even in his most exaggerated assertions. Everyone was willing to listen to him because he was older and his pedigree was impeccable: a miner's son, kicked out of Hornsey Art College for his political activities, he had been working on building sites ever since. In any case, that sheer imperturbable male certainty was intriguing to women in those days. They felt in the face of it a complex mix of thrilled abjection with a desire to batter at it with their fists; also, probably strongest, they believed that given the chance they would be able to find out through their feminine sexuality the weaknesses and vulnerable places behind the imperturbable male front. (This last intuition was all too often accurate.)

Eventually Caro found sleeping bags for everybody and they distributed themselves around mattresses and sofas and floors in the high-ceilinged damp-smelling rooms. And then at some point in the night Keith must have got up again and wandered about until he found not Caro, who had half expected him, but her sister Penny, who happened to be staying with her for a few days. Penny was a year older than Caro but didn't look it: most people took her to be the younger sister. She was smaller, softer-seeming, prettier. Caro found them in the morning twined round each other in their zipped-together sleeping bags. All she could make out at first was the mess of Keith's dark curls and his naked young shoulders, tanned and muscular from the work he did; and then she saw that down inside the bag Penny's head with its swirl of auburn hair like a fox's brush was wrapped in his brown arms against his chest.

She remembered that she had felt a stinging shock. Not heartbreak or serious sorrow: she hadn't had time to do anything like fall in love with Keith, and, anyway, love didn't seem to be quite what it was that could have happened, if things had gone differently between them. It was more as if she felt that, if you put the two of them alongside Keith Reid, it was in some obvious way she and not Penny who was his match, his mate. Penny all through the loud debate of the night before had sat quietly while Caro met him, point for point, and smoked joint for joint with him. Also, there was unfinished business between her and him: some contest he had begun and had now abruptly – it made him seem almost cowardly – broken off. Even as Caro recoiled, just for that first moment, in the shock of finding them, she knew she was learning from it something essential she needed to know for her survival, something about the way that men chose women.

Penny had given up after one year at art college and was living at home again with their parents in Banbury. She was thinking about going to do teacher training. Instead, she embarked on the relationship with Keith: it did almost seem, in retrospect, like a career choice. That whole long middle section of Penny's life, twenty years, was taken up in the struggle with him: pursued by him; dedicating herself to him; counselling him through his creative agonies when he was writing; bearing his children; supporting his infidelities, his drinking, his disappearances, his contempts; making every effort to tame him, to turn him into a decent, acceptable partner and father. It seemed an irony that, when Penny had finally finished with him once and for all, he slipped without a protest into cosy domesticity with his second wife, as if there had never been any problem. 'I was just the warm-up act,' Penny joked about it now. 'Softening him up ready for the show with her.'

Through all of it, Caro had supported her sister: sometimes literally, with money, mostly just with listening and company and sympathy. When Keith went back to live in Wales and got Welsh Arts Council funding to make the first film, Penny had two small babies. Instead of finding a house in Cardiff, or even in Pontypridd, Keith had insisted – on principle – on taking her to live in a council house on the edge of a huge, bleak estate on the side of a mountain in Merthyr Tydfil where she didn't know anyone, and no one liked her because she was posh and English. It was half an hour's walk with the pushchair down to the nearest shops. Caro left a job in London and came to live in Cardiff to be near her, and every weekend after work drove up to Merthyr to help her out, and drive her to the nearest supermarket, and try to persuade her to pack her things and leave. Penny had made the house inside gorgeous on next to nothing, with rush mats and big embroidered cushions and mobiles and chimes pinned to the ceiling; she painted the lids of instant coffee jars in rainbow colours and kept brown rice and lentils and dried kidney beans in them. But the wind seemed never to stop whistling round the corners of the house, and in round the ill-fitting window frames, setting the mobiles swinging.

Keith usually wasn't there, and if he was he and Caro hardly spoke. One strange Saturday evening he had had a gun for some reason: perhaps it was to do with the film, she couldn't remember, although that wouldn't have explained why he also had live ammunition. He had claimed that he knew how to dismantle it, had taken bits off it and spread them out on the tablecloth in the corner of the room where the children were watching television: he was drinking whisky, and erupted with raucous contempt when Penny said 'she didn't want that horrible thing in her home'. He picked the gun up and held it to Penny's head while she struggled away from him and told him not to be so silly.

'Don't be such a bloody idiot, Keith,' Caro said.

'Shut it, sister-bitch,' he said in an absurd fake cockney accent, swinging round, squinting, pretending to take aim at her across the room. Presumably without its bits the gun wasn't dangerous, but they couldn't be sure. They hurried the protesting children upstairs improbably early, bathed them with shaking hands, singing and playing games so as not to frighten them, staring at one another in mute communication of their predicament.

'Put the kids in the car and drive to my place,' Caro said, wrapping a towel around her wriggling, wet niece, kissing the dark curls, which were just like Keith's.

'Wait and see,' said Penny, 'if it gets any worse.'

In the end Keith had not been able to put the gun back together, and had fallen asleep in front of the television:

Penny hid the ammunition in her Tampax box before she went to bed. She had been right not to overreact: Keith wasn't the kind of man who fired guns and shot people, he was the kind who liked the dark glamour of the idea of doing it.

Caro could remember going to see Keith's film at the arts centre in Cardiff – not at the premiere (she hadn't wanted to see him fêted and basking in it, and had made her excuses) but in the week after – and it had made her so angry that she had wanted to stand up in the cinema and explain to all those admiring people in the audience how unforgivably he used real things that mattered and milked them to make them touching, and that in truth whenever he was home on the estate that he made so much of in the film, he was bored and longing to get away to talk with his filmmaking friends. Actually, the audience probably weren't really all that admiring, the film got mixed reviews. She had seen it again recently when the arts centre did a Welsh film season, and had thought about it differently: only twenty years on it seemed innocent and archaic, and its stern establishing shots of pithead and winding gear were a nostalgic evocation of a lost landscape. The one he did afterwards about the miners' strike was his best, she thought: it was the bleakest, most unsentimental account she ever saw of the whole business, capturing its honour and its errors; the ensemble work was very funny and complex (apart from the leads, he had used non-professional actors, mostly ex-miners and their wives). His career had neither failed nor taken off since then: there always seemed to be work, but it was always precarious (it was a good job Lynne made money with her photography).

In the end Penny made friends with some of the women from the estate she met in the school playground, and got involved with the tenants' association, and had her third baby in Prince Charles Hospital in Merthyr, and probably looked back now on her time on the estate with some affection. She grew very close, too, to Keith's parents in

Cwmbach: she saw more of his father in his last illness than Keith did; she really seemed to love the reticent, neat old man, who had been an electrician at the Phurnacite plant and in his retirement pottered about his DIY tasks in their immaculate big postwar council house, putting in a heated towel rail in the bathroom, making a patio for the garden. She stayed good friends with his mother and his sister even after she and Keith were separated.

When Penny eventually decided that he and she should go their different ways, she did the teacher training she had put off for so long, and met her present partner, a biologist working in conservation who was everything suitable and reasonable that Keith was not. They lived in the country near Banbury, not far from where Penny and Caro had grown up. Meanwhile Keith met Lynne, and they shared their time between London and the Dordogne. So that in the end it was Caro who was left living in Wales, and if she thought sometimes that it was because of Keith Reid that she had ended up making her life there she didn't mind, she just thought that it was funny.

She turned out all the lights in the flat; she could see well enough in the light that came from the street lamp outside her front window to pour herself a whisky in hopes that it would help her to sleep. She sat to drink it with her feet tucked under her on the end of the sofa where she had sat an hour or so before listening to Keith; she heard a soft pattering of rain and a police siren, too far off to think about. In the half-dark, awareness of the familiar fond shapes of the furniture of her present life – modest but carefully chosen, tasteful and feminine and comfortable – was like a soft blanket settled round her shoulders; she should have felt safe and complete; it annoyed her that she was still gnawed by some unfinished business just because Keith Reid was asleep in her spare room. There were other men who had been much more important in her life, and yet when they came to stay (sometimes in his spare room bed and sometimes in hers), it didn't bother her this way.

Her heart had sunk when halfway down the second bottle he began to wax nostalgic and maudlin about the Sixties and the decay of the socialist dream. You heard this everywhere these days, in the newspapers and on television; usually, of course, from people who had been young then. The formula, surely inadequate to the complicated facts, was always the same: that what had been 'idealism' then had declined sadly into 'disillusion' now.

'But remember,' she had insisted, 'that in 1968 when we marched round Trafalgar Square we were chanting "Ho, Ho, Ho Chi Minh"! I mean, for Chrissake! Ho Chi Minh! And at that Revolutionary Festival there were Coca-Cola bottles with French riot police helmets you could knock off with tennis balls. And remember us getting up at the crack of dawn to go and try and sell *Socialist Worker* to workers in that clothing factory in Shacklewell Lane. Expecting them to spend their hard-earned money on that rag with its dreary doctrine and all its factional infighting. And I used to go back to bed afterwards, when I got home, because I hated getting up so early. Remember that we spoke with respect of Lenin, and Trotsky, and Chairman Mao, all those mass murderers. Remember that we had contempt for the welfare state, as a piece of bourgeois revisionism.'

'There were excesses,' Keith conceded fondly. 'But then, excess was in the air. Anything could have happened. That's what's missing now. Caro, you sound so New Labour. I'm still a revolutionary, aren't *you*? Don't you still want socialism?'

She shrugged. 'Oh, well, yes, *socialism*, I suppose...'

That conversation had ended awkwardly, each embarrassed by what they thought of as the other's false position. Keith probably thought Caro had sold out (he might even have put it in those words, perhaps to Lynne). She worked as personal assistant to a Labour MP, a man she

379

mostly liked and respected. (Before that she had worked for Panasonic.) On the second and fourth Mondays of every month she went to Amnesty International meetings in a shabby upstairs room of the Friends' Meeting House and was currently involved in a campaign for the release of a postgraduate student imprisoned in China for his research into ethnic Uighur history. This compromising pragmatic liberalism might in time turn out to be as absolutely beside the point as the articles she had once written for *Black Dwarf*: who could tell? Your ethical life was a shallow bowl brimming impossibly; however dedicatedly you carried it about with you there were bound to be spills, or you found out that the dedication you brought wasn't needed, or that you had brought it to the wrong place.

While Caro was tidying up she had had to go into the spare room to put away her grandmother's nineteen-twenties water jug, painted with blue irises, in its place on the lace mat on top of the bureau. This could have waited until the morning when Keith was gone; perhaps she had just made it an excuse to go in and take the measure of him uninhibitedly, free of the wakeful obligation to smile and reassure. She swung the door quietly behind her to admit just a narrow ribbon of light, then stood waiting for her eyes to adjust, breathing in the slight, not unpleasant fug of his smell: good French soap and cologne and a tang of his sweat and of gas flavoured with the garlic she had put in her cooking. He slept on his side with his face pressed in the pillow, frowning; his chest with its plume of grey-black hair down the breastbone was bare, the duvet lay decorously across his waist; under it he seemed to have his hands squeezed between his jackknifed knees; his mouth was open, he made noises sucking in air. She wondered all the time she stood there whether he wasn't aware of her presence and faking sleep.

He didn't look too bad. He took good care of himself (or Lynne took care of him): he hadn't put on much weight, although where he had been lean and hard he was nowadays rangy and slack, with jutting, bowed shoulders under his T-shirt and a small, soft pouch of belly above his belt. He was almost certainly still sexually attractive, which Caro supposed she wasn't any more, although she, too, took care of herself (that was an old gender inequity, probably less to do with patriarchal systems than with desires hardwired into human evolutionary biology). He had opted to deal with his advancing baldness by cutting very short even the rim of hair he had left growing behind his ears and at the back; this was a good move, she thought, pre-empting pretence and turning what might have looked like a vulnerability into an assertion of style. However, it made the starkness of his craggy head shocking. All the years of his age, all the drinking, all the history and difficulty of the man, was concentrated in the face laid bare: its eaten-out hollows, the high, exposed bony bridge of his nose, which rode him like the prow of his ship, the deep, closed folds of flesh, the huge, drooped purple eyelids flickering with sensitivity.

She sat thinking now about the time when Keith was the most attractive man in the room, the man you couldn't afford to turn your eyes away from, careless and dangerous with his young strength. It hadn't been a good or tender thing exactly; it hadn't had much joy in it for Caro. None the less she quaked at the power of this enemy, stronger than either of them, who had slipped in under her roof and was stealing everything away.

When Keith had telephoned from France to say that he had to come over for a couple of days to talk to some people in Cardiff about a new film project, Caro had planned and shopped for an elaborate meal. She didn't make anything heavy or indigestible, but unusual things which took careful preparation: little Russian cheese pastries for starters, then fillet of lamb with dried maraschino cherries and spinach, and for dessert gooseberry sorbet with home-made almond tuiles. Living alone, she didn't get much chance to cook.

She had spent all day getting ready what they had eaten in an hour or so. And of course the food had taken second place to their talk, with so much to catch up on; although Keith had helped himself hungrily and appreciatively. In her thirties she had resented furiously this disproportion between the time spent cooking and eating; it had seemed to her characteristic of women's work, exploitative and invisible and without lasting results. She had even given up cooking for a while. Now she felt about it quite differently, the disproportion seeming part of the right rhythm of all pleasure: a long, difficult, and testing preparation for a few moments' consummation.

She had learnt to love all the invisible work, the life that fell away and left no traces. She used her mother's rolling pin to roll out her pastry; she kept Keith's mother's recipes for Welsh cakes and bara brith. In her tasks around the flat – polishing furniture, bleaching dishcloths, vacuuming, taking cuttings from her geraniums, ironing towels and putting them away in the airing cupboard – she often thought about her mother and grandmother having done these same things before her, was aware of a soothing continuity of movements and competence, working alone in quiet rooms, or with the radio for company. She had had, in fact, a stormy relationship with her parents, and used to think of her mother's domesticated life as thwarted and wasted. But this was how change happened, always obliquely to the plans you laid for it, leaving behind as dead husks all the preparations you none the less had to make in order to bring it about.

WE HAVE BEEN
TO THE MOON

Huw Lawrence

Just in the last four days the Spar had closed. Ten o'clock, late morning, still as a cemetery. Except Pentre Foundry's gates were swinging. A crisp packet blew along the gutter by my feet. In our street the Harrises had finished moving, their removal van out of the way well in time, as promised, another two neighbours less. Breeze-block windows made up a quarter of the street by now. Our house looked no different from always, except for the cars, but appearances are deceiving. I couldn't know it at the time, but it, too, would soon be empty. He lay in the front room, the 'parlour'. The coffin had been closed. Four days ago he had lain in view, cushioned in purple, hands crossed, eyes shut. With the lid down he was all but gone.

Auntie Laura spotted me as I entered and came forward. Even on a day like this she wore too much make-up. I kissed her and shook hands with Uncle Wyn in his dark suit, the quiet opposite of his wife, blue scar not quite hidden by his hair. Then I shook hands with Uncle Col, on my mother's side, alert enough to scare the hands off a clock. He taught physical education at the secondary school, where he was a deputy head, thanks to Uncle Glyn, who shook my hand next. My plump, grey-haired mother bustled forward and led me into my father's study, closing the door behind us. On the inside of the door Dad had pinned a note:

Tu lascerai ogni cosa diletta
Più caramente

On the desk lay books on ecological crisis and alternative economics, and Nigel Lawson's *The View From No. 11*, all library books that would have to be returned. Scribbled notes lay on the desk. I picked one up.

> ...*our unique brain freed us from the bare purpose of survival, enabling us to share collective goals, develop economy and civilised society, think abstractly, conceive the very idea of purpose. Are we to be persuaded we have no more control over ourselves than creatures that have not changed their behaviour in thousands of years?*

My mother stood waiting so I didn't finish it, stuffing it in my pocket without thinking. Before saying her piece, she asked me what the Italian meant. 'He only just put it there,' she explained.

'"You shall abandon everything beloved most dearly",' I translated.

Tears came to her eyes.

'He meant what was happening here, not us. I think it's Dante,' I said, producing my handkerchief, but it was too dirty to offer.

'Tut, tut, tut', she went, snatching it away from me. 'That bloody protest. Down Cwmffynnon every day, when he wasn't going on the wireless. Getting himself worked up. It wasn't even his bloody school.' She might have gone on if someone hadn't called to her. 'Wait,' she commanded. 'I want to talk to you.'

On the turntable was *Nabucco*. My father still played vinyl records. A tenor himself, he had learned Italian in his youth to understand opera librettos, and in my childhood he had made it a secret language between the two us. In one of the desk drawers I found packets of different indigestion tablets. He never realised he had angina. I scanned the 'Education' shelf for a book mentioned to me by a contemporary of his I'd met at a job interview, *The Rainbow Bridge*, but it wasn't there among those long-forgotten volumes by the likes of Dewey, Illych and Neill. I smiled at the booklets on teaching arithmetic with Cuisinaire rods, or the Dean's Apparatus. He had tried out everything when he first returned to Ystrad to teach the children of his former workmates, testing most of it on me first. He had me doing enormous calculations using different colour bits of Lego, and only then bought abacuses for the school. My mother had worked, helping to put him through college. He ended up headmaster of the school he'd attended as a pupil. Not bad for a boy who went down the pit at fifteen. Last thing I wanted was to remember the arguments we'd had. But I guessed I was going to be reminded.

When my mother returned she put a clean white handkerchief in my hand and got to the point. 'Uncle Glyn will be sure to talk to you after the funeral. Listen to him, please, will you? If only to be polite. I want you to promise me that, right now.'

'OK, I promise.'

Local control, my father had called it, and I had called it corruption. Those arguments were history now and I was alone, without his footsteps to question or follow. He had died before I'd had a chance to tell him how much I thought of him. Hell, did I really care about nepotism in these dead valleys? Did I even care if they closed Cwmffynnon School?

'It's not a day for quarrelling,' my mother pleaded.

'I know. I'll listen to Uncle Glyn. I'll be polite,' I assured her.

'He's trying to help you. Isn't that what family is for?'

'Mam, please—'

'You wouldn't have to stay around here long, love. Once you're appointed you can move on. It makes sense in times like these, Gavin. Everyone needs a start.'

'I'll be polite.'

In the living room Uncle Glyn was calling for attention, so we went back there and listened while he told everyone which car to ride in. Tall as I, he looked like a stout chief of police. He was a man with one face and one voice for all occasions. I found myself in the first car sitting between him and my mother. My mother's sister, Dorothy, sat in front of us with Auntie Laura and Wyn. Auntie Laura's ginger curls tumbled down the back of her black dress. 'Well preserved,' my mother always said. 'And so she should be,' my father would reply.

Gone the days when funerals crept along. We sped through the rain behind a hearse that seemed intent on losing its cortege. Funerals fitted into thirty-minute slots and ten of those minutes were for arrival and departure. The chapel doors were open, we found, because of the numbers. I was amazed to see so many people. The rain stopped as we arrived and the sun came out briefly as if just for us. People were lowering and shaking umbrellas. The tarmac gleamed like anthracite.

Reverend Watcyn Pritchard was inside, the only man for the job, my father's friend since schooldays, cheeks like red slippers, nose knitted out of biro refills. His bulky figure was behind the lectern waiting as the coffin with its shiny handles was placed to his left.

We began, not with a hymn, but a song in Welsh, chosen by my mother because my father used to sing it around the house. His favourite verse:

> *When I see the collier's scar*
> *Or blood on the blue slate's face*
> *Then I know what love is*
> *For a people and a race*

After that I went up and read from Corinthians about eternal life. We sang in Welsh, 'Give me the peace the world knows nothing of.'

Then, shifting between our two languages, Watcyn delivered the tribute. Even back then, in 1993, it sounded like history.

'How many memories of Aneurin have been brought here by so large a number of mourners, I wonder. He was a man who thought it was human nature to help those in need, who agreed with Gandhi that poverty is the worst kind of violence and that small communities are the best; a man who spent the last year of his life fighting to save Cwmffynnon school from closure, because he believed young children should go to school where they are loved and feel secure. Fighting for justice, that is the story of Aneurin's life.' Watcyn reeled off a list of battles fought, half of which I knew nothing of.

Watcyn shook his large head sadly. 'Some of you may remember that less than four years ago I stood in this place saying similar things about Aneurin's brother, Dafydd.' He shook his head again, abstractly this time, looking genuinely moved. 'An old Welsh proverb comes to mind, *Ni wyr werth y ffynnon nes elo hi'n hesb*: "The value of the spring isn't known till it runs dry." We are in bleak times. We may wonder who today or tomorrow, will be willing to give selflessly, without profit to himself, out of a sense of humanity and justice. My friends, Aneurin would never let himself think that man's humanity can run dry. So why not let ourselves be led by him?

'Soon we will sing the 23rd psalm: "My soul it doth restore again and me to walk doth make among the paths of righteousness." Paths are there because those who tread them mark the way for those who follow, who maybe carry a different light and speak different words, but are nonetheless on the same journey.

'Perhaps you wonder if it is a journey made in vain.

'I know what Aneurin's answer would be. He would remind us of those who fought the injustices of their day in these valleys, out of a conviction that it is man's nature to cooperate and contribute, and improve things. However bad times may get, goodness remains, because it does not come from the times or the system under which we live, but exists within us. It is "the true light that lighteth everyone that cometh into this world," whatever our beliefs. It is a light that cannot be extinguished. Aneurin is lost to us, and we grieve, but in our human, grieving hearts we know his journey was not in vain.'

As I said, Watcyn was the man for the job. But who saw any paths anymore?

The Watcyn who drank tea in our house, talking politics, was as devastated was as everyone else by what had befallen us, so I wondered if he fully believed what he said. In the fullness of time new people would repopulate this valley, no doubt, but it would not be the same valley. The young were already gone, like me. My own kids would probably end up further from me than I from here. Relocation was the only way now, not just in Wales but everywhere. It was no longer called 'exile'. It was 'relocation'. There was a certain conflict beween that future and Watcyn's tribute, with its suggestions of heritage. *Tu lascerai ogni cosa diletta più caramente.*

We prayed. We sang 'The Lord is my Shepherd'.

Then Watcyn offered the committal and my heart flew to my throat as the coffin started moving. Suddenly, his words were poignant, relevant and true. They were all that prevented this being just a horrible, mechanical conjuring trick.

The family led the way out to the sound of canned music, a song by Schumann, called 'Dreaming'. The hearse was gone and the cars were turned around facing the exit.

A woman detached herself briefly from the crowd: 'We could never repay what he did for us,' she said to my mother. 'Nobody else would have helped us.'

Glyn, a widower with no children, was visibly affected by the service. Maybe feeling his own mortality, he presided over silence in the car on the way back. Feeling something rustle in my pocket, I found the scrap of paper from my father's desk, and read the rest of it. *We are light years ahead of other life forms. We have been to the moon.*

Back in the house, when the reception was underway, Uncle Glyn asked me to step into my father's study. I remember thinking how someone was going to have to go through everything in the study, encounter all those memories. I was aware of my mother watching. Without preliminaries, Glyn got to the point. He puckered the skin between his heavy brows, fixing me with his eyes: 'This may not be the best time, but you'll be going back, and maybe I won't see you. How are your applications going?'

'I've still got two to hear from,' I replied.

I had applied for over three dozen full-time posts.

'You'll probably be waiting till next April, now.'

'There'll be the odd one coming up.'

'There will,' he agreed. 'Indeed, there will be one right here.' He lowered his voice. 'There'll be a vacancy in Ystrad School after Christmas. It'll be advertised as a Scale 1 this November. I can guarantee you'll be on Scale 2 within two years. I don't see anything else coming up for quite a while.'

There was an awkward silence.

'It's not that I am ungrateful, Uncle Glyn...'

'This is the worse slump since the Thirties, Gavin.'

'I'm really trying, Glyn. I'm well qualified, and I'll be getting experience. I've got a few hours part-time at the FE college.'

'I don't want to be a wet blanket, but you are rowing against a strong tide. Every job has more applications that you can shake a stick at. I am not saying you have to stay, Gavin. I am saying that it's a start. In times like these, a start is hard to get.'

There was more silence.

We had been through it before and Glyn didn't let it go on too long. 'All right,' he sighed, putting a friendly hand on my shoulder. 'But at least say you'll think about it. Think hard about it. This could be a long recession. Your mother worries. Your father did, too. You know your father would have wanted this.' He dropped his voice. 'Think about that Scale 2. It'll establish you. After that you can move on to whatever you want, anywhere.'

I promised I would think about it.

Glyn added: 'It is a lot easier to get a job when you are already in one.'

'I'll be teaching part-time,' I reassured him, 'and I'm hoping to earn a bit extra, correcting PhDs by foreign students.'

'All right,' he said, resignedly. 'I'll be here if you need me, for as long as I am alive and well.'

'Thank you, Glyn, I appreciate that,' I said, and meant it.

I meant it for the first time in my life, and I think he recognised it. He went back to the reception.

I stayed and looked around the study. I flicked though a file of cuttings, things my father had published, mostly in the local paper.

> Wales has national plans for Health and Education, so why not planning? Should not towns and villages have a say over what development should overtake them? Get rid of the County Councils and let the Welsh Assembly fund our town and district and community councils. That would be devolution.

You'd have thought he'd have made enemies among the powers that be, but he never seemed to. If he'd lived eleven years longer he'd have seen the localities he defended deprived by a planning act of any say in their own development, and a lot more, too, that he wouldn't have liked.

My mother fetched Dad's retirement present from work, his Omega self-winding watch.

'Here, Gavin,' she said. 'You should have this. It's rightfully yours, now.'

I sat sipping drinks with my mother and Dorothy, remembering my father and wearing his watch. What we remembered was how ordinary he was, how he kept his false teeth in his pocket, slipping them into his mouth if he saw someone he knew, how he sang arias above the sound of the vacuum cleaner, hated baked beans, never walked under ladders, was too superstitious to have a picture of birds in the house, and how anyone could approach him, how he always managed to find time. What a unique amalgam of qualities was a person, and, indeed, the age he lived through. How essential and irreplaceable, and gone.

POD

Stevie Davies

Three kids in four years. I suppose it could be worse: four in three years would be biologically feasible, she's murder, is Mother Nature, considering the diameter of the head to come out and the narrowness of the tunnel to be shoved through, all due to our calamitous bipedal status with no regard for ease of parturition, a design fault that...

Just stop it, Aneurin, stop it now. Put the magazines back. I said... put them back.

...is nearly as bloody woeful as situating the vagina next door to the anus, because next to childbirth cystitis has to be the worst pain, doesn't it, the very worst, I slew in my chair just to think of it and my urinary passage winces, flinches, ouch, as if it remembered, but can tissue actually be said to remember, the delicate, delicate place where such gross pains come to pass and searing pleasures, such violence, such throes...

That's right, come and sit here next to Mami, Magdalena, that's right, you snuggle up ... and the dentally immaculate suited guy reading the *Financial Times* flashes us a surprising grin, very nice, very sweet, given the trauma we're subjecting him to, and Dr Up-his-own-Arse Williams from the Institute (he doesn't deign to recognise me, I'm just the ex-academic mother of three human nuisances, well stuff you, Williams, stuff you all) reluctantly simpers at Magdalena, and the ginger biddy grins too, and suddenly everyone's smiling, a festival of sunlight breaks in on us, while Magdalena turns and whispers breathily behind her dimply hand, *Dat man's got hairs up his nose, Mami.*

Shush Magdalena.

She's got an unusually carrying whisper. Oh God, Christ, what a darling she is, what a precious beauty, I ache for her, for her father in her, for those wormy little fingers and her mass of brown soft curls against my face and lips. Treorchy-Gran had seven living children, two stillborn, goodness knows how many miscarriages, shucked like a peapod once a year she was, but what's my excuse, educated with the toffs at Cambridge, criminal casualness, I just love fucking, I love it in the way nature intended: pity ratbag nature pays you back with this excess fecundity, this fat billowingness, and there are times I've felt like a pod, a gourd, a clay pot just abjectly mindless brooding on its own rotundity, so damned conspicuous, not human any more...

I said, Aneurin, put them down now, stop annoying the people, I won't tell you again.

Oh what's the use? Marie Stopes might as well not have existed for all the notice I've taken and I *don't* like condoms and I *do* like risks, I expect it's something Freudian, I've impaled and imperilled myself and these little loons are the result. Viola wants feeding, my Christ, does her nappy smell ripe, so, Dr Williams, you're going to get a sight of tittie, that'll put the fear of God in you if the dentist doesn't, watch him vanish up his own arse, old poker-face: remember him chairing the library committee and me wandering in from sunbathing with the third-year students, and I slid in beside him, what was it he said? *At long last we are quorate.* How solemnly he said it, what reproof for female lecturers gassing with a bunch of lads on the grass, sucking from a Coke bottle, in a strappy sundress. *At long last we are quorate.* Shuddering with aroused distaste.

And they got rid of me, the wankers. *You have hardly produced at all, Dr Powell.* That's a joke: I'm a one-woman

Harvest Festival. *A total of one article in five years shows a certain lack of commitment*, said the Dean. *Well, look on the bright side*, I sealed my fate, *I score with the students*.

Out flops my tittie, pop it in your mouth, Viola, and let sucking commence. She makes such a noise about it too. Little guzzler. All that lip-smacking, slurping, dribbling from the corner of her mouth, her small palm on my breast, Jesus it's still so sensual, the sensations radiating out in a star, ley lines to pleasure, the sweet drag on the womb, I've had many a happy secret orgasm through this, just cross my legs, so, and...

That's right, Aneurin, you read the nice article...

Aneurin has a premature interest in Things Sexual and Experimental, especially when someone's having a suck, he'll be fingering his willy or, as now, his little blond head (hair wants cutting but I can't be arsed, my God, three scalps, thirty fingernails and eke toenails, the maths of the thing goes into a dimension that's truly round the bend, and that's without adding in the teeth) and you, you snorting, snotty little brat, you're spoiling my fun, you seem to have needles in your gums and want to sink them into my tit when you batten on, Mother Nature has a lot to answer for.

How old are the little ones, may I ask? enquires the foreign guy sitting nearest to our menagerie. Magdalena is standing with one hand lightly on his knee, the other bunched against her lips, just staring. Is she all right in the head, I sometimes wonder?

Four, three and ten months.

Well, really, they are peautiful children.

Thank you. I think they're peautiful children too, I can't resist mimicking. *It's a pain waiting around with them though. I hope we're not disturbing you?*

Not in the world.

This I like. *Not in the world.* Meanwhile there's a flurry of coming and going: Old Williams and Ginger have had their jabs and been put out to freeze, and the girl on reception is sneezing away remorselessly over the queue. Give them one, girl, that's the spirit.

Wot you speak for like dat, Old Man? Magdalena is enquiring.

Well, I come from Chermany. In Chermany we speak Cherman. Not Inklish.

Magdalena is fascinated. Then, without warning or seeking permission, she clambers on to the German knee and gazes into the German eyes.

Oh glory. Do you mind?

I am honoured, he says. *Let us read a book together, Magdalena.* Off she trots to fetch one. *Such a charming name. Is she musical?*

Very. On the drum.

The drum is a very robust instrument.

Especially at five in the morning.

I swap Viola to the other breast. By God, I'll be a sad, saggy woman after all this suckling which I do *not* do, please note, Eternal Powers, do *not* do to protect my little darlings with my antibodies, no way, though, OK, sure, it makes sense and saves them and me a load of hassle, but because I personally happen to enjoy it, the tender, dragging, horny feeling that puts the light on in your body even when you're overworked, which by Christ you are, you're nine tenths dead by bedtime and feel fifty.

Williams is fingering his jaw in bewildered dismay. Asks Ginger in an undertone how her injection is taking. Blimey Charlie, the old goat, I'm sure he's got the hots for her, shouldn't she be warned about *being at long last quorate?*

He was on that panel that gave me the push. They all fiddled with their ties, while Dean Dai Thomas (whose fingers have been lubriciously active in generations of girls' knickers, pantihose, jeans, right back to corselettes and whalebone bras if the truth were known) enquired was I was a mite overburdened? Not wholly suited temperamentally to...? *No!* I should have said. *No way mister are you taking my livelihood!* But Viola chose that moment to wrench round, grinding her unborn bum on my bladder. My belly stretched so taut I gasped and felt I'd split. Uncharacteristic tears sparked. I fatally crumbled, under bombardment without and battery within. Lumbered up, said, *Sod the lot of you, you dessicated load of coconuts. I resign.*

Pure folly. I heard their basso profundo murmurings behind me. Knew it for a catastrophic mistake the moment I was through the door but at the same time there was an exhilaration, a punching of the air.

I'll reintroduce myself to Colleague Williams. When this little sprog of my loins has sucked me dry – oh for someone to fuck me dry, it's an age since I had a proper shag, by which I mean a shag where you see stars, you can hardly move afterwards and your flesh is so tender and lax that your pee scalds, your legs tremble, oh gorgeous, and the guy is still up for another go – oh for that fuck – anyhow, in the absence (temporary, I trust) of such, when Viola has sucked her fill, I'll introduce myself to old Quorate and watch him squirm. With any luck Viola can do a projectile vomit, I'll aim her at him, she's spectacular at those, I kid you not.

No, Aneurin, you'll just have to hold on I'm afraid.

He's whining for a widdle but you can bet, the moment we get into the loo, our names will be called and we'll miss our turn. When I get home I'll dump them for a nap and have a wank. How pathetic is that? Keeps you going, needs must.

Wow, you are pongy, I tell Viola. *You are one ripe stinky malodorous lass.* And she suddenly and surprisingly topples her head back like a heavy chrysanthemum and falls fast asleep, dead weight on my left arm. With the burp still in her.

Dr Williams has been called. He looks confounded and doesn't respond. As if by some Kafkaesque turn of events, he found himself transformed into a dental emergency in the middle of a seminar pontificating about his favourite, I don't know, *Welsh adverb*, and suddenly all his stained teeth sprayed out, revelatory, over the somnolent beery students.

Hi, I buttonhole him as he picks his way past my bratlings, *remember me?* He pretends not to hear my *Hi*, not to see my little Peauties. I should have set them on to him while I had the chance. Why keep a weapon of mass destruction to yourself? But he's gone. So that means we've got to wait for him to be drilled before we get our turn. And all we're in for is examinations.

Excuse me, I petition the crazed-looking receptionist. *Can't my kids go in first? Then you'll have a nice quiet place to sneeze and the other patients can rest in peace.*

Not if 'E says no. What 'E says, goes. Sorry, Mrs Powell.

Miss, Ms or Dr, I say. *Take your pick. But married I ain't. Doesn't matter about the wait. They might as well run riot here as anywhere. Aneurin, come and sit on Ms, Miss or Dr's lap, you yowling little sod.* I yank him by his dungarees.

The guy next to me who's been used and spurned by Magdalena looks at his watch. He read her something about Janet and John, of which she heard not one word, gazing with forensic curiosity into his face, squirming her behind on his knee until she got tired of it and announced her botty was itching. She'd sucked all the juice out of her prey, ground him around a bit on the squeezer and left his skin. If she goes on like that she'll turn into a mantis, either that or she'll have a bun in her oven before she's fifteen. Now they scramble for my lap. It's a conflict Magdalena's bound to win, since I've strapped Viola into the pushchair and Aneurin, for all his cheek, is a coward. When Magdalena comes at him punchy fists flying, with her stocky body, thick little legs and arms, eyes on fire like Boadicea, he has to bow to superior force. I adore her, I adore her. I see Aaron's face in her face swimming up to the surface as the baby plumpness of her cheeks recedes.

Come here, gorgeous, angelic, peautiful. I kiss her cheeks and she snares my neck with both arms, lovely and solid, kneeling up on my lap. And she kisses back, with rapture, her mouth open and wet on my cheek. How I cried for Aaron, how I drained my self in tears for Aaron, but ah-ha little did Aaron know, he'd left me with you, my Magdalena.

I have two children pack in Chermany, my neighbour confides *Two lovely little kirls. Rosa and Gabi. May I show you a picture?*

They're dear.

Yes, aren't they already?

He says no more. I ask no more. Funny, pictures of people's children: what can you say? His thin, fastidious fingers restore the two-dimensional girls to his wallet, tucking them into the compartment where they are housed. Nice quiet, paper children who don't require to be fed, potted, washed, hugged, lugged upstairs on your back and lullabyed half the night. Got it easy, haven't you, mister. And what a wallet. Fancy, swanky. Any number of pockets and receptacles. Now that we're on benefit our purse is notably light.

So you come to us complaining you're skint, are you, having thrown away all your advantages? Don't you know we scrimped for your education, and what have you done with it?

Given you grandchildren?

Any fool can do that. And Magdalena being, well, coffee-coloured. Aren't you ashamed?

Proud, I said quietly. *Proud. Magdalena is my life.*

I'd hoped for more sense from an educated woman. But I suppose you're after money, is it?

I grabbed the cheque, mortified. Done for myself good and proper. Still there was something mysteriously thrilling about being a pod. Going with my tummy spherical, like Plato's all-round men who rolled around without the need of legs, they were so perfect, and the babe-enclosing skin tight as a drum: well, that doesn't sound too pleasant, but...

That's the way, Aneurin, you go sleepy-byes, curl up like a kitten... yes, I know you're hungry, we're all hungry...

...but it was a feeling of being ripe, fruity, and lusciously mindless, just drifting on a current, thinking of nothing but the next meal because, talk about hungry, I snaffled Mars bars galore, I was a frigging Mars bar, and I said to Aaron that time, *I'll have your child, Aaron. Then I'll be content. You'll not be able to hurt me, no one will hurt me then, I'll be.*

Be what?

Just be.

He made no reply but I could see him chewing it over. Well I got over him. And the others. Problem with kids is, you can't put them away in your wallet until convenient. Because I am ravenous for life. For pleasure. So, Dr Powell, why did you not insure against inconvenience by investing in the pill? Haven't a frigging clue. I seem to have lived in a dream.

Wish I hadn't blown it at the Institute. Good feeling, that was, perched on the desk, swinging my legs in the tiniest skirt and the highest heels whilst confiding the obscene habits of Caligula to an agog packed lecture theatre. Invented novel and ingenious vices on the spur of the moment, on the best scholarly principles. They lapped it up. Gives you a buzz to wow a couple of hundred guys at a sitting. Not wowing anyone much now with my tall tales, my svelte figure. I mean, pods don't, do they? Two a penny in every supermarket. God I could get maudlin if I let myself, I could be hangdog.

Williams reels out. Looks fit to puke. Excellent. So it's our turn? But of course we're all in the land of nod. Some of us are even snoring. We've red cheeks and a sleep-sweat. We're curled up like kittens, we're sucking our thumbs, we're an army that has fallen corporately asleep on the watch. And we are deep asleep, make no bones about that, the waters have closed over our heads and we are full fadom five. Thus it is, Mr Dentist Davies, that you have robbed me of my postprandial wank, which these characters would have granted me by toppling asleep en masse after their beans on toast. Thus it is that your ears will be assailed by God awful roaring when you wake them up from dreamland. You have buggered up our day, Mr Davies, good and proper, and you will suffer.

Williams totters, a pitiful crock, with flecks of blood on his chin. Obviously one tooth lighter than when he went in. Relief suffuses his face at the sight of Ginger. Salvation is nigh. A female person to moan to, lean on, leech from. And oh is she asking for it. *Leech me! Leech me!* You daft bugger.

Mrs Powell, would you all like to come through?

Ms, Miss or Dr.

Oh, yes, right, Mrs Powell.

I'm not married, you see. Powell is my name. I'm not Mrs

Well, anyhow, would you like to come through?

Oh yes, that will be very easy, won't it, now that they're all fast asleep.

Well, I'm sorry, Mrs Powell, we've been running late as you know, what with sickness and understaffing, we do our best.

I'm – not – Mrs.

Tell you what, if I take the little one, you could carry the little boy and … we could come back for …

Allow me, says the Teutonic white knight. *Allow me to transport my, if I may so style her, little friend Magdalena.*

So my trinity of young souls trumpet-voluntaries its outraged dolour, its berserk triumph over the forces of fogeyness, bellowing fit to wake the dead, which, as Mr Davies jests, is handy, since it serves to pop open everyone's mouth for inspection, without need of coaxing or bribery, and all at once we are out in the street and headed for home, fish fingers and an hour's serious solace under the duvet.

BLOOD ETC.

Gee Williams

The house, Carousel – a piss-poor, schmaltzy, inappropriate name for a buff-brick nineteen-thirties house, he thought – stood at a bit of a crossroads. Not a roundabout, which might at least have made explicable the overlarge sign they were always meaning to get changed. Just a crossroads. A crossing of two unimportant minor roads, neither of which provided the best or shortest route to the built-up areas they joined together. Tatten Lane passed under Carousel's front wall. It brought sporadic traffic to annoy anyone attempting to read in the sitting room or sleep in the guest bedroom, before it wandered off in the direction of the river and the old packhorse bridge. Only an ugly bungalow (dwarfed by stables the size and shape of a modern factory unit) stood between Carousel and where Dial Green petered out. The wider Old Wrexham Road ran along the side of the house. It made for the country town with more obvious brio but was kept at bay by a large, shrubby garden and the remains of an ancient orchard. In season its ripe fruit, spurned by the inhabitants of Carousel, still fell from the branches, rolled onto the tarmac and were pulped by passing cars…

Or were snatched up by the more quick-witted of the animals being chivvied to and from Tatten Livery by a succession of lithe, young riders. All female.

When they moved in Mel must've been one of the first locals he'd become aware of: a young girl – that's the mistake he'd made and only when already close enough for speech had Alun clocked how, under the hat – the *helmet* – there was a girl/woman.

Round, fresh face. Dark, slightly protuberant eyes under fleshy lids. Freckles across the nose and upper cheekbones. When she smiled it was with rows of small regular teeth, though a shade too ivory for perfection. When she swept off the hat, whose black silk cover had slipped askew giving her a bit of a tipsy air, the red hair sprang shocking out.

Sixteen he reckoned. (Afterwards, after the accident and the passing around of fragments of that day's happening as though they were a new currency the whole neighbourhood had gone over to, he'd found she was nearer twenty.)

'Let him have it!' he'd suggested as he saw the huge horse snatch at the bit, lunge forward in its quest for fruit and the rider with equal determination haul on the reins. 'Let him have an apple. They're only going to waste.'

'That's not the point!' Mel had snapped back.

'Isn't it?'

The horse swung immense, brown hindquarters at Alun's face and he dodged back to the sanctuary of steps up to his gate. A spark was kindled as the iron shoe struck a stone where an instant ago his own feet had stood. He'd never seen that before, but then he'd not had much to do with horses before. 'Why isn't it?'

Breathing hard with the effort the girl circled the horse and its threatening hooves out into the lane before turning its head in Alun's direction as though the animal were a boat in a heavy swell and Alun waiting on the dockside. 'Because,' she said, still panting, 'he mustn't think – stand up, Samson, stand up! – he mustn't think when he's working he can just stop for something to eat. When he wants. He has to—' but in giving her attention to Alun for the moment it took to frame the reply, Samson had shot out his muzzle and grabbed up a half-apple from the gutter. The blunt lower jaw slid from side to side as the fruit was pulverised and the juice ran. And there was nothing Mel could do to hinder it.

'Seems to me,' said Alun, 'that's exactly what he can do.' Mel had let out a hoot of laughter and slapped the blissfully masticating brute on its arched neck. 'I know! He's a greedy sod. Just look at the weight on him.'

It gave him a thrill that voice. Not because it was anything special. Not because of its light, girly tone and easy half-Welsh, half-English border accent. But because it was not the voice of a three-year-old boy – the only other, apart from his own, he heard all day. Not that looking after the child, his child, was bad – how could he ever allow himself to think that? Or if it was, when it was, it couldn't be blamed on Charlie. That day, the day he'd first spoken to Mel, he'd retraced his steps and picked the boy from the lawn and hoisting him onto his shoulders had said, 'Come and see the big horse, Charlie,' and Charlie had shrieked with excitement at the movement and new elevation.

'Hor-orse! Hor-orse!' the child demanded.

'D'you want a ride Charlie, hey? A ride on the horse? Can he?' he added almost as a formality and in the act of passing the small body from his own shoulders to the animal's neck.

Samson's head jerked towards his massive chest as he reined back one stride, two strides, out of reach. 'No, sorry,' Mel said. The action had seemed like a rejection from the horse itself but now he realised it was just a trick, a manoeuvre inspired by some signal of hand and heel that he'd missed. 'Too dangerous. The kid could get hurt.' She sent further directions to the beast – ah, yes, he saw that one: the left boot tap, the right rein twitched – and away they went leaving him standing, the child still offered up in his arms.

The kid? Alun's temper kindled at the slight. *The kid*? Immersed for the better part of Charlie's short life in Charlie's care, his desire to indulge the boy was affectively maternal though masculine in sheer force. His own belief in

Charlie's status as a small but priceless household god was rarely subject to challenge.

'Miserable bitch,' he muttered.

But she was right. Imagine the possibilities, the explanations and Holly's face, angry, flushed and incredulous. *You did what*? *And then what*? *Christ Alun, what the fuck were you thinking of*?

What the fuck had he been thinking of? Of course she was right.

And a good thing not to have taken against Mel, newcomer as he was. No one the length of the straggling, half-pretty place had a word to say against Mel and he soon learned why. She and Samson were local celebrities. Twice daily they'd make their way though the alarums and excursions of The Square to gain access to the old bridleway running over the hill, mile after mile. Local lads – rough as they looked – raised unironic open bottles to them as they passed in front of the Pendy Arms or the Full Moon. *Mel and Samson had once been on television.* You don't go disrespecting someone who's been interviewed for nearly a minute on *Wales Today.* And Mel acknowledged them. Though she came from The Old Rectory, though her father was a consultant at Maelor Ears, Nose and Throat – and wealthy enough to keep a jobless daughter and a vast, money-munching horse – Mel acknowledged them. (*Hi- yer, Scott! See you, then, Tim!* The first time Alun witnessed it, he found himself troubled with unaccountable pain). She nodded to Scott and Tim and the weaselly Neil. She nodded to the driver of the ad-daubed single-decker bus that backed up onto the garage forecourt rather than crowd Dial Green's star. In the store, Mel and Samson's success at the last Royal Welsh Show remained prominent, if yellowing, in the window. The horse's bulk improbably hovered over a construction of striped poles and Mel's small figure, well out of the saddle, hovered above him. Gravity, the picture demonstrated, gravity – for those with the knack – was a sometime force.

On local radio, one endless afternoon, 'a young Dial Green rider proves unbeatable' was actually the before-these-and-other-stories headline. Or it was until an explosion at the soap-powder plant knocked it out of its slot.

One endless afternoon...

In the city where he and Holly'd met, in the tight, modern flat they'd brought Charlie home to, the afternoons hadn't had so many hours in them. It was something to do with the view, he decided. In the city you were connected to a squirming vista, opening up and closed down by high-sided traffic so that pass the window on your way to the kitchen and a whole Victorian canyon of buildings terminated only in the distant prospect of the Cathedral – look again on your return trip and the Japanese tourists in a coach not ten feet away smiled up at you, edgily courteous. Beyond your window, in any half-day period (the time between Holly popping in to breastfeed Charlie his lunch, say, and the first hope of her return) – beyond your window was bound to offer something in the way of a buzz. A rear-ending with or without rage, an assisted fall from a bike... a dog's suicidal dash into the carriageway, lead flapping. He had enjoyed a bag-snatch, a police car's totalling against a concrete bollard and an old lady's collapse and removal by paramedics without accompanying siren – so a probable death right there as he watched.

'How awful!' Holly had murmured over her pasta.

A jolt. Yes, it was awful, wasn't it, another human being subsiding beneath you, breathing her last next to the teak-effect structure holding communal bins?

In Dial Green there was no movie running constantly within the window frame. No free, chaotic fringe-show. There was a painting. The trees in the redundant orchard made him cranky with their sluggard ways. 'When are we going to see some apples on those things?'

'Don't be impatient – the blossom's only just fallen.' Holly was country-bred as Charlie was going to be. Holly had been accurate in this as in most else. Apples had appeared in pointless, messy profusion – and he'd spoken to Mel.

Was it the height of the horse that meant she always had him at a disadvantage? It was a couple of weeks later. The boy was having a nap and Alun was released into the September sunshine and free from the nagging vigilance of care. Mel had surprised him on his own property. He was caught examining fruit still attached to a squat, cankerous branch of apple that was becoming lost in an unpruned briar.

'I'll bet you've got enough there for a ton of jam.'

He spun round to see her head and shoulders above the hedge. Slowly, weirdly, the disembodied living bust slid along the shaggy hedge-top, turned and slid back to its original position but facing the other way.

'*Jam?*'

The fruit already picked that was in his free hand he dropped to the grass.

'Well if it was me, I'd do cider. I think the old bid lived here before you did cider. Always had a smile on her face.'

He shrugged. Beyond the hawthorn the horse snorted and a V-sign of brown ears flicked up.

He could play the townie: 'All this – it needs cutting back. I thought – probably get someone in to do it. Someone who knows what they're doing. Not my thing – all this.'

It was the truth – the near truth. That morning Holly had suggested he harvest and stew fruit for Charlie's tea. ('They must be organic, right? I mean we've been here since the spring. Nobody's sprayed them.') Patiently, whilst fending off his help to zip up the grey dress, shaking out the black jacket, matador-style, she'd explained. How you just peeled a good big apple, cut it up, cooked it in a pan, stirred in that Manuka honey she's just managed to get hold of that was going to be good for Charlie's gripy tummy. How it wasn't rocket science for Chrissake.

But what was a good apple? Not bruised... not already

home to a tetchy wasp. Even on the tree every fruit he examined had some sort of mark or excavation. Did this mean it was not good?

'So what is your thing then?'

'Well – what do I do, d'you mean?'

'If you like.'

'I'm on a break at the moment.'

'Sick leave is it?' It was said, he felt, with a challenge in the tone even though it hadn't made it onto the face.

Cow! He really didn't want to get into this. But where was the refuge from the smiling down, provocative child – yes, child he still thought her. This must be innocence rather than goading – surely? A misreading. Of something not meant or not understood. Not yet experienced. In your thirties you were about as far away from teenagers as you were going to get: twice their years, off the pace of their culture but still with only babies and toddlers amongst your friends and in your own house – so no new perspective there either...

'A career break. We've got the little fellow in there.' *Bollocksfuckingbollocks*. 'We-er had the kid, you know and one of us had to take a break. Holly, that's my partner, she helps run a business. It's a leather factory, if you know what that is. They deal in all types of leather. It's in the city – in Chester. She runs it really. So it was easier for me to... just till we get him off to school. It's good. It's been good. I...'

'Yeah? See you.'

The truck that was suddenly there beside him on the Wrexham Road, its air brakes hissing, was a sort of comfort. It drove off Samson with his inquisitive passenger and allowed Alun to get inside, though appleless... Charlie, must check on Charlie.

Up in the small bed with its racing-car modelling, the boy slept on, one finger hooked into his light brown curls. He knelt beside him and gently pulled down the child's hand and, though gummed with chocolate, tucked it beneath the quilt – for what reason? Did he want to wake him? No, of course not and yes, he needed to have Charlie awake so that he could make amends in play or treats. He needed to make up to Charlie for the disquiet that had come over him out there in the orchard, being questioned by that brainless girl. *Sick leave*! But the boy, though he stirred, burrowed down again into sleep. Against the weight of the covering, the sticky fingers flapped uselessly and stilled. He ought to wake him – tonight as they attempted to eat off their separate trays, Charlie, alert and demanding, would give the game away. Cantering laps of the room, pretending to showjump Holly's outstretched legs and failing – and delighting in the failure with thought-numbing screams.

How long did you leave this child down?

That afternoon he found a machete-type thing in one of the locked outhouses they had yet to clear out. With the boy still sleeping soundly he took it to the briars in the hedge and several other overgrown bushes he couldn't identify; he hacked and decapitated with wired intensity. *Sick leave*. As though hawking around cheap (slash) fucking rancid (slash) hides was such a big deal. As though minding (slash) your own child (slash) was so (slash) fuckingoffthefuckingwall. As though sticking manfully to the cause of Durward (slash) Leather Ltd was going to find the cure for cancer.

'And is it all chugging along as normal at Skin City?' he asked Holly almost before she'd put down her keys and looked around for Charlie, 'He's that heap of sand, by the way, driving the fire engine.'

'Oh, well done Alun!' Holly was out of the back door, picking her way down the uneven path in black five-inch heels. 'Hello yuk-mush!' She picked the giggling Charlie up and carried him in at arm's length. 'You could get him cleaned up when you know I'm coming home. What time is it? It's gone seven for FS.'

'You like to bath him on a Friday. You said…'

'I know. *I know*. But you could have given him a lick and a promise first.'

408

'I'll do it now. Just give him to me.'

'Doesn't matt...'

The pair disappeared up the stairs. Ten minutes later, changed, different, all smiles, they were back... Charlie standing on the rug between them, his unclouded blue eyes fixed on Holly's face – *as they did the instant the very instant the exact instant she came into a room.*

'Early frost, eh?' This from the student working out the summer's end at the garage, behind armoured glass. Alun had spoken to him a couple of times, knew more than he needed to know, now, about his parents' giving up the farm, his course in Forestry at Bangor, his debts. No name.

'Is it?'

'Well – yeah. Don't usually get it white over, not October, do we?'

He pocketed the card – 'To be honest, I haven't a clue' – never for a second taking his attention from the VW out on the forecourt, from Charlie, trapped in his seat, staring good-naturedly about him.

An October frost – that was meant to mean something was it? Put on the spot, he realised, he couldn't have told the exact date and would've had to grope for the month. As he sat, feet up on the kitchen table and the Driving section of last Sunday's paper open before him, he made a point of noting *October 10, 2004.* So – today was the 12th... a date completely without significance of any sort. It wasn't a day away from that important decision on his productivity bonus. No new and fragile contact at The Club Chair Company needed to be inveigled out to lunch. And as for that flight to Stuttgart the lamebrain Julie had forgotten to book, it had turned out to be no bad thing because that had been the week World of Bags had come back to him with the biggest, single...

Swinging down numbed legs he was straight up onto his feet. The paper slipped into its constituent pages onto the floor and he crumpled it for the recyc rather than bother with reassembly. How pathetically easy it was for the brain to stumble into this sort of thing! Present events, hateful as they unfold but their edges gradually smoothed over by memory to become cosy, funny: to become *Well, of course, at the time, while you're doing it, it can be an absolute nightmare but you get a real rush when you pull off a...*

An early frost, was it? OK. A spur to replacing those broken flags before the weather worsened, before Holly in her beautiful brush-dyed, scarlet leather knee-highs went arse over tit. Charlie was uncomplaining as, rebuttoned into a jacket, he was piggybacked outside. 'Right, Charles William Mann, your mission, should you chose to accept it, is to lever up these broken bits, stack them out of sight behind the outhouse because Daddy has no idea what you're meant to do with spare bits of path and then bring those four new slabs that have been sitting round the front for over a month and drop then neatly into place. They will of course be a perfect fit.'

Charlie, nodding, made a move to pick up the crowbar (another outhouse find) but when Alun said, 'No! That's for Daddy to use,' a cynical look crossed his three-year-old face. He trotted off in the direction of the swing singing 'Per-erflect fit, per-erflect fit' in his clear treble.

'Don't worry there'll be something for you in a minute...' Alun couldn't think what though. 'And then you can help me with the really hard part, yeah?' The child didn't even favour this one with a backward glance. The path was history. Down the garden, that's where it was happening... determination to be there was written into his spine, in his arms swinging, despite the padded coat. But small for his age: the observation came accompanied by a slight niggle, a psychic pinprick. Was Charlie destined to be not only light-boned and pale as Holly but also more Holly-beneath-the-skin? Attention easily focused and biddable as a tuning button, cutting from this to that message, the fuzzy to the sharp. Nothing ever got to

Holly, as they said at the Chester office, because Holly *didn't let it*.

The stack of four flags – no five flags, one for breakages, of course – was nestling in its fringe of long grass behind the front hedge. Misjudging size Alun rammed them with the wheelbarrow – and did it again. He could at least have offered Charlie a ride around in the barrow, something that never failed to delight. When he'd got this first one shifted, he'd do it for the next and the next. He bent to the task.

From beyond the hedge, there were three distinct sounds. (Later he'd be able to work out that these were the incident itself and everything else its aftermath.) First came a female voice: a shout that began as 'Whoah-h!' but carried on beyond the word as 'oh-oh-oh!' until drowned out by the second noise, an easily identifiable squeal of brakes. This ended in a thud, dull but with metallic overtones. There were a few seconds of silence during which Alun let go the slab almost trapping his own fingers and stood up. Just over the hedge, but very close to it, was the silver roof of an estate car. He had a moment to recognise it (he was good on cars) as a Mercedes when a new sound started up. It was the worst thing he had heard in his life: a deep, throaty bellow that rose and slackened, rocketed up to an almost unbearable pitch before subsiding into a thick gurgle. Another bellow – more gurgling – a blessed pause – and a horrible human-like scream.

The steps down onto the road were almost blocked by the car's bonnet but he fought the hawthorn to get out. Hidden by the car but now directly ahead of him he came across Mel. She was lying on her side, one arm beneath her head, which was turned toward him. Her eyes were wide open and apparently staring into his. Her hat was still in place though pushed back so that strands of bright red hair were on show and there was a long black mark across her cheek. As he knelt down to touch her face and speak a word to her, the offside door of the Mercedes (with its dented panel) began to swing open. It would, he saw, catch the unmoving Mel in its arc. Angrily he placed both fists on the door and slammed it shut. A face behind the glass – with an open mouth – registered with him as nobody, neither man nor woman.

'Stay in!' he shouted at it. Dimly he was aware that in the vehicle's interior someone had begun to cry.

Mel blinked.

'It's all right but you shouldn't move,' he said to her. He patted the arm that lay along the road surface – in fact, had become a part of the road's surface. The green material of her sleeve was ripped away and her lower arm embedded with gravel. A terrible mewling rose again from somewhere beyond them and Mel screwed up her eyes as though wishing someone, somewhere would just turn it down. She groaned and flopped over onto her back. 'Oh fuck,' she breathed but managed to straighten out her legs.

'You really have got to keep still…'

'Sam-son.'

'What?'

Her hand, its palm dark with grit and blood gestured to somewhere else, somewhere vaguely in the direction of town. 'The fucking horse!' she shouted furiously.

'But…'

'I'm all… right. *Listen*! Go!'

It didn't occur to him to do anything but follow such fierce instructions. Certainly not to turn back to the car and its occupants. Around the corner he found the animal, half of it lying across the grass verge, the rest (the brown heap of its hindquarters and a pair of threshing back legs) sticking out into Wrexham Road. Across the way a motorcyclist had dismounted but stood, visor down, his back to his machine, not moving. Ahead a white van was pulled up on the opposite verge and its driver just getting out. 'D'you have a mobile?' he had to shout above the horse's terrific bellows which had grown at his approach. The man nodded and fumbled at his belt unable to look away from the animal on the ground. 'Call the police and ambulance and – and a vet. Say people hurt – and a horse. Badly injured. OK? Yes? Corner of Old Wrexham Road and Tatten Lane. Yes?' In a wide curve he walked to the front of Samson. To the approaching van driver he said. 'Can you go into the lane and check on the girl – the rider – and whoever's in that fucking car? Can you, please?' Just as he had felt impelled to do with Mel, he knelt down and patted what was closest – in this case a thick, twitching foreleg with its white sock. Samson rolled his eyes and screamed and a violent shudder travelled along his body. Two iron shoes clattered on the tarmac. Alun pulled his hand away. He could see now the explanation of the creature's complaint. The upper right foreleg and right shoulder were not so much injured as mashed: there was a reduction to a bloody ragout of tissue where a robust, load-bearing joint had once been. What had become of the hide in this area with its cover of brown hair was a mystery. No sign of it. It was as though this had been completely dissolved in the impact: the guard was off the machine and the works were on show. Creamy subcutaneous fat and the humps of muscle, grey wires connecting this with that, white and pearly-pink shards of bone, all had come spilling out. Incredible that such a blunt-instrument as a car had done this... easier to believe in a shotgun, a bomb blast, a mauling by lions.

The waxing and waning of distress was the result of the animal's attempt to rise. With stupid persistence, Samson drew his hind legs under him and tried to heave himself up to a comical sitting position. The left foreleg straightened but wasn't anywhere near up to the job of raising such a weight alone. Repeatedly he slumped back onto the turf as blood and gobbets from the gaping hole in his right side sprayed out. Alun thought of catching at the broken rein that hung from the bit, wondering if he had the strength to hold the suffering horse down. Never having so much as touched Samson in the weeks of their acquaintance (having been threatened, in fact, by his wayward nature and size) dare he take charge of the animal now, in its last few minutes of life?

Suddenly Mel was beside him. The flayed arm hung by her side and either she or someone else had taken off her hat.

'Christ, you shouldn't be up.'

Her face was the colour of plaster and seemed to set as she looked down. 'I'm all right – just my wrist. Can you help me get this jacket off?'

'Why don't you wait for the ambulance? Let them decide...'

Already she had the good arm free. 'Are you going to help or what?'

Gently as he could, Alun pulled the stiff garment off her. She dropped onto the grass, not able to kneel, and took hold of the bridle. Surely she lacked the strength to hold the head in place? And yet from her touch, beginning in her fingers, some new force flowed. Through the leather of noseband and cheekpieces it shot, through the half-dead-half-living fabric of the straps and into the horse's jagged nerves. It was as though the animal paused, just for an instant, in its simple program of flight: Mel let go the rein and carefully placed part of the olive stuff of her jacket across Samson's eyes. The long rasping in his throat continued and he began to grind his teeth, horribly – Alun felt he must be sheering off the enamel with the force of it – but the great legs stilled.

'Is that what you're meant to do? To keep them quiet?'

'I don't know – how the fuck do I know? It's just something I've seen on the TV.'

Apart from the slowing of the occasional car – to be waved away by Alun – a sort of peace descended on the three of them. Mel sat bare-armed, pale but not crying, not shivering or moving much at all, one usable hand on the horse's forehead and its blindfold. Her arms, he saw, were nothing like Holly's; they were more like a boy's or a younger version of his own, rounded and strong.

Chat was out of the question, surely. Low voices could just

be made out, back in the lane; they'd be huddled around the car, Alun guessed. He dreaded the appearance of anyone else. Certainly to have the driver, the perpetrator of this carnage, come walking up now with explanations, apologies, recriminations... with anything, just any speech at all: Alun felt if that happened he'd be on the bastard straightaway – it was what he could do to stop Mel having to think about it, having to reply.

'Shush-sh.'

Mel was whispering softly to the horse presumably as she felt each agitation beneath her fingers. 'Shush, Samson.' She breathed the comfortable words but stared straight ahead into the empty road. Beneath the jacket Samson's head jerked.

'I couldn't understand,' Alun said, 'why he kept trying to get up. I mean it must hurt him to...'

'It's not in their nature, to be down like this.'

Another spasm wracked Samson's frame; the rounded mass of dark ribcage and belly, overshadowing the covered head, had taken on the look of something helpless, something blubbery and aquatic now stranded on a dry shore.

'Christ, is he?' 'No,' Mel said.

'I thought then – you know.'

'He's going into shock, I think. A horse is a big thing.' Still not looking, still letting the breeze take the brilliant spirals of hair and irritate her dirty cheek with them. 'They're big so they take a while to die.' (So Samson *was* dying. There was relief in this at least, because Mel's surety meant that there was nothing *he* ought to be doing. There were no actions – messy, difficult, are you up to this? – that if performed might save the horse and if not...) 'They live in their bodies, horses, you know? What their bodies are doing, that's them at that moment. That's where they're at. If you don't ride, you can't understand. It's a good way to be. That's what I try to be – as much as I can. You just are what you're doing and that's it. If you can do that, you can lose all the other stuff – the crap. All the crap with my mum and dad, it's been going on for years and even now – she lives in France now, yeah? With her new bloke. She lives in another country and it can still kick off over nothing. Me... what I'm doing or what she thinks I should be up to. Who owns this really gross painting – that was last thing. He finds it's gone. Two years, then he notices the space on the wall and he's all for going over to get it back because...'

For a moment they could both ignore it and then neither of them could: a siren in the distance but homing in on them, threatening their brittle stasis. Samson heard it, stirred and twitched.

'Shush-sh. I'm not going – if that's the ambulance. I can't leave him till...'

'There's a vet coming,' he said pointlessly.

'I know. Motorbike man said. Thanks.'

A police car, lights flashing but siren now off, drew up a respectful distance away. The policeman who approached was paunchy and near retirement age by the looks of him, sweating as though attending the scene on foot.

'Oh dear.'

Alun stood up and met him on the road to keep between this new intruding figure and the horse. 'She needs to go to hospital. Broken arm at least, I think – God, I don't know, she could be really hurt. But she won't go till someone's dealt with the horse.'

The policeman glanced down at Samson and up again to Alun. What was the matter with the idiot? What didn't he understand? Alun, his back to Mel, raised his index finger to his own temples. 'OK?'

He nodded. 'The other – I mean the vehicle involved in this, sir. Has it been driven off?'

'Just round the corner. You'll find it in front of my house. But stir up that bloody vet will you?'

They sat for what seemed another couple of hours easily,

but was probably only minutes. At one point the policeman came back out of Tatten Lane, talking all the time to a distant agent, removed something from the police car that Alun couldn't see and went back with it in the direction of Carousel. When a Landrover arrived from the opposite direction to that of the police car it was Mel who saw it.

'Hello Peter. I was hoping it'd be you.'

'Hello Mel. You um, hanging in there?'

'Yep.'

Peter was tall and wiry and, dressed in a khaki boiler suit, could have passed for a mechanic, one of those we'll-fix-you-by-the-road-types that Alun had been forced to rely on more than once. Feeling very much the spare part, Alun made space for the vet to kneel between the horse's bent knee and its shrouded head. Peter seemed to ignore the terrible wound from which blood still leaked; he put his hand on the animal's muzzle and pulled at the lower lip. 'Membranes are a poor colour. He's deeply in shock.'

'I know,' Mel said.

'From just what I can see from here,' Peter's contortionist's frame enabled a head-cocked, half-balanced peek into the hole in Samson, 'it looks like lateral head of triceps damage – severe damage... huge amount of tissue loss in the area. Bone fragments might be from the sternum or the ulna or both.' He rocked back and away on his heels but the squeak of rubber boots now failed to set off anything more than a long rattling exhalation from the horse.

'Can you do it now, please?'

'Yes. I think that's the thing to do. Yes. Right, Mel. If you're able to stay there, I'll get my stuff.'

Alun might not have been present: this was to be accomplished by Mel, Peter and Samson, of course. Once Peter had shaved a patch on Samson's neck to insert his lethal injection Alun, more out of curiosity than any distinct purpose, wandered back into Tatten Lane. What met him was an extraordinary scene: across from Carousel on the narrow grass strip it seemed a family picnic was in progress. A young woman sat on a travel-rug, a grizzling baby ignored in her lap while an older, white-haired woman bent to hand her – to hand her very shakily – a steaming plastic top from a thermos flask. The paunchy policeman stood talking to the seated woman whilst being pulled about and interrupted by a small boy who had him by the hand...

So Samson's executioner: not male, as he'd been convinced for absolutely no reason, but one of these ashen-faced, miserable women trying to explain themselves, failing to care for that baby and that little boy who couldn't be much more than Charlie's age...

Who was Charlie!

'Charlie! What are you doing out here?'

'Policeman, Daddy! I had his hat!'

In confusion, the policeman turned a suspicious face to Alun, 'So is this your car, sir?'

'What? No! I live here. That's my son – we live in this house and I know the girl. The girl who was hit,' he finished for the benefit of the women.

Charlie's cold little hand was passed across to him without a word.

'I didn't see the accident, just heard it from the garden – then when I went out, there was Mel in the road...'

'That's fine, then. Perhaps you'd like to take your little boy inside and I'll have a word with you when I'm sorted here?'

'I think I'll go back and see how she's doing if it's all the same to you. The vet's...' he looked at the seated woman, who looked away. 'Well, the vet's putting the horse down now. Mel might need someone.'

He regretted it as soon as the words were out. Of course he couldn't take Charlie with him back around that corner, where Samson was dying – or dead, by now – was nothing more than a giant shocking carcass beneath the inadequate cover of a Barbour jacket. But as the policeman was about to argue the point an ambulance, its blue light flashing to the further delight of Charlie, finally arrived. Alun picked the boy up and made to edge past the Merc still half-blocking Carousel's gateway. He should, he knew, offer to take the women and the whimpering baby with him but he clutched the boy hard against his own chest and, 'Come on, Charlie, let's go and get you warmed up,' he said.

'Samson's dead,' Charlie told Holly. 'Who?'

Charlie was curled against her in the chair. Holly's eyes quizzed Alun above the bright, splayed pages of *Billy Penny's Pig*.

'What's he saying?'

'I was going to tell you about it – when he's gone up, though.'

'Oh?'

'Something – not good.'

'Did Charlie see it?'

'Yes, Mummy! Samson's all dead,' Charlie chipped in. '*No*. Tell you later... What's that you two are reading? What's the story, Charlie?'

Billy Penny was displayed on the cover astride his flying pig and the advantages of being the owner of a pig that could fly thoroughly enlarged upon. Strangely, although the book had been about the house for over a year and he knew the story by rote, so often had it been a bedtime request, only now did Alun notice the name of the book's author: Don Kellett. When he'd been first employed by Durward's as a new graduate in marketing, the company had been run by a Don Kells. Pushing seventy, Don remembered when Durward's had been a *real leather company* – when it had owned tanneries out in Cheshire and Wales, stench-lapped horror stories of workplaces, cosying up to the friendly neighbourhood abattoirs, that were also no more. It was Don who'd insisted Alun accompany him to the last Durward tannery just before it closed...

...down a scabby little sideroad, it was. The inhabitants

of a just-visible council estate had left along its length offerings of mattresses, gaping fridges and carpet offcuts: fair exchange for the miasma in which they lived. By the time Don nosed the car into the tannery yard, Alun believed the stink of anything could not be more intense – it was overwhelming his ability to choose words, to think even – but it could. Inside. Inside the tannery building the atmosphere was laden to a level of pungency that was intolerable – and yet men stood about in it, men came forward and joked with Don about *sammying* and *perching* in it. Men said, 'All right?' in it to him when he was introduced.

Don Kells: 'Tanning, it's got to be the oldest profession bar one, lad. We were at this before farming.'

Don Kells: 'Nothing like leather, nothing else like it – it'll keep the water out and yet let the vapour through. Seems like it's dead but it still *breathes*.'

Don Kells: 'How long will it last? How long? Well it lasted the beast a lifetime, eh?'

That tannery-stink was back in his nostrils now and on it had risen Don Kells.

The old man would probably be dead. But Alun found he was reluctant to ask Holly though she'd know. Instead he said, 'Isn't that book a bit babyish for Charlie now? He seems to have had it for ages. Shouldn't he be moving on?'

'But we love Billy Penny, don't we Charlie? *Mummy* loves Billy Penny. And we do *wish* we had a flying pig.'

'Did you notice, it's a bloke's written it?'

'Yes, I know.'

'Don Kellett. Reminded me of old Don Kells.' Holly had no answer it seemed.

'Anyway, what sort of life is that for a bloke, writing baby books?'

'So what happened?'

'Just like Charlie said, I'm afraid. The horse – it belongs

to, you know... Mel Gethin? I told you about her. She's the girl always stops and lets Charlie feed the horse?' Alun lied, not even sure why he was lying as he did it. 'Well 'bout lunchtime some bitch in a big Merc decides she's turning into the lane and the fact that Mel and this bloody great horse are in the way doesn't slow her down one bit.'

'Christ! Where were you? Is the girl all right?'

'I was gardening with Himself. I heard the crunch. I knew it was going to be bad so I popped him in front of Postman Pat and went out. There's the girl in the road – broken arm, I think but really banged about as well. There's this stupid bloody woman – more worried about the car than anything else by the looks of it. And of course there's this mangled horse. It was obvious they'd have to shoot it – half its chest was hanging out, broken leg – but not dead, that's the bummer.'

'Oh, yuk! So what about the driver?'

'What d'you mean? Police breathalysed her but she hadn't been drinking. Just a naturally rubbish driver.'

'Was she hurt?'

'No. Who cares? I was more into trying to clear up her mess.'

A long pause during which Holly got to her feet and began tidying away Charlie's bright detritus into the pine chest, kept in the corner of the sitting room for just that purpose: somewhere in the series of actions there seemed like a reproach.

'You should have seen it! Mel lying in the road – for a moment I thought she must've had it. Then there's this horse, foaming at the mouth – terrible pain it must have been in. Blood, etc. everywhere... Sorry, is this too much detail or something?'

'No. I was listening.' She swept the light fringe from her forehead in a familiar gesture of fatigue. 'I'm glad Charlie... I wondered what he meant about the policeman. He was chattering on about a policeman all the time he was in the bath... I'm just glad that you managed to keep Charlie out of it.'

'Well I did.'

'Yes.'

'Yes.'

'Perhaps you could take him out tomorrow? For a trip somewhere, just to take his mind off anything he *might* have...'

'But I've said, he didn't. Anyway I thought you wanted the path done, before the winter?'

'I do – of course, I do. It's just one day, though. And it's Wednesday – I'll be late tomorrow. I've got that bloke from Bolton coming in. I told you. He's had two shipments from Pakistan he can't use. Full grain for tooling, you see, but what he's getting isn't taking up the water...'

Alun realised something in his face had caused her to tail off.

In the morning the lane outside Carousel seemed untouched by Tuesday's commotion: a solitary bit of broken hawthorn straggled out over the lane. Then he noticed a series of scrapes on the tarmac – marks that disappeared around the corner along the track of the collapsing Samson – and ghoulishly found he must follow them. A magpie flapped up from the spot on the grass where the horse had dropped and died. 'One for sorrow, two for joy,' he said out loud, as though he had Charlie by the hand and with him, instead of back in the kitchen, wide-eyed at *Pingu* the Penguin, missing his aim with the fingers of toast.

Managing to thorn his hand, he pulled off the broken branch and threw it into the stubble-field across from the house. Briefly he considered getting out the hose and washing away the gobbets of brown blood on the grass; at the tap he saw the impracticality of the plan. No amount of garden hose was going to stretch from the back door of the garage, across the lawn, through the orchard and all the way out into Wrexham Road.

He was unwilling to touch the flagstones or barrow. The only alternative seemed to be to back the VW out with extra care although, today, there wasn't a single other road user in either direction. The uncomplaining Charlie was soon bundled into the back and they were off – but where?

They'd visit Mel – of course, it was the obvious thing to do – it was a five minute drive in the direction of the town centre and The Old Rectory was unmissable in its own little close next to the church... but when he drew up outside the high brick wall and stared up at five sash windows, most of them with pulled blinds, he failed to switch off the engine, made no move to get out.

'What you think, Charlie? D'you think Mel's there? Or in hospital?'

'Where?' Charlie demanded.

'In there. That's where Mel lives. Is she there?'

'Yes!' Charlie shrieked.

'I don't know – I think they'll have kept her in. Her fath... her daddy's a doctor. They'll have kept her in.' Checking his mirror, letting an elderly woman cross in front of him and gain the pavement and checking again, he drove away. 'Let's go to Pendinas,' he said, 'feed the ducks, eh, Charlie?'

It involved a U-turn on an A-road. Bad start.

Opening and dutifully closing the green gate, he drove up through the trees and stopped beneath a sign that read DEEP COLD WATER – STAY WELL BACK FROM EDGE. They were on an area of hard standing right next to the reservoir where only fishermen parked but there were no fishermen today though the air was bright and crisp. It had been a 'white-over' again he realised but the landscape had relaxed now under a low Autumn sun. Alun was glad for the emptiness. No old men or the work-shy, glaring at Charlie's high-pitched yells. The water was smooth enough to show the pattern of the far, wooded shore in its depths and a pair of swans paddled across submerged treetops. Small islands had poked up through the reservoir's surface since their last visit and gave it now the look of a real lake, a more pleasing place than he recalled. Close in, a handful of mallards gathered into a convoy and made straight for them.

'Bread for ducks,' pleaded Charlie. 'Quick, daddy, quick!' Of course he had nothing to give the child.

'*Bread!*'

'I'm sorry. Daddy's forgotten it. Nothing for ducks today.'

'Yes, Daddy! Bread. Now.'

Alun walked parallel to the stone edge of the water letting the boy follow. 'Bread, Daddy, bread-daddy, bread-daddy' lessened into low-level whinging – but when he made the mistake of turning around and offering his attention, Charlie seized a piece of fir tree from the path and lunged at the ducks who had been keeping pace. Once sure of being watched he threw the stick at the bobbing birds. They in turn levered their bodies half out of the water to avoid it and scattered. The missile landed harmlessly but Alun's fury came up like a dark malodorous bubble.

'Don't you do that!' He towered over the child. 'Don't you ever do that! How would you like it, if I threw a stick at you?'

Charlie's eyes grew huge. Any second now the trembling lips would part, the wailing-in-earnest begin.

In one bit of his mind he saw the ridiculousness of it, shouting at the child like that. As a boy, he'd done much the same and worse... and he'd have been older than Charlie – old enough to remember, old enough to know better. Ridiculous. But he didn't reach down for the sobbing child, just taking his hand for a sullen stroll along the path of the earth dam.

There's the place, Charlie, look – look through there and you can watch the water running under the bridge! Look between the sleepers! There it goes. Oh, don't then if you don't want to see...

He watched a long, thin branch – bleached heartwood, white as an arm – waving beneath the surface, seeming to cling to its chosen position, before being swept down from sight. In a few minutes more they were back at the car.

Charlie picked at his lunch and went red-eyed to his nap.

That afternoon Alun had a surprise visitor. He was wheeling the last flagstone along the side of the house when he heard the gate open. By the time he'd lowered the barrow a short, linen-suited man was approaching him, one hand held out, offering to shake. 'Alun, is it?'

'That's right.'

'I'm Cliff Gethin, Mel's father.'

'Oh, right.' Clifford Gethin's hand was small but the grip very firm. 'Nice to meet you. I was going to call to ask how she was but I don't have your number. I was going to walk down to the stables when my son gets up – to ask there. How is she?'

'She'... OK.' Mel's father might be slim and neat and looking at him out of Mel's dark eyes but there the resemblance ran out. He was completely bald, sunburnt and with a patch of peeling in progress above tinted glasses; the impression was of someone stopping by on his drive back from the airport. 'She's better physically than mentally.' Very much the doctor, that tone, clipped and professional and a place or two higher up the class league than his daughter's soft local burr. 'The arm was a clean break, the rest's just lacerations. Head's fine because I've always made sure she had a damn good hat on it. But the horse, you know?' Alun nodded. 'I gather from Peter it was grim?'

'Shocking.'

'Exactly. Anyway, she said you were a big help and to say thanks.'

'It wasn't anything. You shouldn't have bothered coming over...'

'No bother. I'm just on my way to the stables. Good old Samson! In death, as in life, he left me with bills to settle.'

Brittany had the wife run off to? Hardly seemed far enough.

'I was beginning to think you'd run off as well,' he challenged Holly. It was nearly nine, freezing and black outside. The *as well* went unnoticed.

'I rang. Had to take it easy – there's fog between here and Chester... black ice.'

She was exhausted: it was obvious in her falling back onto the sofa cushions and wriggling half out of her coat where she sat... in making no move to dash straight up to Charlie.

'Mel's father's Elvis Costello but completely slaphead,' he told her, just after telling her that he thought Charlie might be sickening for something.

'Glasses?'

'Certainly glasses.'

'You didn't take to him?'

'Too right I didn't. His daughter's nearly killed... her horse, well, I won't bore you with going over that again... and all he can talk about is what it's costing him?'

'Well I suppose he's had to pay out a small fortune over the years. But she's OK, you said. Just a broken arm?'

'If that's OK.'

'Oh you know what I mean!' She hauled herself to her feet leaving her impression in the leather of the sofa seat and the creased silk lining of her coat. 'I'll just look in on him – is it a bug, d'you think? It's not like you to make a big deal of things – the girl getting knocked off her horse, I mean. I couldn't get a cup of tea, could I?'

Perhaps real events could be fashioned through fiction. Perhaps Charlie was coming down with something after all. The child was fretful and uncooperative, seeming to become feverish mid afternoons only to cool and sweeten both days at Holly's walking in. Magically the symptoms vanished for the weekend, returned, as did the nuisance early morning fog, for Monday.

'Take him in to the surgery, will you?'

'I don't think there's anything wrong, Hol.'

'Just to check, then. Oh, it'll probably be nearer seven if the weather's bad.' She swept up her keys from the worktop and had one last scan of the kitchen for anything that still connected her with home, even as her mind wandered out to the car and the journey and beyond the journey. '*Please*. What harm can it do?'

To the young locum Alun said, 'If it was me, I wouldn't be here. My wife's bothered.' Charlie sat on a folded blanket on the examination table, not flushed, not crying, not cowed in the least by his surroundings.

'Well, you were bothered enough to have time off to bring him – let's have a look-see, shall we?'

But the *look-see* revealed nothing other than a touch of inflammation around a late-erupting second molar.

And then there was Mel: when they came out, her brilliant red hair was startling amongst the grey and white heads of those seated around her. So unused was he to seeing her dissociated from Samson, Mel struck him as much smaller than he recalled. A child again, after the adult stoicism he'd witnessed. She was slumped in a corner, her legs drawn in tight and one arm cradling the other in its splint. Only a few days and already the cast, that began at the elbow, was grubby and frayed-looking about the wrist. There was time to note – before she glanced up and recognised him – the darkening of scabs on her hands and the bruise just above her jaw-line, where he'd seen the dirty streak on that day...

'Hello Alun.'

'How you doing?'

'On the mend.'

'You're not having the cast off already?'

'No, worse luck. Fracture clinic in another week.' She stood up and moved toward the door, out of earshot of the assembled sick. 'To be honest I don't know what I'm doing here, really. I'm not sleeping – it's probably just the arm and everything else aching but Dad said – he won't give you anything of course! – he said to come and get something...'

427

'Right.'

'I feel stupid now I'm here.'

'I'm really sorry – about what happened.'

'Yeah.'

He saw her swallow hard but she wasn't going to cry on him. Then – horribly – he felt prickling in his own eyes. He was sorry. *He was so sorry. Just a second sooner or a second later and... it shouldn't have happened.* Only swinging Charlie up into his arms gave him cover to turn away, to say, 'Well, I'm glad I've seen you. I hope... things... work out better. I'm sure your father's right though. You should get something, just to see you through it.'

Charlie slipped over in the surgery car park: Holly had been right about that black ice. On the dark, dependable-seeming surface his sturdy little legs had buckled and shot him flat onto hands and chin. 'Come on now! I'll rub it, shall I? No? Well don't make a meal of it, then. Be a brave boy. You're not hurt.' It set the tone for another day: the child, miserable, complaining, continually badly-done-to and himself, cajoling, snapping, sticking at none of the tasks he began.

What was wrong?

While he scrabbled in the freezer to exhume fish for the evening meal, while he sanded down a square of panelling in the hall, he asked himself: what the fuck's up, Alun? For three years, almost, he'd cared for Charlie and now for whatever reason – for no reason at all – it was as though they'd fallen out of love. Or what he felt for Charlie was getting shot through with needle all the time, just spikelets of annoyance that were enough to... but, of course he loved the child and the child loved him.

His son! A new person, different from himself, Alun, certainly but with Alun as the pattern. A son... a virtual copy, as he was of his father – but closer, more adequately expressed. Him and his father – don't even go *there*, Alun – it was going to be a hundred times better than it was with his own father. *And it could only get easier*! As Charlie's boyishness grew, as his gender took a positive form it was Holly that'd find her patience tested. Now when he thought back to the incident at the reservoir it was possible to see it reversed: an omen. The cabinet scraper slipped from his fingers. Rather than retrieve it he ran up to Charlie's bright-painted room and wakened him with stroking his hair. 'Hello Charlie! Are you going to get up, now? Banana and milk – how about that? And then help Daddy paint that fence?' But the child hadn't slept for long enough: Charlie's eyes flickered and he moaned but he turned again beneath his quilt, clutching it to him with two small fists – and Alun found he had to resist the temptation to prise the bunched material from them, to break their grip.

Meaning to fetch milk for his tea, he found a couple of bottles of Becks in the fridge and sat with them out in the garden, his back against the house wall, his buttocks and legs on the modest expanse of terrace he'd managed to lay in that first flush of summer enthusiasm. It was too cold for sitting but not quite chilly enough to force immediate movement. The sun had pierced the white mist at last, somewhere a blackbird (the only bird he could recognise) was cackling boastfully over its possession of the orchard's rotten produce. When the glow of the first bottle hit and the second was started, he saw Charlie out here again, hooting with delight at the newly-arrived pile of red sand, rolling down from the top, gathering a coating as though it were breadcrumbs...

Unidentifiable weeds sprouted from the near face of the heap now and the thrill of rolling was all worn out.

Somehow the brown, fermenting pulp had got into the house. No – not into the house, *through the house*. 'You've trodden it through the house,' Holly said. 'It must've come in on your boots – it's all up the stairs.' It was the weekend (nearly) again, two days he anticipated with pathetic eagerness and they were going to begin it with a Friday night bicker about this?

Alun walked out into the hall. The pale carpet, left by Carousel's previous owners, now showed the partial-prints of his boots. 'It's in Charlie's room, as well, next to his bed,' Holly called after him, 'I thought it was dog shit at first...'

'Oh it could've been worse then.'

'But it's rotten apple.'

'I'll get rid of it.' 'How?'

'I don't know – clean it off – hire one of those machines, if that's what it takes.'

Later they ate across from each other without speaking, the kitchen television showing a sluggish documentary about a party of ologists, trekking through some... where on the trail of some lost... thing. Alun reached to click it off.

'You've started on the panelling – in the hall.'

'Yeah.'

'You don't seem to have got very far.'

'Charlie woke up.'

'Oh.'

He could always tell her about Mel, he thought, how he and Charlie'd met Mel in the waiting room – and later on, how the kid at the garage had said she was going to her mother's in France to get over the accident. How everybody in the shop was saying she'd never get on a horse again – and not because she'd lost her nerve (because Mel was a local byword for nerve) but because *they reckon Samson getting killed like that has broken her heart*. But Holly had had no part in the accident, Holly had no part in what went on in Dial Green, though she'd wanted to come and live out here, no part in the house though it'd been her choice. He stayed quiet and cleared their plates away, topped up their glasses...

'You OK?'

'In what way, OK?'

'Oh come off it, Alun! You're not exactly Mr Chatty, are you?' Eyebrows raised she watched him fill his own glass and stop short just at the point of overflowing. 'And your hands are shaking?'

'Perhaps I'm coming down with whatever Charlie's got.'

'But Charlie hasn't got anything – you said.'

'So he hasn't.' He'd genuinely forgotten.

The evening dragged on: Dial Green time, that was the way he thought of it. He'd noticed this weird slowing of the hours in the afternoons and now the infection had spread. The evenings were going the same way, stretched out and thinned. There'd been a schools programme on recently, a twenty-minute Janet-and-John exposé of Relativity with a road, a country lane, pulled out and deformed like chewing gum, never reaching the place the signpost indicated but 'still infinitely long'.

He stood, about to draw the bedroom curtains, but not drawing them, looking down to the dark corner of orchard and beyond to the street light in Wrexham Road. No fog: now that it didn't matter and Holly was safely home it was all icily clear. A single car passed and after a wait, another in the same direction. Back in Dial Green, the Pendy and the Full Moon were emptying out...

'*Alun?*' Holly was there, behind him, her warm breasts pressed into his back, the scent of her filling the space between himself and the bay window, her arms locking across his chest. He guessed she was waiting for him to speak or react in some way but he was under water – too much trouble to contest it – too much of an effort not to sink down – too tired to... to... no, that was Holly – it was Holly always too tired to but making a huge effort to...

She said, 'I didn't know you'd come up to bed.'

'Do you remember that time – we were in the flat and we were just looking out, just like this and we saw the bag-snatch? That boy, swiping the woman's bag? And the big bloke chased him for it?'

'Yes... I remember,' Holly said.

'Whose side were you on? I mean did you hope they caught him or he got away?'

There was a long pause while she rubbed her forehead into the nape of his neck. 'Um-m. Well, the man who was chasing him, I suppose. Yes, of course. The boy had stolen something – and it did look like a *really* good leather bag. Might have been one of ours.'

Jesus Hol, you're meant to be just five years ahead of me, not twenty-five!

Or was she joking? He had no idea. Heart hammering! Suddenly and when he'd asked it for no effort – was it expecting to have to fuel a fight? An escape from something that he didn't know was close? And here was Holly hanging about him, impeding his movements… it was all he could do not to pull her off, push her away. 'I was standing here and I just realised. How I was on the side of the bloke then – but now I wish the kid had made it – got away with it, you know?'

'What on earth are you on about?' She let her arms drop and stepped back.

'I don't know. But… something's got to change, Hol.'

'I can see that.'

'Really change.'

'Yes. I think you're right. I can really see it. Can we go to bed, though? I'm dead on my feet. We've got the weekend ahead of us. And nothing's happened – what I mean is, we haven't done anything we can't go back on. We're lucky. There's nothing we can't fix.'

He peeled off his clothes, left them where they fell and got into bed. Later he felt her slip in beside him in the dark and her hand on his shoulder. Later still, her regular breathing. Sleep wouldn't come; instead the scene played out again, this time with Holly not answering his question (or not answering quickly enough) and his turning and shaking her by the shoulders till she cried in pain, till she pleaded, 'I don't know Alun! Whose side do you want me to be on? The kid running away or the bloke after him? Which one?' Her fear of him was new and thrilling. It kept his fingers digging into her thin shoulders. It made him want to keep shaking her as long as it lasted.

It could have so easily gone that way.

FRESH APPLES

Rachel Trezise

When you get oil from a locomotive engine all over the arse of your best blue jeans, it looks like shit, black and sticky. I can see it's black, even in the dark. I stand on the sty and try to brush it away with the back of my hand, bent awkward over the fence, but it sticks to my skin, and then there's nowhere to wipe my hands. Laugh, they would, Rhys Davies and Kristian if they could see me now. Don't know why I wore my best stuff. 'Wear clean knickers,' my mother'd say, 'in case you have an accident.' She'd say *knickers* even when she meant pants. She's a feminist, see. But it's not like anyone would notice if I was wearing pants or not. Johnny Mental from up the street, he said when he was at school the police would pay him at the end of the day to look for bits of fingers and bits of intestines here, before he went home for tea. If it can do that, if it can slice your tubes like green beans, who's going to notice if you had skid marks in your kecks? I can still hear the train chugging away, or perhaps it's my imagination. Over in the town I can hear drunk people singing but closer, I can hear cicadas – that noise you think only exists in American films to show you that something horrific is about to happen – it's real. It's hot too. Even in the night it's still hot and I'm panting like a dog. I'm sure it's this weather that's making me fucking crazy. I'm alive anyway; I can feel my blood pumping so it's all been a waste of time. Forget it now, that's the thing to do. Oh, you want to know about it, of course you do. Nosy bastard you are. Well I'll tell you and then I'll forget it, and you can forget it too. And just remember this: I'm not proud of it. Let's get that straight from the outset. The whole thing is a bloody encumbrance. (New word that, encumbrance. I found it in my father's things this morning.)

Thursday night it started, but the summer has been going on forever, for years it seems like, the sun visors down on the cafés and fruiterer's in town, the smell of barbecued food wafting on the air, and never going away. And the smell of mountain fires, of timber crumbling and being swallowed by a rolling wave of orange flame. On the Bwlch we were, at the entrance of the forestry. There used to be a climbing frame and a set of swings made from the logs from the trees. It's gone now but we still go there, us and the car and van shaggers. Sitting on a picnic table with my legs hanging over the edge so I could see down Holly's top when she leaned forward on the bench, her coffee-colour skin going into two perfect, hard spheres, like snooker balls, or drawer knobs, poking the cartoon on her T-shirt out at either side. She was drinking blackcurrant, the plastic bottle to her mouth, the purple liquid inside it swishing back and fore. I asked her for some. I wouldn't normally – I'm shy, I'd lose my tongue, but my mouth was dry and scratchy from the sun. Yes, she said, but when I gave the bottle back she wiped the rim on the hem of her skirt like I had AIDS. Kristian and Rhys Davies John Davies, they had handfuls of stone chippings, throwing them at Escorts when they went past, their techno music jumping. Jealous they are, of the cars and the stereos but fuck that dance music, it's Metallica for me. (Don't tell them that.) It's his real name by the way, Rhys Davies John Davies, the first part after some gay Welsh poet, the second after his armed-robber father, shacked up in Swansea prison.

Every time something passed us, a lorry or a motorbike, it grated on the cattle grid in the road. That's how Kristian came up with the cow tipping idea. Only we couldn't go cow tipping because you can only tip cows when they're sleeping, in the middle of the night and it'd take ten of us to move one, so Holly had to go one better.

'Let's go and start a fire!' she said.

'Don't be stupid,' I said. 'We should be proud of this mountain, Hol. They haven't got mountains like this in England. And you'll kill all the nature.'

'Nature!?' she said. She rolled her eyes at Jaime and Angharad. 'It's not the fuckin' Amazonian rain forest, Matt,' she said. She can be a cow when she wants, see. 'C'mon girls,' she said and she flicked her curly hair out of her face. 'When there's a fire, what else is there?'

'A fire engine?' Jaime said.

'Exactly. Firemen. Proper men!' And she started up off into the trees, shaking her tiny denim arse at us. The girls followed her and then the boys followed the girls. So that just left me. And Sarah.

Sarah, Jaime's cerebral palsy kid sister. She's not abnormal or ugly, just a little bit fat, and she rocks back and fore slightly, and she has a spasm in her hand that makes her look like she's doing something sexual to herself all the time. But she's brighter than Jaime gives her credit for, even when she's got that big, green chewing gum bubble coming out of her mouth and hiding her whole face. I just never knew what to say to her – how to start a conversation. I smiled at her clumsily and tried to giggle at the silence. We stayed like that, her sitting on her hands, chewing her gum loudly so I could hear her saliva swish around in her mouth, until a fireman came with thick, black stubble over his face, fanning the burning ferns out with a giant fly squat because he couldn't get his engine up onto the mountain.

'Come and get me you sexy fucker,' Holly was shouting at him, hiding her face behind a tree. That's when I went home.

On Friday morning, on the portable TV in the kitchen there was an appeal from Rhymney Valley Fire Service for kids to stop setting fire to the mountains.

'Nine times out of ten it's arson,' the man's voice boomed. 'It's children with matches.' The volume's broke, see, either it has to be on full, or it has to be on mute.

'That's kids, is it?' my mother said, hanging over the draining board, a red gingham cloth stuffed into a tall, transparent cylinder. 'I always thought it was bits of glass left in the ground starting it. It can happen like that when it's hot can't it?' My father ignored her, standing at arm's length from the frying pan, turning sausages over with his chef's tongs. She gave up pushing the cloth down into the glass and washed the bubbles out under the cold tap. I watched the rest of the announcement, spooning Coco Pops into my mouth, the milk around them yellowy and sweet.

'The mountains are tinder-dry,' the man said, 'so please don't go near them with matches. While we're attending to an arson attack there could be a serious house fire in the town.' I remembered the look of helplessness on the fireman's face while he sweated over the ferns, Holly asking him to fuck her. He knew that as soon as he'd gone we'd start it again so he'd have to come back, sweating again. I opened one of the blue cover English exercise books my father was marking at the kitchen table before he got up to cook breakfast, and I read some kid's modern version of *Hamlet*. Crap it was, but I found two new words, *psychodrama* and *necromancy*.

Later, at Rhys Davies' house, his mother was still cleaning spew off plastic beer-garden tables, and his father was still in jail, so Kristian and Rhys, they were drinking a box of cheap red wine.

'Matt,' Kristian said, dropping the PlayStation pad on the carpet. 'Holly got her tits out last night.'

'No she fuckin' didn't,' I said.

'She fuckin' did and you missed it,' he said.

'No she didn't,' Rhys said.

They offered me the wine but I didn't want it. I went to the kitchen and scoured it for Mrs Davies' chocolate. She had a shitload hidden from Rhys' sister in Mr Davies' old lunch box, under the basket-weave cutlery tray.

'I wouldn't poke 'er anyway,' Kristian was saying when I went back. 'She's a snobby bitch. She's the only form five girl I haven't poked and I don't want to poke 'er. She's frigid, inshee?'

I didn't know what frigid meant but I made a note in my head to find out and another one to remember to poke some girl before people started to think I was gay.

'Imagine all the new girls when we start tech!' Kristian said. We were starting tech in a month. Kristian wanted to be a plumber. His father told him, with some prison guard standing nearby, that he'd always have money if he was a plumber. Strange, because Mr Davies was a plumber but he tried to rob an all-night garage with a stick in a black bag. Kristian and me, we were doing a bricklaying NVQ because the careers teacher said it was a good course.

'The girls from the church school'll be starting the same time and none of them 'ave got pinhole pussies,' Kristian said. 'Johnny Mental told me, they're all slags.'

I was leaning out of the window watching the elderly woman next door feeding lettuce to her tortoise. It was still really hot but she was wearing a cream-colour Aran cardigan. I was wondering if there was a job somewhere which involved collecting words to put into a dictionary or something, or a course which taught you to play drums like Tommy Lee so I could throw sticks into the air after a roll and catch them in my teeth because I didn't find bricks and girls with big fannies that exciting. I unwrapped the chocolate but it had already melted.

That night we were on the mountain again, standing on the roof of the old brick caretaker's hut, looking down into town at the small groups of women walking like matchstick people pubs in their sunburn, their too-tight trousers and gold strap sandals, the men in blue jeans and ironed shirts. Holly, Angharad and Jaime, they came up via the new road because they had Holly's collie dog on a lead. There's a farm across the road, see, with a sheepdog in the field, a white one with black patches around its eyes like a canine panda. It barks at the sight of another dog and keeps barking until the farmer comes over and tells us to fuck off before he shoots us. He thinks anyone under the age of eighteen is committing some heinous crime just by breathing. So we missed looking down into Holly's cheesecloth blouse as she passed underneath us. Sarah was five minutes behind them, wobbling over the banking, her thick white shins shining, her short yellow hair bouncing on her fat, pink head. There was some kind of in joke going on with Kristian and Rhys and Angharad and Holly and Jaime. They all seemed to be winking at one another, or talking to one another but with no words coming out of their mouths. I thought I caught Kristian doing a wanker signal behind my back but I passed it off as a hallucination, with the sun being so fucking hot. Then the dog began to cough.

'Holly, there's something wrong with your dog,' I said.

'I think it's dying.'

'Take her to the dam,' Holly said, because she thinks I'm some kind of PA, put on the planet to look after her. I took the dog to the dam, watched it lap up the slimy water and when I came back everyone had gone. You get used to that when you're a teacher's son, your friends disappearing to smoke fags or sniff glue and aerosol canisters without you.

It had been an hour before I thought of something to say to Sarah and even then I didn't say anything. She blew a great big bubble; I saw it growing from the corner of my eye where I was sitting next to her on the grass. I put my finger straight up to her face and burst it. For a second everything smelt like fresh apples. That's what made me want to kiss her. I just pinned her to the ground and kissed her, my eyes wide open, her tiny blue eyes smiling up at me. Inside her mouth the chewing gum tasted more like cider. I found her tits under a thick vest but there was no shape to them. Her whole chest

was like an old continental quilt, all soft and lumpy under
its duvet cover. I kept on kissing her, my front teeth bashing
against hers. She didn't flex a muscle, just lay there looking
amused by me. When I had her bush in my hand, her pubes
rough and scratchy, that's when I noticed the dog looking at
me funny, its brown eyes staring down its long snout. I tidied
Sarah's clothes up the best I could and ran away sniffing my
fingers and I thought that was the end of it.

On Saturday morning – the next day – Kristian, Rhys
Davies and me, we were sitting on the pavement in the street
flipping two and five pence coins. It's the main thoroughfare,
see, for the town. When it's sunny we just sit there watching
women going shopping in cotton dresses, pushing prams
with big, bald babies inside. Our street was built during the
coal boom, my father said, a terrace with a row of small
houses for the miners and their families on our side, and a
row of bigger ones with front gardens opposite for the mine
managers and supervisors. Johnny Mental was sitting on his
porch wearing sunglasses, drinking lager, his teeth orange
and wonky. Someone was painting their front door a few
yards away, with a portable radio playing soul music, Diana
Ross or some shit. A big burgundy Vauxhall Cavalier came
around the corner, real slow like an old man on a hill, until
it stopped next to us and I saw Jaime in the back looking
worried, her eyes tiny and sinking back into her head. Her
father got out, a tall broad man who looked like Tom Baker
in *Doctor Who*, and he picked Kristian up by the collar of
his best Kangol T-shirt because that's who he was closest to.

'You raped my daughter, you little prick,' he said. My
stomach did a somersault inside me and got all twisted up. I
looked at Jaime through the smoked glass of the car but she
had the back of her head to me, looking at Johnny Mental.
He'd stood up and was watching us; the lager can tilted in
mid air towards his chin. Jaime's father punched Kristian in
the midriff, cleverly so that none of us could see it, but we
all knew it. 'Look at you – you dirty fuckin' paedophile,' he

said to Rhys Davies and he spat on the pavement next to his feet. 'Won't be long until you're eating breakfast with your father, will it?' he said, but he didn't touch him. He picked me up by my ears, *by my ears*. My heart stopped beating then and my blood drained away. I don't know where it went but I felt it go. 'Was it you?' he said, and he knocked the back of my head against the brick wall of the house. 'Did you rape my daughter, you sick little cunt?' I could feel myself disappearing in his grasp when I heard Jaime shouting, 'C'mon. C'mon Dad, get in the car.' I heard the door slam behind him but it didn't sound anything like relief.

'You've gone all fuckin' white,' Rhys said, looking down at me when the burgundy car had been out of the street for a good two minutes.

'So have you,' I said, even though I couldn't see him properly. All I could really see was the bright yellow light of the sun but I imagined Johnny Mental smirking at me from across the road. I was thinking that if a stick in a bag was actually armed robbery then just having a cock could make a kiss and a crap fumble into a rape. I tried to look as confused as Kristian and Rhys were, as we all looked at each other, pale-skinned and speechless, and I tried to drift back to myself.

I never really got there. My parents went to the town hall that night to watch a play about an old writer dying of the consumption. I went walking. I walked through the comprehensive school, even though I thought I'd done that for the last time after my exams three months ago. I didn't have the energy to lift my feet but at the same time they seemed to lift all by themselves. Over the running track I kept thinking about Sarah. I tried not to. I tried to think about words but the only ones which came were the ones that came out of Tom Baker's mouth with a spray of bitter saliva: *sick* and *paedophile* and *rape*. And underneath them I could see Sarah on the grass, smiling at me, her skirt hitched up her fat legs. There was no way it was rape or even molestation, she was fucking smiling at me, and she's fourteen, not a child. I'm not a paedophile. Jaime's sixteen and she's sucked the whole village's dick – that's what I told myself. But the longer I looked at the picture the more her smile turned into a frown, like looking at the Mona Lisa too long, and she was starting to shake, her arms flailing on the ends of her wrists. Then I was here, on the railway track, lying down, the rails cutting into my hamstrings and the small of my back. I wasn't sure if I wanted to die. No, I didn't want to die. Not forever anyway, only until it was over, until it was all forgotten. I remembered Geography classes in school, where the teacher would talk about physics instead because he was a physics teacher really and we'd get bored and stare down here to the track and talk about how many people had died here. Kristian said there was a woman who tied herself in a black bag and rolled onto the track so that when the train came she wouldn't be able to get up and run. I didn't need to do that. I stayed perfectly still. Didn't even slap the gnats biting my face. When the train came, the clacketyclack rhythm it made froze me to the spot. I just closed my eyes. When I opened them again the train had gone, gone right past me on the opposite track and splashed my legs with black oil. I don't know now if I'm brave or just stupid. It isn't easy to be sixteen, see, and it isn't that easy to die.

WASTE FLESH

Gee Williams

When Vinny came home and turned the corner into Melidan Street just for a second he saw it as a stranger might: two rows of identical dolls' houses psyching each other out over a strip of new tarmac. The council must've made it No Parking because there was a brace of acid-yellow lines now painted on top. Gary Bithel's old Norton 500 was breaking them up across from Vinny's mam and dad's.

The Crawfords', two doors down, had been pebble-dashed as a late riposte to the Flynns' stuck-on stone... while Mam and Dad... oh, shit! Mam and Dad had new white plastic windows with diamond-shaped leaded lights and the excess mortar still coating some of the old Ruabon bricks like badly applied coffee icing.

Once Vinny started thinking about the people who lived there the street clicked back into its old remembered form. He couldn't really see it anymore. Eighteen years opened up the buildings, spewing out their inhabitants, past and present, the Bithels, Vaughans, Crawfords, Lanes, Wynns, Flynns – and himself and parents at different ages... so that when Number Six really did open and Gaynor Flynn stepped in front of him with kids and a big mongrel dog on a chain and a black bin bag clutched in her bare, round arm he felt crowded.

''ello Vinny,' she said, ' not more bloody 'olidays, is it?'

Gaynor was only a year or so older than Vinny and to

hear her talking in the tones of Grandma Crawford while her bright hair shone like a torch against the dark interior gave Vinny the instant blues.

'That's right. Easter vac.'

He watched her take in his new goatee, well-worn boots and the camera slung about his neck. 'Lucky sod.'

'I know.'

'You photographing all them top models yet?'

'No. Not interested in fashion.'

'Oh I can see that... well just you let me know when you want me to pose Vinny... get my kit off, yes?'

'I will.'

'Yeah – you let me know when... and I won't be in.'

The little group made off at Gaynor's brisk pace with only the dog turning to look back at him. Regretful, it seemed.

Vinny had to knock at his own home because his key wouldn't fit the unfamiliar mahogany-panelled monstrosity.

'Hi, Mam. Bit of a change, huh?'

'I know. Kept it as a surprise – that's what your dad said to do. D'you like it?'

'No.'

'What d'you mean, no? Cost three thousand pound that did, what with security locks throughout and the bit of stained glass. Look at that!' Vinny's mam made the door pivot to catch the late-afternoon light. 'Look at that. Red tulips – see the red on the wall? Lovely they are. Your dad wanted roses – you know, for the Labour – but they didn't have none in stock.'

'It could've been worse, then.'

'Oh, so you've come back a Tory, this time?' His mam couldn't stop playing with the coloured refractions ... back and forth, back and forth as though she were being hypnotised by them – or trying to hypnotise her son. 'D'you 'ear that Col? Doesn't like the new door and he's pining for Benny Potts!'

Sir Benjamin Potts was the local Conservative, put in for

years by the regiment of the retired living along the coast. The Bungalow Fascists, his dad called them. Vinny could glimpse his dad now at the far end of the house, eating at the kitchen table, framed by two doorways but offset to the left.

Radiance from an unseen source caught the pottery mug, the aluminium teapot, his big, pale hands. ''ello there,' he called to Vinny in that odd tone he'd always brought out for greeting his son. It was the tone people used when they met someone they didn't really know for the second time.

Vinny's dad was the handsomest man in North Wales – now that he'd travelled a bit, Vinny thought it might well be in the whole of Britain – this darkly dangerous James Dean with the brains not to kill himself before reaching forty-three. 'Looking good, Dad.'

His dad nodded. The perfect lines of his face held sepia shadows beneath brow and cheek-bones so that whatever he did, wherever he went, he always managed to look like a movie star playing the part of husband, father, miner, union activist… security guard.

'Catch you in a minute, Dad.'

Vinny vaulted up the stairs and bashed his way into his room using the bag. A new plastic window with stick-on leaded lights looked out over the strip of dandelions and lawn. 'Last Shift at Point of Ayr', a two-by-four blow-up, semi-matt finish, had fallen off the wall and lay rolled on the bed. Gently he unslung the old Canon Program and laid it on the quilt. In next door's garden Mrs Lane walked into shot shouting abuse at her hyperactive grandchild but no voice filtered through Vinny's double-glazed lens on the world.

Down in the kitchen while his mother washed lettuce and sliced cheese he said, 'I've got this project to do. Photo-journalism it's called. I thought I'd do this place. What d'you think?' He mimed the camera's focus and click, missing the familiar weight of the Canon against his breastbone.

'What? How we've done it up, you mean? Like in one of those magazines?'

'Na... not the house. The whole place.' Vinny turned away so as not to have to catch her disappointment. 'Thought I'd do a portrait of the... er community. You know, the end of the Flintshire coalfield... unemployment. Social problems... decay. Vandalism.'

'Oh well, if it's vandalism you want you better go to Rhyl. Wrecked the bus shelter, they 'ave... and paint – all up Undersea World! But I don't think you should be taking pictures of that. Just encourages them. Makes them think it's clever... and they're selling drugs in that little café me and your dad did our courting in. Smack... right opposite the Sun Centre.'

'It'll be a few spliffs, Mam, if you've seen them at it.'

'It's all drugs. You take their photos and these druggies think they're somebody.'

'Mam if I started taking smackheads' pictures I'd end up in the Marine Lake.'

'That's what I said,' said his mam.

'No,' said Vinny, 'it's not about deciding to make some things look important – that's not why ... I just want to show what's here... there's the mine – or there was – which was work and the seaside which was... well holidays, the opposite... and this village, with no real reason to exist anymore.'

'Oh, thanks very much.'

'I didn't mean it like that.'

He tried to make eye contact with his Dad wanting to share some feeling about his mam that he had no word for. 'We have this tutor – he did a whole book on the Shotton Steel works when that went. Black and white – thirty-eight full-page bleeds using only natural light.' His mam stared uncomprehendingly.

'Sounds like it's all been done, then,' his dad said. 'Been done to death, that sort of stuff... down South. Big thing,

445

mining and steel was to them. They'd got nothing else at the time.' Vinny tried not to smile: down South meant London to him. 'Still haven't. Anyway, nice to see you back… I'm off up the road for a couple of hours – committee meeting… keep an eye out for some social problems for you, shall I?' He was looking sharp – well defined – in black denims and a blue shirt, which somehow made it sound even more ridiculous.

Vinny waited until the door slammed and sprinted upstairs. He was back out in the street in time to freeze his dad against a bright grey sky. Gary had sportingly moved his wreck of a Norton and the bare terraces held the retreating figure – wide shoulders, straight back – as it sliced the horizon.

'You know,' he said to his mam who was still muttering on about how he mustn't mind his dad as though if both parents got into a who-could-get-furthest-up-your-nose competition, she wouldn't always be an outright winner.

'You know, it's really weird – eighteen years underground and Dad never got a stoop.'

'Your grandad had a stoop,' his mam offered, 'and tiny he was – only my height… like a garden gnome, Colin used to say. I think he'd had rickets when he was a boy.'

'But he's dead… and he was on the railway. He's no use. I can't photograph him.'

He mulled it over while he cruised with the Canon, trying to work out what it was his Dad's silhouette brought to mind… up Melidan and into Ash Grove catching an old woman in fluffy white slippers walking a Westie, wearing its relatives for the camera. Two boys sprawled across the bonnet of a parked car, the smaller shouting, 'It's me brovers' an' 'e don't mind so piss off!' as Vinny snapped them.

He finished the film in the street: one of the Crawford girls rehanging her grandmother's net curtains, tomcats fighting on the footpath behind the scruffy strips of garden and a portrait of Les Lewis in his aviary with budgies fluttering about his head. Les had to clap to get them airborne and

Vinny was allowed just one shot. 'Doin' it more than once,' said Les, ''ll leave the poor little buggers without a feather to their names.'

Les' prize bird was called Tony after Tony Blair.

'Nice looker,' Vinny ragged him, 'but can he perform?'

Les was the Labour Party agent. He didn't rise. 'You on the roll at y'mam an' dad's?'

'Yeah, I guess... on the roll but not on a roll.'

Les wasn't interested in Vinny's problems. 'Proxy vote is what you want then, for the local elections. Those Liberal Democrats always sniffin' round, you know.' He favoured a bright yellow bird with a vicious look. 'Even that Plaid! And then there's this Assembly. Mind you, I reckon old Benny Potts won't live to run. Pickled.'

Vinny grinned. Whatever his mam said, booze remained the drug of choice round here.

'It's true! He could go at any time. Mervyn Price says he fears for the safety of the Crematorium if they get the job. "Abide With Me" – and then one hell of a big bang! Anyhow we don't want to get caught short and you off at that college. What you doin' there?'

'Photography ... with journalism. It's a sort of combined—'

'George Orwell,' said Les, 'he's the boy. Greatest journalist that ever lived. Got all his books upstairs ... if you want a lend.'

'Thanks. Got most of them for A-level. *Inside the Whale*, *Animal Farm*, *Nineteen Eighty-four*...' Vinny popped the lens-cap on: the only coda in his waking life. 'I'll get these developed tonight. Bring you a copy of you and the birds, eh? I'm gonna put captions on them all or a slice of text – "Socialist attacked by true-blue budgies!"... "Hitchcock comes to the arse-end of Flint!"'

Les turned away, his mind on millet. 'Remind your dad there's a committee meeting tomorrow. He's missed the last two.'

He could've corrected Les but didn't. With people Les' age

you could lose good time out of your allocation putting them right.

'You just keep watching the birdies,' he said.

Vinny had to share his dark room with the Hoover, the ironing board and linen basket, a pile of old suitcases and a half-dismembered shopper-bike. His spine ached. His elbows needed to be pinned close to his sides to prevent damage. If he straightened up one of the stairs grazed the crown of his head.

Even before the print was out of the fixing bath Vinny's brain closed on what it had been ferreting around for: those two lines of black italics that he could thread across the page.

George Orwell.

It was as if the long-dead writer had lain in his grave just waiting for Vinny Morris to capture the image of his words. 'Noble bodies' Orwell had said, 'wide shoulders tapering to slender supple waists' and 'not an ounce of waste flesh anywhere.' This was Orwell's picture of miners: confident, athletic beings, physiques made beautiful in the performance of masculine function.

Not an ounce of waste flesh.

In Vinny's picture Karen or Carly or Ceri Crawford – whatever her name was – fought with the veil of nylon lace on her grandmother's glass… but next door the bedroom was uncurtained and Gaynor Flynn's plump arms wrapped the hard muscles of his dad's torso and Gaynor Flynn's face hid itself in the hollow of his dad's neck.

"Looking good, Dad," Vinny said.

DALTON'S BOX

Des Barry

'You remember Mick Dalton, don't you?' my brother said.
'Tall feller with spiky black hair. Always fancied himself as
a bit of a Godfather type, right?'

'Aye,' I said. 'Great bloke. Played cricket with you, didn't
he? For Glyn Taf Engineering?'

'Aye, before he went in jail the last time.'

My brother took a big swallow of his Brains SA and then
set the pint down on the table in front of him.

'Anyway,' my brother said. 'Four months ago, he wins
three thousand quid on the National Lottery.'

'Never.'

'Aye. So I says to him, right, "What you gonna do with
the winnings then, Mick?"'

'"Invest it," he says.'

'Oh, fuck,' I said. 'What was it this time?'

'Import-export,' my brother said.

'Not again,' I said.

'He's got a better plan now. He says, "I'll pay off the
debts, about five hundred quid, then I got just the scheme
for a three-hundred-per-cent return on the initial outlay, like.
But nothing too heavy. Nothing the dogs can sniff out, like.
So it's fags."'

'Fags?' I said.

'Aye. Fags. Contraband Marlboro cigarettes. Two
thousand five hundred quid's worth. So Mick gets on the

449

phone to Spain where his mates are now, and asks this bloke, Harry Smalls, if he can get him these fags, right? So Harry says, "Aye, I can get them for you, but you have to do this right, innit? Set up a company, see. If I try to send through a bloody big box addressed to you, personally, the Customs are bound to open it up to have a look inside."'

'"Fair enough," Mick says. So he thinks a bit. "Oh, right," he says, "I know just the thing. I'll register a company called British Drain. You can ship the box with a load of pipe on top so, even if they open it it'll look legit, unless they really dig down."

'"Brilliant," Harry says.

'So off goes Mick, registers the company, then he rents a prefab unit on the Bryn Morlais Industrial Estate for a hundred quid a week: a minor additional investment, like. He's got a chair in the office and the mobile phone and he sits there waiting for the delivery. Two weeks go by, right? Then this big lorry pulls into the car park: International Express. Must be the fags. Out goes Mick.

'"British Drain," he shouts, "You got a delivery for British Drain?"

'Aye,' says the driver. "There's a box in the back."

'"I'll take it," says Mick.

'The driver looks at him. "You'll take it, will you?"

'"Aye," says Mick.

'"Well it's four hundred kilos, mate. Fetch us the forklift."

'So Mick says, "Oh damn! The forklift! I had to put it in the garage this morning. Hydraulics are fucked."

'The driver says, "Well, how'm I supposed to get it off, then?"

'"Hang on, mate," Mick says, "No problem, I'll get in the motor and have my mate next door come over and give us a hand."

'Car keys outta the pocket. Into the old Polo. He shoots across to Wesley's Builders Supplies where his mate works in the yard. He pulls in, and there's this mate of his, already on the forklift, stacking pallets of bricks.

'"Evan," Mick says, "bring the forklift next door a minute. I got a delivery."

'Evan is that long-haired bloke with thick glasses, lives up on Quarry Row. Anyway, Evan, cool as you please, lays a brick pallet down, reverses the forklift, and swings it round next to Mick's car.

'"Not a fucking chance, son," he says. "Knowing you, it's prob'ly fucking red-hot."

'"I swear to God," Mick says. "It's just pipe."

'"Just pipe?" he says.

'"Swear to God."

'Evan says, "Look, get the lorry round here, and I'll take it off for you. At least you won't be holding the driver up, then. But Wesley'll sack me if I drive the forklift out of the yard."

'So Mick goes back to his unit at the industrial estate and persuades the driver to pull into Wesley's. Well, Evan unloads it, and there it is: a big fucking wooden box in the middle of the yard. And the lorry drives off.

'"Keep it here," Mick says. "Coupla days, no more."

'"Not a fucking chance," Evan says. "I don't know what the fuck is in there, but get it outta here before Wesley sees it. Or the cops show up."

'Mick is fucking gutted, like. Evan won't budge. Nothing for it but to hire a flatbed lorry, a small, unforeseen addition to the investment, but what the fuck? Got to be done. Off he drives, down to Baker's Garage and rents one for the day. Hundred fucking quid, just to get the box from Wesley's yard to his unit. Anyway, long story short, Evan puts the box on the back of the flatbed. Mick drives it round to the unit and reverses the lorry into the bay. He pulls the roller doors shut and gets up on the flatbed to sort the box out. Crowbar. Creak creak. Pull back the straw and what's in the box? Pipe. Fucking loads of plastic pipe. Piece by piece, faster and faster, he tosses it out on to the concrete floor of the unit, pipe plunking everywhere, and then, about halfway down, he comes across a box of fags, then another one. He counts twenty-five boxes of a hundred fags. Marlboros, right? And then there was more black pipe. So all he's got is two thousand five hundred fags.

'What the fuck is this all about, like? He doesn't even jump off the back of the lorry. Straight on the mobile. Top-dollar international phone call.

'"Harry," he says. "What the fuck is going on, son? I asked for two thousand five hundred quid's worth of fags, not two thousand five hundred fags in packets."

'"No problem, son," Harry says. "Dry run, see. Had to know if they'd get through Customs and that. Next delivery, you get the full hog."

'"Next delivery?" Mick says, "When'll that be?"

'"Coupla weeks, no more."

'Coupla weeks. Well, the unit is costing him a hundred quid a week. So he has to get some casual work. He asks Evan next door at Wesley's to keep an eye out for the delivery and call him on the mobile when it comes. Plenty of fucking casual on the railway these days. That's it. Labourer for Railtrack, fixing the lines.

'So there he is now, Mick, out under the pissing rain humping railway sleepers and levering steel rails about for the next four weeks, getting more and more para that Harry's stiffed him. Anyway, it's a Wednesday afternoon and the mobile finally rings.

'"You better get up here fast, son," Evan says. "There's a fucking big box sitting outside the unit. I assume it's for you."

'"Thanks for taking it off the lorry, mate," Mick says.

'"I didn't take it off," Evan says. "It was there at two o'clock, after I got back from the canteen."

'"Oh aye?" Mick says. "Well, anyway, thanks for ringing, Ev."

'Now how did the box get there without a forklift? Mick smells a rat, like. So he puts the phone back in his pocket and yells to the foreman, who's about fifty yards up the tracks.

'"My mother's had an accident," he says. "Gotta go up the hospital straight away. My father on the mobile."

'So the foreman is like, "Is she all right?"

'"Car accident," Mick says. "Don't fucking know, mate. I gotta go."

'Fair enough. The foreman lets him go. So Mick runs down to where he's parked his car. Over the fence, into the Polo, and he takes off. But he doesn't drive straight up to the unit, right? He goes the long way round through Pant Gerrig, so that he can approach the industrial estate from the top of the mountain. Better view of the whole scene like that. And sure enough, he comes over the top of the hill by the cemetery, and there's the box sitting in the car park. But what does he see on a side road by the ICI rugby field? There's these two bloody great Ford vans: a white one with two big bruisers inside, and a black one with blacked-out windows with three more bruisers on the bench seat. He memorises the black van's number plate, drives across the overpass, round the roundabout and out of sight into the Brychan Housing Estate. He parks down on Second Avenue. Out with the mobile. He has to check the number. So he calls up this girl he knows, Jillian Rees – he's shagged her a few times – works for the Driver and Vehicle Licensing Agency. All the contacts, like, Mick.

'"Hiya, Jill," he says. "Check this number for me, love."

'"Hang on," she says.

'A couple of minutes later, she's back on the line.

'"Her Majesty's Customs and Excise, love."

'"Thanks, Jill," he says and he closes the phone.

'Well, that's it, innit? What's he gonna do now, like? He doesn't want to deal with any fucking box of contraband fags. Or the Customs. So he goes off to the pub. He has about four pints in the Cross Hands before Evan shows up for his after-work beer.

'"What about that fucking box, then?" Evan says, setting his pint down.

'"Leaving it there." Mick says. "Customs are all over it. Waiting for me to pick it up."

'"Thought you said it isn't dope," Evan says.

'"It isn't," Mick says. "It's fags."

'"Fags," Evan says. "Fucking hell."

'They sit there a minute in silence.

'"But look," Evan says, "that box is sitting in your car park, addressed to British Drain, which is registered in your name, innit? Sooner or later, they'll come looking for you anyway. And another thing – you can't leave that box there. It's right next to Brychan Housing Estate, home to three thousand fucking burglars, junkies and con artists. Some thieving bastard is bound to notice that box before long and that's the fucking end of it. Customs or no customs, they'll have it out of there. Either way, like, you're fucked."

'"Ah, Evan!" says Mick. "You're a fucking genius, son. Someone is indeed going to steal that box. And I know just the man to do it. Ikey Pearse, the best fucking burglar on the Brychan Estate. He'd do it for a couple of hundred quid."

'So right away, Mick gets on the mobile to Ikey. Tells him about the box. And the fucking Customs, fair play.

'"Look," says Mick. "It could be red-hot. Give it a few days, right. Wait till them Customs blokes get sick of staking it out, then get it outta there. Even if they pick you up, they can't do you, 'cause I'm not going to press charges, am I?"

'"Brilliant," Ikey says.

'"Thing is," says Mick, "you'll need a fucking forklift."

'"No problem," Ikey says. "I got a mate. This gypsy. Up on the Bogie Road. Got a fucking flatbed, son. With a big fucking Hiab hoist on it."

'"Brilliant," Mick says.

'"It'll cost you five hundred quid," Ikey says.

'Five hundred quid! Fucking hell. More investment in the project, like, but Mick still makes a profit if Ikey pulls it off.

And if anyone can pull it off, Ikey Pearse can. "Done," says Mick and closes the phone.

'So Ikey waits for four days before he does the business. A fucking moonless, wet and cloudy night, as they say. Normal for the town of Blaentaff, innit? Ikey gets the gyppo with his truck. Mick drives around the industrial estate first for a recce. No sign of either one of the vans. They must have got fed up. After all, it's only fags, innit? Mick drives back into the Brychan Estate and tells Ikey the score. Then he goes off to wait for him in the pub.

'Ikey, the gyppo, and two of his mates get in the lorry. They come out of the estate, drive round the roundabout, and down the steep hill. There's the box in the car park, right outside the unit. They pull in. Out of the cab. The gyppo swings the cable down from the Hiab. Ikey and one of his boys fasten it around the box, the gyppo works the levers, and the box swings up on to the flatbed. They undo the cables, then they're back in the cab, and away they go. No sign of any Customs. Going up the hill, back towards the housing estate, they hear this scraping sound, then a hideous thump, and Ikey looks behind. The box is sitting in the middle of the road. They hadn't tied it down, had they? And it had slid off the back of the flatbed.'

'Oh fuck,' I said.

'Nothing else for it. Ikey and the gyppo jump out of the cab to get to the hoist, and the next the thing they know, right out of nowhere, there's about sixty fucking Customs men all over them, blue lights flashing on their unmarked cars, like a major fucking drugs bust.'

'All over, like.'

'Well, they haven't got Mick, but anyway, they take Ikey and each one of his boys to a different district police station, right? And they use the gyppo's lorry and the hoist to get the box back on the flatbed and down the station they go with the box.

'Then these two Customs hard cases come into the

interrogation room to get into Ikey. One of them's a cockney, right?

'"You are going down for fifteen years, my son," the cockney says.

'Ikey shakes his head. "Fifteen fucking years? What are you talking about?"

'"Fifteen years, my son. That's a major offence you were caught doing."

'"Major offence?" Ikey says. "It's just a wooden box. Sitting next to the Brychan Housing Estate for five days. If I hadn't got it, somebody else would have. I can't get fifteen years for salvaging a fucking box."

'"Do you know what's in that box?" this cockney says.

'"Not a fucking clue," Ikey says.

'"Two million pounds' worth of Moroccan cannabis," the copper says.

'"Fuck off," Ikey says, totally fucking incredulous.

'"I kid you not," says the Customs bloke. "Come on, Ikey boy. Let's go 'n 'ave a look."

'Out they go. Ikey in tow. And the sergeant comes behind with the crowbar. There's the box in the basement garage of the cop shop. Creak creak. Up come the slats, and the sergeant pulls back the straw. Out comes the first piece of black pipe, then the next, then the next. Then they find the contraband. One box of fags. Another box of fags. And on and on until they get to the next bit of black pipe. Not even a fucking gram of cannabis.

'"Fags," says the sergeant.

'"Oh, fags, is it?" Ikey says. "I never would have guessed."

'"You bastard," the cockney says. "You knew all along, didn't you?"

'"I knew fuck all," Ikey says.

'Red as a fucking beetroot, the old cockney. "Get this fucker out of here," he says.

'What a fucking embarrassment, like. Think about it. Sixty fucking Customs men, for five days, sitting in unmarked cars and two vans watching a box full of fags. What did that cost Her Majesty's Government? Too much to make it worth taking Ikey and his mates or Mick to court. The cockney bastard wouldn't be able to look a fucking judge in the eye, would he? All that money, men and resources for a few thousand fags, like. So they all get away. Scot-fucking-free. Well, scot-fucking-free – not exactly.'

My brother took a sip of his pint.

'What happened to the fags?' I said.

'Customs kept the ones that they seized, right? And the first lot, well, with the initial outlay of two thousand five hundred quid, plus the rent on the unit, the hire of the flatbed truck, and the five hundred quid Mick still owes to Ikey, at the end of the day, like, each of those fags is worth well over a quid and a half, right? Mick's got no choice, has he? At that price, he won't give one to nobody. He's in his house on the Brychan Estate, smoking every one of them fucking fags by himself.'

Mrs Kuroda
on Penyfan

Nigel Jarrett

Solemn over fertile country floats the white cloud.

Mrs Kuroda remembered those words from the diary she had kept as a teenager, and now they seemed to be written in the skies, signalling to her personally a truth so long untold. In those days, she kept lots of similar things: newspaper cuttings, snippets from books, tattered pictures of the Western world. Each will come true, she had told herself, each will materialise.

Smithereens. She had learnt that word from Bill while they were underground at the mining museum. Ichiro, her husband, hadn't been bothered at all. 'Look after her, Bill,' he had said, emphasising the man's name as though he had been practising it all night for some important leave-taking ceremony at which his face would be creased, all-smiling. That was why he had done so well for himself, Mrs Kuroda thought. His determination to succeed in that windswept, hilly land among its emotional people would see them through. Forty years before, in Nagasaki, these were the qualities which mothers-to-be seemed to will on their unborn children in the anguish of bringing them into the world. Mothers who had survived, of course. 'Blown to smithereens,' Bill had said while recounting the tail of the pit disaster. It was almost as if Ichiro had instructed him to mention it, in order to impress on his wife the triumph of similarity over difference.

Alone in their house in the Vale, she stared at her face in the dressing-table mirror, vaguely aware of the double reflection looking in from its two side panels. In front of her was the photograph. The whole effect was that of a shrine, in which she and her mirror images were fixed; not the gazer but the gazed upon. Ichiro had taken the picture with one of his firm's remote-control cameras just before they came to Wales. 'Sachi, my dearest', he had written on it. That was what he called her in private. Now, in their new country, he used it in public instead of Sachiko, which seemed to her like something cast off by another against her will, or something surrendered reluctantly at Customs.

She collected her walking boots, so tiny they made her grin, and placed them on the back seat of her car with the bobble hat and the windcheater. The company had provided them with a big house on its own in the country. It was too big, really, but there was a lot of entertaining involved in being Mrs Kuroda. Ichiro had taken ages to choose. At each likely property, in similar locations to the one he had finally picked, he would race to the first upstairs window, then to the highest point in the garden if it weren't flat, and train his binoculars on the horizon. Only at their chosen site did he obtain a view of a green landscape unfolding tumultuously into purple-saddled hills and jagged spoil heaps. One wintry morning, not long after their arrival, Ichiro woke her and led her excitedly to the bedroom window, offering her the glasses. The tip above distant Pantmoel was snow-capped. 'Mount Fuji!' he cried.

Mrs Kuroda's Mazda showed the beginnings of rust at its hem. She drove it through the gates and let it roll down the slope, through the tunnel of trees. It had been another one of Ichiro's ideas for her to buy a second-hand car which would demonstrate that she was neither ostentatious nor concerned to present all things Japanese as faultless. 'In any case,' he had told her, 'this is the car of our people' – our people meaning the workers at his Pantmoel electronics factory. She went along with these harmless subterfuges. Ichiro's energy made her breathless. He was so sure of himself that she was swept along by his enthusiasm. She had the feeling of always being in his wake, but an affectionate smile over his shoulder every so often would reassure her. He knew all this; he was conscious of having to look back every time he craved her sweet, doll-like features. That was how the sinecure had come about. That was why he had placed her in charge of the Home Club, for the company's middle management and their families.

Tears were welling as she pulled up at the city junction ready to drive north to the Beacons, and they broke like dammed waters as she giggled at the small roadside hoarding. BILL POSTERS WILL BE PROSECUTED it said in bold multiples. Bill had explained the joke, which hadn't been all that difficult to understand with her good command of English, but she had not found it as funny as he had. It wasn't all so unproductive where she and Bill were concerned. He had begun by telling her about the past of Wales and the need to embrace a different Welsh future. He'd told her that her face was like the dawn, on the afternoon he'd introduced her to the story of the ill-fated Gelert. She laughed again through her tears as she recalled her comical attempts at pronunciation. 'Smith-er-reens, Mab-in-og-ion,' she had repeated between her little high-pitched cries of glee. Ichiro had heard her practising the words in the kitchen.

'What's that, Sachi?' he had called from the doorway, lowering his opened newspaper to waist height.

'Oh nothing,' she had replied. 'More English sayings.'

Mrs Kuroda worked hard at her job. Turning up the valley parallel to the one where Ichiro was at that moment addressing his assembled workforce on the impending need for redundancies, she heard the Home Club documents on the back seat cascade to the floor like a column of slates. She didn't care. Her tears were as much for poor Dr Kagoshima, due to arrive from the Osaka plant at the weekend as for anyone else, including herself. Even Dr Kagoshima, coming with bad news from the East but due to be confronted with all that was positive in his Western empire, even the modest Pantmoel Home Club, could not take her far enough back. She remembered a scene from a film in which a teenage boy waited in vain for the return of the suicide pilots before clambering into the cockpit himself, white headband trailing, only for the engine to fail. It might have been old Dr Kagoshima. Both of them in their own ways had been born too late for the big events.

She pulled in at a lay-by which led down to the side of a small reservoir. It was where she and Bill had gone after the visit to the museum. 'My recent past,' he had called it. How thrilled she had been at the success of those first meetings. Ideas and suggestions drifted against the Club's slender administrative structure, almost suffocating it with potential. In the dark evenings, she would sit at home under the standard lamp with her glasses balanced on the tip of her nose and map out the Club's course, while her husband, stretched out on the settee, examined the *Financial Times* in microscopic detail. She felt there was a sense in which he had found her something with which to occupy herself and was loath to intrude unduly.

One night, after a committee member had resigned through illness, she had written the name of William Posters in a vacant space in her minutes book. The surname was a deliberate mistake, and she had stifled a smile. She told her husband his real name. 'Do you know him, Ichiro?' she had asked, without looking up. 'No – oh, yes,' he had replied, and turned the page of his newspaper.

There were three ducks on the choppy waters, bobbing together against a stiff wind. A thousand wavelets broke together. Hers was the only car in the gravelled parking bay.

She put on her hat and walked towards the water's edge, wrapping her arms around her to keep warm. For every wave a thought, collapsing to make room for another. The endless succession wearied her; the wind almost carried her away. She remembered giving Bill that first lift home after they had stayed late to discuss the Club's summer programme. It was he who had suggested the Japanese evening, the slide show, the tea ceremony. Then there was the time she had grabbed his arm as the cage plunged down the shaft at the museum. Then the phone calls to the Vale when Ichiro was at work, the vast silence of the house save for the wind chimes.

She looked up at the sloping main road high above the reservoir and saw one of Ichiro's transporters, sleek in its blue and silver livery and catching the sun as it slid down from the hills towards the border with England. She could barely keep up with Ichiro's explanations of what was happening. She knew nothing could be done about his mother and her father, independently growing frail back home. Each time Dr Kagoshima came over, he reminded her with his hunched shoulders and thinning grey hair of the widow and widower, sitting silent in the groves of Wakamatsu.

Shivering as the wind rattled down from the Heads of the Valleys, she wondered what Ichiro would think of her acting independently beyond the space he had created. What would anyone think, come to that? On his first visit to the house, so long ago that its heart-thumping excitement had been transferred to thoughts of the future, their future, Bill had warned of the perils of being a woman alone in a remote house, describing a Wales in which all slept with their doors bolted at night, unlike the old days. She thought that her small stature made him overprotective. They certainly made an odd-looking pair: he big and brawny yet considerate and gentle of voice; she for ever on tiptoe, as if peering over a ridge, the better to catch sight of some forbidden territory.

Perhaps it was out of bounds because Ichiro had already identified places which would remind her of home, sites of gaping dereliction with kids mimicking aeroplanes in flight, just like the black, water-filled 'bumps' of Nagasaki, where the aged saw their own ruination mirrored in the endless rubble.

She walked back to the car with her head bowed. Her tiny feet made scarcely a sound on the stones. Such lightness she felt now, as though she were disappearing into pure memory, out of range of all that might do her harm. She and Bill had exchanged old photographs of themselves at one of the Home Club's late sittings, while they waited for Ichiro to pick her up in his own car, hers having broken down impressively. The Japanese wives had changed into kimonos for the evening, and she recalled how, quickstepping, they had fluttered colourfully across the play area of the leisure centre, where the Club's monthly-hired room made perfect neutral ground among the learners. In one of the pictures, Bill was a lively nine-year-old, straining forwards as a snow-haired great aunt held him in check for the photographer. Hers, too, were from an equally austere time. All was innocence then, in the days of struggle. As they shuffled the photos, passed them to each other and let them slip into a pile on the table between them, they took on the chaotic shape of destiny in the making. 'Little did they know,' she had thought, 'little did they know.'

While waiting to pull out on to the main road, she thought she spotted one of the wives – there were just five of them in the district – driving in the opposite direction. Her heart quivered like a momentarily trapped bird. But it was too late to be worried by ostracism. In fact, she wished something like that would happen, some trickle of evidence to release the pressure of all her piled-up pain and frustration. She even cursed the old car as it laboured up the slope towards the Beacons, its low gears groaning. Ichiro's success had not made the other wives particularly friendly. As appendages of their go-getting husbands, they were saturated with the influence of ambition, the prospect of once more moving on. This was not the engagement with Western ways she had yearned for as a girl; it was the old behaviour simply transferred to another place. In it she recognised the selfless but rough-shodden manner which, Bill said, had created so much ferment among the miners. He'd welcomed the arrival of Ichiro's factory but she knew when he had sighed so heavily at the museum's coalface – a huge black arrowhead, caught pincer-like by crushing stone above and below – that reality was one thing and dignity quite another. Now that his workmates all wore overalls with their names on, it seemed easier to dispense with their services. She imagined someone ripping off the old tags and sewing on new ones.

At the Storey Arms, she parked opposite the hostel and read Bill's letter again. He had handed it to her at the last Club meeting. (The old formality had been perishing beside her zeal for the new customs, so that even faint-heartedness could barely masquerade as shyness.) She ran her fingertips over the clear, steady handwriting. He had addressed her as 'Dear Sachiko'. She remembered how someone had described Bill as a 'gentleman'. What had that meant? Discretion, good manners, consideration for the feelings of others? In Nagasaki he would be considered a good match for someone like her. On the afternoon of his visit to the house, when Ichiro had phoned minutes earlier to say he had arrived safely in Doncaster for a meeting with Dr Kagoshima's team, she had almost crumbled under the weight of duplicity in a foreign land. Yet there had been a peculiar thrill attached to its shared nature, as though it were a rite of passage to a higher plane of happiness, some fresh and sanctioned departure in a new country. In Bill's embrace she might have been burying herself in the protective folds of the landscape he had commended to her with such pride of possession. She had lain on her bed in Nagasaki, reading of hills and valleys and a people moved instinctively to song. 'Dear Sachiko,'

Bill's letter had said. 'We cannot go on. There is too much in the way.'

The long, worn path beckoned her to the summit. She closed her ears to the siren wind. How the other wives had giggled at the opera in Cardiff as Madama Butterfly tortured herself with ridiculous, old-fashioned feelings and Western music splashed everywhere like breakers on a strange but exciting shore. In the costly seats, sitting together with the others, the strangeness was not on stage but in her mind, reclothing the confusion of her thoughts.

She balanced nervously at the edge of the escarpment and gazed into the void. Her arms shot out. In the gardens of Wakamatsu the trees shivered and a wheelchair turned sharply on a polished floor.

THE FERRYMAN'S DAUGHTER

Alun Richards

I

There had been a preponderance of women in the memorial service, including a uniformed policewoman who had sat with one of Hywel's former secretaries at the rear of the improvised concert hall where friends and colleagues had gathered in embarrassingly small numbers when you compared the occasion to other such services held of late. Of course, Hywel had been much younger than the other distinguished broadcasters who had been similarly honoured, but that was not all, Delyth knew, not by a long chalk.

She sat at home in complete silence on the window seat of the drawing room, her small white face completely immobile as Hywel's mother began the attack.

'I expect it's taken you until now to realise the enormity of what you did?'

'The enormity of what I did?'

'You know very well what I mean. The time will come when even the children will realise. As it is, if there's a trust fund set up, none of the family will contribute unless you have no power over it whatsoever. T.J. told me himself this morning. He was horrified. He couldn't understand how you could have been so brutally callous.'

Delyth did not reply. Hywel's mother, like Hywel himself, had a way of speaking English that was so precise that you knew she was vain of her ability to choose such wounding words with care. T.J. hadn't said 'brutally callous', Delyth was sure. T.J. was a namby-pamby, the elder statesman of Hywel's family, a former university vice-principal who'd inherited a good deal of money and kept it by shrewd investments and a private life of almost peasant simplicity. Having had no children of his own, he had spoiled his nephew all his life, Delyth knew, and T.J., who was over seventy, would understand nothing and provide everything when the time came, she was sure. He had nothing else to do. He also had a shrewder idea of Hywel's character than Hywel's mother. He could be managed but it was Hywel's mother whom Delyth was going to have to remove from the house. Today was the last time she would allow her inside the door and if she thought she was going to spend the night, she was mistaken. The last three days had been bad enough.

But before expelling the second body, there were still things to be done, the odd jobs that followed a sudden death like removing Hywel's clothes from the wardrobe. Although only in his early forties, he had never dressed like a television producer but spent extravagantly on clothes as if he had been some kind of executive (which, of course, he'd hoped to be) and there were at least half a dozen expensive suits from Austen Reed and Daks which would have to be given to someone. There was also a Dunhill cigarette lighter, various items of gold jewellery, sets of cufflinks and one or two masonic watch chain decorations he'd inherited from his father, together with an assortment of ancient silver cigarette cases, propelling pencils, even a snuffbox, which were in the drawer where he'd kept his valuables. Each one of them would have to go, Delyth had decided. Before Hywel's mother said anything, she would make it clear that at present she did not want either of the children to have a single memento of their father. She would cleanse the house of him immediately and deal with the family when the occasion arose.

First, however, there was his mother whom she had never liked and had always refused to call by her Christian name of Morfydd even when continually asked to do so. The Mason-Morgans were a grand lot anyway by Delyth's standards. Hywel's father had been an army padre. Morfydd herself, as she would tell anyone within minutes of meeting them, was the first woman to get a first-class honours degree in geography at Aberystwyth, the family returning to Wales from the sumptuous grandeur of Aldershot (according to Morfydd) only when Hywel's father retired. That Hywel had needed all T.J.'s influence to get him into any kind of educational establishment after a childhood spent on the move from one army establishment to the next, that he had learnt Welsh only when it profited him, while his elder brother had run away from home and spent half his life in the Far East moving from country to country only a few steps ahead of the law – all these were Mason-Morgan problems, undeniable facts that would have buried themselves like slivers of glass into the conscience of any woman other than the woman who now sat preparing a second onslaught, having drawn not so much as a flicker of an eyelid upon Delyth's face with the first.

'I must do something about Hywel's clothes,' Delyth said.

'His clothes?'

'I thought you might take them with you tonight? There's a lot of junk as well. I don't want any of it in the house.'

Throughout the memorial service, Morfydd Mason-Morgan had sat like a ramrod, her stiff back erect, her size dwarfing Delyth who had no alternative but to sit next to her. Morfydd had not cried as she threatened to do but as the eulogies were uttered by the controller of the broadcasting station, she had nodded her head frequently, occasionally giving forth with a curious grunting assent like a sermon-tasting chapel deacon hearing familiar words of praise. She was a tall, striking woman with angular features, sharp eyes and pronounced cheekbones with a kind of statuesque dignity that was emphasized by her severe mourning clothes. A cartoonist would have drawn her with a mere two or three lines, that ramrod of a back, the flinty beak of a nose, the parabola of her downturned mouth, but the cartoonist would have missed the extraordinary brightness of her narrow-set eyes which were blue like her late son's and gave to her face a look of singular intelligence. This was a woman who missed nothing you might think, and even in her seventies, there was not a hint of weakness or frailty about her. She had an abundance of white hair swept up in a neat bun and since she wore no jewellery, you had but to look at her and your gaze was somehow automatically swept up into her face. It was as if there was only the face and the forbidding image it presented, like that of an elderly warden of an unduly strict women's hostel where promiscuous girls were constantly under surveillance. What was extraordinary was that you could never imagine her being a girl herself and the few photographs Delyth had seen, seemed to be of another person altogether, as if that face had somehow been obtained halfway through life and bore no relation to anything that had gone before, certainly not to youth or frailty, or normal human weaknesses. The face, as Hywel might have said himself, was a production number!

Now the chin rose as Delyth's meaning was made clear.

'I wasn't thinking of leaving tonight.'

'I'm sure it would be much better if you did. And if you could take the clothes and things?'

'We normally give these things to the Salvation Army.'

'I don't even want to go through the pockets of his suits,' Delyth said firmly. But she bit her lips. She was already weakening. At first, she'd determined to leave nothing unsaid. She should have told her straight. 'God knows what's in the pockets!' But let her find out, she thought. Thank goodness the children had gone away to friends straight after the service and wouldn't be coming home for at least a day.

'I just want to be on my own tonight, that's all.'

'I thought, in the next few days...'

'*And* the next few days if you don't mind.'

'Are you sure that's wise?'

Here we go, Delyth thought, hardening again. She hadn't forgotten the accusation of brutal callousness.

'There are some large cardboard boxes in the garage. They'll fit into the boot of T.J.'s car. If you'd just take the clothes, I'll deal with everything else before the children get home. We can pack them now.'

'I'm not certain T.J.'s coming.'

'Yes, he is. I asked him especially.'

'Without consulting me?'

'I thought you were too upset.'

That was a lie again. What she should have said, was 'Get out of my house, my life!'

'I don't understand you, I really don't. It's beyond me. You've changed out of all recognition. One of the things I was going to ask you was, how long is it since you've had any kind of medical check-up?'

'I'll get the boxes,' Delyth said, standing.

'Very well, but before you do, I should tell you that T.J. feels exactly the same as I do. We were all horrified. Horrified! How the French authorities allowed it, I do not know!'

'It's very simple. I asked them. I was his wife.'

'But was there no religious service? Didn't you think I'd want to be there? His mother?'

'I didn't want anyone to be there.'

'But what if it got into the Press?'

'He wasn't important enough for that. Anyway, there was no service and I brought the ashes home. Now it's all over, I just want to be on my own. I'll put the boxes in the drive. You know where the bedroom is.'

'Give her something to do,' Hywel had always said. 'It's the only way to deal with her.' Delyth concealed a smile and left the room.

Soon she opened the garage doors, turning instinctively to find Morfydd had wandered out into the drive after her. By now, the pleasantries were entirely dispensed with and in the evening breeze, Morfydd's hair was ruffled and her striking figure reduced. Now she was about to break.

'I can't think what he ever saw in you,' she said querously.

Delyth smiled. That was the whole point. 'Someone unlike you,' was the true answer. But the hardest question was in reverse. Why, oh why, had she herself not seen through him, all of them for that matter, at the very beginning? What they had done – give or take a month or two – was their very best to ruin her life.

II

'Blame the Welsh!' Hywel would have said. It was what he always said when anything went wrong. 'The most paranoid people in Europe apart from the Lapps but at least they have the climate to contend with!' Hywel was never stuck for something to say and, for a short time, was often quite amusing. He had been so from the start whereas she herself was such a mouse and had once actually dressed up as the Walt Disney character Minnie Mouse in a college rag. The girl he had married was often tongue-tied and no match for the grandeur of the Mason-Morgans whose youngest son had quite swept her off her feet. Hywel, of course, had a sports car while still a student. Apart from T.J. there were other uncles who also spoiled him, and the sight of him, his dark tousled hair and fresh complexion under a variety of sporty caps and wearing the kind of expensive sheepskin coat with the cuffs rolled back, made him stand out as a student pacesetter. He was never short of friends then and was already prominent as a leader, casting a kind of glow upon those who were accepted into his company. He had a laughing way of dismissing the responsibilities which blighted other people's lives. He was always laughing, his jutting family eyebrows often raised in jest, his rather thick lips invariably amused; indeed he treated everything as an entertainment. He did not so much arrive as descend, bringing with him an aura of gaiety so that nothing seemed quite as it was before he'd come. It was a very difficult thing to explain, and perhaps the answer really was that she was such a simpleton at the time.

She'd taken him home, his car, his clothes, his family name, and the street was agog. Her father was a bosun on the Irish Ferry and she and her sister lived with their semi-invalid mother in a terraced house without a view of the harbour, their upbringing hardly rural as Hywel had once suggested since they were bound by tides and there was never much to spare as long as Delyth could remember. But they managed, both girls became teachers, although, of course, beside the Mason-Morgans, the academics, the magistrates, the auctioneers, the landowners, all her people were out of a different drawer, despite the fact that Hywel always insisted that there were no class distinctions among the Welsh. Somehow, all the memories of the past always got mixed up with what Hywel had said and he was quite likely to make such statements when they suited him in the face of any number of incontrovertible facts. He had, for example, gone to public school, one of the few in Wales and although the standards there raised a good few knowledgeable eyebrows, there was about Hywel that engaging charm that came from a kind of rootlessness for he seemed then to be free of the marks of any kind of place whereas she herself was a simple small-town girl, the kind who was quite thrilled to meet anyone from the BBC or any of the Welsh television stations. She was in awe of such people and the family joke was that if she'd have been a boy and of another generation, she was the kind who might have run off with the circus, she was that impressed by anything that came from outside her own happy little world.

Like him, of course. He was slightly older than most of

the students at the training college which they attended. There were unexplained gaps in his education, but he had ambitions even then. He was the kind who thought himself much too good for teaching. The children merely existed as material for him to show off his skills. Teaching was going to be a step towards the media from the very beginning. There was then as ever always an intangible hint of quite exceptional promise, of other, always unspecified things.

But it took her father to see through him at a glance.

'Well?' she'd asked after that first visit.

'It's up to you, my girl.'

'No, come on! None of that.'

'Up to you.'

'Don't you like him? What is it?'

'Your life's your own.'

Her father wouldn't be drawn. And it upset her terribly. Like herself, her father was small but broader with immensely strong arms and wrists, the kind of weather-beaten, sure-footed man who is seldom seen out of a jersey and who seemed to spend half his life with a tool bag under his arm, his wizened face under a crop of short white hair eternally sunburnt, a grin never far away. As a little girl, she'd thought he could do anything. He'd once cast the broken eye of a doll in perspex and set it so that it would wink at the press of a button, the tiniest eye of the tiniest doll and when he had handed it to her, she knew there was no other doll like it in all the world. And he was of the world too, a real traveller with tattoos to show for it. But he removed his cap when Hywel came into the room and she was mortified.

Then Hywel started speaking to him as if he were a local character, one of those old men who sat on the bench in the park, sucking their pipes and spitting on dandelion leaves. And Hywel wouldn't even let him buy a round in the pub.

'No, this is on me,' Hywel said, but everything about him said, 'I am aware that you are living in impoverished circumstances.' So much for the Mason-Morgan view of Wales and its absence of class distinctions.

But at the time, she'd blamed her father! He'd retreated into a shell she never knew existed. He made no effort, he was merely dangerously polite. And said nothing. Nothing at all while her mother waited on Hywel hand and foot and her sister was very matter-of-fact. Her sister was going with a boy who lost his foot in a motorcycle accident but soon after, her sister shrugged her shoulders and married him just the same. Her sister had her father's calm, but there was no doubt that it was she, Delyth, the youngest, who was her father's favourite. And it was her father whom she had hurt the most. When Hywel came to the house afterwards, he seemed to have acquired a knowledge of the tides, unerringly picking the times when her father was away. It was as if he had known what her father knew, had seen in a glance, a knowledge which had taken her the rest of her youth to acquire.

There followed the oldest of stories. Pregnant when she married in the summer they qualified as teachers, she did not know that Hywel already had an illegitimate child. What she did know was that the Mason-Morgans were extraordinarily welcoming. And Hywel would not leave her alone. It was a time when, like an exhausted traveller in the desert, she felt blotted out by the sun.

Later, she had many nights in which to reflect upon it all, those brief months, in particular the totality of his physical presence. Whatever you read, or viewed, there was nothing that ever explained the ferocity of sexual attraction, and there had never been anybody with whom she could discuss it, but years later, she believed her father had seen that there was in Hywel the kind of maleness that belonged in stable yards and while it excited her, it also upset her, in particular, the total dependence which it awakened in her.

'My legs are shaking!' she'd cried one night. 'They're shaking!'

She supposed in her ignorance that it was because she was so small and he was so big, but there was more than that. There was something about him that came alive in her presence. He couldn't wait to look at her, to touch her and it was as if his eyes fed on her – as if every part of her must be scrutinised as well as owned. And he made her limp. She seemed to have no will and things seemed to be happening to her that she could tell no one about. And then she was pregnant and immediately overwhelmed because not for a second did he hesitate and there was not the slightest regret on his part.

They would marry at once. The Mason-Morgans too were equally welcoming, Morfydd clapping her hands when they announced the date of the wedding and Hywel's father who was still alive then, hoped very much that her family would allow him to take part in the service. Within a month she was whisked around the family and met them all, including T.J, who made it his business to call on her parents to tell her father what a lovely boy Hywel was and how pleased they all were. The pregnancy was not at all obvious but she got the feeling that they were so relieved to see Hywel married that they wouldn't have minded even if they'd known. And that was that, the invasion of the little chapel, the day over as quickly as a flower carnival, the honeymoon in Rhodes where she miscarried, a house immediately provided for them together with a job for Hywel in a nearby Welsh county town and the march towards the media had begun.

And she'd thought she was as happy as it was possible to be!

There were, however, as ever, things she did not know, little items on the agenda that added up to make her education a total experience. What she did not know then was the Hywel had been given an ultimatum. Marriage was very much on the Mason-Morgan agenda. Morfydd had had her difficulties with her children. There had been problems with the vanished elder brother, little peccadilloes involving cheques, but since most of them had taken place in England they did not concern the family in quite the same way. The brother was no longer mentioned. Now it was Hywel who needed to settle down. Fortunately, Morfydd saw nothing wrong in getting married at a young age. She thought Delyth a pretty little thing and said so. So did T.J., who spent half the reception yarning with her father. And the whole tribe appraised her jovially, the ferryman's daughter. They were delighted she could speak Welsh and thought the fact that she was a qualified domestic science teacher an accomplishment that provided her with a reason for living.

'There'll come a time when Hywel will want to entertain,' Morfydd said warmly.

And her father said nothing.

She was pregnant again when she learned about the ultimatum. They were living then in a comfortable terraced house, purchased through an estate agent who was also a relative. Jobs were hard to come by but Hywel had experienced no difficulty and had walked out of the interview saying that after a few years in a comprehensive school, he could begin to look for something better. He was a well-connected young man with a young wife and an old way with him, and, as ever, there was a feeling that he was at the start of a very distinguished career. Far from feeling he had been given a chance, he gave his seniors the impression that he was allowing them an opportunity to participate in a wondrous future. Of course, there were governors as well as politicians on the selection committee, but even the politicians were impressed and the estate agent had been quietly confident.

In fact, he said so.

'I won't say any more, Morfydd, but I am quietly confident. You can tell T.J. from me. Quietly confident...'

Three months later, Hywel was working late on a school drama production when T.J. rang, his voice betraying the urgency of the call. At first, she'd thought it was Hywel's father who Hywel said was suffering from a deliberately undiagnosed cirrhosis of the liver, but it was not, and T.J. would not leave any message except to ask that Hywel should ring back the moment he came in. As it happened, Hywel was already saying he was being delayed by various production difficulties even then, and she was asleep when he came in so that T.J. rang again on the following morning, missed him, and then asked for the number of the school. It was the first time she'd heard the strain in T.J.'s voice.

When Hywel got home that night, there was a weariness on his face which he could not conceal. He was still slim then, handsome in an old-fashioned swarthy way with dark, smouldering good looks, but his voice was slightly hoarse when he answered her questions. He said he was using his voice a good deal in school.

'What was it?'

'Oh, T.J.'s fussing. We've got some shares in an investment bank and he thinks my brother's after them.'

It sounded plausible enough. Delyth knew nothing about money. The brother existed as a shadowy spectre, and anything could be attributed to a spectre. Now Hywel seemed troubled, so she did not ask any questions, although much later she became very curious for different reasons altogether. But that night T.J. rang again. She could not help overhearing the conversation since the telephone was at the foot of the stairs in the little hallway.

It seemed the family had offered something and something was not enough. But the irritation in Hywel's voice increased until he was saying simple words like 'yes' and 'no' in a screaming frenzy. Then it appeared that T.J. had mentioned a likely visit.

'How has she got my address?' Hywel said hollowly. This time there was defeat in his voice.

At the time, Delyth had no inkling of anything untoward. Hywel's ardour had not cooled. After the miscarriage, their

GP had laughingly suggested 'a little bit of what you fancy', but pregnant again, she had never felt stronger. She also looked stronger. She had lost the bewildered look which Hywel's attentions seemed to have induced. She had once been a competitive gymnast and now went to Keep Fit classes where her figure won admiring glances and she had started to teach on several afternoons a week before she found she was pregnant again. Hywel was glad and, as usual, they seemed to be unduly well off. He dealt with all financial matters and she had not yet learned to drive. In all respects, she supposed she was an old-fashioned wife in the way her mother had been, leaving everything important to her husband. They had been given the house, which made Delyth a little ashamed when she heard other young couples complaining about mortgages, but she was enough of a realist not to let it weigh on her conscience. If she had any complaint, it was that she had not yet had the opportunity of showing off her domestic skills. No one came for a meal, Hywel explaining that he had not yet met anyone worth inviting.

Now when he came in from the hallway, the colour had left his cheeks. He was clearly shaken by something. She'd been ironing one of his shirts on the large Harrods' ironing board which yet another of his relatives had given them and she put the iron down on an asbestos mat.

She attempted a joke.

'Don't tell me T.J.'s lost all his money?'

He looked at her blankly. It was only later that he developed the faculty for remembering his own lies.

'The investment?' she said. 'Is it shares or something?'

'I was hoping not to have to tell you.'

'What?' she laughed. 'We're broke?'

'No, no, it's me... Well, it's a spot of bother I got into a few years ago. It's going to come as a bit of a shock, I'm afraid.'

Years later, she would learn that his brother used such

phrases, 'a spot of bother', 'a touch of the deficits'. They both sounded so un-Welsh, but then Hywel's normal speaking voice had convinced the people they met in Rhodes that he was English. The spot of bother was an illegitimate child, an Irish nurse who refused to be silenced and for whom a financial settlement had been arranged, a settlement that now had to be improved on the advice of her brother who was a solicitor and who had only just learned of it. It seemed that Hywel had a past.

Somehow she understood her father's look at that very moment but Hywel was very plausible and she was soon convinced. Wasn't it possible for him to have got involved with some hard-faced Irish hussy who knew exactly what she was doing? He'd never seen the child. He thought it his duty to marry her but then someone had told him that she'd been married before. There was even some doubt about the paternity. He said he'd broken down and confessed to his mother and T.J. had been sent to fix things. You would not think even T.J. could be so foolish but at the time, it had seemed as if everyone were anxious for a settlement. It had been made, Hywel said, for the child's benefit. It was not as if it had been a lasting relationship. But now she was determined to screw every penny she could from them. Hywel hoped he'd done the right thing in telling her at last.

She remembered sitting motionless on the arm of the chair the iron still switched on, its red warning light blinking like a traffic beacon – it was a Harrods' iron with every safety device. She didn't know what to say. She'd felt herself go cold at first, but then, very soon, she had every sympathy for him. It was the way he had of putting things.

'I wish you'd told me before. I wouldn't have minded then.' She meant, before they were married.

'I know. I should have told you.'

'And not lie to me, an investment.'

'Don't you see? I didn't want to hurt you.'

All the time, he had never relaxed the pressure of his hand

and very soon, they made love on the floor, the red light of the iron winking like a warning beacon above her. The woman did not come, Hywel's father died, his death releasing certain funds in mysterious ways and everything was settled. Later, she suspected that once she had been told the threat of exposure vanished, but anyway, the matter was closed. Hywel's drama group won the county championships and at a staff party, the deputy headmistress told her that Hywel was doing wonders with the children, but the headmaster, who had opposed Hywel's appointment, was not so forthcoming. Then a month later, their son was born, a difficult birth necessitating a caesarian and she felt her body would never be the same again. Three months later, the headmaster visited when Hywel was ill with flu. Hywel tried to order him out of the house, but the headmaster was grey-faced.

'If any charges are brought, it'll concern the two of you.'

The parents of a seventeen-year-old sixth-former had complained. Hywel had spent the night with the girl at a hotel after a drama competition and from that night, Delyth took away the ugliest phrase which remained in her mind like a talisman and which she frequently recalled every time Hywel went off on one of his long explanations. Again, after denying the accusation, he attempted to describe a half-caste girl who would not leave him alone, but the headmaster who'd either seen a medical report or had one quoted to him, said, 'There was vaginal haemorrhaging for several days'.

This time she could not speak. She knew. Fortunately, or unfortunately, there were no charges brought and Hywel left the school at the end of term, and they moved to the capital city where Hywel found a job in a deprived area, a dockside school where, despite all expectations, he was very successful.

'Why didn't you leave him then?' a friend had once asked her.

It was very simple.

'I'd just had a baby.'

But the truth was, she didn't want to meet her father's eyes, didn't want to confess failure. It would have been more understandable if her father had argued or if there had been some terrible scene, but he'd never said a word, just that single glancing look before he covered his own hurt. It was quite extraordinary but her feeling for her father kept her chained to a sense of duty which she could never have defended. So she made the best of things. Later, thinking of her father's influence, she compared it with the disastrous effect Hywel's mother had on her sons, but she could make no sense of it, any of it.

And once in Cardiff, everything changed for a while. 'Blame the Welsh!' Hywel would say every time anything went wrong. But he didn't include Cardiff. Its very cosmopolitan nature was as strange to him as it was to her and while they discovered it, it was as if, for the first time, they were doing things together, like foreigners in a new land. Or so it had seemed at the time. There were even – dare she admit it? – days when she was happy.

III

After three years of marriage during which a second child, a daughter, was born, the birth equally difficult, Delyth began to take stock. At twenty-four with two small children, she still felt bruised enough. But she'd recovered her natural optimism. They were still young. She hadn't, as her father would have said, jumped ship at the first sign of trouble, in exactly the same way as her sister stood by her fiancé when he lost a limb. Neither of them were that kind of people. Now Hywel came home nightly full of tales of the school where he taught. He spent most of his day in a condemned secondary modern building incorporated into a comprehensive complex which was still in the process of construction. It was a grim, prison-like building with an asphalt yard backing on to a glue factory. The staffroom had been in use as a morgue during the First World War and some of the classrooms were merely spaces in an ancient assembly hall separated by wooden partitions so that you could never escape from noise and it seemed the things the teachers said were quite as outrageous as the unruly behaviour of the pupils. Thus he would report on the scripture teacher's latest gem. 'God doesn't want you to be a clock-watcher boy!' Another member of staff, on being introduced to Hywel, made no comment but remained seated at the staffroom table with his head held in his hands, later to announce mysteriously that he was 'Up before the Committee on Thursday'. Thinking he was applying for a new post, Hywel politely offered his good wishes, only to be stared at. 'No,' his new colleague said, 'Whitchurch British Legion. Fighting, foul language and threats!'

Daily there was some such anecdote which Hywel reported and it seemed he had found himself a niche amongst a collection of derelicts, many of whom, like himself, had things to hide, but far from becoming resigned, he now began to plunge himself into school activities with an enthusiasm that immediately brought a response from children who had long been deprived. It wasn't long before his drama groups and clubs came to the notice of the Authority and when he reported that the Inspectorate were interested in what he was doing, she knew that it wouldn't be long before he turned things to his own advantage.

For her own part, when she looked back on this time, her sole problem seemed to be to get enough sleep. Both children were fractious and she would later say that Siân, their youngest, did not have an unbroken night's sleep in three years. Days seemed to pass in a blur, days that she could never after recall, but days nevertheless when their lives seemed to have an entrancing normality about them. Then, she was just like everyone else when her only companions, apart from the children, were the other young mothers whom she met in parks, tied like herself. What was odd was that she and Hywel seemed to avoid those who were Welsh-speaking like themselves and for a time, Hywel deliberately kept away from anyone who might remotely have any knowledge of that incident in the Welsh county town they had left. It was as if he was doing penance in the worst area of the docks and although it was never mentioned again, she noticed how disinterested he had become in things Welsh. There had been a time when he was at the centre of various nationalist groups, when many of his conversations were political, when he could be relied upon to give his support to the multiplying Welsh causes, but now he, like herself, seemed to be deliberately removed from almost everything they had known. She herself was so busy and involved with the children and the house that it was understandable, but Hywel even avoided the pub which were becoming increasingly colonised by outsiders as the Welsh language media grew in strength and little areas of the city seemed to be taken over by people from much the same background as themselves. It was as if he was dropping out of sight and awaiting his chance.

The chance came with yet another telephone call from T.J. Now there were magical words uttered for the first time, 'Educational broadcasting'. It seemed that a Welsh broadcasting station was looking for production assistants with teaching experience and T.J. happened to be speaking to the newly appointed Controller about his nephew who was doing missionary work in the docks and quite wasted from the point of view of the nation's needs as a whole. T.J. always spoke in this way and although Delyth was inclined, at last, to bite her lip when he said anything at all, she was well aware of the implications. The young mothers whom she met daily in the park always referred to Welsh language television as 'Telly Welly' and never watched it, but of course, she knew that while they might regard it as a joke, they were quite wrong and she herself was a warm supporter of all the causes which Hywel had seemingly abandoned. If she was not as active as she might have been, it was because she was preoccupied.

But one night she felt a particular apprehension. Hywel had gone to talk to a cousin who had carved a niche for himself in religious broadcasting on T.J.'s advice. She had a feeling that the cousin would emulate the role played by the estate agent previously. She had no doubt that Hywel was interested and while they discussed the post about to be advertised, they had thought merely in terms of salary which was expected to be more than his present meagre teacher's wage. With the children and the recent purchase of a car, they were not as well off as they had been and although they did not have to pay rent, things were still tight. She was not sure but it seemed that the Mason-Morgan benevolence was not quite so forthcoming, partly, she suspected, because she always put off Hywel's mother from visiting. Now, more than ever before they were on their own.

But that was not the cause of her apprehension. The proposed job would, it seemed, involve irregular hours of work and periods away from home and now, for most of their married life, she had got used to Hywel's regular habits. There was no doubt he worked hard, no doubt he was appreciated, no doubt that he had done well and the very fact of sticking a job in that terrible area was itself a mark of character. Sometimes when she had to get up in the middle of the night to attend to one or other of the children, she did so without disturbing him and often when feeding the baby, she would sit in the armchair with a strange feeling of contentment, knowing that he was asleep upstairs with the front door locked against the outside world. She imagined her mother must have felt like this when her father was home from sea and the more she thought about it, the more she began to appreciate the regularity of their lives. But, of course, there was more to it again. For some reason, she did not see Hywel as a man behind the scenes despite the fact that he was considering a lowly production assistant's job – she didn't quite know what that meant exactly – but instead she saw him as a performer, a personality, one of those household names who were steadily increasing in number. And it was not just the regulars who crossed her mind, those instant opinion givers who appeared on programme after programme with monotonous regularity, but the real stars, those professionals who fronted programmes of every kind and had a kind of glamour that was evident in the way they dressed, the company they kept, their habit of attaching themselves to more famous people, particularly actors or singers, their attitudes seldom critical and often displaying that lugubrious fawning servility which somehow seemed to her the hallmark of such people. It was very noticeable on the Welsh language channels as if minor stars were seeking some of the glow cast by those who populated the major constellations. But she simply thought it greasy and unpleasant. She wouldn't want Hywel mixed up with anything like that. To tell the truth, despite everything, she was rather proud of him for having done so well at a very ordinary job. In a way, it was rather like being a bosun. In Tiger Bay too, she thought. Her father had mentioned that with a wry smile, very surprised when she'd told him.

So she completed her chores and awaited Hywel's return, deciding at the last minute to wash her hair, finally using a blow-dryer and ruefully fingering a clutch of grey hairs and noticing for the umpteenth time that although she had recovered her figure, there were marks appearing in the corners of her eyes, the pronounced crowsfoot lines that would one day become permanent. She remained a bit of a Minnie Mouse, especially when she was tired and the wrinkles showed.

She was seated in a dressing gown when Hywel came in.

'Well?'

'I'm not sure.'

She felt an immediate relief.

'It's for you to decide eventually.'

Her relief vanished.

Of late the old ebullient Hywel had returned, the air of promise and unspoken things to come, and with it, a filling out of his stocky frame. He was not only beginning to put on weight, he was putting it on in the wrong places and when he sat, poised on the edge of the settee as he did now, he reminded her of his father, that mysterious simpering grey-faced man who agreed with everything everybody said, whom she had met so briefly. But where his full face was long-suffering, Hywel's was eager for approval.

'It's not just that the money's more, it's the long term prospects. I'm not going to get much further in teaching without much better qualifications.'

It sounded reasonable. He went on to describe the likely growth of Welsh television and very soon, it was as if he was rehearsing a speech for his interview. There were things he felt he could contribute, and then she knew, he had already decided. Of course he would be starting at the bottom, he said. There would be difficulties, but they had the children to think about. They lived in what by middle-class standards was rather a shabby neighbourhood. Very soon, they would have to think of schools for the children. Whatever course the future took, it was only right that he should do the best he could for them. But it was for her to decide.

Much later, she would think that half of what he said to her on such occasions was like a private sharing of what would later be a public utterance, and yet, she still listened, still felt that she mattered, still went along with him. But later still, she realised that this going back to what he thought were his own kind, far from being a healthy thing, was a death sentence. They were not his own kind, they were a new kind and he was entering a world which had never existed before. That night, and the night he came home to tell her that he had, of course, been successful, she felt an apprehension that she could not precisely articulate at the time. It was very odd but she felt there was an immediate parallel in the sudden departure of a Methodist minister from the town they had just left. Thought by most of his flock to be a complete nonentity and a backslider, he had suddenly emerged a television personality and was constantly seen on arts programmes, his face flushed and gestures expansive, rumours about his drinking and private life circulating freely while he became more and more prominent. It was laughable in some ways, disgraceful in others, and yet she could not help but feel that the very act of becoming such a public man was in some way an act of frenzy – as if the urge to be on public display was a new disease. It was what her father would have said. There was also the strange feeling that Hywel would be leaving something decent for something indecent. Above all, what was quite extraordinary, was that now for the first time she seemed to be thinking for herself.

IV

The suicide attempt came five years later. They'd moved again. Everything promised had been realised as far as Hywel was concerned. With the expansion in Welsh language broadcasting, there was a sudden demand for personnel, despite the fact that more and more aerials in the city were becoming permanently tuned in to English programmes transmitted from Bristol and the West Country. But Hywel had been in the right place at the right time. Now regular programmes were beginning to go out with his name prominent amongst the credits. The children were growing up. She learned to drive in order to transport them to a distant school where Welsh was the medium of instruction. Now she had different friends, among them the wives of people who worked with Hywel. Now they spoke Welsh constantly, and Hywel had been on a crash course to improve his knowledge of his mother tongue. They were part of a group largely composed of people much like themselves.

'Upwardly mobile', Hywel said, but it was a very exclusive curious world and she did not quite feel at home in it for reasons that took some time to become clear. Sometimes she went across to the park where she had earlier wheeled the pram and met some of her old acquaintances, the young mothers who had lived near them previously. A few of them were rather jealous of her, the new house separated her from the old neighbourhood, but others were welcoming. For other reasons which she could not explain, she was sometimes glad to get away from Welsh-speaking people, or rather, the wives of media people, for she was becoming aware of a certain condescension which some of them invariably showed her – as if, despite Hywel's success, there was something about her which had not kept pace with him. Or that was what she at first thought. It was a feeling shared by Hywel's mother who now, more than ever, had to be kept from visiting. It was not just the extra work involved since she was the kind who ran her gloves under window ledges in search of dust, nor even her complete spoiling of the children, but this view she had of Delyth as a pretty little thing, the emphasis always being on the 'little'.

It was not only patronising, but as if she was being compartmentalised as a person, hopelessly cast in the role of *little* wife from whom nothing much else could be expected. The entertaining they hoped to do never quite materialised. If they went to dinner parties, they were invariably media people and the only people Hywel ever suggested inviting back were much older than them, invariably men who might advance his career and although Hywel thought about the invitations, he was not quite secure enough to press them with the result that the few people they entertained tended to be rather boring. Very soon, Hywel began to travel the length and breadth of the country and it was then that the condescending looks of the wives of his colleagues began. Only a fool wouldn't have put two and two together, she thought later, but then, that was how she thought herself for a period of time that seemed never-ending – the fool and the victim.

One day when Hywel was away directing some programme in Builth Wells, she had safely delivered the children to school and was driving home through an unfamiliar district when she saw Hywel, or somebody who looked exactly like Hywel, emerging from a house and getting into a taxi at the corner of the street. It was but a second's glance and when she looked into the driving mirror, she could not verify her impression because the taxi immediately pulled away in the opposite direction. Hywel had now put on weight and his regular drinking had begun, but above all, his appetite had become gargantuan with the result that slim figure of old was already quite unrecognisable. Since he had specialised in making programmes about agriculture recently, he also at this time affected a countrified look, frequently wearing thick tweeds and sports jackets which made him look even more overweight and it was the thick herringbone tweed of the overcoat which had caught her eye more than anything else. It was not the kind of coat you saw often in the city, and, as it happened, Hywel had regretted buying it when there were much more serviceable coats available. It was somehow typical of him to make such a foolish purchase, she'd thought, as if once more, he was taking on the colour of his surroundings. The expensive sheepskin had gone with the sports car, then in school he had for a time worn tracksuits and trainers even though he was the most unathletic man imaginable, but he felt they had given him a certain image as an active drama teacher which no one but himself could have explained. It was the coat that caught her attention, the coat with which she taxed him when the opportunity arose.

But that night, he telephoned as usual from the hotel in Builth Wells as he had done on the previous evening. This was at a time when he telephoned home nightly.

There were the usual pleasantries, the dutiful enquiries

after the children, his apologies because he might have to be away over the weekend.

'What's the weather like?' she said lightly, the casualness of her enquiry the first act of deception in her entire life.

'Quite mild. What's it like with you?'

'The same.'

'Is anything the matter?'

'No, no, I just wondered.'

There was a coolness about her which later disappeared altogether. It was not that she wasn't sure, but that some part of her wanted to confront him in person. She wanted to see his face when she challenged him. And this time, she wouldn't allow him to touch her. Somehow the touching was a part of her defencelessness. So her calm was a progression from the simple casualness of his first question.

'Are you sure you don't mind about the weekend?'

'If you have to be there…'

'If there's any chance of me getting away, I will.'

'Not if it means spoiling the programme.'

Now she felt like an actress! When he rang off, she went downstairs and poured herself a stiff whisky but the unfamiliar taste revolted her and nearly made her sick. What was strange was that there was no doubt in her mind at all. She just sat there motionless and it wasn't long before she began to wonder what she would do when her suspicions were confirmed. Again, she thought of her father but now there were the children to be considered. There were problems. Both were small like herself, Geraint the eldest had inherited her mother's asthma, and already showed signs of frailty, but more than anything she had a horror of divorce that was quite unreasonable. In the first place, she could not see herself returning home, an abandoned wife with two children and all the talk that would involve, and secondly, there was a dismal feeling that getting money out of Hywel would be a tortuous process and she had a vivid memory of one of her park acquaintances who was in just that position, legally separated and made ill by the simple business of staying alive. At the same time, there was a further thought, one that would later amaze her, and this was the incredible perception that a divorce would not help Hywel's career since there remained vestiges of the old puritanical traditions to which his bosses still paid lip-service. She was even at this moment still thinking of him.

But oh, how could he? she thought. She wept finally, tasting her own tears in the whisky. That was the first night without sleep. When the second followed after a day of losing her temper with the children, she spent a night trying to put faces to the half-caste teenager and the Irish nurse and before long she thought she'd begun to understand some of the condescending looks which the media wives had given her. Of course, they knew him, or knew about him. Everything was known. Wales was such a small place, there were no secrets, and she had heard enough talk about others, the real celebrities some of whom had the morals of farmyard animals, she'd heard somebody once say. But that put her in mind of Hywel again. It was not just that there was something in him that couldn't leave any woman alone, it was more; he couldn't exist without the kind of admiration that she had given him, the total belief and abandonment of everything else for no matter how long, an hour, a night, a week. And it would go on and on, no matter what she said or what he promised. That was Hywel and how he functioned.

When he finally returned, he had not come in through the door before he announced that he had to return. There were camera problems, lighting problems. They'd got nothing in the can, he said. He'd only come home for a change of clothes, and, of course, to see if she was all right.

But she clearly wasn't all right. She wore no make-up. There were black patches under her eyes as if she had some kidney disease. She was haggard and pale. When she spoke her voice was tremulous and her hands shook. She couldn't even conceal her distress from the children. He had not noticed in the darkness of the hallway but when he came into the living room, busily shuffling through his mail, he looked up and saw her gripping the edge of the table.

'What is it?'

'I saw you on Thursday.'

'Thursday?'

'In Cardiff. When you were supposed to be in Builth. I saw you get into a taxi. Who was it this time?'

There was not even a flicker of annoyance in his eyes, certainly, not surprise either. He was merely irritated.

'Barbara,' he said. 'We didn't get back till three and I didn't want to wake you. '

Barbara was his secretary, a rather drab spinster who was temporarily allocated to his department.

Unfortunately, he'd forgotten that he'd telephoned that night and the previous night, saying he was actually in Builth Wells. She told him, but just before he could answer, the telephone rang. This time it was Builth Wells and there were problems.

'Real problems,' he said. 'Look, can't this wait? I've got to go. I've driven two hundred miles today already.'

She stood motionless by the kitchen table, then Siân fell over in the yard, the telephone rang again and he was gone, forgetting the change of clothes he'd originally come for, gone, hurrying away back to the car and away from her, sweating in that huge tweed coat, she could see. There was no doubt whatsoever.

Then the children's questions began, as usual making her feel guilty for the way she looked, for not covering up, for communicating her own misery to them. It was not that night but the next night, the fourth without sleep that she took the soneryl tablets and the whisky which were conveniently to hand. They were his tablets and his whisky and her exhaustion was of his doing. But fortunately, she did not take enough, vomited in her sleep and awoke in the middle of the morning to find his mother downstairs ringing at the front doorbell. She'd come unexpectedly on a coach with a party of women on a shopping expedition and also to see *The Sound of Music*. The film was apparently receiving its fifth showing.

'Of course, it's very sentimental but it gave me the opportunity to pop in and see how you all were!'

The children, still in their nightclothes, were huddled like casualties in the corner of the kitchen, a trail of milk and cornflakes across the floor. At the time, she'd thought they hadn't been into her bedroom.

Covering up automatically, Delyth knew that Mrs Mason-Morgan thought she'd taken to the bottle and when Hywel came home later that week, he said there were certain things she had to understand about his job. He was suddenly hard and cool. He did not touch her. She could take it or leave it, he implied. He knew of some marriages that had been ruined by constant unnecessary accusations. The world was changing, he said, and he was changing with it. She sat and listened in a dumb silence. There was neither rhyme nor reason to her acceptance of everything he said, but accept it she did, and it was only when the children were older that he actually started to make excuses again, his lies then aimed at them as much as at her. It was as if something in her had snapped, as if she had forfeited the right to be a human being at all. She went about her daily chores like an automaton. She simply got on with things, a shell hardening about her, as they moved further and further away from each other until in the end, she neither cared where he was, not what he did.

V

It was at this time that she began to discover the city. She'd already explored the nearest parks, and now she was at last able to get some supply teaching, invariably moving as Hywel had done to the roughest schools in the worst neighbourhoods. It gave her a purpose and she slowly began to discover a long-forgotten self. But it took an age to make up her mind. Most of all, she lacked self-confidence.

There was a time when she couldn't even see herself standing up in front of a group of unruly children. She couldn't control herself, never mind anybody else. There were problems with references, referees, the Ministry of Education itself since she'd never even completed a probationary year. Then she became preoccupied with her appearance. She might have passed muster in some country school but now there came a time when she couldn't bear to look into the mirror. It was not just her scarred body, it was her face. She was already greying, the crowsfoot lines were becoming permanent and her thick eyebrows arched above her startled black eyes and her sharp, pointed chin giving her the look of some tiny forest animal in a permanent state of fear. If she was not actually always on edge, she looked it. The Minnie Mouse tag returned to her consciousness. She felt she could never muster any authority and there were such louts of children about.

Then a bizarre happening occurred. There was a long wardrobe mirror in their bedroom and she was changing one morning in preparation for a visit to an old college friend when she could not get her skirt to hang properly. It was a pleated skirt but she had altered the hem line and there was something she'd done which made it irregular so at the last minute she'd decided on a complete change, removing her blouse and examining her hips in the mirror. She was not completely naked but she turned once or twice in what she supposed might be a rather provocative way had she been in view when she suddenly noticed that she was observed. Resting against the window, and appreciatively puffing at a cigarette was the window cleaner, a tousled ginger youth with a pockmarked face and a denim cap jauntily perched on the back of his head.

Startled, she jumped, but the grin on his face and his

appreciative nod might have been that of a spectator at a horse show. The window was open and before she could say anything, he winked in as friendly a way as could be imagined.

'Very nice too!' he said with all the authority of a connoisseur. 'Off out, are we?'

It was not in her to tell him off.

'Make sure you do the children's windows,' she told him.

'Oh, I don't come all the way up here to pick my nose, Missus!'

She pulled down her sweater examining herself, conscious that his eyes were still on her, finally slipped into her shoes with a flush settling on her cheeks. There was no logic to it, but it was as if everything had changed and after that the window cleaner often teased her, 'Not into the Miss Worlds this week then?' Whenever she saw him, she felt cheered as if he was an ambassador of another world out there.

It was the same when she finally began to get the supply teaching jobs which she eventually sought. It was not the problem she imagined, and although her fears remained, eventually she found, as Hywel had, that she was needed. She soon developed a brisk, no-nonsense way of keeping children busy, and by preparing everything thoroughly, broke her day down into small achievable tasks. Eventually, she found herself being asked to return to the same schools and while she did not immediately think of a permanent job, she began to feel more and more optimistic. She had recovered her independence. More than that, her conversations with some of the children brought her into contact with other lives, some of them so disturbed and fraught with difficulties that she had a further sense of the ills of the world. There were those who were maimed and deprived, there was a shiftless seedy other-world where vile happenings and cruelties were daily events. Whatever had happened to her, she was not alone. She was not too badly off.

Within the space of a year it was as if this other world was giving her names. She was Minnie Mouse, Miss World and Our Miss, but then a series of minor ailments caused her to stay home with her own children and this broken winter was capped by a car accident when she broke her ankle. No sooner had she begun to make another half-life for herself when she was returned to the old. Now Hywel was promoted. Now Hywel had reached a point, he said, where he could not go on without her support. What he meant was that he could not stand her coolness. Other people were noticing. His promotion also meant, she suspected, that for a long time he would have a desk job. It was at this time when she had begun to attempt some understanding of the Mason-Morgans and their children that she had begun to worry about her own. She was now sure that Hywel's childhood had been a kind of battleground with several wars being fought at the same time. Whatever had passed between Morfydd and her husband was somehow beyond comprehension at this distance of time. That weak silent man and the domineering, forceful woman, always insisting on her accomplishments, should by all logic have been the result of some inferiority or insecurity but there was no evidence of it. Unless the padre too had constantly strayed? It was an alarming thought. Then the simple primitive concepts of right and wrong, obviously hammered into the children at every possible opportunity seemed to have had no effect whatsoever. Normally, people had a conscience, they suffered guilty feelings in varying degrees. Delyth herself could not lie. She simply couldn't. It was unthinkable and while she was not averse to winning people's affections and scoring off her sister, for example, she was ever-after conscious of her sister's hurt. But Hywel was completely different and she knew now that he was different even when he was articulating precisely the things he thought she wanted to hear. He could describe anything, any single feeling, and over the years, he had become even more expert than when she had first met him. When he was there, he was marvellous with the children. He had the capacity to seem genuinely interested in what they were doing. At the drop of a hat, he could become a child and see things from the child's point of view. It was the same with people, she supposed. He had the habit of intense concentration on other people's wishes, needs, their aspirations for themselves. He gave them his full attention and he never forgot important details, but only when he wanted something. Perhaps he had learnt it, practicing on his mother and on T.J., on all of them since people like that encouraged it. She did not know.

What she did know was that he was on a Welsh bandwagon, and he was a clear example of what one of her sardonic colleagues had described as the contemporary disease. He suffered from Wales-in-the-head. This consciousness affected his every idea and dominated his life which was understandable as far as his work was concerned, she supposed, but she was beginning to realise that it had very little to do with the daily realities of most people's lives. But like every other idea Hywel held in his mind for long, it was very profitable, although she had a longing for someone to stand up and say there was no such thing as a purely Welsh germ! Except Hywel himself, of course. This was how she thought now. He wasn't going to get round her, and one day, coming across an old school geography textbook which dated to the 1930s, she found that the word 'Empire' was mentioned so frequently that it struck a chord in her mind. People then, it seemed, were always doing things for the Empire. They built roads, bridges, sacrificed their lives, their health, their children, all for the Empire. If you substituted the word Wales for Empire it was almost exactly the same kind of thinking. It was quite extraordinary for her to have noticed something like that, but she didn't dare say anything to anybody. She hoarded it all away.

She said he wouldn't get round her. The way he got round her was by asking her things now in front of the children so that any refusal on her part put her in the wrong. He had now reached the stage where there were people he wanted to invite to dinner, and they suddenly began to receive more and more invitations as if those on the echelon below them had also realised that Hywel was worth cultivating. Some of them were the same wives who had given her such looks previously. But now there was a more obvious regard for Hywel, a slightly different appraisal of her but always as if she had somehow miraculously survived and kept pace, quite a surprising little thing. She had gone to one or two houses with the grime of the classroom barely removed from her fingernails. It was at a time when confidential record cards were introduced in schools and she was aware of daily realities in a way she never had been before, in particular of the crimes visited upon children, the beatings, the sexual assaults, the shouted scenes behind locked doors, the visible evidence of hurt, worst of all the silent children who said very little but whose eyes confirmed things she would never have believed possible. And she would sit smiling as the conversation buzzed around her, seldom contributing but saying to herself, 'Ah yes, the Empire. We must keep the Empire, the jolly old Empire!'

'Delyth teaches,' Hywel would say, and then he would say where, naming the shabby districts as if she, in T.J.'s words, was doing valuable missionary work and people were suitably impressed. What nobody understood was that her teaching was the lifeline from the lot of them!

On some nights Hywel would look at her with warm regard as if he too was in some way infected by this view of her as a person who had come on. Now they slept in separate beds. If he touched her, she turned away. But soon, he was wooing her again. But it was the one thing he could not do in front of the children, so he had no chance.

Entertaining was another matter, however. Entertaining was part of his career now. So, it seemed, was keeping on the straight and narrow for he seldom went away and even offered to take her with him on one or two trips. He'd used the children as blackmail before they went on holiday, and she'd been available, as she'd learnt to put it, only because she knew that the children wouldn't have had a father on holiday with them otherwise. That was one for the record cards, but her lack of response made him drink all the more and she didn't care. But entertaining outsiders was not like entertaining him in her bed. That was no longer part of the grand design. But entertaining would produce him another colony.

So again, she went along with it, shrugging her shoulders and setting out to prove something to herself. She was not a prude but gluttony seemed to be an undiagnosed industrial hazard of the media people Hywel knew. It was no good doing wonders with coriander or traipsing to the market to get fresh artichokes, they didn't want subtlety, they wanted quantity, stuffing themselves over Normandy pork with rich puddings to follow, all the things she despised. And they drank like fish, one or two often using Company drivers as they went about their hogging, and just as Hywel had years ago been a great maker of statements about the Welsh (he'd dropped it recently), now she took up the same irreverent strain.

Like her Empire thoughts, these other irreverences remained buried, although in one of the schools in which she taught there was an old, exhausted, permanently hungover Welsh teacher, a Cardi like herself who could not face a class until he had read the *Western Mail* from cover to cover and was the last exponent of 'silent reading' and to whom she often reported on the young notables who now began to come to her house. Like T.J., he was also known by his initials, a white-haired old soak with a country turn of phrase.

'Well?' O.O. would say, 'who did you have last night?'

She would report whereupon O.O. would shake his head in mock sadness. 'That beauty! The pee's not dry on his legs yet!'

And of another, he would add, 'I knew his father. Very few

ministers could empty a chapel, but by God, one look at him was enough!'

She was never without one friend.

The entertaining continued, so did the entertainment. Now Hywel, portly and preposterous, began to cultivate even more important people. He affected waistcoats on occasions and got out his father's gold watch chain and once, when she was required to attend the memorial service held for a famous sporting personality, she'd trotted beside him wearing a cloche hat and feeling like the maid. This was the final period before he got the job he really wanted when the lies began again, and eventually he had become so gross that she could not imagine any woman, certainly a woman younger than him, being interested in the least. His belly sagged and his thickly bearded face had now begun to resemble that of some debauched Old Testament prophet, the eyes often inflamed for, despite his workload, he was never without a glass in his hand. Now the wives looked at her with sympathy once more but also with a certain unmentionable curiosity as if they could not imagine how she endured such a gross physical presence.

But she had already calculated a date for leaving him when he died.

VI

She faced them all in the memorial service like a celebrity. No one could understand why. She wore a sheath dress, patent leather shoes, her highest heels, a black suspender belt, and sheer, seamed stockings, the tiny bulge of the clip of the suspender belt visible through the material of the dress when she sat. She knew because she could see Hywel's mother staring at it. She also wore a hat which was hardly a hat, more like a half-formed butterfly perched on the top of her head with her hair, neatly curled up, coiled around it. She'd recently been to a beauty parlour in France and had her eyebrows plucked and she wore the slightest tint of dove-grey eye shadow, all of which gave her face an altogether more interesting aspect. If anything, it looked thinner, but since she was handsomely tanned, not only had she never looked healthier (as some people remarked) but there was now, for the first time in her life, a certain air about her, a chic that was quite devastating. Had she been a model, you would have expected the ferryman's daughter to appear soon demonstrating what could be done next with a fisherman's slinky jersey! And now her face was quite inscrutable. The reshaped eyebrows had removed the Minnie Mouse look completely and the marks etched below her eyes merely made her look experienced. There was not a hint of her former self.

She'd told her father and sister not to come and she hoped there was no one there from her family. Up until the last minute, she wasn't certain she would go herself, and, as usual, it was only for the sake of the children that she'd agreed, one of the many problems faced by the harrassed controller of the broadcasting station who wasn't at all sure that the memorial service should be held, but had given way himself to departmental pressures. He seemed to be aware of his mistake since there were so few people present and began the customary eulogy with a nervous clearing of the throat, his thick north Walian accent making his ill chosen words seem all the more ponderous. Once you got these people away from their desks you realised how inadequate they were. Throughout, Delyth kept her eyes riveted on the bridge of his spectacles, her chin tilted pertly, allowing herself neither a glance to right or left. The gist of his peroration was soon revealed. Hywel was a man who had given Wales to the world. Of late, his speciality as a producer was what might be called The Welsh Connection, with distinguished exiles, with foreign lands, with those industries that had taken Welsh people the length and breadth of the globe, not forgetting Hywel's other preoccupation with the vanishing past.

But Delyth soon stopped listening. It was the mixture as before. It might even have been Hywel speaking himself. The Vanishing Past, she thought. By it, the controller meant images concocted from obscure farm ploughs or the hulks of derelict schooners which had once plied their trade to long forgotten harbours. As for crossing and recrossing the length and breadth of the world, while it was quite true, what he should have said was that if Hywel had found a Chicago gangster involved in the St Valentine's Day Massacre with a name like Evans, it too would be good for a programme, together with the expenses and the month-long booze-up that went with it. They would do anything rather than address themselves to the present. Later, during the final hymn, Morfydd clutching her throat beside her as she sang querulously, Delyth stole a glance at the assembled congregation. Besides the top brass – the Empire builders – there seemed an unusually large number of women which was a surprise. He couldn't have gone through them all, especially the policewoman, she thought ironically. At last, she felt uninvolved.

When the service ended and the procession of people came over to greet her, she had but one image in her mind and had she revealed it, she would have horrified everyone. She knew exactly what everyone was saying. 'Isn't she bearing up splendidly? She's looking so well considering... I always knew she was a brave little thing!'

But it was all she could do not to giggle. She'd fixed the lot of them. What had upset Morfydd so much, was not just the suddenness of her son's death, but the fact that she had not been informed of it for several weeks. They'd gone on holiday to the south of France and on the very first morning, Hywel had been playing football on the beach with the children when he'd suddenly put his hand to his heart and dropped down dead. There'd been a doctor nearby who told her he'd had a massive stroke. Then with three weeks of the holiday remaining, she determined to carry on with it, making up her mind on the spot since they were touring and had a number of places booked. They'd not had a family holiday for four years; by now Hywel scarcely saw his own children for any period longer than half an hour so she'd come to an abrupt decision. The hotel had been marvellous, arranging the crematorium in Marseilles and eventually, she'd driven home, refreshed and tanned with Hywel's ashes in the back of the car, only informing his mother a few days before they'd got on the ferry. But although it was a decision taken quickly, it was not taken lightly and she had no regrets whatsoever. She'd even had a laugh that she could never communicate to a living soul. Hywel's ashes had been placed in a plastic urn and once, when she'd been stopped for speeding, she'd inadvertently produced the cremation certificate with the other documents and the incredulous look on the faces of the gendarmerie had made her feel like a celebrity. The gendarmes had asked to see the urn and when they did, saluted with that thrilling French precision, even escorting her away from the intersection.

That was the last of Hywel really, sliding about in the boot of the car.

THE FARE

Lewis Davies

Naz had been waiting. The clock clicked forward, timing the day, his fare. Rain traced lines between the droplets on the windscreen, tugging each one down. The wipers swept forward, then back. He checked his watch; the fare was for four-thirty. He wanted to finish by six. He was hungry. He hadn't eaten for nine hours. He didn't like getting up before it was light to eat. It didn't suit him. The days were longer with no food.

He hoped the boy would eat tonight. It had been nine days now. He could see the heat inside his son as it rose to his skin in sweat. But his eyes were still quiet, looking beyond them to somewhere else. The hospital was clean, white and efficient, and it frightened him. The single room surrounded them, hushed.

He needed to finish. Time to eat. Time to visit.

He turned the engine on. A light in the hallway of the house caught him before he could drive the car away. Then the door opened and a man ran from the doorway down the path to the waiting cab.

A rush of cold air filled the car as the man clambered into the back seat. He was out of breath, his coat ruffled up. Naz watched the man as he tried to settle himself and his briefcase into the seat. The man took off his glasses to wipe the steam and rain from the lenses. He peered into the front, up at the mirror, his eyes squinting with the effort.

'Crickhowell House.'

The man spoke with an accent that Naz found difficult.

'Sorry, say again.'

'The Assembly building.'

'Ah, no problem. The bay, yes.'

The man just nodded and turned to face away from the mirror.

Naz concentrated on the traffic ahead as he pulled wide into Cathedral Road. The cars were lined tight, nudging each other out of the city for the weekend. This was a city that dozed through the evenings, only coming awake for a brief few hours between eleven and three, alcohol lowering its inhibitions. It pulled tight to itself during the day. The churches still blistered the city, still calling to it through empty pews. There wasn't enough here yet to break with its past.

Naz had lived in Manchester. It was a real city, full of people, full of the swirl of imagination. There were secret places in that city. Even for him, there were places to drink, to meet women. It was OK to pay for it then. He was a single man. There were necessities he couldn't ignore. He could remember his male friends on the streets at home, holding hands. Frustration dripping between them and not a woman in sight. Death and marriage had saved him from that.

His father had always expected him to give in and come home. The old man was still expecting his son's defeat when he cut into his leg with a cleaver. An accident but still death. Naz had looked for the memory, searched through its corners, even though it couldn't be his. The street thick with the smell of meat. The gutters running with rats and the crows ready to pick scraps from the bones. The panic for a taxi. The blood pouring from the severed artery as his father had seen it pour from so many dying animals, knowing he was dying. Naz had escaped that. His father had died in a taxi on the way to hospital.

The youngest son, he was allowed a chance, a chance to

become himself. His brothers had paid for a marriage then. Sure he wasn't coming back. Insuring against him coming back. A proper respectable girl. A good name. Her family lived in Cardiff. They were cousins of a cousin. He would have to move from Manchester. Too many memories, connections for a man about to marry. It was another city, a smaller city.

There were fewer cars going back into the city. It was a straight run, Cathedral Road, Riverside, Grangetown, Butetown, Docks. He could see the faces and houses change colour as he followed the river to the sea.

The man in the back shuffled the papers in his briefcase. He caught Naz looking at him in the mirror and smiled unsurely back.

'I'm late.'

Naz smiled. 'Can't go any faster. The traffic.'

'No, don't suppose you can.' He looked forlorn.

'Important meeting?'

The man looked as if he didn't quite understand the question.

'At the Assembly?' prompted Naz.

'No, not really. A commission.'

'You're an important man?'

The man straightened himself in the back seat. He looked to see if Naz was mocking him. It was a straight question.

'Er, no, I don't suppose I am.'

'What's the rush then?'

The man looked away. He watched the river rush below him and the space where there had once been factories now filled with cleared land. A sign marked the opportunity: 'Open to offers!'

The radio crackled through. Naz picked it up. A voice told him he had another call at the university. He could go home then. Narine would be waiting for him. She had been at the hospital for days. They allowed her to sleep there at first. Waiting. But she couldn't sleep and she just spent the nights staring out across the lights that marked the limits of the city. Naz liked the view from the ward. It was the only thing he liked about the hospital. At nights he could see the towns on the far side of the estuary and imagine what it would be like living there. Anywhere but here, now, while his dreams struggled through in the bed beneath him. It was a strange country, this. A country trying to find its way. There was nothing he could see that wasn't just smaller than Manchester.

He had taken Narine, the boy and the baby out to the coast last summer. The little boy had played in the waves as if they were something new and unique, especially provided for him. Narine had prepared dahl and chappattis which they ate on a rug placed over the sand. He could feel the stares; unease or novelty, he couldn't be sure. He tried to ignore them. The beach was packed with children, kites, dogs, sandcastles, the debris of a day out. Naz had been filled with the wealth of summer, the God-willing luck that had provided him with a wife and child. Narine couldn't swim, but she went into the water in her suit. The boy had played with the ball, and the waves had played with him. It had been a good day. He would be a father again in the spring, but that was a long way back through the winter now.

The traffic lights held him on the corner of Bute and James Street. An ambulance streaked past. Blue lights flooding the cab. The man in the back leaned over to get a better look at the road.

'I didn't think it was going to be like this?'

Naz looked up at the mirror to see the man's face. Lines of stress seemed to have cut into him.

'It's the time of night.'

'No, not the traffic. The city, this country. I don't understand it.'

The lights allowed the car to move forward. Naz checked his watch.

'What time is your meeting?'

'It doesn't matter.'

The man seemed to collapse back into himself.

'It is your country?'

'Yes, but I can't escape from it.' The man struggled in his pockets for money.

The edifice of the Assembly building rose out of the rain. It was spotlighted but seemed unsure of itself on the stage in this new half-country.

Naz pulled the car into a lay-by opposite the building. Four pounds forty was displayed on the clock. The man handed him a five pound note. Naz knew he would require change.

'Can I have a receipt, please?'

Naz scribbled the amount on the back of a card. His writing had never been as good as his speech, but he was OK on the numbers. The man pocketed his change and the receipt. He got out of the cab and shut the door. Naz pulled the car back onto the road and headed into town.

He didn't like calls at the university. They were usually students. There were too many students in the city. The city swelled with them every October, gorging itself on their easy money. But by December he was tired of their jokes, their endless enthusiasm and the way they threw up in his car. Today was the last day of term. He kept up with these events. He used them to mark his time in the city. Six years now. Six years with a new wife and now two children. The first one was a boy, that was good. The next a girl. That was good also but maybe more expensive. Still he loved girls and the way she opened her eyes to him. He would earn enough money. He would be successful in this city. His father-in-law had offered to lend him some money to start a business. It was good to be in business. In business for yourself. He knew about the cars. There would be younger men keen to work longer hours as the city expanded. He wouldn't be a younger man much longer. Then he would need to make a business.

The car pushed itself along the flyover that cut back into the centre of the city. The road rose steeply, soaring above the railway line and the units that lined its route out to the east. From the top the city was all briefly visible before the road crashed into the walls of the prison and the horizon reduced itself to streets again. The traffic slowed him again at the law courts. He wasn't sure if the fare would still be waiting at the university. People called through then forgot about it.

The students reminded him. There had been a ripple of meningitis cases last winter. He had seen their faces in *The Echo*. Bright, young, hopeful, dead. It took them so quickly. A few days of coughs and headaches and then a sharp coma. There had been a man working in a restaurant he had heard about, a Hindu. He was working on Monday night, in hospital by Tuesday. He had only lasted two days. There was a picture of him behind the counter in the restaurant. A big smiling man. The boy was a fighter. A strong boy. He could feel the determination in his arms as he clambered around his shoulders, mouthing words in two languages. It had been too many days, the dark days of winter in the city. He called back into the radio. He was signing off for the night. There was a brief complaint from the operator on the far side of the call. Then he put the handset down.

A month ago he had followed the cars to the cemetery. They had been given a plot out in Ely, a few miles to the west of the city. The graves were new. They had been cut deeply into the soft Welsh loam. Each new mound, a life ending out here, many miles from the start in a dusty village on the Indus plain, or the crumbling walls of Lahore or Karachi. The cities themselves had changed their names, as if able to disown their children. They couldn't return to a place that no longer existed. They had cut themselves off and would now be the first to die in this new place where it rained through the long winters. He had thought of their hopes. Many of the graves carried pictures of them as young men. Faded, overexposed pictures of dark men in poor new suits, eager for a go at the world. Most had thought they would go back.

They had listened solemnly in the mosque off Crwys Road. The walls dripped with the sounds of his childhood and the cool mornings in Peshawar before the sun got too high. The time to work. His father had been keen on education, avoided politics. The future was commerce.

The new mosque had been a factory, making clothes. They bought it with donations and optimism. He never attended much himself. The community was growing. He could buy Halal meat now and vegetables he hadn't seen since he left Manchester. His wife bought clothes from people who could speak Urdu.

The meat was good but to be avoided in memory of his father. But it was there, fresh and available. They had some strength now, numbers, a community. The boy would be starting school in a year. He would learn English properly then.

There were casualties. His closest friend ran a chip shop in Llanrumney and was living with a woman called Ruth. He had given up the cars. He was too old for the abuse and the girls who wouldn't pay you and the men who simply walked away. He would trust in Allah, he had claimed, and now he was sending money to a woman he had married and living with one he hadn't. But Naz couldn't leave the faith. It was part of him. The inscription above the door convinced him. Allah is good. Allah is great. And indeed he had been. But now, with his son at the hospital, he wasn't so sure. The little boy had committed no sin, but then he remembered his own nights on the riverside in Manchester.

He drove the car along Richmond Road, across the junction. The lights favouring his flight. He pulled up at number forty-seven Mackintosh Place. The lights were on in the front room. He could feel the tension in his fingers as he cut the engine and opened the car door. The door to his house was ajar; he could smell the good smells of cooking flood through him. He found Narine in the kitchen. She was sitting at the table slumped over, her head resting. He touched her hair. She stood up and folded into him. He knew his daughter was being cared for; he knew the boy had gone.

MUSCLES CAME EASY

Aled Islwyn

Muscles came easy, I said. *Looked like a bulldog at eight, size fourteen collar at thirteen and captain of the senior school rugby team at sixteen.*

He was impressed. I could tell. Shuffled his arse on those pussy-sized stools they have at the bar at Cuffs and offered to buy me a drink.

Now normally, I don't. Don't talk. Don't look 'em in the eye. Don't do nothing once I've fucked 'em in the darkroom. Them's the rules. Walk straight out of there. Maybe have a drink on my own, or talk to Serge behind the bar, as I did tonight. Then go back a little later to see if it's busy in there by then.

Guess this guy just happened to see me there at the bar. Well! Let's face it. You can't miss me.

French, apparently. From Lyon. A businessman on his way down to Tarragona. Married. I wouldn't be surprised. But no ring. Not your usual Cuffs customer at all.

Asked me if he could see me tomorrow. How naïve can you get? Didn't disillusion the sad fart. Didn't seem right to, somehow. Said my day job at the gym kept me busy. Wanted to know the name of the gym. And I told him. Said he'd look it up next time he was in Barcelona.

Yes, do that, mate, I said. But, frankly, I wouldn't recognise him if he pole-vaulted onto this balcony right now.

Then – big mistake! – he grabbed me by my upper arm

and tried to lean over to kiss me. Jesus, man! How gross can you get? But I still didn't have the heart to tell him to fuck off, or that Serge paid me to prance around in the darkroom with no shorts on. It's Serge's way of making sure the facilities get well used if it's been quiet in there for a couple of nights. I start the ball rolling in there if they seem a bit on the shy side. Pick someone I'd normally go for and give him a blow job. Sometimes it develops into a free-for-all. Sometimes not. But they've got to feel they've had a good night out, these saddos. That's what they're there for... supposedly.

For the most part they've got to grope around in the dark for themselves and find their own bit of fun, but Serge reckons someone like me making himself available for a while helps get things going. And it's always the start of the week he calls me. By Thursday, apparently, they need no encouragement. Never get these club jobs on a weekend.

Wouldn' t have touched that French guy with a bargepole in my own time. Just didn't have the heart to tell him the truth. Should have really. I'm just too soft. Always have been, see!

Got up and left him after the kissing fiasco. Went straight back in there and fucked two more. Condoms worn both times, of course. Part of the game ever since I've been at it. Surprised how many of the older ones still ask and check. Guess they remember a time when it wasn't the norm.

Seeing the traffic going backwards and forwards kept Serge happy, I could tell.

Then the last dumb trick I pulled must have had this thing for armpits. Licked me sore he did, the bastard. Not really my thing. But he was good at it, I'll give him that.

Glad of that shower though.

First thing I always do when I come in from these club jobs. Check Mike's asleep (and he always is) then get cleaned up. Check myself over. Thorough. All part of the routine. Important. Never fail.

And so's this brandy. Part of the routine, like. Just a small one. Few minutes to myself out here in the fresh air. Mull things over. How it all went and that. Well-toned body. Well-honed mind. All that shit they pumped into you at college. Well! When all's said and done, it's right, like, isn't it? When you really think it over. Has to be... for the life I lead.

I refused point blank. Told him straight. I'm not dressing up in cowboy boots and stetsons for nobody – and no amount of extra euros.

O, si, he said, *but line dancing is all the craze now!*

That may be so, I said back, but I told him straight... he's running a great little health studio there, Raul. Legit. The genuine McCoy. Not some poof's palace where a lot of poseurs prance around pretending to lift weights and keep fit.

I'm strictly a one-on-one guy. Personal Trainer is what I'm employed as and that's what I am. Press-ups. Rowing machine. Circuit training. All the stuff I know really works. I work with clients individually. One-to-one. Assessments. Supervision. Even down to diets and lifestyle choices. A proper trainer.

OK, I do some aerobic stuff with the women clients, I grant you. But they just like to hear the word used often. Don' t think half of them know what the hell aerobics means. And told him that's all the pampering to fashion he'll get from me.

Oh Joel, you not mean it! You think it over, Joel... please... for Raul!

Love the way Raul says my name. And he knows it. They're not used to it here – Joel – which is strange. I always find. Spain being a Catholic country and all. You'd think they'd know their Bible.

He makes it sound like Hywel. Reminds me of home. Our geography teacher was called Hywel Gordon. Had a hell of a crush on him at one time. He'd been a very promising full back, but some injury had put paid to that. No sign of injury on him from what I could see. But there you go! Guess it was the bits of him I never did get to see which needed scrutinising the most.

Raul's been good to me these last four years. Him and his missus. Helped me with my Spanish when I first arrived. Fed me. Gave me a job. *I only want best people work with me in my fitness studio*, he'd say. *And I want you.*

They speak Catalan together. Raul and his wife. And their kid gets taught in it at school. Like they do with Welsh back home, I suppose.

Not me, of course.

My nanna could speak Welsh quite a bit. Chapel and that. But I couldn't sing a single hymn at her funeral. And felt a right nerd. If there's anything of value to lose, you can bet your life my mam'll be the first to do so.

Couldn't be arsed with all that, really, were her thoughts on Welsh.

Then one day she lost her purse on the bus. Huge kerfuffle in our house. A whole week's wages gone. No wonder my dad left. *I'd have been OK if it wasn't for her with the glass eye from Tonypandy confusing me with all that talk about her Cyril!* The only explanation anybody ever got from her on that little incident.

Poor cow has even managed to lose a breast. *You're one nipple short of a pair of tits, Mam!* I tease her rotten sometimes. She laughs.

You've got to laugh in the face of adversity, she says... except sometimes 'adversity' slips out as 'anniversary'. It's a miracle I'm as well-adjusted as I am.

And I bet Raul has me taking these bloody line dancing classes any day now. I can see it coming!

Don't know why you won't get yourself a tidy job, she said.

I knew as soon as I picked up the phone she was going to take a long time coming to the point.

Come back home and be a teacher. Papers always say they're crying out for them round here. And there's you there with all them qualifications…

I already got a tidy job, I said. Why I bother explaining every time, I don't know. She'd never heard of a Personal Training Instructor 'til I started calling myself one – as she'll happily tell anyone who's sad enough to listen.

Didn't take a blind bit of notice. She never does. High as a kite 'cos of something. I knew it when she first came on the line. I could always tell, even as a child. Her voice almost croaking with that hysterical shriek she puts on when she's dying to tell you something.

Our Joanne's pregnant again. At last she came out with it. In one great torrent. *The washing machine's on the blink.* And to cap it all, the real biggy was her final punch: *Oh, yes…! And Dan Llywellyn has cancer.*

Then silence.

I felt nothing, really.

Said I was sorry to hear that, like you do without thinking. But I couldn't honestly say I'd thought of him at all for several years.

She didn't know where it was. *Somewhere painful*, is all she'd heard. The talk of Talbot Green Tesco's last Saturday, apparently.

He had it coming, I suppose. But I couldn't tell Mam that. Wasn't glad. Wasn't sad. Felt nothing.

Still don't know why you started calling him Dan Dracula. She was chipping away on an old bone, hoping she'd catch me on the hop. *Always thought it was cruel of you, that, after all he'd done for you.*

It's because of all he's done to me, Mam. That's what I wanted to tell her. But didn't.

He's also the one who introduced me to weights. Saw my potential. *Dan Llywellyn is the one who saw our Joel's full potential.* That's what he'll always be credited with. Showed me the ropes. Gave me definition.

You're everything you are today 'cos of that man, she declared with conviction.

She was right, of course. And she meant it at face value. Wouldn't know what irony was. Not my mam. If she can't get it cheap on Ponty market, she doesn't want to know.

Her kitchen floor was completely flooded, apparently. Took three bucketfuls of mopping to clean it up. And today it rained there all day.

You call me a Muscle Mary one more time and I'll fucking give you a good hiding, I said.

I haven't called you a Muscle Mary once yet, he replied, playing child-like with my left bicep.

Well! To be fair he hadn't. Not during today's debacle.

Pussy-boys are so predictable, I said. *I always know what's coming next with you.*

You're just a slave to your ego, Joel, he retorted. *And that's a very subservient place to be for a man of your physical stature.*

On the bed, Mike rolled on his stomach as he spoke, and lowered his voice to that detached level which always places him beyond any further verbal bruising. It's a ploy he's mastered to perfection. The aim is to intimidate me and exonerate himself. It's a tactical illusion, of course, rather than a sign of true superiority. It's a part of our game. A futile duel fought in a darkened room, while our neighbours, all around us, bathe in a siesta of rest and serenity.

Maybe that's why we laughed. Lying there bickering in our Calvin Kleins on that vast double bed this afternoon. It was the only thing to do. Our last hope of not looking ridiculous, even to ourselves.

We've lived together long enough to be both comfortable and bored with each other in equal measure.

I slapped his arse and told him to go make a cup of tea. And that's when my mobile rang, just as he opened the door to the living room and let the light in.

This guy's from Valencia, right. The one who rang. Owns a club, it seems, and wants me down there next Tuesday night to work his back room. Personal recommendation from Serge, apparently.

I jumped off the bed and stood upright to talk.

Two things, I said. One: Valencia's too far, man. Must be four hundred kilometres, easily. Don't know how much that is in miles. Gave up converting long time ago. But then relented when he mentioned the fee. Said I'd think it over. Oh, yes! And the second thing, I said: *I'm strictly a top. Hope Serge made that clear. This boy's arse is an exit only. Period.*

Silence! Think the aggro in my voice had been too much for him. All I could hear was the amount of money on offer being repeated down the line. And the sound of water boiling in the kitchen where Mike was doing what he does best. Being English.

I've tried to talk to Mike. But I can't.

The news of Dan Llywellyn's imminent demise has followed me around for days. Ever since Mam told me. *And all the memories slogged me in the guts!*

That's the last line of this poem by a guy called Harri Webb. We did him at college – *You see, it wasn't all boys running around in muddy fields and pumping iron*, I told Mike earlier – and I really loved his stuff.

Mike's painting at the time. What I still call the small bedroom is now his studio. Looks more like a clinic if you ask me. I've never heard of anyone being creative and so tidy at the same time. Whilst the canvas is awash with colour, Mike remains immaculate. But that's Mike for you.

He was only half listening to me, I could tell. He then informs me that he's never heard of Harri Webb. *Another one of your trivial poets*, he insists. But inside I know that he takes it as a personal affront to his dignity as an English lecturer that I've managed once again to draw attention to a lapse in his supposedly superior education.

He was still at it when Mam rang in the early evening. Painting that is.

Things are worse than first thought, apparently. For old Dan. He's at home. But he's shrivelled to a nothing and his hair's all fallen out. Sick every other minute, it seems. All over the bus back from town. So she said.

And what's his wife got to say on the situation? I chipped in. *The usual fuck-all, no doubt.*

Mam tells me to wash my mouth out with soap and water, but I tell you, that woman should have had 'I see nothing, I hear nothing, I say nothing' tattooed across her forehead years ago. She must have known what was going on. Wasn't deaf, dumb and blind through ignorance, I'm almost sure. And I don't think it was fear either. Doubt if Dan Llywellyn ever touched her. It was just indifference. She'd sit there like a beached whale in front of the telly, stuffing chocolates in her mouth, oblivious to the tip around her. And all I ever did was mumble some banality as I passed her on the way to the bottom of their stairs. Dan upstairs before me, usually.

You go on up, love, she'd urge me. And up I'd go.

Twp she was, I reckon. Probably still sitting there right now, incarcerated by her cholesterol consumption and jellied in cellulite, flicking from channel to channel in order to shut out the outrages going on around her.

I reckon our Joanne will go the same way. Already showing early signs of abandonment, despite all this breeding she's intent on inflicting on the world. In fact, I'm convinced it's part of it. All these brats of hers are only an excuse for doing less and less. That's the reality. She has no creative aspirations in her at all. Not for herself. Not for her kids. Never did.

Leave her alone. She only wants to give me more grandchildren, pleads Mam on her behalf. *Since you clearly don't intend to give me any.*

Joanne and Dean already have three. *That was my point*, I said. Why the hell would they want more? Going by the evidence so far, the possibility that some hidden pearl of genius is hiding away in their shared gene pool is pretty remote.

They scream a lot. Mam spoils them. Dean disappears down the pub. And Joanne gets fatter by the day, only admitting when pushed that she doesn' t really care what the hell they do with their lives... *so long as they're happy*. This is the happy heterosexual life we're all supposed to aspire to, as lived halfway up a Welsh mountain. I swear the sheep have more fun.

It's all over the *Observer* apparently. The latest Rhondda bombshell. Dan Llywellyn arrested amidst allegations of child abuse. They've torn his house apart. Even removed the telly and the video. So it's a real crisis as far as his missus is concerned.

I chuckled to myself, but felt nothing. Said even less.

You used to spend hours down that gym with him.

I let her do the talking and grunted in agreement.

And round his house! Some weekends, you practically lived there.

Her hysteria was muted for once. I knew there was so much else she wanted to ask, but never would. Some places are too raw for even my mam to venture. I simply coughed. (This cold I've caught has made me croak incoherently when I speak, making my silence sound less guilty than it might otherwise have done.) Mam's voice cracked in unison.

The mirror by the phone was briefly my only comfort. I flexed my free arm. And smiled at myself in approval. For a moment I remember wishing Mike had been there with me. But he wasn't. It was just me and Mam... the mirror and the memories.

Got a worse drenching that night than I thought at the time. Must have. 'Cos I'm convinced that's where I caught this lot. OK! I know I said I definitely wouldn't do that job. But did in the end, didn't I?

Fancied the run. That's what clinched it, not the money. When you consider that it emerged he wasn't paying mileage for the petrol, it wasn't really that much. But I hadn't been for a seriously long run on the bike for months. So, Valencia, I thought, why not?

The evening went well. Tidy little bar. Changed into my cut-off shorts and leather harness and did a few tricks.

Hadn't even realised it was raining until I came out the back at 4 a.m. If I'd had any sense, would have asked that guy for somewhere to stop over. But in my mind, I'd been looking forward to those empty roads along the Costas in the middle of the night. So wiped the seat, got on and revved my way out of there.

How was I to know the 'Med' was due to have its worst storm for five years that night?

Bloody exhausted by the time I got back here. Had to keep my speed right down, see. Made the journey longer, which meant I got even wetter. Thunder sounding off all around me. Lightning. Hailstones the size of golf balls. Could feel her sliding underneath me. Probably should have checked the pressure before setting out. But didn't. Could feel them tyres fighting the torrent for supremacy of the tarmac on certain corners.

Exhilarating at the time. But glad to get home, I can tell you. It was already light. The sun all bright in the sky as though nothing had happened. Mike still asleep, thank God. Squelched my way to the bathroom to strip out of my bike leathers.

Well! It's been a week and I'm hardly any better. Still coughing my guts up. Sneezing. But the shivering's gone. That was the only hopeful news I could give Raul when he called earlier. Wanted to give the man some glimmer of hope I might return to work before the end of the week.

The things you do, not to do the line dancing, he teased, accusing me of being a fraud.

Cheeky bugger! I leaned forward and pinched his nipple through his T-shirt.

I'm as honest as my prick is long, I said, choking as I coughed as I laughed.

He didn't flinch. Just laughed along. I'm sure he'd be a kinky little bastard given half a chance. He knows I'm gay, of course. Always has. But we've never really discussed it.

That's what made it rather embarrassing when the phone rang. Raul was still here in the lounge when they called. Over there across the table from me. He could tell I'd sobered up pretty quick after picking up the phone.

It was some bloody detective from the central police station at Pontypridd. Well! You don't expect it, do you? Not in Barcelona during siesta on a Sunday afternoon.

It's another world, you see. That's what I keep telling Mam.

Nice for a week, love, but wouldn't want to live there, she keeping replying.

She must have been the one to give them my number. Didn't think to ask him where he got it from. And looking back on it, he didn't really ask me anything either. Confirmed who I was. That I knew Dan Llywellyn. That I'd agree to see them when they came over. And that was it.

Must be serious, mind… coming all that way just to see me.

This coming Wednesday? asked Mike in disbelief when I told him. *They are in a hurry.*

Guess they have to be if Dan is fading fast. They'll want to get their summons served before the death certificate is signed.

Explained very little to Raul after I'd put the receiver down. He had the sense to down the whisky I'd poured him pretty sharpish. Said he hoped I'd be better soon.

So do I. It's no fun, this sickness lark!

I guess I should have. But I couldn't, could I? Don't ask me why, just knew I wasn't going to before they rang that bell. And all that talk of 'substantial financial compensation' he kept dangling like a carrot in front of my eyes throughout our 'little chat' didn't make a difference either.

This isn't a formal interview, Joel, he said. *I'm not obliged to caution you and you're obviously not suspected of committing any criminal activity yourself. We just want a little chat.*

He didn't have a Valleys accent. Couldn't really tell where he was from, the young burly one who talked. Impressive thighs though. He was lean and well-muscled. Not in my league, like. But I knew he was a fit bastard and guessed he probably punched above his weight. Wore a pair of safari shorts, which looked great on him. And a kind of pink cotton shirt, which didn't.

Found the heat oppressive, he said. Never been to this part of Spain before. Investigating serious allegations made against Mr Daniel Llywellyn who ran the Junior Gym and Recreational Club down Bethel Street for many years.

Well, I knew why he was there! He could have saved his breath on that score.

How is he? I found myself asking.

Poorly, came the reply. God knows why, but somehow I'd expected more.

He already knew I was gay. He told me so when he first arrived.

Yes and very happily so, I fired back with confidence. Thought afterwards that I must have sounded defensive and regretted saying anything.

So I see. Beautiful city. Lovely apartment. Must be a very nice lifestyle.

I like it. I found myself agreeing like a sheep. He was setting me up for compliance and I wasn't having any of it.

He also knew I was now working at a health studio myself. *A bit different from your old haunts back in Wales*, he sneered.

Told him I'd taken time off work especially to see them. He said he was grateful. But inside I knew every word he spoke meant something else.

Should have dropped Dan Dracula right in it, I suppose. The stupid bastard. But just couldn't bring myself to do it, see.

Then he said he knew it was difficult to talk about such things.

His mate, meantime – the little short-arse git who hardly said a word – is still sitting in that armchair over by the door to the spare bedroom. Fascinated by art, it seems. Had a good look inside and his eyes devoured every painting we have hanging here in the lounge too.

It seems I can get back in touch with them anytime... or so the talkative one kept reminding me. No problem... day or night. When I'd thought it over. If I could remember any little incident when I'd felt uncomfortable... I shouldn't hesitate. *Any time. You just call me, Joel.* Like all the other lads had done... the ones who'd come forward and were now in line for *substantial financial compensation.*

Wants us to meet again before they go back. Tomorrow evening after the gym closes. For a drink.

I suggested the Zanzibar bar on Las Ramblas. His tourist attire should look at home there.

We shook hands as they left. And I looked him in the eye. For the first time. Didn't want him to think I was scared of doing that. But it's not something I've ever been good at. Looking people in the eye.

Still have his card here in my hand. Detective Sergeant Gavin Hughes BSc. Can't remember the name of the other one. He never left a card. But I told Mike how besotted he'd been with his paintings.

You see the truth doesn't always come easily in this life, Joel. That must be his mantra. It's his favourite sentence, most definitely. Heard it so many times this evening, it's spinning round my brain. Which would make him happy back in his little hotel bedroom if he knew.

That was obviously his intention – to plant the seeds that

would get me to spill the beans. But the truth doesn't always come that easy in this life, does it?

Should have thrown the sentence back in his face... and added 'Gavin' at the end, like he kept adding 'Joel' to the end of everything he said to me. Like one big strapping full stop.

Still, he got more than he bargained for one way or another!

A strange evening really. Don't quite know what to make of it.

Sorry! I just don't do guided tours of gay Barcelona, I said.

Oh, don't be like that, Joel! he pleaded. A wry, old-fashioned smile lit his face.

I gave in in the end. We ended up in Cuffs. Introduced him to Serge.

Shouldn't have really. Gone round clubs drinking, I mean. I'm still taking the antibiotics for my chest infection. Don't finish them till Saturday.

Added to which, Mike went ballistic when he heard I'd shown him some of the nightlife here. *He's a cop, for God's sake!*

He's so paranoid, that boy! It's unbelievable.

I know he's a cop, don't I?

I've done my share of hanging around in gay bars, Gavin assured me.

That was much earlier in the evening, when we're sitting outside the Zanzibar, watching the world walk by on Las Ramblas. It's a warm evening. (Aren't they all, out here?) We down a few drinks. Just me and Gavin. His fat-git partner made his excuses after downing two beers in a hurry. Then headed back to their hotel. Needed his beauty sleep, he said.

Slugs do, I thought.

So that left me and good old Gavin, who proceeded to assure me that he didn't intend to talk about Dan Llywellyn all evening. But then again... *the truth doesn't always come easy in this life...* and he knew what I must be going through... how I mustn't feel disloyal... how wishing to put the past behind me was natural... but how I never would until I had all this off my chest. Oh yes, he understood!

Which amused me, really. He was jolly about it all. One of the lads. Leaning over. Sharing a joke, where appropriate. His hand on my knee when occasion allowed. All textbook, 'You can trust me, I'm a policeman', stuff. I knew his game and went along with it all.

Why shouldn't I let him ply me with drinks? Buy me a meal? As far as he was to know, my tongue might have started to loosen at any second. The one right word from him could have triggered an avalanche of juicy memories at any moment. My guard could be down. Floods of steamy recollections could be streaming from my lips. Salacious anecdotes. Times and dates and sordid details. All the conclusive evidence that would put Dan Llywellyn away for many years.

I'm the big fish he wants to haul. Worked that one out after he rang to ask to see me. And he virtually admitted as much this evening. I was, after all, Dan Llywellyn's 'star boy'. Played for the county at almost everything. Boxed for Wales as a schoolboy. Very nearly made the British Olympic wrestling team. Got to represent Wales in some World Federation weightlifting tournament in Budapest at the age of eighteen. More trophies than my mam could cope with. Which is why half of them ended up in Nanna's house.

So it's down to me.

You're the man who can nail Dan Llywellyn, he tells me.

Seems to me the undertaker will do that soon enough, I said back to him.

He laughs at that and slaps me on the back. Furious inside, I reckon, 'cos he knows I'm making light of his mission. But he's enough of a professional to know he mustn't lose it. I would, after all, be the dream witness for him, if only I'd play ball. The ending of this dark chapter in the annals of Welsh crime lays in my hands. And maybe old Gavin needs this one for his CV to secure promotion or boost his self-confidence or his reputation amongst his colleagues or whatever else he feels is missing in his saddo life. He knows he mustn't blow it with me.

Daft sod! Does he really think I'm going to dish the dirt on Dan?

Seven-thirty! The traffic's buzzing. And the sun is up.

I'm not exactly suffering. But I can't get going either. This coffee is just about enough to revive my mouth. The rest of me can follow later, once I'm doing some warm-ups down the gym.

Raul will already be there. Cleaning. Setting everything up for the day. He works hard.

It must have been two o'clock when we left Cuffs. Early really, by Barcelona standards. The place was hardly getting going. But I told him I had work to go to in five hours' time and that he was also flying home today.

All in all, he must have been resigned to the fact that his tactics hadn't worked.

Guess I can't break you tonight, Joel, he joked half seriously over our last drink.

You'll never break me, man. All these sad wannabees who made these allegations against Dan, don't know what they're talking about.

Talking about tears in some instances, Joel, he comes straight back at me. *The tales some of those boys had to tell have left them emotionally scared for life.*

You'll never find me crying, mate, I proclaimed adamantly.

Ah, Joel, the world is full of men like you who've lived to swallow bitter tears.

Tears are totally feminine things, I tell him. *They're void of any maleness. It's a clinically proven fact. No traces of testosterone have ever been found in a man's tears. Only feminine hormones.*

He was stunned for a moment and didn't know whether to laugh or not.

Oh! Men have the capacity to produce them, I said, *but no means of instilling them with any masculine traits. It's a fact.*

When the taxi pulled up outside, he placed his hand on my knee once more. just as I was about to open the door. He half turned to face me full on and willing sincerity into his eyes with all the power he could muster, he said, *Remember, Joel, I'm on your side.*

I'm convinced the line about 'truth not always being easy' is about to get another airing and in a sublime moment of panic, I kissed him. A smacker on the lips.

Think I meant it as a joke. Can't really remember.

Well! Yes, I can. It was and it wasn't. A joke, that is. I was confused. And high. And horny. And he responded. Old Gavin. There, last night, in that taxi his lips went 'Open sesame' and his hand moved up my thigh.

The taxi driver just sat there not caring a damn. He's seen it all before. And besides, the meter was still running. Why would he mind?

Eventually, my tongue slid free and I got out without a word. Just stood there gobsmacked on the pavement as he's driven away. My hand clutching the card I'd felt him slip into my pocket. It's the second one he's given me. I now have a pair. Only on that second one he's written his personal e-mail address in biro on the back.

It's here in my wallet, hidden away.

I've no idea how he got my e-mail address. My mam is off the hook this time. Telephones are an integral part of her communications system. It's a well-known fact. But an e-mail remains a mystery to her.

However he got it, there it was this evening. Waiting for me.

Thanks for seeing me. I appreciated it and respect your position. But if you ever want to relieve yourself of anything, you know how to get hold of me. My investigations continue. It's a sad and sensitive business. Hope we get to meet again, especially if things get clearer in your mind. Regards, Gavin.

I couldn't reply immediately. What a relief!

Mike has had several of his paintings accepted by some prestigious gallery. He needed the computer urgently. I was banished out here on the balcony. No! Correction. I banished myself.

Hate these days when I've been for a check-up. So fucking humiliating. And six months seem to come around so quickly. Condoms and care are all well and good. But I'm wise to stick to my routine.

Mike pointed out that I wouldn't need to go if I didn't play around. The darkroom work really bugs him. He suffers from selective memory. *We met in a bloody darkroom. Mike,* I said. *Remember?*

You're thirty-three now, was his response. *Time you grew up.*

Perhaps he doesn't want to remember. It was ten years ago. Not here, of course. Not Cuffs. Ibiza. Another club. A holiday. Our first shag. No condom. No cares.

And now, it's not even a memory.

He'll still want me to accompany him to the opening of his exhibition. He told me all about it as he broke the news. 'Launch party' it's called. More of a small reception. apparently. Just critics and friends. He told me the date and to be sure to keep it free.

I'm still good for wheeling out as the trophy boyfriend, it seems. And don't get me wrong, that's fine by me. So long as Mike doesn't forget at which bring-and-buy he picked me up.

Being told you're all clear should give you a high, I suppose. But curiously, it doesn't. There's relief. And then this empty feeling takes over inside, as you stop off in reception before leaving to make your next appointment in another six months' time.

Raul's missus made such a fuss of Mike last night it was almost embarrassing. Her wonderful meal was already enough of a contribution to the celebrations. She's generous to a fault and I can understand why Raul lives in awe of her every act of kindness. I have never in my life lived with anyone who oozes so much goodness with such grace and I understand that it can't always be easy.

It's only two paintings, Mike insisted repeatedly every time she mentioned his triumph.

Still two more than Van Gogh ever sold in his lifetime, I kept chipping in, playing the proud partner.

We'd taken the champagne, of course. Not cava, Raul noted, tossing the bottle in the air when we first got there and catching it again behind his back, much to Mike's relief.

Things are pretty tight on old Raul, I think. His overheads are high and with another bambino on the way he can't have much money to throw around.

As we sat down to eat in their tiny kitchen, Mike ceremoniously popped open the bottle. And the kid starts throwing his pasta across the room in excitement. The rest of us just laughed and made a toast of Mike's success and cleared off that first bottle without a care in the world.

Raul suggested a spot of line dancing to follow and I told him to bugger off.

I flexed my biceps to amuse the kid and he in turn tried to knock the muscles back into place with a plastic hammer which must have come with the set of plastic blocks I kept tripping over underfoot.

As the evening drew on, we all seemed bloated and bubbly and larger than life. And I really hated the moment when I knew I had to tell Raul I'd be away another week. It seems so soon after the week I lost when that bug laid me low.

Needless to say. I needn't have worried. His handshake was flamboyant in his sympathies. He knew. He cared. He caressed.

Si, si! You must, you must, he said. And with that he

fetched the second bottle from the fridge, saying such sadness had to be drowned immediately.

He indulges you something rotten, was Mike's verdict on the way home last night. *You're like a great big toy he just can't get enough of.*

You used to be like that towards me once, I replied. *What happened?*

It's not good that it's back.

Mike made all the right noises last night after Joanne rang, it's true, but he's so buoyed by his newfound success, his words just sounded empty and devoid of any feeling.

Even Joanne's voice rang hollow as she tried to speak through the tears. A combination of the waterworks and the Welsh in her voice. Like a drunken sailor trying to sing a shanty aboard a sinking ship on a stormy sea. The meaning made no sense at all, but you could still taste the salt on your lips as the song slapped your face.

It will be two years since I was last at home. That's the trouble. I've started to forget.

She won't come over to see me. Our Joanne. I've asked her. But she won't. Says she doesn't like the food.

Bloody ridiculous excuse!

The truth is, she's never been anywhere much, our Joanne. No further than the prenatal clinic. And even then, our mam has had to go with her every time.

Not the next time, though! The thought struck me like a left hook. Not if it's back.

Knew immediately I had to do the same. Go back. Take charge.

I had no chance to even ask how Mam was. Dean has a go at me as soon as he picks up the receiver. It was late, apparently, and I'd woken up the kids. He's always hated my guts. Likes to think he's something special with his fists. And he'd love to take a pop at me one day, I know. But the sad wimp has never quite been able to pluck up the courage, 'cos he knows I've won prizes for it. So it's hands buried deep, whenever we meet. Pocket billiards and a mouthful of abuse.

I know I wind him up, which doesn't help, but he's such an easy match to light, I can't resist!

What are you doing sleeping round Mam's house, any road? I said. *Can't you provide a house of your own for your family?*

Very compassionate, Joel, he retorts, except he can't really do sarcasm. He has to scream it at me, thereby missing the advantage of the higher moral ground which had subtly been his for his taking if only he'd played his cards right.

You boys fighting again? You'll be the death of me!

Mam could be heard almost physically wrestling the receiver from Dean's hand as she talked. Her voice was full of sniffing. More tears. I sighed and start to feel depressed.

It seems that she hasn't had the test results yet. I tried to interrupt the moist flow of pessimism by looking on the bright side, but she was having none of it. Easier to wallow in anticipation of the worse scenario than hanging on to hope, it seems.

I was glad to get off the phone.

So much for 'The old town looks the same...' It doesn't.

They've knocked half of it down. And the other half's boarded up.

I'll be next, said Mam. *Already feel as though I've been knocked down by a bus. And I'll soon be boarded up. Eight nails in the lid should do it nicely... with some lily of the valleys from you and Joanne resting on top just to set it all off!*

She chokes me when she speaks like that.

Don't go wasting your money on me now, mind, she continued. *So long as you keep it dignified, that's all I ask. I don't want anything tacky. And make sure your father doesn't put in an appearance at the last moment. Don't want him ruining my big day. He ruined the last one I had in that chapel.*

Mam, don't talk like that, I said.

Well, the bastard turned up, didn't he? Her loud voice brings high camp comedy to the cancer ward. *And don't think I'm the only woman who's ever wished her husband had jilted her at the altar with the benefit of hindsight. The world is full of us.*

And if you hadn't married him, I wouldn't be here now, would I? Have you thought of that? I said.

She's only trying to be cheerful, she answered, expecting me to laugh along. But of course, I don't. I didn't. And I can't. Can't cry either. Won't allow myself. I never can. Ended up just sitting there, telling her not to be so daft.

Had a long chat with the doctor a little later.

He'd no office to take me to. We stood out in the corridor out of earshot, keeping our voices down and shifting sideways whenever anyone walked past. The staff use that corridor as a short cut to the car park when they go for their illicit fags. It sees a lot of traffic. Our whispers had to blend in furtively with a sea of uniforms, camouflaged by smiles and the slight whiff of smoke.

She's been slightly overly pessimistic, apparently. That's what he told me. It turns out he's more worried by her mental state than by the cancer. Well, not more, maybe, but as much.

You're going to be OK. I tried to reassure her when I finally returned to the ward to sit with her a little while longer.

The doctor had just told me her depression manifested itself in laughter, so my heart sank as she roared hysterically in response. She lunged at me sitting in my chair, before throwing her arms around my neck and all but falling out of bed.

It's back, my boy, she howled. *It's back. And so are you.*

Listen to the darkness.

You can't, of course. That bloody clock won't let you. Like it won't let me sleep. Five nights I've been back home and five nights I've just been lying here contemplating how much I hate that clock. I've always hated it. When it chimed away in Nanna's house, I hated it. And now I hate it here.

To put it in boxing terms, it seems to punch above its weight. Stands there in the corner. Looking petit. A wallflower with time on its hands. Delicate casing and a poofy face. Calls itself a grandmother clock. *The only thing of any value I ever got from my mother*, Mam says. It may be old, but I doubt it's worth much. Just a clock with attitude. A wedding present to my grandparents, in the days when even the cheap pressies outlived the marriage.

Hear that tick-tock measuring the emptiness; its tenacity audible above all the other anxieties throbbing in my brain. Like a bantam fighter, it just keeps coming at you. Wearing you down. Numbing your pain. Making you oblivious to the killer punch that's about to get you on the blind side.

Curiously, Mam asked about it tonight. The clock. She wants everything to be in full working order if she's allowed home tomorrow. Had I wound it up?

No, but it's winding me up plenty! I replied.

She laughed that exaggerated laugh the doctor seemed to find so worrying.

I've thought about it. That chat I had with him yesterday. She's not suppressing depression. More like celebrating her inherent over-optimism.

Mam will always laugh. She always has. It's what pulls her through.

I've made her bed up. Ready for tomorrow. Hoovered round a little. Even wound up that bloody clock for her. Well! It's what she wanted.

It hasn't happened, has it? Mam isn't home tonight, as planned. I'm still here on my own. Just me and the clock.

More tests are needed, apparently. They want to be absolutely certain. Of what, I'm not too sure. But it seems they can't decide what to do. The consultant has been consulted and the specialist has had his say. And the doubts that are mostly left unsaid are deafening.

I could tell she was down, bless her. And when I rang Mike earlier, he said I sounded down myself.

I can feel the despondency in your voice, he said. How profound is that?

Well, is it any bloody wonder? I bellowed back.

He always has to use big words to deal with any gut feeling anyone may ever have. It's his defence against any genuine raw emotion. Yes, I was pleased to hear the exhibition continues to be a great success... and no, he doesn't really care a damn about what I'm going through here. I could tell by his voice. He never has cared. That's the truth. Not about me, where I come from, or my family.

The trouble is. I don't really miss him. It's been ten days and I've only made contact with him twice. Both times, what I really needed to find out was how everyone was doing; Raul and the gang, etc. Things in the flat. Not Mike.

Dan Llywellyn turned up a lot tonight. Not in the flesh, of course – what's left of it! In conversation. A verbal resurrection from Mam.

I know he's there, of course. Same hospital, different wards. He's in a lot worse state than her. She kept repeating that. Never mentioned dying, but I knew that's what she meant.

He'd love to see you. Why don't you pop along and have a chat?

She needn't have bothered naming the ward. I've known which one it is since I first went to visit Mam. lt's where the terminally ill are kept. 'God's waiting room' the staff call it on the sly. It's out on a limb. The ground-floor ward nearest the gardens.

One of the cleaners I got talking to the other day told me it was to enable the earth's gravity to make their journey

535

easier at the end. Dust to dust, earth to earth, ashes to ashes... she could quote the lot.

By the sound of her, she'd caught religion and I didn't have the heart to tell her it was probably more to do with the fact that they built the mortuary round the back.

I wound that clock in vain last night. And now I wish I hadn't. Really only did it for her. And she's not here.

A torture for my own insomnia. Should have left it to its own devices. Do unto time as time does unto all of us.

When I next see that cleaner, I'll tell her that. She looked easily impressed.

It's all right for you, Joel, he said. *You're one of the lucky ones. You got out. Looked after yourself. Made something of yourself.*

I told him to go to hell.

I know you don't mean that, he said, eyeballing me like a pneumatic drill as he spoke.

Then he went straight into this sob story about Darren Howley.

That was his name apparently; this gawping, chubby geek I'd noticed in Spar this afternoon. Looked around forty. A beer-bellied no-hoper. The valley's full of them. Except this one had a real talent for staring. I wasn't flattered. I wasn't angry. I just wanted Mam to recover quickly so I could catch the first plane back to Barcelona.

Well! It seems he was once a promising football player. Went to Dan Llywellyn for coaching. Ended up on drugs and off the rails.

A life blighted, Gavin called it.

It seems this Darren called him on his mobile after stalking me round Spar.

I keep in touch with many of those boys, Gavin explained. *Or at least I allow them to keep in touch with me. Feel protective towards them, you see. Seen so many lives destroyed.*

Mine's not destroyed, I started to protest.

No, quite, he interjects. *Like I said, you're one of the lucky ones.*

Made things happen for myself, I said. *No luck about it. Stuck at it in school. Went to college. Learnt Spanish. I'm a self-made man. Made things happen for myself.*

The trouble is, the Darren Howleys of this world are wondering why the hell you didn't make things happen for them as well, Joel, Gavin continues. *Or stopped things happening to them, is more to the point. Do you know what I mean?*

I knew by now that he was intent on saying his piece, so I stood there with my back to the wall and my hands deep in my tracky bottoms.

They know you see. They know what you went through. The verbal assault continued. I held my ground in silence. *And they can't for the life of them work out why you didn't put a stop to it. Back then, they didn't have your balls, Joel. They didn't have your brains. They were dependent on a bright lad like you to speak up and save them further misery. Speak up and break Dan Llywellyn's vicious circle. But you didn't, did you, Joel? Why is that, Joel?*

I still don't know what you're talking about, I said. *No one ever messed with me I didn't want to mess with me.*

I know you, Joel. I just know.

You don't, mate! You don't know me at all…

And I'll get it all out of you too, one day – the hard way if I have to. But it will out. You listen to me good… he paused a moment while a distraught-looking relative went scuttling past in pursuit of a member of the medical staff. His half-turned eyes judged when she'd be out of earshot and, before continuing, his voice lowered an octave, just to be on the safe side. *One day, I'll have you there in front of me, just like you are now. Only it won't be a fuckin' hospital corridor. And you won't be looking so smug. You'll be crying your fuckin' eyes out, Joel. Just like all those other sad bastards I've met on this investigation. You'll be so relieved to have all that shit of years ago out of your system, you won't know whether they're tears of joy or anguish sobbing down your cheeks and nostrils. You'll just know that you've wrenched out a gutful of pus that's been there hiding inside you all those years, Joel. And I'll be the one you'll be grateful to for giving you the best feeling of relief you'll ever know in your life.*

Dream on, sunshine, I said. And he sort of smiled. Knowing it wasn't the place or the time to pursue it further.

The worried lady was making her way back from the smokers' den, the nurse she'd managed to collar barely hiding her annoyance at having her fag curtailed.

Can't pretend it's not good to see you again, he chips in casually as the two women made their way back towards the wards.

Really? Gee, thanks!

How's your mother?

As if you cared! I retorted sharply.

Well, I sort of do, really, Joel, he replied. He'd moved from menace mode to vague benevolence with barely a facial distortion, only the subtle shifting of the balance of his body weight conveying his newfound mood of conviviality. *How is she?*

If the mood had changed, the persistence hadn't.

You're only here 'cos Darren what's-his-name's call reminded you that I'm still in town, I said. Equally calm. Equally polite. I put a jokey lilt in my voice to neutralise the tension. *You knew I'd be up here at visiting time.*

So how is she?

Coming out day after tomorrow, I replied. It was like giving in, really. Telling him that which I'd only just heard myself from Mam. But what could I do?

So you have tomorrow to yourself then?

Found myself agreeing that I did, without thinking through any implications.

Come play a game of squash with me tomorrow afternoon, he says. *At my club. I'll sign you in.*

Played a little at college, but not really a game I ever got into. I'm built for bulk sports, not speed. Had to say yes though, didn't I?

The trouble is, these old routines of mine don't work here. This view's all wrong. This brandy doesn't even work the same. Not like it does when I unwind in the early hours at home in Barcelona.

Mam's lean-to isn't quite the same as our balcony. No warm night breeze. No sound of a city still throbbing somewhere in the distance. Just Welsh rain on the windows, so lacking in force or purpose, you can see how it leaves the bird-shit untouched.

Beyond Mam's ramshackle excuse for a garden, I can glimpse the dawn creeping its way up the mountain. Typical of life here – all routine and no passion.

Except old Gavin's left me knackered tonight. So I guess the passion's always there, if you know where to look for it.

He thrashed me at squash, of course. No surprises there. I could barely remember the rules. Not that that mattered much. When you play with Gavin there are no rules, it seems.

Almost five when I got in. Coming out of his car, I could see some lights just going on in other houses. People getting up for work, I suppose. Routines.

As we drove back from Cardiff, I told him all that heavy stuff he tried the other day in the hospital wouldn't work with me.

He laughed with condescending candour and said, *No, I know*, as though none of it mattered after all.

God, his wife must be a tolerant woman, I told him.

He didn't say a word to that. Didn't even smile. Just drove.

You never said nothing.

The police had apparently told him of my reluctance to

testify against him. And that was the most he had to say to me. Almost all he had to say to me. An anticlimax in the end. It was bound to be.

I knew it had to be today or never. Mam came home this afternoon. And no way am I going back to that place just to visit Dan Llywellyn... even a dying Dan Llywellyn.

I don't know why you don't do the decent thing and go see him, Mam's been nagging ever since I came home to see her. *After all he did for you...*

Sat her down in that foyer place. The concourse they call it. Large waste of space designed to delude you into thinking you're entering or leaving a grand hotel. Placed her bag by her side and told her I wouldn't be long.

The taxi was already late.

The bus would have done me, of course, she proceeds to tell anyone within earshot daft enough to listen. *But our Joel wouldn't have it. He's very good to me. Come all the way from Spain to look after me, he 'ave.*

I tell her to wait. Though God knows where I thought she was going to go without me.

Such a sensitive boy. He loves poetry and all that stuff, you know. Won prizes for all sorts of things at school. Don't be fooled by all that brawn... he's a sensitive boy.

Mercifully, her voice drifts to nothing as I disappear down the corridor. The relief I feel is short-lived, as I see Mrs Llywellyn coming towards me. On her way to sneak a fag, apparently. After years of chocolates and the telly, she's succumbed to the joy of a new source of brain death, it seems. A packet of twenty and a gaudy-looking lighter were clutched in her fat hand.

Oh! What a good boy you are! She oozed all over me. The sentence that followed the most she's ever said to me. *Your mam said you'd go to come see 'im before he goes. I know you'll do him no end of good. In there, sixth door along.*

All those visits to her house! Out the back with Dan. Upstairs with Dan. Picking up some piece of kit I'd left there.

Dropping off some piece of sports equipment I'd borrowed to work on at home. He and me in our man's world. Her, silent and redundant.

She shuffled down the corridor towards the smokers' yard.

Won't be here long, are the first words I say to him. Could have kicked myself, of course. But take comfort in the fact that he never has had much sense of humour. ('Getting to be perfect is no laughing matter,' he'd say to me as a boy whenever I started messing around during any sort of training.) So the irony, like so much else, is lost.

He didn't really seem to be suffering. I felt a little cheated. But he's gone to nothing. That much is true. Just a sad shadow staring at me from the pillow.

You didn't squeal. He made his voice as loud as he could muster. *You never told 'em any of our little secrets.*

It's a long time ago now, butt! I said.

He struggled to move his right hand from where it lay on top of the bed, finally lunging for what he thought would be the safety of my forearm. When I pulled my arm away in rejection, it fell back on the blanket again without a murmur.

His face remained unmoved. No sign of disappointment touched those dark sunken eyes. He'd managed to sense my meaning without as much as a lilt of the head. All shows of remorse were held in reserve, ready for the big one.

You moved far away, didn't you? Spain, is it? They told me you were far away… and wouldn't talk…

Each little verbal outburst came shrouded in a silence with which he seemed ill at ease. Like memories of a life once fully lived. Once vibrant and clandestine. Now, dribbled onto pale pillows. Like small deaths.

They kept me there. Transfixed by curiosity. Those little words of nothing.

A gargle from his throat made me lower my gaze for a moment from his hollow eyes to his dead man's lips. The two thin lines quivered slightly, but remained perfectly dry. And I remembered the time he'd tried to kiss me. The only time.

I'd flinched in repulsion and lashed out with my fists.

Kisses were for girls and proper poofs, I'd thought.

Today, I know differently. My stomach muscles tightened, squirming at my adolescent reasoning. I drew in breath. The way I would before a lift.

There was no one there to see me. He has a room to himself. The dying do, it seems. It's a private affair.

When the taxi finally drops us off, it turns out Joanne's long since let herself in. What you call a surprise party, apparently.

The kids ran around like idiots and shouted, *Welcome home, Nanna!* when prompted.

To crown it all, when Dean arrived from work at the end of the afternoon, a dirty big cake appears. It's candles. And streamers. And most of all, it's a load of bollocks.

She's in cancer remission, not joined the circus, I shouted.

Mam didn't want that crap. I could tell.

But she's laughing as I went upstairs to change into my jogging suit.

Four hours later, it's her and me again. The remnants of a cake and a pile of dirty dishes in the kitchen.

She's gone to bed, exhausted. And I'm lying here in the bath.

It rained solid for the two hours I was out. And Gavin had his mobile phone switched off, it seems.

He caught me unawares. I'll give him that.

That first punch to my belly stopped me in my tracks. And I never saw the second coming, either. His fist colliding with my face with such clarity its terrifying thunder still throbs from the pit of my jaw to the top of my skull.

Floored in one fell sweep, he towered over me, asking repeatedly. *You were abused, weren't you?* His voice intense and calm. The emphasis placed on a different word with almost every repetition. It isn't a passion on his behalf; it's a technique put into practice.

In intent, my *Yes* was a defiant shout, but gasping as I was for breath, I know that the reality of my utterance was nothing more that a whisper in the autumn air.

Barely a mile down the hillside from the scene of my humiliation, Dan Llywellyn's remains were burning in the municipally-approved manner. Even as I lay there, stunned into neo-silence, I remember noting that I was thinking that thought.

Conspicuous contempt had been the motivation for our run. Or so I thought. His idea, of course. *Let's run while old Dan burns? I'll pick you up!*

Our fun run through the Pencwm woods high above the crematorium was planned to coincide with the very hour of his funeral. A show of disrespect. A symbol of indifference.

In reality, it was nothing of the sort, of course. It was his planned revenge. Now that it's too late for me to add a gold star to his CV. Now he's been humiliated by a high-profile investigation that's come to nothing. Now that promotion is that much more difficult to achieve.

Yes. I desperately tried to articulate a second time as I felt his trainers thundering into my ribs.

And he buggered you? Go on! Say it! Tell me what I already know, you piece of shit.

At that point, my hands tried to stabilise the floor. And failed.

I flinched as I saw his right foot raised again and aiming for my face this time.

Once again, *Yes* formed submissively in my brain. The trees above me swayed. The sky-blue faded. Pain was all around. Rolling over on the earth, my capacity for thought was consumed by it.

Then why the fuck wouldn't you tell me? This time, his voice doesn't come from far away. He's in my ear. I smell him close. Feel him grab me by my vest, dragging me to my feet... *You stubborn Welsh bastard!*

Instinctively, I aimed a fist to ward him off. But one arm

was already planted round his neck for balance and, staggering backwards, I dragged us both down. Drops of blood spraying both his face and the leaves beneath.

It's a long time later that I laughed. His outstretched arm ignored as I fumbled on the ground for a wristwatch that somehow managed to get dislodged in the assault.

He only allowed himself a smile.

Finding the watch, I stagger to my feet of my own accord and follow him to the car. We're both mute.

My senses remain disconnected. Even now, hours later, the pervading pain is the only message any of them will carry to my brain with any conviction. All else is fluff. Pain stands alone. Still throbbing, black and sore. Thorough and unrelenting. Worse than anything my memories of a bruising youth can bring to mind.

Mirrors have always been my friends. Until tonight. The wardrobe door's been left unlocked, allowing the reflective façade to swing away from the sight of me.

I can bear no light. I can bear no blanket. Tonight, I lick wounds. And curse.

Just leave it there… and… and go away, I said, straining to be civil to her.

If I've said I tripped and fell while out on my run then that is what she will accept as truth. That is what she'll tell the world. After all, that's what she told Mike. I know how Mam works.

What exactly happened? he asked in that tone of voice he reserves for cynicism.

Oh! Mam exaggerated as usual, I said when I eventually decided to ring him back. *You know what she's like. It's just a scratch.*

It was two days ago that he spoke to my mother. He just happened to ring almost as soon as I'd come into the house. Bad timing. I'd hardly had time to hobble to the bathroom to clean up before Mam could take a proper look when I heard the ringing.

Made the effort to take myself downstairs last night to ring him back. My mobile won't stretch as far as Spain. But I'm struggling for normality.

That's what you get when you hide yourself away in a darkened room. Self-absorption becomes self-destroying. Self-pity dulling your ability to deal with the world.

The telephone rings. Not often. Just once or twice a day. Joanne. Some of Mam's cronies. Mike. A social worker. The front door bell goes too. But that's an even rarer event. No symbolic roses have arrived to put my bruises in the shade. No perfumed bloom has been forthcoming to make tender my unsated nose.

A good bottle of brandy might have been the manly gesture. But, no. Nothing has been forthcoming from him. All I get are trays. Left on the landing by my mother as instructed. A knock on my bedroom door heralding each arrival. Mere supplies for a self-imposed prisoner.

I'm OK. Honestly. Just leave me alone. Had to shout at her several times before I heard her footsteps retracting that last time.

To all the world, I'm here to look after her. But the will to nurse anything except my own ego has left me. I just lay here on this bed, thinking that after this fiasco's over, I never want to come back to Wales again.

OK! I'll go back for Mam's funeral, I conceded. *But that's all.*

Mike just smiled over his cup of tea. I smiled back.

He doesn't believe me regarding almost anything I've told him since my return. But it's all true.

We were both up early this morning, Mike and I.

He had some faculty meeting at the university. Wanted to know if I'd met Gavin back in Wales. *You know, your gay detective friend,* he said, pretending not to remember his name. *The one who came here that time with his fat colleague with a taste for fine art.*

545

Oh him! I replied. *We collided once or twice in the corridor. But he never got what he wanted from me.*

Serge wouldn't believe me either at first, when I said I wouldn't work the darkroom for him any more. But wasn't too concerned.

Don't worry. I find someone else.

Maybe I wasn't that sensational after all. But maybe it's just that there are always others. Others who'll come do what we do after we've long since given up. Moved away. Moved on.

I figure darkrooms are like Wales. I won't go there again. Well! Only in my memories.

Running Out

Siân Preece

My mother once told me of a village that drowned.

'The people were all right,' she said quickly; I was small then, and it was important to me that people be all right. 'They moved away.'

'Where did they go?'

'Scattered far and wide.'

She looked towards the window as if they would be out there, walking down the street with their suitcases. It sounded like a story, but she said it was true.

'Did the people want to go?'

'No, they didn't want to go.'

'Why did they, then?'

'They had to. The valley was needed for a reservoir. A big lake,' she explained. 'To keep water in, for people to use.'

'The people in the village?'

'No, English people,' and she frowned.

'But what happened to the houses?'

'The houses are still there, under the water.'

I tried to imagine it; a house like my Nan's, with the china dogs still fierce on the mantelpiece, and seaweed curtains waving in the green water. Tea cosies like jellyfish, rugs like rays swimming over coral-bed sofas. There would be no point in closing the doors; you could just float out of the window and look down on the map of your garden, at the whole village underwater like a present from the seaside.

Tryweryn. Cwm Atlantis. A tap turns in Liverpool, and a church steeple breaks the surface of a Welsh lake.

I hear a chime like a church bell under water... it's the chain of the bath plug, dancing under the hot tumble at my feet. I turn off the tap and lean back, relax. At the other end of the bath, my toes bob up, white in the red water; ten little croutons in a bowl of tomato soup. I feel hot and weak. I feel as if I will be in this water forever.

At first I felt like a pervert, walking the streets of Cardiff at dusk with a Welsh costume concealed under my mac. Red skirt, checked shawl and apron. A scaled-up version of my St David's Day outfit at school; but no pungent, dusty daffodil pinned to my chest, just a flattened yellow fake. I kept my tall black hat in a carrier bag, swinging it like a bucket, until I got to work. Our boss had no shame, making us dress like that.

In the alley behind the restaurant, I told Jackie: 'The Welsh costume's all made up anyway.'

'Oh aye?' She picked a wad of chewing gum from her mouth and held it in her fingers while she dragged on her fag. Her face was pointed and modern over the white pussycat bow at her chin.

'Aye, it was all invented by this English woman. We used to wear little round bonnets like everyone else. I remember it from history.'

'Well, don't tell Alwyn.' Alwyn was the restaurant owner. 'He've only just found one to fit your big head.'

'Well, that's 'cause I've got big brains. Your hat must be titchy.' I pretended to read a label at the back. 'Look! "Age five!"'

'Ha bloody ha.'

In the kitchen window, froggy, pink fingers appeared and rubbed a squeaky hole in the steam. It was Fat Benny, the bald, wordless washer-up, spying on us. Fat Benny was in love with girls.

'Hiya darlin'!' Jackie tinkled piano fingers at him. 'Meet you behind the bins after for a snog!'

Fat Benny's eye winked shyly in the peephole he had made. He pressed soft, round kisses on the window; wrinkled Os.

'Aw, Jackie, don't tease him.'

'Why not? He's a creepy git.'

I shushed her with my hands. 'He's not creepy. He's just sad.'

Fat Benny bobbed around in the kitchen window, looking quite happy to be sad.

Alwyn pounced out of the kitchen door.

'Have you laid them tables yet? Come on girls, chop chop.'

We had laid the tables when we got in, but Alwyn hated to see us doing nothing. In the kitchen he tried to arrange the two of us into a line, then stood before us with his tiny feet, in their tasselled shoes, at a perfect ten-to-two.

'Jackie, you're meeting and greeting and taking orders. Rhian, you're taking coats and showing to tables. And Rhian,' he added, 'better not do any serving, is it? Not with the way you dish out soup.'

He was being bitchy and I stared at him under the brim of my hat, giving him attitude, but he turned away.

It was getting that Alwyn took another job off me every night. He was right about the soup, though. If I was carrying it, there was no point putting it in a bowl; it always ended up in the serving plate, with the doily drinking it like a Kleenex. And I couldn't manage vegetables that were too round; the peas would make a break for it, and I could only keep the potatoes on the plate if they were mashed. I spent most of my time in the kitchen, scraping butter from a big plastic vat into individual china pots. The trick to getting the butter smooth on top was to breathe on it, to warm it, but I didn't let Alwyn see that.

At the end of the night, Chef would give us leftovers to take home. Fat Benny would only take bread.

'Go on, Fat Benny, there's a lonely Glamorgan sausage

here without a butty. Or how about this salmon steak? Lovely bit of fish; the skin's come off is all.'

But Fat Benny would shake his head and look as if he were going to cry.

'All right. Bread it is.'

And we would tumble the brown, floury rolls into Fat Benny's Adidas bag.

'He do look all right on it, though,' said Jackie.

'He looks like an autopsy,' said Chef; and these two things meant that Jackie didn't like Benny, and Chef did.

There's a bottle of vodka on the edge of the bath, incongruous beside the two shampoos. Mine is Plus-Conditioner-for-Damaged-Hair, with a picture of, I think, a vitamin on the side. Dad's is Anti-Dandruff, with a static dribble of turquoise paste obscuring the letters. His razors are rusty and leaking, sitting in a pool of their own orange blood.

Tonight I showed Fat Benny how to make napkins into shapes.

'Want to see a crown?'

He nodded, wedged in the corner, keeping his bum warm on the oven. I flapped the napkin open, folded and pinched, folded again.

Jackie was serving in the restaurant and Alwyn was going round the tables, talking to the customers. He did it to emphasise that he was the owner; a businessman, crachach, not an employee like his little waitresses. When he said, 'We hope you enjoy your meal', the 'we' was practically royal.

Alwyn divided the customers into two categories: the first was the Smart Regulars, who were rich, and used to eating out, and didn't bother to dress up for it. Alwyn would rub his hands and smile at them like he had greased his teeth.

His second category was the Special Occasions. These

were the people who had saved up, and came dressed in their best, most uncomfortable clothes for the treat. The men had big hands with scrubbed, raw knuckles. The women wore perfume that made me sneeze. They cringed silently in their seats, spooked by the sound of their plain conversation in this *chichi*, unfamiliar place. When Alwyn talked to them, they stared at him like cats, and whispered when he'd gone: 'That was the owner.' He always sat the Special Occasions by the toilets.

Jackie's categories were Good Tippers and Bad Tippers.

My categories were Human and Inhuman, depending on how they treated us.

I was supposed to be microwaving the Welsh cakes so they'd feel fresh-from-the-oven warm. Chef had disabled the timer to stop it going 'ping' and giving the game away, so you had to watch it.

'There you go.'

I gave Fat Benny the napkin crown and he perched it on his shiny head, did a little dance. His big, melon face split into a ripe smile and he made his laugh sound, a high-pitched, soprano wheeze.

'Now we've both got hats,' I said, and we grinned at each other.

Chef had finished up and gone home by this time. I had nothing to do except wait until Alwyn called for the Welsh cakes. I checked the bow on my hat so I'd be ready straight away; Alwyn was always saying, 'It's not the customers' job to wait; it's our job to wait on them.'

I used to complain to Jackie that, if I found the restaurant management book where he read that, I'd burn it. But tonight, when I looked around the kitchen at the white tiles streaked with rainbows of detergent, and the family of knives hanging from Grandpa to Baby on the wall, I thought: I wouldn't mind doing this. Creating this order, this cleanliness. I could go back to college and do Hotel and Restaurant Management. Food Hygiene. Catering.

'What do you think, Benny? Could I do Restaurant Management?'

Benny widened his eyes. He breathed in as if about to cough and, in a high, girl's whisper, said:

'The bread's not for me, it's for my mam. She do soak it in milk. It's her teeth, see.'

He put his hand to his mouth, astonished at himself, and we stared at each other. I had never heard him speak before, and now I realised with surprise that he was quite young: perhaps nineteen or twenty. I didn't know what to do. Did he want me to congratulate him, or would it just make him shy? It felt like giving someone a card when you're not sure it's their birthday.

'Benny,' I said, unfolding another napkin, 'Do you want to see a swan?'

Benny's mam.

She has Benny's ham arms, encased in the sleeves of a floral dress, and the same bald head in a curly wig. She is as silent as her son; they communicate telepathically, watch sitcoms with the sound down, and laugh so only dogs can hear.

When my own mother left, I used to imagine her going back to her drowned village. Walking into the water in her dress, the skirts billowing around her as she dived and searched for her house; or crying on the shore like a mermaid, her hair streaming. But my dad said she'd found a new boyfriend in Merthyr.

Alwyn came into the kitchen, rubbing his hands together briskly like a fly.

'Where have all the napkins gone?' he said, then, 'Ah, Rhian, have you done with them Welsh cakes?'

I pressed the catch and the microwave door sprang open as if the Welsh cakes had rebelled and were kicking their way out. But they were safe, tanned and toasty under the hygienic kitchen neon. They slid wilfully on the plate, but I corralled them against my chest, sprinkled them and my daffodil with a shower of sugar, and offered them for Alwyn's inspection.

'Well, they look fine,' he said. He chose one, snapped it open, and we watched as a currant gave up its last puff of moisture. The cakes were burnt, dry, as solid as shortcake.

'Oh no! Oh Alwyn, I'm sorry!'

Alwyn took the plate from me. He tipped the cakes and their greasy, sugared doily into the pedal bin, and we heard them scuttling like coal to the bottom. Without looking at Benny, Alwyn handed him the plate for washing and, when he finally spoke, flecks of spittle sparked from his mouth.

'Look, Rhian...'

'I'll do some more! It won't take a minute.'

'No, no, don't bother. Just... take the dessert trolley out, will you?'

There was only one table left now, or rather two, pushed together for a party; businessmen from London, in Cardiff for a conference. We got more English customers here than Welsh. They came for the lovespoons decorating the wall, the spinning wheel in the corner, for Jackie and me sweating in our tall hats. There must have been photographs of us all over the country: two life-size peg dollies with eyes scalded red by the camera flash.

'Say cheese!'

'No, say "caws"! That's Welsh for "cheese!"' Alwyn was taking an evening class at the university.

I had taken the businessmen's coats to the cloakroom and, alone in the dark, stroked the collars and cuffs, slotted my hands into the flat, empty pockets. Next to those tiny stitches, my own clothes felt as clumsy as a doll's.

Jackie had smelt money, and now I heard her laughing with the men, responding to their banter; giggling for tips where I would have tried for a smart answer. I wobbled the trolley towards them, the thick carpet catching in its wheels, jingling the dishes and making the trifle tremble as if it were afraid. The noise seemed vulgar. I was ashamed.

'Here's Blodwen Mark Two!,' shouted a man at the head of the table.

'Hello, Blodwen!'

Jackie muttered to me through her clenched smile, 'We've got a right lot here; they're calling me Blodwen too,' then; 'You've got cream all up your shawl.'

The shawls got into everything. I wiped the cream off with my apron and parked the trolley.

'Good evening! Tonight we have sherry trifle, lemon meringue pie, apple tart and custard…'

One of the men pulled me by the strings of my apron to stand next to him.

'Never mind the meringues, Blodwen; give us a song!' He smelt of brandy and cigars, and rich-food farts. There was a splash of dried gravy on his chin.

'I can't sing!' I smiled to soften the refusal.

'Nonsense; all you Welsh can sing. Come on!' He started banging the table, waved at the others to join in:

'Song! Song! Song!'

I glanced around the table in a panic; the faces of the men ran together, became a film, a flicker picture of one man ageing. In his twenties, the shoulders still firm, the hint of a squash racquet in the back of the company car. Then the weight of seniority silting down through the years, the tailoring becoming more careful to hide the bulk. A daring, last-chance moustache at fifty, the word 'distinguished' starting to apply, then the silver hair, the golden handshake, and first-name terms with the doctor. The same man, the same men; a row of grey cloth with a shared mission statement – only the coloured ties, like a Warhol print, to tell them apart.

One of the men spoke, and the picture refracted again.

'Steady on!' he said slowly, his words chewy with alcohol. 'The girlie's trying to do her job.'

The first man replied as if I wasn't there: 'Don't worry. I'll leave her an enormous tip.'

I heard myself shout, in a furious rush, 'All right! I'll give you a song!'

They cheered, with no idea that I was angry, or even that I could be. I folded my hands across my apron like a trembling bird, and began to sing:

'There was an old farmer who sat on a rock,

'A-waving and shaking his big hairy...'

I was into the second verse when Alwyn came screaming out of the kitchen like a fire engine in tasselled shoes and dragged me away.

'What do you think you're doing!' A purple vein twitched on his red temple.

'They asked for a song.'

'Good God!' He threw his arms in the air and I flinched, although he'd had no intention of hitting me. Benny cowered in the corner, frantically washing and rewashing a clean plate, as Alwyn marched up and down the kitchen, his little feet pit-patting on the tiles, repeating his mantra: 'The good restaurateur remains calm at all times.' Then he turned to me and took a deep breath.

'Listen,' he said, 'This job, well, it hasn't really been working out, has it?'

I felt sick and serious. My hands filled with sweat, dripping cold between my hot fingers.

'I'm sorry!' I said, 'I'll do better in future, honest I will!'

He shook his head. 'I'm sorry,' he said, echoing me, 'I've already spoken to another girl who worked here before. See, her husband's left her and she needs the money. We're having her back.' He looked at me and added slowly, to be sure that I understood, 'Instead of you.' The way he said it, I knew he'd practised it. I knew it was a lie.

'I need the money,' I said, but Alwyn had already turned his eyes down, dismissing me.

'You're young,' he said, 'You'll find another job, easy. I'll put a bit extra in your last wage packet. OK? All right? All right, then. Off you go now, and bring the uniform back any time you like. By Thursday, at least. And have it cleaned, will you? There's cream all up the shawl.'

I saw Benny's face like a snapshot, mournful and melting in the background. My bag was hanging on the back of the door, hidden in a row of coats on their hooks, and I pulled at it, tugged in sudden fury until the whole lot came down with a sound like snow falling from a roof. I saw my own mac sprawled under the pile of headless bodies and hauled it out. Its empty arms embraced me as I ran.

I saw a postcard once; a woman lying in a river with all her clothes on, and flowers. Now I unpin my fake daffodil, the pin resisting in the wet tweed, and hold it to my chest. The shawl is heavy with water, I feel its weight when I move my shoulders. It has become crimson where it was white before.

The water has cooled again. I let it out and run more hot, and swill my skirt around to see the dye billowing scarlet. The best, though, is the hat; the steam has broken it down, the brim is collapsing onto my face. Little flecks of black felt are breaking off and floating in the water, like the specks you see in your eye when you're tired; or like water boatmen, who dent the smooth, wet light with their insect feet. They scatter in the breath of my laughter. Even a smile seems to move them.

I stand up in the bath and the water pours from me in a loud wave, then slows to a trickle. The clothes are heavy, but supporting their weight makes me feel strong, defiant.

I pull the plug, and the red water starts running out.

Miss Grey of Market Street

Robert Nisbet

It was around three o'clock on a Saturday afternoon and
Market Street lay grey and wet under the half-hearted shafts
of sunlight which only occasionally broke the cloud. A
tentative snowfall that morning had turned to slush, and
splashed up now and again from passing cars.

The shop fronts were bright enough though, and the
delicatessen at the bottom end of the street sparkled just a
little with the warming ranges of spirits, liqueurs and
chocolates stacked along the window, with the cheese, yogurt,
teas and coffees behind. Miss Grey, pecking, tripping, daintily
white-haired, made her way towards the shop.

She fluttered into it in a rather delicate way, a slight
presence, her sharp, bird-like features softening just
occasionally. Now, as habitually, she stepped neatly and
precisely over to the stacked rows of Oriental teas, where
she pottered long and quietly, in a rapt and quizzical
absorption.

It was nearly fifteen years since she'd retired as founder
and principal of a small prep school in the town. And more
than that, she was Miss Grey, one of the Greys of Market
Street, and the Greys had been for many years one of the
more prosperous local business families. The grocery had
been founded by her father before the First World War.

Continued and expanded by Miss Grey's brother Denzil, it survived into the age of the supermarket as, to quote Denzil's official designation, 'the quality grocery'. Only with Denzil's retirement in the mid-70s did the shop pass to a Swansea firm who, much to Miss Grey's relief, had preserved Denzil's original byline: 'quality grocery'.

Miss Grey was shopping for tea. To the girl at the counter, this was all part of a rather quaint ritual, conducted regularly once a fortnight. Around three o'clock on a Saturday afternoon the old lady would wander in, her main shopping for the week being done in the morning, and would gaze along the rows of Oriental teas. She'd turn the small wooden boxes, read from their inscriptions, linger for quite a while before eventually selecting one and proceeding with it to the counter. It was all so habitual and so harmless as to create little, if any attention.

But to Miss Grey it was important. She was shopping for tea. She wasn't that well off: the prep school had left her with little by way of profit, and, despite Denzil's devotion to the idea of quality – or perhaps because of it – the business hadn't thrived. Miss Grey had inherited little on Denzil's death a couple of years earlier. But still, cramped though she was by a genteel poverty, she looked for quality, and was satisfied, in the last resort, if she could find it in just one area of her domestic life. Her gaze ranged over the titles on the boxes: Keemun China, Russian Caravan, Earl Grey, Gunpowder Green, Orange Pekoe, Ceylon Breakfast. There was a whole wealth there, of dreams and suggested gentility. After some thought, or some dreaming, she picked down a box of Russian Caravan, and made her way to the counter. She wanted a good blend. Terry would be coming to tea again, and she wanted things nice for him.

Terry, Miss Grey's nephew, arrived about five o'clock, spruce in his Saturday suit, just back from the football match, scrupulously wiping the mud from his shoes in the doorway, before perching on the edge of a stiff and ancient armchair.

He looked like her relative. The same bird-like features were exaggerated by soft pecking movements of his head, a slight squint and an occasional nervous twitch. He would jab and squint a curious half-quizzical assent to everything Miss Grey said, but he was still ill at ease in the gentility of her drawing room. It was only six months since he'd started going there, since his return from Margam. And yet: he had come home, he'd wanted to come home, and Miss Grey was part of home. He wanted to get to like it there.

After they'd finished the cakes and sandwiches and were drinking tea, Miss Grey motioned to Terry to stay where he was and went to the kitchen. She came back with the wooden box of Russian Caravan tea which she'd emptied into a tea caddy.

'I thought you'd like to see this, Terry.' She passed it over. Terry's large and rather clumsy hands fumbled the box awkwardly as he gazed at it in determined concentration.

'It's the box the tea was packed in,' said Miss Grey. 'Russian Caravan. Do you see?'

Terry's reply was stammered and clumsy. 'It's nice. It's nice tea.'

Miss Grey smiled with a pecking eagerness. 'There's a story about the tea, on the side of the box. Shall I read it to you?' Terry blushed, but nodded.

Miss Grey was suddenly self-conscious, but caught by a gust of enthusiasm at the same time. She told him the story of the Empress Elizabeth of Russia who in 1735 had set up the first caravan tea trade between Russia and the Far East.

Terry broke into a happy grin. 'That's a nice story.' He looked in awe at the fragile little box in his large and clumsy hands. 'It's a nice box.'

Miss Grey flushed a little with excitement. 'Would you like it, Terry? Or the label, perhaps? Would you like to collect them?' Terry nodded eagerly, fired vaguely with the feeling that this was something personal, a family thing. 'I wouldn't mind,' he said. 'I wouldn't mind saving them. Some of the boys saves cards from the Corn Flakes, and things like that. One boy's got some beer mats.'

'Terry,' Miss Grey was suddenly excited and insistent. 'We're a trading family, the Greys. And trade is travel, Terry, very often. Foreign places, strange places. You could collect these labels. There are lots of different ones, with stories of where they're from. Ceylon and India. Russia.' She paused. 'I get a new box every fortnight. When you come, after the football match, you can have the labels.'

Carefully, she peeled the Russian Caravan label from its place and gave it to him. He folded it up, slowly and carefully, and put it neatly into his wallet.

After he'd gone, Miss Grey let her mind run on: Russian Caravan, Gunpowder Green, Formosa Oolong, Earl Grey, Queen Mary, Ceylon Breakfast. A delicate strangeness lay about her mind, the thoughts of the quality grocery between the wars, of the times as a little girl when she'd played in her father's storeroom behind the shop, looking at the labels on the packagings: London, Bristol, Manchester, a strange wide world stretching its beckoning call into the little market town. Phrases and images spun through her mind: of tea merchants in the Strand, established in 1788. Quality grocery: London and Bristol. This was what it meant to Miss Grey to be part of a trading family.

Terry was Denzil's son and had been mentally retarded since an attack of meningitis early in life. His mother had died when he was still in his teens, so that neither Denzil who had the business to run nor Miss Grey, with her prep school, had been able to keep him at home. For over twenty years, he'd been in Margam hospital. It was only recently, with the opening of a residential home for the handicapped in the town, that Terry had come back.

Margam loomed still, in Miss Grey's mind, as something ugly. The residents in the home where Terry was now staying were variously odd, shambling and confused, but the mood was different to Margam. To her, Margam was part of a harsh and howling urban landscape. Patients had been howling, very often, in Terry's ward, when she and Denzil had driven him back after short stays at home. The place was cramped and understaffed – perhaps it was that; perhaps it was the sheer fact of its urban setting. Cities, in Miss Grey's mental romance of trading forays and travellers' tales, meant India and Ceylon, the Empress Elizabeth linking Russia with the Far East; at the very least, the London and Bristol her father had traded with. But the urban world of Margam, the first-hand contact, was a howling, baying nightmare. There'd been that sad and sour journey across South Wales to take Terry back. And then, quite recently, after Denzil's death a couple of years before, the new home had been opened in Haverfordwest, and Terry had come home.

Terry used to come regularly now, on Saturday afternoons, after his trip to the football match. Regularly, once a fortnight, Miss Grey would peel the label from a small wooden tea box and read him the story before passing on the label for his collection. He must have felt by now the need to reciprocate, for the next Saturday, just before leaving, he passed a small leaflet across to Miss Grey, saying, blushing, 'Got you something.'

She looked. It was a football programme. Haverfordwest versus Ammanford Town. As she gazed in puzzlement, Terry crowded in his clumsy explanations. 'See. It shows you who they was playing.' He blushed. 'I thought you'd like them. Save them up, like.'

Miss Grey could only wonder at the strangeness of the thing. Of course it was nice of the boy, it was kind. So, scrupulously and carefully, she assembled, week by week, her collection of football programmes, read them even, puzzling a little over the names and the jargon. She was touched and pleased by the gesture.

But lurking underneath it was an odd, irrelevant undercurrent of discomfort. In her mind Miss Grey would roll out lists of names of Oriental teas: Gunpowder Green, Darjeeling, Russian Caravan, Earl Grey – lists replete with a magical aura of distant strangeness. But as she collected her football programmes, another list assembled itself: names of opponents and other towns. Carmarthen Town, Llanelli, Ammanford, Briton Ferry, Swansea City, Port Talbot. This list made Miss Grey unhappy. At first she thought it was simply due to how mundane a list it seemed. And then, shuffling a few programmes casually one Saturday, just after Terry had left, she realised the reason for her unease. Carmarthen, Swansea City, Port Talbot. It was the very road to Margam. She realised herself it was a silly objection, no sort of objection at all. She went on saving the football programmes just the same. And all the time she was fighting down her sense of the drabness of the whole affair.

Unease with Terry's visits to the football ground crept upon her in another way. He was getting used to the team and its players by now, and had for a while enthused about a goalkeeper called Cy Morgan, at first perhaps because, as goalkeeper, Cy wore a differently coloured jersey and was easier to identify. Then, one Saturday, he burst out excitedly.

'Auntie. That Cy Morgan. In goal. He's my cousin. I never knew, till today.'

Miss Grey puzzled. 'Cy Morgan? Oh. Cyril. Good heavens. Does Cyril play football? I hadn't realised. Good heavens, yes. Cyril's father is your mother's brother. I honestly hadn't realised Cyril played football. I'm a little out of touch with that branch of the family.'

Terry pressed on eagerly. 'I never knew, like. Not till today. That bloke told me. Uncle Randall. Bloke that sells the programmes.'

Miss Grey nodded. 'That's right. Your Uncle Randall. He did go to the football club quite a bit. He was quite keen on football, I believe. Dear me. I just hadn't realised.'

Her unease deepened at this piece of news. There was no rancour, no family feud, simply the feeling there'd always been, among the Greys, that when Denzil had married one of the Morgan girls from Castle Back, he'd rather married beneath him. But Helen Morgan had been loyal and considerate enough, in a rather humdrum and inconspicuous way, and even her brother Randall, known though he was as something of a town loafer, had little that could seriously be levelled against him. Denzil had employed him briefly, as a storeman, and Randall had effectively drifted out of the job rather than actually getting fired. He was a plump, sandy, faded sort of man with sleepy eyes, lounging around town without doing any particular harm. Perhaps Miss Grey just felt that he wasn't ideal as a relative for the Greys, not ideal company for Terry. But there it was. He liked the football matches, and they were probably kind enough to him down there.

Time passed, and Terry seemed to be settling ever more contentedly into the rhythm of his new life at home. The summer brought the football season to an end, but on one occasion Randall Morgan took Terry down to Milford on the bus to see Glamorgan seconds playing cricket, and Terry brought Miss Grey back a programme from that match. It was signed by a couple of Glamorgan players. As the new season got under way, Miss Grey became aware that the Haverfordwest football team were in a different division or something – Terry said they'd been relegated – and the names on the programme now were of more obscure little townships, off the main road to Margam. Names like Abercynon, Blaenavon and Lewistown were hardly exotic, but had at least the neutral virtue of being unknown.

At Christmas approached, Miss Grey felt she'd like to buy Terry something to do with football for a Christmas present. It would be the right thing to do. By now she'd exhausted the range of Oriental tea labels and she felt there was something a shade selfish in expecting the boy to get involved in her own rather esoteric preoccupation. She couldn't buy him an actual ball: he didn't play himself, as far as she knew;

child though he seemed, in many ways, he was a man of over forty, after all. Then she thought of a football scarf, a supporters' scarf. She asked Terry about the colours.

'They're blue, they wear. Blue and white. Only Cy don't, he wears green. He's the goalie.' He blushed with pleasure. Miss Grey nodded. Blue and white. She'd have to see. Terry went on talking excitedly about Cy. 'He done well today. Stopped a penalty. This bloke shot, like, smacked it, and Cy dived right over. Dived across. Knocked it away, like. They won two-nothing, after that.'

Miss Grey had never taken to knitting, although latterly, in her retirement, she'd often wished she had some such attainment as an interest. Somehow though, it had seemed vaguely at odds with her picture of herself: *Headmistress, Miss Grey of Market Street.* So she searched the shops until she did in fact find a blue and white supporters' scarf. She wrapped it carefully and put it away until Christmas time.

On the Saturday afternoon directly before Christmas, Terry was a little late arriving after the football match. When he arrived, a little breathless, he pushed a parcel clumsily wrapped in untied brown paper, into her hands. 'I got you something. A present, like. For Christmas.' It was a wooden box of Russian Caravan tea. Miss Grey was startled. 'Terry. How kind. That really is nice. But it's expensive, dear, very expensive.'

She wondered vaguely how he could have afforded it on the limited pocket money he had at the home. It was only when the man from the social services department called the next day that she found out that Terry had stolen it.

The same man called again, a week later, to explain the transfer. Terry would be going back to Margam, for an indefinite period, but she mustn't distress herself. Perhaps three months, maybe six. They'd have to see how things worked out. No, it wasn't a punishment, exactly. And yes, he did realise that Margam was different from the residential home. Well, that was the point in a way. Less freedom. Well, yes, that was the point. The need for supervision. You see, the point with fairly easy access to the community was that they had to feel they could trust a patient. Or resident. But the scheme depended on its not being abused. They'd see how he settled down. He should be able to come back. Three months. Six months. She mustn't distress herself.

The following Saturday, at the football ground, Randall Morgan was casting a pale and amiable gaze about him, when he was aware of a quiet voice, and Miss Grey beside him.

'Good afternoon, Randall. Have you a programme you could sell me?'

'Well, by damn. Miss Grey. Long time, no see. Programme? Sure.' She'd always called him 'Randall'; he'd always addressed her as 'Miss Grey'. It was something quite expected and accepted between them. They were left standing side by side for about half an hour, saying little, shuffling uneasily from time to time. Once Randall spoke, to enquire awkwardly after Terry.

'I'm sure he's settling down,' said Miss Grey. 'I'll be writing to him tonight.'

'Send him my regards,' said Randall.

'Surely.'

It was the sort of wet, heavy January day which gets dominated, at football grounds, by the dank smell of mud. Miss Grey, perky still, quite strikingly white-haired, looked cold and out of place, incongruously genteel amidst the confused and sporadic noise of about 150 supporters. She turned to Randall after a while: 'How is Cyril playing, would you say?'

'Boy's doing well. Dominating the box today. Caught everything this side of the six-yard line.'

Miss Grey nodded.

'Where can I find out the result of the match, Randall?'

'Be on the Welsh news, half past six. Or you could phone the clubhouse, like. 3511. They'd tell you.' He gazed in bewilderment at her.

Miss Grey nodded politely and, shortly afterwards, left for home. She listened to the news at six-thirty, to get the result, then settled down to write a letter to Terry. One of the nurses could read it to him, if some of it was a little difficult.

My dear Terry. I hope you're settling into your new way of life. We all hope, dear, very much, to have you back home soon. I saw your Uncle Randall this afternoon and he sent his regards. The football team played Treharris today and won two-nil. Cyril played a very good game in goal. He was dominating the box, and catching everything this side of the six yard line. I'm sending you a programme for you to look at...

She would be back there, at the football ground, at every match, till Terry came home.

THE STARS ABOVE
THE CITY

Lewis Davies

The piano was old. The lid shut, smeared with dust. Thin light cut into the foyer from the bay beyond. Anthony had spent months dreaming of the Intercontinental. Its green shuttered terraces looking down onto the port. He had arrived at the site of one of his dreams.

A porter appeared and picked up his rucksack. It was light and the man smiled. He indicated that Anthony should follow him. The hotel opened out along wide corridors. He noticed with some disappointment that the carpets were worn, and there were prints of palaces on the walls and an English huntsman with hounds. The room was on the second floor. It opened onto a balcony guarded by iron railings. He looked out over the bay, which curved away to the south. There were fishing boats out beyond the headland. The porter was waiting in the room. Anthony fumbled in his pocket. He only had euros. The man smiled. He passed him two euros.

'Euros are good here.'

He waited for the stillness of the room to reach him. He wasn't quite ready to face the city again, but he had promised a man at the port who claimed to be a good guide – 'official, sir' – to meet him at 5 p.m. There was enough time to sleep. He tried to imagine himself back, as the sounds of the port rose up past the balconies. Gulls, lorries reversing, a ship leaving. The sounds of a world moving.

He woke to a loud knocking at the door. He spun, unsure of the room. His hands grasping at the sheets. Then his memory caught him. He waited as his heart calmed. There was a knock again.

'Monsieur, your guide?'

He was aware of his crumpled trousers and shirt as he answered the door. He blinked at the porter. The sun was hurting his eyes.

'*Dix minutes, d'accord?*'

The porter smiled and turned away.

The medina proved more than expected. More than he had read about. He didn't realise that a return to the past could be so swift. A surge of life swept into him. The flux of people, living, eating, working in the shaded passages cut out of what seemed the solid life of the city. He had a few offers of things he didn't need but the guide seemed to deflect most of the attention. He appeared to know many of the people who smiled at him. It seemed he had been telling the truth about being an official guide. The guide's name was Mohammed. At least it was one of his names. Anthony suspected he had used it as the easiest one a European might pronounce. He was an old man. Over sixty with tight-cut silver hair. He wore a well-tailored suit and carried an umbrella to protect himself from the sun. He kept it furled in the medina but carried it with a quiet grace that seemed to protect him from the rush of the city.

Mohammed recommended a restaurant and waited while Anthony was served a 'traditional meal'. He was the only customer of the restaurant.

'You are too early for dinner and too late for lunch, but we'll serve you anyway,' the waiter laughed.

The tour continued after the meal.

'It is quiet in the afternoon. Evenings are better. Now people rest. But I will take you to an emporium.'

At the emporium he was introduced as 'Mr Anthony', as if they should know who he was. A silver tray carrying a heavily sugared glass of mint tea was presented to him. He sipped delicately. He wasn't sure of the etiquette. There must be an etiquette. He was invited to sit down as the theatre of carpets was revealed to him. A thrilling display of four different types of rug and carpet was presented by a tall lithe man in a black singlet. His muscles flexed as he unfurled each new display. The commentary was provided by the head of the emporium. Anthony kept his eyes down, trying not to give himself away. He wanted to buy a carpet. It would look good in the flat. There was more space now. He wondered what Jac would have done. Anthony had never been good with salesmen. They sensed a weakness in him. A desire to please. To be helpful almost whatever it cost him. He looked at the man in the vest. There was a sheen on his skin from the heat even in the cool of the emporium. But he knew he simply couldn't buy a carpet on his first day. He bought a blanket. It was the cheapest woollen item in the shop. The man who had served him the tea shook his head sadly as he took his money. He could sense that what Anthony really wanted was a full-scale, two-hundred-and-fifty-thousand knot, five-hundred-euro carpet. Jac always said he wasn't assertive enough, didn't make demands. Anthony had always found when he made demands he lost things, friends, lovers. He had lost Jac. Jac would have bartered the carpet down to two hundred euros and made the salesmen feel he was doing them all a favour by buying it from them.

He paid the guide off after the third carpet shop.

He followed one of the alleyways back to centre of the medina. It was a Sunday night and children were playing football in the small spaces between the houses. As he walked he had glimpses of lives he could never see in the veiled portals, warm kitchens, the flavours of food high in the air.

He remembered their kitchen in Cardiff. He had loved to fill it with recipes from countries he had never visited as if with alchemy he could produce them to share on order. He loved the programmes on the television that told you how to eat and live. He liked that. He liked the surety of it.

The night was beginning to fold around the city. He walked down the Petit Socco. The chairs were filled with dark men looking out at the moving street, just looking. A shudder went through him. He found a chair at Café Tingis. He looked out. Watching. Men in hooded gowns. Women clothed tightly against the world of men, pale Europeans in the coloured clothes of the young and rootless.

A waiter brought him a coffee. He had asked for it in French. He could order food in French. It was a small miracle of his education that he could actually remember words from a classroom twenty years before. The evening filled in the spaces. He began a postcard in his mind. Dear Jac. On the Petit Socco, you would like it here... Dark men with smiles in their eyes. I'm speaking French badly again... sorry, bad French.

Jac had always laughed at his pronunciation. He would write the postcard in the morning. He should be able to get stamps in the city.

A man in a white shirt smiled at him from the crowd. Anthony smiled back. The man waved and began walking towards him.

Sun filtered into the room early. He remembered the bar he had been persuaded to try for one drink. Hardwood, dusty sawdust floor. The smell of hashish. He checked his face. No marks. He could walk away from this.

He packed quickly. The man at the reception took his money without comment. They had refused his credit card, so he'd been forced to withdraw money from a cashpoint. He walked back up the Petit Socco, through the medina to the new town. It had been new in the 1920s when the French had planned it. There was a Café de Paris, and Café de France, along a Boulevard Pasteur. He was tight with sweat from the climb up the hill with his rucksack. There were no offers in the early morning. It was too early for business. He settled into a dark leather chair and withdrew into an order for black coffee with a croissant. He had always liked croissants since his first visit to Paris as a sixteen-year-old. To him they tasted of opportunity and a delicious sense of guilt in the morning. He had visited the *cimetière* with Jonathan. He was rather horrified when Jonathan produced a lipstick from his pocket, covered his lips with the darkest red and kissed the statue above the grave they had both come to see. He had heard Jonathan stayed in Newcastle after university. They had kept in touch for a few years. It seemed a long way back now.

He wrote a postcard to Jac. It didn't say anything. He signed it, *With love from Anthony, Always.*

The bus was half-full. He had expected it to be old and battered, but it was new with good seats and air conditioning. He sat next to a man who spoke good English. He was going to Chefchaouen. He worked for the Banc de Maroc. He was going to explain a new computer system to the manager in Chefchaouen. He usually travelled by train, but there was no train to Chefchaouen. Anthony was glad of the information. The man had two children. His wife was expecting a third. Life was good. You worked hard, you enjoyed life. What did Anthony do? Anthony wasn't sure about that. I write – write what? For the television. Films? No. Not films. I write down ideas for television. Shows. Programmes. You get paid for that? Usually. Are they popular? They don't usually get made – I just come up with the ideas.

The man looked at him. He wrote ideas for shows that never got made.

The open fields passed the windows. Men riding donkeys, sunflowers about to open, a grey reservoir. Travel made him think of home. His work. Jac.

571

He had started writing plays for the theatre. They had been well received. He was young and the reviewers were generous in small papers. He would get better, write better plays with more complex plots. But he didn't get better. He found that after the third he had very little more to say. He worked for television instead. He wrote treatments for new shows that went into development or were offered to digital channels that no one watched. It had allowed him to live for six years in the city he had shared with Jac. It had paid for holidays to Barcelona and New York. It had never felt like much money. But he was happy. Jac was with him. They had partied. They had friends around to dinner. He felt like he was living the life he had wanted as that sixteen-year-old in Paris.

That was nine months ago. Before the money came. A treatment had been made into a show. It was called *Fantasy Shop*. It allowed people to indulge. That was its hook. It had been franchised. He had had to employ an agent, and the agent had employed a lawyer on his behalf. He had earned money. A lot of it, very quickly. There was still a cheque for $260,000 due to be paid. His accountant had suggested waiting until the new financial year to accept payment. His tax bill had frightened him. Surely he couldn't be giving that much money away in tax? Where would he get it from? The accountant had reassured him. Then Jac had left him.

The man took out pictures of his two healthy children. Their bright eyes stared out at the bright lights in the photographer's studio. He noticed they were well lit. The photographer had known how to light children, how to get the best from their youth and clear skin. A kind of hopefulness.

The bus stopped at a service station on the brow of a hill. The man from the bank invited him to share a table.

'My name is Abdul. Yours?'

'Anthony.'

'As in Cleopatra, yes?'

Anthony looked blankly at the man.

'The play. Shakespeare?'

'Sorry, of course. I was... a bit out of context.'

The station was crowded, full with families and travellers. The man from the bank had a certain stature that Anthony found attractive. He seemed at ease. A waiter arrived promptly to take their order. Abdul switched into Arabic to order his food. There was a rush of words Anthony found strangely familiar. The sound of the language was rather beautiful. The two men then looked expectantly at him. There was no menu: the butchered side of a cow hung down from the rafters next to the kitchen. Anthony didn't eat meat. He had given up meat five years before on one of Jac's fad diets. But he had surprised himself and stuck to it, which was more than Jac did.

'The fish is very good. Trout.'

Anthony was grateful for the advice. He smiled up at the waiter.

'*Un poisson, un café au lait, s'il vous plaît.*'

The waiter retreated to the kitchen.

'*Parlez-vous francais?*'

'*Non. Un peu.*'

'It is a fine language. I lived in Marseille for two years. Before I was married of course.'

'You were able to travel there?'

'To work, yes. *La vie est très cher là bas.*' He looked at Anthony and then added. 'Otherwise it is too expensive.'

'You didn't think of staying?'

'No. Why should I? My family is here. I was a young man. I wanted to see another country, that is all.'

The fish arrived. It was grilled dark under a fine spiced flour.

The afternoon lengthened as the bus climbed through the valleys that fed into the mountains. He was surprised how green the land was. He saw people on the land, farmers and shepherds, and they were making the most of the land. Cultivated plots stretched up into the hills. Small herds of goats and sheep tended by a shepherd seemed to be travelling up and down the valley. He had expected Morocco to be red with sand dunes. It was ridiculous, he knew, but everyone had a mental image of a country built on something, words and pictures, and through these the country had been categorised, the deserts, palaces, dark men. He could see the men.

The night in Tanger. The bar was not what he was expecting. The man at Tingis had suggested they should go for a real drink at Deen's.

'My name is Haroun. You will like Deen's. It is for you.'

He knew the name. It was in the *Spartacus* guide: 'Just the most lively place in Tanger. Bank clerks and diplomats. Careful after dark.'

He followed Haroun up the Petit Socco and across the square. The road narrowed, and they cut back on themselves down a side alley. A simple sign marked 'Deen's – Prix 10 Euro'. He thought about turning back. Jac blamed him for giving up on things. He took out his wallet and passed the money to the man on the door. Haroun didn't pay anything. The light was low and a heavy Europop beat pushed through the air. There was red lighting and flashing fairy lights. He could just make out the rows of men sitting at the fringes of the room. He could feel their eyes on him. He shouldn't have come in. Haroun took him to a table.

'I'll get us a drink?'

Anthony nodded and Haroun disappeared into the gloom. The music began to eat into him. He wished himself smaller.

A man sat down opposite Anthony. He spoke in what could have been German. Anthony smiled back nervously.

'You are English?'

Anthony nodded. He had explained too many times the subtle differences between Welsh and English.

'I am sorry. I thought you were German. My name is Rashid.' He smiled.

'Anthony.'

'You are here on vacation.'

'Yes.'

'Good. I like to meet people on vacation. I get to improve my English. I work in a bank. I need to speak to people. You are a very attractive man.'

Anthony blushed. He had never been called that before. People were usually more subtle or honest.

'Do you have a boyfriend in England?'

A waiter arrived with two drinks. They looked like spirits, probably vodka. Anthony took one of the glasses. His new companion waved the waiter away.

'I don't drink. Because I am a Muslim.' He laughed. 'Maybe I shouldn't be doing this either.' The man raised his eyebrows in a way that sent a shiver down Anthony's spine. He had never been good at this part of the game. He took a sip of the drink. It was vodka. He then swallowed the remainder. He felt the liquid caress his throat, urging him forward.

In the alley he kissed Rashid. There was no one around. He could feel the urgency in the man's caress. In the club Rashid had been confident but now, back in the reality of his city, he was scared. They could both go to jail for this. As Anthony pushed his hand hard onto the man's cock, he could feel the soft, wet warmth of his semen immediately, the tensing of his body as he came, lost in the desire and finality of the moment. Rashid pulled away.

'I am sorry.'

'It's OK. It's my turn now, though.'

The man shook his head. The situation catching up with him. He straightened his trousers, re-zipping his fly.

'I go now.'

'No, not yet.' The man turned and began walking away. 'You can't.'

But he quickly merged into the shadows. A cat scuttled

past him. Anthony looked up. He could see the stars above the city.

Money had always been difficult for Anthony. His father worked at the steelworks. He had been a chemist. Anthony was twelve before he realised his father had more money than other boys' fathers who also worked at the steelworks. His family holidays were package tours to hot places in Spain he couldn't remember the names of. His father changed the family car every few years for a new model. Always something built by Leyland. His father had attempted to push him towards science. Medicine would have been a good career option. Anthony was 'being offered chances that I couldn't dream of'. Anthony had wanted to go to art college. They compromised; English with Drama at Leeds. University was fun but not too serious. After Anthony finished the degree he forgot about money. He wanted to write plays. His father wanted him to get a proper job. Something with a career plan and a pension. Playwright seemed impossible. There were no playwrights in Llanelli. Surely he could write plays in his spare time. The Llanelli Players were always looking for new people.

Anthony forced his way through a series of grim restaurant jobs until he was finally made assistant manager at Pizza Express. He had been good at it. His father saw hope in the title of Assistant Manager. Anthony was now in the restaurant business. When he visited his mother in Llanelli, people still asked him how the restaurant business was going.

He met Jac at Pizza Express. They had both been serving tables. sharing the tips. One night after work they ended up back at his dreary flat off Cowbridge Road. They opened a bottle of Mezcal. Jac had stayed. He wanted to know what Anthony was going to do. Anthony showed him his work.

Jac forced him to request an interview with the literary manager of the Sherman Theatre. It had a reputation for new plays. He had sent a play in six months previously but had received no reply. The literary manager was a thin uninspired man in his early thirties. He flirted hopelessly, almost desperately, with Anthony. A week later they offered him a contract of production. Sometimes you simply had to stand up for yourself. It seemed a long time ago. Anthony knew Jac had changed his life.

His father had never really accepted Jac. He was civil but cold. It was all a bit beyond his experience. He had wanted grandchildren. Anthony was his only child. Anthony didn't hold it against him. His father was a good man. There were a lot of people at his funeral.

Then there were six years of each other. Their own world.

The money had come as a surprise. The unexpected rush of it. His first commissioned play was worth six thousand pounds. He had lived for a year and a half on the money. Now in Asilah he was embarrassed by it. He had recently bought himself a new car. A Volkswagen Beetle with huge headlamps that looked like eyes. He looked at the car in a way that unnerved him, the sixteen thousand pounds of shine, curves and metal transferring itself into an expression of his wealth and well-being. He'd heard Jac's new boyfriend drove an Astra. This knowledge gave him a perverse enjoyment he was deeply worried by.

The bus had passed men on the side of the road. They were riding donkeys or herding goats. They didn't seem as if they could be part of the same world.

They arrived in Chefchaouen in the late afternoon. It was a town trapped at the blind head of a valley. The mountains continued up into the clouds beyond the blue terraced streets. His hotel was optimistically called The Parador. It had a swimming pool that was tacked onto a slope beyond the garden with a view down into the valley. But a thin mist drifted down from the mountains and no one used it. Anthony shared the breakfast room each morning with a party of Americans. They were old but seemed healthy with fine skin and bones carrying them well into their seventies. They talked to each other but ignored Anthony. He attempted to start a conversation each morning but was met with only polite short replies.

The town reminded him of a hill station he had visited for a week in India. It had the same narrow, terraced streets. But here there was more space, fewer people. He was offered more mint tea and a lot of grass. Most of the young Westerners seemed to be here for the marijuana. He had avoided it in college. It was a type of penance he was happy with. Jac had sometimes brought some home, and they smoked it late at night with the windows open, listening to the sounds of the city at night. He always felt slightly ridiculous smoking. The unusual touch of the rolled paper filled with dried plants. He liked the smell better. The sweet promise of it. But here he refused the offers.

He bought more things he didn't need, copper bangles, postcards, odd-looking wooden boxes that reminded him of cuckoo clocks without the bird. He was reduced to giving some away to the children who accosted him for money. The begging here was only half-serious. Here the children had homes to go back to.

He met the man from the bank for tea. The visit was going well for him. He had finished the training and had a day spare to be a tourist.

'Sometimes it is good to have nothing to do. Just to be? Don't you think?'

After three days he caught another bus back down to the coast at Asilah. It had an appealing write-up in his *Lonely Planet* guide, although no mention in *Spartacus*. He wrote another postcard to Jac but didn't post it. He found a hotel on the seafront. Huge blue waves rushed in across a wide-open beach. He could feel the sea in the air and the history in the stones of the old town. Portuguese, British, Spanish and French had all fought over this piece of the world. He had often stayed in places where the Portuguese had built forts. They had a lovely way with stones and the sea. The town had charm. Tree-lined boulevards backing away from a promenade lined with restaurants that served fine French coffee.

He spent a day on the beach. He was resisting the urge to check his email account. He was hoping Jac had written but was afraid he had not. It was a couple of weeks now. He had come to see him off on Cardiff station. It was as if he were performing some last duty. A final leaving. Jac had taken a day off from the new Coffee Republic he was managing. Anthony couldn't believe how miserable he felt. He had watched Jac from the train. He could see Jac's relief, as if he had become a burden. The whole thing had become a burden. The expectations of happiness. Maybe he wasn't meant to be happy.

A group of students were playing football on the beach. A sharp wind blew in off the water. But the players seemed to be able to tease the ball between them, as if it were an object of their own will. They were all lithe men who moved with a grace that was beautiful.

The ease with which he could remove himself from his world caught him. The money he had at home was enough. Here it seemed like too much. He thought about Rashid. The first night in a new country, a strange new man. He had been waiting for him at the top of the alleyway. He was more composed. His suit pulled tight around him. He could sense he wanted more.

'Maybe we can walk together?'

He had taken him back to the hotel.

'No one will know you.'

It hadn't taken long in the room. He was young, inexperienced, still scared. Anthony had brought his own condoms. Rashid's skin was rather beautiful, brown and tight across his chest, his buttocks small, feeling full in his hands. Anthony felt desire even as he was thinking of Jac.

Rashid lay on the bed afterwards covered in the smells of sex, smiling, open. Anthony felt the guilt swallow him again. He walked into the bathroom, closed the door, took a shower. When he returned to the room Rashid was dressed.

'You want me to go?'

'It is probably best.'

His face lost its hopefulness.

'Wait, I will give you something.' Anthony reached for his trousers on the floor. He took out his wallet. As he offered Rashid fifty euros he felt the sting of his hand sharp across his face.

'I am not your boy.' He spat at his feet and left.

In the afternoon he returned to his hotel room. He made love to Jac's memory, the white, starched sheets sharp and exciting on his own skin. It was a relief to come on his own, without any guilt. He fell asleep into the deep heat of the afternoon. The music of God woke him. It was a beautiful sound. He began to cry.

THE LAST JUMPSHOT

Leonora Brito

Xtra practice? say the old laggers, the old leg timbers Parish and Bo. You mean xtra on top of xtra?

Well, practice makes perfect, I point out cheerfully. And anyway, Coach wants us there. For one last run-out.

S'all right for you – Captain Fantastic.

Yeah, Mr Campbell Jones!

But what about us, man? says Chip. We're whacked out.

No! No! I got plenty left in the tank, says Id, the Valleys Boy. Let's go for it!

Silence.

I vote we go for it—?

Everyone looks at the white boy 'gone off'. As if they've just been dealt a kick to their collective sensitivities.

Then Chip-chip jumps to his feet, suddenly re-energised, resurrected, almost. Yo, let's go, he says, breezing past Id #1, as if Id #1 had never spoken. Come on guys, what're we waiting for, yeah?

The guys jump up. Yo, let's go!

Great, I say. Now we're all agreed.

Bouncing the orange basketball I follow them out of the flat, thinking, smiling. It's because of me that Idris #1 got involved with the A team in the first place, along with his sub and namesake Idris #2. I recommended them to the new Coach, Mulrooney. The two Ids, bible-black and paper-white. Outside competition. Works like clock.

Standing by the bus stop. Waiting. Fooling around, waiting, in an afternoon sun that gives off plenty of light, but no heat. Maybe it's too late for heat this time of year. Even so, we six black guys (one honorary) standing on the green hill, under the lone, battle-scarred bus shelter must appear potent. Sunlit. At least in the sunken eyes of elderly shoppers on the supermarket free-bus, which hoves into view before we've been standing there five minutes.

Hey look what's coming, says Chip. *FAZZDERS!*

And the guys start yelling *fazzder! fazzder! fazzder!* as the bus crawls up the hill. The uniformed peaked cap behind the wheel looks as though he'd like to drive straight past. But we step out into the road, all six of us and flag him down. A shade uncool for young gods lately fingered by the sun, agreed. But we can brazen this out. Easy. After all, why pay more, as *FAZZDER* says?

Thank you, driver!

Yeah, thanks, drive!

You boyz all goin' shoppin'?

We are, drive, says Chip. Gonna buy… washing powder. Ain' we, guys?

S' right, yeah. Big bogzz size!

Inside the bus, the chit-chat drops to a murmur as we crowd on board. Then a few bold whispers follow us up. Whispering, all the way up the winding stairs: look… look how many… Somalis?

Innit Somalis?

All praise be to God I say, seeing the upper deck empty; like a breath of fresh air.

Old fogies. Though that type of misidentification doesn't bother me at all. Because I'm secure in my Keltic black heritage, come whatever? But it riles the hell out of Parish and Bo, because Parish and Bo are Docks. And being 5th or 6th generation Docks Boyz (from 'Old Doggz' as they kindly explain to the rest of us) means being black in a way that is

knee-high to royalty. At least the way they tell it. Though
Lisha – who knows – reckons the nearest Parish and Bo come
to being royal, is when they're sat on their butts in the Big
Windsor holding forth. There the guys get serious admiration
and respect (from flocks of daredevil scribes, tourists and
whatnots) simply for sitting and being: Old Doggz.

Which is why they feel particularly hurt now, and
aggrieved.

D'fuckin dee-crepts, says Bo. I'd like to punch their lights
out. One by one.

Yeah, dee-crepts, says Parish. One arf of em are wearin
NHS eye glass an they still carn see! I mean, do I look
Zomali, me?

The two Ids seated down the front of the bus throw a
quick look back. Then they make cartoon-type eyes at one
another, and burst out laughing. *Zeeong!*

Oi, shouts Bo. What you got to laugh about, *Warrior Boy?*

The cut in his voice is directed at Idris #2, who is indeed
Somali, and very tall timber. Which fact perhaps Bo has
forgotten as Id is seated. Now the Somali boy shoots his long
legs from under the seat and thunders down the aisle of the
bus.

I'm Warsangeli, he yells, right up in Bo's face. You get it
right, OK? Warsangeli Welsh!

Guys, I raise my hand peaceably. Let's all remember we're
a team, OK?

The only response to this is a simmering, mutinous silence.

And then my mobile goes off. And suddenly everyone is
transfixed as this wondrous new ringtone hits the air.

Orr, man, now that is just—just—

Awwsome, supplies Id #2.

Aye, *awwsome!* agrees Bo. I mean, d'fuckin US Cavalry
Charge?

S' what they use on the NBA clockshot, innit? says Id.

Correct, Mr Hassan. Grinning, I let the mobile play on,
unwilling to break its spell. And when Lisha gives up and rings

off, the famous US bugle call continues to root and toot in our headspace. Like mood music. Linking us, each and every one of us six guys sat there on the *FAZZDA free-bus,* to the place where we know we wanna be, which is Planet NBA!

Though the bus actually drops us off at the out-of-town shopping complex. And while the pensioners shuffle forward with their bags and four-wheel trolleys, we're down the stairs, off the bus and out, into the sunshine. Green fields. The guys look round. Birds and shit. For them, this is always, *always,* the back of beyond. But not for me, I grew up here. I'm Pontprennau through and through.

Dotted across the fields are the familiar black and white splotches, sturdy young calves chewing up the grass. It's like those pretty pictures you get on cartons of *Ben & Jerry's* ice cream. Except that these are male, Bobbi calves and therefore useless for dairy; but great for kebab meat. Nowadays donner kebab is all these big-eyed spindly legged guys are good for, apparently.

So it's Friday afternoon still. And very late in the afternoon for some of us, standing around courtside, kitted up and ready to go. At only 5 feet 8 inches tall, and with the *Big Two* O approaching fast, it's beginning to dawn on me – that I'm only growing older, not taller. While lags like Parish and Bo are even further down the hill.

But right now? Our spirits are sky. Keyed. Because incredibly, this last-minute run-out has coincided with a VIP visit. Up and coming Councillor Ms Susannah somebody, has turned up here at the sports centre (actually a discontinued warehouse) with a TV camera crew in tow.

And while the Councillor lady and Coach Mulrooney talk to the cameras about disaffected youth and the need for *blah blah blah,* we await the whistle. Excited, expectant and more than ready to roll. Then, unfortunately the Councillor lady trips over her tongue, and starts talking about *disinfected* youth. And they have to start over again.

Orr, man!

The guys fall out, and begin to goof around a little.

Hi there, whispers Chip, pretending he's on camera. My name is Michael Jeffrey Jordan an I'm not *disinfected*, bold-assed bitch. Y'hear? I'm still catchin!

Yeah, he's catchin, he's catchin—

An we catchin!

Orr, c'mon guys, behave—

OK. Hi, I'm Kobe, whispers Id the Valleys Boy. And everyone cracks up laughing.

Including me. Until I note that Coach Mulrooney, all black beetling eyebrows and Irish-American red face, is looking hard across the floor. At us, at me? Immediately I'm reminded of the need to keep a serious head on here. I mean, once we get to London and tomorrow's final – who is to say who's out there? Watching? But for now Coach Mulrooney, the man who successfully rebranded us from the Karbulls to the Crows (post-9/11) is calling the shots.

OK guys, let's keep it down, now, I say briskly. Just 24 on the clock, and it will be the *Big One!*

Yeah!

When Kardiff Crows go toe to toe with the London boyz.

D'cocker knee boyz?

Yeah, d'cocker knee boyz! Suddenly I slam the air with my fist and yell out loud: Hey, no con-test!

At last Coach Mulrooney blows his whistle. That heart-stopping shriek. And for half a nanosecond I freeze – like a five-year-old, back on the school playground. Until I break free, shake free from the loop of time and go charging forward—

Great shot there, Campbell! shouts Coach Mulrooney, as we go three on three for the cameras, and I make the first basket.

Great jumpshot!

Then everything spools forward for me. Faster and faster. And despite my best efforts to play it cool, (keep it for tomorrow, play it cool) I'm suddenly on fire. Smoking. The heat is in the house, as they say. And what a fantastic house it is! This echoey space we're running in; this *huge* aluminium-walled warehouse, that we still call Goodz 4-U. Once it housed an empire of wonderful, wonderful things: like Nike Classic, Air Force, Converse, Zoomerific; and the sneakers I favour today, which are Jumbo Lift-Off.

And again, we have lift-off, because I'm playing out of my skin! Hey where's the D? shouts Coach Mulrooney, abruptly switching sides. Watch Campbell! he shouts in irritation. Stop *Soup* Campbell! (Is *Soup* some jokey kind of put-down, I wonder, designed to halt my flow?) Too bad if it is. And too late. My feet push off the ground, my arm comes up. I grab the orange rock and it's a steal.

They're stealing it! cries Coach Mulrooney. *They are stealing it!* As Id #1 and I rotate the glowing orange rock between us. Tossing it back and forth, back and forth between us. Like a magic ball on invisible string. Invincible as we gallop up court for the nth time. Throwing a fake on Parish, throwing a fake on Chip. We thunder for the line, dropping Bo's D-fence for dead, as Id #2 pops up on the inside. And I toss the ball to Idris, that tall Somali timber. And get it back *smack!* as I run into space and stop. Right foot slam on the edge of the paint.

All at once, the famous US bugle call rings through my head. Fifteen seconds I calculate coolly, or one last jumpshot. And everyone out there will know who I am. I will alchemise my name Campbell Jones. ID-ing it. Gold-plating it to *Campbell*. Period. Aka the Can Man, aka the first Welsh Black who is destined to blaze a trail through the NBA!

The Bible tells us that your old men shall dream dreams, while your young men shall see visions. And when I finally make the shot, the ball leaves my hands and soars through the air. Like a vision. Spinning into space, like a dazzling orange sun that arcs, then fades. Drops and fades... fades...

fades. Until… hey, hey hey! *It's BIG BASKET and another three pointer!*

But, I thought I caught a sound back there? As the ball dropped on its way through hoop and net. *It hit the rim.* It hit the rim! So naturally, I have to try again. And again. Leap on the glowing ball and try again. For the perfect throw, the perfect throw. Until united to a man, the guys grab a hold of my arms, just to make me stop. Stop! Then Coach Mulrooney comes rushing up, and thrusting his angry red peasant face right in front of my eyes, he screams: *Are you crazy, or what?*

I suppose crazy must be the answer. No question. Because when he tells me I'm relegated to the bench for tomorrow's final, all I can think to do, right there in front of the cameras, the Councillor lady and everyone, is to throw my head back. Right back, and just… bellow out my misery, like a bull calf in a field. Then bring my head down hard, in a replicating action and nut the guy… and nut the guy… and nut the guy…

CHICKENS

Rachel Trezise

As a playmate my grandfather was like a cheetah. His energy
came in fast swoops but it rolled away again without
warning and he'd need to rest again until his boring fatigue
had passed over like a black cloud. He'd begun to wave his
NHS walking stick in front of him, to detect potholes and
kerbs, like a blind man, frowning perpetually, as though
everything confused him. Ever since his knee joints had
become inflamed, which seemed like forever ago, his stick
had become a talisman, used once at Longleat Wildlife Park
to gently push the roaming monkeys from peeling the
rubbery windscreen seal from his gold car, only for the
ringleader monkey to grab it and start hammering dents into
his bonnet. The monkey seemed to smile in at us with his
crinkled eyes, and laugh with a breathy cackle, like Muttley
the dog, while I held onto my mother's hand so tight her
fingernails began to bite into my skin, and everyone stared
at the back of Tad's grey head, wondering why he didn't
jump out and throttle it.

'Chelle bach,' he said, 'we'll need to go home soon. Mam-
gu Blod will be looking for us.' He patted the flat top of my
head, between my sprouting bunches and squinted at the
goldfish he'd won aiming darts. 'And mind that fish now,
don't drop him. Don't squeeze him too tight.'

'Just one more ride,' I said, looking through the murky
water of the plastic bag at the red fish not swimming but

floating inside. 'Just one more.' The fun-fair seemed to become more glamorous as the warm day turned into a cool and fuzzy evening.

Eventually my grandfather began to bribe me. He promised lashings of *Mr Creemy's* Neapolitan after roast dinner on Sunday; a return visit with two pounds spending money on Saturday and that evening, a glass of Brains SA beer he affectionately called 'whoosh', none of which interested me. But then he mentioned chickens. 'I'm going all the way to Glyn Neath tomorrow,' he said, 'because my chickens are getting old.'

'Why?' I said. I wasn't particularly asking why he was going to Glyn Neath or particularly asking why his chickens, like him, were getting old, but using the word as a prompt to prolong my time at the fair like the word *discuss* in an essay question keeps a student in his examination chair, his brain ticking.

'They don't lay eggs anymore, bach,' he said ignoring this question, 'and Mam-gu Blod needs eggs to bake sweetmeats for you kids. I'll have to get more. We need more chickens Chelle!' He stamped the grey rubber tip of his stick against the floor as though this confirmed his statement. 'If we go home for tea now you can come with me, all the way to Glyn Neath, tomorrow!' He struggled to smile through his pain.

I gritted my teeth and walked as slowly and as stubbornly as I could, without actually stopping. Getting to the fair in the first place had seemed like such a coup, it was a travesty, a tragedy, to leave. Every May holiday it stopped in our town for a week, the men with moustaches, rippling arms and tattoos sprawling over their naked chests dismantled and erected their vast metal contraptions on the wasteland in front of the rugby pitch, dog ends balancing in their lips. 'Gyppos', my grandmother called them, spitting, as though to shake off her own Romany ancestry. From her front window you could see the thin figures dance around the lot, transforming steel girders and cuts of canvas into rotating waltzers and ferris wheel cars. I'd patiently watch until the flashing neon lights were on, and then cry to go down. At this point Mam-gu would try to scare me, telling me that the men were thieves, and sometimes cannibals, and I gave up, frightened not by the travelling people but by my own grandmother's determination not to be in any way associated with them.

I was staying at my grandparents' house because my mother had gone away. 'Gone away', is all they said, which inevitably meant that there was more to it. In the six and three-quarter years I'd been alive, she had never 'gone away'. I was clumsily shelling peas from their pods and dropping them into a ceramic bowl. I'd watched the dodgem track appear, and then the teapots, and then the red and white striped roof of the shooting gallery. My grandfather had merrily ventured into the living room while Mam-gu prepared gammon with pepper and butter in the scullery, singing 'Calon Lân' loudly, warbling through the high notes, holding her hand flat on her big, left boob.

'Chelle bach,' Tad-cu said, seeing me stare out over the terraced rooftops. 'Shall I take you down there? Shall I?' He put his finger to his lips, instructing me not to shriek. He took my small hand with his stiff, square fingers and happily, repeatedly shrugged his shoulders, like Tommy Cooper about to do a trick. I heard Mam-gu bellow as the front gate sprung closed behind us.

'Danny? DANNY?'

Danny was Tad-cu's real name. For a long time I'd thought the Irish song 'Danny Boy' was written about him because he lived at the foot of a mountain side, and often, as though to deliberately exacerbate this, he'd cock his head and tell me he could hear the pipes calling. I ignored Mam-gu and struggled with Tad's inflamed knees down the hill towards the fair. At first he was delighted to be there.

'What do we want to go on first, bach?' he said, swinging his stick like a dance routine. We'd sat in a spangly red dodgem car and he'd steered it into a blue one a travelling boy was driving, the force throwing me into a mild shock and sending a series of blue and silver sparks across the circuit ceiling. I laughed wildly at his spectacles smoothing down his nose and his fine hair thrashing in the air. He eagerly reversed for good measure and rammed right into the boy's big shining backside again.

But now it was time to go. As we walked over the bridge, Tad, who needed support now from the handrail as well as his walking stick, noticed the ducklings in the river below. Five brown baby ducks followed their brown mother duck in single file, waddling along the pebbles at the edge of the water, the oncoming wind ruffling their soft feathers. They looked like little girls trying to walk in their mother's stilettos, as I had done years before, but got smacked for scuffing the heels, or fell over and grew scabs on my elbows which my auntie checked daily to see I hadn't picked.

'Look Chelle!' he said, halting, 'ducklings. Have we got bread? What have we got?' Forgetting his sore bones, he knelt to the floor and fumbled with the bags in my hand, gently uncurling my digits, one by one, little by little to lift the candy floss out of my grasp, leaving only the fish. He scratched the cellophane open and broke cotton wool balls from the spun sugar. I frowned, hiding my eyes from the other children leaving the fair, my hands held like horse blinkers either side of my head. As a child, nothing can embarrass you as much as an adult to whom you are related.

'They're hungry, bach!' Tad said. He lifted me up over the railing so I could watch my clouds of floss blow like snow into the darkening river. The animals' beady, black eyes followed the pink flakes from the sky to the water but they did not move from the river bank.

'They're not eating it,' I pleaded. 'Look Tad, it's just vanishing in the water.'

'That's their choice,' he said releasing me. 'The important thing is that we offered.'

I sulked all the way across the road, past the Red Cow pub and into Mam-gu Blod's parlour, my right thumb planted between my lips. Like her, I'd learned to roll my eyes at Tad's impromptu Dr Dolittle impressions but secretly I was impressed with Tad's ability to tolerate his own suffering when he thought he sensed suffering elsewhere, and I kept quiet, reminding myself to remember his strangely noble gesture.

My cousin Anna was sitting at the fold-out dining table in a velveteen pedal-pusher set, the colour of my absent candyfloss, her cutlery set out before her and opposite, another place was set for me.

'Danny?' My grandmother roared like steam from behind the bead curtain in the scullery doorway. 'Where the hell have you been with that child?' She made *hell* sound like it had jumped from the mouth of a nun. A saucepan slammed on the draining board. 'I've been worried sick.'

'Never mind that, Blodwyn woman,' Tad said, taking the only bag we had left into the kitchen. 'Where's the salt? This goldfish has got white-spot.'

I sat down cautiously at the table looking at the crochet cloth instead of up at my cousin. I hated Anna, mostly for aesthetic reasons, her plaits were longer and lighter than my own, her dresses prettier. That weekend I hated her more than ever. The night before, I'd heard Mam-gu fretting through the bedroom wall. 'Oh Danny,' she'd said, 'what are we going to do? If she goes to prison?' her voice a low, unfamiliar hum. They talked about the details of the situation in Welsh and the most I could decipher was that my mother was on remand for stealing my estranged father's new car. 'We'll look after Michelle,' Tad had said, 'that's what we'll do.' I heard him drop his teeth into his tumbler of water. I didn't know what prison was exactly, only that robbers went there and I knew it was bad if it worried my grandmother. She had a nervous system like titanium. What was plain, was that it wasn't simply a case of going away, which had sounded nicer, albeit selfish. Now Anna reminded me of it all. She was there because she wanted to be. At night she'd go home again.

Mam-gu put our plates of ham, peas and salad down in front of us, her apron still tied round her waist, her tightly-permed grey hair flattened with sweat. She carried my grandfather's and her own meal through to the living room. I ate in silence, the pungent spring-onions smell rising from the plate to tease tears from my eyeballs. After a while I noticed Anna was watching me carefully and slowly, mirroring my actions, even down to the foodstuff I chose to lift with my fork. She pushed her peas and shallots around in circles, her pink ham gone except for the soft, white rinds lying limp like dead snakes.

'Don't you like jibbons?' I said quietly, waiting for her taunt, or the punch line to her joke, knowing I'd be the butt of it.

'No,' she said dramatically, 'can't stand them.' She suavely popped a sweet pickle into her mouth. She was good at performing; she was going to be an actress. She was already Snow White at the Parc and Dare amateur theatre group. 'That's it,' she said, chewing it. 'I have finished.'

'You have to eat it,' I said.

'I don't, I'm going to throw it in the bin.' She shook her head so her gold braids danced.

'You can't,' I said, whispering.

'We can,' she said, 'watch.' Very slowly, as though the parlour was a safe in a bank, protected by laser alarms, she tiptoed to the bin in the corner and scraped her greens down into the rubbish with her fingertips. 'Now give me your plate.' I sat looking dumbly at her empty plate. Her hand gripped its edge, eclipsing the brown, floral pattern around the rim. It had to be some nasty prank in which she'd turn the blame on me.

'No,' I said.

'Do you want to have to eat all that?' She nodded at my

mound of leaves as they turned purple with beetroot pickling juice. I passed my plate to her uncertainly. As she silently flicked stubborn lettuce from the plate I noticed my colouring book on the spare dining chair. Cleverly I ripped pages from its stapled centre and crumpled them into balls of yellowing paper, precisely placing them in the bin to obscure the awful food. According to my grandmother, oxygen was useless without a well-prepared meal to go with it, so getting caught disposing of fresh produce was not an option. She would have smothered me.

'Oh good, girls,' she said coming into the parlour and eyeing our progress, her tea tray loaded with crockery. As she passed, she stopped, as though able to sniff our nefariousness in the air and manoeuvred herself toward the bin. She stepped on its pedal, her enormous, round bum spreading oval as she bent to look inside. I held my breath as Anna's green eyes widened to the point of rolling out of their sockets. Immediately afterward, as though realising how silly an accusation it was, she stepped off the pedal and the lid crashed down. She shuffled into the scullery where I heard the oven door open. The hot, inviting aroma of strawberry jam tarts wafted out, choking the watery smell of salad.

Anna and I sat on the settee, Scruffy, our grandparents' three-legged Yorkshire Terrier separating us on the middle cushion like a pillow between reluctant lovers. Mam-gu was drinking Guinness from a pint glass. She was a feminist through and through, her fiery French mother's genes bubbling around inside her as she worked and scolded and cared, but if you had ever told her, she wouldn't have known what the word meant. Tad slept, blinking during his lucid moments at the recovering fish in its bowl on the table, or the television where Steve Davis was playing snooker. After bedtime I heard my grandparents make an aggressive argument out of which cushion of the billiard table was the bottom, boasting a long and patience-sapping marriage with continuous ebbs of annoyance and easy flows of acceptance.

Tad-cu's garden stretched for an acre up along the uneven edges of Maerdy Mountain. The stray cats scattered from their tinned stewed steak breakfasts left in rows on the clear, corrugated scullery roof, their triangular ears sent back on their heads by cautious irritation as I climbed the steps in my yellow wellies. Dew glistened on the grass blades. I hiked to the top of the garden, pulling on fern stems for support, avoiding the pet cemetery hidden behind a holly bush, which on less eventful mornings was my castle. Tad was in the chicken run, two small, freckled eggs caked in muck and ginger feathers balancing in his open palm.

'Tad,' I shouted, 'we have to get new chickens, remember!'

'After breakfast, bach,' he said clipping the gate behind him as the army of birds hopped towards us, jutting their funny heads quizzically. I didn't like chickens very much. What I was really looking forward to was a long journey. I loved being in transit because that somehow meant that life was on pause, and that was quite exhilarating. He gave me an egg to hold and we steadied one another back to the house.

'Are we going to eat those chickens when we get new ones?' I said.

He didn't answer me but scoffed as though it was a ridiculous suggestion. This after all was a man who trapped rats only to carry them in their cages to the top of the mountain and release them unscathed. He ate chicken, but never one of his own. They all died of old age.

'Know what I'm going to do?' he said. 'When you marry a prince I'll dig this whole garden over and find enough Welsh gold for your wedding ring! C'mon, let's give these eggs to Mam.'

In Glyn Neath, the egg factory sat unremarkable like a massive brown crate at the back of an industrial estate, the paint chipped from its zinc walls.

'Now hold my hand Chelle,' Tad said in a squeaky wheeze, his nostrils tightened to black slits. Inside there was only the sound of machinery although hens lined the walls in box cages, balancing on one another in stacks, like Barbie dolls in Toys R Us. Fluorescent lights gave the warehouse a blunt and unnatural appearance. Tad talked with his new, high voice to a boy in an overall while I stared at the birds. They hadn't enough room to stretch their wings, let alone fly, and reminded me of the *Return to Oz* wicked witch's hundred heads, dead and locked in a cabinet, each one individual and capable of living, if only given the freedom.

'Why aren't they squawking?' I said as Tad pulled me away.

'They're probably too tired, bach,' he said.

'What's that smell?'

'Fear. Fear and poo and death.'

We walked back to the gold car and the boy in the overall followed, a twill brown sack clutched in his fist which moved of its own accord like a bag of magic potatoes. He passed it to my grandfather.

'Fiver,' he said. 'Not much use for eggs, them, but there's a fair bit of meat there.'

'You'd be surprised what a chicken can do when it's given free range,' Tad said dryly, although many of his chickens never laid eggs. They were left to live as normal with the ones that did. He put the bag in the boot of the car and paid the boy. We sat in the car for a minute, listening to the soft creaking a hen makes when it uses its legs for the first time. Then Tad leaned over into the hatchback and whipped the brown sack out of the gathering of heedful chickens. As he did, one small hen which had still been inside fell out flaccidly, its fleshy mohican which should have been red, was white.

'Is it dead?' I said.

'Michelle,' Tad said, taking it in his hands like a baby, 'it's not dead but I'm going to have to kill it. I have to put it out of its misery or it'll die in pain by the time we get home.' As he spoke he deftly twisted the hen's neck between his thumb and forefinger as though giving it a massage, which he did sometimes on my grandmother's big, knotty shoulders. 'It's for his own good Chelle,' he said, looking at me mysteriously for a moment as though wondering if I still loved him. He reached past me to the glove box for a plastic bag and wrapped the chicken inside it. He always had plastic bags on him, for collecting dandelion leaves for the rabbits. 'We'll bury it in the garden.'

'Is it dead?' I said again.

He nodded and started the engine.

My grandfather drove slowly over the peak of the dusty mountain. He drove slowly anyway on account of the infamous accident. When I was just a newborn he'd backed his green Mini over the edge of a cliff with Mam-gu beside him. Neither of them were hurt but Mam never forgave him for having lost her knitting. (She'd been making a white cardigan with pearls encrusted around the cuffs and it flew out of the window. The wool was an offcut from Ponty market and she never, ever matched its ivory colour.) After a jolt, Tad'd check in the mirror that the chickens were OK. I could see them through my wing mirror. They huddled stiffly like one body of balding, pimply skin with ten legs. Their eyes seemed to be focused on me, whichever direction they looked.

We stopped at the top of the valley for petrol and Tad left me in the car while he paid for it. I'd been sitting in the passenger seat for two minutes when one of the hens moaned from deep down behind its dirty feathers. There was a moment of silence before another hen followed suit. Collectively their noise sounded like a mass complaint, voiced with a woman's yelp. Volume seemed to give them confidence and they parted, pecking one another, like death warming up. The smallest pale and shaking chicken didn't move at all. It sat in the middle of the boot while the others began to prod and butt it, its orange pupils fixed on me. Sometimes, animals instinctively knew when one of their brood was ill. Before my father became estranged, there was a fish tank in the living room and if one angel fish inside it became diseased, the others would push it to the surface of the water, like aquatic undertakers. I reached for the chicken, lifting it easily, like a toy.

Swiftly, I wrung its neck, as my grandfather had done. He made it look easy. In actual fact it was easy but I could feel its warm muscles moving and its life jumped from it with a bustling start.

Then the other chickens noticed me. The largest came towards the seat, flapping its wings and bucking like a frightened she-cat. The others followed, cocking their heads one way then the other as though they saw me through their ears, which I couldn't see but I guessed were situated somewhere around their popping, wan heads. At first I covered my own head and waited for it to stop, but it didn't, the other chickens joined in, wailing and striking my hands with their sharp and brittle beaks. It was important not to cry, because that meant I'd never collect chickens again. There was only one other solution.

'What have you done?' Tad said, his eyes circling the car anxiously where dead birds and emaciated feathers lay like litter. He lifted his fingertips to his temples.

'It was for their own good Tad,' I said. 'They were howling. They were in pain.'

'MICHELLE,' he said, and he was about to continue shouting, like the chickens, attacking me with thunderous nonsense, but words did not come. He sat down in his seat, placing his stick beside him, breathing quickly; his energy seemed to spill out of his pores, as his face turned somnolent in seconds. I gazed at the dry red mud on my sunflower-yellow wellies. After a while his jaw dropped and he spoke. 'I suppose they won't be much use for eggs after all,' he said calmly and he started the engine again.

One day in the playground I overheard Anna tell her theatre friends that the judge had thrown the book at my mother, not for her crime but for her insolence. 'Cheeky cow', she'd called her, her own auntie. I was never really sure if she had been acting, or repeating what the family said when I was out of earshot, or both. A year passed while she served her sentence, or as I preferred to think of it, tanned herself on a beach in the south of France. My grandfather didn't go back to Glyn Neath for any more chickens. Gradually the ones that were left stopped laying altogether. On the Monday after my failed gesture of nobleness, I asked Mam-gu for jam tarts.

'Oh Chelle,' she said, as though remembering something, 'we can't have tarts, there's no eggs.'

'There aren't any eggs in jam tarts,' I said.

'But there is, bach,' Tad said, 'in the pastry.'

'Can't we buy some eggs?' I said.

'Tad spent all his money on those chickens, cariad,' Mam said.

We had similar conversations for months on end. There was no scrambled egg for breakfast, no pies to go with our chips and malt vinegar on a Saturday, no quiche lorraine for days out, no Yorkshire pudding with our dinners, no hard-boiled eggs in our summer salads and no Christmas cake at Christmas. Even at Easter when all the children in my class took eggs to school for the teacher to blow and then paint stripy with primary colours, I wasn't allowed to participate. It was amazing how much of life's foundation was made from egg. All along I had admired the way Tad had punished me. I realised how we needed to appreciate the things that provided for us, even down to the lowly battery hen, but I never thought he'd keep it going for so long.

At May when the fair was due again, an odd woman walked up our front path.

'Chelle, baby,' she said, 'come to Mammy.'

'My mammy has got blonde hair,' I said backing away. Janet Goodwin, who lived in Anna's street, had escaped from a kidnapper the week previous and we'd had talks at school about not bothering with strangers.

She pulled me to her chest and smelt my scalp.

'I used to have blonde hair,' she said. Tears were welling on her bottom eyelids and I could hear them too, in her words. 'God I've missed you. What do you want?' she said. 'You can have anything; let me get you a treat, anything in the world, a doll? A knickerbockerglory from Ted's Supper Bar? Say, what do you want?'

I wanted to push her away. '*Welsh gold for my wedding ring*,' I was going to say. '*My grandfather'll get it, I don't need you.*'

'Come on Chelle, baby, say,' she said, pulling me tighter so I was hugging her without really wanting to. 'What do you want?'

I looked at my brunette mother. 'An omelette please,' I said.

BUNTING

Jon Gower

My, she could whistle! After shedding the trappings of
language, my eighty-year-old mother, Alaw, took to
whistling, and not any old whistling either. She draped
nightingale melodies around the utilitarian, steeped-in-piss
furniture at the old people's home and it was so, well,
appropriate. I am here, this is my place, observe me.

Luscinia megarhynchos. The nightingale. 'A medium sized
songbird of shy and secretive habits with a discretely rufous
tail.' A bird that sings so enthusiastically during moonlit
hours it's been known to die in mid-warble.

It rated high as entertainment. If ever Tony Bennett cancelled
a gig at Caesars Palace you could have booked her in his place,
although God only knows what the Las Vegas punters would
have made of a fragile and rickety woman creaking her way
onto the stage as an augmented orchestra struck up with
something brassy. But if they'd been patient for just two
minutes while she got her breath and adjusted her sticks – if
they'd just sipped their cosmos and margaritas and their
industrial-strength rusty nails, and just shut the fuck up, simply
offered the old dear that much good grace – they'd have been
transported. They'd have actually heard the music of the
spheres, leaving the empty husks of their bodies behind to fly
as iridescent dragonflies around the chandelier-lit room – swear
to God they would – which surely had to be worth the price of
admission? Worth five hundred bucks of anyone's money.

But her melodic brilliance – those glimmering notes, those pitch perfect descants, the rising scales that could be soundtracks for epiphanies – was confined to the tightly hemmed-in quarters of the home, where she was loved by residents and staff alike, but loved especially when she whistled. Whoo-ee-oo. Whoo-ee-oo.

There was never much silence in Noddfa, what with the barkers and shouters and screamers – all the cacophonous soundtrack of the Elderly Mentally Infirm. It was worse at night and worst on moonlit nights. The place sounded like a shearwater colony. In west Wales they call shearwaters cocklollies, to mimic their macabre calls. Someone once described the shearwater's call as it returns to land under cover of darkness as a rooster in full cry seconds after its throat has been cut. Imagine tens of thousands of seabirds all making that sound and you begin to hear what the caterwauling was like when all the crazies at Noddfa started up. But during a rare lull, when all the shearwaters had flown away, my mother's aspirated notes could command wonder. Nurses would put down their urine pans. Rapt inmates would listen as if to the sound of a pin dropping.

She had never whistled before, not that I remember. And she hardly sang either, only in chapel, where the only real audience was the woman standing next to you. In Gerazim my mother stood next to a woman called Hetty who was as deaf as a post, which left my mother just singing to God. She did so with gusto – that entire back catalogue of dirgeful Methodist hits – which collectively assembled more Welsh rhymes than you'd countenance for words such as redemption and pity. Imagine trying to find a rhyme for 'anuwioldeb'. Her favourite hymn was 'Wele'n Sefyll Rhwng y Myrtwydd', not least because it had been written by a woman. She liked the emptiness in the tune, the chasmic space between the notes. And she liked the simple language, homilies expressed in a minor key.

Before the whistling started there'd been a severe decline

in her ability to express herself through words. Syntax splintered. Grammar was wrestled out of shape. Order dismantled. Day by day she lost the world. And she was also spatially confused. When my aunt went to see her she alleged she was in Russia and her descriptions of St Petersburg's Nevsky Prospekt – that grand thoroughfare's busy acts of caretaking and commerce – were as vivid as a marionette show, until you remembered that the old woman had never been there. She had been to Bulgaria once, on a package holiday, but that would only explain a certain foreignness of vision.

When does a person die in your mind? When his or her name is finally forgotten, flashing away like a trout upriver or when you have no recall of a single moment you shared together? No single moment. I cannot pinpoint when things really started to go awry for her, when her world was cut loose like a balloon. Maybe the notes in loose scrawl reminding her of things she had to do. Pay gas. Bring keys. Empty cupboard.

I wanted her to find herself a bower, a shaded settlement among dark leaves where she could build a nest of comfort about her, but that wasn't to be.

On the January day I spotted a glaucous gull near the Cardiff heliport, one of the staff from Noddfa phoned me up to tell me that she'd been fighting. It's not a call you expect to have, ever, let me tell you. About your mother, fighting! Some old collier had taken a pop at her in the dining room – an altercation about digestive biscuits apparently – and she had slugged him one on the nose in return. My mother – the biffer, the bopper, the old scrapper. At least she won the bout. That's a new species of pride. The octogenarian pugilist. The woman who nursed me.

If only she could build a nest for herself. If only those chicken-bone fingers could gain enough dexterity to start to weave again. She could then gather spiders' webs, from the undusted nooks and arachnid corners of Noddfa and with that gossamer – strong enough to strangulate bluebottles, delicate enough to trap wisps of dew – she could knit-one-purl-one, give shape to her bower. She could line it with the fine grey hair that candy flosses out of her yellowing skull.

A strong nest, that's what she needs. Consider the long-tailed tit, that busy grey and pink denizen of the willow world. It builds a nest made of moss, hair feathers and silvery threads of gossamer which it shapes into a gourd, strong enough to hold the weight of two birds, and then more eggs, in fact as many as sixteen eggs, and then the rapidly growing chicks and finally the fledgling birds. The whole extraordinary architecture – shaped using as many as two thousand feathers – lasts just the length of a season and then falls apart as if it's never been. So my mother's nest could be one of gossamer, and she could sit contentedly within its silvery threads. Snug as eggs. Her eyes are meshed with red flecks, like a jackdaw's egg.

It took me until I was a fully-grown man, somewhere in my early forties, before I could tell my mother I loved her. I'd visit her every week, without fail, and would take her shopping to the Carmarthen Safeway before it became Morrison's where she would display all the parsimonious skills of someone who lived through a world war, finding every discount sticker and always taking the newest yoghurt pots from the back of the display. We'd always stop for lunch on the way back home in a village so off the beaten track it probably had werewolves scouting round the refuse bins at night. It was in a sharp sided cwm, which never saw daylight, exacerbated by swathes of Sitka spruce that had been planted twenty years ago and now seemed to lay siege to the place. The old lady would eat an enormous mixed grill of chops, eggs and kidneys with all the avidity of a gannet downing mackerel.

The next time I visit Noddfa someone has installed double glazing over her eyes, and poured liquid cement down her ear canal. She is a shop window dummy and a very sad display at that. Like a down-at-heel florists' showing a wilted tulip in a vase of green water. Zombification doesn't suit her one jot. It's all a matter of meds. You'd have thought that the mighty pharmaceutical industry with its concrete acres of laboratories and infinite profit horizons could devise something to take an old gal's anxiety away without buggering up her locomotive functions. But there doesn't seem to be a magic pill to stop her fretting, to control her hallucinations. One experimental concoction, a mix of chemical stun gun and elephant tranquilliser, knocked her clean into a mini-coma for five days.

I know this guy, Billy Wired down in Burry Port, who claims to have tried every drug in the world: injected ketamine between his toes, snorted peyote in such quantity that he became a pterodactyl for four days and subsisted on nothing more than the occasional Mesozoic fish. He once tried a narcotic from New Guinea that turned his skin permanently green. Even now his skin has a sickly hue. So my guess is that Billy would be able to rustle up something to banish all her anxiety. But at the moment she's at the mercy of the rattling pill trolley in the care home, doomed to a whirling world of hallucinations so powerful that, were I still a drug-hungry student with a penchant for nightly brain alterations, I'd be more than mildly envious of her – someone who could conjure up visions at will, like a starving saint in a cave.

One day Alaw believed a gang had kidnapped her two sons. They had them gagged and bound in the coalhouse and there was dark muttering about being inventive about the torture. Another day she took a sled out over the pack ice to where prowling polar bears scouted for seal cubs, but she could explain little of this, only rounding her lips into a perfect 'O' and making the sound of a tiny hiss. Then, one day, her mind was just one enormous rapture, as colours danced in kaleidoscopic choreography: lilac, diesel blue, mango green shimmying with powder grey, pea green melding with black of night, aquamarine melting into sunflower and milky cream, and, more luminous than the others, queen of the dance, a shimmering titanium white, executing some dazzling disco to the strobe of her own liquid skin. Billy Wired would have envied her the brain-cinema.

The day we met the consultant at Brynmeillion hospital was a day of cheery weather, with a pearl sun in a Mediterranean blue sky. When he showed us the scan results I thought immediately of tetrads, those kilometre squares I used when mapping breeding birds, from greenshank, spotted by satellite in the Flow Country, to buzzards pinpointed in the Cornish countryside. Spots on the charts marked strokes she's had. The consultant held the sheets as if they were on fire.

'Do you understand?' he asked her.

'Does she understand?' he asked me, noting the vacancy of her stare.

I looked at her head – the fine nose and the blood-flecked eyes. Despite her growing confusion these past months there had been nothing to intimate this moment. This demented moment. What goes through that imploding mind?

On a willow wand, serenading the settling dusk, the nightingale pens its solitary symphony. Its liquid voice is a rivulet of delight. But in her nun's room, stripped of decoration, Mam's eyes are wide with fear. They are coming for her. They will get her for certain. She knows. Her bird-like body is a cocoon of tightening feathers, as invisible wires pull her ribcage together, close to bursting point.

In a country she has never seen, the cancer-sickened President has ordered a meal for his penultimate night at the helm. He wants to taste guilt, and it comes in the shape of *l'ortolan*, the bright little bunting. *Emberiza hortulana*, to give it its Latin name.

The birds have been trapped deep in the south of this cruel country by men with lime sticks and near-invisible nets made of horsehair string. They were then blinded in keeping with centuries of tradition and kept in a small bamboo box for a month where they were fed a steady supply of figs, millet and grapes. The ortolan. The fig pecker. When the fig pecker has grown to four times its normal size it is drowned in Armagnac. Steeped to death.

The gluttonous President is also having oysters, foie gras and capons but the tongue's great prize is the tiny bird. The erstwhile President tucks his bib into his tight collar, and despite his illness he begins to salivate like a puppy. He then covers his head with a white cloth as the small birds are placed in the oven. A priest with a penchant for finches and catamites started this gourmet tradition long centuries ago as a way of masking his disgusting gluttony from God, away from divine reprimand.

'Father, forgive me for I have eaten everything in the Ark apart from the tortoiseshell...'

The cook, called Fabien, busies himself with the diminutive main course. He reads his notes, because this is an uncommon meal and it is for the President. 'Place in oven at incinerating temperature for four or five minutes. L'ortolan should be served immediately; it is meant to be so hot that you must rest it on your tongue while inhaling rapidly through your mouth. This cools the bird, but its real purpose is to force you to release the tiny cascade of ambrosial fat.' Sounds tricky, thinks Fabien, who likes Indian food himself. Especially chicken vindaloo.

Under his shroud Francois Maurice Adrien Marie Mitterrand, the first socialist president of the Fifth Republic, places the entire four-ounce bird into his mouth, its head jutting pathetically between his lips. He bites off the marble-sized head and discards it on the salver provided. It will amuse the cat. He tries to savour his memory of a historic role as the first president for two full terms, his mouth full of bird-body. He knows the rules of history: how they will try to besmirch his name. Not that he thought of that when it came to Rwanda, or blowing up the *Rainbow Warrior*, or dealing arms to Iran, or running wiretaps or keeping his fig-pecker in his pants.

'When cool, begin to chew. It should take about fifteen minutes to work your way through the breast and wings, the delicately crackling bones, and on to the inner organs.'

Tonight this is the loneliest table in the world, even though there are guests aplenty and an animated chatter resounding throughout the dining room. But at the head of the table is the President, marooned on a glacier of self-pity.

He can taste the bird's entire life as he chews in the clouded light: the sibilant wheat fields in the shadows of the Atlas mountains, the salt 'n' seaweed tang of the Mediterranean air, the warm draughts of lavender and pear scent blown by a mistral over Provence and on to the Loire. The pulpy lips and time-stained teeth crunch down with a guillotine certainty toward the pea-sized lungs and heart, thoroughly saturated with liqueur. The tiny organs burst with a sherbet fizz. Quiet, the President is masticating! Listen to the crunch of bird bone. Listen to his loneliness.

Tomorrow is his last night as tour guide of the lost republic and tomorrow he will taste nightingale. Fabien has been given this special request. His men, slinky hunters, assured of success, are already deep in the green woods. They will bring him one, trussed in a net. With this much notice they were lucky to get one.

Fabien, brilliant in his kitchen habitat, will know what to do. He remembers his grandmother and her macabre lullabies:

'Lark's tongue in aspic, thrush in a pie, all the birds that ever sang, sing better as they die...'

The songbird's last serenade will be as short as a gasp. In the kitchen, a man will strop his knife on the whetstone. It will glint, as if alive. He will enjoin his sous-chef to start a suitable sauce, let it simmer overnight. Let the flavours meld and intensify. Wild eyed on a twig, the songbird cannot so much as blow a thin note, such is its fear. The hunters' boots crackle like fire through the dry understory. They are pacing out what remains of her terrified life. She knows they are coming, with all of heart.

I Say a Little Prayer

Robert Minhinnick

It's dark now and the Greyhound station is out of town. I sit in the waiting room with the Mennonites in their black bonnets and cloaks. These Mennonite men have square beards like Abraham Lincoln. The Mennonite children seem sad. I wink at one of the girls who looks away and then glances back. I smile at her. She looks away. A little girl, head to toe in black. We're all waiting for the circular.

I used to know a poet who wrote about bus stations. Did a gig with him and he read a doleful piece. We are in it together, he read, until the last buses go out. In it together. He had looked around a bus station and seen Pakistani and Chinese people and he wondered what they were doing. In Bridgend. And what he was doing there. I kissed him on his stubbly mouth and he whispered he was in love with me.

Buy me a drink first, he said. Then we'll run away together.

But not all Mennonites wear uniforms. Years ago, me and my guitarist were booked into the students union of a Mennonite college, way out in rural Indiana. We arrived early, checked out the PA, ordered a beer.

We don't do beverages, Miss, was the response from this big black bursar in the refectory.

No way, I thought. So we asked a student about the closest bar. Hey, I'll take you, he said. Fancy a walk?

What a walk. Along these narrow roads in the cornfields,

the maize ten feet high, the cobs in their purple sheaths still closed against the stems. And us trudging like pilgrims through the Mennonite corn. After two miles we came to a crossroads. And there was a bar there. Right there. 'The Country' it was called. Well we had a good old chinwag about music, and then took some Moosehead back with us and sat in the woods in the college grounds. Drank out of bottles which we kept in brown paper bags. Very respectful. It was a quiet gig. As I remember, some of the women there wore black. But not the men.

That was just after I'd met Amir, and he did the booking. Now Amir, he always says I talk too much. Which is true. But there is a flickering home movie in my head, starring Amir himself and my parents and characters from *Seinfeld* and *Bleak House*, and the Bible, and 'Polythene Pam' and the 'Girl from the North Country' and everyone who has never existed anywhere but my mind.

They're all there. In Barry Island and Inwood and imaginary places that are real to me. So if all that's playing non-stop, I have to talk about it. Yeah, too much. But my mind's an exchequer of dreams. OK, I had that line ready. I've fitted it into a song and sing it about every third gig.

There's this other song too that I've been trying to write, called '38 Cents'. That's what Stephen Foster had in his pocket when he died. Don't tell me you've never heard of Stephen Foster? Best American songwriter ever. 'Beautiful Dreamer'? Boy, he was far ahead. He just wasn't made for those times. He died in 1864 and his last address was 30, The Bowery, at the North American Hotel.

I went down there once to look around because I was doing this unplugged thing at the Bowery Poetry Club. I told the club owner he should do a Stephen Foster tribute night. He said it was a great idea. I looked at him and spoke a verse.

Gorgeous, he said. So I sang it that night as part of my set, and I've done it ever since. And you know what? People simply love it. God bless you, Stephen Foster. And I'm not joking when I say you belong in the Rock and Roll Hall of Fame. These days it's full of crap like Aerosmith. No class.

It's Tuesday I think. But who knows where the time goes? Last Tuesday it was raining. Icy veils were blowing off the Hudson. I had nothing much on so I took the train to meet Amir at JFK. All the way down on the 1 from 207 to 59, then the A out to Howard Beach, then the airport shuttle to Terminal 4. Now, that's fourteen dollars return. Wasted. But I wanted to surprise him. Yet it was me who was shocked.

Amir had been in Amman for two weeks to see his parents. I waited at arrivals long after everyone else had come through. Then I asked at Royal Jordanian. Amir was still at customs. Correction. Amir had been detained by Immigration. Correction. Amir was being interviewed by Homeland Security. They were putting him on the next flight back.

But this is his home, I said. He lives in the city. He's a US passport holder.

Did no good. I kept ringing but his phone was off. Cell phone? The words give me the creeps. But there was nothing to do but go back to Inwood. That night the phone rang and it was Amir. Before he said a word I recited our little joke. 'If ye cannot bring good news, then don't bring any.' That's what we always said to one another. It was a philosophy. Courtesy of the wicked messenger.

Amir was still stunned. Denied entry, he said. Even with a US passport they put their fingers up his ass. He's back in Amman.

I could see him there. I'd visited with Amir, about ten years previously. We'd just met. Of course his parents thought I was the one. Amir's intended. Made me feel a little queasy because Amir's gay as a lark. In New York, before he found our Inwood studio, we often slept together. But only out of necessity. I'd tease him by kissing his neck but he never came on to me. He had these freckles like cappuccino chocolate on his back and black fur on his belly. Dark little cock like a dufflecoat toggle. Sweet and unthreatening. Now I could picture him on the landline in his father's house, the desert dawn streaming through.

One evening we were eating supper there, flatbreads and humus with lemon and thyme. I looked up and saw a lizard on the ceiling. Then Amir's dad caught my eye and everything went crazy. They found an aerosol and a stepladder and started squirting that lizard till the room stank of pine forests.

Amir's mother was hard work. Grievously melancholic. She had sold her business, a nursery school, and now was missing the routine. The new owners were making a success of it and she felt she had nothing. So Amir became even more important to her. She treated me like the betrothed. The special one. She never once asked my age, but I was over thirty-five then, five years older than Amir. OK, I'm forty-eight. And dealing with it.

I had my own bedroom. At night you could feel the tension. The parents were waiting for Amir to sneak in. I could hear them listening. A man must make his move.

But it never occurred to him. I think they were disappointed. But one of his brothers, a fat kid with a moustache, tried it. Came into my boudoir. By mistake. I told him to leave or I'd tell Daddy. So what we did on that visit was to sit around the TV and watch the Bill Clinton impeachment interviews. It was hard for me to credit. I was in Amman and we had satellite TV and Amir's brothers were lying on the floor, sniggering at stories about blowjobs. The most powerful man on the planet, humiliated. Silver hair. Red cheeks. I thought the world was ending. How could they treat a president like that?

What we gonna do? I asked Amir on the phone.

You do the gigs, he said. I'll talk to the US embassy. It's just the usual paranoia.

I like Inwood. It's cheap. Two coffees and two English muffins in the Capital restaurant for four dollars. But it's being discovered, just like Williamsburg. Sometimes we walk up to The Cloisters where Sting did that lute concert and look at the jays and those incredible incarnadine cardinals in the bushes. Yeah, Macbeth rocks. We call that path our Blue Jay Way. Once we decided to trek all down Broadway. Now that's a hike. Went through Harlem and this gang of black kids were jeering 'Sugar Hill, Sugar Hill' at us. Thought we were dissing them. But we kept going, past Colombia where Dylan used to serenade the students, and came to the Broadway Dive on 101. We'd walked over one hundred blocks.

End of the road, Amir said. We went in, had Guinness and french fries, put Aretha on the jukebox, and just sang along. *Forever, forever, you'll…* whatever. Then we took the train back.

So I've begun the tour that Amir had organised. Started yesterday morning. After that call he hasn't rung again, but I have all the contacts. The six gigs are guaranteed. The PA is guaranteed. The amps are there. All I have to do is turn up and tune the Tanglewood.

Normally, Amir would drive. But driving over here is a challenge for me. So I caught a noon Trailways from the Port Authority, reckoning to be in Binghamton by five. The Brandywine Bowl would be just over the road, as would the motel.

What can I say? It's only rock and roll but I like it. Only I don't. What do you see when you hear the word Bowl? That's Bowl with a capital B. I see the Rose Bowl. I even see the Hollywood Bowl. I thought the Brandywine Bowl would be a modest concert arena. But it's not.

It's a bowling alley. Amir had booked me into the café of a bowling alley in the boondocks. Christ, Binghamton has seen better days. Derelict buildings, grey snow. Men in plaid shirts and ball caps. Everything like a bleached out video. But I survived the Brandywine Bowl. Hallelujah, as Leonard Cohen would say. And I spent the fee on a bus ride.

One of my stranger gigs. I did three twenty minute sets, all interspersed with the skittles flying and the bowling balls crashing along the gutters. No, not skittles. Pins. And dorks ordering pizza in the café and just chit chit chattering. Like starlings. I did 'Days' by The Kinks, which went down well. I sang that once at a crematorium for a friend who OD'd. Twelve of us there in a concrete box in the rain. At the Bowl I also tried out Radiohead's 'Creep', which was maybe ambitious. I haven't got enough chords to make it as weird as it should be, and a bowling alley is no place for a tune like that. That's right. I like slow songs. Sometimes Amir tells me to rock it up but songs are poetry. And I'm not Motorhead.

I sold twelve of my 'On the Brink' CDs. Afterwards the manager took me out to dinner. Ravioli with a cream sauce. Real all-American glop. Earlier on, I'd changed in his office and he saw me in my bra. So he gets protective. Which quickly becomes proprietorial. Doesn't it girls?

I googled you, he said. Was a teensy bit disappointed.

Why? I asked.

Thought there'd be more *stuff* about you, he said. And your site's down.

But he liked the YouTube songs, 'Beautiful Dreamer' done extra dreamily, and 'Island Girl'. No, not the Elton song or the Beach Boys song. My own song. About Barry Island. Redbrink Crescent to be exact. That's where I was brought up. *I was always on the brink – well that's what people think* is the chorus. My ever plaintive side. Then he bought me a cocktail. It was blue. I'd have preferred a Guinness.

You got nice hair, he said.

I just laughed. No I don't, I said.

I was tired. My mouth felt like I was getting a cold sore. He walked me to my room and put his hand on my elbow. Kind of steering me.

Hey, I laughed, I'm not that ancient. And I locked the door.

Creep. No. Just a kid. A kid doing well at the Brandywine Bowl, and maybe the only person duking it out in Binghamton.

I took a long soak. I could see the telly in the next room and *Sons of Anarchy* was on, about middle-aged Hells Angels who probably come from this part of the world. Utica, with its Vietnamese triads. Albany. But the room's not bad. I've poured all the shower gel into the water and it's like a Hollywood bubble bath. But the site's down. That's grievous.

Amir's spent a lot of time rebuilding my site, including new pictures. I told him to keep the gypsies. He can't understand that but had to agree. We took that shot in a suq in Amman, when we were finally sick of watching Clinton squirm in his blue suit. There was a couple selling tea out of a silver pot, all dented and blackened. Amir spoke Arabic to them but he said they weren't Palestinian. Gypsies, he supposed. The woman had the moon and stars embroidered on her skirt. The man smiled like a goat. And you know, they spoke some English to me, this couple serving us tea. English in that ancient place.

So speak some of your own language, I said. But they wouldn't. They sort of withdrew then. Amir said their language was the dark language. Only for the clan. A private speech that wasn't Arabic. I suppose I have my own dark language too. But I never got round to learning it.

You know the most Welsh I ever felt? I was about sixteen and me and two friends had a free double period. We left school and went walking in the lanes. It was cold and under the hedgerows were these scarves of frost. Ice in the hoof prints. But roses were flowering too. Haggard but still there. We drifted on, all in our uniforms, me and Jane and Michael. And we came to Barry Zoo. We'd never been that way before. But there, as usual, was the tiger in his cage, standing on his concrete floor. The tiger that would never look at us. In his shame he couldn't meet our eyes. A tiger in the frost standing on this piss-stained concrete. Surrounded by slaughterhouse bones. We mooched around a bit and went back through the fields. Then a man passed us. In that lonely place. There was no one else about.

Bore da, the man said.

He startled us.

Bore da, said Jane.

And then I did too. I spoke the dark language. Or it spoke me. Bore da, said the dark language.

Michael just giggled. Wanker, he whispered.

Jane and Michael had an argument and I joined in. Because for the first time in my life, I mean outside the classroom, I had spoken another language. But I was really thinking about the manky tiger. His feet were the colour of those roses in the frost.

I'd already taken the gypsies' pictures on the Sony digital Amir had bought. And it's on the site, this couple squinting through the steam, the woman with a red scarf, the man bareheaded. I still think it's one of my best. I wrote about them, of course. A song called 'Lost Tribe', and I'm doing it on this tour. Tonight, in fact. At the Blue Tusk.

Good tea, I had said. The woman laughed and looked me up and down, while the man grinned with his big tobacco-coloured teeth. Hey, gyp. Long may you run.

I slept well. And on the dot of ten Mr Manager Man knocked on the door. He was taking me for breakfast, and then to the Greyhound stop which he claimed was not a good place.

Binghamton is sort of depressed, I said, over the Special, which was eggs, bacon, sausage, hash browns, orange juice and endless coffee. And me a vegetarian. Yeah, breakfast in America. You can't beat it. Then I told mine host about the UK, to make him feel better.

I was travelling with this band, The Dodgems, in a van on the M62. Say, two years ago. We'd just done the Upper George in Halifax together and the boys were giving me a lift south. But there'd been an accident and we had to leave the motorway and head into Manchester. It was wet and misty and the driver didn't have a clue. So we're amongst these redbrick streets. I was riding shotgun and could feel it getting dodgy. Well moody.

Women in burkhas, old men with their devout beards. Yeah, I pity the poor immigrant. Then it changed. There were groups of boys on the corners. Not Muslims, these boys were white. White as corpses they looked to me. In their Adidas uniforms. Their murder clothes. Then this one street had a sofa in the middle, like a throne, with a black kid sitting on it, his weapons on display around him. Including, I shit you not, a sword.

Around us now were burned out shops and houses with metal frames over the windows. That country's children were just one vicious sect after another. Real gang land. How it's going to be everywhere when the banks finally collapse.

So what does the driver do? The driver is the drummer, so what can you expect? The driver stops and asks how we get to the M6. Immediately there's a hammering on the sides of the van. Sound of breaking glass.

Christ, shouts the singer in the back, just get the hell out. And so we're haring through this maze and I stick 'Milk and Alcohol' on the CD player. Doctor Feelgood were the best road band ever and Wilko Johnson is still my favourite R&B guitarist. And we're all singing along to the track and laughing and generally pissing ourselves, and I even sang Memphis Minnie's 'Me and My Chauffeur Blues' for the drummer. Those boys had never heard it before. They thought it was a driving song. Bless their hearts.

What a strange brew on the Greyhound. Old codgers, Chinese girls. All gone to look for America. We were driving past these dismal swamps, and sometimes I could see a hunter in an orange jacket out in the trees, but people were rare. All around us were these reeds in the wall-eyed ice. I saw a programme about how those reeds are invading the country. I think they're Chinese, and they're tall and pale and everywhere. The reeds that are burying America. Then I glimpsed a hawk on a fence post, hunched like one of those hoodies in the Manchester rain.

About 4 p.m. we swung into a Burger King. I bought a

coffee and studied the men at the next table. Six old geezers, all looking eighty plus. And I thought, Jesus Christ, this must be their local pub. They meet here every Tuesday afternoon because there's nowhere else. Polystyrene cups and garbage on telly. They should be around a real fire with glasses of Saranac or tots of bourbon, telling tales of brave Ulysses. But when I listened in, it was all about rheumatism.

And the TV? It's a never-ending epitaph for this country. I did an unkind thing once. Woke up one day and Tom Jones was on Good Morning America. Live at 9 a.m. and still belting it out. Christ, I thought. Won't that man ever stop? So I wrote these words as a joke. Called the song 'Past It' and took the tune from Lennon's 'Crippled Inside', which I usually jump on my iPod. Slowed it down a shade. Yeah, I slow everything down. First verse was *Used to say about Tom / Was a real sex bomb /But since women's lib / He's been a damp squib.*

I did it in the KGB Club in the East Village. Some people laughed. At the end of the set this guy sidles up.

Liked the Tom Jones thing, he said.

Great, I said.

But I gotta question. What's that damp squid line all about?

Some things don't travel. Language doesn't always travel. They've never heard of a damp squib over here. Killed it as far as I'm concerned. So it's the UK only for that mother.

The Blue Tusk is going to be another nightmare. What was Amir playing at? It's a big bar in downtown Syracuse, boasting about its real ales and rare wines and whiskies. But it's a strange U shape without a proper stage. Not as bad as the Bowl but still a poor venue for someone like me. I need intimacy. Which I'll get in spades, but I mean tolerant intimacy. I know Amir's losing interest in the whole music business. It's film now. That's where the excitement is. Film it yourself, edit it yourself, be in control. Better than the same old songs done for drunks talking trash.

But seeing those old timers made me think of Dad. I'll try to ring him tomorrow. You see, I live with him. With my dad. I'm forty-eight, he's sixty-eight. And he's a heroin addict. When he's up for it he drives a shoprider around Asda. Like a demon. Got banned once and it was on the news. He was flying the skull and crossbones and blasting out 'I Wanna be Your Dog' by Iggy and the Stooges. He's been on the methadone but now he favours codeine in lemonade.

It was the drugs that made Mum leave. They'd been classic hippies, following the music from school, living in a commune. Mum had money from her parents so anything was possible. But Dad got in too deep. Did acid, then brown. Now he's a victim, a rock and roll suicide, who needs a carer. Usually me. He's sixty-eight and he's wasted.

Anyway, when I'm gigging, and it's not as often these days, the council takes over. As to Mum, she met this retired fellah, Brian. He had sold his building business and bought a house in the most southerly street in Wales, on the coast at Rhoose Point. She lives there most of the time. They've got the Bentley, the golf club membership, the apartment in Marbella, whilst me and Dad are in a flat in Topaz Street, Cardiff.

Sometimes we go down to the Millennium Stadium, him on the shoprider, or over to the Roath Cottage or The Canadian. I once did a set in the Cottage, especially for Dad. My 'Blues for Johnny Owen' always makes him cry. *Never been kissed, Johnny. Never been kissed.* And I looked at Dad and his eyes were alive for once. In that shrunken face. *And now you'll never know what it was you missed.*

Once or twice I take him to Spiller's to look at the records. But it's getting strange down there. All those apartments they've built block the light. Cardiff used to have this wonderful maritime glow. But it's lost. Cardiff has sold its soul. Like New York.

I showed Dad Bob Dylan's 'Bootleg Series: Volume 8, Rare and Unreleased'. You know what he said? Not really, he said.

I know what he means. Everything comes in a boxed set these days. All the mystery's gone. We never used to think about what was hidden in the vaults. Never used to bother. Or if we did, it was with this thrill of unknowing. Because little known is best known. The mystery was a mystery because it was a fucking mystery. Never demystify life. At least I've learned that. Now every muso's so self-aware they're hoarding their own shit and thinking it's gold bars.

I had dinner with Mum and her new hubby when I was last over. Really heavy cutlery but chicken from the house of pain. Free range was the least I expected. Christ, she used to be a vegan. I've changed, she hissed. And so should you.

We'd both had a drink. At least that stays the same. The house is on a promontory and the sea was filling the room. We held each other and looked into the spray coming over the cliff. We're like sisters really. There was a piano there and I plinked out a couple of tunes. Just stay in C, girl, and you can't go wrong. I did 'Imagine'. Yes, imagine that. And Mum sang along. She sang along with a crystal goblet in her hand and this hideous jewellery all over her beautiful skin. And we cried. We both cried. Brian stood there bewildered. With his brickie's hands. His red-brick face.

He wants to take her on cruises with retired bankers. The bankers who have destroyed the world. I went to the downstairs bathroom. There was a bidet there they wouldn't know how to use. A whirlpool bath with gold taps. Christ, Mum used to like the Incredible String Band. Time to grow up, Rhiannon, she hissed, when Brian went to get more valpolicella. Time to grow up, girl.

Yes, Rhiannon. I was about fourteen when the song came out. Stevie Nicks and the reincarnated Fleetwood Mac. Just a gorgeous tune. Mum and Dad used to sing it at me. Not to me. And of course I pretended to hate it. But it's been part of my set for years, a slower tempo, just me and the guitar. Some people at gigs think I wrote it.

Tonight I was going to do 'I Would Rather Go Blind', that

Christine Perfect thing. Just listen to her sing it and you can tell it's real. A woman's perfect pain. But the chords need to be sustained, like with an organ, so it's out. But it's a real bus station song. And I might do that Duffy tune, 'Warwick Avenue'. Christ, where did that chick come from? Newest kid on the block. And there are so many of them now. The bluesy girls. The winsome girls. Yes, here come the girls.

Maybe the world's trying to tell me something. My visa's up in three months and one of my front teeth is loose. So I eat with a limp. Proclivity they call my problem. Teeth are Dad's problem too. They're down to nasty brown stubs. The junkie's giveaway.

You know why he takes codeine? And all that H? To take away the feeling. The feeling of life. He lies on his bed, comfortably, unutterably numb, while the world slinks past on the Jeremy Kyle Show. His bed's in the front room of our downstairs flat. The shoprider is parked in the hall. Peer through the lace curtain and you'll see him, spark out most of the time. But dreaming. I'm sure he's still dreaming.

In front of me in the queue for the circular the little Mennonite girl looks round. She takes in my guitar case, then my leather jacket. I whisper *Beautiful dreamer, wake unto me, starlight and dewdrops are waiting for thee.*

That kid's got a hard face. Kind of flat. The words don't seem to register, but she goes on looking, keeps peeking at me from under her black bonnet, the hem of her cloak dragging in the wet. Such a serious child. Aw, honey. It's too early for you to be in mourning for the world.

Old People Are a Problem

Emyr Humphreys

I

Old people are a problem. What other conclusion could he come to? It seemed as though nothing on earth would persuade Mary Keturah Parry to move out of the chilly squalor of Soar chapel cottage into a comfortable room, or even a suite of rooms, in Cartref Residential Home. Alderman Parry-Paylin felt responsible for her. She was ninety-three and his mother's only surviving sister. And there was the question of how much time he could afford to spend on such a fruitless enterprise. He wasn't feeling too young himself. That very morning he had exhausted his strength trying to break in and then stable one of his mountain ponies. He was pushing sixty and made to realise how much stronger the pony was than himself. There was the depressing possibility, on such a bright summer morning, that he might have to give up this hobby. Then as if to demonstrate further the strength and intractability of youth, no sooner had he succeeded in stabling the wild animal than his only daughter turned up, breathless with triumph, from demonstrating and protesting in Genoa. And in tow, like campaign trophies, she brought a wispy unmarried mother and her snivelling offspring.

'Thought we could put them up for a while,' Iola said. 'A bit of rest and recuperation.'

It becomes clear that the young are a problem too. When your daughter corners you, it is hard to decide whether this world is too big or too small.

'Where has she been this time?'

His aunt was glaring at him as she crouched over a small fire, cooking peppermint cake in a dirty little saucepan. At the heart of the glare lay the congealed reproach of a lifetime. He had gone over to the enemy and she would never allow him to forget that that was still the way she looked at it. All he had done in effect was marry the daughter of Penllwyn Hall, in her view the pretentious home of a family of turncoats. At some stage well within Keturah Parry's copious memory, his late wife's grandfather, a mean and grasping quarry owner, had deserted Methodism for the established church. These fragments of local history did not concern him much, except to remind him, on occasions such as this, of the appalling narrowness of his aunt's views. They were no more relevant to modern living than her working wig that rested low over her forehead like an inverted bird's nest. He could never venture to laugh at her. She knew too much. He had a perfect right after his marriage to abandon primary school teaching, and to go into business in a limited way as a property developer, but she had a way of referring to the transformation as something vaguely discreditable. As far back as he could remember there was always accusation in her glance. When he was small in chapel, if he became restless during the service, she would never fail to transfix him with a glare across an expanse of sparsely populated pews.

'Genoa,' Mihangel Parry-Paylin said.

He pronounced the name clearly for the benefit of her hearing. She took quiet pleasure in getting it wrong.

'Geneva,' she said. '*From Bala to Geneva*. Nice little book. Things were so much more civilised in those days.'

623

She had acquired the perverse habit of appropriating the life experience of her parents' generation as her own. The world had taken a definite wrong turning in 1914. The Alderman said that may well have been the case: but since Keturah was only seven at the time, there would have been very little she could have done about it.

'Genoa,' he said. 'Where those terrible riots took place. A young lad was shot dead there.'

'I haven't got a television,' she said. 'You know that.'

She had a wireless that was fifty years old but she only heard what she wanted to hear. She liked to complain about Radio Cymru. Too much noise and not enough sermons.

'I've been telling you for years, Mihangel Paylin,' she said. 'You spoil that girl.'

He could only agree with her. On the other hand, what else could he have done? She was still in school when she lost her mother and he lost a wonderful wife. Easy enough for an old witch to talk. What had she ever lived for except the chapel and the good name of her family: and both these were no more, he suspected, than extended aspects of her own absorption in herself. All these things he thought and could never really tell anyone since Laura died. His closest friend Morus had moved to live in the Dordogne. His daughter Iola had driven off Charlotte Sinclair, who with a great deal of persuading, might have become his second wife, on the grounds that she was too English and should never be allowed to defile her mother's bed or Penllwyn, which was in fact her mother's inheritance.

'You want to bring her to heel,' Auntie Keturah said. 'I've told you before. Her mother was weak enough with her. Spare the rod and spoil the child.'

Mihangel Paylin sat in the uncomfortable wooden chair despairing of his situation. No movement seemed possible on any front. His only daughter was impervious to argument. This old woman would never budge. She loved squatting in her squalor, so what could he do about it? He looked up at the shelf above the open fireplace and stared at a tin with Mr Gladstone's stern features painted on it, staring back at him. That was where she kept her pennies for the Foreign Mission. They were still there long after pennies had ceased to be legal tender. That's the kind of woman she was. Wedded to the past. Like one of those clothed and crowned skeletons that hang in the crypts of Sicilian churches. A bride of silence. If the chapel was to be sold somehow or other she had to be moved out. As things stood she would only leave feet first in a box.

And how are things at home he asked himself. Will somebody tell me exactly what is happening?

II

The first thing he noticed in the dining room was the absence of his framed photograph on the Welsh dresser. It was taken when he was the youngest mayor ever to be elected by the County Council. He wore the splendid mayoral robes. The chain itself was worth several thousand pounds. A colour photograph, tastefully lit, demanded a substantial frame. There was no good reason why a man should not be allowed to take a certain pride in his appearance and achievements. People had been known to remark he was a fine figure of a man.

'Where's my picture?'

Iola was fussing about helping the unmarried mother to feed her little son who seemed to be rejecting unfamiliar food.

'In the drawer, with your albums. Standing behind the Queen opening the new bypass. Church parade in full regalia. It's all there. Safe and sound.'

'What did you want to do that for?'

'Well it's a bit out of date, isn't it? And you wouldn't want people to think you were self-important, would you?'

Who were 'people'? This wretched girl and her wretched

boy. Iola said her name was Maristella and the boy she called Nino. What were they to him that his daughter should remove his mayoral portrait from its place of honour on the dresser? The furnishing at Penllwyn was unchanged since his wife died. And she in her day had cherished her family antiques with a religious care. They still stood as memorials of her quiet devotion – in such contrast to his daughter's iconoclastic inclinations. Did the girl do anything these days except protest, and when she could spare the time, call the whole purpose of his way of life into question? It was his habit to be genial and generous. They were essential qualities for public life. Smiles all round. You needed to work the familiar streets, dispensing cheerful greetings and armed with pockets full of goodwill. Did that mean he had to be genial and generous to this unlikely pair? He had a legal right to turn them out. Flotsam and jetsam didn't have a vote. There were facts to be established. He addressed his daughter in a tongue the new arrivals could not understand.

'Where did you find this one?' he said.

He made a stiff effort to be judicious and impartial.

'On the ground,' Iola said. 'A policeman was kicking her. And hitting her with a truncheon.'

He knew these things happened. Outside the limits of his council's administration there existed a dangerous world. There was his regular evening television viewing to demonstrate this ferocious fact. But why should his only daughter want to plunge into the heart of it? Such a perfect quiet child. She was twelve when she lost her mother and a light went out of his life. She grieved so quietly. So intense. So determined. It was only worrying about her, and the increasing demands of public life – he would tell sympathetic colleagues when they were inclined to listen – that kept him sane. She showed every sign of academic brilliance. And then just before her sixteenth birthday a police car brought her home from some large-scale language protest. Her forehead was bleeding and he had never seen her look happier. That had to be the take-off of a great career of protest. For years it was something to tolerate. From prison or from foreign parts she would come limping home to recuperate. He could not but welcome her. She was his only daughter. Remonstration proved ineffective. Iola was an excellent cook and it became her practice to prepare a celebration supper as soon as she felt she had recovered. This, however was a new departure and it made him nervous. This was his home; his citadel. He needed the privacy, the space; the relaxation that belongs to a proprietor at the heart of his estate. Did she propose to turn it into a refugee centre?

'We won't be in your way, Mici Paylin.'

She had a way of creating a variety of versions of his name and using them, in the first instance, as badges of affection. As time went on and he felt her character toughen, it would all depend on her tone of voice: it could vary from habitual affection to thinly veiled contempt. With both these women, as it were at both ends of his life's candle, he was obliged to be so circumspect. They had never much taken to each other. His theory used to be, because they were too alike: stubborn and intractable. Even when Iola was small her great-aunt was displeased with her prolonged stubborn silences. 'I don't understand this girl at all,' she would say, as if her inability to fathom Iola's hidden depths was entirely the little girl's fault. And now when Keturah Parry was clinging so stubbornly to her unhygienic and desperately independent life, he had noticed how little interest and sympathy his daughter had with the old woman's predicament. 'Go and visit your aunt,' he would say. 'She doesn't want to see me,' she would answer. 'We don't have anything to say to each other. We live in two different worlds. It's your problem, Alderman Paylin,' she would say. As if it were only one more of his civic responsibilities instead of a family problem that reached in fact, right back to his childhood and even to his birth. With all her capacity for indignation, Iola could be quite heartless.

'I need help in the house and in the garden. There's an awful lot to be done. You'll be free to attend even more committees, Mici P. Think how much more good you'll be able to do.'

Was that snide or was it sincere? These were the questions that beset him latterly almost whenever his daughter spoke. How much good in fact did he do? Public Health, Education, Ways and Means, Planning. Why should there always be a question mark over Planning? There was a crying need for better housing and it had been no more than coincidental that the three barren fields below the closed quarry were part of the Penllwyn estate. It was a social necessity, and the purchase price came at a crucial time.

'I think you ought to know, Alderman Paylin. Maristella and your darling daughter have been through the fire together.'

He inquired more closely. It transpired that Maristella had been tear-gassed at the EU summit in Nice. This had aroused her ire and stiffened her sinews. Protesters of the world unite! You have nothing to lose except your unemployment benefit. The world was disintegrating and there were fragments flying in all directions and what good was that supposed to do? There was a string of sarcastic remarks he could make that remained stillborn in his brain. He managed to mutter a question in Welsh about the identity of the little boy's father.

'She was raped.'

Iola snapped her answer out rather than saying it. For a moment she seemed to be the voice of women through the ages. It was up to him to accept the universal guilt of his sex.

'By a Corsican.'

And that was that. The subject was closed. He could not inquire whether there were black Corsicans. Any further enquiry would have been unpardonably indelicate. He had his own thoughts to cultivate. What was this girl any more than one of those decorative drifters who hung about Riviera resorts? She knew how to be still and unobtrusive like a piece of furniture. It was possible to discern that, in her own fragile way, she had once been decorative. And here they were, old comrades in arms, who couldn't have known each other more than three weeks or possibly a month: and Iola using a blowlamp flame of enthusiasm to create twin souls. Strangers were settling under his roof protected and patronised by his only daughter and there was so little he could do about it. At what point would he be able to inquire more closely into her motives and purposes?

'I thought I'd make a bread and butter pudding, Tada. Would you like that?'

The least he could do was show he was melted for the time being by the warmth of her smile.

III

In the damp vestry of Soar chapel Mihangel Paylin marvelled at the transformation in his aunt's appearance. And in her manner. She was no longer an ancient witch, crouching over a bunch of hot cinders, stirring a brew in a battered saucepan. In some way she was more alarming. A lighter wig was mostly concealed by a black hat of ancient vintage trimmed with a skimpy veil. The black costume she wore had a green tinge and a square shouldered wartime cut. He saw her as an emaciated simulacrum of the stern deacon and Sunday School teacher who had tyrannised his childhood. The washing facilities in Soar cottage across the road were limited. In any case it was possible that in old age Keturah had got out of the habit. The creases on her neck and the wrinkles on her face seemed lined with venerable grime. She had unlocked a safe and was laying out documents on the green baize of the deacon's table.

'You will be fascinated by this, Dr Derwyn. A membership paper. Or ticket should I say? Dated April 15th 1819. "Let it be known that Jane Amelia Parry who bears this paper is a full member of the Christian Society gathered in Soar chapel, Llandawel." Isn't it wonderful?'

Dr Derwyn Dexter had no choice but to agree. He was a tall thin man with a prominent nose and a small mouth set in a propitiating smile. Since he had been placed in charge of the university archive he had cultivated a manner of inoffensive shrewdness.

'Well yes indeed,' he said. 'Yes indeed.'

He clasped his hands behind his back and bent to scrutinise the faded paper more closely.

'My great great-great-grandmother,' Keturah said. 'She thought nothing of walking thirty miles to a preaching meeting.'

Her voice was loud with triumph. Dr Dexter half turned to indicate that by the same token Jane Amelia would have been related to Alderman Paylin too, since his late mother was Keturah's sister. To Keturah in her present elevated mood this could be no more than a peripheral detail.

'1822 this sanctuary was built on the foundation of the original chapel which had been a barn. "A delightful wayside temple," Dr Peate called it. I was standing just there when he said it. "If I had the funds," he said, "I would love to transport this chapel stone by stone all the way to the Folk Museum at St Fagans." "No indeed," old William Cae Clai said. "Indeed not, Dr Peate. This is a place of worship and it shall remain so as long as I live." "Well of course William Jones" Dr Peate said. "Quite right too". Poor William did not live so long after that.'

Dr Derwyn saw a chance for a pleasant diversion.

'Ah, Dr Peate,' he said. 'He put me in the second class for the Crown Poem in '74 was it? He was dead against *vers libre*. "If this competitor is under twenty-one, there is still hope for him." I was twenty-seven at the time so I gave up competing. No crown for me. He knew his stuff though. About architecture. And about poetry if it comes to that. I was never meant to be a poet.'

Keturah Parry paid little attention to the archivist's anecdote. She had the pressing anxiety of a peasant woman who has arrived late at the market to display her wares. From a drawer in the deacon's table she extracted a rusty key that opened the stiff door of a wall cupboard. Inside there were stacks of notebooks.

'Now this is something,' she said. 'Really something. The sermons of five generations of ministers. And all of them notable preachers. Just look at them.'

Mihangel Parry-Paylin shuffled to one side and left the responsibility of looking to the archivist. Keturah took down a notebook as if to display a sample. She opened it and held it at a distance to read the handwriting.

'"*Beloved, now are we the sons of God, and it doth not appear what we shall be*"... John Jones' last sermon. My grandmother remembered it you know. The chapel was full to overflowing and they sang, she said, full of joy and thanksgiving for the blessing of holy eloquence. It all happened here. Those were the days, Dr Derwyn. Those were the days. They had something to sing about.'

Keturah stared at each of the men in turn defying them to disagree with her assessment.

'A better world inside these walls,' she said. 'Simple people wrapped in love and righteousness.'

Dr Derwyn felt obliged to make a judicious comment.

'A simpler world certainly,' he said. 'Less complex. Less loaded with distractions.'

'It will come again,' the old woman said. 'It will come again. Only if we keep the flame alight. John Jones had a wonderful sermon you know on the parable of the ten virgins. The church is One you see. The living and the dead keep the lamp burning. We need money Dr Derwyn. There's the roof you see and other repairs. Now then. If you take this wonderful collection of documents into your care, the question is how far could you help us?'

Dr Derwyn's small mouth opened and shut as he pondered

631

a sufficiently tactful reply. Keturah made a visible effort to contain her impatience.

'Men like to talk business,' she said. 'Mihangel here is a Trustee. We have to save this place one way or another. I'll go and make a cup of tea.'

Leaning on her stick she moved carefully to the small kitchen and scullery attached to the vestry. She opened the rear door to empty the teapot of a previous infusion. An early section of the graveyard stretched between this rear door and the lean-to toilets that needed painting. The headstones were mostly in slate and dated from the nineteenth century.

Alderman Parry-Paylin took hold of Dr Derwyn's arm and led him into the body of the chapel. They were in solemn mood, both very conscious of their responsibilities. They sat close to each other in the shadow of the mahogany pulpit, so that they could exchange views without being overheard by the old woman. Because of the reverberation in the chapel their voices barely rose above a whisper.

'Don't think I am unsympathetic,' the Alderman said. 'But you can see my difficulty, can't you?'

'Difficulty?'

Dr Derwyn repeated the word slowly as if he were trying to give himself more time to think. He found himself in a situation far more awkward than he had anticipated. His best defence was an air of unworldly detachment. Mihangel's whisper grew more vehement. It seemed to whistle through his clenched teeth.

'What are we reduced to?' he said. 'This place has more trustees than members. Could this be described as a building of distinction? I hardly think so. I expect Dr Peate was just being nice to the old people. He could see how much Soar meant to them. In any case, it was a long time ago. I was never all that happy here myself. She was a bit of a tyrant you know in her day. A fierce spinster. She disapproved of my father. He was a sailor and he had no business to go and get himself torpedoed. She doesn't really approve of me either. Just because I married into a family of better off Methodists. Talk about sectarianism. Makes you think, doesn't it?'

Dr Derwyn had come to a decision.

'We could take those papers and all the written records,' he said. 'And care for them properly. But we couldn't pay for them. A courtesy *ex gratia* maybe, but nothing more than that. As you well know these things are regulated by market forces. I don't suppose there is an overwhelming demand for handwritten sermons in our dear old language.'

The acoustic was too sensitive to allow them to chuckle at his mild academic joke. Alderman Mihangel Parry-Paylin clenched his fist under his moustache to demonstrate the intensity of his sincerity.

'I try to be understanding,' he said. 'And tolerant. It's no use being in public life without being tolerant on a wide range of issues. The truth is she lives in the past.'

He made a sweeping gesture to implicate the rows of empty pews in front of them.

'She still sees this place filled with God-fearing peasants. A whole world away. And what kept them in good order? Fear. The fear of death. Weren't they dropping like flies under things like typhoid and tuberculosis? The NHS with all its faults has done away with that, for God's sake. So what is she on about? I used to sit over there you know and sit as still as a graven image while some old preacher went droning on, just in case she should catch me fidgeting or sucking a sweet. She could glare like a basilisk. She still can when she feels like it. You can see what she's like can't you?'

This was a whispered appeal for sympathetic understanding. Dr Derwyn was minded to be put in possession of more of the facts before he could unreservedly extend it. He knew the Alderman was Chairman of the County Council Planning committee as well as a Trustee of the chapel.

'Forgive me for asking but am I right in thinking this chapel is scheduled for demolition?'

Mihangel Parry-Paylin could only lean forward to bury his face in both hands. Dr Derwyn was moved by the strength of his reaction.

'I'm sorry,' he said. 'I didn't wish to be inquisitive. It is widely rumoured. And these things are happening. I read something in the *Chronicle* that said they were still coming down throughout the Principality at the rate of one a fortnight.'

He submitted this as a melancholy statistic from which the Alderman might derive some comfort. The moving finger of history had written and in its own roughshod manner was moving on.

'It isn't that,' Parry-Paylin said.

He stared into the middle distance as if it were inhabited by a seething multitude of problems.

'It wouldn't worry me all that much to see the place come down. It's the vested interests involved. You are lucky, Doctor Derwyn. You don't have to deal with vested interests.'

'Oh I wouldn't say that...' The archivist was unwilling to have the difficulties of his profession diminished.

'People can be very sentimental,' Parry-Paylin said. 'You can't ignore that. And yet in public life the guiding principle must be the greater good of the greatest number. The road needs widening. There can be no question about that. On the grounds of public safety. On grounds of commercial and industrial necessity. There are jobs involved. And progress. There's always progress isn't there with a capital 'P'. Politicians can't survive without visible Progress. She's ninety-three. She can't live for ever. The roof is leaking. Who is going to pay? Should we let the weather and neglect finish the job. You see my difficulty?'

His jaw froze as he heard his aunt's measured approach. She appeared in the open door to practice a gesture of old-fashioned hospitality.

'Now come along, gentlemen. What about a nice cup of tea?'

IV

The sun shone and the verandah's sharp shadow spread across the drive as far as the first herbaceous border. The Alderman paced back and forth somewhat in the manner of a captain on the bridge of his ship. In the bright light of morning the problems that beset him had to be more amenable to solution. There had to be a residue of authority in the very place where he stood. His late wife's great-grandfather had been far sighted enough to build his mansion on the brow of a hill that commanded a view of a magnificent mountain range, as well as the slate quarry he needed to keep an eye on. The quarry had long been closed and the bitter criticisms Mary Keturah made about the old minister's hypocrisy and bogus religiosity were no longer in any way relevant: nevertheless the owner of Penllwyn (the 'Hall' had been dropped on the insistence of his dear wife who found it insufferably pretentious) was in an ideal position to lift up his eyes to the hills from which help and inspiration were bound to come to a man of goodwill such as himself, devoted to public service.

He stretched himself and blinked in the sunlight. There were interesting smells wafting through the open kitchen window where his daughter Iola was busying herself with baking cakes. From the walled garden he could hear the little boy Nino laughing as he dodged about the raspberry canes while his mother picked the fruit. Iola had persisted in drawing his attention to how phenomenally well behaved the little boy was; not to mention his mother who seemed to tremble gently in her anxiety to please.

Iola insisted that a great movement of peoples was taking place: not unlike the great waves of emigration that gave the nineteenth century its special character. He smiled as he took in her youthful exaggerations. At the same time he acknowledged it was wise for a man in public life to lend an ear to what the young were saying. There were great unseen forces at work as difficult to fathom and control as the world's weather. And since his house had nine bedrooms he had to admit he was in a privileged position. He had to accept that it was her benevolent intention to lead him gently into the new paths and patterns of positive existence. 'You are never too old to learn, Mici?' she said. Her innovations, surprising as they were, he had to believe would in no way detract from his civic responsibilities; it was up to him to make sure that, if anything, they would enhance them. It was not impossible at any rate while the sun shone, that he would come to be proud of his daughter's colourful eccentricities.

The little boy's laugh provided the amenities of Penllwyn with a new and pleasant dimension. It was Parry-Paylin's habit before committee meetings to take a walk in the wooded area above the house in order to rehearse arguments and sometimes test oratorical phrases aloud. Primroses grew among the trees in the spring and crocuses in the autumn. He was always ready to enthuse about the views he could enjoy throughout the changing seasons. Yesterday he had looked down at a wild corner of the gardens and saw the little boy chasing butterflies among the overgrown buddleia bushes. He was raising his little arms and trying to fly himself. The Alderman was so pleased with what he saw he wanted to race down the slope and chase the butterflies himself.

Bicycle wheels crunched across the drive and a young man braked and skidded with a flourish, to pull up in front of where the Alderman was standing with his hands behind his back enjoying the undisturbed beauty of the morning.

'Lovely day, isn't it?'

The Alderman had little choice but to agree. The young man's hair was dyed yellow and sprouted around in indiscriminate directions. It wasn't a spectacle that he could contemplate with pleasure and he was obliged to look up at the sky as though a sudden thought had occurred to him he needed to hold on to.

'Iola back then? Hell of a girl, isn't she?'

This wasn't a statement he could disagree with either. This was Moi Twm, Iola's friend and devoted admirer. Not a suitor he had long been given to understand by his only daughter. This only brought limited relief. They were, Iola said, 'partners in crime'. What could that mean except, an unappetising procession of raucous protests? Moi Twm kept a bookshop in an unfrequented corner of the market town. The books in the window were fading in spite of the cellophane he wrapped around them. He lived behind the shop among heaps of magazines and papers and flags and slogans of protests gone by. It was his way of life he said. Living on a pittance was the best guarantee of eternal youth. This light-heartedness might fill his daughter with admiration; all it brought him was suspicion and foreboding. He had an Uncle Ted who wrote a muckraking column in the local weekly. Uncle Ted followed the proceedings of the Council with relentless diligence. The more so because he had failed to get on the Council himself. There was always the possibility Moi Twm could wheedle secrets out of Iola; which meant he had to take extra care when talking to his own daughter: and that in itself was an unnatural curtailment on the resources of family life. If he couldn't talk to his own daughter, who else could he confide in? It all made the business of local government more irksome than it needed to be. And this thin and hungry-looking young man with his silly hair a less than welcome visitor.

'I wanted to see you too, Alderman, Sir. If you can spare a moment.'

Moi Twm had a trick of cackling merrily as though the simplest statements he came out with were potentially a huge joke. Iola had said she couldn't be sure whether this was evidence of a depth of insecurity, a need for affection or just a nervous tick; whenever he heard it the Alderman closed his eyes and racked his brain for an avenue of escape.

'About Soar chapel, Alderman Paylin. I've got just the answer. A rescue operation.'

The alderman restrained himself from saying Soar chapel was none of his business. His long experience of public life had taught him the value of a judicious silence.

'It could make a lovely bookshop of course,' Moi Twm said. 'But Miss Parry would never allow that would she? She's a hell of a girl, I have to say, but we have to respect her wishes.'

Parry-Paylin winced in anticipation of another cheerful cackle.

'You must know this,' Moi Twm said. 'Being one of the children of Soar yourself. But I have to say it came as a complete surprise to me. R. J. Cethin was the minister at Soar for ten months in 1889.'

The alderman did not know this and saw no reason why he should have known. The name of R. J. Cethin meant little to him. Moi Twm was an amateur antiquarian as well as a bookseller and he had an irritating habit of displaying his arcane knowledge at inopportune moments. It often came with a brief cackle.

'A deep dark secret,' he said. 'At Soar I mean. You wouldn't have heard Miss Keturah mention it, I expect?'

'I wouldn't be sure,' the alderman said.

He resented being cross-examined. A shuffle of his feet on the verandah floor suggested he had more important matters calling for his attention.

'I dug into it,' Moi Twm said. 'Nothing I enjoy more than a bit of research. There was just a paragraph in the old *North Wales Gazette* for February 1890. But it was enough to give the game away. The fact is he got the organist's daughter pregnant. They fled and started a new life in the United Sates. He became pastor of a Unitarian Church in Toledo, Ohio. And began to write pamphlets in English about workers' rights and female emancipation and all that sort of thing. Author of *Christ the Socialist*, *The Church against Poverty*, and *The Land for the Poor and the Poor for the Land*. He's very well known over there now. As a pioneer. Not much honour for a prophet in his own country though. The old story Alderman Paylin.'

There was a powerful cackle.

'Anyway, I don't want to keep you. Now this is my idea. Why not turn Soar into a nice little museum? A tourist attraction you could call it on the lowest level, so to speak. But in the true interest of culture and local history it could really be made into something. With your personal associations, it could be a jewel in your crown. So to speak. Don't take any notice of my frivolous manner, Mr Paylin. It's a silly habit I can't get out of. I'm making a serious suggestion. And who would have thought of it. The great R. J. Cethin the minister of Soar chapel Llandawel. Ten months or ten years. What does it matter? And the organist's daughter into the bargain. I haven't investigated her background yet. But it's bound to have interesting local connections. As you said in the council last month. We needed to diversify. In the face of the decline of agriculture and the quarries closed and being too remote to attract new industry. Tourism is our best chance. Our best resource if handled properly. With taste and discretion of course. How else?'

The alderman gave so deep a sigh, the young man grew apologetic. For the first time his enthusiasm subsided sufficiently for him to become aware of another person's reactions. For the alderman, he had taken the bloom off the morning.

'It's only an idea,' Moi Twm said. 'I just thought I'd mention it. A contribution. People ought to know about these things.'

The alderman's silence implied he was wondering whether in fact they should. He was startled by a yelp of delight as his daughter rushed out of the house. Down on the drive below him, Moi Twm and Iola became locked in a fierce embrace. They were like two footballers who had managed to pierce the defence and score the winning goal. He had to look away. He was always embarrassed by too much explicit emotion. And it was hardly right that these young things should be so close. People were talking freely about 'partners' these days. In that case could someone tell him what was to become of the family? It was as if he had to live with a veiled threat of being thrust out of his own nest.

'You little devil,' Moi Twm was saying. 'You just shot off without telling me. Without a word. I'm furious with you. You know that, don't you?'

'Listen you old bookworm. I've got a surprise for you. A lovely surprise.'

'Chocolates? Pearls? Green bananas?'

She took his hand and dragged him towards the walled garden.

'Something you've been looking for, for ages. The nicest girl you could ever wish to meet.'

V

In a matter of days Iola established a routine at Penllwyn that her father found moderately reassuring. Price the gardener who came three half-days a week remarked, not for the first time, how much she reminded him of her dear mother and how Iola had always been a young lady who had a way with her. This was the kind of music the alderman liked to hear and he heard it again from Mrs Twigg the diminutive cleaner who was ever faithful but had a chronic inability to detect dust anywhere higher than her eye level. Maristella and the boy Nino were proving satisfyingly low-pitched and even docile. It amused him to detect that when they passed his study they moved on tiptoe. The flow of chatter through the house did not disturb him unduly. When he stopped to listen it was invariably Iola that was doing most of the talking. The guidelines of dispensation had been laid down skilfully enough to avoid disrupting in any way his own focused way of life.

It was summer and the new arrivals had contrived to make themselves pleasing figures in the landscape. Maristella had a knowledge of plants and was very willing to go on her knees and do some weeding, even without gloves. In the orchard, Price the gardener put up a primitive swing for the little boy and Iola drew her father's attention to the child's remarkable capacity for amusing himself for hours on end. 'It's the Garden of Eden for the child,' she said in a subdued tone that was loaded with darker implications. It suggested too that her father could derive satisfaction from the knowledge that he had helped to rescue a child from an unmentionable fate. The Corsican father was a gendarme in Marseilles notorious for his brutality. The Alderman would have liked to learn more. He had to be content with the knowledge that Maristella, in spite of her courageous nature was extraordinarily naive. Her father must have noticed, Iola said with a passing sigh, how often it happened that nice girls were taken in by the most awful shits. It was in the end a phenomenon that could only be attributed to some obscure force that surfaced from a primaeval past in the animal kingdom.

Supper time became a pleasing occasion. The strangers were transformed into guests and out of courtesy the Alderman spoke more English. Maristella for her part clenched her small fist and declared her firm intention to dysgu Cymraeg. This caused much pleasant laughter. The Alderman was especially pleased when Iola prepared a lamb stew with mixed herbs in exactly the way her mother used to do. It was in the middle of this meal, he could only assume for want of a fresh crusade, that she returned to the attack.

'I hear there are plans afoot to bury toxic waste at the bottom of Cloddfa Quarry.'

Alderman Paylin looked longingly at his plate. There was a lot of delicious stew left and he would have liked to enjoy it in peace.

'In a democracy I suppose we have to put up with

incredibly stupid and vulgar politicians. At least until the population arrives at a higher level of education: and that seems a long way off. But you are in a position of authority, Tada. You can make decisions. Or see to it that decisions are made. Whose idea was it?'

Public life could never be that easy. The blonde bookseller, and his daughter's bosom friend, had this horrid uncle who wrote a column in the local paper and haunted council meetings in search of scandal and the raw material of muckraking.

'Planning.'

He answered briefly, in the vain hope of heading off further discussion.

'Well, that's your committee, isn't it? Your special baby!'

'We are running out of landfill sites,' he said. 'In a high consumption society, this is becoming a problem.'

'Everything is a problem with you Alderman Paylin. It's not problems we need. It's solutions. What about this cyanide business?'

'Cyanide? Who said anything about cyanide?'

He was provoked and his stew had gone cold.

'Moi Twm's Uncle Ted. And when Ted's your uncle you can smell monkey business a mile off. Who is the Treasurer of the golf club these days?'

'Ennis Taft. And has been for years. As you well know.'

'Taft Bronco Products. With cyanide drums to dispose of before they can sell their redundant premises for redevelopment.'

The Alderman raised his hand to his brow and Maristella looked at him anxiously. Plainly her genial benefactor had been struck by a sudden headache. The Alderman rubbed his forehead and wondered why the resemblance between his dear wife and only daughter should be so superficial. Laura was a romantic and an idealist in her own way. She had none of this unwholesome passion for smelling rats and conspiracies all over the place. It had to be a generational change of consciousness. This was just the kind of philosophic thing his friend Morus loved discussing. Perhaps it was time to take a holiday in the Dordogne. Summer should be a time to relax and reflect and recuperate. Perhaps he was getting too old and shouldering too many responsibilities.

'It's up to you to put a stop to it, Tada. They're our quarries after all.'

Did 'our' mean she was anticipating her inheritance? Why should she make these hints and threats when all he had done, all his life, was cherish her. At the first opportunity he excused himself and made for an early bed. Whichever way he laid his pillows, sleep eluded him. This was an annoyance in itself. He was a man who depended on and cherished eight hours solid sleep. His window was open and as the sun went down there was a noisy commotion among the crows' nests in the tallest trees above the house.

It seemed as if he could cope with anything except what was left of his own family. Long ago the family had been a source of strength and encouragement. He had his mother's resolve and courage to emulate. When his father was lost at sea, she went out to work as a daily domestic in order that her Mihangel should enjoy a proper education. They had lived in a small terrace house with his grandmother and both women had seen to it he was well fed and given peace and quiet to study before the open fire in the little parlour. The initial objections to his marriage to the heiress of Penllwyn Hall were overcome and the family background and family backing were enlarged and immensely strengthened. His father-in-law became his mentor and patron. Now it was all gone. All that remained was a cantankerous maiden aunt and a headstrong daughter.

The sad fact was that he enjoyed more encouragement and companionship in the golf club than in his own home. After a prolonged tussle in the Ways and Means committee where else could he turn to for a drink and a joke and a measure of innocent relaxation? Old Ennis Taft would be waiting there at the bar, ready to slap him on the back or on the shoulder and say things like, 'Now then San Fihangel, what are you going to have?' Ennis was on all the committees raising funds for all the charities God sends. It helped to soothe his conscience. He said so himself. 'Not that I've got all that much. It's drinks and laughter and fair play and decency. And a bit of a sing-song. Those are things that mark the man of goodwill, San Fihangel. Now then, how about another?'

It was possibly Ennis' whisky-soaked lips that let those wretched drums of cyanide out of the bag. He was too fond of boasting about his wealth and influence. Uncle Ted had his spies in the golf club. What harm could a few drums of cyanide do buried deep in the bottom of the quarry? Poison the water supply once the drums had rusted away. Always ready with an answer, Iola. How could a man sleep in peace in his own bed in his own house?

In the end he fell into a trouble-haunted sleep only to be awakened by a piercing scream and then the wail and whimper of a child crying. He sat up in bed seething with indignation. There was a full moon and in the wardrobe mirror he could see a white ghost that was nothing more than his own dishevelled image. A man devoted to public service deserved a decent night's sleep. There were more committees tomorrow and he would need all his wits about him to steer through a minefield of amendments. There were enemies on all sides ready to oppose the creation of positive compromise. He was in the chair precisely because of his ability to steer though the waves of controversy to the calm water of any other business. Was there singing going on as well as wailing? He could never get back to sleep. He was the victim of his own benevolence.

There was a piercing scream, he swore, sufficient to shatter the universe. He had to get up and register stern disapproval. This was the kind of disturbance that should not be allowed to continue. It may be a city was going up in flames and his mother was lying unconscious in the street and the tentacles of anarchy were tightening around his little throat so he had to scream; but it had to stop. Down a moonlit corridor he saw Maristella sitting on the floor outside the door of the little boy's bedroom. She was in a skimpy nightdress, nursing a large white bath towel. She said she was waiting there in case little Nino woke up again.

'They come sometimes,' she said. 'These nightmares. Soaking in sweat. I think it is my fault.'

He could only respond with a sympathetic stance.

'I'm afraid he will disturb Iola,' Maristella said. 'Iola can't function without her eight hours' sleep.'

The phrase was so obviously his daughter's. Repeated in this soft exotic accent it sounded like a confession of faith. He was abruptly reminded of his own long-suffering mother and his own childhood.

'I had nightmares,' he said. 'When I was small. I used to think I was drowning. Sinking to the very bottom of the sea.'

This was another mother trying to bring up a fatherless son. An emblem of anxiety, patience, and suffering.

'If it is my fault,' she said. 'He may grow up to hate me.'

The alderman smiled to reassure her.

'I don't think so,' he said. 'I don't think so at all.'

She raised a hand to let it rest on his arm. The scent of tender feminine concern was a comfort he had forgotten.

'You are so good to us,' Maristella said. 'So good. We thank you.'

When he returned to his bedroom it seemed emptier than when he left it. There were forms of consolation, beyond language, that could still exist.

VI

A series of meetings of local government specialists called the alderman first to Cardiff and then to London. He fussed over the preparation but it was a relief to get away. At meal times when he was inclined to make polite inquiries into the kind of life that his guests had emerged from, it seemed incredible that such a docile creature as Maristella had been turned out of a prosperous home in Bordighera. Iola would commandeer the conversation with more probing questions about the Council's planning policies and particularly about the extension of the landfill in Cloddfa Quarry. When Iola spoke Maristella lapsed into respectful silence. It was difficult too for him to establish any reaction on her part to Iola's sporadic and rather crude efforts to push the unmarried mother in Moi Twm's direction. Could both the creatures be so much under his daughter's thumb that they would go to any length to please her? It was none of his business and yet he had a right to know what was going on under his own roof. He found Moi Twm's increasingly frequent visits distinctly nerve-racking. He claimed now to have established contact with a R. J. Cethin Society, in Toledo, Ohio, through the internet. He also claimed that Dr Derwyn the college archivist was showing a keen interest in his discoveries. He even had the temerity to suggest he interviewed Miss Keturah Parry. He was certain the old woman would have more information about the affair with the organist's daughter. In such a closed society, he argued, knowledge of such a scandal would be vigorously suppressed but not forgotten. There could even be papers still kept under lock and key.

The meetings in Cardiff and London were pleasant occasions. His expenses were paid and comfortable accommodation provided. There was the mild excitement of brief conversations with celebrated politicians. Old acquaintances were renewed and new friendships made warm with promises of being useful in the future. An old farmer who used to accompany him earlier in his civic career called the process 'setting out mole traps.' A more recent phrase he learnt was 'networking.' The meetings resembled social occasions enlivened with a measure of pomp and conviviality. Consensus or a genial agreement to postpone were both easy to arrive at. This led him to observe to jovial colleagues that government on the larger scale was infinitely more tractable than squabbles on the home patch.

However diverting the excursion, he was always glad to catch the first glimpse of Penllwyn in the taxi from the station. The old minister had set that stark strong square house on the brow of the hill and it still exuded its own endowment of mid-Victorian confidence. He had designed the place himself, and in a sense it would have been true to say he was monarch of all he surveyed: the theocratic ruler of pulpit and workplace, composing sermons and hymn tunes, and opening quarries and investing in ships that seemed to have gone down in storms with monotonous regularity. There was something about the old man's arrogance that made the Alderman shudder slightly and he had been relieved when his late wife removed the full-length portrait in oil from the drawing room to the attic. The past was to muse upon at leisure, the present was alive with problems that cried out to be solved. There were clouds scudding along high in the blue sky above the hill and he was glad to be home.

The house was empty and it was the sound of the little boy's laughter that led him to the orchard. There his mother was rocking him to and fro in the swing Price the gardener had put up for him. She pushed the swing with one hand and with the other held on to a floppy hat that threatened to fly away in the breeze. She wore a thin pink and white frock, and mother and son together made an attractive picture. He took his time before making his presence known.

'Where is everyone?'

It was something to say. He didn't really want to know. It was agreeable to have the place to themselves.

'They have gone to the Rally in Caernarfon,' she said. 'In support of the coffee workers of Nicaragua. Iola leaves me to look after your house. And my son of course.'

'You mean Iola and her partners in crime.'

Maristella took time to interpret the phrase and decide whether or not the alderman was joking. She offered to make tea and he was pleased to accept. She was a good listener whether or not she understood everything he was saying. For too long the house had lacked the attentions of a woman prepared to listen to a man of some consequence who returns from a conference primed with telltale fragments of the gossip of high politics. Ministers spoke more freely in a convivial social context. Would Maristella be interested to know that the minister had pulled a grim face and said something needed to be done about the Teachers Union? Her response would be more satisfying than his daughter's. All he would have got from Iola would be yet another disparaging remark.

'Alderman...'

She had something to ask. Was it too soon to suggest she used a less formal mode of address? Was there too wide a gap between his title and his first name? Would she have been able to pronounce Mihangel? Iola's frivolous modes of address could well have confused her, which was a great pity. Youth was so obviously the antidote to all the uncomfortable premonitions of old age.

'I have seen the piano in the drawing room,' Maristella said. 'Would you allow me to give my Nino music lessons? He is not too young to learn.'

'But of course.'

It was such a pleasure to be generous and gracious. This would be an opportunity to inquire more closely into her background. It was an operation that needed to be conducted with a degree of delicacy and expertise. He had a reputation for success in interviewing candidates for all sorts of posts. These enquiries of course would be far more friendly and intimate. Maristella had gone to the kitchen to make tea and left the Alderman and the little boy gazing at each other in a state of benevolent neutrality. There was the sound of tyres on the gravel outside. Parry-Paylin saw Dr

Derwyn emerge in some haste from his economical little car. He became aware instantly of trouble afoot. Derwyn was not his usual restrained and urbane self. Something serious had ruffled the slippery smoothness of his feathers.

'I'm so glad you are back,' Dr Derwyn said. 'Something of a crisis I fear. Keturah Parry has locked herself in the chapel.'

Derwyn's small mouth was twitching. Under different circumstances, at a distance perhaps, the disclosure could have been amusing. A nonagenerian had caught up with the methods of the age of protest.

'I have to admit, to some extent, the fault was mine. That notion of Moi Twm Thomas' about a museum for R. J. Cethin. Professor Dwight Edelberg of Toledo was quite enthusiastic about it. On the e-mail. Americans when they're enthusiastic are always in a hurry, aren't they? They like to get things done. He was all for a joint operation by his department and mine. I told Moi Twm Thomas to wait until you got back. But your daughter was all for striking while the iron was hot. And they made matters worse, you see. I told them the approach was too crude. Turn Soar into an R. J. Cethin Museum or see it demolished for the new road scheme. This is her response. She's locked herself in the chapel.'

Maristella appeared from the kitchen with the tea tray.

'Shall I get another cup?' she said.

The alderman was too angry to answer. He stalked out of the house. Dr Derwyn hurried after him.

'I'm sorry to be the bearer of bad news,' he said. 'She's taken her paraffin stove into the chapel. A lamp on the communion table. And blankets. And a chamber pot. She's ready for a long siege.'

'That woman is the bane of my life.'

Dr Derwyn stepped back in the face of such a blaze of indignation.

'And that young devil... mischief makers have made matters worse.'

'I did stress that it would be wiser to wait until you got back. I did stress that.'

Alderman Paylin raised both arms and let them fall again. This academic had no idea how to handle people. He was just the type to rush in where any sensible experienced angel would fear to tread.

'She's mad,' the Alderman said. 'And she's been mad for years. Do you realise we had an electric stove installed in that cottage thirty years ago? She had it taken out. She sold it and gave the miserable price she got for it to the LMS. She lives in a nineteenth-century time warp. You've seen it for yourself. She's completely out of touch with reality.'

He waved a hand to specify the unique solidity of their surroundings, the house and the gardens and the woodland above them: the view of the noble mountain range: the honourable scars of the quarries: the sea on the western horizon. This was reality.

'Did you speak to her yourself? What did she have to say? As if I couldn't guess.'

'She said R. J. Cethin was a heretic and a scoundrel and the sooner his name was forgotten the better. She said I should be ashamed of myself not giving the sermons of five glorious ministers a place of honour. She said I had joined the worshippers of the Golden Calf. Both of them she said. The English Calf and the Money Calf. It was quite upsetting.'

The Alderman allowed himself a grim smile.

'She said something else too. The organist's daughter was one of your family. On her mother's side. It was a terrible secret!'

'One of her hobbies. Making family trees. I used to tell her if we went back far enough we'd find we were all related.'

'Will you speak to her Alderman Parry-Paylin? She's in quite a state.'

The Alderman shook his head. At least he could give the archivist a brief lesson in the exercise of authority and the management of people.

'Let her stew in her own juice,' he said. 'She'll soon get fed up in there. Chamber pot and all.'

VII

Iola was the first to point out that in the kind of community in which they lived people would soon start talking. Since when may he ask had she and her ilk worried about what people were saying? He slumped in his chair at the head of the table as though he were sitting for a portrait of a brooding monarch. He could see that his bad mood was disturbing Maristella and her little son; whereas Iola was just treating the whole affair as a joke. The only way he could wipe the grin off her face would be to threaten to turn the strangers out of the house. That would be worse than a futile gesture. It would deprive him of the few crumbs of comfort available. In the worst possible case if he tried to turn his only daughter out she would go around the place screaming that he had deprived her of her mother's heritage. And that would cause more talk than the scandal of the old woman locking herself up in Soar chapel. The only measure of discipline he had been able to impose was to insist that Moi Twm be kept out of his sight. However this did nothing to diminish the frequent mutterings and chatterings that took place at the back of the house or down by the road gate.

Within twenty-four hours he was perched precariously on top of a tombstone trying to communicate with his aunt through a chapel side-window above the level of green opaque glass. To maintain his balance and make himself heard he was obliged to lean forward and place his hands on a stone sill that was covered with green slime. The grass grew high between the gravestones. He was made to realise that the volunteer caretakers had become too old to cut the grass. A cloudy drizzle was looming to put a damper on everything. Soon the place would be overrun by creeping brambles and briers and what on earth was he to do about it?

'You are breaking the law!'

Against his better judgement he had to shout. It was the only way he could make himself heard. The old woman seemed to treat his warning as a joke. From the end of the pew where she sat she was raising her hands to warm them above the paraffin stove in the aisle.

'The moral law, Mihangel Paylin,' she said. 'That's something you don't know too much about.'

'I offered you rooms in Penllwyn years and years ago. You know that as well as I do.'

In his uncomfortable position he made a strenuous effort not to sound cross.

'Your poor grandfather would turn in his grave if he knew you were living in the enemy's citadel. That's what he called your precious Penllwyn. The enemy's citadel.'

The old woman was enjoying the reverberations of her own voice in the empty chapel. The sound was an incentive to preaching. She stood up and placed a hand on the back of the pew in front to support herself. She was ready to address an invisible congregation.

'That was your grandfather, auntie. I said your grandfather. It was a very long time ago!'

He struggled to maintain his balance as he raised his voice. His aunt persisted with her litany.

'Persecuted he was. Gruffydd Owen Parry. Driven out of his smallholding by a vicious landlord for voting against him. Driven to work in the quarry and driven out of Cloddfa by that old monster of Penllwyn. Driven to work as a farm labourer and walking ten miles a day there and back for fourpence a day. But he never soured in spirit. He was the leader of song in this chapel for forty years.'

She started to sing in a quavering voice, '*Driven out of Eden and its blessings I came to kneel before the Cross...*'

The effort was too much for her. She sat back in the pew

to mumble the words of the hymn to herself. For his part Mihangel could no longer hold his precarious position. A drizzle was beginning to fall.

'I'll be back.'

He shouted as he waded through the long grass.

'I'll be back. We've got to be sensible about this. It's got to be settled.'

In reality he had little idea how. The weather wouldn't allow him to pace to and fro among the trees above the house and Penllwyn itself was being given a thorough cleaning by Iola assisted by Maristella and Mrs Twigg. There would be no peace there. In any case they had no idea of the depth of his problem.

He repaired to the golf club. Ennis Taft was already there enjoying, he said, his first Dubonnet before a light lunch. He insisted Saint Mihangel should join him. Didn't they have a whole agenda to discuss? Over fish, he said, which was good for the old ticker and a bottle of white wine, in no time at all they could set the world to rights. He was full of a new scheme to deal with industrial waste products and make a healthy profit. There was also an amusing crisis at the Comprehensive school where the kitchen staff were threatening to go on strike. It took Ennis Taft some time to apprehend that Parry-Paylin was weighed down with a critical trouble of his own. After an initial burst of amusement, which included an embarrassing rendition of a vulgar ditty about two old ladies locked in the lavatory, Ennis Taft became serious and intensely resourceful.

'The poor old biddy,' he said. 'She must be suffering from senile dementia. There's only one thing to do, San Fihangel. Section her. Or whatever it is they call it. All they need to do is ask her a few questions. What's the name of the Prime Minister of New Zealand? What day is it the day after tomorrow? That sort of thing.'

He grew excited with the sharpness of his own intelligence and the fumes of the white wine. Parry-Paylin had to beg him to keep his voice down. This was a family matter and he found it intensely embarrassing. His friend and colleague was not to be put off his brilliant line of thinking. He continued in a fierce whisper that was hardly less audible than his raucous laughter.

'A doctor and a policeman,' he said. 'That's all you need. And a court order maybe. That should be easy. You're a serving magistrate. I don't want to be callous but you've got to look ahead. Have her put away and you could have the chapel demolished in the twinkling of an eye. And the road widened and the lorries rolling by and everything in the garden will be lovely.'

There was no comfort anywhere. Certainly not in the voice of Ennis Taft. The Alderman sat at the wheel of his car in the spacious golf club car park, stricken with paralysis and the sense of no longer being in charge of anything. This ludicrous crisis called the whole romance of his career into question. In his heart of hearts it had always been a romance: the sacrifices his mother and his grandmother made to ensure his higher education. He was never all that academically bright and he would be the first to admit it, but he had worked hard and overcoming obstacles that in this more comfortable age would have been counted daunting. His greatest triumph had been his marriage. It couldn't be seen as less than a triumph. The daughter of the big house giving him the courage to confront her formidable father to ask for her hand in the most charming old-fashioned manner, with nothing to offer in return except a decent measure of good looks, a winning smile and a manner that, again in this day and age, would be counted a touch too ingratiating. But it was good for politics and his father-in-law set him on the right road. Laura said that was what fathers-in-law were for.

If only Laura were with him now. Their life together was a wonder and a marvel. Laura had presided over a golden age. She knew how to handle everybody. In the case of Mary Keturah she plied her with delicious home-made cakes and jam and praised her grubby mintcake as though it were manna from Heaven. She did more than that. Chauffeuring the surly spinster from one eisteddfod or singing festival or preaching meeting to another. The centre of gravity of his existence had been lost since the day Laura died and in some baffling way both his daughter and this impossible aunt seemed determined to hold him responsible for a loss that he felt far more keenly than either of them were ever capable of doing. There seemed to be very little left for him to do except feel acutely sorry for himself.

VIII

It did not take long for the substance of Ennis Taft's advice to her father to reach Iola's ears. While the Alderman brooded in his study, she bustled about the place increasingly excited by the notion of nurturing a plan of her own. She tried to explain the background of the situation and the opportunities it offered to Maristella, and became impatient with her when she was slow to understand.

'Taft Bronco is hardly the World Trade Organisation,' she said. 'But the principle is the same. A chance to wake up the community. Get the people to reassess their sense of values. If we plan this carefully and get Moi Twm's Uncle Ted to write it all up in his column we could start a home-grown revolution.'

'What are you going to do?'

Maristella would at least understand action and showed that she was as ready as ever to take part in it. She had every confidence in Iola's leadership. This was a woman who knew how to act and bring about satisfactory change. She owed her a great debt and was ever ready to pay it.

'We'll join her,' Iola said. 'We'll have a sit-in strike in Soar. The only thing is we have to keep Moi Twm well away from the place.'

Maristella frowned hard as she struggled to follow Iola's line of reasoning.

'They rubbed her up all the wrong way. All that half-baked nonsense about a museum to the memory of R J. Cethin. It was a daft idea.'

'But you encouraged, I think...'

'Well it didn't work did it. And things have moved on. The essence of revolutionary practice is to seize the moment. I'll get Mrs Twigg to look after Nino and we'll go and talk to her. Right away. There isn't a moment to lose.'

Maristella felt obliged to listen intently while Iola communicated with Moi Twm on her mobile phone in a language she didn't understand. Somehow or other troops of protesters, mostly from the student body of the colleges within a reasonable radius, were to be put on standby. When Iola gave the signal, the ancient bus that Moi Twm used to collect support for rallies would rumble into action and collect enough bodies to lie in the road when the local authority and the police attempted to take possession of Soar chapel. Iola switched off and waved the mobile phone under Maristella's nose.

'Democracy is a fine thing,' she said. 'We've just got to learn how to manage it.'

She became so excited with the potential of her gift for management that she could no longer keep still. They would go now and she would make immediate contact with her great-aunt herself.

In the car she turned to make Maristella appreciate that a dialogue with Mary Keturah would not be all that easy. There were historical difficulties that had to be overcome. Sectarian difficulties in fact. Did Maristella have any idea of what sectarian difficulties could be like? Her best hope she supposed was that blood in the end would be thicker than the bitter waters of contention. That much Maristella could understand. They stared at the unpretentious façade of the chapel. The west wall was slated from roof to the overgrown path.

'Soar,' Maristella said. 'Like soar up to heaven, yes?'

Iola was so amused she embraced her friend and shook with the effort of controlling her laughter.

'Is it Welsh then?'

Iola breathed deeply to stop laughing.

'Hebrew, you ignorant Papist. Did you never read your Bible? Soar was saved from the destruction of Sodom and Gomorrah.'

Iola embraced her again.

'Don't look so worried. Now then. Here we go.'

Iola grasped the iron ring on the main door.

'My ancestors built this,' she said. 'Some of them did anyway. Quite a lot of them are buried over on the left there. Those gravestones buried in the long grass.'

She began to bang the door determinedly.

'Auntie! Auntie Ket! It's Iola. Let me in, won't you? Let me in!'

She realised she spoke with too much authority as if she had automatic right of entry. With an effort she injected a note of pleading into her voice.

'Auntie. It's Iola. Please Auntie. I want to speak to you.'

Mary Keturah's voice was harsh but noticeably feeble when at last she spoke with her face close to the closed door.

'Who's there with you? Not that Moi Twm Thomas? You keep him well away from this place.'

'Are you all right Auntie Ket. I've brought you some milk and fresh bread.'

'Men do not live by bread alone,' Mary Keturah said. 'She was your great-grandfather's cousin.'

'Who was?'

Iola beckoned Maristella to bring her ear closer to the door. Maristella shrugged and shook her head to show she couldn't understand a word either were saying.

'That girl who ran away with that false prophet R. J. Cethin. So you be careful.'

'I don't care about R. J. Cethin, Auntie. I only care about you. And Soar of course.'

'If you marry that stupid Moi Twm Thomas you'll be making the biggest mistake of your life.'

'I wouldn't dream of marrying him, Auntie. People aren't getting married any more.'

Iola pulled herself up and tried to turn the dangerous observation into a joke.

'It's gone out of fashion. So there you are. You were well ahead of your time, Auntie Keturah.'

There was no response to her attempt at humour. For an old woman who attached so much importance to family how could the demise of marriage be something to laugh at? What would become of the family tree that hung in her bedroom and stretched back generations? And what about the first chapter of the gospel according to St Matthew?

'There's got to be a succession,' the old woman said. 'Things can't carry on without a succession. If you were as old as I am, you would know that. Where's your father?'

'We want to come in, Auntie Keturah. We want to join you. We want to support you.'

'Do you indeed.'

'Really we do. We want to save Soar.'

'I've never seen you darken these doors before. Dashing about the world getting into trouble. That's what I hear. You run off now, child, and get your father. He is a Trustee. It's his responsibility. He's let the whole fabric of this building run down. It's his job to repair it. And the sooner he starts the better. You go and tell him that. Him and his precious County Council. And tell him I'm not budging out of this chapel until they start repairing it. You tell him that.'

'Won't you let me in? Please.'

'No, I won't. Go and get your father.'

IX

Iola was too furious to speak. The old woman had left her to glower at a closed door. Maristella was standing behind her, a model of patience, waiting for some form of explanation. She was no more than a refugee in a foreign country, without the language or any acquaintance with local custom. All she could gather was that her champion and benefactor and friend was hugely displeased. On the way home Iola kept repeating the same imprecations under her breath.

'The old witch. She's impossible. She always was impossible. Who wants families anyway? They should be done away with.'

A cloud of gloom and despondency descended on Penllwyn. There was a sharp and unforgiving exchange between the Alderman and his only daughter that Maristella could not follow and from then on they stopped speaking to each other. Mealtimes were particularly uncomfortable. Nino was quick to sense an atmosphere of discord and clung more closely to his mother. His large eyes scanned the faces of father and daughter at either end of the table. The Alderman, when he thought Iola wasn't looking, extended an open hand in Maristella's direction as though looking for sympathy and then closed it abruptly. He was cut off from his habitual source of consolation and comfort at the golf club by a compelling desire to avoid Ennis Taft's poking and probing. Iola, for her part was reluctant to contact Moi Twm. She would have to admit her scheme was a total failure and she had put him to great trouble for nothing. It seemed as if they could not agree what to do about Mary Keturah, they would never be able to agree about anything.

After lunch, Maristella led Nino to the drawing room to give him a music lesson. It was something he had already begun to enjoy. He had two or three notes he could strike in the treble clef so that his mother could tell him they were playing a duet. He hammered away delighted with his own efforts and his mother was pleased too. The volume of sound increased. Iola marched into the room.

'For God's sake, won't you stop that row?'

When she saw how much she had startled them she clapped a hand to her brow.

'I'm afraid I've got a horrible headache,' she said. 'It's not at all my day. I tell you what. Why don't you go and visit Moi Twm in his precious shop. Tell him the sorry tale. You can stick Nino in front of the telly. I'll keep an eye on him.'

Maristella was reluctant to accept the suggestion.

'I don't know what to tell him,' she said. 'I find it difficult to talk to him. He speaks so quickly. I don't really understand what he say. Most of the time.'

'Not good enough for you, is he?'

'Good. He is good of course. Very good.'

'You prefer to be knocked about a bit. Bit of a masochist aren't you, on the quiet?'

Maristella was slow to understand that Iola in her frustrated mood was looking for a fight. She grew pale and took what comfort she could from the little boy clinging to her side.

'Just you remember, if you don't like it here, you can leave tomorrow. I can turn you out the minute you feel like that.'

Her display of nasty temper seemed to bring her some temporary relief. When she saw that both the mother and child were crying, she left the room. It seemed large and empty when she had gone. In the corner of a sofa Maristella nursed and comforted her little boy. They were only here on sufferance. They were isolated in a cold unfriendly world. Within less than half an hour Iola was back again, contrite and full of apologies.

'I'm so sorry my dear. I'm such a nasty spoilt bitch. I know I am. I try to control it. I'm one of those miserable creatures trapped in their own nature.'

She came around the back of the sofa and laid her cheek on the top of Maristella's head. The little boy shrank closer inside his mother's arms. Iola whispered more urgently.

'It comes bursting out sometimes. You do forgive me don't you? Say you forgive me.'

When Maristella nodded she stroked her cheek tenderly.

'We've been through so much together. You are so good for me, Maristella, my guiding star. You help me escape from myself. I mean that. Doing good is more than a backstairs method of getting your own way. You taught me that.'

She moved around the sofa to sit on the floor at Maristella's feet. She took hold of her hand to squeeze it. The little boy gazed at her with his mouth open, wondering what she would do next.

'The Dominican Republic,' she said. 'There's enormous work to be done there. Shelter are very keen on starting a housing project. It's something to think about Maristella, isn't it? You can speak Spanish?'

'Only very badly.'

Maristella sighed deeply. She was anxious to please Iola, but there were simple facts that had to be faced.

'It's an idea anyway. Something to think about. I have to get away from this place. There's so little I can do about it. You can see that for yourself. It's my home of course. I have a deep deep attachment. But what good can I do? It's sunk so deep in a morass of complacency. There's nothing I can do about it.'

Her father and her great-aunt only seemed to exist to make her uncomfortable. She shifted up to the sofa from the floor and sat so close to Maristella that Nino was crushed between them. He gave a little squeak of protest and this amused her.

'Go and bang at the piano,' she said. 'Bang it as hard as you like.'

Once he had more space, the little boy was reluctant to leave his mother's side.

'You do what you like,' Iola said. 'Don't ever let people bully you, especially me. We've got to think about what to do next, haven't we, Maristella? Whatever happens we've got to be in the same boat.'

X

At four o'clock in the morning Alderman Parry-Paylin was woken up by a loud cry. He studied his wristwatch on the bedside table trying to decide whether it was part of a dream, or the little boy having another nightmare: considering the oppressive atmosphere in the house the previous day, it would not have been surprising. He had seriously considered the possibility of asking the little boy's mother to act as some sort of go-between or mediator, between his difficult daughter and himself, only to conclude that such a move would have been too ridiculous. Since when had a foreign girl been able to intercede between a widowed father and his only daughter, who in any case had no excuse to be harbouring imagined wrongs. As so often happened in these matters, it was a case of sitting it out: just waiting until all the parties concerned came to their senses. In all his dealings throughout his life, he had relied on common sense to prevail.

He was slow to become aware of a blue light outside revolving in the grey mist of early morning. He saw the police car in the drive. In a state of agitation he stumbled around the bedroom aware of an impending emergency but uncertain how to prepare for it. Half-dressed and carrying a raincoat he walked down the stairs to be met by Inspector Owen Evans a police officer with whom he had good relations. In their dressing gowns Iola and Maristella stood in silence on either side of the bottom of the staircase. Iola reached out to take her father's hand. He had to assume she was prepared to offer him comfort. In any event, it looked right. The Inspector was a large avuncular figure who liked to say that he was a farmer's son from Meirionydd, who had to make a choice between the ministry and the police force, and had settled the matter in his own mind by making his professional manner a mixture of both.

'Sad news, Alderman. And bad news. I've already

informed these young ladies. A fire at Soar. I'm very sorry to
tell you Alderman Parry-Paylin your dear old aunt has
passed away.'

'A fire?'

The Alderman gripped the curved balustrade to steady
himself.

'Yes. Well now then, I thought it was the least I could do
to come and tell you myself.'

Iola reached out to take his hand.

'Daddy. I'm so sorry. I really am.'

Her sympathy was a form of reconciliation and he smiled
at her. The Inspector placed his large hand on the Alderman's
shoulder, and Mihangel Parry-Paylin lowered his head in
gratitude for so much thoughtfulness and consideration. The
Inspector looked at Iola and she bestirred herself to make
some tea. The Inspector and the Alderman made their way
at a solemn pace to take tea in the study.

'A nasty accident,' the Inspector said. 'It's too soon to jump
to conclusions but I suspect it was that paraffin stove. It is a
great sadness of course, but in my job, alas, we have to deal
with these tragedies every day. At least here, my friend, there
was a touch of heroism in the story and good deeds are
bright lights in a wicked violent world. Nick Jenkin the
postman was on his way to work and saw the smoke
billowing out of one of the windows and from under the
door. He didn't hesitate. He soaked his jacket in the river,
put it over his head, smashed the door open with the jack
from his van and dragged the old woman out. Too late of
course, but a fine gallant action. She was dead of course,
overcome with the fumes.'

They shook their heads and contemplated the postman's
courageous action as they sipped their hot tea.

'They put the fire out,' the Inspector said. 'But the dear
little chapel is little more than a smouldering ruin. There was
a lamp you know on the communion table. Was it the lamp
or the paraffin stove? Did she knock it over? Was she

desperate to escape? She was very old of course. But old people are still people, aren't they? I know how upsetting it must be for you. I know you thought the world of Soar. All those family associations. When you have recovered sufficiently I want you to come with me and look at the damage. Not much we can save I'm afraid. Plenty of scorched papers fluttering around. You, more than anyone else will have to decide what is to be done. And of course, when you feel up to it, we shall need to identify the body.'

XI

In the portico of Moriah, one of the largest chapels in the county town, Uncle Ted drew on the fag end of his cigarette while Moi Twm stood alongside him anxious to find a seat inside. The chapel was filling up rapidly.

'There'll be room in the gallery,' Uncle Ted said. 'Above the clock. That's where I like to sit. Keep an eye on things.'

Moi Twm was embarrassed by the note of cynicism in his Uncle Ted's rasping voice. There was a limit to the extent you could suspect everyone and everything. The death of the old woman and the destruction of the chapel had touched him deeply. He had washed the colour out of his hair and had his head shaved like a Buddhist monk. He hoped people would take his transformation seriously. It was not such a big step, he said, from protest to pilgrimage. Uncle Ted's comment he found thoughtless to the point of being hurtful. He said it made him look like an overpaid professional footballer.

'Here they come.'

Uncle Ted's small eyes ferreted about.

'Two by two the animals enter the ecumenical ark.'

He threw his fag end away and pushed Moi Twm forward to climb the gallery steps on the left side of the vestibule. The weather had taken a turn for the worst. Umbrellas and raincoats abounded and a steamy atmosphere gave the impression that the chapel was packed. In the gallery there was more room, and from his chosen vantage point above the clock, Uncle Ted and Moi Twm could take a close view of the proceedings. The coffin, mounted on a wheeled chromium-plated bier, was parked under the elaborately carved pulpit, where the communion table usually stood. It was adorned with one large wreath of white lilies and red roses. The pulpit itself was overshadowed by the shining mountain of pipes of the powered organ. The curved deacon's pew was occupied by ministers of all the denominations, including the Anglican Archdeacon and the Roman Catholic priest.

'I wonder what the old girl would have had to say about that...'

Uncle Ted fidgeted about the pew so that he could get closer to Moi Twm's ear. There was ceaseless comment he wanted to make for his nephew's edification.

'Quite a bing-bang you know at the Ecumenical Council. How best to take advantage of the occasion. The Bishop was there you know. Agreed to Moriah, provided the Archdeacon made an address all designed to prove the old girl died to prove the church was One and indivisible.'

Moi Twm made an effort to shift further away from the buzz of his uncle's excited whispers. The organ had begun to play low sonorous music. He wanted to be left alone with his own solemn thoughts. Uncle Ted had too much to say for himself. This wasn't the place to be dishing dirt.

'The Press is here you know. We are on the verge of a mini-media event. Jones Llandudno Junction has been trying to get the tabloids interested. Working himself up no end concocting tasty headlines – *Nonconformist spinster sets fire to herself.*

He began to shake as a sequence of witty elaborations occurred to him. In the end he had to clap his hand over his loose dentures to stop them slipping out. He seemed incapable of sitting still. He leaned over the edge of the gallery in case persons of importance might be sitting at the back of the chapel. Moi Twm tugged fiercely at the tail of the black coat his uncle wore to attend funerals.

The two front pews according to custom had been left vacant for the immediate family. Mihangel Parry-Paylin and his daughter Iola occupied the first.

'Not much of a family.'

Uncle Ted felt obliged to comment. He was surprised almost to the point of outrage when Maristella and her little boy took their place in the second pew. Before she sat down Maristella genuflected in the direction of the coffin and crossed herself.

'Good Lord! Did you see that Moi Twm? Did you see that?'

It was a neat and unobtrusive gesture, but surprising in a nonconformist chapel.

'What do you expect her to do?'

Moi Twm was fed up with his uncle's prattle. The man was tied to his bad habits like a wayside goat on a tether.

'She's a Latin, isn't she? It's a mark of respect. We could do with a little more of it around here.'

In a brief address, the Archdeacon said that he was speaking on behalf of the county branch of the Ecumenical Movement. This was a special occasion. By her sacrifice this lonely old lady had brought the whole community closer together and made it aware of all the present dangers that threatened its Christian roots. The fate of our little nation, he said, was inextricably interwoven with the faith that gave it birth in the first place. There was such a thing as an apostolic succession on the humblest level and by her untimely death, Mary Keturah Parry had made a whole community more aware of this vital fact. Uncle Ted made notes in his own peculiar form of shorthand and grunted full approval of the Archdeacon's eloquence.

Mary Keturah Parry was buried in the new cemetery plot opposite the ruin of Soar chapel. For this service the mourners were far fewer in number. When the interment was over, Alderman Parry-Paylin stretched out a hand to hold back Maristella.

'I wonder if I could have a word,' he said.

They stood still on the wet grass as the straggle of mourners went past them. There was some curiosity to take a closer look at the ruins of the chapel. Someone said the pews were still smouldering.

'Something I've been wanting to say.'

The Alderman breathed more deeply to gain courage to speak.

'If you and your little boy wanted to make Penllwyn your home, I would be very glad for you to stay.'

Maristella looked down as if she were measuring the degree of tenderness in the proposal.

'You are very kind,' she said. 'You have been very kind to us both.'

'Will you stay?'

There was a level of pleading in his voice. He had his own problem, being obliged to grow old alone. This gentle unmarried mother could be the answer. He had to make the offer.

'I don't know,' she said. 'I shall have to ask Iola.'

'Ah well, Maristella. I am sure you will find life more comfortable in Penllwyn than wandering the wildernesses of this world. Much easier you know.'

'I don't think my life was ever meant to be easy,' Maristella said.

In her deep black, Iola was approaching to ask them what they had stopped to talk about.

Author Biographies

Gwyn Thomas

Gwyn Thomas was born in 1913 in the Rhondda Valley. He studied Spanish at Oxford and spent time in Spain during the early 1930s. He obtained part-time lecturing jobs across England before deciding to become a schoolteacher in Wales. He retired from that profession in 1962 to work full-time as a writer and broadcaster. He wrote extensively across several genres including essays, short stories, novels and plays, and was widely translated. His fictional works include *The Dark Philosophers* (1946) and *All Things Betray Thee* (1949), the drama *The Keep* (1962) and an autobiography, *A Few Selected Exits* (1968). Gwyn Thomas was given the Honour for Lifetime Achievement by Arts Council Wales in 1976. He died in 1981.

Richard Burton

Richard Burton was born in 1925 in the Afan Valley. He is remembered predominantly for his illustrious stage and screen work, as well as his turbulent private life, but he also wrote copious articles, diary entries and stories during his lifetime. One of these, 'A Christmas Story', was published in 1964. He died in 1984. An edited version of his extensive diaries was published in 2012.

Ron Berry

Ron Berry was born in 1920 in Blaenycwm in the Rhondda Valley. The son of a coal miner, he worked in mining until the outbreak of war saw him serving in both the British Army and the Merchant Navy. He studied at the adult education college Coleg Harlech in the 1950s but had further spells in mining and as a carpenter as his writing was never entirely successful enough to sustain him. His fictional output, which included works such as the novels *Flame and Slag* (1968) and *So Long, Hector Bebb* (1970), depicted a hard but positive view of the industrial Welsh valleys, entirely bereft of sentimentality and the hype which he scornfully left to others. He died in 1997.

Leslie Norris

Leslie Norris was born in 1921 in Merthyr Tydfil. In 1948, he enrolled in teacher training, and by 1958 had risen to the position of college lecturer. From 1974 onwards, he earned his living by combining full-time writing with residencies at academic institutions on both sides of the Atlantic. Aside from a dozen books of poems, his prose works include two volumes of short stories, *Sliding* (1978), which won the David Higham Award, and *The Girl from Cardigan* (1988), as well as a compilation, *Collected Stories*, released in 1996. He died in 2006.

Roland Mathias

Roland Mathias was born in 1915 in Talybont-on-Usk, Breconshire, and read modern history at Jesus College, Oxford. He taught in schools until 1969, when he resigned from his job as a headmaster and settled in Brecon in order to write full-time. His contribution to the study of Welsh writing in English, as editor, critic, anthologist, historian, poet and short-story writer, is substantial. He helped to found *Dock Leaves*, later the *Anglo-Welsh Review*, which he edited from 1961 to 1976. He published one collection of short stories and nine volumes of poetry. The majority of his writing has to do with the history, people and topography of Wales, especially the border areas. He died in 2007.

Sally Roberts Jones

Sally Roberts Jones was born in 1935 in London. She studied history at University College Bangor, and worked as a librarian before becoming a founding member of the English Language Section of Yr Academi Gymreig, of which she later served as honorary joint Secretary and as Chair from 1993 to 1997. She founded the Alun Books publisher in 1977. She has published a wide variety of books, one of which, 1969's *Turning Away*, won the Welsh Arts Council Prize. She has also written for radio, as well as both writing and lecturing on Wales' cultural and industrial history.

Tony Curtis

An award-winning poet, critic and short-story writer, Tony Curtis was born in Carmarthen in 1946, and studied in both the UK and US before embarking on a career teaching in higher education. He was the first Professor of Poetry at the University of Glamorgan. His books include *War Voices* (1995) and *Heaven's Gate* (2001). He has also published works of literary criticism, both as author and editor. He is a Fellow of both the Royal Society of Literature and the Welsh Academy.

Tristan Hughes

Tristan Hughes was born in 1972 in Atikokan, Canada, and was brought up in Llangoed, Ynys Môn. He was educated at the Universities of York and Edinburgh, and at King's College, Cambridge, where he completed a PhD thesis on Pacific and American literature. He won the Rhys Davies Short Story Award in 2001 for his work 'A Sort of Homecoming', and his first book of fiction, *The Tower*, was published in 2003. His fourth novel, *Eye Lake*, was released in 2012.

Raymond Williams

Raymond Williams was born in 1921 in Pandy, near Abergavenny in Monmouthshire. He was educated locally and at Trinity College, Cambridge from 1939. After the war, he taught in adult education before returning to Cambridge, from where he retired as Professor of Drama in 1983. Although most well known for his academic and critical works, such as *Culture and Society* (1958) and *The Long Revolution* (1961), he also published seven novels, setting them largely in the land of his childhood: the Welsh border country, which inspired the title of his first, and perhaps greatest novel, *Border Country* (1960). He died in 1988.

Alun Richards

Alun Richards was born in 1929 in Pontypridd. After spells as a schoolteacher, probation officer and as an instructor in the Royal Navy, from the 1960s he was, and successfully so, a full-time writer. He lived near the Mumbles, close to the sea which, coupled with the hills of the South Wales Valleys, was the landscape of his fiction. Alongside plays for stage and radio, screenplays and adaptations for television, a biography and a memoir, he wrote six novels and two collections of short stories, *Dai Country* (1973) and *The Former Miss Merthyr Tydfil* (1976). As editor, he produced bestselling editions of Welsh short stories and tales of the sea for Penguin. He died in 2004.

Sîan James

Sîan James was born in 1932 in Llandysul, Carmarthenshire. After attending the University of Wales, Aberystwyth, she has gone on to on to write and publish a number of acclaimed novels and short-story collections, several of which have won awards, including the Wales Book of the Year Award in 1997 for *Not Singing Exactly* (1996) and the Yorkshire Post Fiction Prize twice. Her third novel, *A Small Country* (1979) was adapted for film as *Calon Gaeth* (2006) by Stan Barstow and Diana Griffiths, winning a BAFTA Cymru award in the process.

Deborah Kay Davies

Deborah Kay Davies was born in 1956 in Pontypool. Her book of stories *Grace, Tamar and Laszlo the Beautiful* (2008) won the Wales Book of the Year award. She has previously published a collection of poems, *Things You Think I Don't Know* (2006), and released her first novel *True Things About Me* in 2010. Her short stories have been published in magazines such as *New Welsh Review* and *Planet*, as well as broadcast on BBC radio.

Glenda Beagan

Glenda Beagan was born in Rhuddlan, where she still lives, and was educated at the University of Wales, Aberystwyth and the University of Lancaster. She has published three collections of short stories, *The Medlar Tree* (1992), *Changes and Dreams* (1996) and *The Great Master of Ecstasy* (2009), as well as a collection of poems, *Vixen* (1996). Her work has appeared in many anthologies, including *The New Penguin Book of Welsh Short Stories* (1993), *The Green Bridge* (1988) and *Magpies* (2000).

Clare Morgan

Clare Morgan was born in 1953 in Monmouthshire, and now lives in Gwynedd. She gained an MA in creative writing from the University of East Anglia and a doctorate in English literature from Oxford University, where she is now director of the graduate programme in creative writing. Her novel, *A Book for All and None*, was published in 2011. Her stories have been commissioned for radio and have been widely anthologised, with such a collection, *An Affair of the Heart*, appearing in 1996. She won the Arts Council of Wales Short Story Prize, and is a regular reviewer for the *Times Literary Supplement*.

Jo Mazelis

Jo Mazelis was born in 1956 in Swansea, where she still lives. Her collection of stories *Diving Girls* (2002) was shortlisted for Commonwealth Best First Book and Welsh Book of the Year. Her second book *Circle Games* was published in 2005 and her short stories have been widely published and broadcast by the BBC. Her first novel, *Significance*, is due to be published in 2014.

Catherine Merriman

Catherine Merriman was born in 1949 in London, but has lived in Wales since 1973. She has published five novels, the first of which, *Leaving the Light On* (1992), won the Ruth Hadden Memorial Award in 1992, and three short-story collections, including *Silly Mothers* in 1991, and many of her short stories have been broadcast on BBC Radio 4 and published in, among others, *New Welsh Review*, *Everywoman* and *Essentials*. She currently teaches writing at the University of South Wales.

Mike Jenkins

Mike Jenkins was born in 1953 in Aberystwyth, and was educated at University College of Wales before becoming an English teacher. He won the 1998 Wales Book of the Year for his short-story collection *Wanting to Belong* (1997), and he has written two novellas – *Barbsmashive* (2002) and *The Fugitive Three* (2008) – and a novel – *Question Island* (2013). He appears frequently on radio and television, and lives in Merthyr Tydfil.

Leonora Brito

Leonora Brito was born in Cardiff. She studied law and history at Cardiff University. Her story 'Dat's Love' won her the 1991 Rhys Davies Short Story Competition. She also wrote for radio and television, providing a unique insight into Afro-Caribbean Welsh society, largely unrepresented in

Welsh writing until her work appeared. She published one collection of stories, *Dat's Love*, in 1996. She died in 2007.

Stevie Davies
Stevie Davies was born in Swansea. She is Professor of Creative Writing at Swansea University and a Fellow of both the Royal Society of Literature and the Welsh Academy. She has published novels and books in the fields of biography, literary criticism and history. Her novels have been longlisted for the Booker and Orange Prizes and *The Element of Water* (2001) won the Wales Book of the Year Award for 2002. Her novel *Awakening* was published in 2013.

Tessa Hadley
Tessa Hadley was born in 1956 in Bristol, and studied English Literature at Cambridge. She has published four novels and one collection of stories, as well as a work of literary criticism. Her short stories appear regularly in, among others, *Granta* and the *New Yorker*. She has lived in Cardiff since 1982.

Huw Lawrence
Huw Lawrence was born in Llanelli, and trained as a teacher in Swansea before resuming his education at Manchester and Cornell Universities. He is a three-time winner of prizes in the Rhys Davies Short Story Competition, a Bridport prize and a runner-up position in the 2009 Tom Gallon Trust Competition. His debut collection of short stories, *Always the Love of Someone*, was published in 2010. He lives in Aberystwyth.

Gee Williams
Gee Williams was born in Saltney, Flintshire, and studied English at Oxford. She was shortlisted for the James Tait Black Memorial Prize for Fiction for *Salvage* (2007). Her short-story collection *Blood, etc.* was published in 2008.

Rachel Trezise

Rachel Trezise was born in 1978 in the Rhondda Valley, where she still lives, and studied at the universities of Glamorgan and Limerick. Her novel *In and Out of the Goldfish Bowl* won an Orange Futures Award in 2002, and her short-story collection, *Fresh Apples* (2005) won the inaugural Dylan Thomas Prize. Her play, *Tonypandemonium* was staged by National Theatre Wales in 2013.

Des Barry

Des Barry was born in 1955 in Merthyr Tydfil, and was educated at University College London. His debut novel, *The Chivalry of Crime* (2001), won the Western Writers of America's Best First Novel of the Year Award. *Cressida's Bed* was published in 2004 and he has had short stories published in *The New Yorker*, *The Big Issue* and *Granta*, as well as in several anthologies. Aside from Wales, he has lived in Italy, the USA and Tibet.

Nigel Jarrett

Nigel Jarrett was born in Llanfrechfa, Cwmbran. He won the Rhys Davies Award for his short story 'Mrs Kuroda on Penyfan'. His debut collection of stories, *Funderland* was published in 2010. He is a former daily-newspaper journalist. Since 1987 he has been music critic of the South Wales Argus and he reviews jazz for *Jazz Journal* and poetry for *Acumen*. He lives in Monmouthshire.

Lewis Davies

Lewis Davies was born in 1967 in Penrhiwtyn. His work includes novels, plays, poetry and essays. He won the Rhys Davies Prize for his story 'Mr Roopratna's Chocolate'. His selected stories *Love and Other Possibilities* was published in 2008. He is one of the founding partners of the publishing company Parthian.

Aled Islwyn

Aled Islwyn was born in 1953 in Port Talbot. He has written and published extensively in Welsh. He won the Daniel Owen Memorial Prize at the National Eisteddfod in 1980 and again in 1985. His collection of short stories, *Unigolion, Unigeddau* (1994) won the Welsh Book of the Year Prize. *Out With It* (2008) is his first collection of stories in English.

Siân Preece

Siân Preece was born in Neath, and has lived for extended periods in Canada and France and Scotland. Her story collection, *From the Life*, was published in 2000. She won first prize in the 2009 Rhys Davies Short Story Competition for her story 'Getting Up'.

Robert Nisbet

Robert Nisbet was born in 1941 in Haverfordwest, and was educated at Milford Haven Grammar School, University College of Swansea and the University of Essex. His stories have been published in a wide range of magazines in Europe and the United States. As well as enjoying a successful career in education, he has been a regular contributor to BBC radio and has edited a number of short-story anthologies. His selected short-story collection, *Downtrain*, was published in 2004.

Jon Gower

Jon Gower was born in 1959 in Llanelli, and read English at Cambridge University. He is a writer, performer and broadcaster. He has written books on non-fictional subjects as diverse as a disappearing island in Chesapeake Bay in *An Island Called Smith* (2001) and a West Wales tour in psycho-geography in *Real Llanelli* (2000), as well as the fiction of *Dala'r Llanw* (2009), *Uncharted* (2010) and *Big Fish* (2000). *Too Cold For Snow*, a collection of short stories, was released in 2012.

Robert Minhinnick

Robert Minhinnick was born in 1952 in Neath. He is a poet, essayist, editor and novelist who has twice won the Wales Book of the Year Award: in 1993 for *Watching the Fire Eater* (1992) and in 2006 for *To Babel and Back* (2005). His poetry has been published internationally and he has won an Eric Gregory Award and the Cholmondeley Prize.

Emyr Humphreys

Emyr Humphreys was born in 1919 in Prestatyn. A former theatre and television director, drama producer and lecturer, in a long and illustrious career he has written and released twenty novels, several short-story and poetry compilations, and a history volume, as well as produced a number of screenplays. He has won several literary prizes during his career – the 1958 Somerset Maugham Prize for *Hear and Forgive* (1952), the 1958 Hawthornden Prize for *A Toy Epic* (1958), and the Welsh Book of the Year Award twice, for *Bonds of Attachment* (1992) and *The Gift of a Daughter* (1999). He lives in Llanfairpwll on Anglesey.

EDITOR BIOGRAPHY

Dai Smith was born in 1945 in the Rhondda. He was educated in South Wales before reading modern history at Balliol College, Oxford and comparative literature at Columbia University, New York. He has been a lecturer at the universities of Lancaster, Swansea and Cardiff, where he was awarded a Personal Chair in 1986, and was subsequently a Pro-Vice Chancellor at the University of Glamorgan. In addition to his academic career, he has also been a regular broadcaster on radio and television since the 1970s, and he became Head of Programmes (English language) in the 1990s at BBC Wales where he commissioned, presented and scripted a number of award-winning documentary programmes and other series. His many publications, which span books, articles and journalism, have centred on the dynamics – culture and society, politics and literature – of his native South Wales, and most recently have expanded into the form of biography (*Raymond Williams: A Warrior's Tale*, 2008), memoir (*In The Frame: Memory in Society*, 2010) and the novel (*Dream On*, 2013).

Dai Smith was the founding editor of the Library of Wales Series. He has led Arts Council Wales as its Chair since 2006. He holds a part-time Research Chair in the Cultural History of Wales at Swansea University. He is now writing more fiction.

Published List

- 'Gazooka' – published in *Gazooka and Other Stories* (Gollancz, 1957)
- 'A Christmas Story' – published in *A Christmas Story* (Heinemann, 1964)
- 'Natives' – published in *Pieces of Eight*, ed. by Robert Nisbet (Gomer, 1982)
- 'A Roman Spring' – published in *The Atlantic Monthly*, issue dated Feb, 1972
- 'A View of the Estuary' – published in *The Collected Short Stories of Roland Mathias*, ed. by Sam Adams (University of Wales Press, 2001)
- 'The Inheritance' published in *Pieces of Eight*, ed. by Robert Nisbet (Gomer, 1982)
- 'The Way Back' – published in *The Anglo-Welsh Review*, No. 67, 1980
- 'A Sort of Homecoming' – published in *Ghosts of The Old Year: New Welsh Short Fiction* (Parthian, 2003)
- 'That Old Black Pasture' – published in *Panurge*, No. 24, 1996
- 'The Writing on the Wall' – published in *Colours of a New Day*, ed. by Sarah Lefanu and Stephen Hayward (Lawrence and Wishart, 1990)
- 'Bowels Jones' – published in *The Former Miss Merthyr Tydfil and Other Stories* (Michael Joseph, 1976)
- 'Strawberry Cream' – published in *New Welsh Review* No. 36, Spring 1997
- 'Whinberries' & 'Stones' – published in *Grace, Tamar and Laszlo the Beautiful* (Parthian, 2008)
- 'November Kill' – published in *New Welsh Review*, No. 1, 1988

- 'Foxy' – published in *Magpies: Short Stories from Wales*, ed. by Robert Nisbet (Gomer, 2000)
- 'Charity' – published in *Planet*, No. 103, 1994
- 'Too Perfect' – published in *Diving Girls* (Parthian, 2002)
- 'Barbecue' – published in *New Welsh Review*, No. 17, Summer 1992
- 'Wanting to Belong' – published in *Wanting to Belong* (Seren, 1997)
- 'Mama's Baby (Papa's Maybe)' – published in *Mama's Baby (Papa's Maybe): New Welsh Short Fiction*, ed. by Lewis Davies and Arthur Smith (Parthian, 1999)
- 'Some Kind o' Beginnin' – published in *Graffiti Narratives: Poems 'n' Stories* (Planet, 1994)
- 'Dat's Love' – published in *Dat's Love* (Seren, 1995)
- 'Woman Recumbent' – published in *Ghosts of the Old Year: New Welsh Short Fiction* (Parthian, 2003)
- 'The Enemy' – *Granta*, No. 86, Summer, 2004
- 'We Have Been to the Moon' – published in *Eagle in the Maze* (Cinnamon Press, 2008)
- 'Pod' – published in *Ghosts of the Old Year: New Welsh Short Fiction* (Parthian, 2003)
- 'Blood etc.' – published in *Blood, etc.* (Parthian, 2008)
- 'Fresh Apples' – published in *Fresh Apples* (Parthian, 2005)
- 'Waste Flesh' – published in *Magic and Other Deceptions* (Gwasg Gee, 2000)
- 'Dalton's Box' – published in *The New Yorker*, issue dated Apr 23, 2001
- 'Mrs Kuroda on Penyfan' – published in *Funderland* (Parthian, 2011)
- 'The Ferryman's Daughter' – published in *New Welsh Review*, No. 4, Spring 1989
- 'The Fare' – published in *Urban Welsh: New Welsh Short Fiction*, ed. by Lewis Davies (Parthian, 2005)
- 'Muscles Came Easy' – published in *Out With It* (Parthian, 2008)

- 'Running Out' – published in *From the Life and Other Stories* (Polygon, 2000)
- 'Miss Grey of Market Street' – published in *Downtrain* (Parthian, 2004)
- 'The Stars Above the City' – published in *Love and Other Possibilities* (Parthian, 2008)
- 'The Last Jumpshot' – published in *Urban Welsh: New Welsh Short Fiction*, ed. by Lewis Davies (Parthian, 2005)
- 'Chickens' – published in *Fresh Apples* (Parthian, 2005)
- 'Bunting' – published in *Too Cold for Snow* (Parthian, 2012)
- 'I Say a Little Prayer' – published in *The Keys of Babylon* (Seren, 2011)
- 'Old People Are a Problem' – published in *Old People Are a Problem* (Seren, 2003)

ACKNOWLEDGEMENTS

PUBLISHER'S ACKNOWLEDGEMENTS

Parthian would like to thank all the writers, estate holders and publishers for their cooperation in the preparation of this volume. We would also like to thank the editor, Dai Smith, for his energy and engagement with the world of the Welsh short story.

Although every effort has been to secure permissions prior to publication this has not always been possible. The publisher apologises for any errors or omissions and will if contacted rectify these at the earliest opportunity.

FURTHER ACKNOWLEDGEMENTS

The publishers would like to thank Mick Felton of Seren Books for assistance in the preparation of this volume. We would also like to thank the estate of Dylan Thomas, David Higham Associates and Liam Hanley for permission to publish the stories of Dylan Thomas and James Hanley. Ravinda Jasser for the estate of Brenda Chamberlain. Meic Stephens for copyright assistance with the estates of Rhys Davies and Leslie Norris. Merryn Hemp for the estate of Raymond Williams. Dr Lesley Coburn for the estate of Ron Berry. Geoffrey Robinson for the estate of Gwyn Thomas. Helen Richards for the estate of Alun Richards. Myfanwy Lumsden for the estate of Geraint Goodwin. Matthew Evans for the estate of George Ewart Evans. Glyn Mathias for the estate of Roland Mathias. Viv Davies for the estate of B.L. Coombes.

Editor's Acknowledgements

First and foremost, as now over a lifetime, to Norette for allowing me (again) to sequester myself away for months on end with other people's lives. And their stories. To particular friends and advisers, especially Meic Stephens; and to Sam Adams, Peter Finch, Tony Brown and Daniel Williams. To the various editors and selectors who stepped out onto these highways and byways before me, and, of course, to the odd (sometimes very odd!) tipster who nudged me into unexpected diversions. All at Parthian have proved as exemplary in the arduous production of these two volumes as they have been since the inception of the Library of Wales Series in 2006. But, here, I need to single out the principal editorial assistance of the indefatigable Robert Harries who, like me, has now read all the words all of the time, and more than once.

LIBRARY of WALES
FUNDED BY

Noddir gan
Lywodraeth Cymru
Sponsored by
Welsh Government

**CYNGOR LLYFRAU CYMRU
WELSH BOOKS COUNCIL**